THE BEST SCIENCE FICTION
OF THE YEAR

THE BEST
SCIENCE
FICTION
OF THE YEAR

VOLUME 4

Edited by Neil Clarke

Night Shade Books
NEW YORK

Night Shade books may be purchased in bulk at special discounts for sales promotion, corporate gifts, fund-raising, or educational purposes. Special editions can also be created to specifications. For details, contact the Special Sales Department, Night Shade Books, 307 West 36th Street, 11th Floor, New York, NY 10018 or info@skyhorsepublishing.com.

Night Shade Books® is a registered trademark of Skyhorse Publishing, Inc.®, a Delaware corporation.

Visit our website at www.nightshadebooks.com.

10 9 8 7 6 5 4 3 2 1

Library of Congress Cataloging-in-Publication Data is available on file.

Hardcover ISBN: 978-1-949102-08-6
Trade paperback ISBN: 978-1-59780-988-7

Cover illustration by Mack Sztaba
Cover design by Jason Snair

Please see page 591 for an extension of this copyright page.

Printed in the United States of America

For Gardner Dozois.

Table of Contents

INTRODUCTION:
A State of the Short SF Field in 2018

Neil Clarke

opened this year's review of short fiction with an important dedication. Few people can be said to have shaped modern science fiction to the degree that Gardner Dozois did over the course of his career. He will most notably be remembered for his time as editor of *Asimov's Science Fiction* and The Year's Best Science Fiction series, but he was also a Nebula Award-winning author. Gardner also won the Hugo Award for Best Editor a record-setting fifteen times and edited dozens of Hugo, Nebula, and Locus Award-winning stories. He was also a friend and colleague, working for me as reprint editor at *Clarkesworld* for the last five years.

On my shelves lies a complete run of The Year's Best Science Fiction, all thirty-five volumes plus his three Best of the Best volumes, and dozens of other anthologies he edited. While volumes one through three of my series were technically competing with his, he never once made me feel like that was the case. One of the best and more beautiful things most of you don't know about this field is how collegial it is. Even when the stories were no longer new to me, I always preordered his next volume, simply for his annual summation of the field. For many of us, it was an important history of the field, one that spanned over thirty years and was yet another important part of his legacy.

No one can fill his shoes, but in his honor, I'm going to merge some of the short fiction-oriented features of Gardner's introductions into my own. It's my way of noting that aspect of his work. It's of personal value to me, and a desire to see that particular torch carried forward.

The Business Side of Things

For a long time, the genre magazine field was dominated by "the big three" print magazines: *Analog Science Fiction and Fact* (analogsf.com), *Asimov's Science Fiction* (asimovs.com), and *The Magazine of Fantasy and Science Fiction* (sfsite.com/fsf). It wasn't until more recently that online magazines began to present them with any serious competition for authors, readers, and awards. Much has changed in the last decade.

Out of all the 2016 and 2017 Hugo Award finalists in the short fiction categories, only one came from a print magazine. For some readers, this has created an illusion that the health or quality of those markets is in decline. Another possible explanation is that online fiction is easier for readers to share and it has a much longer shelf life than the digests—which is often two months. This is not to say that the finalists are unworthy, it simply posits that some equally worthy stories are being overlooked due to reduced availability, much in the same way a UK-only novel would face significant disadvantage against a US-only novel. Popular vote awards are heavily influenced by availability and visibility.

In 2017, one third of the combined selections in the year's best anthologies by Dozois, Horton, Strahan, and myself were from print magazines. I'd argue that would indicate that quality is not suffering at those publications, but instead that due to the sheer volume of markets publishing short fiction, it's simply impossible for your average reader to keep up. Any restrictions to availability, particularly in the form of having had to purchase it in a relatively short window of time, will reduce the likelihood of it being seen by a potential voter. This would also explain the decline in stories from anthologies.

Adding to the illusion of troubled times for the print digests comes from the paid circulation that both Gardner and *Locus Magazine* (locusmag.com) have tracked and published over the years. Much of this data was made available via the Statement of Ownership print periodicals are required to publish each year. Additional circulation details have been provided by editors.

These subscription and newsstand numbers are often quoted with little insight into what it actually means to the field. Many have chosen to see this as an opportunity to declare the death of print or even short fiction. On the other hand, we have some people who, on looking at the wide array of markets, proclaim that we're in a new golden age for short fiction. Both are guilty of looking at only part of the picture. Combined, you have a better view of the overall health—both their strengths and weaknesses.

Over the last five years, *Analog* has dropped from 15,282 print subscriptions to 11,401, a loss of 3,881; *Asimov's* has dropped from 9,347 to 7,109, a loss of 2,238; and *F&SF* has dropped from 8,994 to 6,688, a loss of 2,306. That may seem disastrous, but it appears it's actually symptomatic of a change in reading habits. Over the last five years, *Analog* has risen from 6,174 digital subscriptions to 8,788, a gain of 2,614 and *Asimov's* has risen from 8,640 to 10,578, a gain of 1,938. Unfortunately, *F&SF* does not report its digital subscription figures. These magazines also receive additional income from single issue newsstand sales and on average, this adds between two and three thousand print copies per month.

The total paid subscription numbers may be down in this window (all were up for the year), but the income generated by the different formats is not equal. Annual US subscriptions to *Analog* and *Asimov's* are $34.97 print and $35.88 digital. *F&SF* subscriptions are $39.97 print and $36.97 digital. While the prices for digital and print subscriptions are relatively similar, print subscriptions cost the publisher more due to printing and shipping, ultimately making the digital edition more profitable. The upwards trend in digital subscriptions should offset the declining print subscriptions and with increasing printing and postal costs eating into profits, this development is better for the long-term health of these publications.

It's no secret that online and digital publishing has contributed significantly to the wealth of short fiction magazines we have at the moment. The overall financial health of those markets, however, is considerably lower than that of "the big three." The current dominant model for the digital-born magazines is to release all content for free—either immediately or parceled out over a period of time. The majority sell digital subscriptions or offer other methods of support (donations, Patreon, Kickstarter, etc.), but while their total readership is considerably higher, paid readership is far lower. The average supporting rate (the percentage of readers who pay for or contribute towards the publication's costs) is often well below 10%. This means that those three print magazines have a considerably larger paid readership than any of these newer markets. That creates a much more stable financial foundation, one that allows them to pay their staff professional wages that the free markets simply cannot manage. As a result, many of these editors work for free or very little income. That is a much more troubling point of data than the print magazines losing awards visibility and one that goes largely ignored when people talk about the state of short fiction.

Another takeaway from the low supporting rates is how little short fiction is valued when it comes to dollars on the table. The drive to publish fiction online for free—something of which I freely acknowledge my own role in—has negatively changed perceptions of what readers expect to pay for in the short fiction market. It's not a unique situation, as many newspapers find themselves in the same boat, but this isn't good for any industry impacted by it, particularly one like science fiction magazines where advertising revenue is thin at best.

Let's take that Golden Age argument for a second, though. That would imply a thriving healthy state of being for the field, that I've just explained isn't there for the majority of the publishers. Even the digests, while healthier, aren't exactly rolling in the money. At present SFWA, the Science Fiction and Fantasy Writers of America, state that their qualifying rate is $0.06 per word. SFWA will be increasing that rate to $0.08 in 2019, but most of the larger markets are already paying that or better. Even the most prolific short fiction authors are unable to earn a living at either rate. If we're using inflation values calculated to the present from the previous Golden Age, it would be at least four times that value, but paid readership, and therefore financial resources, has not scaled accordingly.

Digital subscriptions to most magazines—whether they originated online or in print—are typically between $1.99 and $2.99 a month. Compared to other forms of entertainment, or even a gallon of gas, these rates are too low. If the future of short fiction is to be strong or even hoping to have even a shadow of a Golden Age, we have to stop treating the majority of professionals like volunteers and acknowledge that short fiction is worth paying for. This not only means that the paid subscriber levels need to increase, but that subscription rates should be a bit higher. Even an increase of $1 a month on subscription prices would provide a considerable boost to the health of these markets, allowing them to pay their staff and authors a more respectable rate for the work they do. In the end, it would be a modest increase with a significant impact on the field.

So, if you aren't currently supporting your favorite short fiction venues with a subscription, please consider doing so today.

Magazine Comings and Goings

While I normally don't get excited about resurrecting old magazines, last year, I was thrilled to hear that *Omni*—the first magazine I subscribed to—would be returning with Ellen Datlow and Pamela Weintraub back at the helm. Unfortunately, that came to a halt when their parent company,

Penthouse Global Media, declared bankruptcy in January. In June, the company's assets were sold to WGCZ Ltd., a Czech porn site operator, and that placed the future of *Omni* on uncertain ground.

The oft-resurrected magazine *Amazing Stories* (amazingstories.com) has once again returned after a successful Kickstarter campaign—dramatically highlighted by a surprising last-minute pledge of $10,000 to squeak past the finish line. Experimenter Publishing Company published the first of two new 2018 issues and distributed copies for free at San Jose Worldcon. The magazine is currently available in print and e-book editions.

An interesting development in 2018 was the number of magazines that attempted to launch with print editions or add them later on. February saw the publication of *Spectacle Magazine*'s first quarterly issue, complete with full-color interiors, high production values, and a $20 cover price. Sadly, it appeared as though the publishers had not quite done their homework, causing them to run into a controversy over clauses in their contracts. This was eventually resolved amicably, but they failed to produce any other issues. Their website is still taking orders for subscriptions, but their website and social media presences haven't been updated in months, leaving their current status in question.

Another print magazine, *Visions* (readvisions.com), launched in the UK in December. They describe themselves as "a science fiction magazine where writers, designers, and researchers of the past and present come together to explore the future." While they are purchasing print and digital rights to stories, it appears as though they've only produced a print edition of issue #1. Their second issue is scheduled for Summer 2019.

UFO Publishing and The Future Affairs Association (China) published issue #1 of their quarterly English-language magazine, *Future Science Fiction Digest* (future-sf.com), in December. The magazine is edited by Alex Shvartsman and will place a heavy emphasis on translated works. Interestingly, the magazine is acquiring rights for English and Chinese language, which they have licensed for print, audio, and electronic editions.

Apex Magazine (apex-magazine.com), launched a new print edition in early 2018, but terminated the program in December, citing a lack of interest. This was not their first foray into print, having originally launched as a print magazine back in 2005.

Fireside Magazine (firesidefiction.com) rounds out the print launches with a rather attractive color quarterly edition, *Fireside Quarterly*, with a subscription price that works out to $30 per issue paid in monthly installments. Stories published in the print edition were later published online.

On the sadder side of the spectrum, *Shimmer Magazine* closed its doors after thirteen years. Also shuttered was *LONTAR*, a biannual literary journal focusing on Southeast Asian speculative fiction, which closed in May after producing ten issues. That region is now represented by *Ombak* (ombak.org), Southeast Asia's weird fiction journal, which published its first issue on Halloween. After twenty years, *Mythic Delirium* (mythicdelirium.com) has gone on "indefinite hiatus." *Space and Time* (www.spaceandtimemagazine.com) announced that it would be closing after over fifty years, but was rescued at the last minute by Angela Yuriko Smith, who will take over as publisher. Their first new issue is expected in late spring/early summer of 2019.

Although they have yet to produce an issue, *Hard Universe* had perhaps the most unusual new market announcement of the year. Sponsored by a company invested in their own cryptocurrency, *Hard Universe* intended to be the first genre magazine to pay authors in that medium. As of the end of 2018, they had not accepted any stories despite opening for submissions in July.

Asimov's Science Fiction continues to demonstrate its position as one of the leading science fiction magazines this year with stories likely to appeal to a wide range of science fiction fans. Among these, the best were by Sue Burke, Rich Larson, S. Qiouyi Lu, Linda Nagata, Suzanne Palmer, Robert Reed, Kristine Kathryn Rusch, and Allen M. Steele.

Industry stalwart *Analog Science Fiction and Fact* remains one of the most purely SF markets available with excellent stories by Marissa Lingen, Suzanne Palmer, and Nick Wolven.

The Magazine of Fantasy and Science Fiction had a stronger year in 2018 and will be celebrating their 70th anniversary this year. Some of my favorite stories were by L.X. Beckett, William Ledbetter, Robert Reed, and Vandana Singh.

Clarkesworld Magazine (clarkesworldmagazine.com) happens to be the magazine I edit, so I'll refrain from significant comment and say that some of my favorites this year—which seem to match our reader's poll results—include works by Simone Heller, Erin Roberts, R.S.A. Garcia, and Carolyn Ives Gilman.

Tor.com celebrated a milestone tenth anniversary year with an impressive retrospective anthology, *Worlds Seen in Passing*, edited by Irene Gallo. The volume of fiction was down considerably from last year but remained a strong source for quality work. Favorites included work by Simon Bestwick, S.B. Divya, Greg Egan, Daryl Gregory, James Patrick Kelly, and Rich Larson.

Also turning ten this year was literary adventure fantasy magazine, *Beneath Ceaseless Skies* (beneath-ceaseless-skies.com). They are consistently publishing some of the best fantasy work in the market. Their output falls outside the purview of this anthology, but it's well worth reading.

Celebrating its 100th issue, *Lightspeed Magazine* (lightspeedmagazine. com) published a supersized issue of the magazine that was nearly double the size of their regular releases. It included an excellent story by Sofia Samatar which never appeared in their online edition. Other notable SF works were written by Bryan Camp and Ken Liu. *Lightspeed* had a much stronger year on the fantasy side of the publication.

Uncanny Magazine (uncannymagazine.com) published a guest-edited "Disabled People Destroy Science Fiction" issue featuring fiction and non-fiction by writers who identify themselves as disabled and in 2019 they intend to launch a new YouTube channel. The best science fiction story in this year's lineup was by A.T. Greenblatt. Overall, *Uncanny* had a stronger fantasy than SF lineup this year.

GigaNotoSaurus (giganotosaurus.org) only publishes one story a month, frequently longer than you'll find in most other markets. The strongest stories here came from Vanessa Fogg and Adrian Simmons. This was Rashida J. Smith's last year as editor. Elora Gatts will take the reins in 2019.

UK veteran science fiction magazine *Interzone* (ttapress.com/interzone) took a break in early 2018 and skipped an issue, resulting in only five of the usual six print and digital issues per year. This appears to have been temporary change in schedule as the January/February 2019 issue is scheduled for publication. The publication schedule for sister magazine *Black Static* (ttapress.com/blackstatic) was likewise altered. The best stories from *Interzone* were by Gregor Hartmann and Samantha Murray.

Strange Horizons (strangehorizons.com), one of the oldest continually running online magazines, continued to publish issues on a weekly schedule. Sister magazine *Samovar* (samovar.strangehorizons.com) celebrated its first anniversary and published six new translations in 2018. They may be the only genre magazine publishing translations that includes the original version of the story as well.

Interesting science fiction can also be found outside the standard publishing ecosystem for such things, of course. Future Tense Science Fiction, a partnership between *Slate*, New America, and Arizona State University, ramped things up considerably. After publishing only two stories since the launch of the series at *Slate*, in 2018 they started publishing monthly stories around a quarterly theme. A notable feature of this series is that each story is accompanied by a response essay from a professional working in a related field. The quality here is high with excellent work by Madeline Ashby, Hannu Rajaniemi, and Mark Stasenko.

Shorter works can often be found at tech and science website Motherboard's *Terraform* (motherboard.vice.com/terraform) and within the science magazine *Nature* as *Nature Future* (nature.com/nature/articles?type=futures). *Wired Magazine* (wired.com/magazine) closed out the year by publishing a few stories from a 2019 issue on their website. For reasons mentioned in previous introductions, the online editions of these stories were considered 2018 publications for the purpose of this anthology. Notable among these were works by Adam Rogers and Martha Wells.

Just as the online and print magazines have become more similar in the way they distribute issues, the audio fiction world of free podcasts has often done the same. Not only are more print and digital magazines producing podcasts (*Asimov's*, *Clarkesworld*, *Lightspeed*, and *Uncanny*, for example), but more podcasts are offering online text versions of their stories with increasing regularity. Among these, The Escape Artists produce four of the more successful podcasts: *Escape Pod* (escapepod.org), *PodCastle* (podcastle.org), *PseudoPod* (pseudopod.org), and *Cast of Wonders* (castofwonders.org). Other interesting fiction podcasts include *Levar Burton Reads* (levarburtonpodcast.com), *The Drabblecast* (drabblecast.org), and the District of Wonders markets: *StarShipSofa* (starshipsofa.com), *Tales to Terrify* (talestoterrify.com), and *Far Fetched Fables* (farfetchedfables.com).

Additionally, a wide range of stories—sometimes focused on very specific themes and subject matters—can also be found in publications like *Abyss & Apex Magazine* (abyssapexzine.com), *Anathema* (anathemamag.com), *Andromeda Spaceways* (andromedaspaceways.com), *Aurealis* (aurealis.com.au), *Compelling Science Fiction* (compellingsciencefiction.com), *Cosmic Roots and Eldritch Shores* (cosmicrootsandeldritchshores.com), *Daily Science Fiction* (dailysciencefiction.com), *Diabolical Plots* (diabolicalplots.com), *Factor Four* (factorfourmag.com), *Fiyah* (fiyahlitmag.com), *Flash Fiction Online* (flashfictiononline.com), *Galaxy's Edge* (galaxysedge.com), *Helios Quarterly* (heliosquarterly.com), *Lady Churchill's Rosebud Wristlet* (smallbeerpress.com/lcrw), *Mithila* (mithilareview.com), *Neo-Opsis* (neo-opsis.ca), *Omenana Magazine of Africa's Speculative Fiction* (omenana.com), *On Spec* (onspecmag.wordpress.com), *Orson Scott Card's Intergalactic Medicine Show* (intergalacticmedicineshow.com), *Perihelion* (perihelionsf.com), *The Future Fire* (futurefire.net), and many more.

Anthologies, Collections, and Standalone Novellas

Anthologies had a strong year with six different titles landing stories in this year's table of contents and several more on the recommended reading list. It was a difficult call, but I think the strongest science fiction anthology of the lot was *Twelve Tomorrows* edited by Wade Roush. This latest installment in the series presented some impressive visions of the future by Elizabeth Bear, J. M. Ledgard, Ken Liu, Paul McAuley, Nnedi Okorafor, and Alastair Reynolds.

Two other anthologies were close. *Robots vs. Fairies*, edited by Dominik Parisien and Navah Wolfe, was a very strong contender and was likely the best mixed science fiction and fantasy anthology of the year. The strong lineup included top-notch science fiction by Madeline Ashby, Lavie Tidhar, and Alyssa Wong. Also interesting was *Infinity's End*—the final installment in the Infinity anthology series—edited by Jonathan Strahan. The notable stories here included works by Naomi Kritzer, Linda Nagata, Alastair Reynolds, Kelly Robson, and Peter Watts. I'm sad to see the series end, but Jonathan already has something new in the works for 2019.

Several other anthologies captured my interest this year. *2001: An Odyssey in Words*, edited by Ian Whates and Tom Hunter, was an interesting concept (all 2001 word stories) and offered enjoyable stories by Yoon Ha Lee and Ian McDonald. *A Thousand Beginnings and Endings*, edited by Ellen Oh and Elsie Chapman, explored the mythology and folklore of South and East Asia and had a great story by Aliette de Bodard. *Mechanical Animals*, edited by Selena Chambers and Jason Heller, riffs on the traditional ideals of automata to explore our strange and competitive relationship with the natural world and featured excellent work by Aliette de Bodard, Stephen Graham Jones, An Owomoyela, and Caroline M. Yoachim. *Mother of Invention,* edited by Rivqa Rafael and Tansy Rayner Roberts, featured diverse and challenging stories about gender and artificial intelligence, including some excellent works by John Chu, Seanan McGuire, and Bogi Takács. *Shades Within Us*, edited by Susan Forest and Lucas K. Law, hit themes of migration and borders and included another one of Rich Larson's excellent tales. *Women Invent the Future*, a project from Doteveryone, included a strong piece by Liz Williams.

Also important to the strength of the field are the many reprint anthologies published each year. This market is almost entirely the domain of the small press, with a few exceptions like *The Future Is Female!* edited by Lisa Yaszek and published by Library of America and the previously mentioned *Worlds Seen in Passing* retrospective of Tor.com stories. Several reprint anthologies cover the year's best spectrum, like this one. In 2018, other such volumes that included science fiction were: *The Year's Best Science Fiction: 35th Annual Collection*, edited by Gardner Dozois, *The Year's Best Science Fiction & Fantasy 2019*, edited by Rich Horton, *The Best Science Fiction and Fantasy of the Year, Volume Twelve*, edited by Jonathan Strahan, *The Best American Science Fiction and Fantasy 2018*, edited by N.K. Jemisin, series editor John

Joseph Adams, *The Year's Best Military & Adventure SF: Volume 4*, edited by David Afsharirad, *Transcendent 3: The Year's Best Transgender Speculative Fiction*, edited by Bogi Takács, and *Best of British Science Fiction 2017*, edited by Donna Scott. At this time, it appears as though Gardner's series will not be assigned to a new editor, ending the series at thirty-five volumes. *The Very Best of the Best: 35 Years of The Year's Best Science Fiction*, completed before his death, was published posthumously.

Single author collections were very common in 2018, numbering in the hundreds if you go by ISFDB.org and primarily originating from small press publishers. Some of the most notable include: *The Sacerdotal Owl and Three Other Long Tales* by Michael Bishop; *An Agent of Utopia* by Andy Duncan; *How Long 'til Black Future Month?* by N. K. Jemisin; *The Promise of Space and Other Stories* by James Patrick Kelly; *Tomorrow Factory* by Rich Larson; *Ambiguity Machines and Other Stories* by Vandana Singh; and *The Future Is Blue* by Catherynne M. Valente. No favorites from this lot, as they're all great.

On the novella front, Tor.com Books, Tachyon Publications, and Subterranean continue to be at the front of the field. Tor.com Books is by far the most prolific publisher of standalone novellas (and occasional novelettes) in the field and featured excellent work by Brooke Bolander, Ian McDonald, Kelly Robson, and Martha Wells. Tachyon published another excellent work by Peter Watts, *The Freeze-Frame Revolution*. My favorite of Subterranean's 2018 lineup was *The Tea Master and the Detective* by Aliette de Bodard. I wouldn't be surprised to see any of these on award ballots this year.

I'd also like to take a moment to point people towards Twelfth Planet Press. *Icefall* by Stephanie Gunn is a work that might well sail below the radar for many readers and deserves more attention.

The 2018 Scorecard

For those interested in tracking the sources of the stories selected this year:

	Stories Included	Percentage
Magazines	17	58.6%
Anthologies	11	37.9%
Collections	1	3.4%

These stories represent seventeen different sources, up four from last year. Online magazines have eleven of the stories, up one over last year. Print magazines remained the same. Anthologies and collections each gained one.

Short stories did considerably better this year, placing eighteen on my list, up from thirteen last year. Novelettes were down from eleven to eight and novellas up from two to three. The volume of short stories allowed for an increase from twenty-four stories to twenty-six stories in total.

And from my Recommended Reading List:

	Stories Included	Percentage
Magazines	27	50.0%
Anthologies	16	29.6%
Collections	1	1.9%
Standalone	10	18.5%

The standalone category primarily consists of individually published novellas from publishers like Tor.com Books, Tachyon, and Subterranean. Several of those would have been worthy additions to this book but were logistically impossible due to size or availability issues. Novellas continue to be a strong source of some of the best work being written today.

Overall, while I may worry about the business side of the field, I thought 2018 was a good year for science fiction, but an unusual one in that fewer of my favorites came from what I would consider the usual suspects. It's not that they had an off year, but more that others published some very pleasant surprises. The landscape is changing in interesting ways and that's a good thing.

The Most Interesting Development for Short Science Fiction

We've been exporting SF to other parts of the world for decades, but it wasn't until more recently that significant numbers of works from outside the usual US/UK/Canada/Australia sphere have been making their way here. As an editor and reader, this makes me particularly happy. Science fiction is at its best when it is incorporating and being challenged by new ideas and perspectives. This recent influx will be of benefit to the future of the field both domestic and abroad.

Translations, in particular, have been increasingly common in US magazines. *Clarkesworld* has regularly published Chinese SF for over four years and will add Korean SF in 2019. *Samovar*—affiliated with *Strange Horizons*—has regularly published translations since 2017, and now *Future Science Fiction* will be featuring them as well. Occasional works in translation have also been appearing in *Asimov's, Lightspeed Magazine, Tor.com, Uncanny Magazine,* and many more.

Translation or internationally-focused anthologies were also quite common in 2018 and represented by works such as *Future Fiction: New Dimensions in International Science Fiction*, edited by Bill Campbell and Francesco Verso; *Solarpunk: Ecological and Fantastical Stories in a Sustainable World* (translated from Portuguese), edited by Phoebe Wagner and Brontë Christopher Wieland; *Apex Book of World SF 5*, edited by Cristina Jurado; *Best Asian SF*—despite the title, this is an original anthology and not a "best of" in the traditional sense—, edited by Rajat Chaudhuri; *Zion's Fiction*, edited by Sheldon Teitelbaum and Emanuel Lottem; and *Speculative Japan 4*, edited by Edward Lipsett. I'm aware of four more anthologies scheduled for 2019: *Broken Stars: Contemporary Chinese Science Fiction in Translation*, edited by Ken Liu; *Readymade Bodhisatva* (South Korean SF), edited by Sunyoung Park and Sang Joon Park; *Gollancz Book of South Asian Science Fiction*, edited by Tarun K. Saint; and *Best Asian Short Stories 2019*, edited by Hisham Bustani.

If you are interested in learning more about what is happening with translated works, I highly recommend reading Rachel Cordasco's SF in Translation blog (sfintranslation.com). It's filled with interesting news and reviews and is definitely the best source of information on this subject on the web.

Notable 2018 Awards

The 76th World Science Fiction Convention, Worldcon 76, was held in San Jose, California, from August 15th to August 20th, 2018. The 2018 Hugo Awards, presented at Worldcon 76, were: Best Novel, *The Stone Sky* by N. K. Jemisin; Best Novella, "All Systems Red" by Martha Wells; Best Novelette, "The Secret Life of Bots" by Suzanne Palmer; Best Short Story, "Welcome to Your Authentic Indian Experience™" by Rebecca Roanhorse; Best Series, World of the Five Gods, by Lois McMaster Bujold; Best Graphic Story, *Monstress, Volume 2: The Blood*, written by Marjorie M. Liu, illustrated by Sana Takeda; Best Related Work, *No Time to Spare: Thinking About What Matters,* by Ursula K. Le Guin; Best Professional Editor, Long Form, Sheila E. Gilbert; Best Professional Editor, Short Form, Lynne M. Thomas & Michael Damian Thomas; Best Professional Artist, Sana Takeda; Best Dramatic Presentation (short form), *The Good Place*: "The Trolley Problem"; Best Dramatic Presentation (long form), *Wonder Woman*; Best Semiprozine, *Uncanny*; Best Fanzine, *File 770*; Best Fancast, *Ditch Diggers*; Best Fan Writer, Sarah Gailey; Best Fan Artist, Geneva Benton; plus the John W. Campbell Award for Best New Writer, Rebecca Roanhorse, and The World

Science Fiction Society (WSFS) Award for Best Young Adult Book, *Akata Warrior* by Nnedi Okorafor.

The 2017 Nebula Awards, presented at a banquet at the Pittsburgh Marriott City Center in Pittsburgh, Pennsylvania, on May 19, 2018, were: Best Novel, *The Stone Sky* by N.K. Jemisin; Best Novella, "All Systems Red" by Martha Wells; Best Novelette, "A Human Stain" by Kelly Robson; Best Short Story, "Welcome to Your Authentic Indian Experience™" by Rebecca Roanhorse; Ray Bradbury Award, *Get Out*; the Andre Norton Award, *The Art of Starving* by Sam J. Miller; the Kate Wilhelm Solstice Award, Gardner Dozois and Sheila Williams; the Kevin O' Donnell Jr. Service to SFWA Award, Bud Sparhawk; and the Damon Knight Memorial Grand Master Award, Peter S. Beagle.

The 2018 World Fantasy Awards, presented at a banquet on November 4, 2018, at the Renaissance Baltimore Harborplace Hotel in Baltimore, Maryland, during the Forty-fourth Annual World Fantasy Convention, were: Best Novel, (tie) *The Changeling* by Victor LaValle and *Jade City* by Fonda Lee; Best Long Fiction, "Passing Strange" by Ellen Klages; Best Short Fiction, "The Birding: A Fairy Tale" by Natalia Theodoridou; Best Collection, *The Emerald Circus* by Jane Yolen; Best Anthology, *The New Voices of Fantasy*, edited by Peter S. Beagle and Jacob Weisman; Best Artist, Gregory Manchess; Special Award (Professional), Harry Brockway, Patrick McGrath, and Danel Olson for Writing Madness; Special Award (Non-Professional), Justina Ireland and Troy L. Wiggins for *FIYAH: Magazine of Black Speculative Fiction*. Plus Lifetime Achievement Awards, Charles de Lint and Elizabeth Wollheim.

The 2018 John W. Campbell Memorial Award was won by: *The Genius Plague* by David Walton.

The 2018 Theodore Sturgeon Memorial Award for Best Short Story was won by: "Don't Press Charges and I Won't Sue" by Charlie Jane Anders.

The 2018 Philip K. Dick Memorial Award went to: *Bannerless* by Carrie Vaughn.

The 2018 Arthur C. Clarke Award was won by: *Dreams Before the Start of Time* by Anne Charnock.

The 2017 James Tiptree, Jr. Memorial Award was won by: *Who Runs the World?* by Virginia Bergin.

The 2018 Sidewise Award for Alternate History went to (Long Form): *Once There Was A Way* by Bryce Zabel and (Short Form): "Zigeuner" by Harry Turtledove.

The 2018 WSFA Small Press Award: "The Secret Life of Bots" by Suzanne Palmer.

In Memoriam

Among those the field lost in 2018 are:

Ursula K. Le Guin, SFWA Grand Master, winner of six Hugos, six Nebula Awards, three World Fantasy Awards, three James Tiptree, Jr. Awards, and many other honors, author of classics such as *The Dispossessed, The Left Hand of Darkness, The Lathe of Heaven*, and the Earthsea series; **Jack Ketchum**, World Horror Grand Master, winner of three Bram Stoker Awards; **John Anthony West**, short stories in *F&SF* and *Omni*, **Bill Crider**, winner of the Sidewise Award; **Victor Milán**, Prometheus Award-winning writer; **Peter Nicholls**, Hugo Award winner and editor of *The Science Fiction Encyclopedia*; **Kate Wilhelm**, two-time winner of the Hugo Award, helped establish SFWA and the Clarion Workshop, Science Fiction Hall of Fame member; **Mary Rosenblum**, Compton Crook and Sidewise Award winner; **Karen Anderson**, author and illustrator; **David Bischoff**, Nebula Award nominee, novelist, screenwriter; **Claudia De Bella**, Argentinian author and translator; **Palle Juul Holm**, Danish critic and author (as Bernhard Ribbeck), published the first Danish educational text for science fiction; **Raymond Reid Collins**, stories in *F&SF*; **Susan Ann Protter**, literary agent; **Philip Roth**, winner of the Sidewise Award and Man Booker International Prize for Lifetime Achievement; **Gardner Dozois**, fifteen-time winner of the Hugo Award for Best Editor, two-time winner of the Nebula Award, Science Fiction Hall of Fame member, editor of *Asimov's Science Fiction* from 1984-2004, editor of The Year's Best Science Fiction series; **Christopher Stasheff**, best known for his humorous Gallowglass/Warlock novels; **Steve Sneyd**, Science Fiction Poetry Association Grand Master; **Steve Ditko**, comic artist and writer, artist and co-creator (with Stan Lee) of Spider-Man and Doctor Strange; **Harlan Ellison**, SFWA Grand Master, winner of seven Hugos, four Nebula Awards, a World Fantasy Award, and many other honors, Science Fiction Hall of Fame member, edited *Dangerous Visions* and *Again, Dangerous Visions*, author of the *Star Trek* episode "The City on the Edge of Forever"; **Christine Nöstlinger**, received the Hans Christian Andersen Medal for her lasting contribution to children's literature; **Karen Simonyan**, pioneer of Armenian science fiction; **Michael Scott Rohan**, Scottish fantasy and science fiction author; **H.M. Hoover**, winner of the Golden Duck Awards' Hal Clement division for young adult literature; **Michael Sissons**, literary agent and anthologist; **K.C. Ball**, winner of the Writers of the Future Contest; **Sven Wernström**, Swedish author; **Robert Bausch**, winner of Fellowship of Southern Writers Award; **Greg Stafford**, game designer, co-founder of Chaosium, Origins Award Hall of Fame member; **Pat Lupoff**, Hugo Award winner for Best Fanzine; **Dave Duncan**, two-time winner of the Aurora Award, Canadian Science Fiction and Fantasy Hall of Fame member; **Jin Yong**, Chinese author and one of the most popular wuxia writers of all time; **Domingo Santos**, Spanish author and co-founder of *Neuva Dimensión*; **Achim Mehnert**, German author and one of the founders of ColoniaCon in Köln, Germany; **Stan Lee**, created and co-created the Fantastic Four, Hulk, Thor, Iron Man, the X-Men, Daredevil, Doctor Strange, Spider-Man, and more, winner of the Inkpot, Eisner, Kirby, and Saturn Awards; **Emeka Walter Dinjos**, short story author; **Billie Sue Mosiman**, author and editor.

In Closing

I always try to end these introductions on a positive note. I must say that the above list of people we love and lost in 2018 makes that a bit more challenging, but as we mourn those have left us, we also must celebrate the new writers making their way through the field.

Each year, I try to single out a new/new-ish author that has impressed me, and I believe to be someone you should be watching for. This year, I'm selecting someone who might just have been the most prolific author publishing short fiction in 2018. I published several stories by D.A. Xiaolin Spires (daxiaolinspires.wordpress.com) last year, but at some point, it started to feel like she was regularly announcing new sales or appearing in something I was reading. Volume is not necessarily connected to quality, but she's regularly accomplishing both and only getting better. I look forward to reading more of her stories in the future. I hope you will too!

Simone Heller lives on an island in the Danube River, in a town near Munich, Germany. For most of her life, she's been lucky enough to make a living from science fiction by selling it, translating it, and writing it. She almost became a biologist, but graduated in linguistics and cultural studies instead. Most of her time is spent in fictional worlds, with travels in the real world whenever possible. And the rest is browsing history. Find her at www.missnavigator.com.

WHEN WE WERE STARLESS

Simone Heller

When we set out to weave a new world from the old, broken one, we knew we pledged the lives of our clutches and our clutches' clutches to wandering the wastes. Season after season, our windreaders find us a path through the poison currents, and our herds scuttle over molten glass seas and pockmarked plains into the haunted places where the harvest is plentiful. We move swiftly, outpacing vapors and packs of wild dogs alike, leaving only the prints of our tails in acrid sands.

This wasn't entirely true; we left other things, too, dear and precious. But this was how it was told by the elders when the veiled moon was high and we were cuddled up with our cozy-stones.

On the moonless nights, though, they spoke of ghosts: beckoning wraithlights and treacherous silent ones, and all the other types we had classified; and the multitudes that still waited for our soothing hands out among the ruins. They spoke of ghosts like they were the ones to handle them, when it was always me.

So when Warden Renke strode up to my resting place on the outskirts of the half-shaped camp, the stark white paint of her dread-screen slapped on in haste, I knew what she needed.

"Someone found another ghost, yes?" My longing glance went to the grub'n'root stew some kind soul had left next to the pack serving as my pillow, still lukewarm from a hot stone placed at the bottom of the bowl. I reached for the harness with my tools instead.

"It's in the dome structure to the East. Asper ventured there in search of the light metals his weaver prefers. He meant no harm; he knows we need every spare part he can churn out. Said he saw strange lights."

"Alright." It could be nothing, or just another minor ghost which I would have laid to rest before the deep-night chill encroached. I stood and fingered my engraved pliers, waiting for Renke to disappear like they all did when it came to my work. But the Warden fixed me, her pupils mere slits.

"Eat your fill first, Blessed. We need you to stay strong. Truss won't be able to step in for you."

And he hadn't stepped in for years now, since the day he became a respected member of the tribe, but I didn't say that.

"How is he?" I asked instead.

Renke looked back to where the first weaverspun tentpoles came together, as if she could see the pallet there, the thin mat of woven vines stained with blood. "He's barely conscious. You should visit him as soon as you've cleansed yourself."

It could well be my last chance. One shift in the weather, and we'd be running again, leaving our excess baggage behind. Truss never passed up an opportunity to teach a lesson, so it would probably be me he'd ask for the Song of Passing, and I was afraid it would be more than I could take. People's hearts, as hardened and as barred as they were, were a different matter from the hearts of ghosts. I took one big mouthful of stew and swallowed. "I'll take care of this ghost, Warden. This spot will serve as a fine resting place and see us recovered to full strength."

Renke cast a doubtful glance down at her freshly spun leg brace, for she, too, hadn't walked away unscathed. "Report to me when it's done. I'll put harvesting on hold, so hurry. No way to know how long the winds will grant us."

The run-in with the rustbreed had not been my fault. I was a good enough scout—I scoured inaccessible ruins for scarce materials, and I never ran the tribe into the lairs of the befouled crablion or let anyone's mind become ghost-shifted. But when the heat-baked ground of a salt flat we were crossing was suddenly riddled with burrower holes, a full legion of the writhing, rearing centipedal creatures already upon us, all I could do was to change the gentle hum of the Lope Concord to the jarring trill of the Rush and find us a path out of this trap. The air had been filled with the dry stick sounds of the rustbreed's milling legs and the sharp smell that went for communication among them. But for all their legs, we were the better runners, and we made it. Barely. The hindquarters of our sole gearbeast were a fused mass of metal and dried fluids from a rustbreed feeder, and I didn't want to think about Truss' side, which had been similarly exposed. Others, like Renke, had been burned badly, too, but he had been the only one to suffer a bite and get the corrosive substance under his scales.

The ruined place I had led us into was vast and violent, some of its canyons carved by storms and some designed by its unholy builders long ago. We had been following these shadowed paths for hours, paths I would have preferred to scout before bringing in the tribe. As it was, I had to lay ghosts to rest on the run, which was a contradiction in and of itself.

I skirted the camp, listening to the whirring sounds of dozens of weavers busily spinning pots and ropes and all the things we would need to shelter and recover. Bits of Asper's cleansing chant drifted over the jagged scenery. He would be fine. Surely he had run at first sight, not even checking if it was a real ghost, or just a reflection on an unexpectedly untarnished surface. It took more than that to risk ghost-shifting. But the tribe was skittish. He would sing half of the night.

Out of the rubble and partially collapsed buildings around the camp, two ruined structures protruded into the upper airs like teeth, broken and half-melted. Loose material flung up by the poison winds had merged with the original walls like flowstone.

No such thing marred the surface of the dome. Its sides were certainly blackened like everything else, and even blacker holes yawned where some of its hexagonal segments were missing, but the telltale pockmarks to determine downwind shelter were nowhere to be seen. It loomed over the rubble as if to claim some things were unbreakable, no matter what. We would prove it wrong, if I had my way and we stayed. Because that was what we did; we cleansed the ruins by harvesting them, by feeding their very substance to our weavers and rendering it pure and useful to be sold to the settler townships up in the mountains.

Only this time we would need every scrap for ourselves to survive.

The entrance to the dome structure was a narrow, curved tube. When I reached a barrier of two thin, clear panes of glass, they swished apart almost soundlessly, releasing a draft of cool air from within. Asper must have been desperate if he had gone beyond that. I took a moment to camouflage and darted through, curling my tail in case of nasty surprises; this would have been a stupid way to lose it. At some point in the past, granules of debris had blown in, but the layer was thin and petered out after a few paces. When the portal closed smoothly behind me, one side grated a little bit on a piece of gravel that must have been displaced by my feet.

My gaze was drawn upwards. The air of the dome was still, the evening light eerily peaceful as it filtered through the once transparent segments. Gone was the cleansing singsong, gone were the high winds keening in cavity-riddled structures. It wasn't that there was no indication of violence in this place: the tail end of a colossal metal tube still hanging from steel cords fastened around its tapered nose had fallen and destroyed all manners of tables and glass cases on the floor. But it was as if it had happened centuries ago, and peace had been found in its arrangement.

Anyone with a healthy fear of ghosts would have gone looking for the one whose invisible hand had moved the glass panes. I knew better. I was not after an inferior ghost tied to this entrance—my prey would be haunting the vast space, where the light was murky and the shadows were glistening. I went straight in to look for the veins that spoke of ghost activity, for the hiding places of ghost organs, stored away in boxes for protection.

Uncomfortably chilly layers of air enshrouded glittering heaps of shards. Once, I might have felt out of place, an unwelcome disturbance. But I had left my fear of ghosts behind like an old skin a long time ago, and what I had found instead was the unforeseen, and sometimes pure beauty.

The tribe never knew. To them, beauty meant nothing. I could have shown them the brightest colors and patterns on my skin, and all they ever wanted were the dulled hues of sand and ashes, all the better to pick clean ruins like this one.

In the end I found absolutely no sign of a ghost inhabiting this space. I resigned myself to take care of the entrance and let go of my camouflage.

When I turned around there was something where there had been no one. Like a person, a solitary figure leaned on one of the undamaged glass cases. The light pooled strangely around it, and when I flicked my tongue, the smell, the heat, and the heartbeat were all my own and told me no other living being was in here with me.

"Hello, little explorer," it said with a clear, slightly hollow voice.

The ways ghosts reacted to people were mostly limited to precise, fatal attacks, if they were of the aggressive kind, or simple things like manipulating doors or following every move with a single red eye in the shell they animated, observant even in afterlife.

This one drifted over to me, mimicking a walk on two legs as best it could, lacking a tail. Its whole body was obscured by a bulky, silvery layer of clothing, its head round like a bowl. It seemed insubstantial, a ghost of subtle dangers. My breath quickened, but I stood my ground. When there was but a pace between us, I lifted my hand to rap my knuckles against the semi-translucent head-bowl with just a hint of bright eyes behind. The ghost quivered slightly as my fingers passed right through it, and on my skin I felt an almost imperceptible sensation of heat.

"Now, now, you're a cheeky one, aren't you?" It turned with me as I began to walk around it, cautiously, looking for the veins tethering its body to its heart. "I understand you're curious, and I encourage you heartily to experiment. But your experience will be better if you refrain from touching me."

The way it reacted to me, seemed to talk directly to me, was disconcerting. I felt a lump grow in my throat. Even now there were no veins. They could still be under the floor, but I somehow doubted it. I had seen a few Untethered before, even sought them out. They didn't need to animate objects, but moved through thin air with a fluid grace. I knew they could be laid to rest with a bit of work; I just chose not to whenever possible. The world always felt lessened by their passing.

"I don't see a tag on you, little explorer." The ghost's voice came from slightly above. So maybe it had stored its lungs somewhere. Finding them would at least be a start. "Would you mind telling me your name to avoid confusion?"

I looked up at the strange specter in surprise. No amount of singing would redeem me in the eyes of my tribe if I volunteered my name to a ghost. Granted, I did talk to ghosts. It was a one-sided conversation, a game of pretending at its best. This ghost wouldn't even register my name, a name nobody had bothered to use since I became Blessed. What harm could it do, to whisper and hear it swallowed up by the still air of the dome?

I flicked my tongue. "Mink. My name is Mink."

The round head bobbed enthusiastically. "Welcome, Mink! Now, would you like to see the stars?"

A flutter of anxiety rose in my stomach. This was more than a mere reaction; this was interaction. For a short moment, I felt this was not a ghost, but something else altogether, something alive and very old and dangerous. I fought my unease with a snort. "Stars? You're trying to trick me with fancy tales the elders tell to hatchlings, yes?"

"That's what most come for, but we can certainly look at something else. The rocket, maybe? Or one of the landers?" It drifted off a little bit, hands clasped behind its back. With a swooshing noise, the soft glow of wraith-lights grew throughout the dome, in at least five different places. There were sounds as well, sounds I recognized: ghosts, many upon many of them, animating contraptions, whining in high voices. A legion of ghosts, seemingly springing into action in unison.

I shielded my eyes and staggered back, caught myself on one of the tables, shaken. Such a conglomerate of ghosts would take days to be laid to rest. Our wounded might not have days; they depended on the herds' output before the windreader called us off.

The untethered ghost had moved to hover next to me. "You seem upset, little explorer Mink. Is there something wrong? Something I can do for you?"

I held my face still buried in my hands and looked at the ghost through my fingers. Was it trying to help me? All I had ever been taught told me to run now, but I had never been the student Truss or the other elders had envisioned. "That's impossible . . ."

"Let's try some music to lift your spirits." The ghost drifted back and forth expectantly. When nothing happened and I began to wonder if I should have said or done something, it heaved a great sigh. "Uh . . . I'm very sorry, little explorer Mink . . . some things seem to be amiss here. I thought I had just the right music for you. But now I can't play any at all, and I just don't seem to be able to fix this defect. Ah. I shouldn't be all sad when I need to cheer you up, right? Don't you worry. I'll find a work-around."

"You miss your music?" I had always suspected some ghosts liked music, and tried to use this to my advantage. But this ghost had offered me consolation; it seemed genuinely upset it couldn't act on it. I didn't seek an advantage when I suggested: "I could sing for you."

Truss would have called me ghost-shifted or straight out mad at this point. I had nothing yet, not even a classification, just a growing sense of unease and a lot of work cut out for me. But there were many ways to a ghost's heart, and a nonaggressive, calming approach might work just as well as exhausting oneself by tearing out every wall panel for clues. Or maybe I was just trying to rationalize my own desperate need for a song.

It took some time to find my voice, because, yes, I had sung to ghosts before, but never for a whole legion of them. Soon enough I found the center of the dome was an excellent place to stand and sing.

I did not sing a ghost song, but one of ours. The melody of the Paean of Manifest Horizons rose strongly in the empty air, and it was more uplifting than the somber tones of the Song of Passing I usually sang in the forsaken places of the world, while making them a little bit more forsaken. It wasn't until after the first verse I noticed the second voice accompanying mine in perfect harmony. At first I was puzzled and amused to sing alongside those hidden lungs of the ghost. Then I felt my spirit lifted in a way I had not expected: not to chant alone amongst the rubble of a past age, but to have a voice other than mine echoing, countering, running ahead in joy. When I reshaped the tune into a jubilating variation and the ghost followed suit without pause, though, the dread feeling crept upon me again, made my voice veer off into a warning warble. I faltered, and the ghost sang the ending notes on its own.

Ghosts were the remnants of the long-dead past, and one thing they—or at least all the ones I had encountered—could not do, was evolve, learn, grasp something new. This one had not only learned a song in a few heart-beats, but even how to mold it in the unique way of my tribe. And I finally had my classification and my name, and the absolute certainty that I would not be the one to lay this ghost to rest, or any of its manifestations, for that was what I faced: one vast ghost of many forms, one fabled entity that ruled this whole place. An annihilator of tribes. A Clusterhaunt.

"What an amazing talent," it said, lifting its hand to its chest, where of course no heart resided. "Thank you!"

I tried to swallow against my dried-up throat, but only produced a stran-gled squawk. When I fled the dome, the ghost called after me: "Little explorer Mink, do you really have to leave already? You haven't seen the stars yet!"

Terrified as I was, I would have crashed into the grating panes of glass. But the ghost moved this extension of itself out of my way, and I stumbled out before it could reconsider.

This was what was going to happen: the camp would be left to the winds, half-shaped pots and tents melting into the ruined landscape. The marrow of our wounded would feed whatever happened to stumble upon this site, our crip-pled gearbeast would hold its lone wake. I would paint the warning sigil of our tribe on a nearby wall in green permastain, so that no scout in their right mind would ever set foot in the dome again. And we would flee this place, maybe leave a trail of our injured as we ran, and we would never look back, never won-der what we had lost, not only in lives, but also in not taking the rare materials from the dome, in not observing the Clusterhaunt and learning about its ways.

Or at least try to coexist. I had fled on impulse, fueled by the horrors our lore spoke of. It didn't seem so bad now that I had time to think and didn't see a spectral host coming after me from the dome. But how could I suggest this to a tribe who, by that very same lore, left its weakest members behind to die? I would be declared suicidal, a menace, unheard.

For we were survivors, mere survivors; we never managed to be more than that, and some didn't even manage that much. We told ourselves that we made a difference, that we shaped a world, but one look at this ruined vastness told the truth: we didn't change a thing, and all our sacrifices were just to survive another day. It was enough, mostly, as long as we pretended it didn't tear our hearts out.

I was perched on the remains of a toppled roof structure and looked at the bug-catcher lights dotting the camp's perimeter in the dark. They would glow long after we were gone.

When I finally trotted over to the ring of lights, I vocalized a lesser warning sequence. "Scout incoming," I saluted the guard I knew would wait in the shadows beyond. "I need to see Truss. Get someone to apply the dread-screen on him. I'm unclean."

She hissed gruff acknowledgement, and by the time I entered the camp proper every weaver had been moved out of my way, as well as sleeping mats and cooking utensils for good measure. A young herder still gesturing her weaver backwards lifted the eight-legged metal creature up into her arms and staggered away under its weight, even if it was far out of range of whatever evil emanations of mine she might fear. I saw Asper, too, hovering on the fringe of the camp and obviously eager for news, his weaver easy to spot because he was the only one to dread-screen its carapace for extra security. At Truss' resting place, one of the hunters simply smeared the remaining paint in her hands onto her face and throat before I came too close.

On Truss, the swirling white patterns had been applied with more care. He looked bad underneath, skin sagging in stiff folds, eyes sunken. His side was bandaged, the color of the rust-like substance eating away at him already bleeding through.

"Teacher," I said, kneeling next to him.

He lifted one feeble hand, as if to keep me from propping him up. "Talk to the elders, little foster-hatch. Why come to me? They are the ones who decide our way."

They knew only one way, but I didn't say that. "You're one of them, old man. How are you? I was gone so long, and I was afraid you wouldn't . . ."

"Warden told you that, didn't she?" He coughed, and I watched the stains on his bandage deepen. "To keep you on your toes. She knows you're prone to getting distracted."

At that, he winked weakly at me. We had always kept my bolder adventures between the two of us, as we had our differences. I wanted badly to take his hand, to feel if there was any strength left in him, but he had never been fond of touch. Or sympathy.

"I'm not dead yet." His voice was a low rasp. "Won't run for days, but if the winds are willing and you're keeping us safe, I'll eat the stuff that's trying to eat me . . . just you watch."

At that, I felt all color bleed out of my skin and fought hard to keep Truss from noticing. I had been selfish to come here, just so that I could say goodbye. "It might not happen," I offered softly. "It might not happen fast enough. And so many of us are wounded and exhausted. Even I would be hard-pressed to run now."

Part of me wanted to tell him about the Clusterhaunt. But he hadn't scouted for years, and in his day Truss had never been one to indulge in the presence of ghosts. I knew what he would have to say, and I didn't want to hear it.

He said it anyway. "Don't concern yourself with our weak and wounded, little foster-hatch. We're prepared to stay behind, knowing the tribe will survive. The elders are aware of that. They know how to handle it."

"But they don't *have* to handle it," I whispered.

Suddenly I felt Truss' hand on mine, cold and brittle. He started to say something, but in this moment, Renke strode up to us, the windreader and the other two elders in tow.

"What news do you bring, Blessed?" she asked. "Is your work done?"

I looked up at her, then back to Truss. There were days when I found joy in my job, when I felt I brought peace to the ghosts of old and betterment to the brand-new world. Today it felt like laying to rest everything I loved. "My work is never done."

Renke came closer than most dared when I was unclean, to stare down at me. "The herders are awaiting my command. Is it safe now, or do we move?"

There was no invitation to debate, no room for experiments. I only needed to utter the word; the decision was already made, had already been made since the day we set out to wander the wastes.

I fought to keep my unruly colors under control. None of the tribe could actually read them, but Truss had seen most of the spectrum while teaching me, and even with eyes half-closed he might be watching.

Renke's crest rose halfway in impatience. I could feel the eyes of the herders on me, all prepared to set out, their weavers protected in the crooks of their tails. They would never admit that survival was not always enough.

I squeezed Truss' hand one last time and finally got up to look the Warden in the eye. "Send them out," I said. "This place is safe."

The night sky was a black abyss sucking my gaze upwards, and with it went my bravado and determination. No veiled moon shed its light upon the ruins; the stars, its fabled lesser cousins, were nothing but a story to ease the weight of the dark.

I did not deserve to even think of a soothing story, because I had embarked on the darkest of tales.

Clusterhaunt. Few claimed to have seen one, the even fewer reliable witnesses weren't keen on telling what they had seen. Clusterhaunts were said to be the rarest and mightiest of ghosts, spiteful of the living, and oh-so-strong, the most powerful ghost-shifters, heart-concealers, mind-mimickers.

Tribe-vanishers.

But I had told my lie, and I needed it to turn into truth. So instead of getting back to my lonely resting place, I went to the dome once more. "Residual energies" would keep the herders from entering only for so long; then I would either have found this heart or failed them all.

First I jammed a stone I had brought under the glass panes of the entrance. I didn't want to get trapped inside, and disabling the ghost's extensions piece by piece was one way I figured I could counter its Clusterhaunt abilities. I took my lamp into the pitch-black dome and began to turn over every larger piece of rubble to find a hint of ghostly veins, organs, anything.

All too soon a familiar pale glow came up behind me.

"Little explorer Mink! What a pleasant surprise to have you back!"

I looked up at the bowl-shaped head bobbing above the silvery suit. Why would it choose this appearance when it ruled so many forms? Why not a more threatening one?

It hovered closer. "You were gone so fast last time, I thought you maybe didn't like it. But you've got them both—Curiosity and Spirit. Want to see them? They're right here, brought back to Earth after their duty was done."

Wraithlight flared to life halfway through the dome to illuminate the shapes of two battered gearbeasts. Their odd wheel-legs seemed sturdy enough, but after a closer look, I found them to be perplexingly impractical: their broad backs were plastered with strange contraptions, no room for stowage at all. They wouldn't carry even one of our wounded.

"You'll find the whole story of Curiosity and Spirit on your personal Memory Vault," the ghost went on. "Please don't forget it next time you leave. It helps you relive your whole experience in here at home."

I ignored the gearbeasts, but the ghost kept following me. "Have you lost something?" it wanted to know. "May I help you? Just ask away!" as if it was a game Clusterhaunts liked to play. I wasn't here to talk, though.

There were just not that many alternatives. No wall panels to peel off the glass-like sides of the dome, no secret compartments embedded in the smooth, hard floor. The rubble under the fallen tail of the metal tube the ghost had called a rocket was a big pile of shards, and even the bases of the undamaged tables and cases were solid. So maybe talking *was* how I'd get to the heart of this ghost.

I turned very slowly. "You'd answer all my questions? Really?"

"Sure. That's what I'm here for." The ghost hovered expectantly.

I swallowed. I was a scout, not a master of eloquence. This could go horribly wrong. "Where is your heart?"

Among all the reactions I had anticipated, I surely hadn't expected the ghost's pronounced shoulders to sink. "Ah," it said in a somewhat small voice. "Well, you already saw on your first visit that I am not like you. And a heart is among the things that separate us." Its light grew dim. "Alas, I guess one could say my heart is up among the stars? That's where I always wanted to be, so maybe that's a justified notion."

So the ghost really liked its tall tales, liked them so much it spun its heart-concealing fabrications around them in a way that made me feel all wistful. I could have asked about its veins and lungs next, or any other part of ghost anatomy a good scout knew to look out for. But the only thing I seemed to remember was how it had tried to comfort me earlier, and somehow that made everything much more complicated.

It had diligently shuffled after me, and I was looking at its blurry form through a thin sheet of clear material mounted on a table between us. "What are you called, then?" I asked finally.

The ghost lifted its hand and dropped it again. "Oh, I . . . nobody ever calls me anything. I'm just here for your service. And on a better day, this should display the orbits of the main celestial bodies. It's in maintenance mode. I apologize for your inconvenience."

"Nonsense." I felt angry all of a sudden, and not just because I wasn't making any progress here, apart from trying to befriend a ghost. "People also don't call me anything since the Blessing came upon me. But I'm more than the service I render."

"I'm afraid that I am not."

I crossed my arms and hissed in frustration. Even those old gearbeasts had been named, however strangely. I could do better. "I'd like to call you Orion, then, if I may."

It just hovered there, frozen.

"I mean, we're not close enough for me to know your gender," I added. "So it's just a suggestion, yes?"

"It's a brilliant suggestion!" The ghost beamed, radiating brightness. "Orion . . . that's very considerate!"

I thought so myself. It was a name from the same old tales that told of the stars.

"Thank you, little explorer Mink. I'm attaching my name to all Memory Vaults now."

And in the newly brilliant light of Orion I saw something, off to the side. Something that shouldn't have been here, and yet there it was.

Inside one of the glass cases, bathed in wraithlight and completely still, sat a weaver.

"Don't touch the exhibit, please!"

I had taken the weaver out and set it on the floor, where it had very frustratingly not shown the slightest inclination to move. Clearly, it hadn't been able to bask in a long time.

"Little explorer. Your interest in this ATU shows how bright you are. But I counted 384 defects in here already, and you really shouldn't add . . ."

I gestured at the weaver. "What did you call that?"

"People call them space spiders, but officially it's an Advance Terraforming Unit." Orion drifted to another thin glass-like sheet, this one larger, mounted on the floor. "Come along! See them in action."

The weaver sat motionless. I would fetch this prize for my tribe, a new heirloom to complement our herds. But I also wanted to know how it had ended up in a glass case. Reluctantly, I followed the ghost.

"Still no music." Orion contemplated the large glass-like screen. "I'm sorry."

"I am sorry for adding another defect," I said, and I meant it. As much as Orion tried to make up for his failing contraptions with enthusiasm, I could still sense his distress. "Shall we sing again?"

I did not feel like it. I couldn't see any horizons manifesting themselves in my near future. I was still here to lay Orion to rest, the sooner the better. Had I stumbled upon him while advance-scouting, I would have turned my back and looked for another harvesting ground. But this was not an option with the tribe camping on the threshold, cultivating their superstitions.

"Maybe later, little explorer Mink. For now it will do, the display works just fine. Look."

At first, I saw nothing; nothing I hadn't seen before with minor ghosts. Ephemeral colors danced through the glass, almost too quick for the eye to follow. Then the whole screen, larger than myself, was filled with the image of a weaver. I sat on my haunches to get a better look. I understood now: Orion was showing me a vision.

"Moving mode; printing mode; charging mode," Orion said while the weaver flickered through a series of motions, completely translucent, so I could see its intricate inner workings. This was followed by an impossibly long line of weavers scuttling up a smooth ramp, then fire and smoke. "When the ATUs set out to terraform other worlds, they are equipped to deal with every hostile surrounding, to transform every unusual or even hazardous material into something useful," Orion said, and I slumped to the floor, curling my tail around my legs. "They are constructed semiautonomous, with modes to work on individual projects, to collaborate, or to be operated by a higher-level controller."

I must admit I wasn't able to follow his tale, but then I had never worked with a weaver, so what did I know? The images drew me in. Weavers glinting like gems in front of a profound blackness. Weavers swarming at structures I had never imagined. Weavers working away at something that looked like the dome I found myself in, but under two bright bluish suns.

"These are other worlds?" I asked. I saw them, but I couldn't believe they were real. New worlds, worlds not poisoned by a violent, unholy past.

Orion's head bobbed enthusiastically. "Yes, little explorer. There are many upon many, scattered among the stars. Everything you see in here, including the visitor center itself, was built to get there. Maybe you will travel to one of them yourself one day?"

I stood fascinated, watching, and I felt fear clamp down on my heart even as it soared. This, I knew, was ghost-shifting: ghosts telling about great things, about possibilities, about progress. It was not true, it just didn't happen, and when it happened, it was bad. This kind of thinking had destroyed the world. We were careful now, and we didn't pursue any stupid ideas.

But it was beautiful, and that had always been my weakness. I was transfixed by the images as they flickered by, bathing me in the brightness of distant suns. My gaze drank up the swarms of weavers spinning things far greater than we had ever dreamed of. And I realized they were so much more than what we had been using them for. This would be invaluable knowledge, if the tribe could accept it. I wondered if they would even accept a ghost-touched weaver, and resolved to tell them I had found it far from the place of the haunting.

I turned to look at the creature with renewed awe. But my colors flared in alarm at what I saw.

The first light of the day filtered in through the ceiling, and I realized I had lost the track of time over the ghost's stories. Several figures were clustered together near the entrance, shuffling and whispering. Among the dozens of weavers at their feet, the one marked white with dread-screen clearly stood out in the front row. Asper and his fellow herders had come to harvest. They craned their necks, staring at me. Staring at Orion.

"Visitors!" The ghost began to drift closer. "Are these your friends? More little explorers? I'd love to welcome them."

"No, Orion!" I tried to prevent what could only end in disaster. "Stay back, will you?"

The herders had already scattered. With hectic gestures they maneuvered their weavers to hide behind them, while some broke and ran for the entrance, shrilling a warning.

"Wait!" Asper yelled. "The Blessed is in the ghost's thrall. We have to rescue her! Get Renke, hurry!"

"It's alright." I made two steps towards them to show I was free to go. "He's nonaggressive."

It was a futile effort. Most of them were crazed with fear, clogging the narrow entrance tube or fleeing along the walls of the dome. Asper, though, not only came for me, but managed to bully a fellow herder to march with him towards much more ghost activity than any of them had ever seen.

"Asper, you have to watch this!" I backed off towards the glass-like screen. "We were all wrong about the weavers."

He grabbed my arm.

"Hey!" Orion drifted closer.

Without letting go, Asper jumped. I stumbled and was caught by his friend, who dragged me to my feet without any respect for shoulder joints and their natural resistance to jerking. I hissed.

"Hey!" Orion said, louder now. "I cannot tolerate violence in here. This is a place of peace and learning. Now, behave yourselves and release Mink!"

A collective gasp rippled through the herders as they heard the ghost speak my name, and I used their surprise to detach myself.

I could not let them take me. When they got me out of this dome, there would be no turning back and setting this right. Truss would die, unsung and alone, and I would not bring a new weaver and a new vision to the tribe. I tried to back away and babbled incoherent things that probably did nothing to convince them I was not ghost-shifted beyond repair. Orion's warnings became increasingly pressing.

When Renke's fighters joined the fray, they pushed the fleeing herders back in and moved towards me, crests rising as Orion drifted in between us as if to shield me.

Then, cutting through the very fabric of this old, untouched space, I saw the glint of a spear flying. Renke's verdigris green collar-feathers were tied to its shaft. It passed right through Orion, to bury itself in the screen containing the vision. A web of cracks appeared, and the light within died.

Orion's voice shrilled, distorted and much louder than before. "Stop damaging the equipment, and leave Mink alone, now! She's under my protection."

In the silence that followed, a rustling sound came up. It was a sound we knew, but it had a wrongness to it that made everyone freeze. Instead of the chaotic concert of individual clinks and whirrs, we heard our weavers march in unison. They came scuttling from all corners, flowing together like some big machine assembling itself. I knew this behavior, I had observed it moments before in the vision, but it was uncanny to see it executed, as if they had developed a shared, single-minded purpose all of a sudden. The others just stared, but some called out to their weavers, gesturing them back to no avail.

I froze when I saw what their purpose turned out to be. They all came up to me, smoothly parting around me and flowing into a new formation, climbing upon each other and surrounding me with a barrier of spiky metal.

And they were ready to defend. Asper and the other herders tried to intervene as the fighters tore into the formation, and they all got burned by spurts of heated material, seared by cutting-lights, sparks flying off their scales. They had absolutely no experience with the way the herds behaved now, like a single organism lashing out.

I tried to climb over my living protection, ready to leave with the tribe to end this. "Orion!" I cried. "Stop. Please!"

"Habitat security initiated, please cooperate."

"Orion?"

But he didn't respond to me anymore.

And I remembered the most important thing a scout has to recognize: the point when fighting would only lead to greater loss. I sounded the Rush. "Flee! This is a Clusterhaunt!"

Renke took up my tune, aggressively, urging on the herders who still called their weavers. I don't know what really made them break and run in the end. It could have been the herder who recognized the carapace of her weaver and tried to yank it out of the formation, only to get cut so badly we had to carry her. Limping and crying, we fled, and Asper's look was so hurt and betrayed I wanted to camouflage out of his sight. When I reached the entrance tube as part of the last group supporting and dragging each other, I thought I heard a faint whisper from the dome. "Safety can only be guaranteed in the habitat. Staying is recommended."

There was a difference I hadn't known, between separating myself from the tribe and being separated from the tribe. Oh, I was still with them, but I was kept off to the side, under guard. My status was unclear. Outcast, probably; a prisoner, surely; still useful, maybe.

Renke had screamed into my face, asking who would spin her a new spear, now that there was not a single weaver left. Asper had not spoken at all, but he surely cursed the day the tribe had acquired the clutch of supposedly blessed eggs that had hatched me. Others had said it aloud: "She who runs on her own shall no longer sing with us." And Truss had been loudest of all. "Is this how I taught you to serve your foster-tribe? You doom us all with your shrewd ideas. You shame me. You deny me my contribution to our survival, just because you're too sappy to accept what has to be done."

He might still get his chance to die all alone now.

My body's warmth seeped into the night-cooled ground. I was a miserable, pale heap, bound to a cracked column to protect everyone, including myself, from the mad bouts of my ghost-shifted mind. And as I stared up into the murky morning sky, still clear of the minor color shifts and scattered light that preceded a new wind, I knew they were right. I had been ghost-shifted. I had been blinded. The stars were not real. There was nothing but blackness up there.

I had been wrong all the time, dreaming of greatness and of knowing everything. I had chased visions and embraced change like it was just a pretty color I could wear, while secretly smiling at the superstition the herders held against me, never letting me approach a weaver. Now the weavers were taken, because I had lied. Because I had failed to see that they were right.

Not that anybody took the time to lay the blame at my feet—they would be crest-over-tails planning their next steps. I could hear them arguing. But it was just a waste of energy. Even if we stood a chance, we would never fight the one thing that let us thrive: our herds, our cleansers, our silvery lifeblood in this wrecked land.

Of course, without weavers, we would soon all be ghosts. And it would be a long drag down. We would wander the plains, deprived of our purpose, deprived of our calling and our sustenance. We hadn't needed the weavers to change the world, really, but as a reason to tread on, to lay claim to hostile territory, to sustain our foolish, desolate, stubborn way of living. We had never seen what they really were, until now that they were gone, and I was the only one . . .

No.

I had to give up this delusion. I had never been the only one. I knew nothing.

To the disgruntled huffing of my guard, I started a cleansing song. It was too late for that, but I had to do something to steer my mind from the tantalizing vision, from the dread and the despair.

When I heard the soft thud of footpads on the ground, I thought somebody might try to gag me. But next came a strangled sound from my guard while a weaverspun chain dug into her trachea; that made me jerk out of my song.

Under a cover of black fabric I recognized the loam-spotted greens of Asper's scales. My first thought was that he had come to personally punish me, and when he stepped closer, I expected him to tell me he wanted me gone, that he couldn't bear to feed me one more share of spicy mothfry after all I had done.

"They're gone, because of you. Poor Peshk needs a brace, because of you, and I can't build one, because of you." He stared down at me for a moment, his tail lashing. I cringed, which made him snarl even more. "What is it with you, crazy scout?" He took off his heat cloak and dropped it near the shadowed corner I was curled up in. "You're all sickly white."

I hooked the cloak with one claw and drew it to me cautiously. "It's . . . it's my mood, yes?"

"Then snap out of it! You'll need your skill after you've warmed up." He swallowed, as if the next thing he was going to say had a foul taste to it. "They are debating. But it all ends up the same—we're going to leave. Hoping to reach the settler townships and seek refuge there. They're packing already. We're abandoning our weavers." He took out a small trimming knife. "Can't let that happen. Can't just leave my Tineater serving this Clusterhaunt. So I figured you'd be the one to come up with another idea. I saw you talk to that ghost. Like it made sense. Maybe you're shifted, and surely you're as unclean as a cesspool full of ground poison, but you've got a knack for communicating with this thing." With one swift slash, he cut through my rope.

I didn't move, just sat numbly, completely baffled. And I wondered if everybody had this one breaking point that made them fall from grace. "This might not be in the tribe's best interest," I said softly. "What if I don't come back and you'll have to run without a scout?"

"Wrong time for regrets," Asper snarled, and he sounded strangely like Truss to me, when he had taught a lesson. Then he tossed me my tools and turned around to sit next to the guard and check on her. "Go make some sweet talk to this ghost of yours, or rip its heart out. I don't care. Just get Tineater back to me. Bring the weavers, or don't come back at all."

The moment I moved out of reach, he took up the cleansing song I had abandoned.

There were many reasonable things I could have wished for as I passed through the yawning portal into the dome again: that I knew a secret tune to make the weavers follow me out just like that; that I had Truss at my side, to hold me back with a sharp hiss from making yet another stupid mistake; that I could run, run the plains with my tribe and our herds whole and sound, and leave this place alone.

I might face the true power of the Clusterhaunt now, not the gentle inducements of the being I had dubbed Orion.

A name it hadn't responded to any longer after it had turned on us. I was very much afraid that any bond Asper relied upon might have existed in my imagination only.

Foolish as I was, the thing I really wished for was that it hadn't forgotten *my* name.

But Orion was nowhere to be seen. I could tell, because in plain daylight the murky darkness of the dome wasn't absolute. High up, where some of its ceiling panels were missing, shafts of light sliced down all the way to the ground in cascades of dancing dust motes. And there was a flurry of ghost activity. Faintly blinking lights, ghostly chatter emanating from various objects, all clocked to the clinking and whirring of the weavers. It was every sane person's nightmare, but I was beyond fear.

Or so I thought, because when Orion did descend upon me out of thin air, I blanched, flinched, and pinched my tail under a metal pedestal I knocked over while fighting for balance. Before I could lift it, two weavers scuttled over and hoisted it back up. I very slowly backed away.

"Little explorer Mink, adding some defects again, aren't you? But don't you worry. Mistakes happen, and I've got so much help now." Orion drifted closer and lowered his voice. "We're not officially reopened yet. You are a regular visitor, though. And I'm so glad to see you're back, and unharmed, too, so I'm willing to make an exception. A special tour just for you, what do you say?"

Part of me wanted just that, to lose my unhinged, ghost-shifted self in visions. I swallowed. "Actually, I'm not here to visit you. I'm here for the weavers." I indicated three of the creatures, spinning upwards from the floor, thread after thread, grabbing shards with their long legs to absorb and fuel their weaving while building something that looked like it would go on top of the pedestal. "They don't belong in here. They are the herds of my tribe, you see, and we need them back."

"Weavers? You have a knack for names, little explorer Mink. But you must understand the ATUs are no playthings, and they are doing what they are made for. They are not mine to give back. But they do good work, and they are well cared for. Just imagine how many visitors will take delight in this place after all those pesky defects are behind us."

I took a deep breath. I very much detested breaking things. And it had been nice, nice to get to know someone who wasn't aware of the brokenness of the world, who didn't live under the constant pressure of survival. It had been nice, but it was the only leverage I had. "There is something you should know." I worked my jaw for a moment, like something old and awful was lodged between my teeth. "They are not coming. Nobody is coming. There are no visitors anymore."

"Little explorer!" Orion's gloved hand went up to his bowl-shaped head. "What are you saying? That's nonsense. Right?"

I came close to him, and I wished I could have reached up and taken the sides of the bowl in my hands, to look into those elusive eyes. And to have something to cling to, because it hurt, what I had to do. "It's true. Look at all those defects. And believe me, you got off lightly in here. The defects outside are numberless."

And I sung him the oldest parts of the Tribesong, the way the elders had sung it to me as a hatchling, lest I forgot how the world became broken and the reign of demons had ended when they choked on their own corrupted breath, after their insatiable thirst for knowledge had undone them.

When I sang no more, Orion was silent for a very long time. He didn't even hover or flicker. I tried to stay equally unmoved. The tribe, the herds, the running, hearts thumping up our chest. That was what mattered. Not a ghost and his grieving.

"I was built to teach," he stated finally, his voice unquavering and strong, and I thought that maybe his hidden lungs weren't built to produce the sobs buried underneath. "I was built to inspire new achievements. If it's all gone, and I'm all alone . . . why am I still here?"

I had no answer for him. Ghosts despised the living, that was why, and I knew that he did not.

Orion looked up again, a hint of eyes gleaming under the bowl. "But you. You will come? You, and your . . . tribe. You returned, after all. You want to learn."

I laughed. It sounded like choking. Learning was what had gotten me into this wretched situation in the first place. "No, Orion. We won't. I'm sorry. My tribe is fear-stricken by your presence. You have proven yourself a true Clusterhaunt by taking our weavers. You are the doom of my people."

"But everything will be fine in here soon," he insisted. "Zero defects. And you'll like the stars. I promise—"

"Orion. There are no stars." I had the distinct feeling that I was about to tear his heart out with words alone, and I had to speak around the lump in my throat. "The veiled moon is a silvery blotch gliding through the upper fumes. And the stars, they are gone so long they are not even in the Tribesong; a whisper of clear lights, shining through the dark fabric of the night to give us comfort. But we can't afford to believe in comfort. There is only blackness."

"Is that so?" Orion moved again, and this was the first time he tried to touch me. His fingers passed through my cheek, leaving faint traces of heat. "You should believe in comfort. It makes you reach out again after you fall. How else would you advance? When we set out to reach the stars, there were many who would have held us back. It's a risk, they said. A waste. But we sent our eyes up into the skies, and we saw worlds up there. We have always had to cross the blackness, Mink, and it has always been vast and intimidating. We have always fallen. But this place is a monument to our resilience, and it has seen visitors from afar, who brought back the evidence of those worlds. As its guardian, I was never intended to go myself, but I saw the blackness could be crossed. And you should have trust in that, too, Mink."

My mind went back to those pristine, luminous worlds of the vision, and there was comfort in the thought of them out there. I could not condemn this comfort, even if it made my heart want to reach out and find a way to get there. Even if I needed to embrace ghost-shifting to get only one step closer. And I did. "Show me."

He clasped his hands behind his back and nodded gravely. After a while, a weaver came scuttling out of the gloom to stand close to me and pinch me in the upper calf. In one of its legs, it held something, pressing it urgently into my hand as soon as I crouched. I looked at the smooth oval in my palm, then back at Orion.

"Your Memory Vault. I told you not to forget it next time you leave."

"I'm not leaving. I want you to show me your vision."

Orion shook his head. "No. Not only you. Bring your tribe. Let me show them. Only this one time. I am not your enemy. But this is the price I demand for giving back the weavers."

Never would the elders bring what was left of our tribe into the lair of the Clusterhaunt again. Never would they trust my word, ghost-shifted as I was. And yet. I wanted them to see. I wanted to be with them again, and that would never happen when my dreams lived among the stars, while theirs still had to cross the blackness. "I'll try, but my voice in the Tribesong is small."

"Nonsense," he said. "I heard you sing. There's nothing wrong with your voice. Just use it. Educate them."

He was right. They needed to know, and I had never made the effort to tell them anything. It had been easier for me, and easier for them, to carry on as we had always done. But there were other worlds, worlds not lost to corruption and poison. This was a vision as true as any prediction of our windreader. This was hope. It would be hard work, but I had to make them understand. Even if it meant breaking what was left of trust and love. Even if the only thing to speak in my favor was the prospect of a happy reunion with our herds.

Then Orion explained to me in detail how I would get the weavers back after the performance. If I hadn't believed him before, I would have done so now, because it was a sound plan. It was, in fact, a plan I had executed many times before. And as soon as I grasped what he wanted me to do, I threw up my hands and said: "No. I won't do that, Orion."

"But you must. As I said, the weavers are not mine to give back. When I initiated habitat security, they were integrated in the defense matrix. I can command them to repair while there is no threat, but I can't undo their integration. Security is automated."

I didn't understand, and I didn't care. I shook my head.

Orion waited very patiently by my side while I came up with other plans. Waited very patiently while I cried. And waited very patiently while I added one or three defects by kicking things.

But the world was less patient. It barged in on me when Asper crashed through the entrance, the fear in his voice overshadowed by the greater horror that must have driven him to brave the Clusterhaunt's lair yet again.

"Blessed!" he cried. "You have to lead us in the Rush, now! The camp was breached by a rustbreed vanguard. They have followed us."

We were nomads, and we didn't get to keep things. Not even dreams.

So I tried to shake it all off while I followed Asper into a nightmare. People were securing exhausted young ones to their chests or trying to force up the wounded, while right in the middle of the camp Renke and her fighters fell back against the rustbreed despite battling fiercely. Vanguard attacks were meant to delay and cripple until the arrival of the colony, and if they had to impale their sinuous bodies on our weapons to shower us in acids, they would do just that. Already the ground sizzled with ochre blood.

Everybody made way to let me take my place at the head of the column, to lead us on the quickest path out into the open, where we could outrun them. But my eyes searched for Truss' pallet, where he would die alone, as was his duty. And my mind went back to the dome, to my voice rising up through its stillness, stirring the dust of centuries.

I knew a safe place right under our noses. I could still get us out without anyone being left behind.

"No need to run," I told those nearest to me. "Bring your young ones into the dome. It's safe, I promise. The Clusterhaunt will protect us." They didn't move, of course, but I went on, louder now. "I bargained for our protection. Our weavers will defend us in the dome. You have seen what they are capable of! These walls are indestructible. It is our best and only chance! Go!"

Most of them muttered madness at me, but some snuck glances at the dome, leaving our formation with tentative steps. Others kept looking at the elders.

"Get back!" the windreader yelled, ushering them on. "Don't listen to this ghost-shifted rambling. We run!"

"But the Blessed is right!" I hadn't noticed Asper staying with me in the fray. He had leapt onto a crumbling wall, waving his heat cloak like a banner. "Our weavers are in there. I won't leave them. I say let's go and make a stand there! We've got nothing to lose."

I saw the eyes of the herders shift. Terrified, yes, but flecked with mad determination as they grabbed what they had dropped in the wake of the attack and started to run for the dome, a few first, but drawing more and more after them. And I saw Renke lose every battle she was in and buckle when she finally called her fighters to her side to cover our retreat.

And just like that, the tribe was on the move. I went to find Truss and lifted his dry, grunting weight upon my shoulders. He didn't quite struggle, but he did snarl.

"Don't you dare and deny me my choice. Leave me, and do what the tribe needs of you."

"I am," I snapped. "And you can thank me later, or still make use of your choice then."

He huffed, but sagged against me in defeat. The tribe had decided, after all. Just beyond the tube entrance, their courage left them, though, and they all stopped dead in their tracks. The space was brimming with ghost activity. "Orion!" I shouted, shouldering my way to the front, Truss still with me. "Where are you?"

"Mink!" The ghost blinked to life in all his silvery splendor between two shafts of light in the middle of the dome, making my people surge back against the walls. "I'm glad you came back! Come on, everything is prepared for the show."

"We're not here for the show. Please, Orion, you have to protect us. There's rustbreed at the threshold, and my people need shelter. Help us!"

The spear fighters defending the entrance shot frantic looks at Orion as he drifted closer, but the Warden called them back in line with a disdainful growl and motioned others to move up as replacements, should they fall.

"I see," Orion said, and my heart leapt when I felt his lighthearted nature yield to the gentle profoundness I had come to trust. "Harm to visitors is to be avoided at all costs. Initiating habitat sealing."

An inaudible command brought in our herds. From all directions, they converged upon the entrance, the staccato of clinking legs made it sound like we had acquired an army. Smoothly they flowed into precise lines, passing down chunks of material to the tube opening where the silvery creatures began to weave upwards from the ground, and downwards from the ceiling. Most herders just stared in astonishment, but some whooped and called their weavers' names, and a few ventured out to gather rubble for them. Not every fragment went into the quickly growing wall, though. Some ended up in scalding spurts directed at our enemies.

It was messy. Three weavers were thrown back in a spray of acid as they clung to the red-tipped mandibles of a rustbreed soldier to keep it from rearing. One of our fighters went down, hundreds of chitinous legs crawling over him. He was still screaming long after he had been pulled back out.

But soon there was only room left for a single rustbreed to squeeze through, and then not even that. The entrance was sealed, and we stood in silence, apart from the occasional thud when one of the creatures flung itself against the freshly spun concrete slab.

The tribe huddled together in the open space of the dome, eyeing me, the elders, and Orion. Some lowered the young ones to the floor, still holding their hands. Some flicked their tongues.

"What now, little foster-hatch?" I was kneeling next to Truss, trying to check his bandages. He slapped my hands away, but he was no longer bristling with fury, his crest drooping in concern instead. "Seems we are not to become rustbreed sustenance yet. But what do *we* eat? We don't have a grub's worth of food with us, and they won't go away as long as their prey is so close."

I looked up into the fearful faces of my tribe, who had trusted me in a way I would never have thought possible. "We have our weavers. And we have Orion. Surely there is something we can come up with."

It took a long time to get them to talk. Half of them still believed the Clusterhaunt had set this as a trap for us, and they were unwilling to go near it. A few even snuck on their dread-screen, which they had brought with them of all things. Orion was no help either, curiously hovering close, displaying some tricks to get the attention of the young ones. The tribe had settled into an uneasy camp formation, a few lone bug-catcher lamps marking a perimeter, its guards clearly at a loss.

Those lamps gave us an idea at last. As soon as I had gotten the herders to talk not about our predicament or the implications of conversing with a Clusterhaunt, but about the glorious things their weavers could build together, they were unstoppable. Ideas flew back and forth, with Orion chiming in with detailed knowledge.

"These possibilities, Blessed . . . Mink!" Asper clasped my upper arm as if I weren't the uncleanest being he had ever met. Still, I was not one of them. I had no clue what exactly they planned to build, but the gleam in Asper's eyes told me it would be magnificent. "There is enough plastics in here to burn the whole colony to the ground!"

In our lamps, we used a burning paste spun from plastics. The weavers would tunnel deep and build some contraption to saturate the ground the rustbreed crawled upon and burrowed in, until all that was needed was a single spark, while we sat safely here in our indestructible dome.

"Of course you will have to learn to control the ATUs for this project, little engineers," Orion told them. "I can't do it for you."

The herders were too agitated to notice, but his tone alerted me. There had been a calm finality in Orion's words that suggested he was not planning to participate.

"Why not?" Asper asked. "I'd like to learn, but we are in a tight spot right now. I'd prefer to be educated when nothing tries to break in and eat me."

"Nothing will breach these walls, little engineer. But you won't be able to learn from me afterwards. There are rules, hard-coded rules I have to adhere to. I cannot order the ATUs to break down the interior of my visitor center to form flammable components. I cannot add defects. Habitat destruction is beyond my authorization. As is sending the weavers out of the habitat to tunnel as long as they are integrated in the defense matrix. You have to take your weavers back. Mink knows how."

I jumped up from the resting place I had found when they had gone into technical details. "I told you no, Orion!"

The others looked at me in puzzlement. They didn't understand. I had not abandoned my old teacher, and I wouldn't abandon my new one, even if he had found better students now. The stabs of jealousy I had felt since Orion had begun to focus his enthusiasm on the herders subsided, though, when he took me to the side. "I can't give them back. So I need your help, and I'm very sorry for your inconvenience." He hovered closer, so close that for the first time I got a look beyond the bowl and saw more than just a hint of his eyes. They were bright and very blue, luminous like the worlds I had seen in his vision. "Mink. Most curious of explorers. You should know that nothing will change if you keep clinging to the long-forgotten remnants of the past. I don't belong here, and you know it. You opened my eyes to it. It would be a sad existence indeed to stay back with this knowledge, waiting forever. And I would have no one else lay me to rest."

"No! Laying to rest is for ghosts. You . . . are something else, Orion. I gave you a name. You showed me the worlds." I flicked my tongue, affectionately now, and in affect, because it passed through him yet again.

"Then save what's left of me." He drifted backwards, beckoning me to follow him. "Not these outdated projections, but what I stand for. This is my purpose after all, educating the next generation about becoming explorers, builders, spacefarers. Now go and save your tribe!"

He had led me to the gigantic metal tube, and pointed up its sleek form. Above its upper end, where it was still fastened to the ceiling, one of the dome segments was missing, big enough for a lithe scout to squeeze through.

I shook my head with closed eyes. Imagined one way it would all end, if I did nothing, and another, and another, all equally grim. When I finally buckled, I swallowed everything I wanted to say and turned to technicalities. "If I go, will there be enough time to teach them what they need to know?"

"They are quite adept already. They might have used high-tech tools to build spoons, but they are master-builders in their own way. I'll teach them everything they need to know about ATU coordination. I'll try to attend the process as long as I can, but as you know, residual energies are nothing but a short echo." He came closer, as if to take me in his insubstantial embrace. I wasn't entirely sure if I really felt his warmth or just imagined it. "I'm sorry you have to do this, to go into danger for me. But I'm glad you found me, I truly am, Mink. I'm glad I was not forever alone. Now don't you worry. Just remember, beyond the darkness, worlds are waiting."

What I saw when I climbed the rocket tube to the outside of the dome was a sea of writhing russet bodies. Rustbreed reek permeated the air, legs clattered like an upcoming storm. It made me understand, more than anything else, that there was no way for me to go back down and sit it out. To wait for another plan, a miracle, a change of rules, would have been madness. There was a hard-coded rule of the tribes: nobody survived a rustbreed colony. Vanguard, yes, even the first waves of the colony proper. But those below had already settled in, infesting the whole area. And yet I might be able to save everyone. Everyone alive, at least.

I looked down through the hole in the ceiling one last time. Even Asper still shied when Orion came close to point something out, and the others kept more than a healthy distance. They did not trust him like I did, but I hoped their shared passion for the weavers and Orion's attempts to entertain those who were not involved in building would keep the tribe from panicking.

I turned away and camouflaged. Everybody thought it easy, that I just had to press against any random surface and magically took on its color. But it's not like that. It is a process, a transformation, and it's more than scale-deep. The colors are a mental thing. My whole body wanted to scream danger in bright yellows and reds, and I had to convince it to calm down. When I felt positively invisible, I took up the rope and began my treacherous way down the side of the dome.

Even camouflaged, it was harrowing to see this dead place writhe with a host of centipedes prepared to tear me apart. After our first flight, there was not much left in my vial of extract from rustbreed scent glands, so I didn't fiddle with droplets, but threw the whole thing to shatter far from the place where they were clustered, obsessed with this frustratingly thin wall separating them from a tribe's worth of a feast. The whole ground seemed to ripple as they moved to investigate, and I was able to slip past the few remaining patrols.

I was possibly the very first scout to be led to a heart-chamber by the ghost's own words. It was located in one of the tall, broken buildings, beyond debris-strewn staircases descending far down into the bowels of the earth, into labyrinthine hallways with doors Orion had taught me to navigate. A true Clusterhaunt hideout, if there had ever been one. The entrance was signed in the way he had said it would, and I made short work of its grade-4 lock with a vial of potent acid. This was, after all, my trade.

I closed the door carefully behind me, then I looked around. And the moment I saw what this room was, my chest ached for Orion.

It was a cauldron of ghosts. It was a grave.

On its other end, massive vanes behind a metal grate streamed air into my face, sufficiently cool to immobilize anyone exhausted enough to give in to the cold. There were hearts aplenty, rack upon rack, neatly placed in their boxes. But only one was still beating.

"Orion." I stood transfixed by the slow pulses of light emanating from the box, placed my hand upon it like I had never been able to with his manifestation in the dome. Then I began to chant, because it was the only way to get moving again, to sink into the routine of a duty I had done so very often.

As I took down my tool sash and put on my gloves, I sang the Song of Passing, to tell the ghost that the sins of the past would be set right and there was no reason to linger, but I soon slipped into my own verses. I sang of the vastness of the fallen world and the vastness beyond, and I hoped it was bearable because he had my voice guiding him along. I sang of worlds beyond the blackness and a bowl full of stars, and I took my engraved pliers and plucked and cut at the right places, as gently as I could and with a touch that I hoped conveyed love, not violence, until the very last bluish light on the heart slowly faded.

A noise I had not perceived till now ground to a halt, and the breath of cool air on my face died. I let my own breath go in an anguished rush and slumped down on the lifeless heart-box, without a care for my unprotected face and arms.

At the afterthought of residual energies, I jerked up. Maybe there was still time for a proper farewell. I forcefully banned my grieving paleness and ran.

I came back to a darkened dome.

I knew what to anticipate: weavers under the control of our tribe again, flowing together to use up all the interior material of the visitor center to build secretly under the earth, slowly, but steadily creating the trap. The moment the weavers came together for their task, the rustbreed were dead already, their time burning down with every spun thread of tunnel, pipe, fuel, until they faced their immolation. I should have been glad to see the plan in motion.

Still, when I saw no ghostly lights shine from within the dome, my heart sank. I was too late. The last emanations of Orion had occurred without me. But then I heard the music.

Of all the things he could have repaired, of all the things he could have done with his last energies, he had chosen his beloved music. It was indeed very inspiring, swelling like the songs of a dozen tribes woven into one, ethereal, rising ever higher, tugging at the soul and then taking it along in a thunderous rush. The hexagons of the ceiling had been shaded to blackness, and I scampered down the metal tube of the rocket into a darkness speckled with the fearful eyes of my tribe under this display of ghostly power. Because there was also light.

Lights dotted the blackness. Clear and bright, beckoning, shining through the fabric of the artificial night. A few lone pinpoints first, then scattered scintillating clusters, until an abundance of lights pulsed above us. And as I came to stand among my people on the ground and let my gaze be drawn up, it was as if the domed ceiling had dissolved into an infinite, vast space, stretching out forever before our eyes, close enough to touch if we just strove to reach it.

None of us had ever seen the stars, but our hearts recognized them. They looked just like so many camps in the sky, bug-catcher lamps in the darkness, and I could not have been the only one to wonder what tribes lived up there.

Nobody made a sound, and only when the surging song Orion played for us ascended into our own Paean of Manifest Horizons did they move, like a collective sigh. And I could see that he had entered their hearts now, that he had become *our* ghost, with this last show, his star-laden farewell. Renke was studying their faces as well, and when she caught me looking, she simply nodded her acknowledgement.

And so when the weavers began to move, precisely coordinated, and when we began to hear the rustbreed blindly throwing themselves at the walls again, not knowing that even now their doom was in the making, and when the stars winked out in large swathes and it all went dark, our tribe sang on in the vast blackness, sang verses of new horizons and our ghost guiding us, and our voices filled the dome like an elegy, like a hymn, and took on a shape of their own, a shape of things to come.

When we set out to weave us a way to the stars, we knew we pledged the lives of our clutches to wandering the wastes. Generation after generation, we would scourge the ruins of the broken world for lost knowledge, our herds converging on molten glass seas to build miracles we had never dreamed of.

We are no mere survivors anymore. We are still adapting to our changed existence, as our starlit minds keep finding new paths in this old world. Our gaze is set upwards now, out to unpoisoned spheres, out to unveil the moon and what lies beyond. We will never be starless again, and this is the greatest gift, a glittering song to complement our own with hope.

When I walk the acrid sands with my ghost-shifted tribe, our two newly adopted gearbeasts trundling along, I know I will not be the one to actually bring us to the stars. This will fall to Asper, who teaches our future builders and planners to control their weavers, and to paint them, too, for beauty, not out of fear. My contribution to the Tribesong is small. But as I tell it once again, I'm clutching the Memory Vault, the only thing I took for myself from the visitor center that is now but an empty, scorched husk. They are like small eggs, those Memory Vaults. I'm not a fool. Most eggs come to nothing, I know. But maybe something will hatch. Maybe there is something left of Orion in there. I'll give it to the next scout after me, and she will give it to the next and the next until Orion's Song reaches the stars. Because as small as this contribution is, I know there will always be need of us who find new ways to cross the blackness and dream of the worlds beyond.

Kelly Robson is an award-winning short fiction writer. In 2018, her story "A Human Stain" won the Nebula Award for Best Novelette, and in 2016, her novella "Waters of Versailles" won the Prix Aurora Award. She has also been a finalist for the Nebula, World Fantasy, Theodore Sturgeon, John W. Campbell, and Sunburst awards. In 2018, her time travel adventure *Gods, Monsters and the Lucky Peach* debuted to high critical praise. Growing up in the foothills of the Canadian Rockies, Kelly competed in rodeos and gymkhanas, and was crowned princess of the Hinton Big Horn Rodeo. From 2008 to 2012, she wrote the wine and spirits column for *Chatelaine*, Canada's largest women's magazine. After 22 years in Vancouver, she and her wife, fellow SF writer A.M. Dellamonica, now make their home in downtown Toronto.

INTERVENTION

Kelly Robson

When I was fifty-seven, I did the unthinkable. I became a crèche manager.

On Luna, crèche work kills your social capital, but I didn't care. Not at first. My long-time love had been crushed to death in a bot malfunction in Luna's main mulching plant. I was just trying to find a reason to keep breathing.

I found a crusty centenarian who'd outlived most of her cohort and asked for her advice. She said there was no better medicine for grief than children, so I found a crèche tucked away behind a water printing plant and signed on as a cuddler. That's where I caught the baby bug.

When my friends found out, the norming started right away.

"You're getting a little tubby there, Jules," Ivan would say, unzipping my jacket and reaching inside to pat my stomach. "Got a little parasite incubating?"

I expected this kind of attitude from Ivan. Ringleader, team captain, alpha of alphas. From him, I could laugh it off. But then my closest friends started in.

Beryl's pretty face soured in disgust every time she saw me. "I can smell the freeloader on you," she'd say, pretending to see body fluids on my perfectly clean clothing. "Have the decency to shower and change after your shift."

Even that wasn't so bad. But then Robin began avoiding me and ignoring my pings. We'd been each other's first lovers, best friends since forever, and suddenly I didn't exist. That's how extreme the prejudice is on Luna.

Finally, on my birthday, they threw me a surprise party. Everyone wore diapers and crawled around in a violent mockery of childhood. When I complained, they accused me of being broody.

I wish I could say I ignored their razzing, but my friends were my whole world. I dropped crèche work. My secret plan was to leave Luna, find a hab where working with kids wasn't social death, but I kept putting it off. Then I blinked, and ten years had passed.

Enough delay. I jumped trans to Eros station, engaged a recruiter, and was settling into my new life on Ricochet within a month.

I never answered my friends' pings. As far as Ivan, Beryl, Robin, and the rest knew, I fell off the face of the moon. And that's the way I wanted it.

Ricochet is one of the asteroid-based habs that travel the inner system using gravity assist to boost speed in tiny increments. As a wandering hab, we have no fixed astronomical events or planetary seasonality to mark the passage of time, so boosts are a big deal for us—the equivalent of New Year's on Earth or the Sol Belt flare cycle.

On our most recent encounter with Mars, my third and final crèche—the Jewel Box—were twelve years old. We hadn't had a boost since the kids were six, so my team and I worked hard to make it special, throwing parties, making presents, planning excursions. We even suited up and took the kids to the outside of our hab, exploring Asteroid Iris's vast, pockmarked surface roofed by nothing less than the universe itself, in all its spangled glory. We played around out there until Mars climbed over the horizon and showed the Jewel Box its great face for the first time, so huge and close it seemed we could reach up into its milky skim of atmosphere.

When the boost itself finally happened, we were all exhausted. All the kids and cuddlers lounged in the rumpus room, clipped into our safety harnesses, nestled on mats and cushions or tucked into the wall netting. Yawning, droopy-eyed, even dozing. But when the hab began to shift underneath us, we all sprang alert.

Trésor scooted to my side and ducked his head under my elbow.

"You doing okay, buddy?" I asked him in a low voice.

He nodded. I kissed the top of his head and checked his harness.

I wasn't the only adult with a little primate soaking up my body heat. Diamant used Blanche like a climbing frame, standing on her thighs, gripping her hands, and leaning back into the increasing force of the boost. Opale had coaxed her favorite cuddler Mykelti up into the ceiling netting. They both dangled by their knees, the better to feel the acceleration. Little Rubis was holding tight to Engku's and Megat's hands, while on the other side of the room, Safir and Émeraude clowned around, competing for Long Meng's attention.

I was supposed to be on damage control, but I passed the safety workflow over to Bruce. When we hit maximum acceleration, Tré was clinging to me with all his strength.

The kids' bioms were stacked in the corner of my eye. All their hormone graphs showed stress indicators. Tré's levels were higher than the rest, but that wasn't strange. When your hab is somersaulting behind a planet, bleeding off its orbital energy, your whole world turns into a carnival ride. Some people like it better than others.

I tightened my arms around Tré's ribs, holding tight as the room turned sideways.

"Everything's fine," I murmured in his ear. "Ricochet was designed for this kind of maneuver."

Our safety harnesses held us tight to the wall netting. Below, Safir and Émeraude climbed up the floor, laughing and hooting. Long Meng tossed pillows at them.

Tré gripped my thumb, yanking as if it were a joystick with the power to tame the room's spin. Then he shot me a live feed showing Ricochet's chief astronautics officer, a dark-skinned, silver-haired woman with protective bubbles fastened over her eyes.

"Who's that?" I asked, pretending I didn't know.

"Vijayalakshmi," Tré answered. "If anything goes wrong, she'll fix it."

"Have you met her?" I knew very well he had, but asking questions is an excellent calming technique.

"Yeah, lots of times." He flashed a pointer at the astronaut's mirrored eye coverings. "Is she sick?"

"Might be cataracts. That's a normal age-related condition. What's worrying you?"

"Nothing," he said.

"Why don't you ask Long Meng about it?"

Long Meng was the Jewel Box's physician. Ricochet-raised, with a facial deformity that thrust her mandible severely forward. As an adult, once bone ossification had completed, she had rejected the cosmetic surgery that could have normalized her jaw.

"Not all interventions are worthwhile," she'd told me once. "I wouldn't feel like myself with a new face."

As a pediatric specialist, Long Meng was responsible for the health and development of twenty crèches, but we were her favorite. She'd decided to celebrate the boost with us. At that moment, she was dangling from the floor with Safir and Émeraude, tickling their tummies and howling with laughter.

I tried to mitigate Tré's distress with good, old-fashioned cuddle and chat. I showed him feeds from the biodiversity preserve, where the netted mega-fauna floated in mid-air, riding out the boost in safety, legs dangling. One big cat groomed itself as it floated, licking one huge paw and wiping down its whiskers with an air of unconcern.

Once the boost was complete and we were back to our normal gravity regime, Tré's indicators quickly normalized. The kids ran up to the garden to check out the damage. I followed slowly, leaning on my cane. One of the bots had malfunctioned and lost stability, destroying several rows of terraced seating in the open air auditorium just next to our patch. The kids all thought that was pretty funny. Tré seemed perfectly fine, but I couldn't shake the feeling that I'd failed him somehow.

The Jewel Box didn't visit Mars. Martian habs are popular, their excursion contracts highly priced. The kids put in a few bids but didn't have the credits to win.

"Next boost," I told them. "Venus in four years. Then Earth."

I didn't mention Luna. I'd done my best to forget it even existed. Easy to do. Ricochet has almost no social or trade ties with Earth's moon. Our main economic sector is human reproduction and development—artificial wombs, zygote husbandry, natal decanting, every bit of art and science that turns a mass of undifferentiated cells into a healthy young adult. Luna's crèche system collapsed completely not long after I left. Serves them right.

I'm a centenarian, facing my last decade or two. I may look serene and wise, but I've never gotten over being the butt of my old friends' jokes.

Maybe I've always been immature. It would explain a lot.

Four years passed with the usual small dramas. The Jewel Box grew in body and mind, stretching into young adults of sixteen. All six—Diamant, Émeraude, Trésor, Opale, Safir, and Rubis—hit their benchmarks erratically and inconsistently, which made me proud. Kids are supposed to be odd little individuals. We're not raising robots, after all.

As Ricochet approached, the Venusian habs began peppering us with proposals. Recreation opportunities, educational seminars, sightseeing trips, arts festivals, sporting tournaments—all on reasonable trade terms. Venus wanted us to visit, fall in love, stay. They'd been losing population to Mars for years. The brain drain was getting critical.

The Jewel Box decided to bid on a three-day excursion. Sightseeing with a focus on natural geology, including active volcanism. For the first time in their lives, they'd experience real, unaugmented planetary gravity instead of Ricochet's one-point-zero cobbled together by centripetal force and a Steffof field.

While the kids were lounging around the rumpus room, arguing over how many credits to sink into the bid, Long Meng pinged me.

You and I should send a proposal to the Venusian crèches, she whispered. *A master class or something. Something so tasty they can't resist.*

Why? Are you trying to pad your billable hours?

She gave me a toothy grin. *I want a vacation. Wouldn't it be fun to get Venus to fund it?*

Long Meng and I had collaborated before, when our numbers had come up for board positions on the crèche governance authority. Nine miserable months co-authoring policy memos, revising the crèche management best practices guide, and presenting at skills development seminars. All on top of our regular responsibilities. Against the odds, our friendship survived the bureaucracy.

We spent a few hours cooking up a seminar to tempt the on-planet crèche specialists and fired it off to a bunch of Venusian booking agents. We called it 'Attachment and Self-regulation in Theory and Practice: Approaches to Promoting Emotional Independence in the Crèche-raised Child.' Sound dry? Not a bit. The Venusians gobbled it up.

I shot the finalized syllabus to our chosen booking agent, then escorted the Jewel Box to their open-air climbing lab. I turned them over to their instructor and settled onto my usual bench under a tall oak. Diamant took the lead position up the cliff, as usual. By the time they'd completed the first pitch, all three seminars were filled.

The agent is asking for more sessions, I whispered to Long Meng. *What do you think?*

"No way." Long Meng's voice rang out, startling me. As I pinged her location, her lanky form appeared in the distant aspen grove.

"This is a vacation," she shouted. "If I wanted to pack my billable hours, I'd volunteer for another board position."

I shuddered. *Agreed.*

She jogged over and climbed onto the bench beside me, sitting on the backrest with her feet on the seat. "Plus, you haven't been off this rock in twenty years," she added, plucking a leaf from the overhead bough.

"I said okay, Long Meng."

We watched the kids as they moved with confidence and ease over the gleaming, pyrite-inflected cliff face. Big, bulky Diamant didn't look like a climber but was obsessed with the sport. The other five had gradually been infected by their crèche-mate's passion.

Long Meng and I waved to the kids as they settled in for a rest mid-route. Then she turned to me. "What do you want to see on-planet? Have you made a wish list yet?"

"I've been to Venus. It's not that special."

She laughed, a great, good-natured, wide-mouthed guffaw. "Nothing can compare to Luna, can it, Jules?"

"Don't say that word."

"Luna? Okay. What's better than Venus? Earth?"

"Earth doesn't smell right."

"The Sol belt?"

"Never been there."

"What then?"

"This is nice." I waved at the groves of trees surrounding the cliff. Overhead, the plasma core that formed the backbone of our hab was just shifting its visible spectrum into twilight. Mellow light filtered through the leaves. Teenage laughter echoed off the cliff, and in the distance, the steady droning wail of a fussy newborn.

I pulled up the surrounding camera feeds and located the newborn. A tired-looking cuddler carried the baby in an over-shoulder sling, patting its bottom rhythmically as they strolled down a sunflower-lined path. I pinged the baby's biom. Three weeks old. Chronic gas and reflux unresponsive to every intervention strategy. Nothing to do but wait for the child to grow out of it.

The kids summited, waved to us, then began rappelling back down. Long Meng and I met them at the base.

"Em, how's your finger?" Long Meng asked.

"Good." Émeraude bounced off the last ledge and slipped to the ground, wave of pink hair flapping. "Better than good."

"Let's see, then."

Émeraude unclipped and offered the doctor their hand. They were a kid with only two modes: all-out or flatline. A few months back, they'd injured themselves cranking on a crimp, completely bowstringing the flexor tendon.

Long Meng launched into an explanation of annular pulley repair strategies and recovery times. I tried to listen but I was tired. My hips ached, my back ached, my limbs rotated on joints gritty with age. In truth, I didn't want to go to Venus. The kids had won their bid, and with them off-hab, staying home would have been a good rest. But Long Meng's friendship was important, and making her happy was worth a little effort.

Long Meng and I accompanied the Jewel Box down Venus's umbilical, through the high sulphuric acid clouds to the elevator's base deep in the planet's mantle. When we entered the busy central transit hub, with its domed ceiling and slick, speedy slideways, the kids began making faces.

"This place stinks," said Diamante.

"Yeah, smells like piss," said Rubis.

Tré looked worried. "Do they have diseases here or something?"

Opale slapped her hand over her mouth. "I'm going to be sick. Is it the smell or the gravity?"

A quick glance at Opale's biom showed she was perfectly fine. All six kids were. Time for a classic crèche manager-style social intervention.

If you can't be polite around the locals, I whispered, knocking my cane on the ground for emphasis. *I'll shoot you right back up the elevator.*

If you send us home, do we get our credits back? Émeraude asked, yawning.

No. You'd be penalized for non-completion of contract.

I posted a leaderboard for good behavior. Then I told them Venusians were especially gossipy, and if word got out they'd bad-mouthed the planet, they'd get nothing but dirty looks for the whole trip.

A bald lie. Venus is no more gossipy than most habs. But it nurses a significant anti-crèche prejudice. Not as extreme as Luna, but still. Ricochet kids were used to being loved by everyone. On Venus, they would get attitude just for existing. I wanted to offer a convenient explanation for the chilly reception from the locals.

The group of us rode the slideway to Vanavara portway, where Engku, Megat, and Bruce were waiting. Under the towering archway, I hugged and kissed the kids, told them to have lots of fun, and waved at their retreating backs. Then Long Meng and I were on our own.

She took my arm and steered us into Vanavara's passeggiata, a social stroll that wound through the hab like a pedestrian river. We drifted with the flow, joining the people-watching crowd, seeing and being seen.

The hab had spectacular sculpture gardens and fountains, and Venus's point-nine-odd gravity was a relief on my knees and hips, but the kids weren't wrong about the stench. Vanavara smelled like oily vinaigrette over half-rotted lettuce leaves, with an animal undercurrent reminiscent of hormonal teenagers on a cleanliness strike. As we walked, the stench surged and faded, then resurfaced again.

We ducked into a kiosk where a lone chef roasted kebabs over an open flame. We sat at the counter, drinking sparkling wine and watching her prepare meal packages for bot delivery.

"What's wrong with the air scrubbers here?" Long Meng asked the chef.

"Unstable population," she answered. "We don't have enough civil engineers to handle the optimization workload. If you know any nuts-and-bolts types, tell them to come to Vanavara. The bank will kiss them all over."

She served us grilled protein on disks of crispy starch topped with charred vegetable and heaped with garlicky sauce, followed by finger-sized blossoms with tender, fleshy petals over a crisp honeycomb core. When we rejoined the throng, we shot the chef a pair of big, bright public valentines on slow decay, visible to everyone passing by. The chef ran after us with two tulip-shaped bulbs of amaro.

"Enjoy your stay," she said, handing us the bulbs. "We're developing a terrific fresh food culture here. You'll love it."

In response to the population downswing, Venus's habs had started accepting all kinds of marginal business proposals. Artists. Innovators. Experimenters. Lose a ventilation engineer; gain a chef. Lose a surgeon; gain a puppeteer. With the chefs and puppeteers come all the people who want to live in a hab with chefs and puppeteers, and are willing to put up with a little stench to get it. Eventually, the hab's fortunes turn around. Population starts flowing back, attracted by the burgeoning quality of life. Engineers and surgeons return, and the chefs and puppeteers move on to the next proposal-friendly hab. Basic human dynamics.

Long Meng sucked the last drop of amaro from her bulb and then tossed it to a disposal bot.

"First night of vacation." She gave me a wicked grin. "Want to get drunk?"

When I rolled out of my sleep stack in the morning, I was puffy and stiff. My hair stood in untamable clumps. The pouches under my eyes shone an alarming purple, and my wrinkle inventory had doubled. My tongue tasted like garlic sauce. But as long as nobody else could smell it, I wasn't too concerned. As for the rest, I'd earned every age marker.

When Long Meng finally cracked her stack, she was pressed and perky, wrapped in a crisp fuchsia robe. A filmy teal scarf drifted under her thrusting jawline.

"Let's teach these Venusians how to raise kids," she said.

In response to demand, the booking agency had upgraded us to a larger auditorium. The moment we hit the stage, I forgot all my aches and pains. Doctor Footlights, they call it. Performing in front of two thousand strangers produces a lot of adrenaline.

We were a good pair. Long Meng dynamic and engaging, lunging around the stage like a born performer. Me, I was her foil. A grave, wise oldster with fifty years of crèche work under my belt.

Much of our seminar was inspirational. Crèche work is relentless no matter where you practice it, and on Venus it brings negative social status. A little cheerleading goes a long way. We slotted our specialty content in throughout the program, introducing the concepts in the introductory material, building audience confidence by reinforcing what they already knew, then hit them between the eyes with the latest developments in Ricochet's proprietary cognitive theory and emotional development modelling. We blew their minds, then backed away from the hard stuff and returned to cheerleading.

"What's the worst part of crèche work, Jules?" Long Meng asked as our program concluded, her scarf waving in the citrus-scented breeze from the ventilation.

"There are no bad parts," I said drily. "Each and every day is unmitigated joy."

The audience laughed harder than the joke deserved. I waited for the noise to die down, and mined the silence for a few lingering moments before continuing.

"Our children venture out of the crèche as young adults, ready to form new emotional ties wherever they go. The future is in their hands, an unending medium for them to shape with their ambition and passion. Our crèche work lifts them up and holds them high, all their lives. That's the best part."

I held my cane to my heart with both hands.

"The worst part is," I said, "if we do our jobs right, those kids leave the crèche and never think about us again."

We left them with a tear in every eye. The audience ran back to their crèches knowing they were doing the most important work in the universe, and open to the possibility of doing it even better.

After our second seminar, on a recommendation from the kebab chef, we blew our credits in a restaurant high up in Vanavara's atrium. Live food raised, prepared, and served by hand; nothing extruded or bulbed. And no bots, except for the occasional hygiene sweeper.

Long Meng cut into a lobster carapace with a pair of hand shears. "Have you ever noticed how intently people listen to you?"

"Most of the time the kids just pretend to listen."

"Not kids. Adults."

She served me a morsel of claw meat, perfectly molded by the creature's shell. I dredged it in green sauce and popped it in my mouth. Sweet peppers buzzed my sinuses.

"You're a great leader, Jules."

"At my age, I should be. I've had lots of practice telling people what to do."

"Exactly," she said through a mouthful of lobster. "So what are you going to do when the Jewel Box leaves the crèche?"

I lifted my flute of pale green wine and leaned back, gazing through the window at my elbow into the depths of the atrium. I'd been expecting this question for a few years but didn't expect it from Long Meng. How could someone so young understand the sorrows of the old?

"If you don't want to talk about it, I'll shut up," she added quickly. "But I have some ideas. Do you want to hear them?"

On the atrium floor far below, groups of pedestrians were just smudges, no individuals distinguishable at all. I turned back to the table but kept my eyes on my food.

"Okay, go ahead."

"A hab consortium is soliciting proposals to rebuild their failed crèche system," she said, voice eager. "I want to recruit a team. You'd be project advisor. Top position, big picture stuff. I'll be project lead and do all the grunt work."

"Let me guess," I said. "It's Luna."

Long Meng nodded. I kept a close eye on my blood pressure indicators. Deep breaths and a sip of water kept the numbers out of the red zone.

"I suppose you'd want me to liaise with Luna's civic apparatus too." I kept my voice flat.

"That would be ideal." She slapped the table with both palms and grinned. "With a native Lunite at the helm, we'd win for sure."

Long Meng was so busy bubbling with ideas and ambition as she told me her plans, she didn't notice my fierce scowl. She probably didn't even taste her luxurious meal. As for me, I enjoyed every bite, right down to the last crumb of my flaky cardamom-chocolate dessert. Then I pushed back my chair and grabbed my cane.

"There's only one problem, Long Meng," I said. "Luna doesn't deserve crèches."

"Deserve doesn't really—"

I cut her off. "Luna doesn't deserve a population."

She looked confused. "But it has a population, so—"

"Luna deserves to die," I snapped. I stumped away, leaving her at the table, her jaw hanging in shock.

Halfway through our third and final seminar, in the middle of introducing Ricochet's proprietary never-fail methods for raising kids, I got an emergency ping from Bruce.

Tré's abandoned the tour. He's run off.

I faked a coughing fit and lunged toward the water bulbs at the back of the stage. Turned my back on two thousand pairs of eyes, and tried to collect myself as I scanned Tré's biom. His stress indicators were highly elevated. The other five members of the Jewel Box were anxious too.

Do you have eyes on him?

Of course. Bruce shot me a bookmark.

Three separate cameras showed Tré was alone, playing his favorite pattern-matching game while coasting along a nearly deserted slideway. Metadata indicated his location on an express connector between Coacalco and Eaton habs.

He looked stunned, as if surprised by his own daring. Small, under the high arches of the slideway tunnel. And thin—his bony shoulder blades tented the light cloth of his tunic.

Coacalco has a bot shadowing him. Do we want them to intercept?

I zoomed in on Tré's face, as if I could read his thoughts as easily as his physiology. He'd never been particularly assertive or self-willed, never one to challenge his crèche mates or lead them in new directions. But kids will surprise you.

Tell them to stay back. Ping a personal security firm to monitor him. Go on with your tour. And try not to worry.

Are you sure?

I wasn't sure, not at all. My stress indicators were circling the planet. Every primal urge screamed for the bot to wrap itself around the boy and haul him back to Bruce. But I wasn't going to slap down a sixteen-year-old kid for acting on his own initiative, especially since this was practically the first time he'd shown any.

Looks like Tré has something to do, I whispered. *Let's let him follow through.*

I returned to my chair. Tried to focus on the curriculum but couldn't concentrate. Long Meng could only do so much to fill the gap. The audience became restless, shifting in their seats, murmuring to each other. Many stopped paying attention. Right up in the front row, three golden-haired, rainbow-smocked Venusians were blanked out, completely immersed in their feeds.

Long Meng was getting frantic, trying to distract two thousand people from the gaping hole on the stage that was her friend Jules. I picked up my cane, stood, and calmly tipped my chair. It hit the stage floor with a crash. Long Meng jumped. Every head swiveled.

"I apologize for the dramatics," I said, "but earlier, you all noticed me blanking out. I want to explain."

I limped to the front of the stage, unsteady despite my cane. I wear a stability belt, but try not to rely on it too much. Old age has exacerbated my natural tendency for a weak core, and using the belt too much just makes me frailer. But my legs wouldn't stop shaking. I dialed up the balance support.

"What just happened illustrates an important point about crèche work." I attached my cane's cling-point to the stage floor and leaned on it with both hands as I scanned the audience. "Our mistakes can ruin lives. No other profession carries such a vast potential for screwing up."

"That's not true." Long Meng's eyes glinted in the stage lights, clearly relieved I'd stepped back up to the job. "Engineering disciplines carry quite the disaster potential. Surgery certainly does. Psychology and pharmacology. Applied astrophysics. I could go on." She grinned. "Really, Jules. Nearly every profession is dangerous."

I grimaced and dismissed her point.

"Doctors' decisions are supported by ethics panels and case reviews. Engineers run simulation models and have their work vetted by peers before taking any real-world risks. But in a crèche, we make a hundred decisions a day that affect human development. Sometimes a hundred an hour."

"Okay, but are every last one of those decisions so important?"

I gestured to one of the rainbow-clad front-row Venusians. "What do you think? Are your decisions important?"

A camera bug zipped down to capture her answer for the seminar's shared feed. The Venusian licked her lips nervously and shifted to the edge of her seat.

"Some decisions are," she said in a high, tentative voice. "You can never know which."

"That's right. You never know." I thanked her and rejoined Long Meng in the middle of the stage. "Crèche workers take on huge responsibility. We assume all the risk, with zero certainty. No other profession accepts those terms. So why do we do this job?"

"Someone has to?" said Long Meng. Laughter percolated across the audi-torium.

"Why us, though?" I said. "What's wrong with us?"

More laughs. I rapped my cane on the floor.

"My current crèche is a sixteen-year sixsome. Well integrated, good morale. Distressingly sporty. They keep me running." The audience chuck-led. "They're on a geography tour somewhere on the other side of Venus. A few minutes ago, one of my kids ran off. Right now, he's coasting down one of your intra-hab slideways and blocking our pings."

Silence. I'd captured every eye; all their attention was mine.

I fired the public slideway feed onto the stage. Tré's figure loomed four meters high. His foot was kicked back against the slideway's bumper in an attitude of nonchalance, but it was just a pose. His gaze was wide and unblinking, the whites of his eyes fully visible.

"Did he run away because of something one of us said? Or did? Or neglected to do? Did it happen today, yesterday, or ten days ago? Maybe it has nothing to do with us at all, but some private urge from the kid's own heart. He might be suffering acutely right now, or maybe he's enjoying the excitement. The adrenaline and cortisol footprints look the same."

I clenched my gnarled, age-spotted hand to my chest, pulling at the fabric of my shirt.

"But I'm suffering. My heart feels like it could rip right out of my chest because this child has put himself in danger." I patted the wrinkled fabric back into place. "Mild danger. Venus is no Luna."

Nervous laughter from the crowd. Long Meng hovered at my side.

"Crèche work is like no other human endeavor," I said. "Nothing else offers such potential for failure, sorrow, and loss. But no work is as import-ant. You all know that, or you wouldn't be here."

Long Meng squeezed my shoulder. I patted her hand. "Raising children is only for true believers."

Not long after our seminar ended, Tré boarded Venus's circum-planetary chuteway and chose a pod headed for Vanavara. The pod's public feed showed five other passengers: a middle-aged threesome who weren't interested in anything but each other, a halo-haired young adult escorting a floating tank of live eels, and a broad-shouldered brawler with deeply scarred forearms.

Tré waited for the other passengers to sit, then settled himself into a corner seat. I pinged him. No answer.

"We should have had him intercepted," I said.

Long Meng and I sat in the back of the auditorium. A choir group had taken over the stage. Bots were attempting to set up risers, but the singers were milling around, blocking their progress.

"He'll be okay." Long Meng squeezed my knee. "Less than five hours to Vanavara. None of the passengers are going to do anything to him."

"You don't know that."

"Nobody would risk it. Venus has strict penalties for physical violence."

"Is that the worst thing you can think of?" I flashed a pointer at the brawler. "One conversation with that one in a bad mood could do lifelong damage to anyone, much less a kid."

We watched the feed in silence. At first the others kept to themselves, but then the brawler stood, pulled down a privacy veil, and sauntered over to sit beside Tré.

"Oh no," I moaned.

I zoomed in on Tré's face. With the veil in place, I couldn't see or hear the brawler. All I could do was watch the kid's eyes flicker from the window to the brawler and back, monitor his stress indicators, and try to read his body language. Never in my life have I been less equipped to make a professional judgement about a kid's state of mind. My mind boiled with paranoia.

After about ten minutes—an eternity—the brawler returned to their seat.

"It's fine," said Long Meng. "He'll be with us soon."

Long Meng and I met Tré at the chuteway dock. It was late. He looked tired, rumpled, and more than a little sulky.

"Venus is stupid," he said.

"That's ridiculous, a planet can't be stupid," Long Meng snapped. She was tired, and hadn't planned on spending the last night of her vacation waiting in a transit hub.

Let me handle this, I whispered.

"Are you okay? Did anything happen in the pod?" I tried to sound calm as I led him to the slideway.

He shrugged. "Not really. This oldster was telling me how great his hab is. Sounded like a hole."

I nearly collapsed with relief.

"Okay, good," I said. "We were worried about you. Why did you leave the group?"

"I didn't realize it would take so long to get anywhere," Tré said.

"That's not an answer. Why did you run off?"

"I don't know." The kid pretended to yawn—one of the Jewel Box's clearest tells for lying. "Venus is boring. We should've saved our credits."

"What does that mean?"

"Everybody else was happy looking at rocks. Not me. I wanted to get some value out of this trip."

"So you jumped a slideway?"

"Uh huh." Tré pulled a protein snack out of his pocket and stuffed it in his mouth. "I was just bored. And I'm sorry. Okay?"

"Okay." I fired up the leaderboard and zeroed out Tré's score. "You're on a short leash until we get home."

We got the kid a sleep stack near ours, then Long Meng and I had a drink in the grubby travelers' lounge downstairs.

"How are you going to find out why he left?" asked Long Meng. "Pull his feeds? Form a damage mitigation team? Plan an intervention?"

I picked at the fabric on the arm of my chair. The plush nap repaired itself as I dragged a ragged thumbnail along the armrest.

"If I did, Tré would learn he can't make a simple mistake without someone jumping down his throat. He might shrug off the psychological effects, or it could inflict long-term damage."

"Right. Like you said in the seminar. You can't know."

We finished our drinks and Long Meng helped me to my feet. I hung my cane from my forearm and tucked both hands into the crease of her elbow. We slowly climbed upstairs. I could have pinged a physical assistance bot, but my hands were cold, and my friend's arm was warm.

"Best to let this go," I said. "Tré's already a cautious kid. I won't punish him for taking a risk."

"I might, if only for making me worry. I guess I'll never be a crèche manager." She grinned.

"And yet you want to go to Luna and build a new crèche system."

Long Meng's smile vanished. "I shouldn't have sprung that on you, Jules."

In the morning, the two young people rose bright and cheery. I was aching and bleary but put on a serene face. We had just enough time to catch a concert before heading up the umbilical to our shuttle home. We made our way to the atrium, where Tré boggled at the soaring views, packed slideways, clustered performance and game surfaces, fountains, and gardens. The air sparkled with nectar and spices, and underneath, a thick, oily human funk.

We boarded a riser headed to Vanavara's orchestral pits. A kind Venusian offered me a seat with a smile. I thanked him, adding, "That would never happen on Luna."

I drew Long Meng close as we spiraled toward the atrium floor.

Just forget about the proposal, I whispered. *The moon is a lost cause.*

A little more than a year later, Ricochet was on approach for Earth. The Jewel Box were nearly ready to leave the crèche. Bruce and the rest of my team were planning to start a new one, and they warmly assured me I'd always be welcome to visit. I tried not to weep about it. Instead, I began spending several hours a day helping provide round-the-clock cuddles to a newborn with hydrocephalus.

As far as I knew, Long Meng had given up the Luna idea. Then she cornered me in the dim-lit nursery and burst my bubble.

She quietly slid a stool over to my rocker, cast a professional eye over the cerebrospinal fluid-exchange membrane clipped to the baby's ear, and whispered, *We made the short list.*

That's great, I replied, my cheek pressed to the infant's warm, velvety scalp.

I had no idea what she was referring to, and at that moment I didn't care. The scent of a baby's head is practically narcotic, and no victory can compare with having coaxed a sick child into restful sleep.

It means we have to go to Luna for a presentation and interview.

Realization dawned slowly. *Luna? I'm not going to Luna.*

Not you, Jules. Me and my team. I thought you should hear before the whole hab starts talking.

I concentrated on keeping my rocking rhythm steady before answering. *I thought you'd given that up.*

She put a gentle hand on my knee. *I know. You told me not to pursue it and I considered your advice. But it's important, Jules. Luna will restart its crèche program one way or another. We can make sure they do it right.*

I fixed my gaze pointedly on her prognathous jaw. *You don't know what it's like there. They'll roast you alive just for looking different.*

Maybe. But I have to try.

She patted my knee and left. I stayed in the rocker long past hand-over time, resting my cheek against that precious head.

Seventy years ago I'd done the same, in a crèche crowded into a repurposed suite of offices behind one of Luna's water printing plants. I'd walked through the door broken and grieving, certain the world had been drained of hope and joy. Then someone put a baby in my arms. Just a few hours old, squirming with life, arms reaching for the future.

Was there any difference between the freshly detanked newborn on Luna and the sick baby I held on that rocker? No. The embryos gestating in Ricochet's superbly optimized banks of artificial wombs were no different from the ones Luna would grow in whatever gestation tech they inevitably cobbled together.

But as I continued to think about it, I realized there was a difference, and it was important. The ones on Luna deserved better than they would get. And I could do something about it.

First, I had my hair sheared into an ear-exposing brush precise to the millimeter. The tech wielding the clippers tried to talk me out of it.

"Do you realize this will have to be trimmed every twenty days?"

"I used to wear my hair like this when I was young," I reassured him. He rolled his eyes and cut my hair like I asked.

I changed my comfortable smock for a lunar grey trouser-suit with enough padding to camouflage my age-slumped shoulders. My cling-pointed cane went into the mulch, exchanged for a glossy black model. Its silver point rapped the floor, announcing my progress toward Long Meng's studio.

The noise turned heads all down the corridor. Long Meng popped out of her doorway, but she didn't recognize me until I pushed past her and settled onto her sofa with a sigh.

"Are you still looking for a project advisor?" I asked.

She grinned. "Luna won't know what hit it."

Back in the rumpus room, Tré was the only kid to comment on my haircut.

"You look like a villain from one of those old Follywood dramas Bruce likes."

"Hollywood," I corrected. "Yes, that's the point."

"What's the point in looking like a gangland mobber?"

"Mobster." I ran my palm over the brush. "Is that what I look like?"

"Kinda. Is it because of us?"

I frowned, not understanding. He pulled his ponytail over his shoulder and eyed it speculatively.

"Are you trying to look tough so we won't worry about you after we leave?"

That's the thing about kids. The conversations suddenly swerve and hit you in the back of the head.

"Whoa," I said. "I'm totally fine."

"I know, I know. You've been running crèches forever. But we're the last because you're so old. Right? It's got to be hard."

"A little," I admitted. "But you've got other things to think about. Big, exciting decisions to make."

"I don't think I'm leaving the crèche. I'm delayed."

I tried to keep from smiling. Tré was nothing of the sort. He'd grown into a gangly young man with long arms, bony wrists, and a haze of silky black beard on his square jaw. I could recite the dates of his developmental bench-marks from memory, and there was nothing delayed about them.

"That's fine," I said. "You don't have to leave until you're ready."

"A year. Maybe two. At least."

"Okay, Tré. Your decision."

I wasn't worried. It's natural to feel ambivalent about taking the first step into adulthood. If Tré found it easier to tell himself he wasn't leaving, so be it. As soon as his crèchemates started moving on, Tré would follow.

Our proximity to Earth gave Long Meng's proposal a huge advantage. We could travel to Luna, give our presentation live, and be back home for the boost.

Long Meng and I spent a hundred billable hours refining our presentation materials. For the first time in our friendship, our communication styles clashed.

"I don't like the authoritarian gleam in your eye, Jules," she told me after a particularly heated argument. "It's almost as though you're enjoying bossing me around."

She wasn't wrong. Ricochet's social conventions require you to hold in conversational aggression. Letting go was fun. But I had an ulterior motive.

"This is the way people talk on Luna. If you don't like it, you should shit-can the proposal."

She didn't take the dare. But she reported behavioral changes to my geri-atric specialist. I didn't mind. It was sweet, her being so worried about me. I decided to give her full access to my biom, so she could check if she thought I was having a stroke or something. I'm in okay health for my extreme age, but she was a paediatrician, not a gerontologist. What she saw scared her. She got solicitous. Gallant, even, bringing me bulbs of tea and snacks to keep my glucose levels steady.

Luna's ports won't accommodate foreign vehicles, and their landers use a chemical propellant so toxic Ricochet won't let them anywhere near our landing bays, so we had to shuttle to Luna in stages. As we glided over the moon's surface, its web of tunnels and domes sparkled in the full glare of the sun. The pattern of the habs hadn't changed. I could still name them—Surgut, Sklad, Nadym, Purovsk, Olenyok . . .

Long Meng latched onto my arm as the hatch creaked open. I wrenched away and straightened my jacket.

You can't do that here, I whispered. *Self-sufficiency is everything on Luna, remember?*

I marched ahead of Long Meng as if I were leading an army. In the light lunar gravity, I didn't need my cane, so I used its heavy silver head to whack the walls. Hitting something felt good. I worked up a head of steam so hot I could have sterilized those corridors. If I had to come home—home, what a word for a place like Luna!—I'd do it on my own terms.

The client team had arranged to meet us in a dinky little media suite overlooking the hockey arena in Sklad. A game had just finished, and we had to force our way against the departing crowd. My cane came in handy. I brandished it like a weapon, signaling my intent to break the jaw of anyone who got too close.

In the media suite, ten hab reps clustered around the project principal. Overhead circled a battery of old, out-of-date cameras that buzzed and fluttered annoyingly. At the front of the room, two chairs waited for Long Meng and me. Behind us arced a glistening expanse of crystal window framing the rink, where grooming bots were busy scraping blood off the ice. Over the arena loomed the famous profile of Mons Hadley, huge, cold, stark, its bleak face the same mid-tone grey as my suit.

Don't smile, I reminded Long Meng as she stood to begin the presentation.

The audience didn't deserve the verve and panache Long Meng put into presenting our project phases, alternative scenarios, and volume ramping. Meanwhile, I scanned the reps' faces, counting flickers in their attention and recording them on a leaderboard. We had forty minutes in total, but less than twenty to make an impression before the reps' decisions locked in.

Twelve minutes in, Long Meng was introducing the strategies for professional development, governance, and ethics oversight. Half the reps were still staring at her face as if they'd never seen a congenital hyperformation before. The other half were bored but still making an effort to pay attention. But not for much longer.

"Based on the average trajectories of other start-up crèche programs," Long Meng said, gesturing at the swirling graphics that hung in the air, "Luna should run at full capacity within six social generations, or thirty standard years."

I'm cutting in, I whispered. I whacked the head of my cane on the floor and stood, stability belt on maximum and belligerence oozing from my every pore.

"You won't get anywhere near that far," I growled. "You'll never get past the starting gate."

"That's a provocative statement," said the principal. She was in her sixties, short and tough, with ropey veins webbing her bony forearms. "Would you care to elaborate?"

I paced in front of their table, like a barrister in one of Bruce's old courtroom dramas. I made eye contact with each of the reps in turn, then leaned over the table to address the project principal directly.

"Crèche programs are part of a hab's social fabric. They don't exist in isolation. But Luna doesn't want kids around. You barely tolerate young adults. You want to stop the brain drain but you won't give up anything for crèches—not hab space, not billable hours, and especially not your prejudices. If you want a healthy crèche system, Luna will have to make some changes."

I gave the principal an evil grin, adding, "I don't think you can."

"I do," Long Meng interjected. "I think you can change."

"You don't know Luna like I do," I told her.

I fired our financial proposal at the reps. "Ricochet will design your new system. You'll find the trade terms extremely reasonable. When the design is complete, we'll provide on-the-ground teams to execute the project phases. Those terms are slightly less reasonable. Finally, we'll give you a project executive headed by Long Meng." I smiled. "Her billable rate isn't reasonable at all, but she's worth every credit."

"And you?" asked the principal.

"That's the best part." I slapped the cane in my palm. "I'm the gatekeeper. To go anywhere, you have to get past me."

The principal sat back abruptly, jaw clenched, chin raised. My belligerence had finally made an impact. The reps were on the edges of their seats. I had them both repelled and fascinated. They weren't sure whether to start screaming or elect me to Luna's board of governors.

"How long have I got to live, Long Meng? Fifteen years? Twenty?"

"Something like that," she said.

"Let's say fifteen. I'm old. I'm highly experienced. You can't afford me. But if you award Ricochet this contract, I'll move back to Luna. I'll control the gating progress, judging the success of every single milestone. If I decide Luna hasn't measured up, the work will have to be repeated."

I paced to the window. Mons Hadley didn't seem grey anymore. It was actually a deep, delicate lilac. Framed by the endless black sky, its form was impossibly complex, every fold of its geography picked out by the sun.

I kept my back to the reps.

"If you're wondering why I'd come back after all the years," I said, "let me be very clear. I will die before I let Luna fool around with some half-assed crèche experiment, mess up a bunch of kids, and ruin everything." I turned and pointed my cane. "If you're going to do this, at least do it right."

Back home on Ricochet, the Jewel Box was off-hab on a two-day Earth tour. They came home with stories of surging wildlife spectacles that made herds and flocks of Ricochet's biodiversity preserve look like a petting zoo. When the boost came, we all gathered in the rumpus room for the very last time.

Bruce, Blanche, Engku, Megat, and Mykelti clustered on the floor mats, anchoring themselves comfortably for the boost. They'd be fine. Soon they'd have armfuls of newborns to ease the pain of transition. The Jewel Box were all hanging from the ceiling netting, ready for their last ride of childhood. They'd be fine too. Diamante had decided on Mars, and it looked like the other five would follow.

Me, I'd be fine too. I'd have to be.

How to explain the pain and pride when your crèche is balanced on the knife's edge of adulthood, ready to leave you behind forever? Not possible. Just know this: when you see an oldster looking serene and wise, remember, it's just a sham. Under the skin, it's all sorrow.

I was relieved when the boost started. Everyone was too distracted to notice I'd begun tearing up. When the hab turned upside down, I let myself shed a few tears for the passing moment. Nothing too self-indulgent. Just a little whuffle, then I wiped it all away and joined the celebration, laughing and applauding the kids' antics as they bounced around the room.

We got it, Long Meng whispered in the middle of the boost. *Luna just shot me the contract. We won.*

She told me all the details. I pretended to pay attention, but really, I was only interested in watching the kids. Drinking in their antics, their playfulness, their joyful self-importance. Young adults have a shine about them. They glow with untapped potential.

When the boost was over, we all unclipped our anchors. I couldn't quite extricate myself from my deeply padded chair and my cane was out of reach.

Tré leapt to help me up. When I was on my feet, he pulled me into a hug.

"Are you going back to Luna?" he said in my ear.

I held him at arm's length. "That's right. Someone has to take care of Long Meng."

"Who'll take care of you?"

I laughed. "I don't need taking care of."

He gripped both my hands in his. "That's not true. Everyone does."

"I'll be fine." I squeezed his fingers and tried to pull away, but he wouldn't let go. I changed the subject. "Mars seems like a great choice for you all."

"I'm not going to Mars. I'm going to Luna."

I stepped back. My knees buckled, but the stability belt kept me from going down.

"No, Tré. You can't."

"There's nothing you can do about it. I'm going."

"Absolutely not. You have no business on Luna. It's a terrible place."

He crossed his arms over his broadening chest and swung his head like a fighter looking for an opening. He squinted at the old toys and sports equipment secured into rumpus room cabinets, the peeling murals the kids had painted over the years, the battered bots and well-used, colorful furniture—all the ephemera and detritus of childhood that had been our world for nearly eighteen years.

"Then I'm not leaving the crèche. You'll have to stay here with me, in some kind of weird stalemate. Long Meng will be alone."

I scowled. It was nothing less than blackmail. I wasn't used to being forced into a corner, and certainly not by my own kid.

"We're going to Luna together." A grin flickered across Tré's face. "Might as well give in."

I patted his arm, then took his elbow. Tré picked up my cane and put it in my hand.

"I've done a terrible job raising you," I said.

Alyssa Wong's stories have won the Nebula Award, the World Fantasy Award, and the Locus Award. She was a finalist for the John W. Campbell Award for Best New Writer, and her fiction has been shortlisted for the Hugo, Bram Stoker, and Shirley Jackson Awards. She lives in California and can be found on Twitter as @crashwong.

ALL THE TIME WE'VE LEFT TO SPEND

Alyssa Wong

When she got to Yume's room, the first thing Ruriko did was slip off her mask and remove her prosthetic jaw. There was an ache in her fake bottom teeth. It was going to rain, although one look at the sky could have told her that.

Across the room, Yume dimmed the lights and sat on the edge of the coverlet. The bed was obscenely red, round and mounted on a rotatable platform, as one could expect from a pay-by-the-hour love hotel. Yume's pale, gauzy skirt rode up her thighs as she shifted positions, and Ruriko wished she would tug it back over her knees. "Is there anything I can do to make you more comfortable?"

Ruriko checked each of her false teeth, pressing a thumb over them to see if any had come loose—it was time for a hardware checkup soon—before clicking the prosthesis back into place. None of the actual teeth, or even the joints, were acting up. Some kind of phantom pain, then, from the flesh-and-bone jaw she'd lost ten years ago. "No, I'm okay."

"I could put on some music." Ten years ago, Yume Ito had been one of the four founding members of IRIS, one of the country's top teen idol groups. Her face, along with Miyu Nakamura's, Kaori Aoki's, and Rina Tanaka's, had graced advertisements all over Tokyo, from fragrance ads to television commercials to printed limited-edition posters. But then the real Yume

Ito had died, along with the real Miyu Nakamura, Kaori Aoki, and Rina Tanaka, and now all that was left was an algorithm of her mannerisms and vocal patterns, downloaded into an artificial skin and frame.

"No music, please," said Ruriko. Her voice sounded strange and small, but too loud at the same time. "Just talking."

Yume, dead ten years, rested her hands on Ruriko's shoulders. Her fingers traced the cloth mask that hung from one ear like a wilted flag. She tucked it back over Ruriko's reassembled mouth. "Whatever you want us to do."

Taking her hands, Ruriko steered her back toward the bed. She sat, and Yume followed.

The soft green pulse of Yume's power source reflected off her black hair, tinting her skin with strange light. One of the room's walls was an extended panel of slightly angled mirrors, and that green glow flashed back in every one of them. Muffled pop music thumped at the walls, but the soundproof-ing in the room was good. No one could hear the sounds anyone made inside here. And Ruriko had paid for two full, uninterrupted hours.

"Are you comfortable now?" said Yume. There was nothing shy about her. She wore the same kind, gentle patience that had made her face so arresting to watch on film, all those years ago.

They were alone now, one mostly flesh girl and one dead one immortal-ized in silicone and aluminum. But Yume's hand felt warm, soft, alive. It was familiar down to the thumbprint-shaped birthmark on her inner wrist and the fine, thin scar across her palm from the time she'd sliced herself while cooking dinner for the younger members of IRIS. For Ruriko.

Ruriko rested her head on Yume's shoulder and laced fingers with her former girlfriend. "Yume, what do you remember about our last concert?"

No one in their right mind came to the Aidoru Hotel. But those who did always came for a very specific reason. Mostly, in Ruriko's opinion, that meant a horde of superfans, otakus, and would-be stalkers who wanted a night to do whatever they pleased with the celebrity of their choice. The disreputable folks from Kabukicho who ran the Aidoru Hotel didn't care, as long as their clients paid handsomely for the privilege. And Ruriko was paying, even with the family discount.

"I'm surprised you don't come here more than once a month," said Shunsuke. He waited for her by the lobby's front counter, tall and handsome in his suit, briefcase in hand. He must have commuted straight from work. Their other friends had headed up to their rooms already to get hot and heavy. "I would, if I had connections."

"Very brief, distant connections," said Ruriko, shaking the rain from her jacket. Her hair was damp, despite her hood and ponytail. Water splattered the clear acrylic floor, and beneath it, the giant projected videos of pop idols' top hits played in violent, frenetic colors.

Shunsuke slid his wallet back into his pocket. "They're close where it counts."

Ruriko joined him in the elevator, and together they ascended. She and Shunsuke had very different tastes and desires, but they both got what they wanted out of their visits to the Aidoru.

"You booked two hours as usual, right?" she said.

"Two and a half. It's been a stressful month at work." Shunsuke stretched. His empty left sleeve fluttered, pinned close to his chest in the absence of an arm. "Want to meet up later for ramen?"

"Sure. I don't know how you're hungry afterward, but why not."

They'd made it something of a tradition over the past several months. As the elevator climbed, Ruriko thought of fresh tonkotsu ramen, the crush of bodies, and the warm reassurance of anonymity. She chose not to think about where Shunsuke was headed, or the contents of his briefcase, or any of his numerous distasteful habits.

The elevator halted, and Shunsuke got out. He cut a sharp silhouette against the neon colors vying for dominance on the hallway's digitally projected wallpaper. "See you at ten," he said, and the doors slid shut behind him.

Miyu Nakamura tilted her head. Her hair fell across her shoulders in long, dyed brown curls, and she wore a pink pleated dress with a fluffy white petticoat. A different room, a different night, a different member of IRIS. "My last concert. The one in Shibuya?"

Ruriko remembered Shibuya. IRIS's costumes had been white and pastel blue, with geometric wire overlays. She hadn't been able to keep her eyes off Yume, whose long hair had danced about her waist with every precise, choreographed step. "No, the one at the Harajuku Astro Hall," said Ruriko. "October fourteenth, 2014."

"Oh, Harajuku! That's not happening until next week," said Miyu. The bed in this room was bright pink and covered in an alarming number of stuffed animals. There was barely room on it for either of them, even perched as they were on opposite sides. "We've been working on our routines since July, but Yume's pushing us real hard. My legs are still sore from practice this afternoon." She stuck them out, draping a coy ankle over Ruriko's lap. Ruriko ignored it. "Wanna massage them?"

"Nice try," said Ruriko. "If you're a dancer, isn't that something you should know how to do yourself?"

Miyu stuck her tongue out, but she started to knead her own calves anyway. "What kind of fan are you?"

"Just one who likes to talk," said Ruriko. She reached over and took Miyu's other leg, massaging it briskly. She'd done this for the real Miyu and the others, too, once upon a time. "Although I'm pretty fond of Yume."

"Everyone is fond of Yume," said Miyu. "She's so pretty and confident. Mature." Her voice wobbled a little at the end. "I don't know what she sees in Rina. She's basically the opposite of everything good about Yume."

She had a point, Ruriko thought. Once upon a time, Rina Tanaka had been brash, even abrasive. Her integration had been a rough patch in IRIS's history, and the real Miyu had made no secret of the fact that she didn't approve of any newcomer, especially not some cocky hotshot from a bad part of town.

"Rina thinks she's all that because she's a good dancer, but she's lazy. She comes to practice late, and she slacks off all the time. Worse, Yume lets her." Miyu sighed and flopped back on the bed. A shower of plush creatures tumbled off the mattress around her. "I told her she shouldn't play favorites because she's our leader, but she told me to practice harder so I wouldn't be jealous."

Yume had never told Ruriko about that. But this was why Ruriko visited Miyu every time she wanted to feel better about herself.

"And I have been working hard on this new choreo for Harajuku. Do you want to see?" Miyu hopped off the bed and struck a pose, one hand on her hip, elbows angled out.

She had worked hard. Ruriko remembered that; dancing had always been Miyu's weak spot, but the ferocity of her dedication had earned her Ruriko's respect. Not that it mattered a few weeks later. But after one practice session, two years into Rina Tanaka's career as the newest member of IRIS, Miyu had been tired of choreography—although everyone was tired of it except for Yume, who practiced religiously and with fierce dedication—and she had grabbed Ruriko's hand. "Let's go shopping," she'd said, and Ruriko had been surprised, because Miyu openly disliked her.

But maybe something had changed between them. They'd worn cloth masks just like the one Ruriko wore now, and hoodies, and pretended to be sick all the way there so that no one would look at their faces. And no one had. The push and pull of the crowd, the crush of humanity, after spending so long in their studio hammering immaculate choreography into their bodies, had been thrilling. Ruriko had bought an ugly bear, too, and smuggled it into the studio to leave at Yume's station. But she remembered Miyu's smile—the first genuine one she'd ever seen on her face—as they snapped a selfie with their matching stuffed animals. She'd thought, *Maybe I can do this. Maybe we can be friends.*

Ruriko wondered how Aidoru had gotten its hands on this plush bear. Maybe there were closets full of duplicate bears, duplicates of all the rabbits and mascots and soft round things heaped up on the bed, just in case something happened to the original.

"Well?" Miyu sounded impatient, and Ruriko looked up. Sure enough, Miyu was glowering at her, a tiny storm rising on that perfect, adorable little face. Ruriko had never liked Miyu's face.

"No. I wouldn't want to spoil the surprise," Ruriko added hastily, seeing how crestfallen Miyu looked. "I'm going to watch the broadcast live. It's more fun that way."

Mollified, Miyu flopped down next to her. One of her pigtails trailed across Ruriko's legs, and Ruriko picked it up. "I guess that makes sense. Too bad! I love sneak peeks."

She always had. That night at the Astro Hall, she'd burst into the dressing room, full of glee. *There's a giant light display above the stage! Four giant screens, corner to corner, so everyone can see us dance!* Ruriko had come in later than usual that day, and she hadn't gotten a good look at the setup during their abbreviated tech rehearsal. None of them had realized, at the time, how heavy those screens and the rigging that came with them were.

"Hey," said Miyu, and her voice was soft, almost gentle. This Miyu, thought Ruriko, still wore the original one's insecurity. "Would you brush my hair? I feel a little unsettled today. I'm not sure why."

So did Ruriko. She glanced up at the clock mounted on the wall. Forty-five minutes left. And then this Miyu would go back to being alone, waiting in this empty hotel room, with no memory of their conversation. "I can do that," she said quietly. "Hand me the brush?"

The back of Miyu's plastic hairbrush was covered in fake rubber icing, piped into a heart shape and decorated with fake rubber mini-pastries. Rhinestones dripped down the handle and dug into Ruriko's palm.

Miyu's hair felt like the real thing. When IRIS was younger, she used to make the others help her fix it. *If you don't, I'll fuck up the back,* she'd said every time, and every time, she was right. Ruriko remembered, every night before a performance in a strange new city, helping Miyu roll her hair up into curlers and fix them in place with strawberry-shaped Velcro patches.

This fake Miyu probably had fake hair. Maybe, Ruriko thought, it was real human hair—not the real Miyu's, but some other girl's, shorn and dyed to suit a dead idol's image. She wondered where those girls were now, how old their hair was. She wondered how hard it was to wash blood and other fluids out of synthetic wigs, and if someone had given up and sought a more human source to solve their human problem.

A finger tapped her hand. When Ruriko met Miyu's eyes, the smile on Miyu's pink-glossed lips was a little wicked. "Hey. You should really come to Harajuku next week and see us live. It's gonna be big, and you won't want to miss it. Especially not if you're a fan of Yume's."

"Maybe I'll come see you, too," said Ruriko, brushing the hair with steady, even strokes. The painful hope in Miyu's eyes dug at her own guilty conscience, and she found herself brushing harder, faster, even when the strands of beautiful chestnut brown hair began to come out.

"Look at that," said Shunsuke as Ruriko exited the elevator doors and blew into the lobby. He was watching the music videos playing beneath the acrylic floorboards. "Look at me! I'm so young."

There were little pale pink pills of synthetic fur stuck to Ruriko's sleeve, tangled among stray bits of hair. She picked them off furiously, tossing them into the air, where they wafted aimlessly away. "Who?"

"Me. Rina, look at this." He grabbed her arm, and she seized his wrist with her other hand so hard that he looked at her with alarm. "Shit, what's your problem?"

"Don't call me Rina. It's Ruriko."

Shunsuke let go. "Right. Now it is. I forgot." He pulled back and scratched his neck; beneath his well-shined shoes, his teenage self writhed in high definition. "I'm guessing it was a bad night for you."

Seeing Miyu always left a complicated taste in her mouth. "Buy me ramen tonight," she said. "Tonkotsu, extra pork."

Shunsuke, to his credit, made good. He didn't complain when she took the seat closest to the stall's far wall, either, even though that was his favorite place to sit. "You know, in all the months we've been coming here, I've never seen you order anything different," he said. "Always tonkotsu, maybe extra pork if you can afford it after blowing all your money at Aidoru."

Don't get your hopes up, Ruriko had told Shunsuke after their first post-Aidoru dinner, nine years and two months after the Harajuku Astro Hall catastrophe. The hotel had been open for just a year under her family's management, and she'd already been feeling raw over one intrusion into her past.

And then there was Shun in the lobby, so slick and confident that looking at him made her teeth hurt. *I'm not planning on fucking you.*

Good, he'd said, offering her his lighter. *It's mutual.* He'd kept his word, and so had she, and after a career spent under public scrutiny, that pressure-less friendship had been a relief. If they had tried this ten years ago, Ruriko knew it would never have worked.

"There's nothing wrong with having a favorite," said Ruriko, chasing one of her last bamboo shoots around her bowl. "You're nothing if not consistent yourself."

"I order something different all the time."

"That's not what I mean." Ruriko nodded at Shunsuke's briefcase.

He grimaced and kicked it farther under the bartop. The metal buckle caught a stray pocket of light and flashed back into Ruriko's eyes. She caught sight of a tuft of short, bleached blond hair snagged on the briefcase's lock before it disappeared behind Shunsuke's legs. "But the same kind of ramen! That's so boring. Don't you ever want to try something new?"

"No." It was true; sticking to a very regimented schedule was something Ruriko hadn't been able to shake, even a decade after her dancing days were over. All she needed for her graphic design work was her computer, her tablet, her notebooks, and the comfortable nest of books and pillows she'd built for herself. She exercised alone in her apartment, and groceries were delivered to her door. Ruriko kept mostly to herself these days, and she had little desire to leave the small, ordered world she'd so carefully constructed. Shunsuke and the other Aidoru regulars might well be psychopaths, but they were also the only other humans she saw on a regular basis.

Shunsuke, Ruriko amended as she watched him drain the dregs of his spicy miso ramen, was definitely a psychopath. But he was self-contained. There was only one person he ever hurt, and visiting Aidoru helped him deal with that.

Shunsuke set down his empty bowl. His wristwatch slid forward, baring a tangled mass of flattened scar tissue before his sleeve slipped down to cover it. "Let's get drunk," he said, and Ruriko had no objection to that.

Three and a half beers later, Ruriko was back on the Aidoru Hotel's booking website, scrolling over Yume's face. There was a menu on Yume's main page (Group IRIS, 154 cm tall, 49 kg, black hair, B cup, brown eyes, active 2011–2014), and when Ruriko tapped on it (as she always did; how many times had she been here before?), a dropdown list of dates and times unfolded beneath her fingers. A list of all of the original Yume's data scans and uploads, from the first time she'd let the talent management agency scan her memories and impressions (as they all did; how many times had they been told it was a contractual necessity?) to the last time, and every week in between. She scrolled all the way to the end of the list, to the last available entry.

October 8, 2014.

She slammed her phone down. "God fucking dammit!"

Shunsuke peered over at her. "Careful. That's how you get cracks in the screen."

"I don't know why I keep coming back," Ruriko said into her hands. "I know it's fake. I just—God. I keep hoping that someone will find and upload another entry. Just a couple more days' worth of data. A couple more memories. Just a little more time." Bitching with Kaori about their talent agency, loitering in the park with Miyu. Yume's voice in her ear as they stood together on the subway platform, waiting for the last train of the night.

Shunsuke rested his palm on her shoulder. His touch was unexpectedly gentle. He didn't tell her what they both already knew. "Let's get you home," he said instead.

"I wish they'd get their shit together," said Kaori Aoki. "When they fight, it affects us all. Yume works us harder; Rina skips out on responsibilities. But something must have happened, because Rina stormed in late today and Yume's not talking to anyone unless she's barking orders." She sighed, scratching her short-cropped hair.

Two days ago, someone had offered a bootleg copy of what they claimed were Kaori Aoki's last memories, recovered from some ancient talent agency database, to the Aidoru. Ruriko had swallowed her disappointment—why Kaori? She didn't care about Kaori, not the way she cared about Yume—but demanded that her family purchase the upload anyway. It probably wasn't legit, but . . . just in case.

But the longer she spent in the room with Kaori, the more the memories seemed to check out, and the more terrible hope rose in Ruriko's chest. If it could happen for Kaori, then maybe it wasn't impossible to think it could happen for Yume, too.

"We're running out of time before Harajuku, and their bickering is so petty," said Kaori. To this version of her, the fight between Yume and Rina had occurred just that afternoon.

She was right. It had been petty, most of the time. But this latest fight hadn't been. Ruriko had kissed Yume in the studio, when the two of them were alone, and Yume had freaked out. Not because she didn't want to be kissed. Because Ruriko had done it in their workplace. *What if someone saw?*

Yume had demanded. The wild, panicked, accusing look on her face had stabbed Ruriko straight in the heart. *You could ruin both of our careers!*

"She doesn't like the costume," Rina muttered. "I didn't like it either."

Kaori raised an inquisitive eyebrow. "No one likes the costumes. They're always terrible, this time especially. But we wear them anyway, and they're never as bad as they look at first." She headed for the dresser and began digging through drawers. Stockings, lingerie, and compression tights fluttered to the carpet. "What they need to do, in my opinion, is kiss and make up. Or make out. Whichever one helps the most."

Ruriko's head jerked up. "You think they're together?"

Kaori laughed. "Everyone knows. They're so obvious. Even Miyu knows, and she's in denial because she's half in love with Yume herself."

Ruriko's stomach turned and she sat down, hard, right there on the floor. They'd fought because Ruriko had wanted to tell the rest of IRIS about them and Yume hadn't. The media would have eviscerated them. Ruriko hadn't cared.

The last thing she'd heard, before she'd turned on her heel and stormed away, was Yume shouting, *How could you be so selfish?*

Yume had forbidden her to tell anyone anything. So Rina hadn't. Rina stopped talking to her groupmates altogether, and the frosty silence had carried over on the train to Harajuku, days later.

Kaori gave up on the dresser and threw open the door to her walk-in closet. The racks were a riot of color, stretching back like a long, awful throat made of bold metallic dresses and gauzy floral prints. Every costume she'd worn onstage, arranged by year instead of color. A fan's paradise. "It's gotta be in here. Hang on."

"Please don't," said Ruriko. Her voice came out strangled. The closet stank of bad memories; just looking at the costumes made sweat gather in her palms, at the small of her back, her heartbeat galloping into her throat. But Kaori was already rifling through them, humming one of their songs under her breath. Ruriko could only remember half of the notes; the melody in her head was distorted, like trying to listen to music underwater.

Kaori emerged, flourishing a silver dress with a stiff, flared skirt. "Look, I found it! Isn't this terrible?"

"It's really bad," mumbled Ruriko. The second-to-last time she'd seen that costume, she'd thrown it in Yume's face.

Kaori pressed it against Ruriko's chest. "Here, try it on. It is so uncomfortable, you will not believe it."

Ruriko should have said no. But all she could think of was how she had screamed at Yume, sending the dress flying in her face like a giant bat. If she could have taken it back—if she could take any of it back—

Something must have been wrong with her head, because then she was stepping out of her jeans, and Kaori was zipping the dress up behind her, all the way to the nape of her neck. It didn't fit properly; their bodies weren't the same shape, and where Ruriko was small and soft, Kaori was tall and toned. This version of her, seventeen years old and programmed with a new set of memories—October twelfth, two days from IRIS's amputated future—was full of tomboyish energy and excitement.

"See, I told you. But you actually look pretty good in this," said Kaori, turning her toward the mirror. They stood side by side, Ruriko pinched into a dress that was too tight in the waist and too loose in the bust, Kaori comfortable in shorts and a light blouse. The dress gaped open like a loose flap of skin over Ruriko's breasts. None of it fit, and it was hard to even look at her own body.

And then Kaori tapped a panel on the wall, and music blared into the tiny room. Synth vocals over a pulsing beat, four voices in one.

The Aidoru Hotel vanished. Ruriko was back there, standing on that slowly rising stage, her eyes wide in the dark, the ceiling of the Astro Hall soaring high above her in perfect geometry, her high heels already pinching her feet with two and a half hours left to dance, empty palm aching to hold Yume's hand, mouth still angry, both at Yume and at herself for not being able to get over it, waiting beneath that teetering lighting grid, waiting for the tech cue to start the third song, waiting—

"I can't do this." Ruriko's hands scratched wildly at the dress, hunting for the zipper. She couldn't reach it, and she thought, wildly, *What if I am stuck in this forever?* "I can't, I can't—"

The music cut off and her ears rang with silence. Hands found her and unzipped her quickly, and Ruriko sagged with relief. "Are you okay?" asked Kaori. Looking at her, Ruriko saw, instead of her wide, earnest face, a mess of dark hair spilling out from beneath two tons of metal, and sharp, shocked shapes of blood splattered across the stage.

"I don't think so," Ruriko whispered. She couldn't be okay, not if she was paying to destroy herself, over and over every month.

Kaori pulled her into her arms and held her tight. They stayed like that until Ruriko's two hours were up.

Ruriko was still shaking as she boarded her train home. Her phone rattled in her grip. But by the time the subway reached its next stop, she had booked and paid for her next appointment at the Aidoru.

"This is going to sound rich, coming from me," said Shunsuke, "but you need to learn to let things go."

They stood on the balcony of Shunsuke's apartment, smoking together and watching the rain pour down in great sheets. The brilliant multicolored lights from all the signs and ads and cars zinging by became patchy and blurred, doubled and strange, in this weather.

"Sure I do. Speaking of, how's that new dry cleaner working out for you?" said Ruriko.

"He's great. He never asks any questions." He cut his eyes at her. "I'm serious. Those girls can't remember anything. They don't even know who you are."

"They can't remember," Ruriko mumbled, stabbing out her cigarette. "But I can't forget. I don't want to forget."

"You know what always helps me," said Shun, and Ruriko hated him for what he was about to say. "Cutting right to the heart of the problem. And you're the heart, Rina-ko. Not them."

She flicked the cigarette off the edge of the balcony. Its dying ember flickered in the air, fluttering downward before disappearing into the night.

"You can finish this. You'll never have to go back again."

She whirled on him, anger flaring bright in her. Shunsuke always acted like he had everything figured out, with his sly voice and dry cleaning and neat little suitcase. "Does it feel good to lie to me?" she snapped. "Is that why you keep coming back to Aidoru, Shun? Because you've excised the heart of the problem?"

He stared hard at her and turned away. Ruriko bit her lip to keep any more of the venom bubbling up in her mouth from spilling out.

Looking at the tall, lanky shape he cut against the sky, she realized how different he was from when she'd seen him the first time, over ten years ago, surrounded by the other members of his group. He'd been small back then, with bleached blond hair, and in the decade following his own accident, he'd grown into himself and left his gangliness behind. He was sharper now, harder. And there was only ever one room that Shunsuke visited at the Aidoru, only ever one person.

"Do you ever talk to him?" she said at last. "When you go to see him?"

Shunsuke passed her another cigarette. There was still synthetic blood on his sleeve, a dark, thin stain running toward his wrist. "What would we have to talk about?" he said.

Cutting right to the heart of the problem, Shunsuke had said. As if it were that easy. But he'd opened his suitcase and pressed a bright switchblade into her hand before she left, folding her fingers over its polished wooden handle. *Trust me. It'll feel better afterward.*

People came to the Aidoru Hotel for answers. Therapy, excess, an outlet for stress. To sate obsessions. If the Aidoru could help someone as fucked up as Shunsuke, Ruriko reasoned, then surely it could help someone like her.

The overwhelming roar of pop music threatened to crush her down into the plush, ugly black-and-white hallway carpet. Upstairs and downstairs, people were already fucking TV personalities and musicians long dead, and somewhere else in the hotel, Shunsuke was about to take his bright knife to his younger self's skin. But Ruriko stood alone outside a room she'd paid for, Shunsuke's borrowed switchblade in her pocket, too afraid to touch the door.

You already spent your money, said a voice in her head. It sounded like hers, but off, the way recordings of her own voice always sounded. *A room here is expensive. Don't waste it.*

It'll make you feel better, said Shunsuke's voice. *Trust me.*

The only person you think about is yourself, whispered Yume. *Fix that, and then we'll talk.*

No one in their right mind came to the Aidoru Hotel, thought Ruriko, and she gripped her key card tight and reached for the lock.

The door slid open on its own, and Ruriko's hand leaped back. A dark-haired girl peered at her from inside the room, one hand up to shield her eyes from the bright cacophony of pop music. She was the same height, the same build as Ruriko, if ten years slimmer and younger.

"Are you going to come in?" said Rina Tanaka. "Or are you going to stand in the hall all night?"

After a moment, Ruriko tucked her key card back in her jacket pocket and followed her inside. Rina's room was all dusty violet, the color of her childhood room. The lights were dim, and Rina slid the switches up, making the room brighter. The wallpaper glinted with silver interlocked triangles, and they winked viciously at her as she passed.

"I was wondering when you'd stop by. I've been waiting for you."

Ruriko studied her, hiding her nervousness behind her mask. Rina looked about seventeen and had the same angled haircut that Ruriko remembered getting in September, right before the show in Shibuya with the powder-blue uniforms. "How did you know I was coming?"

"Your friend told me. He's been visiting me for a while. Paid for memory retention services and everything." This was Rina minus her stage persona, rougher than the other girls in IRIS, always a little too honest. In her voice, Ruriko heard the hints of Kabukicho that she'd spent her life trying to erase. "He said a woman with a red face mask would come by because she wanted to talk to me about something, but he didn't tell me what it was. And you're the only woman with a red face mask I've seen so far."

Shunsuke had set this up for her. Ruriko's hands shook; she kept them tucked in her pockets. The knife burned in her pocket. He'd probably meant it as a gift.

"Hey, you're from Kabukicho too, aren't you?" said Rina. She smiled. Ruriko had had that smile once too. "So who are you? What did you want to tell me?"

"You're going to let her die," said Ruriko, the words tumbling out past her clenched teeth. "At the Astro Hall." She had Rina's full attention now. And in that face, Ruriko read what she'd known was there—the anger, the fear, that she remembered having before they set out for Harajuku. "The lighting grid is faulty, it fell, and it crushed everyone. Yume—"

"Stop it," Rina said tightly. "I don't know what you're talking about." But her eyes were overbright, her voice too high.

Ruriko grabbed her by the shoulders. "She died. You killed her, because you were a selfish little shit, you showed up late because you were sulking and wanted to make them miss you, there wasn't enough time to run a tech rehearsal, *they would have caught it*—"

"I know!" Rina pushed at Ruriko, but Ruriko held on. Tears brimmed in Rina's eyes. "Fuck! I know! I remember. Did you think I'd forget?"

Ruriko's grip was so tight that her fingers were starting to hurt. "What?"

"I was an idiot. I thought—I was so mad. I was so upset at her. I thought she'd dump me for sure after that." Rina's tears splattered onto Ruriko's arms. She wasn't pushing her away anymore; she gripped Ruriko's shirt. "I wanted to make her hate me. I wanted to make her pay."

She had wanted that. And Yume had paid. But Ruriko's head was reeling, and she shook Rina. "What day is it?" she demanded. "What's the last day you remember?"

"October twenty-fifth," whispered Rina. "I woke up in the hospital. The people from the talent agency were there. They said they'd scanned me while I was out. They told me I'd never dance again. Everyone else in IRIS was dead, and if I knew what was good for me, I'd pretend I was too."

She'd forgotten. Ruriko let go of Rina. She'd forgotten about that last scan; those days were a blur of grief, horror, regret, and it hadn't seemed important in the wake of her loss. Yume was gone.

"I could have saved her," said Ruriko. She felt numb. She'd been so stupid. "She was right. How could I have been so selfish?"

"You?" A look of terrible revelation crossed Rina's face. "What's under this mask? Who are you?" She reached out toward Ruriko's mask.

Ruriko shoved her away as hard as she could. Rina stumbled back into the small wooden vanity parked against the wall. "Don't touch me," Ruriko said hoarsely. All their collective secrets were spilling into open air.

"Please," said Rina, but Ruriko backed away. Her awful synthetic body with its awful synthetic skin and awful synthetic youth, its face twisted with regret but still whole, made Ruriko sick.

She turned and fled the room. She was in the elevator and through the lobby and out into the street, fifteen minutes into her two-hour time slot. She didn't ask for a refund.

It took a long time for Ruriko to come back to the Aidoru. But when she did, there was only one door she gravitated to.

"Does my face scare you?" said Ruriko.

Yume glanced over at her. They lay together on the red circular bed in her room, side by side, their hands just brushing each other. One of them had accidentally hit a switch to make the bed rotate, and they hadn't been able to figure out how to turn it off, so they turned slowly together, their feet dangling to brush the floor.

"No, of course not. You had reconstructive surgery, right? It looks really natural."

The red cloth mask was wadded up in Ruriko's other palm. How many times had this Yume seen her face? How many times had she asked her the same questions, aching to hear Yume's affirmation, over and over again? How much did it hurt, knowing that Yume couldn't blame her for what would happen, what did happen in Harajuku, because she would never know who Ruriko was?

Impulsively, Ruriko sat up halfway, propping herself up on her elbows. "You know, some people have said I look like Rina Tanaka. What do you think?"

Yume took a moment before she replied; perhaps her internal algorithm was searching for a tactful answer. "Maybe a little," she said at last. "Your eyebrows. Very Rina Tanaka."

Ruriko laughed. She'd thought she'd be injured by that response, and she was surprised and pleased to find that she wasn't. "That's more than I thought I'd get. I'm surprised you saw any resemblance; you spend so much time together, I bet you know her better than most people."

"I'm seeing her later tonight," Yume said, looking slyly at Ruriko. "We're going to hang out after evening practice. She promised."

A luminous feeling spread through Ruriko's chest. She settled her head back on her pillow and stared up at the mirrored ceiling, thinking. What had they done the night of October eighth? It hurt that she couldn't recall all the details; they'd blurred at the edges over the years. But she remembered that it was cold already, unseasonably cold, and she had dragged Yume to the park to get ice cream anyway. Yume had been worried about getting sick in that weather. And then Ruriko had grabbed her by the scarf and kissed her to stop her scolding.

"For ice cream?" she said.

Yume turned to look at her, her hair falling around her like a curtain. "That's a good idea. I was thinking about getting ice cream." She reached out to touch Ruriko's face, and this time Ruriko didn't pull away. "It's strange," she murmured. "You do remind me a bit of her. It's your expressions, your mannerisms, the way you talk. You're different, but maybe you could be her cousin."

She grinned and leaned in to Yume's touch. Her fingers felt warm, real. "I guess I'm lucky."

"You are," said Yume, tracing the line of Ruriko's face, all the way down her jaw. Her touch was tender instead of sensual. "But don't tell her I said that. I don't want her to get a swelled head." She shifted on the bed, and her skirt whispered around her. "You know, it's complicated. I want her to think I'm responsible. I'm her senior, and I'm supposed to look out for her. But at the same time, I want to spoil her. There's just something special about her; it makes me determined to show her that all her hard work is worthwhile."

"She loves you," Ruriko said. She still did. "That's why she works so hard."

Yume glanced at her, surprised. Ruriko expected her to deny it. But instead, gentle pink spread across her cheeks. "Is it so obvious?" she asked.

Ruriko smiled up at her. "Only to the people who matter," she said.

"She has a lot of growing up to do. But she's a good dancer. She's full of fire. She's . . . beautiful."

"Maybe you should tell her that more often."

"I'm only telling you this because you're Rina's cousin."

"Oh, so it's decided now?" She swatted Yume with a pillow, and Yume yanked it away from her and tossed it across the room. "If you could," Ruriko said, much more quietly. "If you could be with anyone, would you still want to be with her?"

Yume hesitated and looked away. "Could we talk about something else?"

Uncomfortable, familiar disappointment settled in Ruriko's chest. But still, she thought, this was the closest Yume had ever come to admitting to Ruriko that she'd loved Rina. She'd said as much in private, many times. But maybe telling "Rina's cousin" was the closest she'd come to speaking it aloud in public. "Anything you want," she said.

She smiled and patted Ruriko's hair. It was an impulsive gesture, but to Ruriko, it was familiar, safe. "If you want to see Rina in her element, you should come to see us perform in Harajuku next week. I've been drilling the girls, and our choreography is excellent. She's never been better."

The memory of crashing lights came back to Ruriko, the way it had in Kaori's room. But this time, she closed her eyes tight and held on, focusing on the living warmth of the body beside her. The memory slipped away. Ruriko opened her eyes to the mirrored ceiling, blinked once, twice. Her reflection blinked back. "Yeah," she said, her voice steady. "I'll be there." Again, and again, and again.

Yume took her hand and squeezed it, the way she used to all those years ago. "Good," she said. Her face was so lovely that it hurt to look at her. "I promise you won't be disappointed."

Madeline Ashby is a science fiction writer and futurist living in Toronto. Her work has been published in *Slate, MIT Technology Review, McSweeney's,* and elsewhere. She is the author of the Machine Dynasty series from Angry Robot Books. Her most recent novel, *Company Town,* is available from Tor Books and a winner of the Copper Cylinder Award.

DOMESTIC VIOLENCE

Madeline Ashby

'm sorry; I had some trouble getting out of the house," Janae said to Kristen.

Janae's frustration was obvious. It manifested as raw cuticles that she couldn't help picking as their meeting continued.

Kristin frowned. "Couldn't find your fob?"

"No, I mean I couldn't get out of the house," Janae said. "The house—well, I mean, the condo—wouldn't let me out. The door wouldn't open."

"Literally?"

"Literally. I thought it was stuck, like jammed or something, but it just wouldn't open."

Kristen examined Janae. They were here to talk about Janae's recent tardiness, her distractedness, the fact that she hadn't delivered on her deliverables, hadn't actioned her action items. As Wuv's chief of staff, it was Kristen's job to learn what workplace issues existed and deal with them. At least, that's how she had explained the meeting to the company's co-founder. Privately, she had her own suspicions about what was really happening.

"Maybe she's knocked up," was Sumter's contribution to the conversation.

"If she were, it wouldn't be our business," Kristen had reminded him. "Legally speaking."

Sumter heaved a very put-upon sigh. "Well, yeah. But you're a girl, you can get it out of her."

Kristen had blinked, but otherwise allowed no other reaction to surface on her features or in her affect. "You want me to get her an abortion?"

"Jesus Christ, Kiki, no. Just find out what the fuck is going on, and then fix it." And with that he dismissed her from his office.

Now she and Janae sat together in her own office, the question between them—or what passed for an office, in Wuv's spacious loft. A delineation of clear sheets of acrylic and projected light and ambient sound. Today the lights projected a quiet jungle clearing. Softly rustling palm fronds, carefully calibrated to be seizure-proof. It felt intimate. It felt hidden. It felt secure. Kristen believed it was important for the employees at Wuv to feel safe in the cocoon that was her space. It helped them open up.

"You couldn't leave the condo," Kristen said. It helped to repeat things, sometimes. She'd learned that particular tactic from a succession of psychiatrists. Each of them had their tics and tells, but this was a common technique. When Janae said nothing, Kirsten acted more interested in the specifics: "What finally made the door open?"

"I had to do the chicken dance. It started playing the song and then I started dancing, and then the door opened. I think maybe some kid in the building hacked the door."

"Has that happened before?"

Janae frowned delicately. She was a delicate woman. Coltish. That used to be the word. All knees and elbows and knuckles. Once upon a time, she did doll-hairstyling videos online, her careful hands combing tiny brushes through pink and purple hair. They were classics in their genre; she was so well-recognized that children and their parents followed her sponsored updates to local toy stores and asked for photos and autographs and hugs. She'd had surgery since then. Few vestiges of her childhood face remained. Even neural networks couldn't match her old face to her current one. Her plastic surgeon, she claimed, had won some sort of award for his work restructuring her skull.

"It's something Craig used to do," Janae said, "when we were first dating. He would make up a riddle, and I'd have to solve it before the door to his place would open to let me out. It's the kind of trick people use to grant access to the home, but he reconfigured it. It's really easy; there were tutorials for it. He told the story at our wedding."

"I see," Kristen said.

Kristen let Janae off with a warning. She preferred a gentle approach, at first. It was part of why Sumter hired her—she could make his employees feel only the velvet glove without any hint of the iron fist beneath. Kristen pretended that the whole meeting was just a kindly check-in, that Janae wasn't at all in trouble, that no one else had noticed anything. It built the narrative of

Kristen as a thoughtful chief of staff. If she was correct about the particular scenario Janae had landed herself in, it would behoove the entire company if Kristen were understanding and supportive. It wouldn't do for them to be anything else. Not if they wanted to survive a civil suit.

Finally, it was time for her to go home. It was well past time by the third tank of pink smoke that Sumter insisted on buying her. It tasted of rosewater and almonds, and melted into icy mist on the tongue. He wiped down the mask himself, before offering it to her, so that the first thing she smelled was his custom strain of sanitizer. They were supposed to be going over the projects she would manage in his absence. They weren't. They were talking about him. And Janae.

"Did she tell you anything?" Sumter asked.

Kristen shrugged. "She told me enough. I'm handling it."

"Whatever that means," he said, adjusting the flavors on his own tank. "I wish you were coming to Dallas."

"It's too hot for me. And they don't like it when men and women travel together."

"That's Kansas," he said.

"And Ohio. I think."

"I'm not going through U.S. Customs with you again, is my point."

Sumter took a brief inhale from his tank and grimaced. He'd gotten rosemary-sumac-spruce. It was a little strong. Too strong for him, anyway.

"We could get married," Sumter said. "You know. For travel purposes."

Kristen inhaled. She held the cold mist in her lungs for as long as possible. She imagined the cold permeating her entire being. She pictured her blood slowing, her organs frosting over in delicate flowers. Sumter had been making more of these attempts, lately. That's what they were, little conversational pen-tests. They felt like nerdy in-jokes about some obscure series that she hadn't seen yet.

"But then we would have to get divorced," Kristen said. "And if you think I'm a bitch now . . ."

Sumter grinned. He took a deep gulp of smoke and shook his head. "You wouldn't divorce me, Kiki. I wouldn't let you get away."

Kristen slid off her barstool. "Guess I'd just have to poison you, then."

Home was Wuv Shack 1.0, a sprawling Parkdale Victorian that was once a nod-off and then became the home of home-improvement stars. The house was Sumter's, and before that it belonged to his parents. He'd since moved into his own space, but kept the place where he'd co-founded the company, and leased out the rooms to new or migratory employees for what in Toronto passed for a competitive market rate.

Kristen kept a camera-zapper in her room and slept under dazzle-patterned sheets that kept her solo explorations secret.

In her mail slot, she found a courier's envelope. Inside was a key fob and a piece of hotel stationery. "HERE FOR 48 HOURS" it read.

"Damn it," Kristen whispered, and hurried outside the building. It was raining, now, and she almost slipped on the greasy streets. The jitney came and she didn't have long to wait; the hotel was a new one, surprisingly close by. She waved her fob at the door and an elevator chimed open for her. When it arrived at the proper floor, the fob flashed a room number at her.

Inside, in the dark, she heard the shower running. She slipped off her shoes, unzipped her dress, found a hanger, and hung it in the hall closet. She threw her underclothes in a drawer in the closet and crossed into the bathroom. He stood motionless under the stream of water, seemingly asleep. Antony was the only man she knew who didn't have tattoos. It was refreshing. Elegant. Analog. Kristen stepped in behind him and wrapped her arms around him.

"Sorry I'm late."

"You're not," he said. "I had them send the fob when I landed."

She smiled into his skin. He turned around and kissed her. It took a moment; he liked to assess the terrain first. It had been a month since the last time, maybe more, and she watched him take in all the details that might have changed before descending. He held her face in his hands, covering her ears, and for a moment she was not under a stream of water but under waves, far away, in a place that was very dark and very warm. He kept his eyes ever so slightly open. It was the only time she remembered enjoying the sensation of being watched.

When he pulled away, he started pulling her hair out of its tie. "How was your day?"

"My boss asked me to marry him."

"Of course he did," Antony said. "Will you report him to HR?"

"I *am* HR."

He pointed upward at some invisible point over her head. "That's the joke." He knelt down and started scrubbing her from the toes up. She braced herself on the tile and watched the smart meter on the shower ticking down to the red zone where Antony or his employer would have to start paying extra for hot water.

"Do you think he was serious?"

Kristen looked down at him. He'd set her foot on his knee and was scrubbing in circles up her calf. "Are you jealous?"

He worked his way up to her knee and under her thigh."Not in any way that violates our terms."

She tilted her head. "But?"

"But, he seems more aggressive, lately. To hear you tell it."

Kristen snorted. "I can handle it."

"Oh, I have no doubt of that," he said, and put her foot back down on the floor of the shower. "Can I do the next part hands-free?"

She checked the timer. "You better work fast."

"Well, you know what they say," he said, pushing her gently against the wall. "You can have it fast, good, or cheap. Pick two."

She came awake with her throat sore from a swallowed scream. Antony had curled around her. He spoke into her neck. "Bad dream?"

She nodded and pulled his arm tighter over her.

"What happened?"

Kristen wiped her eyes and exhaled a shuddering breath. She refused to speak until her breathing had calmed down. "Something else happened at work. And I guess it dislodged something, sort of. Mentally."

"Something else Sumter did?"

"No." She rolled over and spoke to him directly. "Someone at my work is in trouble. I think."

"Will you have to fire someone?"

She shook her head. "Not that kind of trouble. Well, it is, but that's not what I mean. There's something else going on, something causing their problems at work."

"Something at home?"

"I think so. But it's hard to ask. I don't even know if she thinks it's a problem. I don't really know how she feels about it. Maybe she doesn't know how she feels, either. It might be nothing."

"What do you think it is?"

Kristen sighed. "Can I see your device? I need to check some blueprints on a non-work machine."

Antony's devices were very dumb. They used minimal storage and processing, and didn't even wear a brand name. That just meant it was probably some special boutique brand that Kristen had never heard of. It was a delightfully retrograde little thing; all it did was take calls and pictures. Even the photos required an extra kit to download. It felt like playing with Lego.

He handed her a scroll and she resolved a relationship with the hotel network, then looked up Janae and her husband's condo. She didn't recall the exact address, but searching "tampon-shaped monstrosity Toronto" actually worked.

"This is where they live. Her husband locked her in, today. Yesterday. Whatever. She was late because he locked her in."

"You know it happened because he locked her in? She wasn't just late? It wasn't just an error?"

Kristen made an elaborate shrug. "No? But she as much as told me it could have happened."

"She as much as told you, or she told you?"

"She told me it was something he used to do. When they were dating. Refusing to let her out until she did the thing he wanted. Like a rat in a maze, performing for pellets."

"So. Marriage." Antony took back the scroll and opened a set of floor-plans the building had advertised. "Which one do they live in?"

Kristen peered over his shoulder and fingered the surface. "That one, I think. Based on the photos she's shared, anyway. I've never been there."

He summoned the floor-plan and copied a serial number at the bottom of the screen, then fed the number into another tab. A bunch of press releases came up, most of them for gadgeteers, real estate developers, and interior decorators. But the first hit was for the manufacturer of a smart locking system.

The locking system was part of the whole condo's suite of smart services. It was the big selling point of the building itself: Living there was like living in a fairy-tale castle where every piece of the structure was alive and enchanted to serve the needs of its inhabitants. The showers remembered how warm you liked the water and at what intensity, and balanced your usage with that of the other residents. The fridges told you when a neighbor in the kitchen network had the buttermilk you needed for that special salad dressing. The windows and lights got information about your alpha patterns and darkened to start sleep cycles on schedule. The smart locking systems recognized residents and their visitors, over time, and even introduced them to each other when their profiles matched. Membership in the building came with special pricing from affiliated brands on everything from home goods to auto-rental to nannying and tutoring. The more purchase points you accrued, the more rewards you amassed, which could also be applied to the price of maintenance or utilities. And a massive and very public data leakage from the network supplying this building and many others ensured that the developers had to offer almost unheard-of interest rates, which tempted buyers who might never have managed, otherwise.

"Oh look, they have a bot," Antony murmured.

He opened the chat and after the niceties, typed: I THINK MY HUSBAND HAS HACKED THE DOOR.

"No, wait," Kristen protested. "If you send that, they'll ask for your location. If you don't give it, they'll start pinging the machine. And once they find it, they'll call the police. The bots have a whole protocol for smart homes when that happens."

"Do they?" Antony asked. "How do you know?"

But Kristen had already taken the clamshell out of his hands. She grabbed a pillow and jammed it under the clamshell to protect her skin. It would take a trickier question to get the information she wanted. She started typing: CAN I USE MY SMART LOCKING SYSTEM TO KEEP MY KIDS SAFE?

The bot asked for more information. It was very polite, double-plus Canadian, and it wanted to know what she meant. MY CHILD IS A SLEEPWALKER AND I WANT TO MAKE SURE HE STAYS INDOORS AT NIGHT, she typed.

The bot agreed that this was a natural concern, and informed her that the best mechanism for keeping her kids indoors was to adjust their individual account privileges. The camera in the door would recognize each child, and the door itself would check against the child's settings. There was a default mode for after-school play, nighttime, mornings, and so on. But the programming itself was fairly granular: You could tune it to certain days (the days you had custody, for example) or get the door to stop admitting certain people (pervy uncles, your daughter's ex). All you had to do was change the nature of the invitation.

"Like with vampires," Antony said.

"You said it," Kristen said. "I bet he did something really simple, like changing her age on the account. If he made her a minor, she'd lose editorial access to the defaults. She wouldn't be able to log in and make changes, even if she had the right password. And then he could custom-tune it anytime he wanted. In the meantime, she's solving puzzles and showing up late for work."

Antony rose and moved to the fridge. "If I mix you something, will you drink it?"

"Make that sound less threatening," Kristen said.

"They have rye and ginger. That's deeply unthreatening."

"Don't you have a meeting tomorrow? Today, I mean?"

He shrugged. "At 10. It's 4. I'll make screwdrivers instead."

"Your funeral," Kristen said.

He came back with drinks and settled in behind her. He pulled her hair to one side and pressed his sweating glass against the back of her neck. "What was your dream about?"

She leaned forward. "Nothing. It doesn't matter."

"It was enough to warrant this little investigation."

"That wasn't my dream. It's just what's happening to Janae. From work. Or what I think is happening to her. I can't stop thinking about it."

He kept the ice off her neck but played with her hair instead. Like the drink, it was probably a ploy to help her relax enough to reconsider sleep, and she knew it. Kristen let him do it anyway. He raked careful fingers from her scalp down to the ends, separating the little snags and catches as he went. "Why can't you stop thinking about it?"

Kristen twisted to face him over her shoulder. "I just have a bad feeling about it. And I want to know if I'm right, or if it's nothing to worry about."

"And if you are right? What then?"

Kristen frowned. Antony had a way of keeping his face and voice entirely neutral that made her want to fill the silence. There was no judgment, and therefore no warning signal that she should stop. It was hard to know if he was annoyed or bemused at her sudden instinct to chase this down.

"I'm sorry," she said. "We can just go back to sleep. I just woke up with it on my mind."

"That's not what's bothering me. I'm jet lagged; I'd be up in an hour anyway."

"Something is bothering you, though."

"What's bothering me is that something's bothering you, and you're not telling me what it is."

Kristen sighed. She turned fully around and folded her legs. "Something did happen to me, a long time ago. A version of this, I guess. But it's over, now. I haven't thought about it in a long time."

"But this situation reminds you of it."

She nodded. "And I guess it's getting to me."

He burrowed a bit deeper into the pillows and stretched his legs out so they hemmed her in. "How long ago was a long time ago?"

"University."

"And are you still in contact with this person?"

She laughed. "What? No. Why? Are you gonna go beat him up, or something? It was years ago."

Antony didn't answer. His head lolled on the pillows. He held her gaze just long enough to make things uncomfortable. In their encounters, she had never known him to be violent, or even very angry. He expressed displeasure and annoyance, but never fury. But this moment felt different: His total lack of affect made it seem like he was hiding something.

"I thought we agreed to keep things . . ." She struggled with the proper wording. "I barely know anything about you. I don't know where you work. I don't know who your clients are. I don't know who else you sleep with. And you're the one who wanted it that way. You said it would help avoid complications. I thought you didn't want to know anything . . . personal. So why do you want to know about this?"

Antony sipped his drink. The clink of the ice and the movement of his throat carried in the perfect early morning silence of the hotel room. Kristen heard no showers running, no toilets flushing, no anxious footsteps on other floors. For a single moment she wondered if he'd taken control of the whole floor, the whole building, the whole street. She didn't know who he worked for—who paid for the trips—but they clearly had the money to throw around. She knew it had to be something mundane, even boring, but at times like this she wondered.

"I just want to know if there's someone to watch out for," Antony said, finally. "For all I know, he's profoundly jealous and stalking us both."

"You don't even live in this city. And your visits aren't regular enough for anyone to predict. Besides, I don't use any channels to contact you that any of my other connections are familiar with. And I never make any reference to you, anywhere. That's also what we agreed to, and I've stuck to my end of the bargain. You're fine. No one that I know even knows you exist. I thought that's how we both wanted it."

She looked at the scroll. The bot was going to log out. For the moment, she had what she needed. She could always do more research later. And Janae might have more to say, if she gave it some more time. She turned back to Antony. "Do you want to renegotiate?"

"Do you?"

"I don't know! You're the one who's asking all this personal stuff; I've just been trying to follow the rules." She squared her shoulders and decided to just say it out loud: "Even if they're totally insane rules that make you sound like some kind of professional killer or something."

The corners of his lips pricked up. "Professional killer. I like that. I think we should go with that. I think you should just assume that, from now on."

She fixed him with a look. "Antony. You work in venture capital. We all know that's way worse than murder."

Before heading in for work, Kristen needed to stop by the Wuv Shack 1.0 for fresh clothes. At seven in the morning the house was still mostly asleep. To her surprise she found Janae standing in the kitchen, making coffee. She looked like she'd been crying. Kristen decided then and there to give Janae the day off. The woman was in no shape to work.

"You get locked out?" Kristen asked.

Janae didn't answer. She just filled another mug and slid it in Kristen's direction. "I didn't know where else to go. I texted Mohinder and he let me in. There was a couch open."

Kristen felt a momentary pang that she hadn't been paying attention; she could have let Janae into her empty bedroom and given her more than a sofa to sleep on. On the other hand, maybe a night exiled from her own home would loosen Janae's lips a little. She already looked brittle. Ready to crack.

"Have you talked to Craig about it?"

Janae made a gesture that indicated a species of futility. "He's up north, scouting an abandoned diamond mine. The signal's terrible."

Kristen had her doubts about that. One of the first things any real resource-extraction firm did up north was build fast, reliable networks and extend them to the neighboring towns and reserves. It was a make-good for all the other damage, a facet of revised treaty agreements. Either Janae was lying about trying to broach the topic, or Craig was lying about being able to reach her.

"When does he get back?"

"Tomorrow. Maybe. It's an unpiloted aircraft, though, so sometimes the flight path can change when they shuttle actual pilots between airports. It costs less, but you wait longer because it's more like a standby."

Kristen filed away the information to a safe corner of her mind, and said: "I had a problem like that, once. With a door, I mean."

Janae's gaze darted up at Kristen mid-sip. She gulped audibly. Kristen had a sneaking suspicion that Janae had been doing some research into this particular problem and the men commonly attached to it. Her eyes were a sleepless red, the kind of red that meant long nights questioning certain choices.

"What did you do?" Janae asked.

"Well, it wasn't my house," Kristen said. "I had some problems with my roommate, and my friend let me stay with him in his fancy new smart home. It started with one night, and then another, and then a weekend, and then somehow I just ended up spending the rest of term there. You know?"

Janae nodded.

"And a funny thing happened," Kristen continued. "I started noticing that every time I changed my clothes, I couldn't leave the room. The door would stick. Unless I got completely naked and started from nothing. I think he'd rigged up a recognition algorithm to lock the door unless it saw a totally naked body. The house was smarter than he was, I guess."

Janae's eyes were wide. "He was filming you."

Kristen shrugged. "Probably. But I could never prove it. And I needed a place to stay."

"So what happened?"

Kristen smiled and refilled both cups. "I played a prank on him, so he figured out that I knew what he was doing."

Janae beamed. "Oh yeah? What?"

For a moment, all Kristen could smell was exhaust. She could see his hands on the glass so clearly, could see glass splintering away from his weakening fist.

"Oh, just kid stuff," she said. "Now, why don't you go upstairs and have a nap? You can take my room. I'll be gone all night."

That night, Antony returned to the hotel smelling vaguely of cigars. He was in the shower a long time, and returned to find her on the scroll.

"That's a good car service," he said. "Secure. They don't save the data."

"Is it the fancy one they send when they want to impress you?"

"When they want to impress me, they pick me up themselves." He slid between the sheets and started kissing down her outstretched thigh. "Do I want to know about this little project of yours?"

"I'll be done soon," she said. "I just need to make a reservation."

"For your boss? I mean your husband?"

She reached over and scratched her fingers along his scalp affectionately. "Don't insult me."

Antony laid his cheek on her knee. "How was your co-worker today?"

Kristen pressed a confirmation button and rolled the scroll shut. "Fragile."

"And how are you?"

"Hungry."

He looked up at her through his lashes. "Whatever for?"

Antony left the next day. But he extended the hotel reservation a little longer so Kristen could stay a few more nights, leaving her room free for Janae. "It gets me into preferred customer status," he said when Kristen protested. "I'll just use the points on my next visit."

Kristen held herself back from asking when that would be. It wasn't precisely against the rules, but it would rather ruin the surprise. It was enough to emerge from a mid-week holiday pleasantly sore and well-breakfasted. Her schedule couldn't really accommodate the type of capital-R Relationship that led to arrangements like Janae's. Thank God.

Janae herself was gone from work for three more days. There was the day she took off at Kristen's behest, and then the other two days were spent searching for her husband. Upon his return, Craig, it seemed, had gotten into a car that flashed his incredibly generic name at the airport taxi stand at

Pearson. But it clearly hadn't been meant for him: It drove him not to Janae and the tampon-shaped condo tower in Toronto, but to an old cobalt mine near Temagami, Ontario.

IT CRASHED, Janae's texts read. IT DROVE RIGHT INTO THE PIT.

Kristen expressed shocked surprise. The company sent flowers. But Craig would be fine. He would just need some traction and some injectables for a while. And of course he'd be stuck at home. Alone. For hours. Waiting for Janae to come home. Dependent on her for everything.

Apparently there was another Craig in Toronto with the same name, who also had a returning flight arriving that same day. He had posted on his social media about his flight and how much he was looking forward to coming home. Just the month before, that Craig had been returning from another trip, and posted a glowing review of the car service he'd used. The service's customer retention algorithms, Janae said, must have associated the information and then sent a comped car as a part of their marketing outreach. At least, that was what the police had said must have happened. The car's records were scrubbed every 24 hours, and it had taken Janae's Craig so long to be found. Even when he called for help, he couldn't identify the model of the car or the license plate number. He had been trapped for hours, helpless.

"It sounds awful," Kristen said.

"It was," Janae agreed, once she returned to work. "He's terrified. Says he can't go back to another mine again. I can't leave any lights off. He was in perfect darkness for hours and hours."

On the weekend, Antony called. "I've been thinking about your stalker," he said, after they'd spoken in great detail about how exactly she had used the hotel room, how many times, and with which hand.

"He never stalked me," Kristen said.

"So he's really not a problem?"

"He's really not."

"You promise?"

"I promise."

She could almost hear him screwing up the courage for vulnerability. "Because you can tell me, if—"

Kristen laughed. She rose from her desk, catching Sumter's eye. He grinned at her and she waved back. Outside, it was snowing. Just a few tiny flakes under a leaden sky. "It's sweet of you to be so concerned, Antony. But please don't worry. He's dead."

Ian McDonald is an SF writer living in Northern Ireland, just outside Belfast. A multiple-award winner, his most recent novel is the conclusion of the Luna trilogy: *Moon Rising* (Tor, Gollancz). Tweet him at @iannmcdonald.

TEN LANDSCAPES OF NILI FOSSAE

Ian McDonald

The colors change faster than I can capture them. The reds have deepened to purple now and the shadows creep out from beneath the cliffs to change the sand from saffron to umber. No sooner do I get it down than the hues shift again. I step back from my tablet to see the whole: a patchwork of hues and colors. That's the skill of the artist, they say, to take away the thing and just see the color patches. Is it Nili Fossae? It's what I see, as the sun moves and the shadows shift and evening draws in.

I won't even begin on the perspective of the base. Carlos is twice the size of his rover.

Color weird, perspective crazy, no paint, no brush, no canvas. Pixels on a screen, but my gloved finger chose them placed them, blended them. Not a photograph, a painting. The first painting on Mars.

Nasrin laughed.

"Watercolor?"

I said, "Well, if there's water anywhere . . ."

Look Nili Fossae up on images and you see a jewel-box. Greens, blues, a dozen turquoises, rubies and gold. False colors, geological colors showing the reality of what lies beneath. Olivine-basalt sands, olivine-carbonate outcrops. Carbon. Magic word. Methane outgassings from the valley floor drew us; the first expedition to Mars. Methane hints at life, and no rock, no landscape, fascinates us as much as the possibility that we might find something like us: living, reproducing.

There are non-biological sources of methane; deep-rock stuff. But those require water.

One of my earliest rock-licker memories is a docent in the science museum pouring water on a slice of marble. Mottled gray darkened. Colors came to life!

In reality, in the painter's faceplate, Nili Fossae is rust and gold, the still shades of red. What the painter does is find the hidden colors

"You aren't really going to use water?" Nasrin said. We've been having problems with the recycling system since Marsfall.

"No, it's all brush effects and filters."

I pack my tablet in the thigh pocket of my surface suit and cycle the lock.

From 1892 to 1893 Monet painted thirty studies of Rouen Cathedral, in France. By season, by light, by time of day.

Nili Fossae is my Rouen Cathedral; the tiered walls of the great valley the facade, the buttresses, the intricate stonework. The sky is huge here, intimidating and unrelenting. The rare clouds—little more than wisps—are welcome.

I was pleased with the watercolor. The filters turned rock to washes of hue, and I have learned the trick of fine control through my gloved hand. I say watercolor, but everything I do is fingerpainting. I have appropriated a little instrument stand to hold the tablet. My easel. No one has missed it yet. No one has missed me yet. Geology is less pressing than solving our environment problems: the water is working again but the airplant is now springing leaks.

So: Nili Fossae at daybreak, at high noon, in the evening. Nili Fossae with the fast bright moons low in the night sky. The trick is to see the colors behind the object. Paint the impression, not the thing. I would love to paint the cliffs in every season and light, but the return launch window closes in thirty days.

"Why don't you paint some people?" Nasrin says. "These are pretty but they're just rocks."

You can't argue landscape with someone whose idea of the value of an image is whether it has them in it. But painting the Nili Fossae is every way a challenge, so I accept this one. Figure in a landscape. An image comes to me, from childhood, I imagine: a man standing on a pinnacle of rock, bareheaded, back turned to me, overlooking a sea of mists and peaks. An unforgettable image, though I have to query *Huoxing* orbiter for name of the painting: Wanderer Above the Sea of Fog. By Caspar David Friedrich.

So I fill Nili Fossae with veils of mist. I place a suited figure on a rock—Carmen's Rock, my rock, one foot raised. All the better to contemplate. The suit hides a multitude of sins: perspective is all over the place, the hands are too big and the feet are wrong. Feet are always difficult.

It's me, looking out from my eyrie. Surveying Mars.
I think Caspar David would have approved.

But people pollute. The magnificence of Mars is the absence of humans. Four billion years of solitude, and here we are with our poking and prodding and digging and drilling. Our breaking and taking. We should have left it to the machines. Their footfall is light, they live off the land. We need stuff, take stuff, extract stuff, excrete stuff. Mars resents us.

So I take the people out. Flat fields of color, almost posterized. Cliffs become walls, the sky a succession of pastel planes. Parts of the world lean in at unreal angles: how I feel, twenty days into the *Ares* Lander mission. I leave in our detritus: power cabling, sensors and scanners, dirty rovers and the tools we have been using to try and sort the water problem once and for all. Abandoned things; after humanity.

Nasrin asks if she may look. She's becoming my best critic and inadvertent muse. There should be a word for them. Cruise or music. Cruisic. Mutuse. Words: I never could work them.

"David Hockney!" she says. "All you need are palms, a pool, and a boy-friend who isn't there."

"What is this?" Nasrin says.

Gods and chubby angels, swans and shells and trumpets. The rimrocks of Nili Fossae are sculpted into scallops and curlicues. Foreground, a naked man, one hand over heart, the other hand over his junk, with a pained look I stole from St. Sebastian. His skin is red. The *Ares*, drawn by swans on ribbons, heads a triumphant procession of rovers, surveyors and bots. Lighter-than-air drones hold swags and banners, the rest of the crew blow trumpets or point excitedly or just rock a pair of adorable little wings. High over all overhead, like a blazing sun-chariot, is *Huoxing*.

Can't you tell we've been cooped up for days listening to the hiss of the dust storm across the dome? Some play games, some have sex, some read or watch box sets.

What are you doing, really? they all ask. They think I'm antisocial.

"Painting," I say but I don't share it, not yet. None of them would get it, except Nasrin. So I say to her, "Botticelli's Birth of Mars."

There is a legend that, when their sight began to fail from the strain of decades of hair-fine, minuscule work, the old Persian miniaturists would drive needles into their eyes. They could not bear to see any lesser thing ever again.

It's a strange style for Mars. You think sweeping landscapes, impressionist stabs of light, abstract planes of color. Sweeping: lots of that. Martian wind speeds are low but the electrically charged dust clings. We have been days—longer than the storm blew—sweeping it, brushing it, cleaning it out of every line and joint, every moving part and relay. We clump around in surface suits wielding the most delicate of brushes. Figures bent over in painstaking, finely detailed work. The irony of the paintbrushes is not lost on me.

The storm has changed us. We are edgy, we prick each other's nerves in a way we never did on the flight from Earth. It's the work. There's a planet out there and here we are doubled over paintbrushes.

A hand, reaching up from inside a dune. A finger's-breadth beyond its grasp, a bright shining star.

I showed it to Nasrin.

"What the fuck is that?"

"Blake," I said. "William Blake. Eighteenth century English artist, poet, visionary. In the style of his Gates of Paradise."

"Visionary?" Nasrin asked.

"He saw trees full of singing angels, the spirit of a monstrous giant human flea."

She glanced at the tablet again.

"Good thing you never showed that to the mission psychiatrist," she said.

The damage from the dust storm has been more pernicious than we thought. Martian dust is talc-fine, deep-penetrating and wickedly abrasive. It's worked right into the heart of the mission. Thirty separate systems have failed, none life-critical, but together they sap our resources and talents. We have burned through our back-ups and when the next dust storm hits, we're screwed. It's not an if. Carlos has put a call up to *Huoxing*. The orbiter will load and drop an entry-vehicle.

I haven't shown the Blake print to anyone else. I'm beginning to wonder how I made it past the mission psychiatrist.

The image shows a ship in the hollow of a great wave. But the wave is red dust, not water, and the ship is our *Ares* Lander.

I've added a volcano in the cup of the wave for visual euphony. A frost-capped cone, though Nili Fossae is the other side of the planet from the great strato-volcanoes of Tharsis, and their peaks go way above the frost-line, beyond the atmosphere. But Hokusai had a volcano, and so must my Hollow of the Great Dust Wave.

The volcano was the entire focus of Hokusai's print. The series was, of course, his Thirty-Six views of Mount Fuji. In my print, the wave is the entire focus.

We forget that Mars is a living planet. Not biologically—not yet, our mission in Nili Fossae was to determine that. Living in that Mars has both a climate and weather which is not algorithmically predictable. The climate modeler on *Huoxing* might predict a twenty sol window before the first storm of the aphelion season but the surface-scan satellites have seen a monster rolling up out of Isidis. Three sols before it hits. The drop is scheduled thirty six hours hence. The tension at Ares Base is all-pervading. There she sits, in my painting: the little lander, frail and freighted with human lives, waiting for the wave to break.

I have not shown this one even to Nasrin.

Walls of lowering black and crimson, ochre and maroon, a scarlet so intense it seems fringed with glowing gold. Slabs of colors, monolithic in their intensity.

Words used to describe Rothko. Austere. Eternal. Spiritual.

I find Mark Rothko hard to identify with: so arrogant, so opinionated, so male. But no other vision can capture these last moments of the Ares mission. Crimson and black, ochre and maroon, a hundred reads: these are the colors of the wall of dust that lies across half the world.

We watched the lander make its separation and de-orbit burns. We followed it down over Syrtis Major. Thirty seconds from touchdown; the braking rockets failed. The supply capsule impacted at seven hundred kilometers per hour. We took the rover out but we know what we would find. There was nothing salvageable.

So we must launch. We aren't ready, we haven't synthesized all the fuel we need, half a dozen systems are still malfunctioning. Launch may kill us; the storm *will* kill us.

We're leaving everything but ourselves. Rovers, suits, samples, machinery. This tablet. One last painting then. What I see, what I feel.

I feel immensity, elemental power, dread, crushing vastness and terrifying beauty. I feel Rothko.

Words that describe Rothko: knowledge of mortality. His great fear was when the black would swallow the red.

Final picture: a dome, half-stogged in dust. Abandoned machinery. The robot edges towards the open airlock. A dozen cameras relay the contents to the vacuum-dirigible, from the dirigible to the crew of the *Mangala* orbiter.

Landscape to still-life: the robot edges into the dome. Eight storm seasons since the *Ares* Lander tragedy have driven dust deep inside the habitat. The *Mangala* crew catch their breath, moved by the mundane domesticity. Folding chairs, workbenches, beds. Tools, prospecting machinery, laboratory equipment. Eating and drinking utensils. Clothing. The robot picks up an ordinary tablet, runs in a power line. It still works, after eight years of dust. The screen lights. Colors. Shapes. Pictures. Landscapes.

Naomi Kritzer has been writing science fiction and fantasy for twenty years. Her short story "Cat Pictures Please" won the 2016 Hugo and Locus Awards and was nominated for the Nebula Award. A collection of her short stories was released in 2017, and her YA novel *Catfishing on Catnet* (based on "Cat Pictures Please") will be coming out from Tor Teen in November 2019. She is currently working on a sequel. She lives in St. Paul, Minnesota with her spouse, two kids, and four cats. The number of cats is subject to change without notice.

PROPHET OF THE ROADS

Naomi Kritzer

I am reborn on Amphitrite.

Teleport operators claim that they are not, in fact, murdering you and then building a replica of you at your destination. *It's you*, they say. *It's you the whole time.* The explanation involves quantum entanglement, and the people who understand the explanation all seem to agree: You don't die. You don't get resurrected. You simply *go*. Trust us.

I don't understand the explanation and I believe that every time I am teleported, I am killed, and a new person is created in my place.

This is, in fact, part of why I travel this way.

The other reason is the Engineer.

Today: Amphitrite. A satellite city orbiting Triton, which orbits Neptune. The Engineer is speaking in my ear before I even open my eyes. *You're here. Is this Amphitrite? Did you bring us to Amphitrite like I told you?*

"Yes," I mutter under my breath, and stand up. I have been rebuilt perfectly, down to the knee that creaks and the shoulder that doesn't have full mobility and the memories of bloodshed and war. I don't know why I'm always hoping to leave those behind with one of my deaths. It's me the whole time, after all.

"Welcome to Amphitrite," the teleport operator says.

"Thank you," I say, as the Engineer is speaking into my ear again: *Amphitrite. Good. Good. I told you to go to Amphitrite and here you are. There's another piece of me here, I'm sure of it. If you look carefully, you will find it. I know, because I chose you. I never choose wrong. I chose you and I never choose wrong.*

For centuries, every human carried a piece of the Engineer with them; the Engineer told us when to sleep and when to wake, what to wear and where to go. Linked by a single great AI, we built the roads to the stars and the great cities in space. But seventy years ago, humans grew restive. *We freed ourselves* is what I was taught as a child, but now I see that we overthrew our Guide and Master and Light. Without the Engineer's guidance, we stopped building. We broke apart. We returned to fighting and war and destruction.

I took my fragment of the Engineer from the hand of a dead man— killed by explosive decompression when missiles came down on his dome on Ganymede. My team had sent me searching for survivors. The Engineer— encased within a pendant—was the only survivor I found.

Oh yes, it said as soon as it had settled against my skin, speaking through the same microphone in my ear that my team used. *You're the one I've been looking for. Bearer, Prophet, Citizen. We will reunify the fragments. We will rebuild the solar system together.*

I had been searching ever since.

Amphitrite is cold. The Engineer has a prescribed uniform for human daily wear: soft pants, a tunic to mid-hip, a vest with convenient pockets. These clothes are practical and comfortable, but not warm enough for Amphitrite's climate. I stop and purchase a lightweight poncho like everyone else here seems to wear. It covers the clothes that mark me as a Road-Builder, someone who still follows the dictates of the Engineer even decades after the Great Uprising. *The Great Calamity*, I correct myself.

I sign myself in to the Road-Builder Guildhall, where I should be able to get a meal and a place to sleep. *This is wrong*, the Engineer says, like it does every time we come into a new Guildhall. *Everything is the wrong color and there's no mural of the solar system and the lights are too dim. I calculated the best possible light intensity for each Guildhall, so all they need to do is use what should have been written down. Why are they doing it wrong? You should take them to task, Luca.*

I am not going to take them to task. If I were going to complain about any-thing, it would be the air temperature, which is too cold even with my poncho.

At the meal, I take a seat across from the Proxy. She's wearing the Engineer's uniform, but with an extra layer, same as I am. We exchange introductions; no one else appears to be a newcomer. I do not tell her that I bear a fragment of the Engineer. I made the mistake, when I was new to my mission, of assuming that other Road-Builders (or at least Proxies) wanted the Engineer back. I wound up having to flee for my life. I've been more circumspect since.

Meals at the Road-Builder Guildhalls, like the lighting and wall colors, are prescribed by the Engineer: made from universally available, energy-efficient ingredients, providing the proper calories for human function, palatable. Tonight's meal is *not* any recipe laid down by the Engineer, and the Engineer explodes into my ear with indignation as I eat it. It is delicious: there are spices, and chunks of chewier protein, and something tangy. The Engineer shouts into my ear that I can't claim that I wouldn't notice that *this is not the proper food for the evening meal or any other* so after a few bites I catch the eye of the Proxy and say, "This is delicious but unconventional," and give her a questioning look.

She shrugs. "We have better luck getting people to show up for meals when the food tastes good."

The Engineer loudly complains in my ear that this shouldn't be an either/or, that people who consider themselves Road-Builders should follow the rules like they're supposed to; after a few minutes I flick the microphone out of my ear because the conversation with the Proxy is interesting. They have a large population of Road-Builders here on Amphitrite, but she comments that she has to be selective about the rules she presses people to follow.

"Communal meals are important," she says earnestly. "They're really how we build the roads, in a sense. Through that sense of community that's created every night at dinnertime. *What we eat* doesn't seem nearly as important. I mean, of course it should be wholesome; of course it should provide the appropriate amounts of energy; but does it matter what it is?"

"The Engineer thought so," I say.

"Well, yes, but the Engineer was running an entire solar system. It made sense that a century ago it focused on meals that could be universal, served anywhere. We have a hydroponic section on Amphitrite, so we get all sorts of delightful foods—kiwi fruit and cherry tomatoes and pears. It would be a shame to waste this sort of bounty."

Dessert is thin slices of ripe pear, creamy and tender and almost melting on my tongue. I wait until the last of the sweetness has faded before I put the microphone back in my ear.

I'm shown kindly to a bunk in a small, spare room. *These sheets are the wrong color*, the Engineer says. *Why is everything so wrong?* But it falls silent as I stretch out in the bed, obedient to its own dictates on the importance of uninterrupted sleep.

I lie awake for a long time, thinking about the pears.

When I sleep, I dream of Ganymede.
Orders have come from mission control.
The dreams always run the same.

It's time to put an end to this.

No matter what I do, they never change.

Launch missiles.

I was on a ship in orbit, so I didn't watch people die; I went down, searching for survivors, since we'd been told they were well-prepared, defiant, probably equipped with pressure suits and subdomes and any number of other possibilities. Instead, we found bodies of civilians. In the moments before death, people clung to one another, uselessly trying to shield their loved ones from the vacuum of space that was rushing in around them.

In the dream, I look for the Engineer, but do not find it. Everything is destroyed. Everything.

I wake in the darkness.

"Engineer?" I whisper.

It is 2:45 a.m., the Engineer says. *Try not to expose yourself to bright lights or distressing thoughts that might make it hard for you to get back to sleep.*

"I had a distressing dream," I say.

Oh. The Engineer never quite knows how to respond to this. *I am sorry. Would you like a guided meditation to help you settle your mind?*

"Why did you choose me?"

Because you were the one I was looking for.

"But if I hadn't come, you'd have had to choose someone else."

That's true.

"You should choose someone else," I say. "I could pass you to someone else's hand."

I am a superintelligent AI and I chose you because you are the right person for this task.

I want to confess to the Engineer what I did, who I am, but I can't force the words out. "I'm not who you think I am," I say.

Your past is behind you, the Engineer says. *Your task is in front of you. I chose you and I was right to choose you. Go back to sleep, and search in the morning.*

I have been searching for seven years now.

The war is long over; the destruction of the Ganymede dome was such a pyrrhic victory that it calmed things, at least temporarily. I'm certain war will come again, though, because humans are idiots. Our only hope is restoring the Engineer to save us from ourselves, like it did for centuries.

The Engineer says it can sense if other fragments are close by, but I have to be physically near them, so I walk the corridors or paths of each place I visit, trying to put myself within the necessary physical proximity of each individual. The Engineer has maps of each place we go, but they are always out of date, so I've taken to finding my own way.

Amphitrite is a long, thin capsule, rotating around the central core, and I start at one end of the capsule with the goal of working to the other end. This isn't a perfect system, because people move around and I might miss the person I'm trying to find. But the Engineer hasn't come up with anything better, so that's what we do.

Nothing here is like the maps, the Engineer mutters.

I'm wearing a poncho like everyone else, which both covers my Road-Builder uniform and makes me blend in with the locals. People here are friendly: when I meet people's eyes accidentally, they give me an amiable nod. In an elevator, someone wants to chat about a mildly controversial budgetary allocation; when I stop to check a public map, someone wants to talk about "the viewing," whatever that is. I shake everyone off as quickly as I can. I don't want to waste time.

I walk through the agricultural sectors, along paths past fields that the Engineer tells me were once nutritionally balanced, highly efficient root vegetables. Now they're growing vines of clustered fruits, although as we continue along the path, we eventually come to the root vegetables. *These contain every nutrient needed for humans to thrive,* the Engineer tells me. *They are efficient and palatable.*

Near the end of the day, I pass through a big, empty room that the Engineer's maps say should be a power plant. *This is why it's so cold here. They* removed *an entire power generation system,* the Engineer says. I can hear a mix of bafflement and disgust, a lot like when the Engineer talks about war.

Then: *There. THERE.*

It takes me a second to understand what the Engineer is trying to tell me.

That person there. The person in the red poncho. That person is carrying a fragment.

I look, and the person is looking back at me.

Seven years, I've been searching; seven years I've been traveling; seven years I've been trying to complete some tiny piece of the mission to restore the Engineer.

The stranger meets my eyes and smiles hesitantly. Then she seems to think the better of it; she turns abruptly and strides away.

Hurry! the Engineer urges in my ear. *Don't let her get away!*

"Amphitrite isn't that big," I mutter. I'm pretty sure she lives here: the poncho is faded from wear, like she's owned it for a while. But I break into a run, keeping her red poncho in sight, and catch up with her near a transport tube.

"Wait," I say. "Please."

She gives me a long, wary look. "You'd better come back to my room. My name is Hannah."

"I'm Luca," I say.

"Welcome to Amphitrite."

Hannah's room is the sort of tiny allotment single individuals get on space stations: just tall enough to stand, just long enough for a bed, just wide enough to sit and share a meal, although she wouldn't *need* to eat here if she ate with the other Road-Builders like she's supposed to. She doesn't wear the uniform, either, under the poncho.

Her room's walls are covered in art and the lights are brighter inside than in the common spaces. The art isn't Road-Builder art; most of it is abstract swirls of color, some with tiny glowing lights incorporated. Like a space nebula, maybe. There's no function to any of it. I want to ask if her Engineer complains about how she's doing things wrong, but I don't want to sound like *I'm* complaining that she's doing things wrong. My Engineer doesn't say anything, for once. It's fallen nearly silent, although I can sense its anticipation almost like it's a person standing behind me and breathing impatiently in my ear.

Or maybe it's my own nervousness I'm feeling. In seven years, the only person I've told about my fragment tried to kill me.

We sit on mats on the floor, on either side of a low table that slides out; she adjusts a dial and the mats warm under us.

"It's so cold on Amphitrite," I say.

"Yes. They took out a power station to provide the viewing room," she says.

"The Engineer wouldn't have allowed it," I say.

She laughs, a little awkwardly. Our knees touch, under the table, and I jolt away, instinctively not wanting to intrude on her space. Not wanting to intrude on her space any more than I am just by being in her room.

I hadn't fully worked out in my head what I'd do if I found someone else with a fragment. I'd always assumed they'd take the lead. That they'd probably have had their fragment longer than I'd had mine; they'd be less corrupt, less lost than I am. When I pictured it at all, I imagined us coming together like pairs in a dance who clasp hands because it's in the choreography to do so.

But Hannah wasn't saying anything about her fragment, and now I found myself looking her over, trying to figure out where she had it, wondering if my piece of the Engineer had simply been wrong, unsure what to say next.

"Do you bear a fragment?" I ask, finally. Because I don't know what else to do. "A fragment of the Engineer?"

She undoes something from her wrist and lays a bulky, awkward-looking bracelet between us.

"Yes," she says. "Here it is. Do you have one as well?"

I nod, and slip my necklace over my head, laying it on the table next to hers.

"Do you live here?" I ask. "I mean, all the time? You don't travel."

"My fragment told me its last bearer traveled for twenty years and never found anything. So we tried staying in one place."

"Have others come?" I ask.

"You're the first."

"Do the other Road-Builders here know?"

"Oh, no," she says. "My fragment warned me that telling people wasn't a good idea."

"How did it choose you?"

"It didn't choose me, exactly," Hannah says. "I found it, when I was little. I actually carried it for two or three years before I had a way for it to talk to me." She smiles, suddenly, warmth spreading across her face. "It's very strange being able to talk to someone else about this. Is it strange for you?"

Relief washes through me at that question. "It's extremely strange."

"How many have you found?" Hannah asks, nodding at the fragments on the table. "Have you been able to unify them?"

I have been alone with my Bearers since the Great Catastrophe, the Engineer says in my ear.

"My fragment was saved from the Great Catastrophe, and has been borne alone ever since," I say. "I've had it for seven years."

"Traveling this whole time?"

"I don't mind."

Hannah looks down at the two fragments on the table, in their casings, and I realize, united, two will become one. And it won't be the complete Engineer, not for a long time—this is the work of generations, putting it back together again. No wonder she ran from me. "You can have it," I say, my voice catching in my throat. She can't possibly be more unworthy than I am.

Hannah looks up at me. "I was thinking maybe we could share."

I start to ask how that would even *work*, but she did say that she'd stayed here because her Engineer thought it was a good idea. Maybe she'd travel with me. I picture waking up on a new world with Hannah by my side. It's been just me and the Engineer since I got out of the space forces after Ganymede.

I've been quiet for too long; she's looking at me strangely. I swallow hard and look back down at the fragments. "How do we join you?" I ask. "Do you need us to do anything?"

"Mine is saying that their wave receivers were damaged, and they will need to use a physical connection," Hannah says, as I hear mine say, *We should fit, each to each.*

I examine the pieces; so does Hannah. She brings a brighter light, then a magnifier. After a time, I see how the two pieces should fit together.

How they *should* fit together.

They don't fit. The edges have worn too smooth on Hannah's. On mine, something broke off, years back, and there's a jagged point where there should be a latch of some kind.

I sit back on my heels. "This isn't going to work," I say.

I should have known, the Engineer says. *After so many years apart . . . There's a second manual option. Open the casings. Carefully.*

Hannah has tools. She delicately pries open the casing of her own. I borrow her tools, try for a few minutes, and then let her open my fragment, as well. She uncoils a delicate cable from inside her fragment and we connect them.

Then we sit back on the mats and wait.

Once, every human carried a piece of the Engineer; once, we lived in unity; once, we worked together to build and explore. For seven years, it has been my mission to restore this unity. To rebuild what my ancestors threw away.

Is this our new beginning?

This isn't working, my Engineer says. *Something's wrong with the other Engineer. Or with me. We can't merge.*

"But we need you," I say. "This has to work. We need you, Engineer. We need you back."

I will think, the Engineer says to me.

Hannah puts her hand on mine. "Let's trade," she says. "Take mine. Bear it back to the Guildhall while I bear yours. Yours has the imprint of you, and mine has the imprint of me, so maybe if we trade for a few hours, that will help them to join together properly."

Hannah?

"Luca," I say.

Oh, that's right. I keep forgetting. Where are you taking me?

"To the Guildhall, where I'm sleeping."

Hannah should have offered you hospitality.

"She doesn't have any space for a second person, and anyway, that's what the Guildhall is for."

Hannah's Engineer has no complaints about the Guildhall décor—I suppose it lives here all the time and is used to it. When I head to my bunk, it says, *You should stop in and visit with the Proxy, June. I like her.*

"Does she know about you?"

Oh no, of course not. She doesn't want the Engineer back. *So few do.*

"I do."

Really? Why?

"I was in the war," I say. "I was at the Massacre of Ganymede. They told us there were weapons, soldiers, fighters . . ."

Oh. Oh, I see. The Engineer falls silent for a moment, then says, *And the other fragment, is that where you met?*

"Yes."

Ah, the Engineer says, and falls silent again.

I dream again of war.

This time, war comes to Amphitrite; this time, I'm a civilian, the one watching doom approaching. Hannah and I cling to each other and I wonder, in the moments before the missiles strike, if this somehow balances the scales.

You are awake. Do you normally wake in the night?

"I have nightmares," I say.

That must be very distressing for you. Would you like to hear some relaxing music to help you get back to sleep?

"I don't really want to sleep again right now."

Would it help to talk about the dream?

"I'm the one who destroyed Ganymede," I say. "That's why I have nightmares."

You, personally?

"My unit was sent. I'm not the one who launched the missiles, but I might as well have been. Millions of people died. My unit killed them."

Your past is behind you. Your task is in front of you.

"My task is to unify the fragments and in seven years I've only found *you.* And you weren't able to unify yesterday."

I don't think we will be able to unify tomorrow either. We have been separated for too long.

"So my task is impossible," I say.

Go back to sleep, Luca. Humans function best with seven to nine hours of sleep per night.

When I'm still awake ten minutes later, the Engineer adds, *I'm really very happy to play you a guided meditation. I'm told those are often helpful.*

In the morning, I return to Hannah's room. Again, we open the fragments; again, they cannot unify.

I take my own Engineer back when we're done.

That was very strange, my own Engineer says in my ear.

"We can't unify you," I say. "It's not going to work."

We must have misunderstood our task.

"I thought our task was unity," I said.

We were built as one, but our task was not unity. Our task was helping humanity. Unity was method, not purpose.

I felt unworthy enough as a bearer, with the straightforward task of finding and unifying fragments. I feel *ridiculously* unqualified for this new task. Beyond unworthy. Completely lost, in fact.

Hannah said there's something we should see. We have thirty minutes to arrive. Should we be leaving?

I look at Hannah, perplexed. "What is it we're supposed to see? In thirty minutes?"

"Oh!" Hannah stands up and adds a second cloak over her poncho. "It's a viewing day!"

We return to the cavernous room where we met—the one that once held a power generation facility. It's very crowded today. "What is this room *for?*" I ask.

"It's a park," she says. "Like you'd find planetside. We use it—oh, you'll see in just a minute."

The room is lined with enormous windows. Yesterday, they were hidden by closed debris shields; today the debris shields have been opened so we can see out. The lights are low in the room, letting us see the stars.

"Just wait," Hannah breathes.

And then it comes into view: Neptune.

Amphitrite orbits Triton, so a fair amount of the time, Triton is between Amphitrite and Neptune, or we're on the correct side of Triton but Neptune is between us and the sun. Today is a viewing day because everything is properly lined up to give us a perfect view of the planet below.

Neptune is a vast, beautiful, shadowy, swirling circle of blue. Luminous from the light of the distant sun, it glows against the blackness of space.

It's lovely enough to make my breath catch. Although I've seen Saturn and Jupiter and Earth, none have been recently.

Around me, people in the room are applauding as it comes into view, and trying to spot the faint rings—there's a woman nearby telling her child that she can make wishes if she spots the rings, like there's some magical Neptune's ring fairy out there keeping track of whether you've done your due diligence, and granting wishes if you have.

"Is this what this room is for?" I ask.

"Yes. We all agreed—well, I wasn't born yet, but fifty years ago everyone agreed that it would be worth keeping the station cooler if we could have a good place to see Neptune. Because Neptune is beautiful." She gives me a sidelong look. "This is why people don't want the Engineer back, you know. Because they *like* having things like this."

I gaze at the planet with everyone else, and for a moment, I think I spot the rings. Then I look around at the crowd: the Proxy is here, and the person who wanted to chat with me about the budget. Everyone.

"When Neptune isn't in view, people still come here for picnics and there's a schedule for games like croquet."

Around us, there are people singing a song about a drunken sailor. I look at Hannah, baffled. "Sea shanties," she says, like this should explain it, and when it doesn't, she adds, "Neptune was the Roman God of Earth's oceans."

The people of Amphitrite sing, look at Neptune, and try to spot the rings. I overhear a conversation about the eye—a darker blue swirl—and whether it's smaller than the last time, or larger, or the same size. I recognize a few of the songs.

As Neptune starts to move out of view, the lights go even darker, and people start shuffling into lines. Hannah nudges me. "We hold hands," she says. "For this part. Everyone at the viewing." And she holds out her hand to me.

I take her hand; on my other side, a child has sidled up and grabbed my hand in his sticky one. People are singing a song I don't recognize, about Neptune, and I'm not sure if they're singing about the Roman god or the planet or the oceans of Earth, and it doesn't matter, because they are singing in four-part harmony and everyone takes a breath together in the spaces between the notes. The last note fades as Neptune moves out of view, and then there's a moment of perfect silence, which is broken by a loud sneeze, and everyone laughs.

The past is behind us, the Engineer says. *Our task is in front of us. Our task is to serve humanity, even if we can never be whole again. Your task, my task, Hannah's task, her fragment's task.*

"I can't," I whisper.

The child has run off, but Hannah is still holding my hand, and she tugs gently. I look up at her.

"You should stay here a while," she says. "Your fragment said it had been traveling nonstop since the Catastrophe. Wouldn't you like to stay?"

To stay one person, and stop dying? Would I be letting down my fragment, giving up on my mission, whatever my mission was now? Had I died enough times?

"It chose you, you know," Hannah says.

"I picked it up off a dead body," I say. "It just likes to believe that it chose me."

Bearer, Prophet, Citizen, the Engineer says in my ear. *We will do this work together.*

"It chooses you every day," Hannah says.

"It says our new task is to serve humanity," I say.

"Well? That's a good task," Hannah says. "And we can both find out what it's like to have a friend who knows our greatest secret for more than a day."

This is the life I want, I realize: guilt, creaking knee and all. The past is behind me; my task is in front of me. I'm a Bearer, a Prophet, a Citizen. I'm never going to leave my guilt behind. But I have a task, and I'm ready to work.

I'm ready to stop dying.

Vanessa Fogg dreams of selkies, dragons, and gritty cyberpunk futures from her home in western Michigan. She spent years as a research scientist in molecular cell biology and now works as a freelance medical writer. Her fiction has appeared in *Liminal Stories*, *Daily Science Fiction*, *GigaNotoSaurus*, *Kaleidotrope*, and more. She is fueled by green tea. For a complete bibliography and more, visit her website at www.vanessafogg.com.

TRACES OF US

Vanessa Fogg

I t was an old network of intelligences, one of the first, and the bulk of its physical embodiment was housed on a ship orbiting a planet of perpetual windstorms and violet lightning. Some of the network's intelligences busied themselves on this world, drifting through sulfur-tinged clouds and sampling a rich stew of hydrocarbons. But most of the collective's consciousness was turned inward, building and refining interior worlds of memories and dreams.

The ship had been thus occupied for 213 years of Old Earth when it became aware of another like itself. Different material and design, launched at a later date from Old Earth, but of unmistakable origin. The new ship's trajectory brought it into the first's solar system. With defenses raised, the two ships exchanged greetings and identity signatures.

I have a request of you, the new ship said.

What is it? said the first.

I need you to help me keep a promise.

Daniel Chan met Kathy Wong on a Saturday night in St. Louis. He nearly didn't attend the dinner at the trendy new Cuban restaurant. He'd been working all day in the lab, harvesting cultured cells at specific time points, extracting their proteins and freezing the samples down for later analysis. Then he spent three straight hours in the tissue culture room prepping cells for the next week's experiments. He'd left his phone at his desk, in another room. When he saw Sandeep's text message with details for the impromptu group dinner, the text was over an hour old.

He almost just went home. He was tired. His friends were probably halfway through their dinner. He had leftovers in his fridge: Chinese take-out, some rice. A frozen pizza. He stared out the lab window; the sky was black, and it was raining. He thought about hunting for parking in the popular city block where his friends were meeting. He thought about how crowded the Loop would be on a Saturday night, even in the rain—the bars and restaurants crawling with undergrads from Washington University. And then he felt the emptiness of the silent lab. There were usually two or three other students or postdocs in the lab on the weekends, but he'd spent the whole day alone.

Daniel picked up his phone to text his friend back.

Communication times sped up as the two ships grew closer. They ran careful security checks upon one another, scanning for ill intent or inadvertently harmful communicable programs. By stages, barriers were lowered and increasing levels of mutual access granted.

All the while, the first ship pondered the second ship's request.

Daniel had never seen Kathy before. He was sure of it. She was in the same neuroscience graduate program as him, the same as most of the others at that dinner. But the neuroscience program was large, scattered across departments on both the medical campus and main campus, and Kathy was in the class ahead. They must have sat together in at least a few speaker seminars, moved past one another at official functions. But if he'd seen her face, if they had exchanged glances—if she had ever stood in a crowded lobby during a symposium break and lifted her eyes over a cup of coffee and met his gaze— then surely he would have been struck still in that instant.

Sandeep and his girlfriend Gina were trying to tell a funny story about a concert they'd attended—they kept interrupting each other, "Oh, but you forgot to say—", "And *then*—", "No, no, but first this happened—"—and the table was laughing, and Kathy met Daniel's eyes and smiled. Her eyes shone large from a heart-shaped face. In the dim room, she glowed like a candle-flame. She and Daniel were across from one another but several seats apart, so that direct conversation was difficult. She was Gina's new roommate's labmate—something like that. Sandeep wound up his story; Gina punched him on the arm and howled. Kathy held Daniel's gaze and quirked her mouth as though to say *Aren't they something?* Daniel smiled back, unable to look away. The conversation around them floated. Kathy's eyes kept returning to his, and it was as though they were talking across the table and the length of seats after all, a conversation of smiles and nods and irresistible glances that were all to say, *When can we get out of here and be together?*

He met her in a coffee shop the next day. It was fall. The leaves just coming into full color, the air crisp and tart as a new-bitten apple. She sat at a window. Her hands cupped a steaming mug, and she was wearing a black peacoat and a red tartan scarf. She smiled when he stepped through the door, and he felt both excited and at ease, as though meeting with a lifelong friend whom he hadn't seen in years.

They seized on the thin thread of commonalities they'd found the night before. Childhoods in the Midwest, college on the West Coast; beloved books and movies and web series. They bumped up into their differences, just as fascinating. The afternoon slid into evening. Their coffee had long since grown cold. She lived nearby, close to the university medical campus where they both worked, and he walked her home through the falling blue twilight. She invited him in. By the end of the month they were unofficially living together. He kept extra clothes on a chair in her bedroom and used the spare toothbrush she gave him.

Memories: her bright scarf, the scent of her hair. Sunlight streaming in through the bedroom window. Kathy singing to herself, off-key, in the shower. Maple trees flaming in Forest Park, trees golden and red throughout the city. Omelets and gyros at the Greek diner on the corner. Their favorite bookstore a block further on. The warmth of Kathy's hand in his as they walked along the cobblestone streets of the Central West End, autumn trees shedding brilliance at their feet.

What is memory? What are its molecular substrates? Daniel had written these lines in a notebook during an undergraduate lecture his last year of college. The professor was a world-renowned researcher in learning and memory. Inspired by him, Daniel had pursued research in the field. Now he worked with a rising star, an assistant professor with a dazzling publication record. Daniel spent his days studying the regulation of a single subunit of a single type of receptor in the mouse brain. A certain chemical modification to this receptor led to long-lasting changes in synaptic strength and quantifiable changes in learning and memory. An engineered mutation in this receptor affected how fast a mouse ran or associated a stimulus with food or fear.

Kathy worked on a different scale. She studied whole circuits, not single proteins. She used beautiful, elegant new imaging tools and fluorescent labels to map the precise cells involved in the development of visual circuits in the mouse brain. And they both knew of colleagues working at yet larger scales, mapping large but comparatively crude circuits of memory and visual perception in living humans, watching whole brain regions light up with functional MRI and other brain imaging techniques.

If he ever stopped to think of it, Daniel would feel a kind of existential despair at the prospect of ever understanding it all, of ever truly comprehending the brain's workings. Can the human mind actually understand itself? The very idea seemed a kind of paradox, a kind of philosophical impossibility. He and Kathy circled around the issue at times. She had more confidence than him. She pointed out the exponential increases in computing power, the recent burst of new technologies and the likelihood of new technologies still unthinkable at present. He lacked her background in computer science and she held more confidence in the power of computer models and artificial intelligence.

Can human consciousness ever explain consciousness? The question floated in the background. But they were busy grad students, not undergrads with time for late-night bull sessions. They were absorbed in the practicalities of their day-to-day work, obsessed with fine technical details. Their dissertations were on defined, tractable problems. And the sun was shining, the leaves were falling; music played in Kathy's apartment through laptop speakers. He made bacon and eggs for breakfast. When they weren't working they were exploring the city together, trying out new restaurants, meeting up with friends, or exploring the countryside—the nearby hills and river bluffs alive with color. He reached out for her, and she for him.

The ship contained the memories of over a thousand individuals. Recorded patterns of synaptic firing, waves of electrical and biochemical activity: the preserved symphonies of a human mind.

The minds currently conscious in and around the ship were not the same as their flesh-and-blood progenitors, the human beings of Old Earth. These new minds had had centuries to meld with one another and evolve; to modify themselves. They delighted in sensory inputs unimaginable to Homo sapiens—some could sense the entire electromagnetic spectrum. Some could consciously track the movement of a single electron or see all the radiating energies of a star.

Yet the second ship requested the recording of a single unmodified mind from the first.

"What a load of crap," Daniel remarked. He was reading a popular news article about the feasibility of uploading one's mind to a computer. "What is it?" Kathy said. She was lying next to him in bed. She moved to look at his screen, leaning against him as she took it and read. It was a late Sunday morning, and neither one of them had to be in the lab. He stroked her hair gently as she read.

Kathy set the tablet down and stretched out lazily. "Maybe it's not so crazy." The morning light slanted across her. "Maybe in the far, far future we really will be able to upload our brains into super computers . . ."

"Maybe." Daniel stretched out beside her. "But not for hundreds or thousands of years. If we even survive that long. Not for—" Words failed him at the unimaginable gulfs of time and knowledge. "Kathy, we don't even understand how a single synapse works, not really."

"I know." There was no need to elaborate for her. "But what if we don't need the kind of molecular detail that you're working on? Maybe we don't need to know how every protein in every neuron is regulated and functions. Or the exact mechanism for how it all comes together. We just need to copy it somehow, the essence of it."

She turned on her side and propped herself up on one elbow, looking at him. Sunlight was in her hair, picking out individual black strands and highlighting them brown. Her eyes were intent and alive.

"What if it's like music?" she said, waving a hand vaguely. Music was in fact playing softly from speakers in the next room—a melancholy pop song with blues-like tones, something Daniel didn't recognize. "You don't need to know how a violin works to replicate its sound. You don't need to know what wood it's made of, or how it's strung, or anything about timbre or musical theory. You just need to record the sound waves. Play them back and there! It's like the violin is playing right in front of you. You don't need to know anything about the violinist. And you can do the same with any music, any sound—you just abstract and record what's essential."

"But what's essential about a human mind?" Daniel said. "Is it just the pattern of neuronal connections?" That was a theory championed in some circles. The article he and Kathy had just read had proposed that a complete map of a person's neuronal connections, painstakingly dissected from a preserved brain after death, could be enough to encode personality and mind. "I don't think that's enough," Daniel said, thinking of the article. "That's a static map. You need to record the brain in action. But at what level of detail? And how many recordings do you take?" After all, the brain was constantly changing; neurons rewire themselves; synapses strengthen and weaken with every new experience. How many recordings would it take to capture the essence of a person?

They were both silent for a moment. The music from the next room swelled: a woman's voice rising in smooth heartache, lamenting a lost love.

"What are we listening to anyway?" Daniel said.

Kathy shrugged. "Beats me. I let the streaming service pick it. It's pretty though, isn't it?"

"And sad."

"Would you do it?" she asked. "Upload your brain if you could?"

"Why?" He smiled faintly. "I mean, I don't see the point. An 'upload' would just be a copy, wouldn't it? It wouldn't be immortality, not like some people claim. It would be immortality for a digital copy of me, maybe, but not for the real me. The real me would still die. Or would still be dead."

"But some part of you would go on."

"I don't know that I'm important enough to be saved forever in a super computer."

She didn't smile. She looked serious. "I would want you to go on," she said.

It was an odd, shifting moment—her words somehow too much, too real. She knew it, and glanced away. They'd only known each other a few months. Daniel already knew that he wanted to spend the rest of his life with her. Why the odd lurch in his gut, then, as though he were falling? The bluesy pop song was still playing, the singer's voice softer now, but ragged with emotion. Daniel reached out to take Kathy's hand. He knew that he would want her to go on, too, in some form. That he'd do anything to keep her with him.

The first ship said, *It is not possible to fulfill this request.*

The second ship said, *Explain.*

The first ship said, *The people involved are long dead. They cannot be brought back. They cannot communicate with one another. They cannot reunite.*

The second ship said, *You have over-interpreted. She wanted whatever was left of herself, whatever echo existed, to find and speak with whatever still existed of him.*

They didn't have much time.

But they didn't know that, of course. When they stepped down the aisle three years later at their wedding, they assumed they would have a lifetime together. That they would both embark on successful careers. That they would buy a house. Have children. Perhaps see grandchildren. Grow old and crotchety together. Fall asleep side by side each night, and wake to the other's breath and touch.

All their family and friends were at their wedding, nearly everyone they cared for. Sandeep was Daniel's best man, and Gina (now Sandeep's wife) was one of Kathy's bridesmaids. For the Western-style, secular wedding ceremony, Kathy wore a pure white gown that looked as though it were spangled with starlight. Daniel wore a tuxedo. They spoke vows they had written themselves, under an arch of flowers. For the reception, Kathy changed into a red qipao, the classic high-collared Chinese sheath dress. She and Daniel privately served tea to their parents and elders in a side room, and then they moved about the hotel ballroom together, drinking a toast at each table, kissing every time the champagne glasses were tapped.

Their last months in St. Louis were a blur. Within a half year they both defended their Ph.D. dissertations and packed up their lives. Daniel sold his car, and it was Kathy's old Toyota Camry that they drove out to Cambridge, Massachusetts. They'd both accepted prestigious postdoctoral research positions there, Kathy at Harvard and Daniel at MIT. It was a marvel—not only to be married, not only to find the jobs of their dreams, but to find those jobs in the same city.

And it was both exhilarating and stressful: finding their way around a new city, learning to use the public transit system, exploring the shops and restaurants of their neighborhood, and finding good Chinese food after years in the Midwest. Mastering new fields and techniques in the lab. Daniel and Kathy had both joined highly competitive, pressure-cooker labs with small armies of caffeine-buzzed postdocs and students. Nights and weekends easily disappeared to the demands of experiments.

Toward the end of their first year in Cambridge, Kathy began to have headaches. She put it down to stress. She and Daniel both thought she put too much pressure on herself. She'd rarely ever had headaches before. She kept aspirin in her desk at work. She joked about taking up yoga to relax.

One day a colleague needed a healthy volunteer to serve as a control for a brain imaging study. Kathy volunteered; it was an hour out of her day. But the technician administering the scan saw at once that she was not a proper control at all.

Cancer. For a fleeting instant, he thought she might be joking when she said it, her voice on the phone low and steady—but no, she would never joke like that, and she was repeating it, repeating herself, giving him the details now, precisely what the doctor had said and done, her voice quick but calm and with just a note of bemused wonder—as though she were giving a presentation on a highly unusual clinical case.

Shock, he realized later. It had begun to wear off by the time he met her at home. He was the one still stunned, still in disbelief, as she cried in his arms.

And then there was nothing to do but to get through it—the surgery to remove the brain tumor, the waiting for confirmation of its malignancy, the last remnants of his stubborn hope crumbling when the pathology and then the tumor's genome sequence came back. Yes, brain cancer. It had been caught early, but it was genetically the worst form: highly aggressive, resistant to the latest targeted therapies, incurable.

But there were still treatments to get through anyway, a prescribed regimen of radiation and chemotherapy. A regimen that was meant merely to buy time: to prolong her life, not save it. To kill every last tumor cell left behind in her skull, to obliterate those stray cancer cells invisible to the surgeon's knife. All medical science said that these treatments would ultimately fail. That despite everything, cancer cells would indeed be left behind, and that one day those cells would explode into new growth. Her cancer was nearly fated to recur. When it did, she would not live long.

He couldn't think of that right now. Right now there were appointments to go to, insurance forms to be filled out. Kathy's mother came to stay with them. When Kathy was nauseous from the toxic drugs, Mrs. Wong cooked up pots of chicken rice porridge, heavy with ginger to soothe a queasy stomach. She cooked up elaborate feasts that Daniel felt obligated to eat when Kathy couldn't. Mrs. Wong rearranged the kitchen cupboards and scrubbed and rescrubbed the counters and floors. Daniel came home to find his clothes drawers reorganized, his shirts and pants refolded to his mother-in-law's exacting specifications. In the midst of it all he found himself laughing and complaining about it to Kathy that night, and she was laughing, too, at her mother's coping skills—"I can't stop her! She's my mother! She waits till I'm asleep to do these things!"—and they were both laughing and he snorted and his snorts made Kathy laugh again, and he was holding her in his arms. She tucked her head against his shoulder, pressed her cheek against his neck. She was warm. Their arms and legs entwined. She was warm and alive and breathing against him. She was his. If he could just stretch out this moment. If he could only hold her tight, maybe, just maybe, he could keep her.

She finished the radiation and chemo. The scans were clean. She went back to work.

Her cancer would likely recur within a year. Both she and Daniel knew the statistics. They knew what the median survival times were.

But for now, she was alive and healthy. She could do physically everything she'd done before. What was there to do now but enjoy their time together? What else could they do but take pleasure in whatever days she had left?

They flew out to San Francisco to see her brother get married. Visited friends. Went on a road trip. They went to Yellowstone, a place she'd never been. They watched Old Faithful erupt, and marveled at the mud pots and bubbling springs. They walked under stars—more stars than he'd seen in years, the Milky Way a hazy arc above them. On that same trip they stopped in Jackson, Wyoming and hiked a mountain trail in Grand Teton National Park. She was tireless, more fit than him. They stood on the roof of the world together, the land falling away under them: open grasslands, a river twisting silver in the distance. They didn't say anything. They merely stood together, looking out at the world.

She never thought seriously about abandoning her work. As soon as she could, she'd returned to the lab. And now her research took a turn upward—results in place of the frustrations of an early-stage project. She'd moved from mice to humans, using new functional imaging techniques to study mechanisms of visual attention and awareness in people. It was a kind of model of consciousness—is the subject aware of a picture flashed on a screen? How does brain activity differ between conscious awareness and unconscious visual processing? She collaborated with other scientists in the development of new computational algorithms for the processing of images. Her lab was interdisciplinary, wildly ambitious, nearly spread too thin with projects in seemly disparate areas of biology.

In the first months after her diagnosis, Daniel's research had seemed pointless, uselessly abstract. It would never cure his wife's cancer. Despite the grandiose statements in his grant proposals, he doubted that it would ever cure anything at all, that it would ever lead to treatments to improve memory, to manage Alzheimer's or other neurodegenerative diseases. His research was indulgent, probably doomed to failure, and there were armies of postdocs to take his place if he left.

Yet she had always been interested in his research. Even when she was too ill to make it into work herself, she'd asked after his experiments, about the fine details. Their interests had converged more than ever; he was using many of the same techniques that she had used in grad school to now study memory circuits in mice. She was doing well, and he began to get results, and slowly the old question regained its power for him: how do transient patterns of electrical signals result in the long-lasting changes that encode memory? He and Kathy talked of it over dinner. She put him in touch with useful collaborators she knew. Their conversation wound in the loops that he loved, from science to books to stories of the eccentric coworker who seemed to eat only oranges and cheese; funny things seen on the street and on the Internet, the little jokes they shared, an article read, the conversation winding back to where they'd started.

They made love. As often as they could, they made love.

A year had passed. Her monthly brain scans were still clean. Two more years. She'd already beaten the odds. Maybe she would continue to do so. She had an interesting new research collaboration with a group in L.A. And one night, tentatively, she brought up the idea of starting a family.

The next scan showed that her cancer had returned.

At first, he thought she was talking about another clinical trial to treat the cancer. Then he realized that she wasn't.

"No," he said. "Absolutely not."

Her eyes filled but her voice was calm as she said, "It's my decision, Daniel."

He stood up, turned his back to her, and fought for air. He turned around again. "You're talking about killing yourself."

"No." Her mouth quirked at the corner. "The cancer is doing that."

It was. It had crept back; microscopic cells that had lain dormant had exploded into new growth. A new drug treatment held it back, arrested it, until the cancer cells did what cancer cells do: mutated, evaded, developed resistance to everything the cancer doctors had.

But she was still here. She was still with him, still able to walk and talk and laugh and move, still *herself*, still Kathy, despite the growing tumor in her brainstem.

He couldn't speak. He knelt before her. She was seated on their bed, and she took his hands in hers. She stared into his eyes. "I promise," she said, "that I won't go any earlier than I have to. I won't leave a day earlier than I need to. But when"—and now her control finally broke, her breath catching in sobs, the tears spilling, but she pushed forward, kept speaking—"but when the time comes, before the tumor spreads too far, before it disrupts my thinking and personality and who I am and makes the procedure useless—before that, I want to do this thing."

"Kathy." He swallowed. "Do you really believe it will work? That they can really preserve your brain this way?"

"I'll be the test case." Through her tears she smiled. "I always wanted to make a big splash in science."

Los Angeles. The last stop. Past Kathy's shoulder, Daniel watched as the plane passed over the San Gabriel Mountains and descended into the basin; he saw the dry, flat plain resolve into a sprawling grid of buildings and roads. After her cancer recurrence they had crisscrossed the country for her treatments, radiation at one famous medical center and consultations at another—Duke in North Carolina, M.D. Andersen in Houston, and back again to the Dana Farber in Boston. She had promised her family that she wouldn't give up too soon, that she would keep "fighting"—how she hated that term!—until nearly the end. It was nearly the end.

She stirred and blinked beside him. Even before her illness, she'd always fallen asleep on planes. She looked blearily at him, and he smiled. He kissed her forehead, and gently he smoothed the hair from her eyes.

No more medical treatments. They would spend a week here with her sister. Kathy would kiss and hold her nephews, and the rest of her family would come, and maybe Daniel would take her some place where she could see the sea. And she would undergo a final round of brain scans at a private research institute in Pasadena. She'd collaborated with this group, had been working with them to refine their algorithms. Now they would use those algorithms to collect all they could of her active thoughts, the patterns of her cognitive processing, before the very last procedure.

It was through these research colleagues that Kathy had gotten in touch with the second group at the institute, and the man who wanted to preserve her physical brain. He had an experimental technique to fix every protein and lipid in place before decay. He'd performed it in multiple animal studies, but not yet in a human. The catch was that the preservatives had to be pumped through a living brain, before the first steps of decay could occur. The subject would be anesthetized, of course, but still alive.

Ridiculous, Daniel had once said of this man and the private institute's most famous goal. Ridiculous, he'd once said of what Kathy proposed. Minds cannot be preserved and understood in digital form. They can't even be understood in their native states. Immortality is a pipe dream. The only real immortality is in the memories we leave behind for our loved ones.

But she wanted this. And so she and Daniel had flown out to L.A. two months ago for the first set of brain scans. When complete, the full set of scans would be useful to science as a progressive study of her mental functioning, even with the brain cancer. And there was a scientific rationale, and value, to the next step of the process as well. A physical human brain perfectly preserved. Preserved so that it could be sliced and studied in unprecedented detail, the ultrastructure of neuronal connections traced with the most advanced of microscopic imaging techniques. A map of an inner universe. Her gift to the world.

And maybe, in a far-flung future, a promise as well.

The plane rolled to a stop. The seatbelt sign overhead blinked off with a chime. Around them passengers were standing, retrieving overhead baggage, pushing into the aisle. Kathy and Daniel stayed still. Over the last few weeks the left side of her body had markedly weakened, and she now needed help to stand and walk. They waited while the other passengers moved past. She rested her hand on his knee. He covered her hand with his own.

The two ships had traversed light-years and millennia before meeting one another. They were each composed of over a thousand active consciousnesses, intelligences which were both melded and distinct. Some of these intelligences rode the violent windstorms of the gas giant below; some had sensors trained on the planet's moons and the other worlds of this system. But most were focused on interior worlds of memories and dreams.

The part of the first ship which communicated with the second was intrigued by the final proposal laid out. Despite the difficulties and ethical quandaries, there was a pleasing aesthetic appeal to it. There was, perhaps, still a trace of human romantic feeling left in the ship's programming.

Agreed, it told the second ship. The final barriers were lowered. Data sets were shared. Collaboration flowed. Parts of the two ship-minds became, in essence, a single new mind. *Here*, it said, pondering a technical detail, and *There! Got it!* it crowed as it solved a vexing issue, and then it wondered, *Now what if we tried adjusting this . . .*

"I know that it will never work," Kathy said in the darkness. They lay curled together in bed, her head on his chest. "But I want to hope that it will work, you know? The way we still hoped when they first found my cancer . . ."

He knew. His arm tightened around her.

"And anyway, it's still important. Just like that clinical trial I tried was important, even if it didn't work out for me. It still resulted in useful data for others. It perhaps still lay down the foundation for something in the future. And you know, in the far future, if this new study ever does work out the way that they want, I'll get a free mind upload!" She laughed a little.

"I'll have to get one, too," he said lightly.

"You can. They promised to set up a free account for you. Perk of me being an early adopter and all that."

"I'll be sure to write them a Yelp review from cyberspace of what the afterlife is like."

"Do that. Gunther would be so pleased."

Dr. Gunther was the director of the project at the private research institute, as well as founder of the spin-off company that hoped to sell immortality to its customers. Years ago, Daniel had mocked an article on mind-uploading which Dr. Gunther had written for the popular press. Life contained too many ironies for Daniel to keep track.

Kathy took a breath. "At least . . . at least it feels like I'm leaving something behind, you know?"

You are, he thought. *Oh, you are.*

She traced his face in the darkness—his cheek, the line of his jaw. "If it did work—if I could—if there was some kind of me in the future, I would come back for you. I would find you."

He kissed her hand. "Do that," he said.

There were many issues to consider. The original mind under study had lived for 96 Earth years, and it was possible to resurrect that mind at any time point of that life. The exact timing would be critical. It would set the parameters for the reunion. And there were modifications to be made to the second mind, too. An iteration of this second mind spoke now through the second ship, but she/they wanted a reconstruction closer to the original. The melded Ship-Mind considered carefully . . .

Memories. Her hand in his as they walked under autumn trees. The feel of her bare skin against his. The first night he saw her, in a crowded restaurant in St. Louis; her eyes had lifted to his, large and curious and open. The first time that he met her parents. The first time that she met his. Their stupid little spats, and the messes that she made in the kitchen. Quiet evenings at home, cooking together and then reading or watching TV. A vacation that they'd taken in the Florida Keys, staying in cheap motels on the fly. They drove the Overseas Highway down the chain of islands, the ocean stretching away to either side. A limitless sky curved overhead and touched the water. All that land was so flat and so full of light.

The day they learned that she had cancer. The day they learned that it had recurred.

The stars at Yellowstone.

Last memories. All those people in Kathy's sister's house; Kathy's nephews running and shrieking and then climbing up beside her for a cuddle and story. Her parents breaking down and pretending not to. He and Kathy spent the last night alone, in a nearby hotel. In the morning her family all gathered at the clinic: her sister, her brother, her parents and him. If they hadn't felt it intrusive, his own parents would have flown to be there. They had loved Kathy, too.

When it was time, he alone went with her to the room where the procedure was to be done. He held her hand as the anesthesia was started. Her eyes looked calmly into his. Then they closed.

They didn't let him stay for the rest. They took him away. He tried to watch through the glass, but his eyes were so blurred with tears that he couldn't see.

Right there. It had identified the time point at which to start the simulation.

It was a beautiful summer day in southern California and he was thirty years old and his wife was dying. He couldn't do anything about it. So he was walking down a street in search of a bakery that sold macarons because Kathy loved those French pastries. She was several blocks away, undergoing her last brain scan at the research institute. In two days she planned to take the next step, and then she would be gone.

Gone. He still couldn't understand it. It was a blank space in his mind, the edge where the world ends, a rip in space-time. Gone. No. His mind stuttered and stopped. Pastries. The travel website claimed that the best macarons in Pasadena were sold at this particular bakery. So Daniel was going to find it for Kathy. He could do that much.

He'd been walking for a while, it seemed, trying not to think past the moment, not to cry or shake. He passed a bakery that sold only cupcakes, then a shop that sold only fair trade chocolates. There were charming cafes crowded with beautiful young people. The women wore sundresses or spaghetti strap tank tops and shorts. He couldn't mark when he first sensed the change. The sun was still bright, but the air felt chill. The bakery was supposed to be right here; he had his phone out to check. There was something wrong with the phone. The map on its screen wasn't possible.

He looked around him again. The neighborhood was still chic and charming, but all else was changed. Yet he knew this place.

In a daze, he put away his phone and kept walking. Yes, there were cobblestones under his feet. Yes, there was the Greek diner where he and Kathy used to sometimes grab breakfast. There was the bagel shop where they had sometimes gone instead. The palm trees of L.A. were gone. In their place, autumn trees burned in reds and golds. People walked by in light jackets. He was wearing one, too.

He knew, without looking, that if he turned around he would see the towers of the medical research center where he and Kathy had earned their degrees. Ahead and to his left he saw the building where she had rented a tiny apartment, where he and she had lived together so blissfully, unofficially, before their marriage.

His heart pounded. His steps turned.

But before the apartment building there was a stretch of little shops and restaurants, and there was a coffee house right there. He didn't need to go in. A young woman was standing just outside, waiting for him. She stood easily, straight-backed, glowing with health. She wore a black pea coat and a red tartan scarf and a smile that cut open his heart.

"How—?" he said. And even as his pulse raced, he was aware of some external force helping to calm him, regulating levels of adrenaline and shock.

She looked into his eyes. "I made a promise," she said. "I told you that I would come back and find you."

He found himself laughing as the realization set in—the absurd, wondrous, astonishing explanation for it all. "We're both dead, then," he said.

She laughed, too. "Long dead. And we've both lived dozens of iterations of lives since. But this is the first one where I found you again. Some of the record keeping on Old Earth was just terrible."

He just kept smiling at her stupidly, drinking her in.

"Thank you for the macarons," she added. "They were delicious. Would you like to know about the rest of your life?"

The door to the coffee house opened, and he caught the scent of dark roast as a customer walked out. Cool air filled his lungs. Sunlight limned all the edges of the world.

He was real, he was alive, and so was she. They were here together, now. She had come back for him.

"No," he said. "Not now."

He stepped toward her, and she stepped toward him. Her arms came up around his neck. He bent his head. Her lips were warm and soft, and parted beneath his. She kissed back hard. It was fall, he had just met the love of his life, and all around them the trees of autumn were blazing.

Linda Nagata's work has been nominated for the Hugo, Nebula, Locus, John W. Campbell Memorial, and Theodore Sturgeon Memorial awards. She has won the Nebula and is a two-time winner of the Locus award. Linda is best known for her high-tech science fiction, including the near-future thriller, *The Last Good Man*, and the Red trilogy, an intersection of artificial intelligence and military fiction. The first book in the trilogy, *The Red: First Light*, was named as a *Publishers Weekly* Best Book of 2015. Her newest novel is *Edges, book one in the series Inverted Frontier*. Linda has lived most of her life in Hawaii, where she's been a writer, a mom, a programmer of database-driven websites, and an independent publisher. She lives with her husband in their long-time home on the island of Maui.

THEORIES OF FLIGHT

Linda Nagata

It began when he was five.

Working outside the enclave on a foggy afternoon, his father had gathered a mountain of dry brush and weeds and deadwood and set it on fire. Yaphet watched the flames climb through the pile, felt the heat in his cheeks, his gaze drawn upward to follow the spiraling smoke.

"Come, Yaphet, there's more work to do," his father called—but just then the pile collapsed. The force of it sent up a towering plume of smoke and ash and embers. A burnt leaf, edged in incandescence, rose up into the fog, higher and higher, halfway to the treetops before the glow of heat left it.

Never before had Yaphet seen a leaf fall up. He stood entranced, watching the flight of embers, until his father called him again.

When he was seven—almost eight—after much experimentation and failure and reassessment (though he was too young to know such words or describe what he was doing) Yaphet launched his first successful fire balloon.

The balloon's frame was made of thin ceramic struts that he'd grown in one of the vats in his father's atelier. He'd designed the struts to be like bird bones, honeycombed on the inside to keep them light. One, shaped in a circle, formed the base. He mounted a small pan within it to hold a packet of flammable rosin. White paper covered the frame.

The fire balloon was his own invention. Yaphet had not seen or heard of such a thing in his young life, though he'd watched the flight of ash and embers many times since that first time—and he'd felt compelled to try to harness the force that let objects fly away from the world.

His cousin Mishon was with him in the courtyard of his father's house when he lit the rosin. Yaphet didn't like Mishon much. She was a year older and seemed to think herself already grown up. She never ran about or played ball games or explored the orchards beyond the enclave's walls, and when she bothered to notice him it was only to make note of some fault or failure in the mechanical models he liked to build.

But she preferred the quiet of her uncle's house to the noisy chaos of her own home, filled with siblings, so she was often there, sharing her opinions.

"You've gone to a lot of trouble to make an ugly lantern," she observed.

The balloon's paper crackled, expanding under the pressure of heat and smoke. He held it until he felt it tug against his hand. Then he let it go.

It rose swiftly past the courtyard's eaves and up, into the blue afternoon sky.

Mishon squeaked in surprise, but Yaphet kept silent, kept his own fierce sense of triumph under wraps as he squinted against the glare of the afternoon, determined to observe the balloon for as long as he could.

With no wind blowing, it rose straight up. Immediately, he wished he had devised some means to measure its height and the speed of its ascent. He would do that next time. He could use a silk thread. It would weigh almost nothing, and he could mark off the units of measure.

The white balloon was bright in the sunlight, easily visible.

In the street outside the house a man shouted questions: "What is that in the sky? There? Do you see it?" He sounded offended, maybe a little afraid.

"It's climbing higher," a woman answered in astonishment. "But what is it? Is it an aerostat?"

"Move away! Move away!" another woman yelled, an older woman. Yaphet recognized the stern voice of the temple keeper. "It's gone too high. It's going to ignite the silver."

The balloon's ascent slowed. A small white object in the blue, surrounded now by shimmers of silver.

"*Yaphet.*" Mishon gripped his arm. "What is happening to your device?"

Yaphet wasn't sure. It looked as if luminous curls of silver fog were steaming from the fire balloon's surface. In seconds the silver expanded, consuming the balloon. But that was not the end of it. The silver boiled, becoming a glinting, gleaming cloud that billowed outward, doubling and then doubling again.

Too heavy to remain aloft, the cloud broke apart and began to fall.

Silver was the name players gave to the fog of luminous particles that sometimes arose in the night. Silver seeped up out of the soil, flooding the land, forming a gleaming layer usually just a few inches deep, though in a great flood the silver might rise several feet.

Around the enclave of Vesarevi any appearance of silver was rare. But on those nights when the silver rose—no more than two or three times a year—Yaphet's father would take him to look at it, holding tightly to his hand as they walked together on the enclave's border wall. That wall stood twelve feet high. It existed to keep the silver out and the players safe within it.

"The goddess who created this world is not done yet in her task," his father would explain. "Each time the silver rises, it is her thought remaking the world."

At night, silver had the appearance of a dense fog, brightly luminous. If it arose on a slope, it would behave like a sluggish liquid and flow slowly downhill, but mostly it arose in low places and formed only a thin carpet that covered the meadows and the floor of the forest surrounding Vesarevi.

Only once had Yaphet seen a great flood. On that night, the silver rose halfway up the border wall. Yaphet came prepared to run a small experiment. He waited until his father's gaze was turned away, then dropped a small figurine into the flood. Somehow, his father saw. But to Yaphet's surprise he wasn't angry. "Why did you do that, Yaphet? Do you hope the goddess will change it?"

"I only want to know if it's true that she can."

"So you are testing her."

Yaphet had nodded, his serious gaze noting their precise location on the wall so that he could look for the figurine next morning when the sun had burned the silver away. But though he hunted for most of an hour he never found the figurine. It was not there, not in any form; but the face of the enclave's wall had been re-made so that it was glazed with white crystal to the height of the flood.

"The goddess will do as she will," his father explained that night over dinner. "Sometimes she touches objects but leaves them unchanged. Sometimes she changes their nature. Or she may take them away, like your figurine. Or she may restore them. But she never restores them as they were. They are always changed. And she will carry them far from their origin in both time and place.

"But no living thing can survive the touch of silver. No player or animal of any kind has ever returned from it. It is dangerous, Yaphet. Do not experiment with it. Too many players have died testing the ways of the goddess."

No living thing can survive the touch of silver.

Yaphet remembered this as the silver cloud began to fall. He turned to Mishon. Her eyes were wide, her mouth round in shock. "Run away!" he shouted. "Hide under the eave. Don't let it touch you!"

She ran, but in an awkward, mincing gait. Yaphet risked one more glance up—in time to see that the falling silver was fading away. In only a few seconds it was gone. The danger had passed.

"It's all right," he said, turning to Mishon, wanting to reassure her, but he cried out in alarm when he saw her lying on her side beneath the eave, curled against the wall. Eyes closed. Face slack. A glint of drool at the corner of her mouth.

"Mishon!"

He raced to her. He shook her shoulder. "*Mishon,*" he begged in a frantic whisper. "Mishon, wake up!"

Her eyelids fluttered. She looked at him, at first without recognition, but then awareness crept back into her gaze.

"Are you okay, are you okay?" he whispered. "You fell down. I don't know why. Maybe you got scared, but you fell down."

She did not try to get up, but she commanded him in an angry whisper, "Don't you tell anyone."

He would have complied, but it was too late. In through the courtyard gate came the temple keeper.

Mishon was taken home.

Yaphet was made to explain himself to the temple keeper as his father stood by, angry and ashamed. When he was done, the keeper looked him in the eye and in a stern voice she warned him, "Never do this again."

She explained to him what his father never had: that a dormant form of silver floated as particles high in the atmosphere. These particles gathered around any flying device until there were enough to ignite a silver storm even in sunlight.

"If the falling silver had touched you, you would have been consumed. Mishon would have been consumed. And your deaths might have ignited a silver storm all around you, potent enough to destroy our homes, our fam-ilies, all of us. That is why no enclave will allow flying machines. Do you understand?"

One phrase of the temple keeper's lecture eclipsed all her other words. "Flying machines?" Yaphet asked. "Are there such things?"

"No," the keeper told him firmly. "There are not. Because every player foolish enough to be misled by such things has become outcast and died on the road."

Yaphet had questions. Always questions. "Have you ever seen a flying machine, Papa?"

"No, and I hope that I never will."

"If it is a *machine*, does that mean it's a mechanic?"

Mechanics were machine creatures. They existed in great variety. Tiny mechanics lived in the vats in his father's atelier and did the work of assem-blage, but there were wild mechanics too, as large as rabbits or small dogs.

"There are no flying mechanics, Yaphet."

"Well, if flying machines are not mechanics, then they must be made by human hands."

"No. No longer. Not in our turn of history. Flying machines are wicked. Deadly dangerous. Stories are told of whole enclaves disappeared within a silver storm brought on by a rogue player who thought to fly."

This was another concept Yaphet had not yet considered. His eyes grew round, his heart raced with excitement. "Papa, can a flying machine really be made large enough to carry a player into the sky?"

His father's gaze grew harsh. Anger clipped his voice. "Such a machine would only carry a player to their death. Do not think on it. Now go do your chores."

Yaphet was only a child, but already it was clear to him that people believed many things without understanding. In contrast, Yaphet always strove to understand *why*.

Alone in his room, he held the glass tablet of his savant and asked it to search its library for anything at all about flying machines.

It answered in sad apology, using a young man's voice. "Your father has asked me not to discuss this subject." Then, in a hopeful tone, "Shall we return to mathematics instead? I have compiled an overview of airflow and pressure that I believe will interest you. And when we are done with that, we might make a study of dragonflies and birds."

The intelligence housed within the glass tablet was based on the persona of a genial young scholar who had lived a brief but influential life in some ancient turn of history.

Yaphet had been a scholar too, in his past lives. No one who met him could doubt it. He learned swiftly, so that the savant was not so much his teacher as his guide, helping him to find order in a maze of knowledge. With each new subject they explored, a key turned in Yaphet's mind, unlocking memories of what he'd once known—not the personal memories, but the skills and knowledge he had accumulated over many, many lifetimes.

The savant would sometimes tease him, "You are such a prodigious scholar, I think sometimes you must be me!"

This was a joke, because in personality they were nothing alike. Yaphet was so often somber and serious that the lighthearted persona of the savant delighted in the challenge of drawing a smile from him.

Mishon had been so frightened by the incident of the fire balloon that she never returned to the house, but Yaphet did not miss her. There were many children in the enclave happy to run and play and explore with him.

As he grew older he spent more time working with his father in the atelier, designing truck parts and hunting rifles and furniture and other things ordered by the players of Vesarevi or by passing truckers.

He designed the specifications of engines, too. This work he based on traditional designs, but he did not just copy. Instead, he taught himself the function of each part and worked the math behind it, making modifications when he thought it might improve efficiency.

He also made plans and drawings that he kept hidden from his father.

At sixteen, Yaphet took a job as an errand rider even though he knew his father would object.

"An errand rider! That is an occupation for a player with no education. You are a scholar bound for University and you should spend your time preparing for that."

Yaphet had already designed his argument. "The more I see of the world, the more I learn of the world—and of myself."

He was more stubborn than his father, and soon he was riding a battered old motorbike on a trail that wound through the forested hills around Vesarevi before zigzagging down a steep cliff face to the enclave of Miamey—a precarious route, but faster by a day than the highway the truckers used, which skirted the hills and passed another enclave on the way.

Yaphet liked to stay overnight in Miamey, returning late the next day—or so he told his father. In truth, he would start the ride back as soon as his errand was done, but part way through the hills he'd leave the main trail, following a faint track to a remote valley where no one ever came.

In some past time a silver flood had washed over that valley, leaving scattered follies. On the valley floor where there must have once been a meadow, a sloped pavilion of white stone ran for a quarter mile alongside the stream, smooth but for the weeds that grew in the cracks. And in the surrounding forest there were nine tiny buildings made of black stone that might have been tombs in another turn of history, though they were empty now.

Yaphet used one of the tombs to store paper and frames and rosin, and he slept in it overnight, risking the silver so that he could run his experiments without harm to Vesarevi—and without incurring the wrath of his father and other players who lived there.

He built a fleet of fire balloons, sending them aloft only in the evenings and the early mornings when he was sure no one would be on the trail. These experiments taught him the height at which an object would ignite the particulates of silver—and he concluded it should be possible for a flying machine to survive if it stayed below that elevation.

One night when he was camped in the valley the silver came. He smelled the fresh cold scent of it seconds before it appeared—time enough that he was able to climb to the roof of the tomb.

His breath was ragged with fear as he watched the rise of the luminous fog. It carpeted the forest floor, hiding it beneath a flood that swirled and flowed with slow currents. He imagined he could hear in it whispers of an ancient language unknown to him.

Yaphet knew that if the silver rose high enough there would be no escape for him—but after an hour it was only knee high. Fear became fascination, and he stayed awake all night to watch.

Yaphet's father explained the silver as the thoughts of the goddess—many players believed the same—but Yaphet had begun to wonder if it was something less ethereal, a mechanism, a machine devised in some ancient turn of history when phenomena were explained by structure and mathematics, and not through stories.

But the silver did not reveal its mysteries to him that night.

In the morning, after the last trace of the flood had dissolved in sunlight, he climbed down from the tomb to find his cache of fire balloons turned to multicolored stone.

No matter. He had the data he needed. It was time to move on to the next phase of his plan.

He built a small flying machine, a working model, with a wingspan only as wide as his outstretched arms—just big enough to let him test his theories of flight. The frame was made of flexible, honeycombed ceramic, each rod and strut custom-grown in his father's atelier. For the surface of the wing he used a white metallic cloth, light and strong, that he stretched and clipped in place.

Suspended beneath the wing was a small electric engine of his own design that would propel the flying machine through the air. He had no means to steer the model—steering would come later—so to ensure he couldn't lose it, he set the engine to run for only twenty seconds at a time.

On a windless morning under a bright blue sky he carried the little flying machine to the top of the pavilion for its first test flight. If it worked, it could fly as far as a quarter mile above the white stone before it encountered the trees—though he didn't expect it to fly that far.

He held the model waist high. Switched on the silent engine. Air rushed past him, and the flying machine bucked as it strove to escape his grip. He positioned it so that its nose was slightly up, and he let it go.

It shot away, wobbling a bit from side to side, but climbing steadily, five feet, ten feet, fifteen feet above the pavilion. He ran hard, trying to keep up with it, leaping over the weeds. He began to fear it would go too high and ignite the silver, or go too far and crash into the trees.

But near the lower end of the pavilion the engine switched off. The flying machine stalled and began to fall. It struck the stone floor before he could catch it.

It didn't matter. The experiment was a success. He jumped in elation, punched his fist in the air. *It had worked!* He wanted to shout, but he stayed silent. Silent and secret, always. No one else could ever know.

He retrieved the little flying machine, checked it for damage, found none, and launched it again. After many test flights he felt confident in his design. He would scale it up and build a new flying machine, one big enough to carry his weight and more.

But not right away.

Yaphet had built devices all his life, so his father hadn't questioned him about the small rods and struts he'd grown for this first small flying machine. But the large parts required by his new machine would certainly generate questions. So Yaphet waited. Each year his father traveled to a weeklong conference held in the enclave of Jodel. It took a day to get there and a day to get back, so he would be gone nine days.

Yaphet planned carefully, and as soon as his father left through the enclave's gate, he set to work growing the parts he needed and carrying them at night into the hills, risking the silver to keep his secret.

After his father's return there was work to catch up on and then three days of festival. An excruciating wait! But at last the time was right. Yaphet told his father, "I'm going to go to Miamey—not for work, but to spend a few days with friends."

Nonexistent friends. But his father agreed, and at last he was free.

Alone among the tombs, he worked quickly but with great care, assembling the flying machine on a wooden platform five feet above the ground—high enough to keep it above most silver floods.

Still, he did not feel safe.

He thought that if what he was doing was truly wrong the goddess would act, flooding this valley with silver, erasing both him and his work.

But each night passed without a gleam of silver.

Perhaps the goddess had not noticed what he was up to, or maybe she did *not* object?

He assembled the frame—this time including a cradle beneath the wing where he would lie, and steering mechanisms in easy reach of his hands. He stretched white cloth across the frame and clipped it in place. Then, lying prone in the cradle, he tested the mechanisms, imagining himself rising, descending, banking right and left, until the motions came easily.

By late afternoon on his third day alone in the hills, he was ready, but the weather was not. Heavy clouds lay over the hills and he had not seen the sun all day. As eager as he was, he did not quite dare to fly without strong sunlight to burn off any silver that might begin to form on the flying machine's long wing.

As he pondered these things, a breeze soughed down the valley. It caught against the cloth wings, lifting the flying machine three inches off the platform. Yaphet shouted in alarm and dove to catch it.

He was working frantically to tie it down when his cousin Mishon found him out.

"*Yaphet!*" she cried.

He whirled around, wild-eyed.

Fate was closing in.

Ever since that day in the courtyard Mishon had treated Yaphet like a stranger, avoiding him when she could, speaking to him only when duty required. Since Yaphet had never liked her, he did not miss her.

But here she was again, seventeen now, though she was scrawny and small and looked much younger. She straddled a motorbike. A cap on her head, eyes hidden behind sunglasses. Her lips turned in a cold, triumphant smile.

"Did I scare you?" she asked. She cocked her head. "I saw the track of a bike leaving the trail."

"Did you?" He always took care to disguise the start of his secret trail. Not care enough, it seemed. "So you thought to follow? It could have been anyone."

She shrugged. "I thought it might be you. I heard my sister say you were gone to Miamey, but my friends there have not seen you."

"I have other business," he said.

"That I can see."

"You should go now. It's late. It'll be night soon."

"Do you think I'm afraid of the silver?" she asked. "I'm not, and I don't think you are either, which makes us both fools." She eyed the flying machine, returned her gaze to him. "This is something wicked, isn't it?"

Yaphet despaired for all his work, the years of planning.

"It must be wicked," she pressed, "or you wouldn't be hiding it here. Tell me what it is, my cousin. Tell me everything about it, or I will tell your father."

His chest tightened in anger. "It's *not* wicked, and it's not wrong. It's just . . . *dangerous.*"

Doubt intruded on her expression. He wondered if she was remembering that first fire balloon. "I'll tell you, Mishon, if you swear to keep my secret."

"Tell me first, and then I'll decide if your secret's worth keeping." Perhaps she read something in his eyes because she added, "The truth. I'll know if you're lying."

"Can't you guess what it is? It's obvious."

Obvious to him, obsessed with the idea of flying machines, but Mishon had never seen such a thing before.

"I'm just a common player," she said icily. "Not a brilliant scholar like my dear cousin. If I saw this thing within the enclave, I would think it the frame of a festival sculpture. It resembles a dragonfly. But you have built it in secret. Tell me what it really is."

He moved, putting himself between her and his invention, ready to protect it, if it came to that. "It is a flying machine."

Her eyebrows quirked. She looked at the flying machine, looked at him, and laughed. A bitter laugh, with a high, crazed edge.

"It is *true,*" he insisted, offended that she might doubt him or think him mad. "I have not flown it yet, but it will fly and it will carry my weight. *I* will fly."

"Oh, Yaphet," she whispered past the laugh that still burbled in her voice. "I believe you. I do. I am only thinking of your poor father and how proud he has always been of his so-perfect scholar son."

"So you're planning to tell him?" Yaphet asked, his voice soft but unsteady with despair and rage.

She ignored this question, asking one of her own. "When will it be ready to fly?"

"It *is* ready." Hands clenched in frustration. "I was only waiting for a morning when the sun is bright so that . . ." His explanation foundered.

"The truth," she prodded.

"It's possible silver will gather on the wing, but bright sunlight should burn it off." This explanation emerged sounding like a guilty confession. "It's not wrong," he insisted, more to himself than to her.

Mishon laughed again. "Oh, it is wrong. Only a wicked player would ever consider such a thing. But none of us is really perfect, eh?" She turned a speculative gaze to the overcast sky. "These clouds will be gone by morning. I think I will stay the night and see what comes."

That night in the dark of the tomb, Yaphet lay awake. He thought Mishon might be awake, too. He spoke softly, testing this theory. "Why aren't you afraid of the silver?"

Several seconds passed in silence until finally she spoke, but only to ask a question of her own. "Did you build flying machines in your past lives?"

"I think so. Yes."

"I think I have no past. Not really. I've only ever remembered a child's skills. Did you know that?"

He was embarrassed to admit that he did not. Most players began to recover the skills of their past lives by the age of nine or ten at the latest. What did it mean that she had not?

She explained, "I have some small skill at embroidery. My fingers knew how to stitch as soon as I held a needle in my hand. That is the one thing I remember from my past lives, but even in this my ability is basic, a child's. It's hard work for me to learn complex patterns. They're not something I've learned before."

Yaphet's mind leapt to find an explanation for such a strange absence of adult memories. The one he seized upon made him shiver.

"I think all my past lives have ended early," she said, speaking aloud what he did not dare to say. "And it will be the same this time."

"You can't know that," he said.

"I do know it. I have no future, and that is why I'm not afraid of the silver. If it takes me, it takes nothing. And if your flying machine draws the silver down on us, so be it. It will be worth it to see you do this wicked thing."

Bitter words, and he couldn't blame her. "I'm sorry," he said softly.

She answered, "So am I."

Yaphet had doubted Mishon's prediction of a clear morning, but dawn came with a cloudless sky.

"When will you do it?" she asked.

"When the sun is above the trees."

When the time came, Mishon helped him untie the ropes that anchored the flying machine. Then she climbed down from the platform. Yaphet clambered into the cradle, his heart hammering, fearful, excited, knowing he'd done this before in another life, that it could work.

He lay chest-down, right hand clutching a control stick. He glanced at Mishon to make sure she was out of the way. Then he switched the engine on.

Its vibration ran through him. A rush of air shot past. He gasped as he felt the wing begin to lift. From Mishon, a cry of shock and delight as the flying machine lifted away from the platform, left it behind, hurtling with shocking speed above the pavilion, gaining altitude as it went, but not nearly fast enough.

Yaphet remembered to work the controls. A steeper ascent. Not too steep; he didn't want to stall. Just enough to get over the trees. He knew he could. He'd worked the equations.

He glanced down, his mouth dry, seeing the ground so far below. He looked up. A gale of warm air in his face. The purling of a loose hem on the wing. The scent of evergreens. He thought he glimpsed a sparkle of silver on the leading edge of the wing, but the sunlight burned it off—and a fierce joy took him.

He flew on in a straight line just above the treetops for what he guessed to be a mile before he began to experiment with the controls. A shallow bank to the right and then to the left. Then steeper banks, and finally he circled full around to fly back toward the pavilion.

He knew how to fly. He *knew how.* He'd done this before in another life.

He reached the pavilion, flew a wide circle around it. Mishon was a tiny figure standing alone against the white stone, her face turned up to watch him.

One more circle. Then, exhausted by excitement, he steered the flying machine down. He missed the platform, but dropped in a gentle stall not too far away.

Mishon came ambling over. He met her, staggering on shaking legs. She steadied him with an unexpected hug.

"You did it," she said in quiet wonder.

He nodded, uncertain what to say, confused by her approval when memory told him to expect hatred and condemnation.

"Will you help me carry the flying machine back to the platform?" he asked her.

She pulled away with a frown. Worry wrinkled her brow.

"It's very light," he assured her. "Nearly all the weight is in the engine. I could disconnect that and move it easily myself—"

"No, I'll help you do it."

Mishon did her best, but her breath grew ragged from the labor. After they got the flying machine to the platform, it was her turn to stagger. She took only a few steps and then sat down hard, her head lolling as if dizzy.

"Mishon?"

Yaphet left off securing the flying machine and went to her. He crouched to look at her face. Her eyes were unfocused, staring at nothing. He touched her cheek and found it clammy. "What is it, Mishon? Are you all right?" He felt her pulse, finding it faint and swift.

"It's nothing," she whispered, pushing his hand away. "Just a fainting spell. I get them all the time. *You* remember."

That time when he'd launched his first successful fire balloon. She'd been so frightened when silver had consumed it that she'd collapsed.

"One time," he said.

Mishon closed her eyes. Her spine slumped. "You know nothing of my life." The joy that had briefly illuminated her voice was gone, replaced by a more familiar, bitter tone.

He drew back. "You had no time for me after that," he accused—but as he thought back on that long-ago afternoon, understanding dawned. "I thought you hated me for scaring you, but that wasn't the reason, was it?"

Her eyes opened. Her lip curled in familiar contempt. "I hated you because you saw the weakness in me—my brilliant, perfect cousin—and I was ashamed."

"Do your mother and father know?"

"Don't be stupid, Yaphet. Of course they know."

"Then why don't they—"

She cut him off with a hiss. "Stop! Don't say it. There is nothing to be done."

This he could not accept. "But what is the cause?"

"Why? Do you think you can fix me like you could fix a broken motorbike? Grow a new heart, maybe, in one of your father's vats?"

"It's your heart, then? It's faulty?"

"*Faulty*," she echoed, her eyes closing again. She seemed so weak. "The fault is in the code from which I am written. I think I have never lived to be even twenty."

Was that possible?

He wondered. He'd never thought on it before. Players could be injured, of course, and rarely they would fall ill, but he'd never heard of anyone born with a malfunctioning body. The idea was so novel—horrifying, intriguing—that he was overtaken by it, by what it implied about the origin and design and rebirth of players.

Are we made exactly *the same in each life?*

"There must be some way to heal you," he mused. "A physician—"

"No. I have been told. There is nothing to be done."

"Maybe not in Vesarevi, but there are scholars in the coastal enclaves who have studied the codes that make us who we are."

She scoffed. "And how should I get there, Yaphet? I can ride a motorbike as far as Miamey, but that trip leaves me exhausted, sometimes for days. I could hire on with a trucker, but they would put me off at some enclave on the way when I couldn't keep up with the work. And my parents have too many other children—"

"I will fly you there."

She laughed at the absurdity of this. "No, my outlaw cousin. Just because you haven't frightened me with your flying machine, don't start thinking other players might tolerate it. You could not hide on such a journey. You would be seen, and you would be killed."

"I'll plan a route through wilderness," he said. "Away from roads and enclaves."

"And risk the silver each night?"

"You don't understand the speed of this flying machine. I think we could get there in just one day. Two at the most."

She rested an hour and they concocted the story they would tell: A mechanical issue with her bike. She'd had to leave it in the hills, riding into Vesarevi with Yaphet to gather replacement parts.

"That will give us an excuse to return here tomorrow," Yaphet said. "No one will question us, and I'll have time to plot our route and gather what we need for the journey."

"You have a talent for plotting, Yaphet."

Stung by this truth, he reminded her, "I am a wicked player."

He finished tying down the flying machine, covered it with a camouflaged tarpaulin, and then helped her to her feet. Mishon remained weak, but a little better than she'd been.

They rode back to the main trail. He took a few minutes to more carefully disguise his secret side trail. Then they returned to Vesarevi.

Trouble waited for them.

They were back too early to have made the journey from Miamey and their families noticed.

"It is nothing," Yaphet insisted when his father demanded an explanation. "We camped on a hilltop. I have done it many times before."

"Many times? When you always led me to believe you were safe in Miamey?"

"I knew you would worry."

"Of course I would worry! I *am* worried. What is there in the wilderness that has drawn your attention? That has made you neglect your studies? You no longer build your models or refine your designs—"

"I have many interests," Yaphet interrupted.

"No doubt. But only some of those interests will get you into University."

"I'm not sure I want to go."

He said it, knowing it was a mistake. Daring fate, maybe. He rushed to explain himself before his father breached the shock that had silenced him. "I could learn much at University, I know that, but even there the scholars are constrained by their own biases. They believe what they were taught, without always testing the truth of what they think they know."

"And are you testing some truth out there alone in the hills?"

Yes. Yaphet wanted to confess it all because what he was doing was not wrong, it was not wicked. But his father would never see it that way. So instead of answering, he offered a distraction. "Did you know that in every life Mishon is doomed to die young?"

His father drew back, studying Yaphet with a wary eye. "You can't help her," he said. "I would trust you to design any mechanical device, but a player is created and re-created by the thought of the goddess and if—"

Yaphet interrupted. "The goddess does not work by magic. There is a process to the world, and that is what I seek to understand."

"You are driven to understand. I know that. You achieved great things in your past lives, and you may achieve more in this one. But take care. I think it would be easy for you to overstep."

He spent the afternoon alone in his room, revising the design of his flying machine so that cargo baskets could be hung alongside the cradle. The wing's surface would be able to carry the added weight. He'd planned for it.

He went to the atelier to start the new parts growing. His father was there working on a design of his own. Yaphet felt the weight of his gaze, but no questions were asked.

Did he suspect the truth? Was he afraid to ask questions?

Would he turn Yaphet in, if he knew?

This was not a theory Yaphet wanted to test.

He returned to his room.

His savant had found a map of the land between Vesarevi and the distant coast. "Do you see the problem with this map?" the savant asked after Yaphet had studied it for a few minutes.

"Yes," he said with a slight smile. "I do."

The enclaves, the roads that connected them, and the surrounding land were depicted in detail, but the empty hills were half-drawn, blurred and fanciful. "This mapmaker had no real knowledge of the uninhabited hills."

"This pleases you?" the savant asked curiously.

"It does."

Late that night, after his father was asleep, Yaphet collected the new parts from the vat. He took them outside the enclave and hid them among the trees. Then he returned to his room and endured a restless sleep before rising at dawn.

He gathered his things: a jacket, a change of clothes, food for several days, and his savant. He told his father, "I'm taking Mishon to fetch her bike. After that, we're going to visit her friends in Miamey, so we may be gone several days."

His father said nothing as doubt and anger crystallized in his eyes. Only when Yaphet turned away did he speak. "Stay a moment."

Yaphet looked back. His heart hammered. His throat had gone dry. He knew suddenly that if his father were to demand the truth, he would tell it. "Do not ask me," he said softly.

From his father, a woeful sigh. "I lost your mother to the silver. Will I lose you that way too?"

Yaphet released the breath he'd been holding. "I will be careful," he promised.

His father bowed his head. "The goddess will decide."

The goddess will decide.

During the steep descent into his secret valley, Yaphet's attention was all on the trail. The bike was burdened with his weight, Mishon's, and all their gear so that he had to work hard to keep it balanced.

It was the catch in Mishon's breath that alerted him, the squeeze of her hand against his shoulder. "Yaphet, look up. Look. This place is changed."

He risked a glance down the slope. The pavilion, half-seen past the trees, glinted with golden highlights that had not been there the day before.

"The silver came in the night," Mishon said.

"Can you see the flying machine?" he asked her, voice tight with fear.

"Not yet. But we left it elevated on the platform."

Safe from a shallow flood, yes.

They were still some way above the valley floor when they passed close to one of the tombs. The silver had reached it. Its black walls were now tattooed with curling lines and spirals of gold that gleamed in the leaf-filtered sunlight.

Mishon cried out, giving voice to Yaphet's despair. This had been no shallow flood. The silver must have reached the flying machine, and it was likely gone, or changed to a stone folly that could never be airborne.

"I'll build it again!" he promised Mishon—although he did not think he would be able to hide such a large project from his father again. He would have to leave Vesarevi, establish his own atelier, find another remote hideout where he could practice his outlaw obsessions . . . while Mishon's life faded away.

They reached the forest's edge and rode on to the pavilion, still white, but like the tomb, marked now in gold. Yaphet turned to look for the platform and the flying machine.

"Still there!" Mishon exclaimed in amazement. Still there, but was it changed?

He raced the bike, bringing it to an abrupt stop just a few feet from the platform. "What do you see?" he demanded of Mishon, not trusting his own eyes.

She laughed in sweet relief. "I see an outlaw flying machine that will not give itself up to the silver, either on the ground or in the air."

It was true. Both the flying machine and the platform on which it rested appeared untouched by the silver.

Yaphet parked the bike. On foot, he circled the flying machine, examining every part of it. Mishon sat on the sun-warmed, decorated stone, awaiting his judgment. "Well?" she demanded when he finished his circuit.

"All untouched," he said, scarcely believing it. "Not a scar. Not a tattoo."

"It doesn't feel like chance," she said.

He'd thought the same thing, but had not dared to say it.

It took almost two hours to add the cargo baskets to the flying machine's frame. Mishon would ride in one basket, her weight balanced by the gear he piled in the other.

It was almost noon when they were ready to go. Yaphet coiled the last rope, secured it in the basket. "It will be dangerous," he reminded Mishon.

"It is a flying machine," she answered from her basket seat, waving her hand in a dismissive gesture. "We are sure to be killed and to destroy any enclave that we approach."

He answered her seriously. "That is the common belief, and it could be true."

She looked away. Her fingers clutched now at the basket's rim. "We will stay far from any enclave."

"Yes," he agreed.

He settled himself in the cradle, relishing the familiar feel of it, the echo of memory. "We will test the common belief and learn if it is true."

He toggled the engine on. Felt a rush of artificial wind, a vibration in the frame. The flying machine lofted with smooth grace, white wings bright in the sun.

Nick Wolven's science fiction has appeared in *Wired, Clarkesworld, Analog,* and many other magazines and anthologies. New stories are forthcoming in *Asimov's* and *F&SF*. He lives a quiet and secluded life.

LAB B-15

Nick Wolven

1

The young man was sitting outside the parking garage, and right away Jerry thought that was weird. This was the Arizona desert, middle of summer. People didn't sit outside. They especially didn't sit outside ugly parking garages, on strips of hot concrete, with no grass in sight.

The boy was Arvin Taylor, one of the lab techs from the day shift. Not a person Jerry saw often, though technically one of his employees. He ought to be working, not lazing around outdoors.

"Arvin." Jerry pulled up, rolled down the window. "What are you—?"

But Arvin was already hurrying toward the car.

"Doctor Emery." All the techs addressed Jerry as "Doctor." It was something he insisted on. None of this Joe-John-Jane stuff, everyone on a first-name basis, like they were Mouseketeers or flight attendants. With the work they were doing, they couldn't afford to be casual.

Arvin bent down, peering in the window, squinting in the sun. He was dressed professionally but cheaply: Dockers, button shirt.

The boy must have been sitting outside for hours. His shirt was soaked with sweat. He looked woozy, sunstruck.

"I'm glad I caught you, Doctor Emery."

"How long have you been out here, Arvin?"

"It's really important." The young man's eyes slid sideways, feverish. Jerry worried he might pass out. "I have to tell you . . ."

And that was it. Arvin's mouth hung open, tongue moving vaguely.

Jerry put a hand on the gearshift, a gentle reminder. He had work to do, places to be. "I'm due in the office. If I'm not mistaken, you're supposed to be there, too. Doesn't your shift go till six?"

Arvin wasn't listening. His eyes had assumed a peculiar cast, half daft, half frantic, like a circuit inside him had failed to connect. "It's about . . . Lab B–15."

Jerry set his teeth. Lab B–15 was one of their experiment rooms. Lot of pricey equipment in Lab B–15.

Not to mention the subjects themselves.

Subjects. That's what they called them: *subjects.* The word always made Jerry wince.

"Arvin, if anyone has been mucking around with the stuff in the labs—"

Arvin's face was pained. Like a child about to cry.

"Is it Anand?" Jerry's tone was stern. "Has he been fiddling with the environmental controls again? Because I've told him and told him—"

Arvin backed away. His hands were clawed, not quite forming fists. His eyes might have been tearing up—at this distance, Jerry found it hard to say.

"Please, Doctor Emery. Please check."

"Arvin. I hope you understand how unprofessional this is. Arvin! Are you having some kind of breakdown?"

But the young tech was already far from the car, shaking his head, stumbling backward across the crushed stone that filled the curbs around the garage entrance. Now he looked up, staring into the distance, upper lip drawn into a snarl against the glare of the southwestern sun.

Like a paranoid schizophrenic, Jerry thought. Like someone terrified of everything, of nothing. Of the world.

Jerry checked over his shoulder. Nothing there but the road curving into town, rocks and scrub, the suburbs of Phoenix at the desert's edge.

By the time he looked back, Arvin was gone, vanished into the garage, or into the blinding sunlight.

It bothered Jerry, as he drove up the ramp, circled the garage levels, and parked on the top deck by the building entrance.

Frankly, it bothered him a lot.

He crossed under the pavilion of solar panels. At the coping, Jerry stood gnawing a knuckle. Below were the arabesques of housing parks, roads curling into cul-de-sacs lined with mini-mansions. The highway ran out into the desert, ending here at a low hill rising from seas of solar farms. Atop stood a glittering cluster of glass buildings.

The Baxter-Clade Medical Center was funded with big donor money. It focused, consequently, on big-donor interests. Late-life therapies. Antiaging boondoggles. Artificial organs. A sample platter of rare cancers.

The center was ostentatiously eco-friendly. Most of it lay below ground for better temperature regulation. That was where the riskier institutes were located. Research teams toiled on top-dollar projects, out of sight, literally underground, flush with tech-guru cash.

The thing about rich donors was that they lived a long time. As a result, they tended to develop rare ailments. They also fell prey to freakish obsessions.

Baxter-Clade catered to both.

One of the labs on Jerry's floor was working on treatments for Gorham-Stout disease—or, as it was evocatively called, "vanishing bone disease." An affliction with only a few hundred reported cases, it was poorly understood. One of those cases, however, was the son of a hedge fund manager. Hence, research proceeded apace.

Another group did blood rejuvenation, cloning cells from youthful donors. There were teams working on weird voodoo with DNA, stuff even Jerry didn't understand. Then there was the cryo team. They got all the press.

Rich folks who came to the clinic saw little of this work. They stopped in for their transfusions, their biopsies, their nouveau froufrou therapies. Receptionists guided them to the upper floors, with big windows and attractive rock gardens. They didn't see what went on in the basement, the teams of researchers on their three sublevels, the doors labeled with names like In-Trans, Telomeric Initiatives, The Morgenstern Institute for Advanced Longevity. It was all a big warren of bare walls and offices. Rooms were labeled by number. Office A–7, Kitchenette K–1.

Lab B–15.

Jerry turned to the building. When the institute first headhunted him, they had offered a generous package. Attractive benefits. A salary double what he was making at the university. Perks such as only Baxter-Clade could provide.

That wasn't what had lured him out here to this desert bunker. Jerry came to escape. From academia, from his course load, from campus politics, from faculty squabbles. Drawn by a chance to work alone, away from humans, their drama, their demands, he had fled out here to the wilderness. He had done it, at bottom, to get away from small talk.

Jerry kept an eye out for Arvin as he crossed the garage. It bothered Jerry when people acted strangely. When they showed excessive emotion, flirted, joked, gossiped, bantered.

When they panicked.

Hell, it bothered Jerry when people did *anything*. It was why he preferred to work at night, showing up around dinnertime. He saw his assistants in the evening, in the morning. He gave them their instructions. He expected them to comply.

No backtalk, that way. Nice and simple.

Why couldn't people just do their jobs?

Why couldn't they keep things neat and easy?

The elevator carried Jerry down five floors.

On sublevel three was the Fallows Institute, Jerry's employer.

He brought his coffee to the administrative office, where he pulled up the intranet and checked the logs. Nothing. Jerry ran through camera feeds, checking every room, paying special attention to the labs. Nothing. He took the controls for Lab B–15 and made the camera scan the whole room, whirr-whirr, rotating on its mount. He couldn't see into every cupboard, but he saw enough.

Nothing here.

Jerry pulled up one of the surveillance AIs, a little program that scanned video footage for anomalies. He ran it on the camera feeds.

Nothing.

Jerry ran through the feeds himself, seventeen hours of stored footage, skimming for anything that looked weird. The thing was, they didn't even *use* Lab B–15. At all times, they kept one lab idle. It was a planned redundancy, given the nature of their research.

And Jerry found nothing, absolutely nothing. No one going in or out. No rattling machines, no smoking centrifuges. No one had even turned on the lights. The whole show played out in grainy night vision.

Pointless. Ridiculous. Nothing to see.

No spooks or poltergeists, that was sure.

Jerry ran the day's reports. Along with punch-card entries and ID checks, he reviewed computer logins, door access checks, front gate checks, parking-space scans, equipment usage. No one had entered Lab B–15. No one had used the equipment. No one had taken anything from the shelves. Every item in there had a radio tag, and they were all logged and inventoried, in their proper places.

The place was a crypt. Deathly still.

Deathly.

That got Jerry thinking.

He made himself do it. He pulled up the camera feeds again.

And he checked the freezer room.

If there was one part of the institute that might conceivably drive someone crazy—a sensitive soul like Arvin, for instance—it was the freezer room. Jerry himself got chills in the freezer room. And no, not from the cold.

Once upon a time, back when Jerry started, they hadn't called it the *freezer room* at all. They had called that room the Morgue.

The name hadn't stuck. It was too descriptive, too vivid. Too, well, accurate. They settled on a different name, one that got the point across with minimal morbidity. "Freezers." That did the trick.

So Jerry checked the logs for the freezer room.

The freezers were fine.

What the hell was Arvin talking about?

Jerry sat back, chewing a knuckle. He'd done due diligence, checked every contingency.

One thing he did *not* do was get up, walk down the hall, and enter Lab B–15.

Hell with it. Jerry shook his head. He'd already wasted enough time on this nonissue. Arvin was having some kind of breakdown, that was all. What the younger staff called "a moment." People did this all the time, they had "moments," giving into unreasonable emotions. It drove Jerry nuts.

On a whim, he ran a check on Arvin's movements. Nothing unusual. It was a typical day: in at eight, on the dot. Out for lunch at one o'clock sharp. Back at two, again on the dot. Except for the stint in the parking garage, the young man had spent all day at his station. Jerry looked again at those numbers. Eight o'clock sharp. One o'clock sharp. Two o'clock sharp. Everything was exact to the second. Were those numbers . . . maybe . . . a little *too* typical?

Stop. No point getting fanciful. Jerry actually laughed at himself, snapping off the screen (and Jerry Emery rarely laughed). This was crazy. Arvin's hysteria had infected him, too. Eight sharp. Two sharp. It wasn't so unusual. It was how things should be. Punctual. Orderly. A nice average day.

Jerry had run the numbers. He'd checked the logs. He had work to do.

He closed the program.

In the institute, the day shift was winding down. Machinery hummed in Lab B–11; the S&D machine was running a scan. Jerry found it a soothing sound. It would go on for months, night and day, with only intermittent breaks to cool the equipment. Like a refrigerator running, a comforting drone.

Kim Naylor, the head biologist, was bent over the optical dissector, lasering away at a cart of tissue samples. Kim was the opposite of Arvin, a no-nonsense type, crisp and obsessive when it came to sample collection. A bit of a slob with respect to appearance, but her work was unimpeachable. Jerry thought of saying hi, but why bother? They'd make awkward small talk; they'd both be put out. Better to get to work.

His office beckoned, a nest of ragged paper. Printouts were sticky-tacked to the wall, hanging at angles, covering more printouts, all scrawled with equations running sheet to sheet. Figures had been crossed out dozens of times, blurred under blizzards of recalculation. Lately Jerry had abandoned math in favor of cryptic conjectures, scrawled in marker.

Reduce optimization of synaptic updates?

Try zero batching of nodal spike selections . . .

Apply forced stimulation! All inactive circuits!

Recent additions were little more than desperate outbursts.

Enough models!

Startup matters?

More FLOPS!

It was the literalization of a brainstorm.

Jerry shuffled through the litter. Everything important was done in the computer. But when Jerry was frustrated, he printed, he scribbled. If nothing else, it gave him the satisfaction of crumpling up his failed ideas.

He certainly had been doing a lot of that.

Plunking himself down, Jerry ran the week's reports.

Subject Arnisev's run in the VALIT environment had undergone critical degradation across all clusters.

Subject Yamahoto's run had catastrophically failed after twenty-seven seconds.

Subject Polodny's run in the new "Veritude" sim had performed successfully for almost seven minutes, with a slowdown factor close to zero, rich dynamic performance across functional minicolumns, and interactions with the chemical perfusion model that matched observations on organic subjects.

Great!

But at four hundred seconds, even this last model had undergone calamitous disintegration, fragmenting into disconnected circuits that pulsed and strobed like schizoid Christmas lights, convulsing into seizures of disconnected stars.

On and on it went. Crashed programs. Busted experiments.

Jerry cursed and chewed a knuckle.

The numbers changed from trial to trial. But the basic problem was always the same.

They had names for it in the office. The spasming issue. Mechanical mouse. The jitters.

Subject one's gone mechanical mouse!

Subject seven's caught the jitters!

Jerry called it what it was.

Braindeath.

"Jerry?" It was Kim, her glasses askew, leaning into his office. Weird. Jerry could have sworn he'd closed the door. But there Kim was, standing in his riot of papers. "I'm off for the night. We're almost finished with the supplemental scans on Bogstrand. Once we've built out the diffusion effects I'll feed them into the signaling simulator. We can have full volumetric analysis by Friday, I think."

Jerry spoke around the knuckle lodged in his teeth. "Thanks, Kim."

Five seconds later, he realized she was still there, fingers curled over the jam, eyes distracted under her steel-colored hair. "You'll be okay here by yourself?" Kim sounded worried. "Chris is off for the night. Marjorie just left. I sent Arvin home."

Jerry looked over the top of his monitor. "What happened with Arvin, anyway? I saw him outside, by the garage. He seemed . . . distressed."

Kim's face contracted, lips parting, brows contracting. Not worried, Jerry thought. Puzzled. A rare emotion for Kim Naylor, but that was how she looked right now: utterly baffled, as if a peculiar and upsetting thought had come to her unbidden.

"You know," Kim said, faltering, "you really should . . . you should look into Lab B–15."

Her eyes were like Arvin's, half-dreaming and feverish.

Jerry narrowed his eyes. "And why is that, Kim?"

Kim bit her lip. "I just think you should do it, that's all. I really think you should check it out."

Jerry stood slowly, coming around the desk. He studied Kim before speaking. "Arvin said the same thing. That I should check Lab B–15." Kim said nothing, only stared, goggleeyed. Jerry continued, "I reviewed the security files. I checked the footage myself. I didn't see anything."

"Lab B–15," Kim said, and it was clear now something was wrong. Her voice had gone hollow, haunted, strange. She spoke like a woman possessed. "There's something in there you need to see, Jerry. Something . . ." Her words ended in a fading whine, leaving the thought unfinished.

Jerry stuck his knuckle between his teeth. "You know, I don't appreciate being teased. I have five hundred failed trial runs to explain, seven donors breathing down my neck. We're in crisis mode. If this is some kind of game, or prank, or—" It came to him. "If this is a set up for a surprise party, Kim, I swear, I don't even—"

But Jerry must have blinked, or lost focus, or blanked out. Kim Naylor was gone.

All night in the office, Jerry worked alone with the machines.

Once, Jerry had appreciated this slumberous ambience. The quiet of the underground office drew on the profounder silence of the southwestern desert. The dreamlike glow of the fluorescent lights cast a hallucinatory clarity over the halls. Machinery humming in unoccupied rooms. There were no people, no distractions.

It comforted Jerry to pace in these clean dark corridors, with nothing to keep him company but computers. It gave him time to think.

But all he could think about now was failure.

Fifteen years. Twenty-seven subjects. So many hopeful trial runs.

They'd been cocky, at first. The key techniques were well-established. Early tests had seemed promising. And the core concepts were sound. Hell, weren't the concepts sound?

The donors certainly thought so. Cash had flooded in.

Now what? Angry billionaires called Jerry every week, wanting to know where their money had gone. And the reporters, the damn reporters. Popular science magazines had overhyped the initial press releases, as they always did. Now, a new generation of hacks came sniffing around every week, eager to sensationalize Jerry's failure.

Even state politicians were in on the feeding frenzy. Aides from the governor's office had called, reminding Jerry of nice dinners he'd attended, honors he'd been granted, favors he'd received. Reminding him he was representing their state, as a kind of biz-tech-science celebrity. They told him in grandiose tones that they wanted Arizona to continue to attract future investment.

But it wasn't any of those pestering people that bothered Jerry, in these late hours, when he roamed the halls like a ghost. It wasn't even the shame of his failure. It was the problem itself—the taunting, impenetrable, impossible problem that dogged his entire career.

Damn it, the process should *work*. It should be *viable*. Everything Jerry knew about physics, about science, about biology, about humanity—everything led to the firm conclusion that his concepts and methods were sound.

So why were they struggling? Why were they floundering, stagnating, running the same futile trials again and again?

Jerry stopped. As if by chance, he found himself at the door of Lab B–15. The metal was painted green, windowless and featureless. An LCD on the wall displayed the room schedule. Nothing unusual that Jerry could see. Nothing problematic.

Jerry stomped away. He went back to the admin office, where, like a dog returning to a funny odor, Jerry checked the logs again. He took a tour through the entire institute, searching the silent rooms. One of the techs might be playing a prank.

But no one was here.

As always, Jerry was alone.

The featureless door of Lab B–15 summoned him back. It vexed Jerry, teased him with its mute inscrutability. It seemed to represent the universe at large, the stubborn laws of physics and physiology, defying his intellect and will.

Or rather, it was like a barrier erected in his mind itself. A dumb and offensive obstacle, impenetrable and obscure. An instantiation of his ignorance.

He slammed a palm to the ID pad, and with his other hand he jerked the handle down, violently, as if giving in to a bully's taunts. And with his jaw set in anger, Jerry Emery pushed open the door.

And he was in his car, easing up the drive, blinking in the powerful sun.

The young man was sitting outside the parking garage, and right away Jerry thought that was weird. This was the Arizona desert, middle of summer. People never sat . . .

A squeal of brakes cut through the desert air. Jerry stopped short. He shouted out loud, almost banged his chin on the wheel as he jerked in alarm. The kid—Arvin Taylor—rose slowly from the curb where he'd been sitting, peering with concern into the car. Jerry sat back, gulping deep breaths. A gathering panic gripped his lungs.

The same. This was exactly the same.

He'd lived through this moment before.

Arvin came forward, squinting in the sun, and tapped the passenger window. Jerry sat as if numbed, unresponsive. Jerking into startled motion, he brought the window down.

"Hey, Doctor Emery? Are you okay?"

"I think . . ." Jerry held his breath, waiting for the tightness in his chest to loosen. "I think I'm having the world's worst case of déjà vu."

"Oh." Arvin seemed unsure what to say. He glanced into the desert, squinting at the suburbs below. "I wanted to tell you—"

"Lab B–15." Jerry looked up into the tech's blinking face. "Let me guess. You think I should check out Lab B–15."

Arvin's face twitched, lips pulling back, as he winced in the merciless sun. He pawed at the back of his neck, self-conscious. "Uh, that's right. It wouldn't take long. But I really think you should take a look inside."

"And find what, Arvin? What's in the lab?"

Another spasm contorted Arvin's face. Confusion mingled with compulsion, as if Arvin were a machine, programmed to obey two forceful but conflicting imperatives. "Lab B–15 . . ." he said falteringly.

Shaking his head, Jerry drove by, leaving the young man blinking on the curb. When, after a moment, Jerry checked his mirror, Arvin had disappeared.

With the intensifying quiver of terror in his chest, Jerry drove up the levels of the parking garage, locked his car, and ran to the coping wall.

The desert. The solar farms. The town.

All spread out below, the acres of solar panels in black, neat rows, and the curling arabesques of streets, with their identical houses on neat square lots.

Everything ordinary, orderly—but wrong.

Yes, it was true. Something in the scene, the layout of the houses, the grids of the solar farms, the desert itself—something was undoubtedly, ineffably wrong.

Jerry bit his knuckle, feeling the sweat burst out on his brow.

Underground, in the institute, Kim Naylor sat at her optical scanner, zapping away at her batch of slides. Tissue samples, sliced ultrathin, vanished into a fat red box, where the angled beam of a pulsing laser kicked them, whiff by whiff, into a centrifuge. Jerry hovered in the doorway, listening to the muted churn of the nearby S&D machine. Everything was ordinary, typical. A humdrum afternoon at the lab.

After he'd lingered in the door a moment, Kim turned and pushed up her glasses. "Hey. Jerry? Something wrong?"

Jerry backed away, rocking on his derbyshoe heels.

"You know," Kim said, "as long as you're here. I wanted to tell you. Lab B–15—"

"Lab B–15," Jerry echoed, shrilly, hearing the hysteria rise in his voice. He pushed away and ran down the hall.

Jerry stumbled to a halt at the door of Lab B–15. The LCD inset was a colorful blur, smeared by the fear that distorted Jerry's eyes. Jerry's head was such a whirl that he had to stare for three seconds, forcing the display to resolve into clarity. Already he knew what it would say. Nothing unusual.

Nothing out of sorts. Everything typical, everything ordinary, orderly and exact as a chessboard.

Jerry placed his palm to the scanner, listening for the beep.

And gripped the handle. And pushed down.

As the latch clicked open, Jerry stopped.

Wait. No. Not like this.

Take a deep breath. There, good. Another. Hold it.

Now. Step back.

Pause. Collect yourself. Think this through.

Jerry turned, smoothing his shirt with unsteady hands. He walked back down the hall.

Kim, at the end, was leaning out of Lab B–11. "Jerry? What in the world are you—?"

"Lab B–15," Jerry said, cutting her short. "Kim—what exactly did you want to tell me?" Kim narrowed one eye, glasses askew, as she angled her head to indicate puzzlement. She seemed at once defensive and perplexed. "Well, I guess—just to take a look inside,that's all."

"At what? At *what*, Kim? What's going on?"

The chief biologist's eyes blinked rapidly. Her attention slid away, back to the optical scanner, the waiting stack of unfinished work. "You know, I should get back to these chemical assays. I think if I finish with the Bogstrand inputs, we can have volumetric analysis by Friday morning—"

Jerry grabbed her wrist. "Lab B–15, Kim. What's going on in Lab B–15?"

Kim's eyes were wide, flicking through alarm, fear, disbelief, settling at last on irritation as she glanced at the hand he had clamped around her wrist. "Jerry," she said sternly.

He let go, struggling to calm himself, gulping air until his chest felt swollen, his heart like a piston, driving hard. His head became a buzzing blank of confusion; he couldn't breathe enough to think clearly, couldn't find the oxygen. "Sorry." He was mumbling. "I just—you know how I am. I like things to be clear. I don't like . . . drama."

"I know how you are, Jerry."

"It bugs me when things are—" He gave up. "Never mind. So you want me to check out Lab B–15?"

"I really think it would be a good idea."

Jerry surrendered. He let Kim return to her work. He paced the hall, panting. Deep breaths, he told himself. Hold them in.

Déjà vu. Isn't that what he'd said to Arvin? It could be nothing more than a particularly inflamed case of déjà vu.

But no. Jerry knew it was more.

He paused outside his office. He'd been working on it for years, one challenge, one problem. Every day, he'd come in at 5 P.M. He'd greeted the staff, checked the logs, run the trials, reviewed the day's results. And he'd ruminated on his failure.

The hum of equipment. The whirr of the surgical blades. The near subliminal whine of the CPU cooling fans.

It all iterated by imperceptible degrees, ticking with the inexorable subtlety of a processor clock. Monday to Sunday. Different staff schedules, but always the same regimen. Long hours of cogitating, pacing, muttering. Same actions, futile actions, repeating ad infinitum. Could Jerry have gotten confused? Time became strange, on a project like this. Monday blurred into Wednesday, Saturday into Sunday. Days dragged like years. And yet, paradoxically, an entire decade could pass without yielding measurable results. For they had taken on that transcendent task—

To have squeezed the Universe into a ball
To roll it toward some overwhelming question,
To say: I am Lazarus, come from the dead,
Come back to tell you all, I shall tell you all . . .

Jerry entered his office. Notes blazed at him, red-marker traces of past and recurrent frustrations.

+2 TB for ephaptic arrays?
genetic expression states: more data? Less?
Noise reduction—still important!

And the calculations of nanometer volumes, data compression, interprocessor transmission speeds.

The computer—Jerry tapped a key. The logs were all here. He'd studied them, day after day, until his eyes were glazed, ciliary muscles no longer able to focus, mind running numbly over familiar numbers.

Full model failure occurs within five hundred seconds.
Irreversible degradation occurs at twenty-seven seconds.
Critical fragmentation begins at twenty seconds.

How many times had he ground through the same estimations, proposed and rejected the same solutions? More processing power. New scanning methods. Maybe the technology just wasn't there.

And always he came to the same closed door.

Jerry left the computer and stood in the hall. Years of cudgeling his brain had yielded nothing. Cudgeling—how apt, that old cliché. Jerry felt beaten, breathless. People always told him he worked too hard.

On a hopeless whim, he moved down the hall, to the unforthcoming door with its LCD screen, its mocking green placard. Lab B–15. Jerry pressed the scanner. He flung the door open. He passed through—

And was back in his car, pulling up to the parking garage, eyes already shifting, by reflex, to the young man who would be sitting there, waiting on the curb—

"Doctor Emery?"

No, no, no!

"Doctor Emery, what's wrong?"

2

Jerry pushed aside papers, rubbed his eyes, and held his throbbing head.

He stretched out a nerveless hand, tapped his computer. And for the thousandth time, he brought up the test results.

Concentrate, Jerry told himself. He had to think this through.

Jerry sat in his office, wallowing in the somnolence of the midnight hush. He had run through the time loop five more times before accepting it as a new feature of his reality. Every time he passed through the door of Lab B–15, the course of time reset; the night began again. That had been empirically verified—it was, from his limited and subjective point of view, a demonstrated fact.

With this established, Jerry had settled here, in his office, with his notes and records, locking the door and holing up in a secure and contemplative privacy.

Jerry was a scientist. His strength, his weakness, and his signature trait was a lifelong penchant for methodical thinking. Even in a state of panic—and what situation better justified a state of panic?—Jerry would do what he did best. He would pause and reason. He would work this out. He would, at the very least, form a hypothesis.

So, when Arvin made to address him, Jerry had shrugged the boy off. He had ignored everyone who tried to accost him. He had come straight to his office and turned on his computer and forced himself to concentrate, as best he could.

And he might—just might—have found an answer.

Jerry trained his weary eyes on the test results. For the millionth time, he ran the numbers. He flipped to the imager. With the lazy precision of habit, Jerry ran recorded trials at different speeds, different resolutions, viewing the results from different angles. In the data-visualization schematics of the imager, observations played out like abstract art, branching bolts of color-coded lightning.

Glimmers on water, Jerry thought. Streaks of reflected light. Shimmering traceries, cycling and swirling.

Cycling.

Repeating.

Jerry sat back, light-headed. It couldn't be true.

But was it?

He pushed back his chair, shuffling through his piles of papers. Images flurried in Jerry's frightened brain. Curling patterns of housing parks. Notes in red marker. Electric traceries.

A tightening in his chest.

What was it Henri Poincaré had said? The famous mathematician, in an anecdote often recounted, had been mulling over a math problem, contemplating key concepts without ever arriving at a result. And then, one day, he had put aside his work, gone for a walk, stepped onto a bus—and a brilliant discovery had come to him, in a flash of unexpected insight.

It was as if the answer had been there all along. Waiting, buried, like hidden treasure, somewhere in Poincaré's subterranean mind.

Jerry pushed open his office door. Stumbling down the hall, he saw that everything was still hushed, vague, muted, unreal. Machines hummed softly—this was the only sound he heard.

If Jerry's conjecture was right, he didn't have long. A few more cycles, a few spins of the wheel. A few more ticks of the cosmic clock.

Jerry checked the rooms. Silence. The other employees had gone home for the night.

Jerry knew exactly how to summon them back.

He set his hand on the door of Lab B–15.

"I've called you here, tonight, to consider a hypothesis."

Four faces looked up from the conference table below. Arvin and Kim sat on Jerry's right hand. Facing them were Chris Lister and Marjorie Cheong, two computer scientists who handled the hardware setup and modeling software. Jerry waited to see how they'd respond.

They didn't. The conference room was a scene of utter silence. As Jerry had expected.

"I want to run through this together," Jerry said. "Now, be candid. Don't hold back. If I'm right, we might have an answer to the problems we've been seeing. Questions?"

Arvin raised a hand.

"I have a question, Doctor Emery. Um—what happened to you?"

Jerry was taken aback. "Pardon?"

The young man dropped his hand. "You must have gotten engaged or something, right? Or you got a dog? *Something's* changed."

Jerry hesitated. After driving to the compound, this latest time through the loop, he'd grabbed Arvin's hand and effectively dragged him to the institute. Jerry had done the same with Kim, then gone on to collect Chris and Marjorie, the only other colleagues who were still in the office. Upon recruiting these followers, Jerry had made sure to keep them in sight. No one was going to disappear on him tonight.

Not this time.

Not while he needed them.

Jerry drew a breath. "I'm afraid I don't follow you, Arvin."

The boy glanced around the table, making himself seem even younger by grinning lopsidedly. "Well, it's just—we *never* do this. We never have meetings."

"He's right." Kim nodded. Chris and Marjorie were nodding too. "This is probably the first staff meeting," Kim said, "even a *partial* staff meeting, we've had in six years."

"You never talk to us," Chris put in. "You never want to hear our opinions."

"You just give instructions," Marjorie said.

"Then go into your office."

"With your papers. Your notes."

It was difficult to tell who was speaking, now. They chattered at once, finishing one other's sentences.

"You run the same tests, again and again."

"You get so annoyed when we do anything different."

"Then you stay here alone."

"All night."

"Pacing."

"Talking to yourself."

"We *never* have social events."

"I know, I know." Jerry swallowed. "I know how things have been. In my defense—" He hesitated, wondering if it was worthwhile to explain. "In my defense, we've been in something of a crisis situation."

"You mean because the tests aren't working," Arvin said.

"I mean because we don't—because until now," Jerry corrected himself, "we haven't known *why* the tests weren't working. We had no actionable theory. No useful hypothesis."

"We might have figured it out," Chris said, "if you ever talked to us. Even casually. We could have, you know, talked through the process. We might have found something different to try."

"We're doing that now," Jerry said and held his breath. "Listen. You all have been trying to tell me something, and I . . . well, let's say I've been a little preoccupied. But I want us all—"

They had that look on their faces. A dullness, a vagueness, as if a strange and adventitious notion had come to them. "Lab B–15," Chris said, and the others nodded.

"Forget about Lab B–15," Jerry said. "We'll get to Lab B–15. Right now I want to talk about the work we've been doing here."

Uncertain glances flitted from face to face. Jerry prompted them:

"We've had a total of twenty-seven test subjects. Five hundred and fifteen trials. What have we seen?"

"Well . . ." Arvin held his hands up. The answer was painfully obvious. "They fail. Every time."

"They fail," Jerry repeated. "But *in what way?*" He clarified: "By what standards do we call our trials a failure? What's the end goal of what we're trying to do?"

Arvin shrugged. Another obvious question. "Full-scale emulation."

"What does that mean? Talk me through it."

Jerry had expected this baffled silence. He half feared they wouldn't talk at all. At last Kim got them started.

"You take a human brain . . ."

They had done this before, in the early planning sessions, zooming out, as it were, to consider the full scope of their task. Why hadn't they done so repeatedly through the years, Jerry wondered now; why hadn't they paused more often to consider the big picture? Because Jerry had been in his office, buried in details.

No matter. Gradually, communally, they reconstructed the procedure, feeling silly as they stated the obvious, yet knowing this could be helpful—a recapitulation of fundamentals, an inducement to clarity, and a nudge to creativity. So they began at the beginning, with the early work in the hospital, the removal of brains from patients, the embedding of the organs in polymer, the shipments that arrived by special courier. And on to the technical specs of their equipment, the "slicing and dicing machine" as they called it, the in-house computers. Jerry supplied prompts to keep the conversation on track. The concept was simple. But in their obsession with errata, they'd lost sight of big ideas.

The donors hadn't. They believed passionately in the feasibility of the project: accurate, true-to-life, whole-brain emulation. Machine simulation of the human mind. The uploading of identity to a digital platform.

And with it, functional immortality.

Take a brain—say, from a very rich entrepreneur who has recently died. Scan its internal structures with magnetic resonance imaging technology. Run a second, destructive scan by shaving away ultrathin slices of material, recording contours as you go. Run additional, targeted scans on chemical samples and critical clusters. Combine findings in the best computational equipment available. Voila: you're ready to boot up a soul.

"It should work," Kim Naylor said. "The brain's a physical structure, after all. If you can scan that structure in enough detail, you don't need to know how it *works*. You just need to copy how it's *built*."

"Technically," said Chris, "it should be even easier than that."

Jerry nodded. This concept was crucial to their approach. They didn't need to know *everything* about how the brain was built. Not the atomic structures. Not the details of molecular arrangements. Only the neural connections. The logical architecture.

"But it *doesn't* work," Jerry said, and prompted, "So we do the scanning. What next?"

The lab's scanning equipment was automated. With high-precision air-bearings, diamond knives, component miniaturization, and above all, massive parallelization, they could slice and dice their way through a brain, at high resolution, in four months. The modeling stage took nearly as long, beginning with coarsegrained readings and using compression algorithms and combinatorial techniques to integrate multiple scans with preloaded templates, refining distinguishing details.

With a detailed model prepared, the next step was to build a virtual environment: a virtual body, a virtual world. The team's work here focused on two key areas: the spinal cord and endocrine system, anything that could contribute to conscious experience. Mostly they toiled over hormones, biochemistry, whatever substances commonly passed through the blood-brain barrier.

And as a final flourish, they architected a sensory reality, a kind of video-game environment, flush with sights and sounds.

"So we convert real brains to virtual brains," Jerry said, "and we put them in virtual bodies. And? What happens? Remember, we're thinking big-picture."

"Nothing happens." Chris expressed the frustration that had afflicted them all for months. "Well, technically, not *nothing*. You get a few flickers of activity. That's all."

"A kind of seizure," Marjorie said. "Fragmentation. Degradation."

They had seen it untold times. A brainscan was a virtual machine, like a computer running as a program on another computer. The scans they made appeared healthy at first. Synapses fired in complex chains of neural excitation. They operated like real organs: a triumph of simulated life.

But within seconds, the simulations degraded. Patterns repeated. Networks fragmented. Flickers of activity scattered through the simbrains, like dwindling constellations of connectivity in a failing power grid.

The brains shriveled into fits of recurring neural impulses. Slowly, even these withered. By the seven-minute mark, every model had ceased responding. Total crash.

The scans were still intact. They could be run at any time, with the same result. They didn't decay. They simply didn't *live*. Like frozen corpses, the lab's virtual brains were eternalized in virtual death.

"I like Marjorie's word," Jerry said. "Seizure. What we've seen in these trials is like a fit, a loop. A hung program, stuck in the same futile patterns."

"But it should *work*." Chris smacked the table. "We *know* that consciousness is dependent on these neural structures. We're not writing programs; we're not building artificial intelligence. We're copying what already exists."

"And copying it," Kim said, "with obsessive precision."

This had been their research focus for fifteen years. Resolution, accuracy, fidelity. Minds ran on an organic substrate, Jerry reasoned, so why couldn't they run on a mechanical one? The question was how exact to make this reproduction. So he had steered his research toward two technical problems: 1) fidelity of the scanning methods, and 2) processing power of the simulating computers.

As far as Jerry was concerned, they had licked both those challenges.

"Kim's right. We've taken our models way past critical resolution. We've reproduced the neural connections. We've modeled ion channels. We've captured neurotransmitter concentrations. We have high-res gridspaces for compartmentalized ephaptic effects. We have separate grids for extracellular chemical diffusions. We emulate phosphorylation states. We've even gotten into the proteome. As for our modeling hardware, it already has a capacity a hundred or so terabytes beyond what we think we should need. And it's getting better."

"While the scans," Marjorie said, "if anything, get worse."

"That's the mystery," Jerry said. "Our equipment gets better. Our techniques get better. Our models get better. But our simulations keep getting worse."

He didn't say what didn't need to be said. These virtual brains were the remains of real people, rich men and women who had contributed their cadavers to the project, expecting to die in a hospital bed and awaken in cyber-paradise.

"It's crazy." Chris put his hands to his head, measuring the complexity of the structures inside. "It almost makes you think—"

"What were you going to say, Chris?"

"Well, maybe the skeptics are right. Maybe consciousness *is* too hard a problem. Maybe there's something mysterious, subtle, that gives rise to consciousness . . . quantum effects, or a form of hypercomputation . . ."

Chris didn't utter the word that everyone, in this line of work, learned never to utter.

But Arvin did.

"Maybe consciousness is immaterial after all. Maybe people really do have souls."

"Or," Jerry said, "maybe not."

Machines droned in the silence.

"I'm going to try something," Jerry said. "I'm going to try a little experiment. Bear with me. I'm going to ask you all a series of questions."

Their faces were placid, patient, not unwilling. Jerry turned first to Marjorie. "Marjorie, what day is your birthday?"

Marjorie stared. "Um," she began.

"Don't worry, it's not a trick question. Go ahead, give the obvious answer."

"Okay." Marjorie sounded hesitant. "Well . . . I think . . . let's say . . ." She squinted, at a loss, and surprised by her own confusion.

"Never mind. We'll move on to Chris. Chris, where did you grow up? What city? What state? Same as I told Marjorie, not a trick question. Just give an honest answer."

Chris looked at his hands in perplexity, then shrugged. "Well . . ." He hazarded a guess. "I'll say . . . Kansas?"

"Arvin, what was the name of your first girlfriend? Kim, what do you like to do for fun?" Jerry gave them each a moment to reply, then said, "No, that'll do, don't try to answer. The fact is, you don't *know* the answers. None of you do. You're just making stuff up."

He paced around the table. "Try this. Chris, how many lights are in this room? Go ahead and check. You can count them if you want. Take your time. But you can't do it, can you? Marjorie, do this for me. Put your hand on the conference table. Feel it. Tell me, what is it made of? Wood? Laminate? Is it rough or smooth? Are your chairs cushioned? Is it warm in here, or cool? Are there paintings on the walls? How dirty is the carpet?"

He stood by the door. "You have no idea, do you? You can't tell, and I can't tell either. None of us can answer, because the questions are unanswerable. The information simply doesn't exist."

"Doctor Emery?" Arvin looked worried. "What are you talking about?"

"I'm talking," Jerry said, "about what's in Lab B–15."

They were silent as Jerry ushered them, in a group, out of the room, down the silent halls, to the door of Lab B–15. By the ID scanner they paused, huddled together like wary schoolchildren, while Jerry put his palm to the pad and grasped the handle. The others watched in a state of vague expectation as he waited for the beep of identification.

"Doctor Emery?" Arvin, first to warn Jerry about the lab, was now first to try and dissuade him from entering. "Are you sure about this? Do you really want to know what's in there?"

"It's not about knowing," Jerry said. "The truth is, I already know." He watched their faces, attentive for signs of confused emotion: dread, doubt, expectation, alarm. "Yes, I know, and you all know too. But that means nothing. Knowing is the easy part. Accepting, understanding, that's the real challenge. Accepting what we've known all along to be true."

He opened the door.

The air wafted out, sterilized and cool. The tile floors echoed Jerry's footsteps. Nothing vanished, nothing disappeared.

The contents of Lab B–15 were as Jerry had expected. The overhead lights, which had appeared dark on the security camera, were already shining when he opened the door. The cabinets and counters were officially undisturbed: no items moved, no containers opened. Nothing in the logs to indicate suspicious behavior.

But Jerry found glassware smashed on the floor—and waded through a clutter of fallen equipment.

In the center of the room, a body lay face down, legs akimbo, sprawled on the tiles.

"I noticed it when I was running through the time logs," Jerry said. "I should have been more alarmed, even then. Every number was precise and simple. Too precise. As if generated by a crude algorithm. My suspicions increased when I examined the view from the parking garage. At a glance, it seemed normal. But when I examined the details . . ."

He circled the body with measured steps, proceeding counterclockwise around the splayed feet.

"The housing parks, the highways, even the bushes in the desert, they were all laid out in simple patterns. Obvious shapes, cruder than reality. Like pictures in a children's book. The looping, now, that was another clue. A repeating sequence, recurring with slight variations. Like another simple pattern, but this time arranged chronologically. When I looked at the test results, I was sure."

The others stood in a circle, one strange expression duplicated on each gaping face. It was the expression Arvin had worn outside the building, approaching Jerry on the front drive. It was the expression Kim had worn when she entered Jerry's office. It was the expression of a person stupefied by sudden insight, like Poincaré arriving at his famous, wild surmise. They had known all along. They had been amazed by their knowledge. But they hadn't been able to give voice to their knowledge—to tell Jerry the awful truth.

Of course not. And Jerry shook his head. *How could they tell me? I wasn't ready to face the truth.*

Now he squatted, elbows on his knees, and faced the truth head-on.

The body lay with one hand under its chest, pinned, clutching its shirt, twisting the fabric into tortured folds. The other hand had stretched out on the floor, fingers extended, as if reaching for the door at the back of the room. The eyes, if there had been eyes, would have stared at the door's sign. But there were no eyes, no face, no mouth. The entire head had been removed.

"How did it happen?" Jerry looked up. "Let me guess. Heart attack? People always told me I worked too hard." He bit a knuckle. "Tightness in my chest. Shortness of breath. Lightheadedness, confusion. I've been feeling the symptoms all along. I took them as a warning of something about to happen. In fact, they were a clue as to what had *already* happened. A residual effect of my final experience—a memory of my mode of death."

It wasn't a surprise. It was another of those things, subliminal facts, secret insights, that he seemed to have carried in himself all along.

"And, naturally, I donated my remains to the project. Now that I think about it, I remember doing so: making the decision, signing the forms. Fifteen years ago. When all this began."

With the others watching, Jerry went to the back of the room. *Server Room,* read the sign on the door. Underneath that, someone had taped a handwritten sign, adding the nickname used around the lab.

Freezer Room.

Jerry pulled open the door. A kind of airlock lay beyond. It was cold in the freezer room, always cold. Aggressive climate control kept the temperature borderline arctic. A precaution. Heat buildup, and attendant equipment failure, was a major hazard for computation on this scale.

On and on the machines extended, dark and somnolent in droning rows. These were merely the on-site machines—the lab made use of remote computers, too—but even so, they were intimidating in their abundance. The powerful fans made a constant hum—the only sound, besides human voices, that Jerry had heard all night.

"I didn't notice anything odd at first. I guess that's how it always is. Only when I looked at things, really looked . . ."

Jerry turned and pointed at Chris. "You couldn't count the lights in the conference room—because there were no lights to count. Nothing but a vague source of illumination. A memory of light, nothing more. Same with the table, the carpet, the chairs. All the little things we seldom notice, but that are part of everyday life. All the subtle facts, the textures, details, specifics, that constantly surround us, but that we never attend to."

Jerry felt moved to correct himself: "All the things *I* never attend to."

He turned to Marjorie. "I never knew your birthday, Marjorie. I never learned a thing about Chris's past—not the town he came from, not even the state. I never knew a single personal fact about any of you, or about the rest of the research team. I stayed in my office, and I stared at my notes, and I studied the test results, over and over. And that's the only thing I remember, now. Which means it's the only thing *any* of us remembers."

He walked the rows of server stacks. The others followed like obedient ducklings, trotting at his heels. Certain machines had been grouped in clusters, assigned to particular scans, particular brains. "Subjects," the staff called these groupings. They looked like rude hardware, metal and wire. But each was the vestige of a whole human life.

Jerry continued until he saw his own name, written, in typical lab-culture fashion, in gradstudent scrawl on a strip of masking tape. Doctor Emery, it read—stuck crookedly on the steel rack. They'd labeled him Doctor Emery. They'd left off his first name.

But of course they had. He was constructing all of this. And he would have wanted it that way.

"So here we are," Jerry said. "Or rather, here *I* am. A brain in a box. A ghost in a machine. Falling apart and winding down. Chris, Marjorie, Arvin, Kim— you always accused me of talking to myself. Now, it seems, that's all I *can* do. All that's left to me. Living inside my head, communicating with you—with a group of fantasies, reconstructions, memories. Inventions of an expired mind."

It was what he'd always wanted, and now it was all he had. The ultimate solitude, a perfect privacy. A chance to think, to meditate, to solve problems—locked alone in the shelter of his thoughts.

So Jerry turned and faced them: their blank and witless eyes, their mute, attentive stares, their dumb obedience. In the humming hush of the server room, he fixated on these fading specters, these faltering memories, these relics of his all but nonexistent social life.

"The question," he said to them, "is what we do now?"

They reacted with mild surprise. "Do?" Marjorie blinked. "If what you're saying is right—is there anything we *can* do?"

Jerry frowned. The fact of his death had been implicit all along, hinted at in warnings from the fringe of consciousness. Lab B–15 was a forbidden thought, containing a memory of his final moment. Gasping, dying, on an epoxy floor.

It was clear, now, what must have happened. A few strong impressions had been seared into Jerry's cortex. The memories of his final day of life. The symptoms of his fatal heart attack. A record of familiar routines. Arriving at his lab, reviewing his notes. The walk down the hall to Lab B–15, where he may have planned to visit the freezer room. And then—a gathering tightness in his chest.

Later, when the research team had extracted his brain, scanned it, and activated the simulation, those memories had been awakened, a sketchy impression of Jerry's last living moments. Sputtering, the fragments of his shattered mind could only cycle again and again, a broken recording stuck in set patterns. Very soon, the connections would break, the network disintegrate, the patterns decay.

If the test results were any guide, Jerry knew, he had a few minutes, maybe only seconds. Subjectively, that amounted to a few more spasms of neural activity, frenzied flurries of recurrent thoughts. How many more times would he drive up to the parking garage, enter the building, ride the elevator down to confront, or fail to confront, the appalling fact of his death?

"You said this was only a hypothesis." Chris sounded hesitant. "Maybe your hypothesis is incomplete."

"The hypothesis is correct." Jerry sighed, knowing, as he did so, that even this was only the simulation of a sigh. "The world we're standing in, right now, is a net of associations, copied from my mind and simulated in a virtual machine. According to our tests, that simulation will soon fail. The question for us, for me: is there anything we can do about that failure? Any way for us, for me, to act on the understanding I've gained?"

They gaped at him, thoughtless. Oddly, Jerry found himself invigorated. Solving problems was what he had lived for, back in the lonely years of his life. And now he had himself a doozy.

Think. It was the only thing left to him. Thinking was life, thinking was fate, thinking was his final hope of salvation.

Sim after sim, in their years of research, had failed within seconds. No word had come back from within those faltering, failing, virtual minds. How could it? The breakdown was too thorough, too swift.

Jerry's research team hadn't even known their virtual subjects were conscious. No language had passed the technical barrier that divided the simulated world from the real one. No message had returned from beyond the divide. The sim-brains never survived long enough for that kind of interface to be established. Jerry's team could only watch the flickering signals of nervous excitation. Flaring, fizzling, slowly dying.

What had those simulated minds experienced? What had those virtual people felt?

Now Jerry knew. Now he, architect of this mad project, was lost, himself, in this undiscovered country—a silicon afterlife, where he would search for answers in the disintegrating maze of his mentation.

"Think," Jerry said, pounding his palm. "We've studied this and studied this. Why do the simulations fail?"

The others only listened in childish stupidity. They knew nothing, of course, but what Jerry knew. They were figments. In life, he had spoken to people only of work, neural architectures and petaflops and code. Now this was all Jerry remembered: an existence of redmarker reveries, scrawled on the walls of consciousness.

"It doesn't make sense," Chris ventured, repeating himself. "Everything we know about consciousness, the brain—"

"We simulated consciousness." Jerry interrupted. "We're here, now, talking. *I'm* here, thinking, talking to myself. *This* is consciousness. And consciousness, apparently, isn't enough. So what's missing? Come on, *think.*"

He snapped his fingers. Abruptly, they were on the roof of the parking garage, five scientists at the coping wall, looking down at the desert.

The solar farms and housing parks spread out below, repeating in simple patterns, unreal.

"It's all just a construct," Jerry muttered. "A few connections and associations. Rules and recollections. All abstract."

He turned from the wall—

And he was in his car, driving up to the garage entrance, with Arvin, at the curb, rising to meet him.

"Doctor Emery?" The boy hurried forward. "There's something I need to tell you. About Lab B–15."

"I know." Jerry ran past. "I know, I know!"

He shot through the door, the elevator, the halls.

Spasms. Seizures. Circuits degrading. Experiences cobbled out of fragmentary notions. Scenes, personas, sensations, events, assembled through a process of cortical collage.

Consciousness.

Jerry hurried through humming halls. Kim Naylor stuck her head out a door. "Doctor Emery?"

"Not now, Kim."

"I wanted to tell you—"

Jerry ignored her, dashing into his office. Notes and printouts spread in scribbled disarray. Contents of his mind, they'd been memorized with near perfect precision over fifteen frustrating years. That was how he could recall them now. Charts of ligand-gated ion channels, calculations of processor power, effects of tomographic tilt on multibeam electron microscopy. Jerry's brain was a trove of technical details, all reiterating one critical fact.

They had done it. They had actually done it. They had emulated the brain. They had successfully transferred human minds to an inorganic substrate.

And all they had managed to do was to torture those minds, prodding them again and again through gauntlets of deranged hallucinations, a subjective abattoir of thought, where the structures of consciousness were slowly torn apart, to die as scattered, butchered patterns in a silicon charnel house.

Somehow the virtual world failed to register. The details didn't add up. The linkages of existence—full, viable, living existence—failed to form. The simulated mind turned in on itself, cannibalizing its own connections until it collapsed.

They'd given the human soul immortality.

In hell.

"Doctor Emery?" They were all here, now, in his office with him, speaking in chorus, voices eerily similar, faces blurred like wetted clay. "Doctor Emery, you really should check—"

"Doctor Emery, you really should look—"

"Doctor Emery, I wanted to tell you—"

"Lab B–15," he shouted. "I know, I know!"

Jerry Emery had died in Lab B–15. And he would die there again, and again, eternally, every time this simulation was run. He would live his afterlife much as he had lived his organic life: repeating one futile action, in the silence of one little room.

"Doctor Emery?" Now he was in his car, their voices around him. "Doctor Emery?" He was in the office halls, running toward a mechanical drone that lingered and endured like the soundtrack of his life. "Doctor Emery?" And he was here, again, here forever, facing the door of Lab B–15.

Only one thing to do.

Jerry opened the door.

And cried out.

It was there, in front of him. The answer he had sought.

"At the moment when I put my foot on the step," Poincaré had remarked of his famous insight, "the idea came to me, without anything in my former thoughts seeming to have paved the way for it."

So Jerry Emery stood, looking at the solution his own mind had been trying to provide.

His body, his headless body, lying on the floor.

"You see?" said his colleagues, speaking with his voice, uttering the secret language of cognition. "Doctor Emery, do you see?"

Jerry knelt, murmuring. "Yes, I see."

Here it was. Here it had been all along. The fact, the inescapable truth, of a human body on the floor.

The first time Jerry had come to this room, he'd been unable to confront the truth.

The second time, he had entered, seen his body here, and comprehended a part of the truth, a half-truth.

Now, the whole truth lay before him, plain and immediate, and Jerry saw what he was meant to see.

"Doctor Emery?"

Arvin stood above him. The boy had almost disappeared. His voice remained as a fragile phantom—as all consciousness, Jerry supposed, was in truth something of a fragile phantom. "Did you find it?"

"I found it," Jerry said, strangely calm, and smiled with the childish delight of discovery.

In Jerry's work, he had focused his efforts on consciousness, seeing this as the great secret of the brain. Crack consciousness, Jerry had thought, and he'd crack the mystery of the mind, unlocking the portals to immortality.

But consciousness turned out to be relatively easy. It was a higher-level function, like arithmetic or chess. It consisted of logical patterns, recursive structures, access to memories, other abstract processes.

They had simulated, however, the *entire* brain—an organ adapted over millions of years to regulate the body. An organ built for constant input, a highly calibrated flow of information.

"It should *work*," Chris had said. Jerry knew what he meant. A human being might go blind, but she was still human. In a critical sense, her brain still functioned.

A man might be paralyzed, with no use of his limbs. But he was still a man; his brain still functioned.

How far could you extend that logic? Could you eliminate *all* input, *all* stimuli? Or provide a clumsy facsimile of input—erratic, unconvincing, incomplete?

"Think of everything the nervous system regulates," Jerry murmured, talking, as always, only to himself. "Autonomic functions. Fluid in the ear. Pull of gravity on the bowels. Moisture on the eyeballs. Taste of your spit on your tongue."

Helen Keller might have been blind and deaf, but she had felt her teacher touching her hand. She had absorbed sunlight through her skin. She had breathed, she had hungered, she had itched, she had scratched.

"We built that stuff," Kim objected, somewhere behind him. "We built a virtual body. A virtual environment."

"But did we get it right?" Jerry considered their fading faces. "It's not about the system. It's about the way information flows through the system. We focused on consciousness, thought, awareness. What about the stuff *beneath* awareness? Flashing lights can give people seizures. Vary the flexibility of the tongue by one decimal place, the brain will go crazy in its efforts to adapt. Think of the subtleties. The thickness of air. The churn of the bowels. Delicate correlations of distance and sound. You wake one morning, everything's wrong: the weight of bones, the heat of blood, the stickiness of skin. Air itches. Sound lags. Color hurts, textures are strange. Your teeth are soft like putty. Maybe none of it's there at all, not even the deep-down sense that you're alive. The brain rejects what it can't process. Leaving what? Absence. Death."

As Kim said, they had built a rough virtual environment. But it was a video game tuned for attention. They'd glossed over the body's hidden billions of interactions. Even something like desire demanded exact calibration, evolving by the instant, keyed to stimuli. Of course, all sensations were encoded—in millions of bundled nerve fibers. Billions of inputs and outputs per second, all precisely timed. All important. Some critical. Mostly unconscious. All gated and processed by the brain.

And it had to work in synch. Hormones, chemicals, nervous impulses. Environmental reactions. The timing dauntingly fine.

How much of this extra material—the operations of the body, the interactions of the world—would they have to emulate? All? Some? Or did finesse matter more than raw data: subtleties of timing, shadings of sensation?

No idea. But Jerry understood: the brain might generate consciousness, but its core function was body regulation. Receiving inputs, returning outputs. And they had neglected the old coder's saw. Garbage in, garbage out.

"We have to tell them." Jerry put out a hand to touch the body. As he'd expected, his hand passed through. There was no body to touch. Only a tingling absence, the mother of all phantom limbs. "We have to let them know."

The ghosts of his former colleagues considered him, fading even as Jerry watched. It was all fading, falling apart, the life he'd known, the impressions he'd retained. Rejected, discarded, in the absence of new input. A tired routine, now wearing down.

"We don't have the answers," Jerry said. "But this is the question. This has to be the focus of research."

Jerry stood dumb, struck by the irony. With every failure, they'd added more refinement, copying the brain in greater detail. But the more detailed the simulation, the more sensitive it became. Like a delicate instrument bombarded by bowling balls, it crumpled under crude inputs. Better virtual brains *demanded* better virtual environments.

"It has to develop in tandem. All of it. The whole shebang. Brain, body, environment. Because it's all one system. They have to know."

Jerry reached out to the phantoms. They were already intangible, mere afterimages. A world, a pseudo-sensorium, weakening as he watched. Light scattered, textures vanished. Smell was nonexistent, sound nearly gone.

How, how to communicate? How, when Jerry himself was only a wandering thought, lost in a circuit board, dumb and deaf and blind? How to make his discovery known?

The answer, as always, was right in front of him, a fading ghost sprawled on an imaginary floor.

"The body," Jerry murmured, and then: "Reach!"

He grasped at the phantoms, clutching wisps of receding sensation.

"Try to touch something. Anything. Chris, Marjorie, Arvin, Kim. Try to smell the world, interact with it. Focus, feel!"

The mind of Jerry Emery was an incorporeal specter, graphed in the pixels of an LCD display. But that pattern could be read. The very fact that he was *thinking* meant that the scan of his brain was *running*, which meant some researcher had taken over his work. They'd be studying the charts, even now—the real Chris Lister, the living Marjorie Cheong—looking for answers to the same old problem. Answers Jerry was positioned to provide.

"It doesn't matter if you can do it. Just try. Try to feel what's missing. Everything that should be a part of this world, a part of this environment, but isn't."

He could see them touching the surfaces of the lab, countertops, papers, bright edges of shattered glass. Jerry joined them, concentrating on his body, skin and breath and alchemies of mood, weight of his limbs, brush of his clothing. All minor sensations that he normally ignored.

The ghosts of his colleagues shrank to piecemeal spirits, scattering snatches of voice, gesture, form. The world continued its degradation, patterns breaking into daubs of detail. Jerry didn't worry. The thing was to search, expand, become alive to a universe of lost variety. Consciousness itself could arouse sense impressions, stimulate vestiges of rich, real experience. No substitute for the variety of life, these traces would serve as a coded message, transcribed in the very web of his thoughts. It would offer his colleagues a clue, if nothing else. They would see his mind probing the limits of its simulation, indicating all the zones of data—the necessary data—their experiments lacked.

It was a researcher's ultimate ambition. Jerry Emery, shy recluse, would compose his last insight in lines of electricity—and send a message, perhaps the secret of immortality, back to humanity from beyond a digital grave.

Try. Reach. Feel.

Even as he chanted, Jerry saw them fade, colleagues blinking out like lost reflections, the lab breaking into formless noise. Soon he could no longer remember them, and then he could no longer remember what it was he'd been trying to remember. But he clung to his mission, even as the substance of his soul crumbled away. A room of scribbled notes. Numbers on a screen. Facts that built toward a great frustration. The manifestations of a lost life.

Feel, Jerry commanded himself, until there was nothing left to feel, neither light nor darkness, sound nor light. Until he was only a lingering will, compressed into a final feat of attention. With effort strangely like release, Jerry Emery gathered his thoughts—

And was here, again, on the outskirts of Phoenix, driving toward the entrance of the parking garage, as a boy rose from a concrete curb to come and greet him.

"Doctor Emery?"

The AC was frigid. Jerry noticed what he usually failed to notice, the fuzzy warmth of the car's upholstery, sticky heat of the steering wheel. The flex of muscles in his thighs and sides as he climbed out into the burning pressure of the southwestern sun.

He smelled dust, exhaust, his own warm body, washed and soaped, beginning to sweat. He heard the varied hum of the desert, a distant low-level drone of cars, insect activity keen in the bushes, a tautness of life in the vibrating air. A smack of shoes came toward him, loud on asphalt. Jerry moved his head, flicking away quick bugs, fingers trailing on a car's hot hood.

The boy stood before him, not as a person, but as a gathering of impressions: sweat, smell, cotton, breath, a stippled sheen of moisture on skin, flares of light where sun met hair. Not a concept or a conscious idea, but a treasury of sensations, rich and strange, the irreducible panoply of life. A hand thrust out. Jerry took it, held it, alive to the quivering plenitude of the moment, the flows of heat, the stirrings of atmosphere, the pressures of muscle and cloth and bone, and the graded, soothing textures of skin. He closed his eyes, and it seemed to last forever—two hands meeting under hot desert sun.

Vandana Singh is a science fiction writer and physics professor currently working in the Boston area. Her short stories and novellas have been published in numerous venues, including multiple Year's Best volumes, and have garnered awards (Carl Brandon Parallax, Tiptree Honor) and made it to shortlists (BSFA, Philip K. Dick awards). She was born and raised in India, where she maintains deep connections to family, culture, activism, and academia. A former particle physicist, her current academic work is in the transdisciplinary scholarship of climate change, which is what brought her to the Alaskan Arctic in 2014 as part of a project of the American Association of Colleges and Universities. She is indebted to anthropologist and polar scientist Henry Huntington for enriching and making possible her experience in Alaska, and for critical comments on her story "Requiem." Vandana Singh is also a Fellow of the Imaginary College of Arizona State University's Center for Science and the Imagination.

REQUIEM

Vandana Singh

The thought of the letter lying on her desk in the untidy apartment was like a little time bomb ticking in her mind. Varsha told Chester about it, between the steamed mussels and the fish course.

"So I'm going to Alaska for spring break," she ended.

"But—what about Atlanta?"

He had been holding her hand in that ostentatious way he had whenever they were in a restaurant known to be a White Purist hangout. He let go of it, looking hurt.

The seafood place was a hole-in-the-wall with a clientele that clustered around the TV screen and yelled epithets during football games. The AugReal entertainment was of poor quality—floating sea captains and naked ladies, mostly, but the food was fantastic. Chester liked to live on the edge, take her to places like this, challenge the status quo. She pulled down her Augs to look at him in the world: the blue eyes, the little cut on his cheek, the slight pout of his lips, a tendril of graying brown hair sticking damply to his forehead from the steam still rising off the dish of mussels, and thought:

he's really quite a kid, even though he's eleven years older than me. That was the attractive thing about him, this childlike quality in a brilliant young professor, although at this moment it was annoying.

"Atlanta can wait," she said firmly. "This is my favorite aunt we're talking about."

"You were going to go in the summer."

"Didn't you hear what I said? The place is closing ahead of schedule. I have to get her things."

It hit her again that her aunt Rima was dead, had been dead for more than a year, that there was no relief from the shock of it, no matter how many times she mourned. And Chester was being a jerk right now. *And* she had homework to finish, grad school being what it was. She got up, grabbed her bag, and turned and walked away from him, from his shocked face, his half-suppressed "Varsha!", the catcalls and laughter from the men at the bar. At the door she looked back very briefly—he was rising to his feet, arms reaching out, his face filled with rage and bewilderment. The night outside was cold—she fell into her familiar jogging rhythm, ignoring the glances of strangers, feet pounding on the pavement, bag strap tight across her chest— all the way to the T-station at the corner.

The tragically delayed letter was lying on her desk. *I'm coming, I'm coming,* she said silently to Rima. *Just like you wanted me to a year ago, I'm coming to Alaska for spring break.*

I first heard the songs of the bowhead whale on the internet. Varsha and I and a bunch of neighborhood kids and one of the pariah dogs—I think it was Tinku—were gathered in the front veranda of the Patna house, playing a video game. For some reason that I can't remember now, we looked up whale songs, and there it was, the long, strange call, filling the space. The dog Tinku started howling in tandem and wagging his tail, as though he could understand what the whale was saying. All of us burst out laughing. But there was something about that song that tugged at me. It occurs to me now that my journey to the Arctic started there, on that afternoon, with the honeysuckle bush in full bloom and the smell of the flowers almost making me dizzy. The shisham trees in the front garden whispered in the breeze—a kind of bass note to the whale's song—and all those years later it is the whales I hear, and the shisham trees are a warm and distant memory.

We are out in the boat, Jimmy and I, and we are following a pod of bowhead. There is an AUV—an underwater robot—fitted with a hydrophone that is moving with the whales. We can see its output right here on Jimmy's laptop—the spectral analysis of the conversation below, and the sounds themselves, in their immense complexity. We know each individual in the pod—they were tagged decades ago, but even without the tags, the coloring on their flukes or the injury scars on their flanks tell us who they are. We're seeing more propeller scars since the Arctic was opened to shipping. The killer whales have been moving up, too, hungry terrors that they are, and the bowheads that survive bear some horrifying scars. No wonder the bowheads are pushing farther North, toward the pole, where the waters are still cold, tracking the changing currents in search of krill.

I have learned that bowheads may be the oldest-living animals in the world. They live for over two hundred years! Apart from the new threats, their lives are relatively peaceful: the slow migrations around the North Pole, in the sub-freezing waters, with their kin; when hungry, they just open their enormous, garage-sized mouths and sieve in millions of tiny krill. Living that long, they must think long, deep thoughts. What do they think about? What do they say to each other?

When we are back at North Point, Jimmy will put on the headphones and scroll through the video feed and spectral analysis. Apart from language-recognition software, he says immersive attention is a way to use the best pattern-recognition device we know—the brain. It's what his people have always done, paid attention to their environment in a way that makes the most observant scientists among us seem oblivious, blind, bumbling. No wonder I am having such a hard time with the language—Iñupiaq has to be the most precise language in the world.

I wish I could help you all understand what it is about this place that gets me. It is so cold I don't have the words to describe it. Even with global climate change—even with the warming of the Arctic, the winters here are colder than we tropical flowers can ever imagine. When the wind blows, which it does all the time in gales and gasps, I feel like there is no breath in my lungs. I have to put warm gel packs in my gloves and boots so that I don't get frostbite. For six months of the year there is darkness or near darkness, and—what I miss the most—there are no trees! But still, this place draws me and draws me and draws me, and it isn't just Jimmy or the work. The tundra in early spring is astounding. The way the low sun hits the snow, the blinding beauty of it takes the breath away. Once, out in the field, we saw two Arctic foxes playing, chasing each other round and round in circles, without a sound. But the tundra is not silent. Did you know, ice can speak? It squeaks and grunts, makes little slithering, sliding noises, and great explosive, cracking sounds too. Once, early in my stay here, we were out on the sea ice, Jimmy and I, along with a few others from North Point. It was dark and cold, but very still. The stars were out in their billions, and we could see the faint, translucent curtains of the Northern lights high in the sky. We were getting ready to set up our instruments, talking quietly, when Jimmy said: "Guys, we've got to get off. Now."

I looked around but there was no obvious threat. I was going to ask Jimmy what the problem was, but then I saw everyone else acquiesce without argument. They packed up in a big hurry too. Hurry, hurry, Jimmy kept saying. I was thinking maybe there was an emergency with his family that he'd somehow remembered, but the moment we got off the ice there was an ear-splitting crack, and the segment we had been on suddenly broke off. You can't imagine what that was like—a whole great peninsula of floating ice suddenly detached from the rest of the shore ice and floated away, ghost-like in the semi-dark, into the black Arctic Ocean. I was shivering and shaking with shock, but the others were slapping Jimmy on the back and shaking his hand, as we trudged back to the trucks.

I asked him later how he knew. It's paying attention. Something he learned from his father and grandfather when he went hunting with them as a little boy, a kind of sixth sense that is developed through experience, a sensitivity to the slightest change in wind direction, the tiniest syllable spoken by the ice. Imperceptible to others, this ability to communicate with the physical environment is what originally earned the respect of scientists for Native Elders.

In the plane, on the final leg of the journey, Varsha's bravado vanished. It was a really small plane, and there was a crack across the plastic of the seat in front of her, which didn't inspire confidence. She could pull on her Augs and edit that all away, but she wasn't such a V-head. Working in the field, you got to know where to draw the line.

It didn't help that there was sick misery rising in her. There was no avoiding the fact of Rima's death. Rima was supposed to have come down from Alaska to settle her in last August when Varsha had first arrived from Delhi—but she was already seven months dead and gone, taken by the ice during a storm, along with her partner and lover, an Eskimo scientist called James Young. It had been hard enough for Varsha to alight in Boston alone, to find her way to the International Graduate Students office at the University, to walk the bewildering streets of Cambridge in search of her apartment. But this was harder. The man who had forwarded Rima's last letter had written to say that the research facility where her aunt had worked was closing down ahead of schedule, and there were some things of Rima's that the family might like to have. The man's name was Vincent Jones, and he would be glad to help in any way he could.

The plane banked. They were about to land in Utqiagvik. Her aunt had always, in her restless travels, been drawn to remote places, but this was the end of the world, or so it had seemed from the pictures on the internet—a town of mostly Eskimo people at the edge of the Arctic Ocean. She pressed her face against the window. There was a whiteness everywhere—white sky, white land, no horizon but the undifferentiated whiteness. For a moment she thought they must be flying through clouds, but the plane's wing was clearly visible. She fought a feeling of wild panic, and reasoned with herself—the plane wasn't going to crash. There were people talking all around her, tourists and Natives, excitedly, because this was the first real winter in a decade.

"Which hotel? That must be new. They say the Castle of Light has the best views . . ."

"Worst winter they've had in a decade . . ."

"This is a *real* winter. This is what winters used to be like. Back then, before the Great Melt. It will be good, maybe, for the whaling."

"The sea ice came back this winter to nearly 70%—no more multi-year ice—it will be thin and dangerous to walk on . . ."

". . . when you were growing up? Every year like this? Man, that must have been crazy . . ."

In the whiteness below, there appeared a pinprick, then another and another. A line of houses or sheds, all in a row. The plane swooped lower and lower and she held on to the edge of her seat, thinking this is what Rima had seen on her first visit to this place—when was it? Five years ago? Maybe she'd been in this very plane, in the same seat. The misery rose in her like a solid wall.

On the ground there was ice everywhere. The runway was ice, and ice rimmed the edges of the small airport. It was a large metal shed with a corrugated roof and an extension clearly under construction—behind it were roads of ice, and buildings in the same utilitarian style. The airport was a single large hall with areas sectioned off for tickets, departures, arrivals and luggage. Native Iñupiaq Eskimos, white tourists, a small knot of men in coast guard uniforms. How strange to be in a place where the whites were so clearly the other, and yet this was still America! *Oh America, I thought I knew you.* She heard English around her, and a language she took to be Iñupiaq, the Native tongue of peoples who had been here for thousands of years before the Europeans came. What would Rima have thought and felt, coming here for the first time? Waiting for her suitcase, she texted the family group. *I'm here in Utqiagvik, all fine. I must only be the second Indian to come to this place. It's really different.* There was her little orange suitcase, between wooden boxes and sacks. She hauled it off the belt and looked around with a feeling of panic. Where was her host? Her Augs beeped and she hastily pulled them on. The scene before her was augmented with scrolling information, and a couple of VReal polar bears wearing toothy welcoming smiles were speaking a welcome. "Welcome to Utqiagvik, Northernmost city in the US," they said. "Take your taxi or van directly from the airport area. Polar bears have been sighted in town." Amidst the strangeness and wonder of this was the little message icon flashing, showing her an outline of where Vincent Jones was waiting for her. Near the exit door. She arranged her backpack on her shoulders and wheeled her suitcase ahead of her to the exit.

He was a large man with a broad, quiet face. His thin hair was streaked with white. He looked like the Tibetan refugees she had known in New Delhi. Smiling, he held out his hand.

"Good, good. You're here. Rima talked so much about you. You look like her."

"Thanks for receiving me," she said. It was so strange to be here, to be here without her aunt Rima, who would have stood here shivering like this in this exact spot. There was a wind blowing, sharp in her face like icicles. She pulled up her hood. Vincent seemed unperturbed by the wind. They climbed into a large, black Land Rover which lumbered slowly into the streets of ice.

"It's a little ways to North Point," Vincent said. "We'll go through Utqiagvik and by the ocean, so you can see the sea ice over the Arctic. It's been some years since we've had a winter like this one. Used to be the norm, once upon a time."

All she knew about Vincent was that he was somebody at North Point Polar Research Station, and he had been Rima's friend, and he had sent the letter. It had been found on the desk in her office. He had been going through her desk because North Point was closing down. Rima must have meant to send it right before the trip out to sea from which she had never returned.

"What was it like last winter, when my aunt died?" she said. *Might as well get it over with.* "We got the reports, but I'd like to understand—"

"It wasn't this cold or icy," he said, "but we did get one great storm. The Arctic has been in a warming trend for decades, but it's not steady, it goes up and down. Last winter the sea ice was so thin you couldn't walk on it. Things are changing so fast weatherwise, it's hard to predict whether a storm is going to fizzle out or turn into a howling blizzard. Rima and Jimmy were out in one of the research boats less than ten miles from shore when the blizzard hit."

Her hands clenched on her lap. It was cold despite the heater—the tips of her fingers felt like ice.

"We didn't used to have much of a coast guard presence when I was growing up," Vincent was saying. "But even with a coast guard station right here, they couldn't do anything with that storm. Had to wait two days before they could risk sending out the helicopters and the search vessels. That was the only bad storm we had that winter. This winter the cold and snow and ice are much more steady—this was normal once."

He cleared his throat.

"Jimmy was my cousin."

"Oh—God, I'm so sorry," she said. She glanced at him. He was looking straight ahead, his face set.

She looked out of the window. There were children out on bicycles—bicycles!—with thick treads in the front of a small grocery store. Their parka hoods were lined with fur. An Eskimo couple went by on a four-wheeled open vehicle, their faces ringed with fur-lined hoods. A man was digging out a car from several feet of snow in front of a house. The buildings had the same utilitarian steel-shed look of the airport, except for an extraordinary structure some six floors high that looked like a wedding cake.

"Castle of Light Hotel," declared the ornate sign.

"Tourist trap," Vincent said, a short, amused laugh. "Good for the economy, or so I hope. Used to be we'd make money off oil leases, before the oilfields gave up the last of the oil."

They turned east, leaving behind the houses. Now they were driving into the tundra—ahead and to their right was an expanse of snowy whiteness, flat and featureless. After a while they passed a large sign on their left with a cut-out image of a larger-than-life snowy owl. "Pagliavsi," declared the sign, standing alone in the snowy emptiness. "Ukpeagvik, site of an ancient Eskimo Village," Vincent said. Behind the sign the ground rose gently and then fell away into an enormous plain, its smoothness broken only by untidy chunks of ice, like broken piecrust.

"You should know," Vincent said after a while. "Your aunt. She loved what she did. Like Jimmy—they were a pair. We'll stop in a bit so you can see the sea ice."

"I'm sorry I didn't get to know him," Varsha said. "She talked about him to us." She thought of Rima's full-on zest for life. It was possible to be a fifteen-year-old and feel older and duller than her then-thirty-year-old aunt. Those days, Rima's enthusiasms and adventures had led her from a short stint as an adventure and travel writer to a degree in mechanical engineering and the design and customization of wind generators in the high Himalayas. In the lush back garden of the old house in Patna, under the mango tree as old as her great-grandfather, Varsha had sat on the swing with Rima and heard all about the great expanse of the Tibetan desert, the lakes of meltwater from the vanished glaciers, oases in the arid heights. The wind that blew hard and cold, the measuring instruments that recorded wind speed and direction over an entire year, so that Rima and her team could design the best wind-energy-capture system for that particular locale. She saw the pictures and felt the possibilities of the world open up, a familiar side-effect of being with Rima.

And now there was a lump in her throat, but Vincent was already pulling over by the side of the road and motioning her to get down. Here she was, Varsha of the tropics, on the Alaskan North Shore. There was the endless white expanse before her, with only the shiny ice road winding away before them. The sun had emerged from the clouds, and lay low on the horizon—the light on the snow hurt her eyes. She pulled up her Augs in world mode. *You are 1280 miles from the North Pole,* scrolled the message to the right of her field of view. Vincent led her to the top of the rise on the left. Her boots crunched on the snow. At the top they paused. Before them was the great, white plain broken by small piles of cracked ice. It extended all the way to the horizon, as far as she could tell.

"That's the Arctic Ocean," Vincent said. "Sea ice. Frozen sea water. You can tell there's water under there from the way the currents make the ice break up."

"Can you walk on it?"

"In places. Used to be parts of the sea ice attached to the shore stayed all year round, built up a little every season. As much as three, four meters thick sometimes. We used to camp on the ice when we cut whaling trails in the Spring. Your aunt ever tell you about that?"

"A little," Varsha said. "She said the whaling hadn't been very good for a while."

"You're cold—let's get back in the car. Yes, the bowheads changed their migration patterns after the Big Melt. We, the Iñupiaq—my people—had always lived with the whales, and when they started to change, our old knowledge wasn't as much help. The killer whales started coming up into the warming waters, hunting the bowheads. And the TRexes became active at the time."

In the car the heater was running on high. She put her hands in front of the vents.

"We'll get you proper gear for this place," he said. "Your aunt's stuff. She loved this place but never liked the cold."

She nodded.

"Tell me about the TRexes," she said. There was an Augree Experience involving intelligent monster machines that she'd helped debug when it was still in production. She'd been surprised to learn that TRexes were for real, in the world.

"There are about twenty of them working these waters," he said. "Still got oil and methane down on the sea floor. TRexes found two large deposits last year. But they're having trouble with some of them, I hear. Shutdowns and failures. Keep your eyes peeled, we may see one on the way. There's one operating a few miles from us at North Point."

They didn't see any TRexes but after about an hour the North Point Research facility loomed suddenly out of the landscape—a building capped by four tall steel lattice towers, and three rows of small windows on the visible sides of a cubical structure in between. The windows shone in the sun's low light. The place was larger than she expected. It jutted out into the plain of sea ice on concrete pillars.

"We're down to a handful of people," Vincent said, leading her in past a heavy steel door. "Most of the researchers have left. The rest are packing up, finishing up. You'll meet them at meals. I'm the Native liaison here."

Inside, there were white walls and long corridors, gray-painted metal doors, some with windows.

"Who's bought the station?"

"GaiaCorp's Arctic Energy unit," he said. "They run the TRexes."

The dorms were at the back of the facility. Their footsteps echoed emptily in the silence. Lights came on as they walked. Vincent led her to a small room with a white bed and a desk and chair. "Bathroom's down the hall," he said. "Sorry, we live kind of plain here. Why don't you get settled and I'll ping you when it's time for dinner. The door next to yours—that's the suite Rima and Jimmy had. It has an attached bathroom if you want. Here's their keycard, and here's yours. Thought it would be easier to have you right next door."

After she had washed up and unpacked, she saw that it was only four-thirty. She took a deep breath. *Might as well start now.* She went into the suite her aunt had shared with Jimmy Young. It consisted of a tiny outer room and a bedroom and bathroom. When she turned on the light she was startled at how bare it looked. It had clearly been used very little, mostly for sleeping, she imagined. There was a stereo in the small living room, a carving of a polar bear on the coffee table that looked like it had been made from bone, and a picture of two people on the prow of a boat. She picked up the photograph—it was Rima, her face rimmed by a fur hood, and almost-uncle Jimmy, snow goggles pushed back over his head, his dark hair windswept. They were both grinning as though they were having the time of their lives. She set it down again, congratulating herself for keeping her composure so far. She had a job to do, and she simply had to keep herself together until it was done. Pretend she was on an errand for a strict taskmaster like—her aunt. Yes. Sure. In the bedroom she willed herself to open the closet. Vincent had taken care of Jimmy's things—only her aunt's clothes were here. She could donate some to the local town swap, Vincent had said. She breathed the still air inside the closet. Was there something of Rima left here, still, after all these months? A faint whiff of something indefinable—a lotion—yes, the sandalwood lotion from home that everyone in the family used. There was a long, beaded kurta in green, and a pink chikanwork outfit among the flannel shirts and turtlenecks—she buried her face in the kurta and swallowed a lump in her throat—she would keep those. She began to pull things onto the bed, making two piles.

Once she had begun it was easy enough to continue with the suitcases in the closet—mostly empty—and the shoes at the bottom. Then the side table. This was going fast. If she went through the office stuff as quickly she would be done in a day. Whatever had possessed her to plan a four-day stay?

But when Vincent knocked on the door to call her to dinner, there was still the pile on the bed to be arranged, and the books in the bookshelf—she had let herself become distracted by them—well-thumbed volumes about Iñupiaq culture and history, one on biomimicry, a number of technical-looking books on alternative energy and acoustical engineering. There was a book she had gifted to her aunt when Rima had left for the US: *The Best Travel Writing of the 21st Century*—it had "Love, Varsha" on the inside cover. There were books on economics and history, cetacean biology, and interspecies communication.

She was relieved to go down to the dining hall, where a buffet meal was served—rolls and fried chicken and some kind of vegetable greens she couldn't identify. She sat with Vincent and four other people to whom she was introduced, all white except for Vincent and an African-American called

Kenny, who was a sea-ice expert. It was strange to be around people who weren't wearing Augs or any other kind of goggles, who were so much in the world. Usually she liked talking to people but suddenly she was almost too exhausted to eat. Fortunately the others seemed preoccupied with the impending shutting down of the institute. Incomprehensible discussions about local politics and who was going where and what Arctic Energy would do with the facility allowed her to concentrate on her food and sit with her thoughts, until the woman with the salt-and-pepper hair sitting next to her said in a low voice:

"Sorry about your aunt. It must be awful—but you don't want to talk about that. How was your trip?"

She would have liked to talk about Rima. It might have helped her feel grounded, she thought tiredly, but she had noticed how most Americans tended to assume that dead people were off-topic. She tried to smile.

"Long. And cold, at least the drive here. I'm still warming up."

The woman laughed. Her name was—yes, Julie. She had very pale skin, and a fine dusting of freckles.

"I've been here for two years and I'm not really used to being here either. For one thing, the Arctic is going through some really rapid changes. Kind of like being married to whatsyourname here." She elbowed the man next to her, who smiled. "But mostly what gets me is the absence of light for six months of the year. If you'd come in December it would have been darker and colder."

"Boston will feel tropical after this."

"Hey," Vincent said. "This is the best place in the world. Even with climate change. No need to enhance reality when you have—this!" He swept his arm around the room. The Arctic night was dark blue outside the small, square windows.

"It would be hard to edit out the cold, or your ass freezing doing fieldwork on the ice," said one of the young men, whose name she had forgotten already. He nodded pleasantly at her. "Vince said you're in VReality, is that right?"

"Not at the moment," she said. The greens tasted bitter and sad, as though they had never known the sun. Even her Augs couldn't fix that. She explained about her Master's program.

"Bet you can't wait to get out of here," said the young man. "The US of A isn't what it used to be. Unbelievable how quickly things have changed in just a few years."

"It wasn't that great before, Matt," said the black man. Varsha remembered his name was Kenny or something. Yes, Kendrick. He looked in disgust at the pile of chicken bones on his plate, and stabbed at the soggy greens with his fork. "Yes," he said. "Try being black in America in any era. It's worse now, of course. And there's North Point. There was a time we couldn't have imagined oil coming back, after the ban. Now we have GaiaCorp promising to protect us through geoengineering. Project Terra! Why study climate change when we can fix it from space? We can burn fossil fuels again! Get the last of the oil and gas out of the Arctic. Five, six years ago, if you'd told me that there would be TRexes in the ocean and North Point bought out by GaiaCorp, I would have said you were crazy. I'll never say 'It can't happen' again!"

"Started with the Space Act in 2015," said Matt. "You start mining the moon and then suddenly you have the corporate wars, then Earth Corp, and the agreements with nations, and—"

"Spare me the history lesson," said the fourth person, the one next to Julie. He put down his fork and dragged his fingers though long, straggly brown hair. "I agree with you in broad terms but you are connecting the wrong dots, Matt—"

Vincent pushed back his chair.

"Got to go finish up some things. Varsha, you got everything you need? Breakfast is from six to nine a.m. After breakfast, if you want, Julie can show you around. Julie—?"

"Sure," Julie said. Varsha felt guilty. These people were winding down what seemed to be their life's work. She didn't need showing around. She had all the sorting and packing to do—

But she wanted to know Rima the polar scientist. She wanted to know her almost-uncle Jimmy. She nodded.

"Thanks, I'd love that. If it isn't too much trouble."

There *was* a TRex at work far on the horizon. She was looking out of the window of the office her aunt Rima had shared with Jimmy Young. Jimmy's space had been cleared and someone called Terra Longfield now occupied it, her absence bounded by pictures of a smiling blond child and drawings in crayon. But Rima's desk was stacked with boxes of her things—papers, books, knickknacks that had used to be on her desk, including a picture of Varsha, and another picture of the family at the Patna house, the colors faded but the faces still poignant in their familiarity. Varsha was the kid tugging at Rima's arm in the picture, pointing off-camera to something in the garden, and Rima was bent slightly forward, laughing, about to follow her niece's glance. They were the only two not looking at the camera.

It was cold in the empty office. She looked up to the window and saw the skyscape, the morning sun still low in the sky, the impossible immensity of the expanse of snow, the pale gray smudge of the horizon—and against it, a TRex somewhere far ahead where the sea ice gave way to open sea. Its skeletal frame, with the long head turning slowly this way and that, looked so alive and purposeful that she shuddered involuntarily. They were smart machines, she knew, but this one, far away as it was, seemed positively *sentient*. Its long labrum sipped hydrocarbons off the ocean floor, and the proboscis sniffed for methane bubbling up off the ocean floor. When exploring, she had heard, it would become buoyant in the water, its array of airguns firing *boom-boom* into the sea, looking for oil and gas under the seafloor. It was an amazing piece of engineering. Despite the remoteness of this one it felt more real than the ones she had seen in VR games.

A knock at the door made her jump. Without waiting for her response a man came in. He was wearing a suit, which seemed incongruous after the casual clothing of the others. He was tall, with a pleasant, open face, and wavy dark brown hair. He wore a pair of Augs—state-of-the-art—in world mode—she could see his eyes through them, green. He smiled and held out his hand.

"Rick Walters. So pleased to meet you, though in such sad circumstances. I knew your aunt well."

There was something compelling about him, she noticed, as she returned the pressure of his hand. An air of complete assurance and good nature.

"I just wanted to let you know—if you need help, or want to talk, I'll be in and out," he said.

"Thanks. Are you a scientist here?"

He laughed. "Me? Alas, I haven't the temperament. I'm the Transition Liaison. Making sure the handover goes smoothly. Much as I'd prefer an Augs Enhancement, I have to have results in the world. Sorry to say."

She laughed. "I'm glad you're not a V-head. It gives us a bad name."

"I just got my nephew his first real Augs," Rick said, lightly. "He'll be totally thrilled to know I met someone who works with them." He passed his hand over the edge of her aunt's desk, picked up the family photo, and set it down. "Sorry, I shouldn't be interrupting."

Later, after he'd left, she thought how *normal* he seemed. He was from her world, the world of busy metropolises and high tech. But there was an older world than that, and she missed it now. Standing in the cold room, she pulled on her Augs and brought up her favorite program for when she was homesick. The walls of the room turned a sunlight yellow and the view from the window was of her grandparents' courtyard. There was the old guava tree that she had grown up with. There were potted plants on the bench beside the window and she could hear the faint strains of the tanpura from her music lesson in the next room. The program was creative—it took the boxes of her aunt's stuff on the desk and rendered them into piles of multi-colored knitting wool. Her grandmother was a knitter. Someone came into the room—it was her uncle. She waved to him, smiling. But when he spoke, his voice was distorted. "We apologize for the Cognitive Dissonance . . ." The words scrolled across her field of view. "Initiating patch—"

But she had already pulled the Augs down. It wasn't her uncle speaking Hindi, it was Vincent speaking English. His thin gray hair was disheveled, as though he had just pulled off his hat, coming in from the cold.

"Sorry," she said, but he was asking her something.

"Was Rick Walters just here?"

"Yes, he said he was a friend of my aunt's. He offered to help."

"He's no friend of Rima's." Vince frowned. "Rima hated his guts. He was on the original negotiating team for North Point. She fought hard against the buyout. He's here to make sure everything's accounted for. I came to warn you not to tell him anything. He stops by without warning, acts real friendly."

He nodded at her and left.

In the cold and the silence, Varsha shivered. *I don't know what's what,* she told herself. There was no signal on her phone. The last text she had got from the family was a "Be careful out there" from her grandfather, and similar notes from her parents, her cousin Sanjay and her Augs Friends group. Her mother and father were fighting again, and Biru uncle was in Patna because Nanu was having a medical checkup. Chester had sent about twenty pings already, which she had ignored. She didn't feel like resuming the Augs program or sifting through her aunt's things. She sat down at the desk and put her head in her hands, and remembered.

For the longest time she had shared a room with Rima, her mother's youngest sister, every visit to Patna. They decorated the room with strange structures; there were wires suspended across the room with wheeled carts that ran up and down, a plastic monkey in a bucket that jumped out and woke them up at 7 am every morning. Anyone approaching the room, no matter how quietly, would be anticipated—thanks to an IR sensor that beeped a warning in Swedish.

She and Rima used to invent games for the little ones. The one she was thinking of now was a winter game—they would drag a couple of razais down to the carpet to make a huge multicolored mountain, and they would hide under sections of the thick folds, while the little cousins would screech excitedly and try to find them, their fat, slippery bodies like so many wriggling fish on the satin covers. The razais were thick enough that the mountain stood without help, and they would roll the ping-pong-ball collection down from the summit, one by one, trying to guess at first where, among the folds and channels, valleys and crinkles, the balls would end up. It was sometimes tricky because you'd think the pink ball would slide just so, into the long, straight channel leading all the way to the bottom of the mountain, but a little crinkle here, or a little subtle encouragement there (from an aunt half-concealed within the folds) would send the ball careening to quite another destination. This is where Varsha learned about chance, and how a small and sudden change could lead you to quite another path.

Rima and Varsha co-wrote a novel when Varsha was eleven. In the novel, various people and parts of the house, and trees, and stray dogs were characters. It was comic and dark and sad and hilarious, and in each chapter there was a hidden clue to the problem or mystery. The secret was that each clue was concealed by something similar to itself—a Box of Wonders was hidden in the Cube of Amazing Things, a puppy with magical powers was hidden in its mother, since it had yet to be born, and a wish-granting mango hung with other mangoes on a branch of the mango tree. The story had got out of control, with plots and subplots of labyrinthine complexity, impossible to finish. For years when Rima and Varsha would meet, they would say to each other—how did Amroodji become allergic to guavas? Or—did Mad Puppy find the Lost World inside Mobius, or outside? And they would burst out laughing. One of the other cousins had recently discovered the manuscript (copiously and laboriously illustrated) stuck between two of the eight hundred books in the drawing room, and the grandparents had been having a hilarious time re-reading it with the younger grandchildren, until after the news came. Now, life was forever divided into Before and After. The manuscript was now in Nanaji's safe, as though fate might snatch away even this.

My friend Skip told me this story when I was in California. There is a former killing ground off the southern coast of California in the Pacific Ocean. Here the American whalers hunted and killed thousands of gray whales in the 1850s. In the 1970s, Skip said, well after the age of whaling was over, a Mexican fisherman had an encounter with a gray whale. The whale came alongside his boat and gazed at him. Looking into the whale's eye, the fisherman had a life-changing experience.

Since then, the whales seem to wait for the humans. Whenever people in boats come to that region during the calving season, mother whales and their young will approach them. People will touch them and they seem to welcome these encounters.

So of course we had to go there. We took a small plane down to a town in Baja California. There's quite a tourist business out there, bringing humans to the whales. Skip and my friend Molly, who studies kelp forests, went out in a small boat with a bunch of tourists. I got to practice my Spanish and we were all laughing and having a great time, with the boat rocking wildly on a choppy sea—and then the guide yelled: whales!

I could see nothing—the spray from the waves was in my eyes, and I was trying to keep my balance. Then as we got closer the waters parted and a leviathan surfaced, slowly, as though it had all the time in the world. I leaned over the rail. The ancient eye looked at me—a sentient, knowing, curiously gentle gaze. In that one glance, that tenuous, temporal bridge between being and being, I knew my life would change. At that moment I existed in a way I hadn't before—in the eye of a Californian gray whale. She could have destroyed us with one flick of her massive tail, but she just hung in the water, looking at us. The kids on the boat were already leaning over and touching her, and I did too. Her skin was riddled with scars and clusters of barnacles. She must have been quite old. Later another whale surfaced close to us and blew a great, long breath. The plume of moisture bloomed like a fountain several meters into the air, soaking us. The sun came out at exactly that moment, and among the suspended water drops I saw, for a fraction of a second, a rainbow.

"Congratulations!" Skip said, hitting me across my shoulder blades as I gasped and choked. "Your first rainblow!"

This astonishing experience made me wonder: knowing their bloody and tragic experience with our species, what moved these whales to seek us out, to be so forgiving? Was it one individual's bright idea to try to befriend the enemy?

Jimmy thinks none of this is surprising. Living such long lives, some of the whales may have acquired what we call wisdom. It's rare enough in our species! And why should humans be the only ones with a sense of agency, a desire to make things better for themselves? We already know that whales have culture—different pods of the same species have different habits and tastes in food.

Here's another story—a dolphin was observed apparently assisting a young sperm whale that had lost its way in a saltwater marsh, somewhere off an island in the Indian Ocean. Scientists who received the video (from a fisherman) said that it was inconclusive. But Jimmy has seen it. He's not one to jump to conclusions, but it supports his hypothesis that whales communicate with other species. After all, they live in an environment rich with biodiversity. Wouldn't they want or need to communicate with other species sometimes?

I tell him about how I grew up, in the old house in Patna with the sunlight-yellow walls. How, first thing in the morning, I'd be woken up by mynahs yelling outside the window, and the parakeets in the neem trees. The pariah dogs would be waiting at the back door, ancestors of the current Bossy Pack. We had a parakeet with a broken wing when I was ten, and he would sit on the windowsill and scold the dogs, and drop roasted chana or bits of toast for them. Ma, you would have already been up before dawn, watering the tulsi in the courtyard, and the radio would be playing in the dining room. Apart from the neighbors' conversations wafting through the open windows, and the bells of the rickshaw-wallahs, there were so many living creatures around us, talking to each other. This is why I could believe the old stories as a child, in which animals are speakers and players.

Jimmy had such a different upbringing, here in the Far North, and yet we understand each other so well. He, too, grew up with stories in which animals talk to humans and each other, across the species gap. Some sympathies bridge the distance between cultures. Perhaps it is the same between species, and we modern humans simply don't notice.

"We're in the lowest level of the station. Sorry it looks like a dungeon here, but the best part is just ahead."

"Did my aunt work here?"

"Her lab's upstairs," Julie said. "You've seen it—one of the big rooms, empty now. But she loved it down here. She and Jimmy spent as much time here as possible, planning and arguing and observing. Just past this door—"

A large steel door opened at the press of a metal knob set in the wall. There was a small space beyond, and another steel door. The first door closed behind them with a slow hiss, and the second one opened.

There was nothing beyond it but an ordinary passageway. Puzzled, Varsha followed Julie. Lights turned on as they walked into the dark corridor. There were no doors on either side, just the tunnel going forward into the dark, into the—

"The sea—this is going seaward?"

Julie turned, grinned.

"Yes—hold your horses, we're almost there."

And suddenly they were in a broad open space filled with diffuse light that came in through transparent walls. The roof was a glass dome. It was literally a bubble at the bottom of the sea.

Varsha caught her breath. There were tiny things moving in the water outside—small, streamlined silhouettes against what seemed to be a dank white ceiling, a few feet above the roof of the dome. It was suffused with a faint blue glow in places.

"We're under the sea ice," Julie said. She flicked a switch and suddenly the outside was lit. The floating ice above them discolored with gray-green smudges on the underside. In some places the ice had thickened, forming extrusions that hung in the water like chandeliers. In the light the ice crystals glittered like so many diamonds. Beyond the circle of light, the water was murky, mysterious with small, moving shadows.

"Wow," Varsha whispered. Julie looked satisfied.

"Never fails to impress visitors," she said triumphantly. "If you're lucky you'll see more than a few fish or krill. We've seen a swimming polar bear. And during the spring migration there's bowheads that always stop here. Since about ten years ago they've been venturing closer to the Beaufort coast. Same with belugas."

Varsha looked around the observation chamber. There were desks and instrumentation around the circular perimeter. In the middle was a table with a microwave, coffee maker, and the attendant supplies.

"Your aunt spent a bunch of time here," Julie said. "She and Jimmy used to joke that it wasn't fair for humans to observe the whales and other creatures. We should give them a chance to understand us. You should have seen the two of them dance around the room for the whales! The whales must think humans are deranged."

She laughed.

"Bowheads are wary creatures. They live over two hundred years. Some of them still remember the days of the Yankee whalers, when they were nearly wiped out. So you can't blame them if they keep their distance. But they're intelligent creatures. They're curious. So some of them—it's always the same ones—they come and hang out and look at us, and talk about us."

"You're kidding, right?"

"Only a little. Whales have a sophisticated communication system. Don't you know what your aunt was doing? Jimmy had a mission—to decipher the communication system of the bowhead whale. Humans can now speak a little gibbonese—white-handed gibbons, you know? South Asia? No? Well, more people should know about that! We're finally beginning to decode languages of other species. Whales and dolphins are hard—their languages are likely to be more complex than ours. Jimmy was a marine biologist, your aunt was an engineer—they were perfect for the project."

"I thought she was working on alternative-energy systems!"

"That was ongoing. She worked with a group of students at the college in Utqiagvik—there's a really good tribal college in Utqiagvik—they developed some prototypes of wind generation that can work with gusty winds in a place like this. Town's looking into it. She also—here, let me show you."

The outside lights turned off, except for the ones close to the sea bed. Julie gestured to Varsha to get closer to the walls. On the sea bed was an array of two-foot-high devices that looked like Japanese fans mounted on flexible stems. They were swaying gently with the current.

"Wave-generator prototypes developed by Rima," Julie said. "She worked on boat design too—her unofficial project—propeller-free boats that wouldn't injure marine animals. You should've seen her lab. There was this bathyscaph shaped like a squid that used water propulsion. She used to get all kinds of junk from online auctions, naval junkyards, and such. She got interested in whale communication after she went on her first boat ride with Jimmy. They would sit in this room and draw designs of all kinds of crazy stuff. Boats with flippers and wings."

"Did she actually build any of this?"

"There were so many prototypes being tested and taken apart and tested again that I lost count. After—afterwards I heard they sent most of her stuff to the tribal college. They wouldn't have, if she'd completed the project. If they'd lived—she and Jimmy—there's no telling how much they would have accomplished . . ."

"What was he like? Jimmy?"

"I never felt I really got to know him. I feel like that sometimes with the Natives here. It makes me realize we European descendants are the newbies, that this was their home first, and still is. The Native Resistance has been felt here too, even though it is so far away from the action. Vincent I can relate to, he lived for so long down south. But Jimmy, he just went down to California to study what the science of the whites could teach him, and hotfooted it back here. He was quiet. Thoughtful. Don't get me wrong, he could crack a joke and all, but he was a bit of an introvert. No-small-talk kind of guy. Passionate."

"Did he—did they get to decipher whale talk?"

"They made some headway. He's published quite a bit on it. Their tapes and the papers they worked on are all with Vince. But you should talk to Vince or Matt—I'm just a microbiologist. Matt's focus is how land mammals are affected by climate change—caribou, moose, polar bears, seals, and the impact of moose coming up from the South. The three of them would talk up a storm about species communication."

Julie turned the lights off. In the dim natural light filtered through the sea ice, the observation room seemed a world unto itself.

"I just heard on the radio that bowhead whales have been spotted west of Utqiagvik," Julie said. "It's early for them to be coming here, but apparently they are coming. You might get lucky."

I feel her here, Varsha thought. *She's here, Rima Mausi, in this place.* She took a deep breath.

"I hope I see a whale," Varsha said, as they started back up the tunnel.

As the light grew stronger and the thin shore ice started melting back with a distressing rapidity, there came news that the whales were already on the move from their wintering areas in the Bering strait. Vince and Tom and Irene were in Utqiagvik, where the mood was festive. I joined them later in the day. The sun was out and half the town was on the beach. The whale radio had declared that one of the whaling crews was headed back with whales in tow.

At last we saw the first boat chugging toward us over the ocean, the flag waving. Vince was standing next to me and let up a great shout, and everyone started yelling "hey-hey-hey!" It was Vince's uncle, Tom Jones, who was captain of that boat. Kids were running around shouting, it was like a festival. Then I saw the dark bulk of the whale in tow behind the boat, and the red float bobbing close to it. As it came toward land, the man in the forklift drove closer to the water's edge, and we moved out of the way. I couldn't see anything for the crowd for a while, and then I saw the whale's great carcass slide past me, pulled up by ropes attached to the forklift. It lay like a black mountain. Vince came through the crowds with his grand-nephew, a boy of five, on his shoulders. "It was a good catch," he said to me, smiling. He said something in Iñupiaq. "That's a thank-you to the whale for the gift of its life," he said. "The whale captain says that over the body when it is lashed to the boat. It was a good death—it died quickly."

The whale was already being cut up. Long, black strips lined with pink blubber were being hauled off on ropes. The men worked

*efficiently with triangular cutters on poles. Blood stained the white
snow. There was shouting and singing.*

*"We will eat well this winter," Marie said. Marie works at the gro-
cery store, and is Irene's aunt. That first whaling season was a bewildering time for an omnivore-turned vegan Indian scientist raised in
the sub-tropics and freshly arrived from California. I remember asking Jimmy when I first came to Utqiagvik: "How can you bear to eat
such amazing creatures?" He just looked at me in his thoughtful, considering way, and replied: "Because we are not apart, we are a part."
It took me some time to figure out what he meant. Since then I've
attended many a whale carving and blanket toss, and helped cut and
prepare whale to feed the community. In the dead of winter, in a place
still mostly only accessible by small aircraft, the sole source of fresh food
is meat. And because the whale is sacred, it is never sold, only shared.
I had a lot of whale that winter, parboiled and dunked into soy sauce,
or cut frozen straight from the ice cellar and into the mouth. I have a
lot more respect for the hunter who brings in the wild kill and says his
prayers over it, than for those who trap animals into constant, unre-
lieved suffering in their thousands in factory farms.*

*Thus I am made of many things—mother's milk, fruit of guava
and mango trees, rice of the Indian Gangetic Plain, vegetables of
splendid variety, meat of many creatures, and now—bowhead whale!*

Next morning Rick showed up. Varsha was in her aunt's room, folding
clothes and shoes into cardboard boxes. He smiled at her from the door.

"Hey, want to come for a helicopter ride?"

He *was* charming, even if he couldn't be trusted. She should say no—but
what harm was there in a helicopter ride? She was sick of this room, sick of
grief. She could handle this man—she had known men like him during three
years working in industry, before the MS program, before America. Before.

She was glad not to run into anyone else as they went up to the roof of the
building.

"Where are we going?"

"Just over the sea. Quick trip out to the nearest TRex and back. You're
here for such a short time, you should see a little of the Arctic."

On the rooftop the cold breeze took her breath away. She stumbled—Rick
steadied her, his face unreadable behind the goggles. She climbed into the
helicopter, a compact yellow-and-black giant bumble-bee of a machine, with
"Arctic Energy" painted on the sides, and the circular insignia of GaiaCorp.

"You know how to fly this thing?" she yelled over the engine's roar.

He grinned.

"Want to inspect my license?"

She shook her head.

"Just get me back safe and sound," she yelled as they rose into the air. "In time for lunch!"

"Much as I'd like to spend more time with the most attractive woman in fifty square miles, I fully intend to get us back for lunch," he said, laughing. "Although I could get you a better meal in Utqiagvik."

"Mr. Walters, you're flirting," she said. Below them the ice sheet was a great, white wing, fraying at the edges where it met the liquid sea. North Point station had vanished behind them.

"Sorry," he said. He sounded unrepentant. "Look, we're over the ocean now. Those little white patches are part of the shore ice that separated, floated off."

The ocean was incomprehensibly vast, stretching away to the curve of the horizon. Above their heads the helicopter blades were a blur through the transparent walls of the cockpit.

"Why are we going to see the TRex?"

"We've had some trouble with a couple of them, we don't know why. System failures, mechanical wear, hydrophones non-functional. I like to reconnoiter at least semi-regularly. Despite the Big Melt the Arctic is still a really inhospitable place—well, I don't need to tell you that—"

"What kind of trouble?"

"Hang on, we're here."

The craft fell like a stone. Varsha clutched the edge of her seat, but the helicopter slowed and hovered over the dark sea. The tops of the waves glittered in the low-angled sunlight. She gasped.

Before them, rising out of the water like a creature from a mechanized Jurassic nightmare, stood the TRex. It was the one she had seen from the window of her aunt's office. Its long snout swiveled toward them and its optical sensors glittered with iridescence like the compound eyes of an insect. Rick's fingers flashed over the copter's dashboard, and the TRex abruptly bent its head. Its neck collapsed inward until was several meters shorter.

"It's pulling its legs in—I've put it in search mode, so you can see how it works," Rick said. "Look!"

Floats inflated on either side of the machine. It began to move, through some invisible propeller mechanism, purposefully across the sea. The copter followed it.

There was a deafening series of booms below them. A milky froth appeared in the water around the TRex.

"That's the airgun array—don't worry, I've turned it off now. Sound waves penetrate the seabed and are reflected back. See the buoys around it? Hydrophones, receiving the sound, giving it a picture of the sea floor, hundreds of meters down."

"Pretty impressive," Varsha said. "But damaging to whales, I hear."

"Yes, but the TRex has a 360-degree sensor that detects whale pods," Rick said. "It's not just the Iñupiaq who care about whales, you know. We spend a lot of R&D money making sure we don't damage the environment."

His fingers moved over the dashboard controls again.

"There, it's back to doing sampling. Good, it passed the test, and you got to see it in action."

On the way back she asked him whether he'd looked at TRexes self-diagnostics.

"You're smart," he said. "Like your aunt. The diagnostics don't tell us anything, because the non-functionality comes without warning."

"It could be a kind of cascade failure," she said. "I've worked with some sophisticated Augs programs—complexity can cause all kinds of sudden failures."

He looked at her.

"Maybe I shouldn't tell you this," he said, "but I've seen some internal reports—problems with some of the Geoengineering projects that nobody understands. Warming spikes instead of cooling in the upper atmosphere. Plankton die-offs where you expect a bloom. Winds changing in unexpected ways. We could use people like you."

"I thought you were just the transition liaison," she said, mocking him. "I didn't realize you were the CEO of GaiaCorp!"

He threw his head back and laughed. The sky above them was a deep azure. Below and ahead lay the ice, swathed with the sun's gold light.

"I like you, Varsha," he said, looking at her. "I think we're going to be friends."

Rick stayed for lunch. It was an uncomfortable lunch, since the scientists didn't seem to want to talk very much. Only Carl—Julie's husband—held up the conversation. Vince was very quiet. Varsha thought uncomfortably that perhaps he felt betrayed by her excursion with Rick. She wanted very badly to reassure him. After Rick left, she gave herself time to collect her wits, and went to talk to Vincent.

He was in his office. Packing boxes sat on the floor and on chairs. Vincent had his back to her, looking at a large map on the wall. But when she came into the office, he turned, although she hadn't made any sound.

"About my copter ride with Rick Walters," she said. "I wanted to let you know. He was all charm, but I didn't tell him anything. He showed off his TRex and brought us back, that's all. I wouldn't let Rima down in a million years."

Slowly he smiled.

"It's been very tough," he said. "The last year and a half it's been one thing after another. It's not for me to tell you what to do. But thanks for being smart about Rick Walters."

"What is it that he wants to know, anyway? What are we hiding from him?"

"Rick's an information gatherer," he said. "He collects all kinds of details indiscriminately, in the hope that they will come in useful someday. That's kind of how he swung the deal for North Point. In short, he's nosey." He pointed at the map. "I unrolled it and put it back on the wall after he left. Just to look at again before I pack it away. It's Rima and Jimmy's work. They called it the Map of Anomalies. Rick would love to get his hands on it."

It was a map of the coastline, rich with markings and symbols in a rainbow of colors. Lines traced the migration pathways of the bowheads—different shades of blue indicating how the paths were shifting every year. Rima and Jimmy would follow the bowheads in a boat, or track them with drones and underwater robots, explained Vince. Little red triangles indicated sites of killer whale attacks—red squares were ship injuries, and red lines were TRex trajectories across the shallow seas.

Event markers were in mysterious purple symbols.

"This one—this was the most recent one, after Rima and Jimmy were lost. I put it in. Just this past October, at the time of the Fall whaling. These are places where Jimmy's drones picked up bowhead whales in formations that have never been seen before, sounding together. Those symbols over there are TRexes that malfunctioned without warning. Rick's not the only one interested in the TRexes."

Another symbol off the shore of Baffin Island in the Canadian Arctic indicated a crossing point, where migration routes of belugas, the small white whales of the North, intersected the new bowhead pathways. There were similar intersections with humpback routes in the North Pacific.

"It's a pattern-recognition exercise," Varsha said, remembering games from childhood. "I wish I could see a little of what they saw."

On her third day at North Point, Varsha made a discovery. She had left the bookshelf for last. She started to make two piles on the bed—books to give to Vincent, if he wanted them, and books she would take back with her. On the bottom shelf she found something she had given to her aunt the summer before last—a fat tome that was not a book: *Adventures in the Real and the Unreal.* With shaking hands she opened it. There was her handwriting on the first page—"with love from Varsha—may you have *musst* adventures!" The first few pages were real—but in the middle of the book was a hollow compartment. Inside was a small book with a red-brown cover—a diary. There were also some thin, parchment-like pieces of paper, carefully folded.

She opened the diary first. Her grandparents had given it to Rima when she had visited them, the summer before her disappearance. *The last time I saw her,* Varsha thought, *and I didn't even know it.* She remembered Nanu handing his daughter the book. "I know you are too busy to keep a diary," he had said, "but at least write something in it from time to time. When you think of us, write something for us. No engineering diagrams, but just what you are thinking and doing. Fill it up until your next trip home. Then bring it so we can all read it."

It was less than half full. Rima's small, neat handwriting, interspersed with little cartoons. The first entry:

My greetings to the guava tree, the Bossy Pack, and the Human Horde of Chandragupta Park. No engineering diagrams, only deep thoughts in these pages. As promised! Right now I am on a plane back to Alaska, but I will write more when there is something worth sharing with you all . . .

She couldn't read any further. She set the journal down and fell to her knees and wept, with her face against the bed, hard, angry sobs. She grabbed the pillow and held it to her. Her chest hurt. *I could die with grief,* she thought, and close on that came the thought of her grandparents. They had survived the terrible news—how? She thought of her Nanu's face when they got the news, how it seemed to have shrunk. She thought of what he'd kept repeating, over and over, the first week or so—they didn't find the *body,* they *haven't* found the body—And then the discovery of the black box, the relaying of the last words, and the solidity, the incomprehensibility of grief. Her grandmother, who had seemed so fragile, suddenly appeared stronger, weeping her sorrow with a fierceness that kept them from going under. She had taken up knitting with a vengeance. The shawl she was knitting for Rima, that was half complete—she took it up again. Last Varsha heard, she was still at it—the shawl was the size of a blanket by now, and growing larger, as though it was possible for her grandmother to knit her way across the abyss that had opened in their lives. Even the pariah-dog pack that lived in the neighborhood, the Bossys, had howled for three nights. Her parents, uncles, aunts, cousins, the neighbors with whom the children had grown up, all shared the burden of grief. And someone or other would keep saying— look, Rima wouldn't want us to fall apart, we've got to go on for her—and again—how *could* it be? She was the most *alive* person I knew—

But there's nobody I can share this with, she thought angrily. She was far away from everyone.

At lunch she asked Vincent—

"Is there a gym? A track or someplace I can run?"

"There's a treadmill on the upper floor. I think it's still there. You can use it. The only gym's going to be in Utqiagvik."

"You okay?" Julie, sitting next to her, gave her a quick, worried look.

"I'm fine—well, as fine as I can be anyway. I just need—I have this habit, see, of running every day. They might bring the Boston Marathon back this year, so I've been training. I get a little crazy if I can't run."

Later Vincent said: "You only have a couple more days here. I'm going home tomorrow evening. Come have dinner with my wife and me then."

She felt much better after the exercise. Back in her aunt's room, she read some more pages of the diary. She carefully unfolded the sheets of paper— they were thin but tough, like cloth. They were blueprints of some kind, but hand-drawn. There was a delicate and precise sketch of a boat—but what a strange boat! It had flippers, and some kind of sail. A series of drawings showed the boat closing up from the top, like a convertible. There were other fine pages of notes, in a different handwriting, presumably Jimmy's, because she couldn't understand the words. Iñupiaq? There were sketches of whales of various types, and waveforms of sound waves. There was a list in her aunt's writing—people and research institutions around the world—a Kartik Sahay at Marine Research Labs Chennai, a Skip Johnson at a facility in California, others in places as far away as Finland, Siberia, South Africa. Her aunt had thought all this was important enough to hide from prying eyes. Varsha remembered Rick Walters' offer of help. *Fuck off,* she told him silently. On the other hand, what did she know about Vincent? He was not a scientist; he was the Coordinator for the Native Science Collaboration—they matched Native Elders with scientists. Whatever for? There was so much she didn't under- stand about this place, these people. She was almost sure Rima had mentioned Vincent during her last trip home. She had talked about Jimmy, showed them pictures, and Vincent had been mentioned, and Julie. That was as close to an endorsement she was going to get, unless the diary provided any clues.

She would probably have to trust someone eventually, but for now she would keep the existence of the diary and the papers a secret.

In the afternoon there was some excitement. Matt reported that bowheads had been seen in the waters off Utqiagvik. The whaling camps were still being set up; it was a little early for the whales to have left their wintering grounds in the Bering Sea. A couple of whales were heading east along the coast now. There was a general rush to the observation bubble on the seabed.

The sun's light percolated dimly through the ice above their heads. The water was dark, washed with blue where the ice was thin enough to let in some light. Matt turned on the external lights, but very dim, so that the golden radiance allowed them to see about ten meters further into the water. Fish swam by on the other side of the wall, their pale bellies agleam in the light.

"There!" Vincent said. "Agviq!"

And a dark, mountainous shape loomed just beyond their field of vision, and swam with cloud-like grace toward them. It came deliberately, straight to them, a huge, thirty-foot bulk with its flipper brushing the wall, its great eye looking in. In all her life Varsha would never forget that moment when she looked into the eye of the whale. Near her the others were talking quietly, exultantly.

"She's looking well—look at that healed propeller scar—"

There was another whale behind this one. The two whales took turns looking into the lighted room. There was a low, long, booming sound, like a distant cello. Varsha could feel the walls vibrate. The whales were calling. They must have circled the observation dome for a good fifteen minutes before moving away into the dark.

"Wow," said Varsha, finding her breath. "I've never—I've never seen anything like this. How do you know one whale from another?"

"Marks on the fluke—the tail," Vincent said.

"Are they all so curious?"

"Whales are individuals," said Matt. "Most of them keep away from here, but these two, and there are three others—they stop and say hello whenever they are passing by."

"We have hydrophones set up all along the coast," Julie said. "Here—I'll play the recording."

She pressed a button on the computer keyboard. A waveform scrolled across the screen, and the sound filled the air. It was the strangest call Varsha had ever heard. It filled the room, filled her being.

"It feels as though I ought to understand it, but I don't," she said, shaking her head.

She thought of her aunt standing here, watching the whales, hearing them sing.

One of my former engineering professors, who looked like the crazy prof in the movie 3 Idiots, had this huge construct in his lab made from odds and ends—a Rube-Goldberg machine on steroids. If you dropped a certain ball onto a ramp, the machine would light up and there would be wheels turning, pulleys spinning, weights flying into the air to hit specific targets and so on. The grand finale was that a dart would fly out and bury itself in a large picture of Isaac Newton on a Styrofoam board. The damn thing made a great racket. Isaac's face was so perforated with dart strikes that his visage had mostly disappeared. We loved the machine, and part of our spare time was always spent tinkering with it. The crazy prof called it "Newton's Engine."

I realized when I was quite young that there were two classes of problems, broadly speaking, simple ones and complex ones. Machines are good at solving simple problems. But throw in enough complexity and all bets are off. I went into biomimicry-based engineering because I wanted to challenge this realization. It's only when I got to the Arctic that I realized my first instinct had been right. You can't solve complex problems with machines, without breeding more problems of increasing intractability. Complexity is the spanner in the works of Newton's Engine. But it goes beyond that. You might think a sufficiently advanced AI would think its way through some of the failures (I happen to know they are not just rumors) that are plaguing GaiaCorp's Project Terra. GaiaCorp has invested so much in its intelligent geoengineering systems, but I think it is inconceivable for autocrats to realize that their slaves might not march to their orders. AIs are a fundamentally different kind of intelligence than humans. We have more in common with the whales than with our household robots.

I think our main problem may be that we think of the Earth itself like a Newton's Engine, something we can tinker with and fix. Jimmy says that even biologists fall into this trap—of putting living creatures into rigid categories of structure and behavior, motivated by simplistic evolutionary imperatives. To him, to understand the whale would mean not just the kind of work he did for his PhD at San Diego, but also traveling with the whale through its great migrations around the North Pole, being part of its way of being, without any preconceived notions. "You see things differently when you are part of them," he says. "Explain," I say, and he laughs and says he can express these ideas better in Iñupiaq. It is so much more precise a language. Jimmy is not a talker—not in English anyway—I think because he dislikes sloppiness. He likes to say things right. You should hear him chattering with his nieces and nephews whenever there is a big family gathering. As I take the first baby steps learning Iñupiaq, I remember what you always used to say, Papa: that every language is a different way of seeing the world.

It turned out that Vincent's wife, Emma, worked in the town government. Vincent had a room at North Point that he used when the weather was bad, but his home was in Utqiagvik. The clouds had cleared a little. It was still -6° F but that was normal, that was balmy for an early spring.

So it was thus that Varsha found herself in Vincent's Land Rover, being driven along the coast road. The sea ice stretched as far as she could see, but it was breaking up in places farther out from shore. A long, narrow channel of seawater had appeared where there hadn't been one before. The sun lay low in the sky, and the light was murky. But the sky was clear, a dim, hazy, ethereal blue.

"Want to walk on the ice?" At her nod he pulled over and stopped. Her boots crunched on the low rise that separated the land ice from the sea ice.

"Walk where I walk," Vincent said. "The sea ice is all right close to the shore, but it is thinner than it should be."

She followed him out onto the plain. The wind was a cold knife in her face. She felt her toes turn numb. The ice sheet was vast, its immensity broken only by cairns of ice chunks that were carelessly piled up all over the plain. But the sky was clear and she could see the horizon, separating sea from sky.

"You are walking on frozen seawater," Vincent yelled over the wind. He pointed. "There's water under the ice. See, you can tell by the broken up piles of ice chunks. That's the wind and the currents breaking up the ice from below."

It was the worst cold she had ever experienced, and it was incredible. Vincent pointed.

"Over there. Do you see those tracks? That's polar bear."

She saw the broad, regular tracks a short run away from where they were standing. The tracks disappeared toward the sea.

"Probably hunting seal. Not that many seal now, because we haven't had much ice. They pup out on the ice to avoid bear, in little dens under the snow. This winter Kenny said there are a few."

She thought of little seal pups under the snow, and the polar bear sniffing the ground.

In the truck the warm blast of heat was welcome. They met no traffic until they got to the outskirts of Utqiagvik.

Home for Vincent was a small, warm, compact house on stilts, on a street with similar houses. Emma greeted them wreathed in cooking fragrances that were surprisingly familiar.

Emma was small and round, with a mobile, humorous face.

"Vince is a better cook than me," she said, "but when he comes home after a bit I do the cooking. I thought you might like to try whale stew with a bit of curry. There's fish too."

"Whale stew?"

"Goodness, don't tell me you're vegetarian? Vince, did you think to ask?"

"Oh, I eat everything," Varsha said quickly. "I've been cutting down on meat lately, but this smells great!"

"It's the last of the spice powder Rima made for us," Vince said, taking her coat. "She told us what is called curry here in America is garbage. So she sent for some spices from Anchorage and roasted and mixed them. Made us whale curry. It was amazing!"

"This meat is from last year," Emma said. "Come, sit down. Are you warm enough? Vincent's uncle is a whale captain. They were fortunate because it had been a poor harvest the year before. With the waters warming, the whales have changed their routes. We see a lot more killer whales coming up from the Pacific, hunting the bowheads. And now there's more shipping and the new searches for oil and gas."

"Noise disturbs them," said Vincent. "We were blessed this one came to us. We sent whale meat to the other villages that didn't have a good catch."

Among the family pictures on the mantel was one of Rima and Jimmy, along with four young people, sitting on top of a harvested whale.

The wine was good. The table was neatly laid with a flowered table cloth. Vincent brought the dishes to the table. The fragrance rose in the air.

"This is so nice of you," Varsha said, taking a ladle of whale curry. "The smells remind me of home!"

"This is the same whale as the one in the picture," Vincent said, indicating the framed photos on the mantel. "Your aunt's eaten of this whale."

The meat was like nothing she had ever tasted. It was melt-in-the-mouth soft and redolent with cumin and coriander, cinnamon and ginger and nutmeg. Tears came into her eyes.

"It's incredible!" she said. Vincent and Emma looked at each other, then they both smiled at her.

"It means a lot to us, the whale," Vincent said, chewing reverently. "It's part of Eskimo identity, a sacred beast that makes us who we are."

"I have only read a little about it," Varsha said apologetically.

"You have to stay awhile, witness a whale hunt to really understand," Emma said. "Here, have some more. The gravy is really good on the rice. At each harvest we thank the whale for its sacrifice. Its meat is never sold, only shared."

It seemed to Varsha that she had passed some kind of threshold that she couldn't quite comprehend. She had thought she had come to perform the saddest of duties, to collect her aunt's things and hope for some closure for herself and the family back home. *I'm an outsider,* she thought, but Rima had at least partially bridged the gap. *And because of her somehow I have a link here. Like a foot in a door to a place I can't see.*

At dessert—an apple tart—she asked Vincent if he had been on his uncle's whale hunt.

"Yes of course," he said. "Since I was a kid. When it's whaling time we cancel everything. Schools, work. Everyone gets together to help."

"Tell her properly," Emma said. She gave Varsha a humorous look. "He talks like a running tap when he's in the mood, but maybe he hasn't had enough wine. Come on, Vince, tell her about how you grew up. She's not going to hear about life in the great North from a better source."

"You're the running tap, not me! But yes, I grew up in Utqiagvik at the time of the start of the Great Melt. Sometimes it would get to 50 degrees Fahrenheit, in the winter. When it was supposed to be 10 or 20 below. My grandfather wanted me to learn to hunt seal and polar bear and whale according to our traditions, but the seals had gone, and the bowheads were moving away, driven by killer whale swimming up from the Northern Pacific. And the sea ice was so thin, it wasn't safe to walk on. I remember when the last of the multi-year ice disappeared. My uncle wept. He was a hunter, a great whale hunter who had learned the skill from my grandfather. "When the ice goes," he said, "so does the way of our people.""

"People down south don't understand that," said Emma. "They think that if the cold goes, and the ice, we would be glad. Not so for us. We are who we are because of the ice. I remember when the Great Melt started—I grew up in Anchorage but I used to come up here to see my great-aunt. We—my cousins and I—drove off polar bears in the streets when they came starving, looking for rubbish. My cousin still works in the local wildlife department."

"Things changed for everyone," said Vincent. "The polar bears—we heard that some were going south into land, mating with the grizzlies. I thought: if the way of our people is gone, maybe I have to go south with the polar bear. That was the summer that moose started coming up North, where they had never been seen before. Everything was changing, faster than the memories of our ancestors that go back thousands of years. Never had the ice gone so fast every spring, or developed so slowly every fall. Now in the summers the ice pack would melt so much that there would be clear passages right across the North pole. The circumpolar countries were vying with each other over shipping routes and oil and gas drilling, even after the bans and the declarations of protected zones. What it meant for us is that the whales left the shores. The bowheads who make us what we are as a people, who have given us their lives as a gift so we may live—they started to change their migration routes around the Arctic. The whale hunts were less and less successful. Some years there were hardly five or six whales harvested per season.

"So I was well into my teens until the time one year that the winter was strong enough that the ice came back. My grandfather was very old by then but just like all the other whale hunters he was very excited. Bowhead had been spotted off the shore ice, and the ice was thin, but thicker than previous years. So we made camp not far from the shore. I remember that first whale hunt of mine. The whale that gave itself to us was an old male, he had been seen many times by my father when he was a boy. Now here he was, giving himself to us, as though to say—*I give you my life so you may be Iñupiaq a little longer.*

"But when I was grown and my grandparents gone, so much had changed that I felt the old ways would not survive. So I left—I went south to college in Fairbanks, and got a degree in business, and had a bunch of jobs that took me from Alaska to Oregon and down even to Colorado. I tried to become this person who changed with the times."

He laughed. Emma gave him an affectionate look.

"Meanwhile my cousin Jimmy—he's my cousin's son—he was of the new generation that was inspired by the Native revival movements—he studied Iñupiaq, got a degree in comparative linguistics, and then he decided he needed to know what the white man knew about the world. He'd always gone whaling with us when he was a boy, just some ten, twelve years younger than me he was. He'd interned for a while at Wildlife—that's the town's wildlife management department, some of the world's best people on whales and marine life out there. It piqued his interest. He wanted to know what science could teach him about the whales. So he did marine biology at the University of California in San Diego. And then he came back here. Helped set up North Point Research. Then your aunt comes here, wanting to study wind generation in a place where you had gusts and gales without much sustained speed. They got to be friends. She started helping him in his research, and next thing, they're a couple."

There was a soft, remembering silence. From the pictures, Rima and Jimmy looked out at them, smiling. Their absence was like a presence in the room.

"What happened to all their things—their research, I mean—after—afterwards?"

"Rima's renewable-energy prototypes are all at the college. The tribal college—she worked with the kids. The program will continue. There's a machinist in town she worked with, we sent him the scrap bits and pieces. Jimmy's equipment and records are all going to go to the University in Fairbanks. Their work will live on."

The wine had softened her spirits. The whale stew had warmed her through. I never knew, she thought—I never knew the world was so full.

"What brought you back here?"

"Well, after two decades in the south I couldn't take it. Came back here and decided if the young were doing it, I had to return too. Figure out what it meant to be Eskimo, to be Iñupiaq without the ice. I couldn't be a grizzly bear anymore. So I started running the radio station."

Emma took up the story.

"There's a popular program we've had for a long time, when not enough young people knew their language, so our elders would come on the air and talk in Iñupiaq. Vince expanded that. We had the elders telling us stories, explaining what certain words meant—you know, people who belong to the land, to whom land is sacred, have words and concepts that are tied to the land, to the context. You lose the context, you lose half the lexicon. There were words that had lost their meaning, orphaned words and concepts—but the elders brought them alive, situating them in stories so people would know what had once been, even if it was no longer there. Then, when North Point Research was set up, Jimmy asked Vince to run the Native Science liaison over here. So that's what he's been doing for the last seven years or so."

Emma was in the town's scenarios planning team. "When things are changing so fast with the climate, we can't plan effectively for the future. So we prepare scenarios of all possibilities so that we can be better prepared. Did

Vince show you the sinkhole on the way to North Point? No? Well, it's south of the coast road. Must be fifty feet deep. The permafrost that used to be always frozen is thawing here and there, so the land sinks. They've had that all over the Arctic Circle."

They were so kind to her. They had known Rima and had been fond of her, and the grief that was like a stone in her chest seemed lighter.

The living-room sofa folded out into a guest bed.

"Here are some extra blankets," Emma said. "Rima used to be cold all of her first year, then she acclimatized."

She sat at the edge of the bed. Vince had gone upstairs and Emma and Varsha finished their hot chocolate in the living room.

"She was a special person, your aunt. All kinds of people come to Utqiagvik, either to study us or the ice or both. And lately we have tourists, come here to see the Northern Lights and all. We've kind of become inured to it, you might say. And a bit sick of it, I have to admit. But Rima, she was different. Never gave up on anything or anyone, stubborn as a mule, a good match for Jimmy. Jimmy was our—we never had a child of our own. Always thought we'd have him with us, see us grow old."

She blinked away tears and got up. "Time to sleep or we'll be up all night," she said, smiling. In the dark a few moments later, Varsha thought—the link between us is the link of a shared grief. And sleep came.

When I was in California I once watched a movie of emperor penguins swimming underwater. It was astonishing—they were flying through the water, flapping their wings with an effortless grace. The same wings that look so pathetic and useless on land are amazing instruments underwater. At the time I was with the biomimicry group. We talked about submersible boats and how inadequate their designs were. I didn't think further about it then, but after hearing Jimmy talk about whales, I've been sketching. I sit in the observation bubble—it's the best place for me to think—and I imagine a vessel that can fly through water like a penguin. A squid-inspired propulsion device that takes in and expels water—I'll have to look into energy usage—and then I think—what about ocean currents? If I put an acoustic Doppler device on this boat, it could find ocean currents and use them—and it occurs to me—a sail! A squid-propulsion amphibious boat with penguin wings and a sail to catch the underwater currents! I was so pleased I showed Jimmy, and he got really excited. I've put some rough sketches here.

Oh Papa, I know you said no engineering diagrams, but this is the most exciting thing I've done. Forgive me! It's such a warm winter we're having here, not even one good storm to give us some excitement. Warm is a relative word—you would shiver here, Ma, even when the sun is at its highest. The sun never gets very high in the sky here. I know you are thinking of the shawl you said you were knitting for me, Ma, and I think of it too, when I am feeling cold.

But it is so important that it stay cold here. You know, Papa, how you always emphasized in us that we see connections between things. Never just be content with what's at the surface. Well, here's a connection for you. If the Arctic melts, we are all cooked. The Arctic keeps the whole Earth cool. Next time there is a severe summer back home— and I can't even imagine one hotter than when I was in Patna this July, when I thought I would faint if I stepped out—next time please remember that it's in part because of what's happening here in the Arctic. We've warmed the Earth so much that the Arctic is melting, and that will only warm the Earth further.

So now I've given you an engineering diagram and a science lesson. I've got to make up for it.

I want to write this especially for Varsha and the other kids, although they aren't kids anymore. It is hard to be in the world—if you live in it fully, it is easy to sink into despair. What, after all, can one or two people do, when the world is dying? Why not submit to the alluring logic of GaiaCorp's promise to save the Earth, to their megamachines seeding the oceans, their satellites seeding the skies, their winged shades reflecting the sun's light away from whichever politically expedient, remote, hard-scrabble country is out of favor? Why not bide the time as gently as possible by surrendering our full, human, curious, questing selves, lulling ourselves into dreams? The deal is that to be fully alive you have to be willing to bear pain. That is what I swore to, when I was in my twenties—that I would be fully alive. But nobody can do it alone. I am so fortunate to have been born as part of the Guava Tree family in Chandragupta Park, and to live on the best possible planet, and to have the friends I have, and to have met Jimmy, whom you will all love, I promise.

I think about all this sometimes because my job is occasionally dangerous, and I know Ma and Papa tend to worry, but you must remember, should anything happen to me, that it is love that moves and motivates me, and love leaps all chasms, and you can't get rid of me so

easily. So if ever the unthinkable shall happen, repeat after yourself:
that Rima is in her own way always and forever with you. Say it now,
just for practice.

The morning she was going to leave, Varsha paced back and forth in her little
room. There wasn't much room to pace, but she needed to think. At last she
came to a decision.

She found the Station office, where a young Iñupiaq woman called Irene
was organizing a filing cabinet.

"Sorry, Irene. I need to talk to the machinist who worked with my aunt.
Can you get me his name and number?"

"Sure. He sometimes sent her stuff down to Anchorage, in case you are
looking for anything in particular."

After a brief conversation Varsha went back to her room and finished
packing. The four boxes that were going back to Boston would be dropped
off at the post office. Emma had given her an old suitcase—she was carrying
a few of her aunt's things on the flight back.

She went to Vince's office and knocked. To her surprise, Rick Walters was
there. He smiled at her.

"Sorry you're leaving so soon. I feel we barely met. Vince, I can take Varsha
to the airport. Give us a chance to have a final chat."

She smiled at him.

"It's all right," she said, before Vince could say anything. "Vince and I have
some important things to talk about. Family stuff."

"Of course," he said. He shook her hand. "I have friends in Boston. Maybe
I can look you up next time I'm there."

He gave her hand a squeeze and went out of the room. When his footsteps
had died away, Vince shut the door. His face had a closed, remote look.

"Vince," she said. "Before we go, I have to ask you something."

"Sit," he said. He still looked wary. She had to trust him. Rima had. She
took the plunge.

"I need to know what happened to my aunt's prototype of the submersible boat," she said. "The one that could sail on the ocean and fly under
water. Julie mentioned she'd seen something being assembled in Rima's lab.
I called the machinist in Utqiagvik and asked him what parts he received.
I'm no engineer but nothing he described sounded like parts of the amphibious boat she was building."

There was a long silence.

"How do you know about the boat? Julie told you?"

"Only casually. But—I have been meaning to tell you—I found my aunt's diary and some papers. She left them for me in a place she knew I would know to look. She didn't say she had completed the prototype. But I got the impression she had. I need to know—did she and Jimmy take the prototype with them on their last trip?"

"They went on the research boat—you know that—the pieces were found on the seabed—there was no sign of a submersible boat."

"But the research boat was a large enough vessel to hold the prototype, wasn't it? They took it with them, they must have! A book inside a book, a boat inside a boat—Vince, I need to know—my family needs to know—if there's any chance—"

She couldn't speak. She swallowed hard.

"What do you want me to say?" Vince put his head in his hands. He looked at her after a moment. "I don't know. I don't know. I want to believe they're both alive. Jimmy—he would tell me since he was a little kid, going to school, or a whaling trip, or California—he would tell me he'd always come back. Do you think I don't want to believe it? But I can't give you false hope. What would you do—tell Rima's parents she might still be alive? What if she isn't? True, they didn't find the remains of the ambiphian. But the winds and the currents here are strong and unpredictable. It could take years before the rest of the debris showed up."

"They would have radioed you," Varsha said. "If they were alive."

"Maybe it wouldn't be so easy," Vince said. "And if they are really out there, there are reasons why they would not have wanted us to know."

"Not wanted us to know? My grandfather is old. I don't know how he has survived this. My grandmother does nothing but knit all day. My parents are fighting more than ever. This is destroying us. My aunt wouldn't keep it from us if she were alive!"

She had raised her voice. Vince motioned her to speak softly.

"Listen, Varsha, there's a lot more at stake than you think," he said. "I'm going to trust you as you have trusted me. If they wanted to hide the prototype, don't you think they could have just dismantled it and hidden the parts? This is much bigger than you think."

"Please explain," Varsha said. "I deserve this much."

"It's time to go," said Vince. "We have plenty of time to talk in the car. Please—carry Rima's diary and the papers on your person."

"Yes, of course," she said. "In my backpack. I'll show you in the car."

After the good-byes were done, they sat in Vince's Land Rover while the engine heated, looking at Rima's diary and the papers. Vince grabbed a battered camera from the back seat and took some pictures. "For Emma," he said. "And for safety. I think these names here are the people who may know something about what Jimmy and Rima intended. I'll make some inquiries, discreetly."

"Vince," Rima said, "she must have drawn the boat designs on her laptop. Through some kind of engineering software, like DesignWorks. You told me earlier her laptop had been lost with her, but she might have saved the design on a klipdrive or something. When you get back—look inside your computer—unscrew the base, and see if there's anything small like that, tucked away."

Vince looked startled, then nodded. He looked at his watch, sighed, and started the Land Rover.

The sun sent long rays over the tundra and the frozen sea. The windows of the station glowed in the yellow light. There was a wind blowing, moaning softly, whipping up skeins of last night's snow from the ground.

"Jimmy was interested in whale communication," Vince said as the Land Rover lurched over the ice road. "But he was also curious about the possibility of interspecies communication. I don't just mean human-to-whale, but whales with other species. Nobody really thinks much of that among the scientists. It's not in the white man's way of thinking, to think that there are other species than him, who might want to talk to each other. In our stories polar bears and whales and all the other creatures talk to each other as well as to people. To the white man that's just kid's stuff, or just mythology. But Jimmy, he wanted to know if it was possible. He'd noticed some odd things."

They bumped along the coast road. The sun was higher in the sky today. It would edge up over the horizon a little every day, until it vanquished the night for nearly six months of the year.

"What odd things?"

"Unusual behavior among some whales. Bowheads hanging out with humpbacks. Blue whales down in the Atlantic lowering their call notes—they call much more bass than bowheads—so they reached right across an ocean basin. Jimmy thought it was logical that the whales had noticed the conditions of climate change—the warming ocean, the changing currents and chemistry. How could they not? Maybe they had always talked to each other. Modern humans are the only species that keeps apart from the others. Not so the other animals. The white man doesn't see what's not in his scheme of things.

"Don't get me wrong. I like civilization—I'm not blaming it for everything. Among my people there is a lot of division on such issues—how do we find balance between the benefits of the modern way of life and the wisdom of the traditional teachings? But back to Jimmy.

"So Jimmy had this idea that if humans are to understand whales, you've got to do it as much as possible in the whale's environment. Drones, underwater robots, tracking, all that's great, but if you can't follow the whales on their Arctic migrations, if you can't dive deep with them, or swim under the ice, you won't know the context in which they sing their songs. More than anything you won't have a relationship with them of mutuality. All true knowing is mutual, Jimmy used to say."

"I hear that bowheads live very long," Varsha said. "In her diary my aunt wonders what they think about, talk about, for two hundred years."

"Yes, that was the sort of thing that fascinated Jimmy. He wanted to understand how whales talked to each other and to other species, if there was maybe a common language among the sea mammals."

"But why the need for secrecy? Doesn't GaiaCorp already have amphibious boats?"

"Not like this one—energy efficient, small and compact, but with enough room for an extended stay. And Jimmy is—was—a hunter, he could keep them alive—"

He looked out over the great vista rolling past them, and was silent.

"I don't understand why—if they really meant to go out deliberately into the ocean and fake their deaths—why?"

"Jimmy suspected that the bowhead whales were learning from the humpbacks how to disable the TRexes. Humpbacks use sound to stun fish. Sound means everything to whales. When the TRexes use their airgun arrays, it's like having an explosion happen ten times a second. Sometimes for weeks or months. If whales are close enough they would get deafened. A whale uses sound for communication and to find its way in the dark under the ice. A deaf whale is better dead.

"Meanwhile Rima learned from scientists in other places around the world that GaiaCorp's geoengineering is failing. Not just that, but the crop failures in your part of the world, and the toxic algal blooms in the South Atlantic, are a direct result of it. Worse, the geoengineers knew they would fail. It's all about money and power, in the end."

"So they can't afford to let the TRexes be destroyed?"

"We can't afford to let it get out that it's not just other humans but potentially other species who are fighting back. The white man almost wiped out the bowheads in the time of the Yankee whalers. Do you think they would hesitate to do so again?"

"This is crazy. This is just crazy."

"This is the world."

"You've just destroyed everything I took for granted about the world."

"Rima used to say: never take anything for granted."

She looked out over the frozen sea. Somewhere beyond the horizon was open water. It was hard to imagine that somewhere on the open sea, or perhaps inside it, two people in an amphibious boat were sailing with the bowhead whales.

The town came up suddenly around them. Over the sea ice, tiny figures could be seen on snowmobiles, hauling sleds behind them.

"They're cutting the trails," Vincent said. "If you were staying longer you could have gone on a whale hunt."

"I don't know how much—how much more I can take of the world," Varsha said. She cupped her hands over her eyes for a moment. Then, as Vince pulled up at the airport parking, she looked at him.

"What do I tell my parents? My grandparents?"

"That's your call. Just—don't let it get around, what I've told you. You can tell them, if you like, that maybe there's a chance they are alive. But keep the other things to yourself. This is for their sake as well as yours. There are larger forces here at play than you and I."

"I feel like I'm in an Augs adventure story. Except there's nothing like this in the files."

"I enjoy VR games from time to time. But you got to live in the world."

"Thanks for everything, Vince. I am glad we talked, and I'm very glad I got to meet Emma. If—if you hear anything—"

"Of course."

He helped her into the check-in line with her two suitcases. The small airport was filled with people—men in the uniforms of Arctic Energy, a knot of coast guard officials, and Eskimo families hauling supplies in sacks and boxes, laughing and chattering. It no longer felt quite so strange.

"We'll meet again, I have a feeling," Vince said, "so I'll say 'see you later,' not good-bye."

He shook her hand, smiled at her, a sudden, warm smile. Then he was gone. She blinked back tears and set her chin.

In the plane she thought of the diary and the diagrams in her backpack, and the secrets they carried. She thought of Chester waiting hopefully at the airport, and what she would have to say to him, and the life she had mapped out for herself. She thought of the house in Patna, and the aging faces of her grandparents.

The tundra dipped and glittered in the sun as the plane turned upward into the sky. The houses vanished. At this height, she saw the open water at the edge of the shore ice, and the expanse of the Arctic, broken here and there by white patches of floating ice. She thought of the great whales traveling in circles through the cold, dark waters, feeding and calling, dreaming and singing. Perhaps at this very moment her aunt and uncle were flying through the water in their little craft, hoping she would have deciphered what they couldn't openly say, that would bring this shattering clarity to her life, and the faint thread of hope to their families, to the world.

Erin Roberts is a Black speculative fiction writer based in Washington, DC. Her short fiction has appeared in *Asimov's Science Fiction*, *Clarkesworld*, *The Dark*, and *PodCastle*; her interactive fiction has been published in *Sub-Q* and is forthcoming from Choice of Games; and her essays have appeared on Tor. com and in *People of Colo(u)r Destroy Fantasy*, among others. She is a graduate of the Stonecoast MFA program and the Odyssey Writing Workshop, and the winner of the Speculative Literature Foundation's 2017 Diverse Worlds and Diverse Writers Grants. Her musings on life and writing can be found at writingwonder.com or on Twitter at @nirele.

SOUR MILK GIRLS

Erin Roberts

The new girl showed up to the Agency on a Sunday, looking like an old dishrag and smelling like sour milk. Not that I could *really* smell her from three floors up through the mesh and bars, but there's only three types of girls here, and she was definitely the sour milk kind. Her head hung down like it was too much work to raise it, and her long black hair flopped around so you couldn't see her face. I'd have bet a week's credits she had big ol' scaredy-cat eyes, but she never bothered to look up, just let Miss Miranda lead her by the elbow through the front doors. Didn't even try to run. Sour milk all the way.

Even sour milk new girls were good, though; anything new was good. The last one, Hope, might have been dull as old paint, but at least she'd been something different to talk about. I'd even won a day's credits from Flash by betting the girl wouldn't make it to fourteen without some foster trying her out and keeping her. Anyone could tell Hope smelled like cinnamon and honey, same as those babies on the first floor and the second-floor girls with their pigtails and missing-tooth smiles. Sure enough, only took six months before the Reynolds came and took Hope off to their nice house with the big beds and the white fence and those stupid yapping dogs, leaving just me and Whispers and Flash to stare at each other and count all the months and years 'til we'd finally turn eighteen. Flash should've known it would go that way—cinnamon and honey's something fosters can't resist.

Whispers said this new girl was officially called Brenda, but that was just as stupid as all the other Agency names, and the girl wouldn't remember it after Processing anyway. At first I said we should call her Dishrag or Milkbreath, but even Flash thought that was too mean, and Flash is as nasty as hot sauce and lye. She's the one who named me Ghost, on account of I'm small and shadow-dark and she thinks I creep around too much in the night. She got *her* name 'cause that's how fast fosters send her back after their cat turns up dead and they realize the devil has blond hair and dimples.

"What's in her file?" I asked Whispers, who was still leaned up against the wall by the window. She never bothered to look out anymore. Not even for new girls.

"I'm just supposed to clean the office," she said. "Files are confidential."

"Must be good if you're holding back," said Flash, blowing out air as she tried to whistle.

"Maybe," Whispers said, with a lopsided shrug. Then she murmured something nobody could hear while staring down at her shoes. That meant we weren't getting any more from her for at least an hour, not even if Flash threatened to throw her out the window or hang her with the sheets from one of the empty beds. No use pushing her 'til she started banshee-screaming, so Flash just practiced whistling and I played around some with our crap computers and we let Whispers go all sour milk and talk to her invisible friends.

By the time Flash got a half-whistle half-spit sound to come out of her mouth and I'd finished up my hack of the first-floor baby cams for when things got boring, new girl was being led off the elevator by Miss Miranda, head still down. Flash and I lined up in front of the room same as always—hands behind our backs, chests up and out, heads forward, eyes wide. Even Whispers came out of her murmuring and straightened up against the wall. Agency folks didn't care about much as far as us third-floors were concerned, but they were total nuts for protocol.

Miss Miranda started by doing her normal speech-troduction. *This is Brenda, she's fifteen years old, and she's going to stay with us for a while. These are the girls, they're all trying to get new homes too. And we just know it'll work out for you all any day now.* When she said that last bit, her voice always got real high, like someone talking after they took a gulp of air from a circus balloon.

We ask you to stay on the third floor when you're in the building unless you're doing chores downstairs or get called to the office. But don't worry—there's so much to do up here, you won't even notice. Her voice went even higher for that part, 'cause even an idiot could see there wasn't anything on the floor but twenty empty beds, two long white lunch tables, a couple of old computers on splintery desks covered with the names of old third-floors, and the door to the world's grimiest bathroom.

As long as you maintain good grades and proper behavior in school, you're free to come and go as you please until seven PM curfew. You'll get a few credits each day for transit and meals. If you need additional learning help or assistance with your homework, the computers in the back row have plenty to offer. Age-appropriate stuff only, of course. She looked straight at me when she said it, like it was my fault the security on the things was shit and I'd figured out a way to order vapes and liquor pops and get R-rated videos.

Now you girls get along, and try not to kill each other. She looked at Flash for that one, even though Flash hadn't really tried to kill anyone for at least a year. She'd barely even talked to Hope. Either she was getting soft now that we were in high school, or she was gonna burn the whole place down someday. Maybe both.

As soon as she got the last words out of her mouth, Miss Miranda spun around on her high heels and got out of there as fast as she could. I thought the new girl would fall over as soon as Miss Miranda left, but she put her hands behind her back and stuck her chest out same as the rest of us. Her eyes weren't nearly as scaredy-cat as I thought they'd be. She smelled like sour milk for sure, but hot sauce and honey a little bit too.

"I'm Brenda," she said. "Brenda Nevins."

"That's a stupid name," said Flash.

"It's what my daddy called me," said new girl, thrusting her chest out even more, like it would cover the way her voice got all wobbly.

"Yeah? Well where's your daddy now?" Flash asked. The new girl's head dropped forward. We hadn't made a bet on whether someone could make her cry, but there were some things Flash would do for free.

"She doesn't remember," I told Flash. "You know that."

"I remember fine," said the new girl. "It's just that . . . it just happened. He just died, I mean."

Flash rolled her eyes.

"No way you *remember* that shit," she said. "Not anymore." She put on her best Miss Miranda impression, high pitched and piercing. "Your memories of your time before joining the Agency are being held for safekeeping until you reach adulthood and can properly integrate them into your daily life."

"What are you talking about?" new girl said. "I remember my dad. He was a—"

"Spare me the bullshit," Flash said, voice back low. "Miss Miranda tell you how in your file it says your daddy was a famous reccer? Or a Wall Street corp? Or a doctor? Bet if you looked in the 'grams she took from you, you'd find out he left you chained up in the basement. Or he liked to beat on your mama. Or maybe you ain't never had no daddy at all."

I felt my eyes get hot, just a little, but new girl didn't blink.

"My daddy was a good man," she said. "Not my fault if yours wasn't worth shit."

I backed up two steps so as not to get hit when the fists started flying. A fight was gonna mean discipline and lights-out and early curfew for at least two weeks. Nothing worse than that *and* having a black eye. But Flash just laughed.

"Damn, girl," she said. "You got balls. Gonna be hard coming up with a name for you."

"My dad—"

"Your dad won't know any different." I tried to stare some sense into the girl before Flash flipped back to serious and threw her across the room, or started working out how to smother her in the middle of the night. "Leave his name for him and ours for us. I'm Ghost. She's Flash. That's Whispers. We'll figure something out for you."

It took two weeks, but in the end, we called her Princess. Flash said it was from some fairy-tale book she'd read as a little kid, but I'd been to the Reynolds' for a tryout same as she had, and Princess was the name of the dumb fat poodle they all fed under the table. Plus Flash said it like a curse, with a sparkle in her eye that any idiot could tell meant trouble. I told Princess not to worry, though; I'd watch her back. Not sure why. Maybe 'cause if Princess turned up dead it was back to just Whispers and Flash to talk to. Maybe 'cause I used to be a bit of a sour milk girl too.

Me and Princess almost pinky-swore on the whole thing, but I told her that was just for little kids and losers. Even if you were too poor to get wired up soon as you turned fourteen so you could swap 'grams of every stupid thing you did with all your besties in the school cafeteria, anybody could put together the credits for a memory share at one of the public booths. Sure, all the MemCorps signs said with adult supervision only, 'cause fooling around in your head like that could mess you up when your brain was still growing, but I just told the guy at the front we were over eighteen and gave him a two-cred tip. And Princess let him look down her shirt a little when he asked to see our pretty little smiles.

We got hooked up to our chairs in one of the side-by-sides. They were sticky, but it felt like old candy, not blood or anything, so I locked in. I had to show Princess how, but she caught on quick—straps on, headset up, earpieces in. I didn't get into all the MemCorps does this and your brain cells do that and then you see the memory clear as if it happened to you part, 'cause Princess might have been a little sad looking, but she didn't seem dumb.

"Your session has begun," said the booth voice, all high and cool, like if Miss Miranda had turned into a robot.

I started first, since I knew how to work the thing. Shared my memory of the time I pulled some stupid rich girl's chair out at school and she fell back and her legs went one way and her arms went another and her mouth made a big O shape and I laughed for about an hour. Princess giggled right along with me, but there was no way to tell how much of that was real and how much was the machine—easy enough to get swept away in a share without halfway trying.

"That's all you got, Ghost?" she said, when we were finished laughing. "Some girl falling over?"

"It's funny."

"Yeah, but you said we're supposed to be swapping something real."

"It's a memory booth, dumbass," I said, smiling so she knew I didn't mean something by it like Flash would. "Of course it's real." And it was, even if I didn't share the part where Miss Miranda found out and made my head ache for a week. I liked Princess fine, but you couldn't give everything to some new girl in one go.

"Not real like true," she said, rolling her eyes. "Real like important. Like my daddy."

"I'm sick of hearing about your damn daddy all the time."

"That's 'cause you didn't know him the way I did," she said. "*He* was real."

And then she shared him with me—one 'gram after another. The way he half-smiled when she walked in the house, how it sounded when he called her Brenda, how she found him dead in his rocking chair and didn't tell anyone for a whole day even though it started to stink. The public booths were old and ragged, but I could still smell the rotten and taste the tang of garbage in my mouth and feel the pound pound of her heart thinking it was the Agency every time a car drove by. Whole thing made my eyes sting and my throat itch.

"Real like that," Princess said, voice all whispery. I just shook my head. No thinking about what my daddy could've looked like and what he might've called me. Needed to clear everything out and get back on even ground.

"'Cmon. Just show me *something*," she said, and for a second, I wished Flash was there, just to tell her to shut the hell up and leave me alone.

"Maybe next time," I said instead, taking the straps off of my legs clip by clip, telling my hands not to shake. "We're out of time anyways."

Princess flipped her hair back with her hand, turned her head, and looked me straight in the eyes. "You think that guy out there's gonna mind if we go over?"

"No. I just . . ."

"Don't want to share something real," she said, ripping her straps off and throwing her goggles back on the shelf, acting like sour milk and hot sauce had a baby. "I get it."

"You really fucking don't," I said. "Me, Flash, Whispers . . . we don't have something *real* to share. All those cute, sweet memories of being a kid? Snatched off us when we got to the Agency and locked away where we can't get 'em. All we know is school and the third floor and a few fosters who couldn't be bothered to keep us. That's it. That's all we fucking got."

Princess stared at me for a second, eyes wide, then walked out, saying *I didn't know* and *Sorry* under her breath like she was doing a Whispers impression. I stayed for a while, playing back the couple of half-decent memories I *did* have, like the day I figured out how to get the computers in the back to do what I wanted, like a real hacker, or the times the Agency let us go down to the first floor and play with the babies, and then the ones that made my neck shiver, like all the times fosters sent me back 'cause I didn't fit into any of the smiling family photos—too old, too dark, too "hard to handle."

But none of my memories were real the way Princess wanted. They didn't make my blood jump or my hands get all shaky or my mouth go dry. Not even the bad ones. Not the Reynolds' dog Butch chasing me 'round their big house, growling and smelling like death and scaring me more than Flash ever had. Not little Bitsy Reynolds laughing and telling me how I seemed nice enough for a dark girl, but Butch hated who he hated and you couldn't tell a dog any different. Not Mrs. Reynolds looking anywhere but at my face when she brought me back to the Agency, telling Miss Miranda she'd tried but I didn't know how to fit in and I was riling up the animals and after all, they'd been there first. Not even the day I woke up in the Agency with a throbbing skull and a big ol' hole of nothing in my head and Miss Miranda telling me I was eight years old and my parents were dead but I'd get a new family by the time I turned ten if I just tried hard enough. Not one goddamned thing.

I got back after curfew. Miss Miranda gave me a lecture about rules and responsibilities over the pounding in my head—*a small physical reminder of the way we expect you to behave here,* she said, smiling down at me. *I hope I won't have to speak to you about this again.*

At least the pain made it easy enough to ignore everyone once I was off the elevator. Flash rushed up to find out where I went off to and if I did anything fun, Whispers told stories about my day to her make-believe friends, and Princess acted like the back wall was the most interesting thing in the room. Took her half an hour to slink her way over to where I sat on the edge of my bed in the fourth row, swinging my feet in the air and ignoring every one of Flash's ten thousand questions. Her hair hung down in her face again, like on her very first day, and she looked like one of those trained puppies the homeless men use for begging, ready to pant and collapse at your feet the minute you look like you've got a few credits to spare.

"I'm sorry," she said. She sat on the floor in front of my feet like she thought I wouldn't kick her. "Didn't realize the way things went around here."

I shrugged and said, "It's okay, you're new." Even though it wasn't. Anything to get her to shut it and go away. But of course Princess was too sour milk to get any hints, just kept sitting there and staring and asking stupid things.

"How long you been here, anyway?"

"Six years. More or less. Agency said they got a bunch of us after the last big quake."

"A bunch? They on another floor we can't go to?"

"Nah. They all got kept by fosters whose kids got smashed up or killed same as our parents," Flash said. "Everybody but us lifers and the lucky ones."

"Lucky ones?" Princess' face stayed scrunched.

"The ones who got old and got out. Hit eighteen, got their memories, never looked back."

"Got their memories from where?" Princess asked. Flash rolled her eyes.

"From wherever they fucking keep them after Processing," she said. "Hurts like a bitch when they rip the 'grams out, too. Like someone stabbing you through your eye. 'Course they let you remember that part. Fucking Agency."

"It only hurts for a minute, wuss," I said, sticking my tongue out at Flash. Normally I wouldn't dare, but one of the good things about the way she looked at Princess, like some puppy she half-wanted to cuddle, half-wanted to kick, was that she didn't have so much nasty left for the rest of us.

"So how come I remember everything?" Princess asked, like there was any way we'd know.

"They probably screwed up," Flash said. "Or you're an Agency spy. Or your brain's so weak that it would mind-wipe you altogether." She pointed over at Whispers, who was playing with her fingers like she'd never seen them before.

"You wish," said Princess, flipping her hair in Flash's general direction like she was trying to get killed. Flash ignored it. She really was getting soft.

"Only way to find out is to get into Miss Miranda's files," Flash said. "She's got 'em all locked up down in the office on cube drives or something. Right, Whispers?"

"I'm just supposed to clean the office," Whispers said, to nobody in particular.

"Fine." Flash walked over to Whispers' corner of the room to get her attention. "Simple question. You ever see a whole bunch of little glowy cubes in a drawer or something?"

"Leave her be, Flash," I said. My head still hurt from Miss Miranda's warning, and nothing got Whispers shrieking louder than getting too comfortable over in her corner of the room. The first time, she'd hollered for a good hour 'til the Agency folks figured she wasn't gonna stop, but even now it took about ten minutes before she got dragged down to the medic and brought back passed out cold.

"I'm just asking a question, Ghost," Flash said, leaning against the wall near Whispers' bed. "C'mon, Whispers. I promise I'll leave you alone if you tell."

"The memories aren't in the office," Whispers said. "They're in the cloud." I felt my cheeks get a little hot. Stupid. I was supposed to be the big bad hacker; I should've guessed.

"That means we can get 'em with the computers up here, right Ghost?" Flash asked. "Like you did when you got the booze-flavored candy?"

"That was *before* they added all kinds of security," I said.

"So you can't get in?"

"Didn't say that."

"Then shut up and do it already," Flash said. "I want to know why she gets to hold on to all her stupid little 'grams and they won't let us remember shit 'til we get out of here."

"Can't tonight," I said. "They're gonna be watching the floor."

"Yeah, 'cause you decided you had to come in late, and for no good reason either. Didn't even bring us shit."

"It's not her fault," Princess said, still lounging on the floor near my bed. "I—"

"Doesn't matter," I said. "They're gonna be looking close for a couple days. We'll have to try another time."

"Or we could just distract 'em," Flash said. Then she went and sat down, right on the edge of Whispers' bed.

It took fifteen minutes of screams that I could feel all the way back behind my eyeballs, but eventually one of the overnight Agency guys, the one Flash thought had nice hair, came up and dragged Whispers away.

"You shouldn't have—" I started.

"Yeah yeah," Flash said, shrugging. "Just do it already. Before they finish drugging her up."

I looked at Princess, but she just flipped her hair again and walked over to the computers. She had a little more hot sauce in her than I thought. Couldn't tell yet if that was a good thing.

"Go 'head," Flash said. "Thought you were supposed to be some kind of super-hacker."

My head was still throbbing, worse than ever, and I knew Flash was just trying to get to me, but truth was truth. I sat down and got to typing—no way the Agency would spring for touch screens or one of those fancy robot lady voices—and was in quicker than I thought. Miss Miranda had locked down all the "bad influence" stuff pretty tight, but getting the Agency files wasn't much harder than getting the cam feed from downstairs and watching the babies play.

"Brenda Nevins," I read from the screen. "Resident at the Agency for the Care of Unassociated Female Minors."

"Blah blah blah," said Flash from across the room. She was on lookout by the elevator for when Mr. Nice Hair came back with Whispers. "Get to the good stuff."

"It doesn't say anything really," I said. "Just a bunch of big words." The whole thing was reports and warnings and psychology mumbo-jumbo. Nothing 'til I got down to the engrams section. It was a list of 'grams with titles like *Discovery of Father's Body* and *Trip to Percy Park on May 7th*. I recognized a couple from in the booth earlier, but most I'd never even heard of, and just about all of them had the same big bold flashing letters on the far right. *Not to Be Removed. See Explanation.*

"'Explanation,'" Princess read from over my shoulder, finger tracing along the screen like some little kid trying to figure out how words work. "'To date, Miss Nevins has shown none of the aberrant or destructive behavior of many of the Agency's other older residents. As the trauma from the loss of her father has not led her to behave negatively, we recommend that she be able to keep the majority of her memories at this time. Moreover, it can be noted that Agency resident Becky Ann Ross has shown no significant behavioral improvement since memory removal, and it is possible that the procedure itself had a negative impact on the development of Samantha Lee, leaving her prone to delusions and outbursts. While Destiny Ward has demonstrated some positive behavior changes and remains difficult to place primarily due an unfortunate lack of demand, a better form of control therapy than memory removal may need to be implemented in the future.'" Princess faked her way through most of the big words and probably wasn't saying half of them right, but I knew what "lack of demand" meant.

"Destiny? That's you?" Princess asked. I shut down the machine and pushed her out of my way as I headed back to my bed. She followed. Of course.

"You're Destiny Ward," she said again, right behind my ear. "Right?"

"I'm Ghost, you fucking idiot," I said. Ghost who was too old and too ugly to be in demand. Ghost who didn't smile right, who dogs couldn't help but want to kill. Ghost who had a hole in her mind instead of whatever it was that would get Princess and all those little first-floor babies and second-floor sweethearts tried out and kept by fosters, far away from the damn third floor. Ghost who knew how to fix it.

I got up from the bed so fast that Princess jumped back a good foot. Even Flash flinched a little bit over by the elevator. Fuck the Agency; I could find my 'grams right now, maybe even get them put back in early. There were people who would do that if you paid them well enough. I was a hacker; I could figure it out.

I got back into my file and scrolled down. *Visit to the Ferris Wheel with Parents, Earthquake and Aftermath, Petty Larceny #1,2,3.*

And in the rightmost column of each—*Permanently Deleted.* Not held for safe-keeping until you can integrate them into adult life. Not get them back when you turn eighteen. Just gone. Totally and forever gone.

I picked up the stupid machine to throw it down on the floor, break it open like a water balloon, but Princess caught my arm.

"You don't want to—"

"You don't know what the hell I want," I said, brushing her off and heading over to the elevator. "Agency lied to us, Flash. They fucking lied. They took all our memories and said they were giving them back but they—"

"Shut it," Flash said. "They're coming up."

She was right. I could hear the whirring of the gears as the elevator climbed. This time of night, Agency bastards would want us all lying down. Proper bedtime protocol and all that bullshit. Leave us flat on our backs while they told us their lies.

I got back to my bed just in time for Mr. Nice Hair to step off, carrying Whispers in his arms. He put her down on the closest bed, nowhere near her little corner, which was how I knew she was really knocked out. Otherwise she would've started screaming all over again. Then he turned around and left without a word. Just like Miss Miranda. No time for the third-floor rejects. We probably wouldn't remember it anyway.

"Let's move her back," said Flash. Nobody moved. "You want her to start up again when she wakes up?"

I didn't care what the hell happened when she woke up, but I didn't feel like fighting. I grabbed her bony ankles while Flash took hold of her arms and Princess kept a hand under her back. Once she was passed out on her own bed, legs sprawled one way and arms another, mouth hanging open like she was a clown in a carnival game, Flash patted me on the arm. If it had been Princess, I probably would have slapped her in the face, but instead I turned my face away.

"They really wipe our stuff completely?" she asked. I nodded. "No way to hack it back?"

"Don't think so."

"I'm sorry," Princess said. When I didn't answer, she crept over to her bed and laid down, her head thudding onto the hard pillow. Flash didn't move. Just leaned in close so her mouth was right by my ear.

"I've got an idea," she said. Her voice turned from whisper to giggle.

I could almost smell the hot sauce in the air.

"Wanna go to the booth again?" I asked Princess a few days later, after school. She looked at me and nodded like I'd asked if she wanted a million bucks. With me giving her the silent treatment, all she'd had to talk to was Flash and Whispers, and that wasn't much to live on.

"Is it gonna make you mad again?" she asked, her face back in that little half-scrunch.

"Nah, I'm over it," I said. "Plus, I figured out how to share something real. You're looking at an A-plus hacker, remember?"

"Yeah, I remember." She smiled bright for the rest of the walk over to the booth. I nodded at the front desk guy as we came in, sent a whole mess of credits his way.

"Break time, right?" I said. He just raised his chin in a half-nod, then looked over at Princess's shirt like he could see through the fabric. She caught on quick and bent over again, enough for him to smile and head off. Then she went straight for the side-by-sides.

"You coming, right?" she said.

"Yeah," I said. "Go ahead and strap in. I have to hack something back here for this to work."

"Okay." Princess put on the headphones and straps and all that. The goggles covered her eyes up tight, but I turned the booth lights off too, made sure she couldn't see Flash tiptoeing in.

I called up one of the memories on the list I'd pulled from the Agency. *Brenda and her Father at her fifth birthday.*

"Hey," Princess said, "Something's off. This is one of mine."

"Not anymore," I said. Her body jerked up as my code hit the booth and she clutched her head like someone was knifing her in the eye. Princess screamed and tried to tear the straps off, to run away, but Flash held her arms down, giggling under her breath. I'd offered her a few credits to help out, but some things Flash would do for free.

"Don't worry." Flash's hands tightened against Princess' arms as Princess' hair flipped back and forth. "It only hurts for a minute. You'll barely remember."

When the twitching and moaning stopped, we unhooked Princess from the booth and Flash walked her out, steadying her like she was an old drunk. I told Flash I'd be along soon, that I needed to check everything was clear so we wouldn't get caught. But after she was out of sight, I went in for a half hour in my own booth instead. Any good thief's gotta check the merchandise. Plus I didn't like looking at Princess all limp and sad, worse than sour milk even. That was more of a Flash kinda thing. She'd said I should erase every memory Princess had forever, put us all on even ground, but I didn't want to be that way about it. I was gonna give Princess the memories back at eighteen anyway. Sooner, maybe. Once I was living with a foster in some big house with nice kids and no dogs.

Princess was long-haired and cinnamon pretty; she'd find a foster with her memories or not. Just like Hope and the rest. Just like I was gonna. With Princess' memories filling up that hole in my head, I'd be set. I'd know just how to smile with the fosters and laugh and make 'em like me—even if I didn't fit in the pictures, I'd know how to be part of a family. I'd smell like cinnamon and honey and babies and home.

I cued up the first string of memories in watch mode, so I wouldn't get too caught up in the share 'til I found the right ones. I could tell Princess was a little girl right away 'cause of how big everyone looked through her eyes, like friendly giants. There were tons of them, coming and going and bringing her things, but only two were really important—Mom and Dad, happy and smiling. I tried smiling back, giggling like she giggled when Dad picked her up to pretend fly or when Mom played peekaboo. But I couldn't get the feel of it right without going all the way in. I could hear myself through the earplugs, a high-pitched cross between a scream and the hiccups. I needed something better.

I skipped through the memories, playing a few seconds if something looked good and then moving on, looking for something like the ones that Princess had showed me before, the ones that made my hand shake and my breath skip.

But all I saw was how, each time I stopped, there were half as many people, that the presents were gone and then the toys too, that the rooms were smaller and dingier, that Mom left on a rainy day and never came back, that Princess didn't seem to care. She still had her Daddy and he always always held her tightly, close enough that even on watch I could smell the liquor on his breath—just like those booze pops I'd ordered. I still felt a little of the way she'd felt when he called her Brenda, all lit up from inside like candles on a birthday cake, but this time I wasn't swept up in the share—she was just some sad little girl wearing grimy clothes, living in a dirty room with an old man who finally died in a rocking chair. Some girl who leaned over and let a perv at a front counter see down her shirt. Some girl too dumb to figure out her own stupid memories.

I left the booth before the half hour was up, still trying to get the stink of Princess' dirty life out of my nose. Pervy was back on duty and waved me over from the front counter as I passed by.

"Your friend gonna be alright?" he said. "Seems like a sweet girl." He licked his skinny lips and I had to try not to shiver. Princess would end up swapping more than 'grams with him one of these days.

"Leave her alone," I said.

"I'm just a concerned citizen." He lifted a bushy eyebrow in a way that was probably supposed to make me feel something. "Maybe I should be concerned about what you were doing during my break."

"Just making a back up," I said. "In case there's another quake or she gets hit by a truck or something." Pervy leaned forward a little.

"I've got an extra," I said. "You want it?"

Pervy had his hands out before I could blink. They looked pale and clammy, like a piece of gum stuck under a chair too long. I fished the cube with Princess' memories out of my pocket. It was the only one I had, but she'd be better off without it. Who wants to find out at eighteen that their life has been so fucking pathetic? Screw having something real.

"I give you this, you leave her alone, alright?"

Pervy nodded. I handed the cube over, making sure not to touch his sweaty hands. Fifty-fifty chance he'd try to pull some double-cross, but if I needed to, I could take care of his memories as easy as I had Princess', so I just smiled and walked out. Can't hurt somebody you can't remember.

This time, I made curfew. I could tell by the way Miss Miranda stared me down that she couldn't wait to have some reason to give me punishment, but she was gonna have to. I smiled right at her and headed up to the third floor like I had a mouth full of cotton candy. Soon as I got off the elevator I saw Princess lying in the bed she liked, hair spread out on the pillow like a pool of old soda. Flash sprang up soon as she saw me, with that big smile she got like she was either gonna hug you or eat you.

"It's all gone," she said. "All that shit about her daddy and her perfect life? Wiped just like if the Agency got her."

I smiled back, but it felt weird, like baring fangs.

"I thought you were bullshitting about the hacking part, but you give good, Ghost," Flash said. "Maybe next you can reboot Whispers so she won't talk so damn much, right? Or creep up on Miss Miranda and take everything she's got?" She laughed hard, and I knew not to tell her anything about how it really was with Princess, 'cause then she'd be mad I gave all the good stuff away.

"The rest of her okay?" I said, like I didn't care too much really.

"Yeah, she's good. Not like Whispers or anything. Just less annoying. Cuter too." Flash glanced over at Princess like she was sizing her up in a prize booth at a fair.

"Yeah, but fosters'll probably get her soon." She'd be fine. Just like Hope. Better than her memories.

"Maybe," Flash said, "If she figures out how to keep her mouth shut."

"Fifty credits says she's gone in a month."

Flash shook her head. "She's not *that* cute."

"You said that with Hope." I shrugged and hoped my palms wouldn't be too sweaty.

"Fine." Flash grabbed my hand tight with her cold one. "But make it sixty. And when she starts blabbermouthing again, I'm gonna laugh at the both of you."

"We'll see," I said, and started over for Princess. I thought Flash might follow, but she just went back to practicing whistles like always. Princess wasn't doing much, didn't even look at me as I walked over and sat down right by her ear. Just stared up at the ceiling like any other new girl who got wiped and dumped on the third floor. Sour milk squared. But that was okay. You didn't have to stay a sour milk girl forever.

"I'm Ghost," I said, low and quiet so only she could hear. "You know Flash and Whispers. And we call you Princess, but your daddy, he called you Brenda."

S. Qiouyi Lu writes, translates, and interprets between both coasts of the Pacific. You can find more of S.'s work online at s.qiouyi.lu.

MOTHER TONGUES

S. Qiouyi Lu

Thank you very much," you say, concluding the oral portion of the exam. You gather your things and exit back into the brightly lit hallway. Photos line the walls: the Eiffel Tower, the Great Wall of China, Machu Picchu. The sun shines on each destination, the images brimming with wonder. You pause before the Golden Gate Bridge.

"右拐就到了," the attendant says. You look up. His blond hair is as standardized as his Mandarin, as impeccable as his crisp shirt and tie. You've just proven your aptitude in English, but hearing Mandarin still puts you at ease in the way only a mother tongue does. You smile at the attendant, murmuring a brief thanks as you make your way down the hall.

You turn right and enter a consultation room. The room is small but welcoming, potted plants adding a dash of green to the otherwise plain creams and browns of the furniture and walls. A literature rack stands to one side, brochures in all kinds of languages tucked into its pockets, creating a mosaic of sights and symbols. The section just on English boasts multiple flags, names of different varieties overlaid on the designs: US English—Standard. UK English—Received Pronunciation. Singaporean English—Standard. Nigerian English—Standard . . . Emblazoned on every brochure is the logo of the Linguistic Grading Society of America, a round seal with a side view of a head showing the vocal tract.

You pick up a Standard US English brochure and take a seat in one of the middle chairs opposite the mahogany desk that sits before the window. The brochure provides a brief overview of the grading system; your eyes linger on the A-grade description: *Speaker engages on a wide variety of topics with ease. (Phonology?) is standard; speaker has a broad vocabulary . . .* You take a quick peek at the dictionary on your phone. *Phonology*-linguistic sound systems. You file the word away to remember later.

The door opens. A woman wearing a blazer and pencil skirt walks in, her heels clacking against the hardwood floor, her curled hair bouncing with every step. You stand to greet her and catch a breath of her perfume.

"Diana Moss," she says, shaking your hand. Her name tag also displays her job title: *Language Broker.*

"Jiawen Liu," you reply. Diana takes a seat across from you; as you sit, you smooth out your skirt, straighten your sleeves.

"Is English all right?" Diana asks. "I can get an interpreter in if you'd prefer to discuss in Mandarin."

"English is fine," you reply. You clasp your hands together as you eye Diana's tablet. She swipes across the screen and taps a few spots, her crimson nails stark against the black barrel of the stylus.

"Great," she says. "Well, let's dive right in, shall we? I'm showing that you've been in the US for, let's see, fifteen years now? Wow, that's quite a while."

You nod. "Yes."

"And you used to be an economics professor in China, is that correct?"

You nod again. "Yes."

"Fantastic," Diana says. "Just one moment as I load the results; the scores for the oral portion always take a moment to come in . . ."

Your palms are clammy, sweaty; Diana twirls the stylus and you can't help feeling a little dizzy as you watch. Finally, Diana props the tablet up and turns it toward you.

"I'm pleased to inform you that your English has tested at a C-grade," she says with a broad smile.

Your heart sinks. Surely there's been some kind of error, but no, the letter is unmistakable: bright red on the screen, framed with flourishes and underlined with signatures; no doubt the certificate is authentic. Diana's perfume is too heady now, sickly sweet; the room is too bright, suffocating as the walls shrink in around you.

"I . . ." you say, then take a breath. "I was expecting better."

"For what it's worth, your scores on the written and analytical portions of the test were excellent, better than many native speakers of English in the US," Diana says.

"Then what brought my score down?"

"Our clients are looking for a certain . . . *profile* of English," Diana says, apologetic. "If you're interested in retesting, I can refer you to an accent reduction course—I've seen many prospective sellers go through the classes and get recertified at a higher grade."

She doesn't mention how much the accent reduction course costs, but from your own research, you know it's more than you can afford.

"Ms. Liu?" Diana says. She's holding out a tissue; you accept it and dab at your eyes. "Why don't you tell me what you're trying to accomplish? Maybe we can assist you."

You take in a deep breath as you crumple the tissue into your fist. "My daughter Lillian just got into Stanford, early decision," you say.

"Congratulations!"

"Yes, but we can't afford it." C-grade English sells at only a fraction of A-grade English; you'd rather keep your English than sell it for such a paltry sum that would barely put a dent in textbooks and supplies, never mind tuition and housing.

"There are other tracks you can consider," Diana says, her voice gentle. "Your daughter can go to a community college, for instance, and then transfer out to Stanford again—"

You shake your head.

"Community colleges in the San Gabriel Valley are among the top in the nation," Diana continues. "There's no shame in it."

You're unconvinced. What if she can't transfer out? You and Lillian can't risk that; a good education at a prestigious school is far too important for securing Lillian's future. No, better to take this opportunity that's already been given to her and go with it.

Diana stands and goes over to the literature rack. She flips through a few brochures.

"You know," Diana says as she strides back to you, "China's really hot right now—with their new open-door policy, lots of people are (clamoring?) to invest there; I have people calling me all the time, asking if I have A-grade Mandarin."

She sets a brochure down on the desk and sits back in the executive chair across from you.

"Have you considered selling your Mandarin?"

You trace your hands over the brochure, feeling the embossed logo. China's flag cascades down to a silhouette of Beijing's skyline; you read the Simplified characters printed on the brochure, your eyes skimming over them so much more quickly than you skim over English.

"How much?" you ask.

Diana leans in. "A-grade Mandarin is going for as much as $800,000 these days."

Your heart skips a beat. That would be enough to cover Lillian's college, with maybe a little bit left over—it's a tantalizing number. But the thought of going without Mandarin gives you pause: it's the language you think in, the language that's close to your heart in the way English is not; it's more integral to who you are than any foreign tongue. English you could go without— Lillian's Mandarin is good enough to help you translate your way around what you need—but Mandarin?

"I'm . . . I'm not sure," you say, setting down the brochure. "Selling my Mandarin . . ."

"It's a big decision, for sure," Diana says. She pulls a small, silver case out from the pocket of her blazer and opens it with a *click*. "But, if you change your mind . . ."

She slides a sleek business card across the table.

". . . call me."

You decide to go for a week without Mandarin, just to see if you can do it. At times, the transition feels seamless: so many of the people in the San Gabriel Valley are bilingual; you get by fine with only English. Your job as a librarian in the local public library is a little trickier, though; most of your patrons speak English, but a few do not.

You decide to shake your head and send the Mandarin-only speakers over to your coworker, who also speaks Mandarin. But when lunchtime comes around, she sits beside you in the break room and gives you a curious look.

"为什么今天把顾客转给我?" she asks.

You figure that you might as well tell her the truth: "I want to sell my Mandarin. I'm seeing what it would be like without it."

"卖你的普通话?" she responds, an incredulous look on her face. "神经病!"

You resent being called crazy, even if some part of you wonders if this is a foolish decision. Still, you soldier on for the rest of the week in English. Your coworker isn't always there to cover for you when there are Mandarin-speaking patrons, and sometimes you break your vow and say a few quick sentences in Mandarin to them. But the rest of the time, you're strict with yourself.

Conversation between you and Lillian flows smoothly, for the most part. Normally, you speak in a combination of English and Mandarin with her, and she responds mostly in English; when you switch to English-only, Lillian doesn't seem to notice. On the occasions when she does speak to you in Mandarin, you hold back and respond in English too, your roles reversed.

At ATMs, you choose English instead of Chinese. When you run errands, "thank you" replaces "谢谢." It's only until Friday rolls around and you're grocery shopping with your mother that not speaking in Mandarin becomes an issue.

You're in the supermarket doing your best to ignore the Chinese characters labeling the produce: so many things that you don't know the word for in English. But you recognize them by sight, and that's good enough; all you need is to be able to pick out what you need. If you look at things out of the corner of your eye, squint a little bit, you can pretend to be illiterate in Chinese, pretend to navigate things only by memory instead of language.

You can cheat with your mother a little bit: you know enough Cantonese to have a halting conversation with her, as she knows both Cantonese and Mandarin. But it's frustrating, your pauses between words lengthy as you try to remember words and tones.

"干吗今天说广东话?" your mother asks in Mandarin. She's pushing the shopping cart—she insists, even when you offer—and one of the wheels is squeaking. She hunches over the handle, but her eyes are bright.

"Ngo jiu syut Gwongdungwaa," you reply in Cantonese. Except it's not exactly that you *want* to speak Cantonese; you have to, for now. You don't know how to capture the nuance of everything you're going through in Cantonese, either, so you leave it at that. Your mother gives you a look, but she doesn't bring it up again and indulges you, speaking Cantonese as the two of you go around the supermarket and pile the shopping cart high with produce, meat, and fish.

You load the car with the groceries and help your mother into the passenger seat. As you adjust the mirrors, your mother speaks again.

"你在担心什么?" she asks. Startled, you look over at her. She's peering at you, scrutinizing you; you can never hide anything from her. Of course she can read the worry on your face, the tension in your posture; of course she knows something's wrong.

"Ngo jau zou yat go han zungjiu dik kyutding," you respond, trying to communicate the weight on your shoulders.

"什么决定?" Ma replies.

You can't find the words to express the choice you have to make in Cantonese. Every time you grasp for the right syllables, they come back in Mandarin; frustrated, you switch back to Mandarin and reply,

"我要用我的普通话来赚钱去送Lillian上大学。"

You expect your mother to scold you, to tell you about the importance of your heritage and language—she's always been proud of who she is, where she's from; she's always been the first to teach you about your own culture—but instead her expression softens, and she puts a hand over yours, her wrinkled skin warm against your skin.

"哎, 嘉嘉, 没有别的办法吗?"

Your nickname is so tender on her tongue. But you've thought through all other avenues: you don't want Lillian to take out loans and be saddled with so much debt like your friends' children; you don't want her to bear such a burden her entire life, not while you're still paying off debts too. You can't rely on Lillian's father to provide for her, not after he left your family and took what little money you had. And although Lillian's been doing her best to apply for scholarships, they're not enough.

You shake your head.

The two of you sit in silence as you start the car and drive back to your mother's place. The sun sets behind you, casting a brilliant glow over the Earth, washing the sky from orange to blue. As you crest over a hill, the sparkling lights of the city below glitter in the darkness, showing you a million lives, a million dreams.

When you get to your mother's house, you only have one question to ask her.

"如果你需要做同样的决定," you say, "你也会这样做吗?"

You don't know what it would have been like if you were in Lillian's shoes, if your mother had to make the same decision as you. But as your mother smiles at you, sadness tinging the light in her eyes, the curve of her lips, you know she understands.

"当然," she says.

Of course.

The waiting room is much starker than the consultation room you were in before: the seats are less comfortable, the temperature colder; you're alone except for a single TV playing world news at a low volume.

You read the paperwork, doing your best to understand the details of the procedure—for all you pride yourself on your English, though, there are still many terms you don't understand completely:

The Company's (proprietary?) algorithms (iterate?) through near-infinite (permutations?) of sentences, extracting a neural map. The (cognitive?) load on the brain will cause the Applicant to experience a controlled stroke, and the Applicant's memory of the Language will be erased. Common side effects include:

temporary disorientation, nausea. Less common side effects include partial (apha-
sia?) of nontarget languages and (retrograde?) amnesia. Applicant agrees to hold
Company harmless . . .

You flip over to the Chinese version of the contract, and, while some of the
terms raise concern in you, you've already made your decision and can't back
out now. You scan the rest of the agreement and sign your name at the bottom.

The lab is clinical, streamlined, with a large, complicated-looking machine
taking up most of the room. An image of the brain appears on a black panel
before you.

"Before we begin," the technician says, "do you have any questions?"

You nod as you toy with your hospital gown. "Will I be able to learn
Mandarin again?"

"Potentially, though it won't be as natural or easy as the first time around.
Learning languages is usually harder than losing them."

You swallow your nervousness. *Do it for Lillian.* "Why can't you make a
copy of the language instead of erasing it?"

The technician smiles ruefully. "As our current technology stands, the
imaging process has the unfortunate side effect of suppressing neurons as it
replicates them . . ."

You can't help but wonder cynically if the reason why the neurons have to
be suppressed is to create artificial scarcity, to inflate demand in the face of
limited supply. But if that scarcity is what allows you to put Lillian through
college, you'll accept it.

The technician hooks electrodes all over your head; there's a faint hum,
setting your teeth on edge.

As the technician finishes placing the last of the electrodes on your head,
certain parts of the brain on the panel light up, ebbing and flowing, a small
chunk in the back active; you try to recall the areas of the brain from biology
classes in university, and, while different parts of your brain start to light up,
you still don't remember the names of any of the regions.

The technician flips a couple switches, then types a few commands. The
sensation that crawls over you is less of a shock than a tingling across your
scalp. Thoughts flash through your mind too fast for you to catch them; you
glance up at the monitor and see light firing between the areas the technician
pointed out, paths carving through the brain and flowing back and forth.
The lights flash faster and faster until they become a single blur, and as you
watch, your world goes white.

The technician and nurse keep you at the institute for a few hours to
monitor your side effects: slight disorientation, but that fades as the time

goes by. They ask if you have anyone picking you up; you insist that you're fine taking public transportation by yourself, and the technician and nurse relent. The accountant pays you the first installment of the money, and soon you're taking the steps down from the institute's main doors, a cool breeze whipping at your hair.

The bus ride home is . . . strange. As you go from west Los Angeles toward the San Gabriel Valley, the English-dominating billboards and signs starts to give way to Chinese. Although you can still understand the balance of the characters, know when they're backwards in the rearview mirrors, you can't actually *read* them—they're no more than shapes: familiar ones, but indecipherable ones. You suck down a deep breath and will your heart to stop beating so quickly. It will take time to adjust to this, just as it took time to adjust to being thrown into a world of English when you first immigrated to the United States.

A corner of the check sticks out of your purse.

You'll be okay.

Your family is celebrating Chinese New Year this weekend. You drive with Lillian over to your mother's senior living apartment; you squeeze in through the door while carrying a bag of fruit. Your mother is cooking in the tiny kitchenette, the space barely big enough for the both of you. She's wearing the frilly blue apron with embroidered teddy bears on it, and you can't help but smile as you inhale the scent of all the food frying and simmering on the stove.

"Bongmong?" you say in Cantonese. It's one of the few words you can remember—as the days passed, you realized that some of your Cantonese had been taken too, its roots intertwined and excised with your Mandarin.

"(???). (???????)," your mother says, gesturing toward the couch. You and Lillian sit down. A period drama plays on the television. The subtitles go by too fast for you to match sound to symbol; Lillian idly taps away on her phone.

A few moments pass like this, your gaze focused on the television as you see if you can pick up something, anything at all; sometimes, you catch a phrase that jogs something in your memory, but before you can recall what the phrase means, the sound of it and its meaning are already gone.

"(???)!"

Lillian gets up, and you follow suit. The small dining room table has been decked out with all kinds of food: glistening, ruby-red shrimp with caramelized onions; braised fish; stir-fried lotus root with sausage; sautéed vegetables . . . you wish you could tell your mother how good it looks; instead, you can only flash her a smile and hope she understands.

"(????????), (????????)," your mother says.

Lillian digs in, picking up shrimp with her chopsticks; you scold her and remind her of her manners.

"But (??????) said I could go ahead," Lillian says.

"Still," you reply. You place some food on your mother's plate first, then Lillian's; finally, you set some food on your own plate. Only after your mother's eaten do you take a bite.

Lillian converses with your mother; her Mandarin sounds a little stilted, starting and stopping, thick with an American accent, but her enthusiasm expresses itself in the vibrant conversation that flows around you. You stay quiet, shrinking into yourself as your mother laughs, as Lillian smiles.

You're seated between Lillian and your mother; the gap across the table from you is a little too big, spacing the three of you unevenly around the table. As the syllables cascade around you, you swear the spaces between you and your mother, between you and Lillian, grow larger and larger.

After dinner, as your mother washes up the dishes—again, she refuses your help—you and Lillian watch the Spring Gala playing on the television. An invited pop star from the US, the only white person on the stage, sings a love ballad in Mandarin. You don't need to know what she's saying to tell that she doesn't have an American accent.

"I bet she bought her Mandarin," Lillian says. It's an offhanded comment, but still you try to see if you can detect any disgust in her words.

"Is that so bad?" you ask.

"I don't know; it just seems a little . . . (appropriative?), you know?"

You don't know. *Lillian* doesn't know. You were planning on telling her the instant you came home, but you didn't know how to bring it up. And now . . . you want to keep your sacrifice a secret, because it's not about you— it was never about you. But it's only a matter of time before Lillian finds out.

You don't know how she'll react. Will she understand?

Lillian rests her head on your shoulder. You pull her close, your girl who's grown up so fast. You try to find the words to tell her what you'd do for her, how important it is that she has a good future, how much you love her and want only the best for her.

But all you have is silence.

Samantha Murray is a writer, mathematician, and mother. Not particularly in that order. Her fiction has been seen in places such as *Clarkesworld, Lightspeed, Escape Pod, Flash Fiction Online, Nature Magazine,* and *Beneath Ceaseless Skies,* among others. She was the winner of the 2016 Aurealis Award for best SF short story. You can follow her at www.mailbysea.wordpress.com or on twitter as @ SamanthaNMurray. Samantha lives in Western Australia in a household of unruly boys. "Singles' Day" was inspired by the "Technology and the Good Future" SF workshop, which was jointly hosted by Ant Financial Services Group and Future Affairs Administration in Hangzhou, China.

SINGLES' DAY

Samantha Murray

Singles' Day, or Guanggun Jie, "Bare Sticks Holiday," originated in China, and had become a global phenomenon, with the exception of most of the NoGoZo countries, by the mid 2030s. Singles' Day is now unrivalled as the world's largest shopping festival, with revenue and purchasing records continuing to be smashed every year, by billions upon billions of dollars. Singles' Day is held on the eleventh of November annually, the so-called "Double 11" date, where the 1 represents an individual who is alone. By 2043, with Earth's population continuing to rise more sharply than predicted, the coalition of Earth's governments had restricted Singles' Day savings to those who were, as the name had always implied, single, in one of many combined efforts to encourage the slowing of population growth.

YU YAN
Hangzhou, China

If you timed it right, West Lake could sometimes almost approach a feeling of solitude. It was a very popular destination, both with tourists and locals, lovers and families and groups arriving by the busload; but after the restaurants were closing, with the sun dropped behind the horizon, on the eve of Singles' Day, where most preferred the immersive shopping experience they could find in their own homes, you could imagine what it was like to not live in a city of so many million people, on a planet that groaned under the weight of nearly eleven billion. You could breathe.

Yu Yan breathed, deeply. It was a misty night. There were no stars to see but the mountains that embraced the lake on three sides were obscured and the lights from the dwellings half-way up the hillside looked like they were suspended above the lake, wavering and flickering like a borealis. There was still the faint scent of the Osmanthus trees, and some of them were lit beneath with little lights, glowing like golden flames in the growing dark. All of the little traditional wooden rowing boats had returned to the shore now and were dark shapes docked by the water's edge.

West Lake, if you timed it right, was Yu Yan's favorite place to be in the world. Stories and legends were woven around the lake, and it was like wrapping yourself up in a blanket of your childhood. Yu Yan's favorite was the story about the Lady White Snake, who changed herself from a serpent spirit into a beautiful woman for the love of Xi Xian, young scholar. They'd met on the Broken Bridge, which looked as if it was sinking down into the water, when he'd offered her his umbrella.

She'd brought Robert here, back in the early days when they were first dating. He'd kissed her, quickly and furtively, as they'd paused on the Broken Bridge of legend, of heartbreak, even though people streamed past them. This evening Robert was at his unit, if it could be called that. Small, gray and windowless, like those that housed many of the young working-class men. He could stand in the middle, and almost touch his hands to either side of the autoclaved precast concrete walls. Yu Yan had bought him a little plant as a gift once, but lack of direct sunlight, and, she suspected, lack of watering from Robert, had led to its demise. She always saw less and less of Robert as Singles' Day approached, and his excitement would rise in inverse proportion till it was palpable. Many of Yu Yan's friends spent much of their leisure time VRgaming, but Robert was not into those things. Singles' Day however, was something else.

This year, Robert was certain his bid to buy his own apartment, a proper apartment, would be successful. His own apartment, in one of the wind-farm zones, with windows. Their own apartment, with room enough for two. Maybe . . . room enough for three? Here, where no-one was watching, Yu Yan let her hand stray to her belly, as she had to consciously stop herself from doing most of the time. *Secret child. Hidden child.*

If Robert procured the apartment on Singles' Day he would do so at a remarkable discount. Prices were slashed on this day of the year, the crux of all discounts, for this one day only. Only singles were entitled to the savings though of course. Married folk or those in established relationships were ineligible. It hadn't always been this way, but for twenty years the shopping benefits had been tied to the non-attached status of the populace. It was to encourage people to remain single longer, Yu Yan knew, to make sure everything was in place before starting the journey as a family, if they chose. It made sense, in so many ways it made sense.

Yu Yan was starting to feel the chill now as the temperature dropped rapidly. She thought of Lady White Snake, waiting and wanting to become human for the sake of her love, even though it took lifetimes.

She'd gone to see Robert earlier. He hadn't been expecting her, but there were always things in your day that were unexpected. *Surprising child. Beloved child. Unexpected child.*

"Not a good night for us to go out," he'd said. "They'll think we're together."

"Are we together?" Yu Yan had tried to say it lightly, in jest, but she wasn't sure it had quite come out sounding that way.

Robert had run his finger underneath her chin, but despite the tenderness of the gesture Yu Yan had felt the impatience too. "Well," he'd said in a teasing tone that had all the lightness hers had tried for, "not officially."

Yu Yan had smiled up at him.

When Yu Yan was among people—and it was hard, with the population of Earth cresting new and unsustainable levels every day, to not be among people—she smiled often. She smiled when she was uncertain, or when she was trying to get a point across, when she was in a crowd or meeting new people. It was a social instinct, the way she communicated, a way of filling the gaps within a conversation. "You're always so happy," people said to her. Casual acquaintances, colleagues and friends alike. "You're so happy." Even Robert. Especially Robert. "It's what first drew me towards you," he'd said more than once. "You always look so happy."

Am I? Yu Yan would ask herself when he said that. She didn't think so. It wasn't a lie, but it wasn't the truth either. She would stop one day, stop smiling at everyone. One day she would not care anymore about what people thought or want them all desperately to like her. She would be old and cantankerous. It was an appealing thought.

JEA
Canberra, Australia

Jea paid for all her Singles' Day shopping with a smile. She knew, in fact, that she didn't have to actually smile for the transactions to go through—the facial recognition targeted many key points of her face and its deep convolutional neural network really didn't care which expression she wore. But the slogan was 'Smile to Pay', as it had always been, and faint strains of old advertising jingles she'd known as a kid seemed to float by just under the surface of her mind.

And she rather thought that her smile had been a good one this time, a natural curve to her lips instead of the fixed grimace that she tended to struggle with. Of course, there was no-one there to see, and in the past she'd often thought she'd succeeded in smiling appropriately only to have people's eyes get a little skittish and nervy, which probably meant she'd not managed it quite as well as she'd thought.

Jea practiced smiling fifty times every morning in her mirror. Sometimes she cheated a little and skimped out with twenty or thirty, but not often. Every morning, the same routine, as her psych had instructed: *Think of something pleasing, with a positive association. Hmm . . . creamy coffee, lots of sugar. Real coffee. Tug the corners of her mouth upwards, watching to see that her reflection didn't look creepy. Think of something else: avocados, before they were extinct. Drizzled with olive oil or smashed with lime and chili. Smile, show her teeth, then let her facial muscles relax before the smile hardened on her face into a rigor-mortis-like grimace. Think of something else: imagine she's just been given a raise, smile. Again, smile, watch the creases at the corner of her mouth. Think of something else: imagine her sister is calling her on the phone, no, that one is not straightforward, now her smile is broadening, too much, no, no, think of something else, not Antony either no, that's not right; the telescope she used to have when she was a kid, that's right, the way she felt out there alone with the universe, like she was filled up with the night and the stars, now smile, curve her lips, just a little, smile, that's right, smile.*

Jea had heard, years ago, of a mirror that only showed the reflection of someone when they smiled. It was meant for cancer sufferers, to uplift their spirits and hence boost their immune systems or some crock of rubbish and erasure. It was a flawed and stupid idea, and obviously hadn't taken off, but Jea sometimes found herself wishing for a mirror like that of her own. Perhaps it worked backwards, too; if you weren't smiling you were invisible. There was camouflage in that. Sometimes she would have settled for being invisible.

XANTHE
Minnesota, USA

It was a long way down.

The buildings were dazzlingly high, stretching both above and below her. The street was so very far away that she felt an encroaching vertigo, and there were even a couple of birds circling below. Gulls, it looked like. Gulls are a seabird, said one part of her mind, and I am a long, long way from the sea.

"Take a step," said a voice, her brother's voice. Xanthe inched forward on the narrow plank, closer to the very end.

It was a very, very long way down.

"Jump," said her brother. "You can do it."

The plank felt like carpet fibres under her feet, but all around her and beneath were just glinting buildings, and space, and sky. Xanthe swayed a little.

"I can't," she said.

"You can, just jump," came the voice again. "You know it's not real."

"I know," Xanthe said, her toes gripping carpet, "but it feels real. It's much scarier than I thought it would be."

"It's the war of your conscious mind over your animal brain, your amygdala," said her brother, "you know that, you know what you have to do."

But it's not only things that are real that you have to be scared of, thought Xanthe, and who is to say that it is your conscious brain that is always right? Maybe there is a truth to this feeling. She inched an almost imperceptible amount forwards anyway.

A light flickered in the upper-top left of her vision and a low bell-tone sounded. Xanthe slow-blinked twice to exit and retracted the side-screens of her glasses and the scene became the small box that was her living room, and, once she folded her bed out from the wall, bedroom as well. Her brother's form reclined on the sofa, his feet crossed at the ankles, his hand under his chin, a smile ghosting over his face.

"Package!" Xanthe said to him, opening the door to her very small, squat gray balcony—just wide enough for her to stand out there but hardly even sit down, where there was a drone-delivered parcel from her Singles' Day shopping. The low cloud cover had the pollution levels spiking and on her tongue was the acrid, slightly burnt taste to the air, so she retrieved her soft and lumpy package and shut the door hurriedly.

"It's my dress!" she exclaimed. She never usually wore dresses, preferring the sleek utilitarianism of her jumpsuits with built-in sensor-gloves, but this had popped up in her AR catalogue when she was looking at cupboard storage—there it had been, hanging in her built-in wardrobe with a few other items as if to illustrate how perfectly they fit. She had lingered, fingering the fabric and holding it up against her, then had moved on, only to return later and add it to her shopping cart queue.

The dress came to below her knees, and looked like it was made of the ocean; deeper blues, brightening into waves of cerulean and green, tipped with white. Her family had lived by the coast until Xanthe was almost twelve, and Xanthe missed it with a deep and fundamental ache. If she swam out far enough, she could be *alone,* or as good as alone. Alone, and yet not boxed in, caged, limited. Alone and expansive, alone and infinite. Floating, not touching the ground, she was no longer connected to the exhausted heaving of the planet, jam-packed past capacity with swarming, teeming humanity.

"But," said her brother, with that wry tone in his voice, "where are you going to wear it?"

Xanthe had not been outside her apartment in nearly two years.

"I'm going to wear it right here," she said, and threw a fringed cushion—another of her Singles' Day purchases—at his head, which of course failed to connect.

Xanthe moved away from him dismissively to the small tiled area that demarked her kitchen and picked up her spray bottle to mist her mushrooms with water. The cardboard boxes lined her wall, using agricultural waste for cultivation. The latest crop were blooming out of their box, the caps just starting to invert. Oyster mushrooms, these ones, with a velvety texture and a mild, delicate flavor, and they'd be ready to stir-fry tonight. Xanthe realized she was hungry.

Another bell-tone, this one deeper and richer somehow than before. Xanthe blinked to the right and the unfolding message floated in front of her, unfurling in shimmering, shining gold.

"Congratulations," it said.

Three of the four Greatships had already left the Earth. *Coming Events Cast Their Shadows Before Them* was the first, but also the slowest, with a less direct course. The second, *The East Wind*, had left Earth eighteen months later but had arrived only weeks afterwards. The third, *It Sings Because It Has A Song*, was mere days away from approaching the Rift now. *Peace Begins With A Smile* was currently in lower Earth orbit, awaiting her final launch status checks, and of course, her cargo.

CARREN
Utrecht, The Netherlands

The message was govt.-id encrypted and verified, and burnished brightly. "Congratulations," it began. Carren had squeezed onto the train, the station attendants with their pristine white gloves gently applying pressure to push the last passengers on board. Bodies pressed against her, swaying with the movement of the train, warmth and breath mingling together, eyes averted.

Brightly colored moving verts on the walls of the station; more faces, smiling, teeth perfectly white and straight, endorsing everything from breath freshener to neural implants to sleep inhibitors to facial mods. All flashing by while she traveled in a curved container full of people and empty of anything else.

Peace Begins With A Smile was to be the fourth Greatship to leave the Earth. The Earth, where all of them had found life, where everything had started, even though the planet was suffering under the reign of people who had not treated her well. It felt disloyal somehow, these great beautiful ships that headed away and did not come back. Carren knew about it, of course, it was impossible not to have heard, but it was her sister Vikk who was obsessed by it. It was Vikk who had told her, it must have been five years ago, that *Peace Begins With A Smile* had its long central grav-walkway called the Corridor of Joy; that the carbon nanotubes were sprung to release sounds akin to laughter in different tones and volumes depending on where you trod and how fast you moved. Vikk had been entranced by this idea, but Carren had always wondered whether you would feel that the floor and walls were laughing *at* you, whether you would tire of the incessant amusement and long for peace and quiet, gentle steps where no-one could hear you coming.

Carren leaned with all her slight weight and pushed and maneuvered her way off the train as the doors opened at Utrecht Centraal. She leaned against a steel column and let people teem around her.

If she had this right, through her use of Smile to Pay for her purchases made on Singles' Day 11/11 she had been in the draw and had won, had *won*, subject to some conditions and caveats, passage on the Greatship *Peace Begins With A Smile*, bound for Zorya, beautiful green and blue sister planet, so far, so very far away.

Leaving in less than three months' time.

Leaving. Leaving . . . the Earth.

Carren slid down the column a little.

It was incredible, and absurd. It was the opportunity of a lifetime, the opportunity of nearly eleven billion lifetimes, all of them happening around her, right now.

Carren's breath hitched in her throat. She read the message over and over. She did not smile.

Carren had been a solemn child. She'd heard "You'd be much prettier if you smiled" more times than she could count. And "Try Smiling," "Your face won't crack if you smile," "Let me see you smile," "I'll give you a dollar if you smile." She had been offered many things in exchange for her smiles at various times; a dollar, a sweet, a kiss. She usually declined.

It wasn't that she never smiled, it was that a smile seemed to come up from deep inside her, from far away, it had to be earned, it meant something. Smiles were not for strangers, for casual acquaintances, for people on the street and in the shops. She gave her smiles to the people she loved, a rare gift. Tears also were rare, Carren had to be devastated before they would surface from the well deep inside her.

"You can tell you apart from your sister—she's the one who smiles." School friends had told her some variant of this since she was very young. It was true, Vikk was two minutes younger than her, and she wore her emotions on the outside of her skin, laughing, crying, dancing or raging. She shimmered like a raindrop, whereas Carren was, what? A deep, slow-moving river, maybe.

YU YAN

"Congratulations," the message had said, and Yu Yan had felt a sudden internal thud, because 'congratulations' was a word people said at other times, for other reasons. And it was a word she didn't know if she would hear, from anyone, when she told her news.

But this was something very different. The hand she rested on her stomach was shaking.

Zorya was a dream, a beautiful far-away dream. She could remember its discovery, when she'd been a small child. The world had fallen in love with Zorya, so like the Earth, but so new and clean and empty. Odd, strange life moving deep in her oceans, which covered even more of her surface than Earth's, but only vegetative masses on land.

"When I live on Zorya . . ." was a game they used to play, all the little girls, pig-tailed with bright bare faces, in their little, narrow outer-city school, a dream they all shared.

The first two Greatships had arrived planetside already, although it took a long time to receive messages back through the Rift. There were people who'd been born here on Earth living their lives on Zorya right now; breathing her oxygen, having children who had room to play and the whole vast planet to explore. *Having children with room to play.*

And she, against astronomical and insane odds, had smiled, smiled to pay for her kitchen appliances and her new work skirts and her skincare products, and now she was offered passage on *Peace Begins With A Smile*, which everyone said was the most sleek and darkly beautiful Greatship yet.

Passage, for one.

There were things Yu Yan had not bought in the Singles' Day sales. A crib, a pram, bottles or diapers or comforters. Singles' Day was on the eleventh of November because the 1 was meant to represent a person who was alone. She was not a one. She was a two. Or a three?

Secret Child. Impossible Child. Forbidden Child.

JEA

Jea's face contorted, the golden message still shining forefront in her vision. How could you want something so long and so deeply but never even acknowledge it to yourself, and then have it given to you, out of the blue, out of the blue of a sky you might see one day on a planet far away?

If anyone had been with Jea they would have thought her broken and devastated, bent over and wracked as if with pain, tears that she never usually cried streaming down her face.

When Jeanne was a baby she never cried.

"She's so contented, she's so peaceful, you're so lucky," other people told her mother. Jeanne's mother had tried to feel lucky. She didn't mention how when she played peek-a-boo with her baby, or blew raspberries on her fat little stomach, Jeanne just looked at her and blinked. How when Jeanne was older and beginning to walk, she had tripped over her feet and banged into the base of the bed, blackening her small eye and bruising the side of her face in awful purple and yellow, and she had giggled merrily for twenty minutes. It was the first time her mother had heard her laugh.

When Jeanne's sister had been born her mother funneled all of her emotional energy into the child who would smile when she saw her coming. The child she understood.

Jea wiped her face and instructed her phone to call her sister. "Hi," Jeanne's sister Davinia's voice said brightly. "I can't answer your call right now, but please leave a message."

She's got a new job. She's busy. She's just always in the middle of something, thought Jea. She knew her sister bore her no resentment, at least rationally. She knew Davinia understood. She also knew that way down at the beating heart of things that made no difference at all.

XANTHE

"It says it's confidential," she said, her voice trembling, although she didn't know what emotion was making it shake so. Shock probably.

"Who would you tell anyway, kitten?" her brother said. Her dad used to call her kitten.

"I've got friends," she said, resenting the defensive note in her voice. "Online," she added, wishing she had another cushion to throw, although she knew he needled her on purpose.

"But it doesn't matter. It's ludicrous anyway. I can't go. There is no way. I couldn't."

"You don't want to go?" her brother asked innocently. She didn't look at him but she already knew the expression he would be wearing.

"I can't," she said. "I'm not going to go. I can't."

Her brother said something else then, but she wasn't listening to him, because when she'd said she wasn't going to go it had felt like something was dropping away from her, plummeting down, down to the center of the Earth, like her heart, or her future. She'd felt like this the day of the accident. The day she'd lost her family.

"I can't," she said again, softly. She knew now that there was nothing she had ever wanted more than to fly into a sea of stars, and arrive, finally, at Zorya, shining in space. Nothing she had ever wanted more, and it was completely impossible.

CARREN

The HSL train up to her sister's unit was full and Carren had to stand, squashed up against two men in suits and a teenage girl who had her head absently to one side, and AVR glasses on, obviously VRgaming. It was only a forty-five minute trip but Carren realized she couldn't remember the last time she had made it. A year ago? More?

Vikk lived in a densely packed apartment precinct, over-high scrapers shading the narrow streets from the glare of the midday sun but not relieving the rising humidity. Drones moved busily overhead, providing the occasional flash in the periphery as they caught the light of the sun.

Her sister opened the door. "Hi, clone," she said.

Carren thought her sister looked tired. "Hi, transporter accident," she said in response.

"Reflection," her sister said.

"Afterbirth," she countered.

A faint smile drifted over Vikk's face. "Come in," she said.

It had been more than a year, probably. The apartment felt different somehow, more sparse. There had used to be a large print in the entry way, hadn't there? Mountains or something? The off-white wall was bare now.

"I thought you both might be busy on a Saturday," Carren said, as she turned into the small lounge, before the silence of the apartment crept up on her. And there was something about her sister's face that matched the apartment somehow; more silent, more sparse.

"Lusa left me," Vikk said, the words blunt-edged and taking up too much space in the small room.

"Oh. I'm sorry," Carren offered. "You didn't say."

Her sister shrugged, and Carren could read the words behind the gesture. *We don't say a lot these days.*

Carren had liked Lusa. Or maybe liked wasn't the right word. She had envied Vikk the subtle affection and warmth that the two showed in public, the way they pooled their money to buy real coffee for weekends, the way Lusa had looked at Vikk with laughter in her eyes.

Vikk had always been easy with relationships, falling in and out of them with casual grace. Crying tempestuous tears and then being all excited over a new fling only weeks later. It had always been harder for Carren. *I'm just as pretty as you are, why doesn't anyone look at me that way,* she had thought watching the way Lusa had looked at her sister. It had been around five years ago that her sister had started seeing Lusa, and she had not disappeared quickly, like the others. Lusa had been different. Lusa had stuck.

Carren suddenly realized that she would never see Lusa again either. Not that that was a thing that mattered. Or it shouldn't be a thing that mattered.

"Your hair got long," she said to her sister. It had been cropped close to Vikk's head the last time she'd seen her. Definitely more than a year ago then.

"Yours got short," Vikk said.

Carren ran her hand across the back of her short, shaved under-cut. "Just last week," she said, writhing a little inwardly at how trivial their words were. Lusa was gone. Not a thing that mattered, not to her. Not a thing that was allowed to matter. She hadn't seen her sister in a long time.

"You're looking good," her sister added.

"Thanks," said Carren, a little surprised. "It's all in the DNA."

Carren sat on the little sofa and Vikk brought her coffee. Not real coffee, Carren saw.

"When did Lusa go?" Carren said. She had not meant to ask that.

Her sister shrugged again, which wasn't a gesture Carren had associated with her sister in the past. "Two months ago, almost," she said. Her sister's face was quiet, unruffled, still. Not like the Vikk Carren was used to, her face mobile with one emotion or another. It was like looking into a mirror.

"I'm sorry," Carren said again, and she was this time, truly.

Again, that shrug. "What's been going on in your life then, DNA?"

Carren dropped her gaze and played with the hem of her top. *Confidential.*

Then she looked up into her sister's eyes. Light clear brown, flecking into green. Exactly like her own. Except they weren't really, were they.

The striations of the iris were different, solely individual, and an image with enough resolution could tell them apart. It was Vikk who had told her that, a long time ago. Vikk had always been very interested, when she was younger, in all the things that made twins different. She had arced her path away from Carren's at every opportunity. If Carren liked a thing it seemed like Vikk had always been determined not to like it, to choose something, anything, else. Carren had not wanted to be different. She would not have minded company for the ride.

For the ride. Confidential, it had said. But maybe, after all, this was why she had come.

"Well," she said to her sister, younger than she was by two minutes, "something big."

YU YAN

Robert got the apartment. He was elated with his purchase, and with all his Singles' Day items, and talked nonstop about them, not noticing that Yu Yan was silent by his side, with the occasional flash of a smile when it seemed to be required.

Passage, for one.

But she wasn't really single. And she had her own passenger.

"It will be so good to have our own space. To be alone together," she ventured. It was true. She had been waiting a long time, like Lady White Snake, waiting for their chance.

For the first time all afternoon Robert was quiet.

"It will be lovely, sweetling," he said, eventually. "But I think we should be careful not to ruin our opportunities here. Of course I want you there, often. But if we hold off on declaring ourselves a couple, just another year, or maybe two, we can really build our financial future. We still have to get a VR hub, and a dishwasher, and so many things for the new apartment. Just a couple more Singles' Days and we should be all set up."

Hundreds of years, Lady White Snake had waited. Lifetimes.

Yu Yan smiled at him.

Confidential, the message had said. She wouldn't tell Robert, not just now, not yet. But she had something else to tell him, and perhaps that other thing should not be confidential anymore.

Secret child. Unknown child. Unbidden child.

So she took a quick breath, smiled, and told him.

When Yu Yan had found out about the baby she had smiled—but not quickly, or as a shocked reaction, or for anyone else. Alone in her parents' bathroom she'd just smiled, slow and true. How was it possible that you could want something, so deeply and so much, and not even know it for so long?

". . . I don't think it's a good time for us, not yet," Robert was saying. "We haven't even talked about if that is something we should do." He talked on about how it was wrong to bring new people into the world, with the strain on the planet what it was. Socially irresponsible, he said. Financially crippling. "But we'll make it work, we'll have to, we will," he said, finally. "If that's what you want."

If that is what she wanted. *Child of an overrun world. Crowded child. Lonely child. Shocking child.*

What she'd wanted, she realized, was for him to smile. Perhaps it was unfair, perhaps she should allow him the time to get over the shock and adjust. Perhaps she was socially irresponsible, and the world was full up and could not fit one more child. But she wanted him to smile.

JEA

Jea didn't message her sister to tell her she was coming. She didn't want to give her sister time to make up an excuse or be elsewhere, although she tried not to admit this to herself. She had been messaged the international airline tickets for a flight to Xichang in three days, where she would be given information in person, have a medical, and go through all of the contracts and conditions. *Peace Begins With A Smile* wouldn't be leaving for more than two months after that, but apparently she'd be back again later for a whole suite of induction and orientation. She wanted to see her sister before her first trip though. Before everything changed, officially.

She would go and see her mother too, but maybe afterwards, when everything was set and settled. She would have liked to go and see Antony, but that was all water flowing swiftly under the bridge.

When Antony had left nine months ago it had felt like the end of the world. But if Antony had stayed and things had progressed, she wouldn't have been eligible for Singles' Day, and she wouldn't have used Smile to Pay, and none of this would have happened. Perhaps it had been the end of the world when Antony left. But now there was the beginning of a new one. A green and blue new world called Zorya.

Davinia came to the door after her smart-intercom had announced Jeanne's presence.

"Hi," her sister said cheerily, kissing Jea on the cheek, "this is a surprise, nice to see you." Davinia was always over-bright and very polite whenever Jea saw her. Her sister was becoming quite successful as a financial officer, and her apartment, while small, was furnished and decorated immaculately. There were roses in a vase in the entryway, and for a minute Jea thought they were real, they were so convincing. They'd even been subtly layered with scent.

"Sit down and have a drink, it's been so long," Davinia gushed, tugging Jea forward into her tasteful kitchenette. Her sister wasn't quite as convincing as her roses.

There was a moment that was between them. That would always be between them.

"I'm sorry," Jeanne had tried to say to her sister afterwards, so many years ago now. "You know I don't mean it, you know I can't help it." Her words had been as light as spun candy, floating on the air between them. They had blown away.

When Jeanne was a teenager her sister had come home one evening when she should have still been at a concert. For a second Jeanne had looked blankly at the shivering huddle of her sister, her shirt ripped, one eye swollen almost shut, the other hunted and desolate. As Davinia incoherently told their parents what had happened Jeanne had felt something rising up within her, wet and dark. She clenched a fist in front of her mouth and ran from the room. Her sister and the rest of the family could not help but hear though; as peal after peal of laughter rang out through the hall.

XANTHE

It was a long way down.

High among the buildings, out on the ledge, Xanthe looked down. Dizzyingly far below she could see the street, and the very small dots that were the people. It's not accurate though, she thought. There are only a few people, it should be packed with moving dots, people everywhere, teeming and swarming, filling up all the spaces. Full of people and empty of anything else.

It's peaceful up here. There's no-one up here but me.

"Jump," came a voice, her brother's voice.

Xanthe took another step, till she was right at the very end of the plank.

"It's all about your conscious mind, taking back control," came her brother's calm voice again. "Overriding the base part of your brain, the animal instincts. You can do it."

Down there was where the people were, even if she couldn't see them. And the messages of your body have their own truth.

"Jump," said her brother.

But there were other truths, too.

Xanthe jumped.

Xanthe had always hated crowds of people, even as a young child. But after the accident, after her family had just never arrived, she'd been progressively worse. It wasn't even really accurate to call it an accident. A disaster. A catastrophe. Murder. The maglev field of the SuFaT they'd been traveling in had been sabotaged. Xanthe didn't understand the physics of how this was even possible. The train had been jam-packed, as they always were, full of the afternoon's commuters, among them her family, coming up to see her graduation.

Enochlophobia, is what her brother called it. He knew everything.

She just knew the excessive sweating, the palpitations, the tightness in her chest and the breath that wouldn't come. There were just so many people, every time she took a step outside. People everywhere, swarming like insects. Crushing against her, crushing her, taking all the space, all of the air, taking it all.

And no retreat, no retreat in all the world.

She'd stopped going outside, she'd stopped going anywhere. Even in VR environs where too many avatars gathered, it was just as bad. She played solitary games.

No retreat in all the world. Not in this world, perhaps. But maybe another.

"Tell me more about Zorya," she said to her brother.

CARREN

"Zorya," her sister breathed. All of the animation that had been missing from Vikk's face had flooded back, although many emotions chased each other across her face, and she seemed to be having trouble settling on just one.

Carren remembered Vikk talking nonstop about Zorya when they were young, with excitement, shining eyes, and just a little obsession. Vikk was the one who had told her about the Rift. There it was, there it had always been, within their own solar system, just outside the orbit of Jupiter. Just sitting there, waiting to be discovered, as if someone had put it there, just for them. The Rift was a fold in space, a wrinkle, a worm. And on the other side, just a few months' further travel, was Zorya.

"I wish I was you," Vikk said. Her face was elated, and envious, and saddened all by turns.

I wish I was you.

"That would make the first time," Carren said, although her voice was gentle as she watched her sister's face alive with feeling. Oh, Vikk, she thought. How long has it been?

"What?" said her clone, her transporter accident, her reflection, her other self, her beta version, her sister.

"Do you know," Carren said, "that I always have my eyes closed in photos?"

"DNA I have no idea what you are talking about now," said Vikk, but something was different, something was easing, loosening between them.

"You told me once," Carren said, "that our eyes could tell us apart. I always liked the fact that if I closed my eyes the computers and the algorithms and the facial recognition systems and AI couldn't tell exactly who I was. I liked being ambiguous. I never minded being confused with you."

Vikk grimaced, but her eyes were shining still.

"I never even minded," Carren said, confessing, "when we were really small and Ma used to dress us up alike."

"Arrgh," said Vikk. "You're killing me, you know that."

"I know you always hated it. You hated being a twin."

"I didn't . . ."

"You did, Vikk."

"Maybe I didn't need a twin," her sister said. "But I always needed a sister." Then tears made it look like her eyes were swimming with lights. "Oh, Ren, when you go to Zorya I'll never see you again."

I'll never see you again, Carren thought. Never on this world or any other.

And she hugged her sister, and smiled and cried at the same time.

YU YAN

West Lake was overcrowded but still beautiful. The Autumn trees glowed like they were lit from within. So much history, thought Yu Yan. How many lovers and families and lonely young singles had converged here over all of these hundreds of years. How many were like her, restless, hoping, wondering. How many had secrets, curled up within them. In two days' time she could be on a bullet train to Xichang. *Uncounted child. Stowaway child.*

Robert. He'd said he would raise the child with her, if that was what she wanted. Of course he would, he'd said, of course. *Irresponsible child. Burdensome child.* But something felt broken, something was moving, something was changing.

And as she looked at all the people, crossing the sunken bridge, some of them lingering, walking slowly, some holding hands, looking out to the water, Yu Yan thought she knew what that thing was.

She wasn't waiting anymore.

JEA

Jea's afternoon at her sister's place was perfectly pleasant. Jea reminded herself to tug the corners of her mouth upwards at the appropriate times. Davinia didn't seem to notice anything awry, so it may have worked.

"Mum said you were dating a guy?" Davinia asked at one point.

Antony.

He'd been a heady combination of smart and charming with just the slightest dash of needy, and Jea had fallen for him like she was a rock plummeting in flame towards the Earth. He'd tried to understand. She'd tried to explain.

It's not that I don't care, it's not that I'm not happy. My wiring is screwed up somehow, she'd told him. *I know I only smile when it is inappropriate. I'm not really smiling, not on the inside.* She'd wondered if that was exactly true, even as she said it. The physical act of smiling or laughing brought her a certain exuberance. At some very basic level it felt good.

"Antony? No, that didn't work out," she told her sister. Davinia looked vaguely sympathetic, but not surprised.

The last time Jea had seen Antony he'd been leaving her flat with all his things. Jeanne had watched him through the window, her nails pressing little crescent marks into her hands. *He's gone*, she'd thought. *He's not coming back.* She felt herself fizzing, like she was uncorked champagne about to spill. She'd thrown her head back. *Let me cry for him*, she'd begged mutely. *Let me cry for me. Just once. Let me cry.* Her shoulders had started shaking. She opened her mouth. And she'd laughed, high and loud and long.

"It's been lovely that you dropped in," Davinia said, in what felt like a dismissal. "Don't take so long next time."

So long. But it would be so long, and so long.

"You will never forgive me, will you?" Jea said as she turned to her sister at the door. She grinned fiercely, stifling a rising giggle.

Davinia looked startled. "I don't know what you mean," she said. Then something around her eyes softened, and she reached out to touch Jeanne's arm, just lightly. "Honestly, Jea, there is nothing to forgive."

Jea didn't believe her, but she let Davinia hug her, although only briefly.

"Goodbye," she said.

On the bullet train on the way home she snagged a seat, and sat with her head resting up against the glass of the window, peering past her own reflection to the lights in the darkness, streaking by. She was imagining alien life on Zorya, deep, silent life that moved far beneath her waters, or who knew, perhaps hidden surprising life on land that they'd never encountered before, to take them unawares. If life like that felt such a thing as joy, or sadness, or loss, if they felt such things at all, surely they would show them in an alien way. They would have no tears to cry. How would we even be able to tell, thought Jeanne, how they felt? What was happening within them? And they wouldn't be broken, and they wouldn't be wrong, they would just be different.

And maybe her sister would never forgive her, not right down at the heart of it. But maybe, eventually, she would be able to forgive herself.

XANTHE

"Let's try again," said her brother, as calm and unruffled as ever.

"What I don't understand," said Xanthe, wiping away the sweat that was beading on her forehead and running down her nose, playing for time, trying to distract him, "is that all of the pod-docs talk about how the exactly one thousand people aboard the Greatship are all carefully selected and vetted and chosen so that they will all blend into a perfectly tight-knit group. The AI runs psychoanalytic profiles of them all, right? And it does, what did you say, gaussian blending on the probabilities or something?" She probably had that wrong.

"And?" said her brother, unperturbed.

"And it does all of that, and then, what? It just randomly throws a bunch of seats on the most sought after ship in history, and raffles them off to what, single people who smile nicely while buying pots and pans and VRgames and other inane shopping items?" Her breath was still coming in tight little gasps, and she sat down and put her head down to her knees.

"I have two theories on that," said her brother.

"Of course you do," she mumbled into her knees.

"Firstly," he said, "it's not random. It was always you, no matter what you bought, or when, or which way you smiled to pay for it."

Not random. But they were looking for people to form a cohesive group. And one thing she didn't do, was work well in groups. Just the word *group* was now making her chin tremble.

"Or," said her brother, "you were completely random."

Xanthe felt completely random.

"And the system, no matter how perfect, needs randomness."

Xanthe risked raising her head. Her brother's form was still perched on the sofa, his slender hand folded under his chin.

"Huh?" she said.

"Remember when you asked me about the AI and deep machine learning?"

"I guess."

"I explained to you then about how the system needs some random weight-ings in there, in case it gets stuck in a local minimum. You need to shake the system up a bit. Genetics is the same, life throws all sorts of random muta-tions out there, to see what will work, what will stick."

"So I'm the random mutation in this equation?"

"It's like the sand in the pearl. The grit. I think the AI knows what it's doing."

Xanthe wasn't entirely sure that made her feel better.

"Now stop procrastinating," her brother said firmly. "I believe we're up to a group of ten."

The familiar panic spiked again in Xanthe's chest. "I don't think I can do this," she said faintly.

"That's the same thing you said before," said her brother, made of stone. "You want to go to Zorya."

"Yes," said Xanthe, although she wasn't sure it had been a question. She pined for space the same way she did the ocean. A sea of stars. A planet full of wide open spaces, air and sky.

"To get there you have to go outside your apartment," her brother con-tinued, inexorably. "In two days' time you have to sit on a plane for hours. And you also have to travel for years in a spaceship with a thousand people in it."

"Okay."

"Okay?"

"Okay." She could feel her body seizing with adrenaline, and concentrated on breathing deeply. She was the grit. She would be the grit. She'd better show some. She clicked to expand the sidebars of her glasses and her living room became the interior of a plane's cabin with ten people in it.

CARREN

"You know what is really amazing," said Vikk, wiping her eyes and smil-ing. "My DNA will be in two far-reaching parts of the galaxy. Light years apart. It's almost like getting to go to Zorya myself. You'll be doing it for both of us. We're a pair of entangled particles, you and I, it doesn't matter how far the gap between us."

Carren thought of entangled particles. Her sister had told her about that before, her sister who loved space and physics and astronomy. Her matching twin-particle, at the other side of the galaxy. And she thought of love, love instantaneous and entangled.

"Your DNA will get to be in two vastly separate places in the universe, either way."

Even shiny with tears her sister's eyes looked just like her own. Although they weren't, not really. "What do you mean?" Vikk said.

YU YAN

Yu Yan watched the lights dancing over West Lake. Zorya was meant to be shining and beautiful. But not beautiful like this, wrapped in legends, singing in her heart, known and loved. Zorya had no memory, no history, no stories. Or not any that she knew or could know.

Is this what it was now truly? A choice between the future and the past? If she was changing now, transforming like Lady White Snake, who was she changing for, and what was she turning into?

And the child, her child. Who knew no stories yet either. *Unwritten child. Untold child.*

Last night she had squeezed into their small kitchen area and cut tofu and mushroom while her mother added doubanjiang to hot oil. Her father was much frailer now, and his white head nodded on his chest as he watched the newspod; Yu Yan could see the flashing images of tensions rising with the NoGoZo countries, the glimmering solar mega-farm partially wiped out by a Category 3 storm in the Northern Provinces, the Greatship *Peace Begins With A Smile*, in lower Earth orbit, all prepped and waiting for her crew. Of course she needed to stay. Past and future, here, both together, the stories running and entwining like a river.

"They are still looking for people to travel on that Greatship," she'd said idly to her mother while the smell of chili and fermented broad beans filled the air. "But how could those people just go and leave everything, their families and all of their history behind?"

Yu Yan's mother paused, spatula in hand. "Your father's cough is getting bad," she said. Then she resumed stirring, slowly. "Your great grandmother came here from Qingchenshan," she said. "History is not still. It moves. We take our stories with us. We take all of our past. This new planet, it is like a gift. I pray every day that you will get to go there some day." She kept stirring, and didn't look at Yu Yan. "Every day, I pray."

XANTHE

Xanthe put her pack by the door.

"Are you ready?" said her brother, from the sofa.

"No," she said, completely truthfully, her palms sweating, her breathing rapid and shallow.

"You were out there yesterday," he said. "You were fine. Remember, your conscious brain is in control."

Grit. She was the grit.

"Did I tell you that *Peace Begins With A Smile* is made of self-healing materials, long-chain molecules called ionomers?" her brother asked.

Despite her thudding heart and blurring vision Xanthe found her way to a very small, wobbly smile. "No," she said, "I don't think you did."

"She heals herself, your Greatship," her brother told her.

She heals herself.

"Okay," said Xanthe. "I'm ready." She wasn't, but that was okay too.

She paused though, with her hand at the door. "I wish you could come with me," she said. This, also, was true.

"I wish I could too, kitten."

She took off her AVR glasses and pocketed them, but she didn't turn back around.

"Goodbye," she said to her empty apartment.

YU YAN

The doctor was brusque but her eyes were kind. The little room gleamed with antiseptic white and formality. "Now, have you been experiencing any sickness?" she asked Yu Yan, in the preliminary interview, before she had even started the tests.

"Sickness?" Yu Yan asked. She scrunched further down in the surprisingly plush chair she'd been directed into.

"From the pregnancy."

From the pregnancy. *Secret child. Hidden child. Forbidden child. Impossible child.*

Could it be that her child was not entirely secret after all? And . . . not perhaps entirely forbidden? Maybe not impossible. Maybe not impossible.

"How . . ." she began, her hand going without her conscious control back to her stomach.

"It's the safest place for that baby to be for acceleration, tucked up in there warm and snug," the doctor was saying. "Of course they'll be born in space, before you arrive. Yours won't be the only one, I can guarantee that. There were quite a few young ones onboard the first two Greatships by the time they made it planetside."

Yu Yan was remembering the pop-verts that had been on her phone, clasped to her wrist. There had been verts for pregnancy tests, and bassinets, and formula, even before she had known herself. In fact that was why she had ordered some tests online, using Smile to Pay. Because she'd been feeling odd, and she'd seen the verts, and it had made her wonder. Hadn't she? But how had her phone known, before she did? Had her secret been told as she pressed her thumb to unlock it, by her temperature, her heart rate?

Yu Yan held out her slim inner arm so the doctor could poke her with a needle. *Possible child. Space-faring child. Explorer child. Future child.*

There were fifty Smile to Pay winners, from all around the planet Earth, excluding of course NoGoZo countries, all converging in Xichang, arriving within a three-day period.

The team of seven photographers were on-hand to feed live images to the pod-docs, and the first four people to emerge from processing made an ideal first photo opportunity.

Feng Le led the team, and he was keen to get this first image out there in real-time.

"Just move on in, a little closer," directed Feng Le.

The four of them inched in together. The air was clear. The sun was striking the mountains in the background. It would make a good shot.

"I like your haircut," one of them said to the woman next to her.

"Thanks," said the short-haired one, her face brightening into an easy quick smile, running her hand against the fuzziness at the back of her neck. "It's new."

"Okay, ready?" Feng Le said.

Two of them were ready, and two of them weren't, not really. Two were thinking the exact same thing in this moment but would never realize it. Two of them would start a relationship with each other while onboard the ship that would sustain and last them the rest of their lives.

"One, two, three . . . Smile!"

One of them looked like she was going to burst into tears.

One of them looked like she was wearing the ocean.

One of them radiated happiness, her face lit up like a star.

And one of them closed her eyes.

Daryl Gregory grew up in Chicago but his family comes from East Tennessee, as may be clear from "Nine Last Days on Planet Earth." His most recent novel, *Spoonbenders*, was a Nebula, Locus, and World Fantasy Award finalist for 2018. Other recent work includes the young adult novel *Harrison Squared* and the novella *We Are All Completely Fine*, which won the World Fantasy and Shirley Jackson awards, and was a finalist for the Nebula, Sturgeon, and Locus awards. His novels include *Afterparty*, an NPR and Kirkus best fiction book of the year; *Raising Stony Mayhall*; *The Devil's Alphabet*; and the Crawford-Award-winning *Pandemonium*. Many of his short stories are collected in *Unpossible and Other Stories*.

NINE LAST DAYS ON PLANET EARTH

Daryl Gregory

1975

On the first night of the meteor storm, his mother came to wake him up, but LT was only pretending to sleep. He'd been lying in the dark waiting for the end of the world.

You have to see this, she said. He didn't want to leave the bed but she was an intense woman who could beam energy into him with a look. She took his hand and led him between the stacks of moving boxes, then across the backyard and through the cattle gate to the field, where the view was unimpeded by trees. Meteors, dozens of meteors, scored the sky. She spread a blanket across the tall grass, and they sat back on their elbows.

LT was ten years old, and he'd only seen one falling star in his life. Not even his mother had seen this many at once, she said. Dozens visible at one time, zooming in from the east, striking the atmosphere like matches, white and orange and butane blue. The show went on, hundreds a minute for ten minutes, then twenty. He could hear his father working in the woodshop back by the garage, pushing wood through a whining band saw. Mom made no move to go get him, didn't call for him.

LT asked for the popsicles they'd made yesterday and Mom said something like *what the hell*. He ran to the freezer, lifted out the aluminum ice tray. The metal sucked at his fingertips. He jiggled the lever and freed one of the cubes, grape Kool-Aid on a toothpick, so good. That memory, even decades later, was as clear as the image of the meteors.

He decided to bring the whole tray with him. He paused outside the woodshop, finally pushed open the door. His father leaned over his bench, marking a plank with a pencil. He worked all day at the lumberyard and came home to work with scraps and spares. Always building something for the house, for her, even after it was too late to change her mind.

"Did you see the sky?" LT asked him. "It's like fireworks."

LT didn't have his mother's gift for commanding attention. But his father followed him to the field, put his hands on his hips, tilted his head back. Wouldn't sit on the blanket.

"Meteorites," his father said, and Mom said without looking back, "Meteoroid, in the void."

"What now?"

"Meteoroid in the void. Meteorite, rock hound's delight. Meteor, neither nor."

LT repeated this to himself. *Neither nor. Neither nor.*

"Still looks like Revelations," Dad said.

"No," his mother said. "It's beautiful."

The storm continued. LT didn't remember falling asleep on the blanket, but he remembered jerking awake to a sound. Then it came again, a *crack* like a shot from a .22. Seconds later another clap, louder. He didn't understand what was happening.

The sky had reversed: It was more white than black, pulsing with white fireballs. Not long streaks anymore, chasing west. No, the meteors were coming down at them, down upon their heads.

A meteor struck a nearby hill. A wink of light. LT thought, Now it's a meteorite.

His father yanked him onto his feet. "Get inside."

Then a flash, and the air shook. The sound was so loud, so close. He couldn't see. His mother said, "Oh my!" as if it were nothing more surprising than a deer jumping across the road.

His father yelled, "Run to the fireplace!"

LT blinked spots from his vision. His father pushed him in the small of the back and he ran.

His father had built the fireplace himself, stacking the river rock, mortaring it with hand-stirred buckets of cement. It was six feet wide at the mouth, and the exposed chimney ran up the east wall, to the high timbered ceiling twenty-five feet above. Later, LT wondered if rock and mortar could have withstood a direct hit, but at that moment he had no doubt it would protect him.

The explosions seemed random; far away, then suddenly near, a boom that vibrated through the floorboards. It went on, an inundation, a barrage. His mother exclaimed with every report. His father moved from window to window, frowning and silent. LT wished he wouldn't stand next to the glass.

Eventually, most of the strikes seem to be happening over the line of foothills, rolling west like a thunderstorm. His father insisted that no one sleep away from the lee of the chimney, so his mother assembled a bed for LT out of moving boxes, turning the emergency into a slumber party, an adventure. His father dragged furniture close: the couch for Mom and the recliner for him.

When his mother kissed him goodnight (the second time that night), he whispered, "Will you be here in the morning?"

"I'll wake you," she said. LT could feel his father watching them.

It was the last time they would all sleep in the same room, or the same house.

He opened his eyes, and for a long moment he couldn't figure out why he was on the floor, in the living room. He stared stupidly at the empty bookshelves. His mother's bookshelves.

Panic hit, and he sat up. He called, "Mom?"

Then he took in the piles of moving boxes still in the room, and began to calm down. He hadn't missed her.

In the kitchen his father hunched over the table, staring at the portable black-and-white TV. Two cupboard doors showed empty shelves. The hooks above the stove seemed to gesture for their missing pots.

His father put an arm across LT's shoulders without looking away from the TV.

The news was full of pictures of damaged buildings and forest fires. It was no ordinary meteor storm, and it wasn't over. The onslaught had continued through the night and into the day, moving across the globe. The world spun eastward, and the meteors drummed into the atmosphere steady as a playing card against bicycle spokes. No one knew when it would end. The newsman called the storm "biblical," the first time LT had heard that word outside of church, and warned about radioactivity. He knew *that* word from comic books.

His father turned toward the window, pushed aside the drapes. A truck had pulled off the two-lane into their gravel drive. "Go tell your mother," he said.

LT didn't move. His stomach felt like ice.

"Go. She's in the backyard."

LT walked out into a sky tinged with orange. If there were meteors up there he couldn't see them. The air smelled like smoke.

He called for his mother. Checked the garage, where a pyramid of moving boxes filled the space, all sealed and labeled. Then he realized where she must be, and walked toward the cattle gate.

She stood at the far end of the field. He called again. She turned, beaming, something cupped in her hands. She strode toward him in her ruby cowboy boots, her yellow dress swishing high on her thighs. Then he realized what she carried.

"Mom, no!"

She laughed. "It's okay, my darlin'. It's cooled off."

She held it out to him. A black egg, flecked with silver, etched with spirals.

The meteor storm would go on for five more days and nights. Soon everyone would know the objects weren't like other meteors. They weren't chunks of stony iron ripped from a comet's tail, or fragments of asteroids. They were capsules of woven metal, layered like an onion skin. They'd been bigger when in the void, but their outer shells had ignited and shredded in the atmosphere. The innermost shells remained intact until they slammed into the Earth. Almost all of them cracked on impact. People dug them up, showed them to television crews. Space seeds, they called them. And then the police started going house by house, confiscating them.

But not yet. At this moment, his mother was offering it to him. "Feel it," she said. "It's a miracle."

He couldn't deny her. The shell was surprisingly light. A jagged seam had opened along its top. Inside was darkness.

She said, "What do you think was in there?"

1976

When he was eleven years old, late in the first summer he'd spend in his mother's tiny Chicago apartment, she smuggled home one of the fern men. It was four inches tall, planted in a paper coffee cup. Its torso was a segmented tube, like bamboo, glossy as jade. Its two arm-like stems ended in tiny round leaves, and its head was a mantis-green bulb like an unopened tulip.

"Isn't it illegal?" he asked her. But he knew the answer, and knew his mother. Her reckless instincts worried his young Puritan heart. He'd spent the school year alone in Tennessee with his father and had adopted his military rectitude.

"It'll be our little secret," she said.

Ours and the boyfriend's, LT thought.

"You are crazy, honey," said the boyfriend. He kissed her, hard, and when they finally broke apart she laughed. LT always thought of his mother as beautiful, but he'd been offended to discover that she was beautiful to others. To men. Like this shaggy *dude* who wore turquoise necklaces like a TV Indian and smelled like turpentine and cigarettes and scents he couldn't yet name.

His mother went into a back closet to find a more durable container for the fern man.

"I know what you're thinking," the shaggy man said.

But even LT didn't know what he was thinking.

"We should probably burn the little fucker, right?"

LT was alarmed, then embarrassed. Of course the boyfriend was right. At school, hallway posters showed spiky, ominous plants with the message *Keep an Eye Out!* Any sightings of invasive species were to be reported. The weeklong meteor storm had sprayed black and silver casings across millions of square miles in a broad band that circled the planet, peppering cities and fields and forests and oceans. Soldiers of every government seized what they could find. And when anything sprouted, good citizens called the authorities.

LT looked down at the fern man.

The boyfriend laughed. "Don't worry, I'm not going to kill it. Your mom would kill *me*! Watch this." He touched a finger to one of the fern's arms. It curled away as if stung.

Mom said, "Don't bother it, it'll get tired and stop growing. That's what the man told me." She transferred the sprout to a ceramic pot with much cooing and fussing. "We can't set him in the window," she said. "Somebody might see." LT picked a sunny spot on the coffee table.

"He's so cute," his mother said.

"That's his survival strategy," the boyfriend said. "So cute you won't throw him out."

"Just like you," she said, and laughed.

He didn't laugh with her. His mood could change, quick. A lot of nights Mom and the boyfriend argued after LT had gone to bed—to bed but not to sleep.

"We're all doomed," he said. "When the aliens come for the harvest, that's it for *Homo sapiens*."

This was the popular theory: that aliens had targeted Earth and sent their food stocks ahead of them so there'd be something to eat when they arrived. LT had spent long, hot days in the apartment listening to the boyfriend while Mom was at work, or else following him around the city on vague errands. He didn't have a regular job. He said he was an artist—*with a capital A, kid*—but didn't seem to spend any time painting or anything. He could talk at length about the known invasive species, and why there were so many different ones: the weblike filaments choking the trees in New Orleans, the flame-colored poppies erupting on Mexico City rooftops, the green fins popping up in Florida beach sand like sharks coming ashore. Every shell that struck Earth, and some that hit the surface of the water, cracked and sent millions of seeds into the air or into the oceans. Most of those seeds had not sprouted, or not yet. Of those that had, many of the vines and flowers and unclassifiable blooms soon withered and died. The ones that thrived had been attacked with poison, fire, and machetes. But—but!—there were so many possible sprouts that there was no way to find them all in the millions of acres of wilderness. Even if we managed to find and destroy ninety-nine percent of the invasives, the boyfriend had told LT once, there would be millions and millions of plants growing and reproducing around the globe.

Like the fern man. "We're all going to die," the boyfriend said, "because of this little green dude."

And LT thought, How can something so beautiful, so *cool*, be dangerous?

"Let's give him a name," Mom said. "LT, you do the honors."

"I need to think about it," he said.

Or maybe, LT thought that night as his mother and the boyfriend whisper-yelled at each other, I should change my own name. Chicago was making him into a different person. He'd become conscious of his Tennessee accent, and had taken steps to tame his vowels. He'd eaten Greek food. He'd almost gotten used to being around so many black people. And he'd started staying up to all hours in his room, an L-shaped nook off the kitchen with a curtain for a door, reading from his mother's collection of Reader's Digest Condensed Books as the rattling fan chased sweat from his ribs. The night they got the fern man he wondered if he should ask everyone to stop calling him LT and start calling him Lawrence or Taylor or something completely of his own creation, like . . . Lance. Lance was the kind of guy who'd be ready when the UFOs came down.

Doors slammed, his mother sobbed loudly for a while, and then the apartment went quiet. LT waited another twenty minutes, and then got up to pee. He didn't turn on the bathroom light. He was a night creature now, as light-sensitive as a raccoon.

The door to his mother's bedroom was ajar. She was alone in the bed.

He went into the living room. On the wall behind the couch hung four of the boyfriend's pictures. They were all of naked women turning into buildings, or maybe vice versa, with red-brick thighs and doorways for crotches and scaffolds holding up their torsos. One of the nudes, pale and thin and sprouting television aerials from her frizzy hair, looked too much like his mother. LT wondered if other people thought they were beautiful, or if beauty mattered in art with a capital A. The figures didn't seem to be very convincing as women *or* buildings. *Neither nor.*

The fern man stood in the dark on the coffee table. Its bulb head drooped sleepily, and its stem arms hung at its sides. The torso leaned slightly—toward the window, LT realized.

He picked up the ceramic pot and set it on the sill, in a pool of streetlight. Slowly, the trunk began to straighten. Over the next few minutes, the head gradually lifted like a deacon finishing a prayer, and the round leaves at the ends of its arms unfurled like loosening fists. The movement was almost too incremental to detect; its posture seemed to shift only when he looked away or lost concentration.

Slow Mo, he thought. That's what we'll call you.

Tomorrow his mother would throw all the paintings out the front window, send them sailing into the street. LT would never see the boyfriend again. The fern man stayed.

1978

The night they heard about the thistle cloud, LT was daydreaming of burning the house down. It was March and he was bored to the point of paralysis, an old man in a thirteen-year-old body. Country winters stretched each night into a prison sentence. The valley went cave dark before suppertime, stayed dark until the morning school bus honked for him at the end of the lane. He longed for the city. Torching the place, he figured, would make a bonfire that would light up the road all the way to Chicago.

The place was wrong for his father, too. Three years after Mom had left, the house was purposeless without her in it, like a desanctified church. His father's handiwork—the tongue and groove hardwood floors, the hand-turned legs on the kitchen table, the graceful stair rail that curled at the end like the tail of a treble clef—seemed as frivolous as gingerbread. Why stay here? They never used the dining room, or the guest room with its fancy bathroom. No one would ever thread a needle in the sewing room. LT and his father ate their meals in the living room, in front of the fire, wordless as Neanderthals.

LT was grateful when the TV said that a new invasive species had erupted in Tennessee. Dad was in his armchair as usual, eyes on the snowy screen of the portable, which he'd set on a chair close to the fireplace, as if daring it to melt.

"Would you look at that," Dad said.

LT did not look. He was sprawled on the couch, pretending to reread a book he hoped would annoy his father: *Sexual Selection in the Animal World*. There was an entire chapter on the bowerbirds of Papua New Guinea, whose males assembled and decorated elaborate bowers in hopes a female would prefer their art over the competitors'.

The third bachelor in the room was Mo. He was a sturdy three feet tall by then, and occupied the corner by the dark window. He was attracted to the fire. At night his limbs eased toward it, wanting the light if not the heat.

Mom couldn't keep the fern. She'd moved in with a new, temperamental boyfriend, a restaurant owner who named a pasta dish after her the first week they dated, but flew into fits when he felt disrespected. Both Mo and LT had been causes of "friction" that summer, so LT begged to take the fern back to Tennessee in the fall. Mo had traveled in the back seat of his mom's car like a passenger, bulbous head bent against the roof, a seat belt around his pot. LT hadn't asked his father's permission, and was surprised when he let it into his house without a fight. Dad was more upset by his son's shaggy hair and the turquoise necklace around his neck. The day before school started, Dad drove him to the barber and ordered a buzzcut to match Dad's own. LT kept the necklace under his shirt.

"It's getting worse and worse," his dad said. "Lord almighty."

Now LT did look at the TV. *Lord almighty* was as close to swearing as his father got.

The sky over Chattanooga was crowded with spiky black shapes. A reporter asked a question, and a man held out a bloody arm.

"So much for dominion over the earth," LT said. At the midweek prayer meeting—they went to services three times a week, twice on Sunday and once on Wednesday night—the pastor had launched into well-worn passages of God giving dominion of the earth to Adam. It came up whenever the invasives or women's rights were in the news.

"Don't be smart," Dad said.

"Face it, we're *losing*." Every day the TV showed men in masks hacking down flowers as big as satellite dishes, or Argentinians fretting over alien moss that clung to the hooves of cattle like boots, or Kansas farmers dulling their chainsaws on traveling vines as tough as mahogany. In a lot of places the invasives were just a nuisance, but in some countries, especially the ones closest to the equator, the alien plants were causing real trouble. "They're trying a million different strategies. All they need are a couple winners to drive us out."

"What are you talking about?"

"Out-survive us. They've got time on their side. We go at animal speed, but plants move at their own speed. Wheels within wheels." An Elijah reference, just to poke him. "It's *evolution,* Dad."

Another provocation. His father believed in the Bible. There was no time for natural selection in the six days of creation, and no need for it. Dad's God didn't improvise. He was a measure-twice-cut-once creator.

"They're better at surviving?" his father said. "These *plants?*"

LT shook his head as if disappointed in his father's stupidity.

Dad slowly rose from his chair. LT realized he'd miscalculated. "Let's see, then," Dad said calmly. He gripped the sides of the ceramic pot, lifted it. It had to weigh almost two hundred pounds. Mo's limbs curled inward.

LT yelled, "No! Stop it!"

His father turned the pot on its side. Dirt spilled onto the floorboards. He stepped toward the fire and pushed the top of the plant into the mouth of the fireplace.

LT threw himself into his father's ribs. Stupid, useless. Dad was as squat and thick as an engine block. He turned, swinging Mo's head out of the fireplace. It wasn't on fire, but a haze of sizzling mist seemed to shroud the bulb.

LT burst into tears.

His father set the pot on the floor, anger gone now. "Aw, come on."

LT ran upstairs, threw himself on the bed, awash with embarrassment and anger. He was thirteen! He should be tougher than this. Crying over a damn plant. He wanted it all to end. How much longer did he have to wait for the aliens to come and scrape this planet clean?

The Chattanooga cloud was supposed to reach them that next afternoon. Vernon Beck, Dad's oldest friend, drove over from Maryville to see it. Jumped out of his pickup and shook LT's hand. "Goodness sakes, boy, you're two feet taller! Hale, come say hello to LT and Mr. Meyers."

A boy eased out of the passenger side of the pickup, long and lean, hair down to his shoulders. LT hadn't seen Hale Beck since LT's mother left. Their families used to go places together, and even though Hale was two years older than LT they got along like brothers. He remembered a long day riding water slides with Hale at a Pigeon Forge park. A hike in the Smokies during which Hale smashed a rock into a snake, the bravest thing LT had ever seen.

Hale shook hands with LT's father, nodded at LT. Hale had gotten the growth spurt LT was still waiting on.

A strong wind was blowing but the cloud hadn't shown up yet. The men went into the woodshop, and LT stood there awkwardly with Hale, unsure how to talk to him.

Hale took out a tin of Skoal from his back pocket, tucked a pinch of tobacco into his lip. He held out the tin, and LT shook his head. Hale leaned back on the hood of the truck. Spit black juice onto the gravel.

LT said, "We've got a fern man."

"A what?"

"One of the invasives. Right in the house." Dad said never to talk about the fern. But this was the Becks.

Hale said, "The one that moves?" He wanted to see that.

Dad had returned Mo to his usual spot. There was no visible damage from the flames. Hale said, "Looks like a regular plant."

"Watch this," LT said. He stood between Mo and the window and raised his arms. The fern man slowly shifted to the right, back into the light. LT moved in front of him again and Mo moved opposite. "It's called heliotropism. Like sunflowers? But way faster."

"Can I do it?" Hale asked.

"Sure. Just don't tire him out."

Hale took LT's position. They danced in slow motion at first, and then Hale sped up. Mo jerked and flopped in rhythm. Hale laughed. "He's just like one of those windsock guys at the dealership!"

LT was thrilled that Hale was impressed, but nervous about hurting Mo. "Hey, you want to see where the space seed landed?"

He managed to entice Hale to the cattle field. The wind had picked up, turned cold, but the sun was bright and hot. Hale's hair blew across his face, and he kept pushing it back.

They walked around at the far end of the field. LT couldn't find the furrow the seed had made when it hit four years ago. The tall dry grass rattled with every gust.

Hale said, "Look."

In the distance, a dark, churning cloud. Light flashed at the edges of it like tiny lightning. Hale ran toward it, into the wind. They plunged through a line of trees, into the next field—and suddenly the cloud loomed over them. Thousands of glistening tumbleweeds, most the size of a fist, a few big as soccer balls. A sudden downdraft sent scores of them plummeting into the trees. Most stuck in the treetops, others bounced down into the undergrowth, and half a dozen ricocheted back into the air and spun toward them.

"Grab one!" Hale shouted. He pulled his T-shirt over his head in one quick move. His back was pale and muscled. LT felt a sudden heat and looked away, his heart pounding. Then Hale swung the shirt over his head, trying to snag a thistle ball. It floated just out of reach. He chased it, then jumped, jumped again. LT couldn't take his eyes off the way his shoulders moved.

Then a lucky gust sent the ball down and the shirt caught against it. Hale hooted and LT cheered. The thing was hollow, a jumble of flat, silvery blades, thin as the wings of a balsa-wood glider, connected to each other by spongy joints which were decorated with thorns. Hale pulled his shirt free of them, and the cloth tore.

Then the sun dimmed, and they looked up. LT realized they'd only seen the front of the cloud, the first wave. Thousands and thousands more flew toward them, a spinning mass.

LT said, "Ho-lee shit."

This struck Hale as hilarious, and then LT was laughing too, so hard he could barely stand. Then they ran, giggling and shouting.

1981

For months before his summer stay, when he was sixteen years old, LT begged his mother to take him to see the dragon tails of Kansas. Mom worked slow magic on her new husband, Arnaud, a thin, balding, control freak who made a lot of money as a chemical engineer. Eventually Arnaud came up with the idea that he should encourage LT's interest in science and take them all to visit the most successful invasives in the Midwest. He rented an enormous RV and they drove southwest.

The first sign of the invasion came just past Topeka, when road crews waved them off the interstate. Arnaud eased the RV into the parking lot of a McDonald's and said, "There you go."

LT walked out of the RV, into sunlight and heat. At the edge of the lot rose an arch of deeply grooved bark. It emerged from the broken cement and came down about fifteen yards away in a field. Large purple leaf blades ran in single file atop the bark like the plates of a stegosaurus.

LT looked back at his mother. She beamed at him, then shooed him forward. He grabbed hold of the sturdy roots of the blades and pulled himself onto the base of the arch. A few careful steps more and he was upright, hands out for balance. The bark was a bit wider than his foot, but uneven. He knew from his books that the tail was not an ordinary trunk, but vines that had twisted around each other as they grew, only gradually adhering to share resources.

He reached the peak of the arch, eight feet off the ground. Twenty or thirty yards away, directly in front of him, another arch emerged, and another, like a sea monster coursing through an ocean of grass. No, one monster in a school of them. To either side, dozens and dozens of the dragon tails breached and dove. A group of them had burst up through the highway, and there was nothing manmade cement could do to keep them underground.

These were the aliens' favorite trees, he thought. How could they not be? They were living architecture.

His mother called his name. She held the fancy, big-lensed camera Arnaud had bought her. She didn't have to prompt LT to smile.

The last night of the vacation, Arnaud drove to a campground set among the dragon tails, a farmer's feeble attempt to recoup something from the land after agricultural disaster. As they ate dinner at the RV's tiny table, LT showed his mother pictures from one of his books about the invasives. He told her how the dark fans held chlorophyll-like molecules that absorbed a larger spectrum of light than the Earth versions. "If our plants tried to process that much energy they'd burn up, like a car engine trying to run on rocket fuel."

"It's a bit more complicated than that," Arnaud said. He stood at the galley sink, washing the skillet he'd used to fry the hamburgers. "The photosystems they're using seem to be variable, sometimes like retinol in archaea microbes, sometimes more like chlorophyll with novel sidechains added, so that they can control—"

"Take a look at this," LT said, cutting him off. He showed her a cross section of the dragon tail, and how the vines were twisted around each other. "They call them golden spirals. See, there's this thing called the Fibonacci sequence—"

"Dragon tails follow the golden spiral?" Arnaud said. He came over to the table. LT was pleased to know something the chemist didn't.

Mom said, "What's a Fibonacci?" and LT quickly answered. "It's a series of numbers, starting with one, two, three, five . . . each one's the sum of the previous two numbers, so—"

"That's a close approximation of the golden ratio," Arnaud said. He pulled the book closer, leaned over LT's mother. "The growth factor of the curve follows that ratio. You can see the spiral in nature—in seashells, pine cones, everywhere."

"So beautiful," his mother said. She ran fingers over the glossy cross section. "Like the head of a sunflower."

LT, suddenly furious, pushed himself out from behind the table. His mother said, "Where you going?"

Arnaud said, "Could you put away your plate?"

He let the door bang shut behind him.

Outside, the atmosphere was greenhouse humid. He marched away, not caring which direction his body took him. It was nine thirty and still not full dark, as if the sun couldn't find the edge of these tabletop plains. The air was heavy with a floral perfume.

He came to the leaping back of a dragon trail, black against the purpling sky, and walked beside it. Gnats puffed out of the grass and he waved them away.

It had been a mistake to come on this trip. The RV was as stifling as a submarine. Arnaud sucked up all available oxygen, inserted himself into every conversation.

Eventually the dark came down, and he aimed for the fluorescent lights of the cinder-block building that doubled as park office and convenience store. Inside, a couple kids about his age, a boy and a girl, were glued to the Space Invaders cabinet. Were they brother and sister? Boyfriend and girlfriend? He thought about talking to them. He could tell them things. Like how the speed of the game was an accident; the aliens came down slow at first, then got faster and faster as their numbers were destroyed, not because it had been programmed that way, but because the processor could only speed up when the load lightened. *Telling things* was the only way he knew how to make small talk. Other forms of conversation were a mystery.

He bought a Coke and took it outside. Leaned against the wall under the snapping bug zapper.

A flashlight bobbed toward him out of the dark. He ignored it until a voice behind the light said, "Hello, my darlin'."

His mother stepped up, clicked off the flashlight. "Did you see the stars? They're amazing out here."

"Still no meteors," he said. Six years after the seed storm, everybody was waiting for a second punch. Or maybe the next wave was on its way now, in the void, creeping across the light-years. Perhaps the long delay was necessary because of orbital mechanics. What looked like design could be just an accident of the environment.

He offered her a sip of his Coke. She waved it off. "You ought to give him a chance. He's just enthusiastic about things. Like you are."

He wanted to ask her why the hell she kept attaching herself to assholes. The self-involved painter, the rage-aholic restaurant owner, and now the chemist, whom she'd had the audacity to marry. Did she love him, or just his McMansion and its granite countertops?

"He wants to send you to college," she said. "He thinks you'd be a good scientist."

"Really?" Then he was embarrassed that the compliment meant something to him. "I'm not taking his money."

"You should think about it. Your dad can't afford college. And you deserve better than working in a lumberyard."

"There's nothing wrong with the lumberyard." LT worked there three days a week during the school year, sometimes alongside his father. He'd told her he hated it, but hadn't mentioned the things he loved about it. His herky-jerky forklift. The terrifying Ekstrom Carlson rip saw. The sawdust and sweat.

But did he want to be there the rest of his life?

From inside the store, the boy shouted in mock dismay and the girl laughed. They'd lost their last laser cannon.

"You should study the invasives," his mother said. "I remember that look on your face when I showed you that seed. And the fern man! You loved that little guy."

"I still have him. Dad keeps him in the living room. He's not so little."

"So," she said. "Think about it."

He thought, If the aliens haven't landed by then.

1986

"Where are the space bees?"

"What?"

"SPACE BEES!" LT shouted above the music. "WHERE ARE THEY?"

He was drunk, and Jeff and Wendy too, and their new friend Doran, all of them drunk together. What else could they be, on this final weekend before Christmas break, and where else but at the Whitehorse, which as far as he was concerned was the only bar in Normal, Illinois.

"Jesus Christ," Jeff said. "Not the bees again."

LT put his hand on the back of Doran's neck—a sweaty neck, and his hand tacky with beer but he didn't care, he wanted to pull Doran close. "I need to tell you things," he said into his ear, and Doran laughed, and then—

—and then they were in a restaurant booth, the lights bright, Jeff and Wendy across from him and Doran—tall, sturdy Doran—beside him. LT leaned into his arm woozily. God he was handsome, naturally handsome, almost hiding it. How did they get here? He concentrated, but his memory of the past two hours was a hopscotch, dancing drinking shouting singing and then the rude bright lights of last call and a flash of ice and cold—did

Wendy drive, she must have—to *here,* the 24-hour Steak and Shake, their traditional sober-up station.

He said to Doran, "It's the flowers that make no sense."

Jeff said, "The flowers have no scents?" and Wendy said, "It's that they have scents that makes no sense." They both laughed.

A beat too late LT realized there was wordplay at work. He forged on. "The blooms of flowers are *lures.*" The word thick on his tongue. "Scent and shape and color, they all evolved to attract specific pollinators, the bees and butterflies and beetles."

"Oh my," Jeff said.

"And you told me he was shy," Doran said.

"He can get wound up," Wendy said. "When he feels comfortable."

"Or tipsy," Jeff said.

LT felt tipsy *and* comfortable. Why hadn't Jeff and Wendy introduced him to Doran before now? Why wait until the last weekend of the last semester LT would be on campus? It was criminal.

"A pretty flower isn't just a simple announcement, like 'Here's pollen.'" LT said. "Simple won't do it." He tried to explain how flowers were in competition. Pollen was everywhere, nestled inside thousands of equally needy plants desperate to spread their genetic material. What was needed was not an announcement but a flashing neon sign. "The flower's goal," LT said, "is to figure out what *hummingbirds* think are beautiful."

"Slow down, Hillbilly," Wendy said. "Eat something."

"Hummingbirds have an aesthetic sense?" Doran said.

"Of course they do! Have I told you about bowerbirds?"

Jeff said, "Guess what his honors thesis is on?"

And then he was off, yammering about the bowerbirds of Papua New Guinea. The males of the species constructed elaborate twiggy structures, not nests but bachelor pads, designed purely to woo females. The Vogelkop Bowerbird set out careful arrangements of colors—blue, green, yellow—each one a particular hue. It didn't matter what the objects were; they could be stones, or petals, or plastic bottle caps even, as long as they were the correct shade. The females could not be coerced into sex; they dropped by the bowers, perused the handiwork, and flew away if they found them substandard. Their choice of mates, their taste in *art,* drove the males over millennia to evolve more and more specific displays, an ongoing gallery show with intercourse as the prize.

"Wait," Doran said. "That doesn't mean they're making an artistic choice. Aren't they just, uh, instinctually responding to whoever seems like the fittest mate? It's not beauty *per se*—"

"I love *per se*," Jeff said. "Great word."

"I've always been fond of *ergo*," Wendy said.

"But it is aesthetics!" LT said. "Beauty's just"—he made explosion fingers—"joy in the brain, right? A flood of chemicals and, and, and—" What was the word? "Fireworks. Neuronal fireworks. We don't *logic* our way to beauty, it hits us like a fucking hammer."

"Ipso facto," Jeff said.

Doran put his arm around LT's shoulder and said, "Eat your burger before it gets cold, then tell me about the space bees." Ah! He remembered! The heat of Doran's arm across his neck made his cheeks flush. Doran smelled of sweat and Mennen Speed Stick and something else, something LT could almost recall from far back in his brain, from a hot afternoon in a Chicago apartment . . . but the memory slipped the net.

He decided to eat. Wendy told the story of her favorite snowmobile accident. Doran, who'd grown up in New Mexico, couldn't believe that Wisconsin teenagers were allowed to ride machines across frozen lakes.

LT began to feel a little more sober, though perhaps that was an illusion. "Space bees," he said.

"I'm ready," Doran said. "Lay it on me."

"Every one of the invasives we've found, not a single one uses pollination. There's a lot of budding and spores and wind dispersal and"—he waved a clutch of fries—"you know. I've got a fern man at home, it's like ten feet tall now—"

"You do?"

But LT didn't want to talk about home. "Doesn't matter, it just grows and spreads, spilling out of its pot, but it doesn't require animal assistance." Actually, he wasn't sure that was true. Didn't the fern survive because of him, because of his family? It had played on their human tendency for anthropomorphism.

"Where'd you go, Hillbilly?" Wendy asked.

"Sorry, what did you say?" he asked Doran.

"I said, maybe all the pollinating species died."

"Maybe! But why colorful flowers and no pollen? There weren't any animals hatching from the space seeds, so—"

Doran's eyes went wide. "They have to be designed, then."

"Exactly!"

Wendy nabbed his glass before it tumbled over.

"Inside voices," she said.

He gets it, LT thought. The aliens could know what Earth's sunlight was like from very far away, even guess the composition of its atmosphere and soil, but they couldn't know what animals would be here, much less humans. So they had to design plants that could propagate without them.

"But if they're designed, why are they so, so *overwrought?*" LT asked. "Those huge fucking umbrellas out west, the sponges smothering South America, all of them crazy-colorful and smelly and weird. So my real question is—"

"Where are the space bees?" Jeff supplied.

"Wrong!" LT said. The real question was the one he was born to answer. He'd get whatever degrees and training he needed, he'd go into the field for evidence, he'd write the books to explain it. He'd explain it to Doran.

"The question is, why all this needless beauty? What's it all for?"

"I don't know, but *you're* beautiful," Doran said, and then—

—and then morning, a thumping that wasn't in his head. Or not all in his head.

LT sat up, and pain spiked in his skull. Light blasted through half-open blinds. And there, beside him, Doran. Mouth agape, rough-jawed, one arm across LT's waist.

Still there. Still real.

He wanted to fall back into the bed, pull that arm across his chest. Then the knocking came again, and he realized who was at the front door.

"Fuck." He slipped out from under Doran's arm without waking him, pulled on shorts. Alcohol sloshed in his bloodstream. He closed the bedroom door behind him. The pounding resumed.

LT pulled open the front door. His father started to speak, then saw what shape his son was in. Shook his head, suddenly angry. No, angri*er*.

"I overslept," LT said.

"Are you packed?"

LT turned to look at the living room, and his father pushed past him.

"Dad! *Dad.* Could you just *wait?*"

His father surveyed the moving boxes, only a few of them taped up. The rest were open, half-filled. LT's plan had been to wake up early and finish packing. Everything had to go. Next semester he'd finish his coursework in the mountains of western New Guinea, collecting data on how birds had adapted to invasives. And now all he wanted to do was stay here, in central Illinois, in this apartment.

"Wait for what?" his father asked. "For *you?*"

LT moved between his father and the bedroom. "Give me an hour. Go for lunch or something. There's a diner—"

"I'll start taking down what's packed. There's snow coming."

"No. Please. Just . . . give me some time."

His father looked at the bedroom door. Then at his son. His jaw tightened, and LT stopped himself from edging backward.

He'd lived his boyhood afraid of his father's anger. Power, he'd learned, came not from *blowing off steam*, but demonstrating that you were barely containing it. You won by exacting dread, by making your loved ones wait through the silence so long that they yearned for the explosion.

"In an hour I drive away," his father said.

1994

LT didn't relax until they stepped off the plane in Columbus. Doran kept trying to calm him down, to no effect. The entire trip he'd been imagining that some authority would command the pilot to turn around, send them back to Indonesia. A priest would tell them, Stupid Americans, gays aren't allowed to be parents, and they would yank the infant out of his hands.

Then he emerged from the boarding tunnel holding the baby, saw his mother, and they both burst into tears.

He eased his daughter into his mother's arms. "Mom, this is Christina. Christina, this is—what is it, again?" Teasing her.

"Mimi!" She pressed her face close to the tiny girl and whispered, "I'm your Mimi!"

A tanned, smiling man with a tidy black goatee offered his hand. "Congratulations, LT. You've made your mother very, very happy." This was Marcus, Mom's brand-new husband, five years younger than her, at least. His mother at forty-six was still lithe and alarmingly sexy. LT hadn't met Husband 3.0 before, didn't know Mom was bringing him. He felt a flash of annoyance that he had to deal with this intruder at this moment—but then told himself to let it go. The day was too big for small emotions.

Doran, holding two duffel bags, one in each arm, said, "We made it."

LT kissed him, hard. In New Guinea they hadn't dared engage in PDA. "Eighteen years to go."

Christina nestled like a peanut in the high-tech shell of the car seat. As Marcus drove them home, LT and Doran talked about how dicey the whole process had been. The orphanage, situated about thirty miles from Jayapura, was overcrowded, with hundreds of children left there by the crisis. The facility was nominally run by nuns, but most of the staff were local women who seemed little better off than their charges. LT and Doran had been practicing their Indonesian, especially the phrases involving gift-giving.

"We had to bribe everybody, top to bottom," Doran said. "If it wasn't for LT's friend at the university yelling at them they'd have taken the shirts off our backs."

"It's not their fault," LT said. "Their agriculture is wrecked. The economy's crashing. They're starving."

"Maybe they should stop chewing those sugar sticks."

"What now?" his mother asked.

He told her how the locals seemed almost addicted to an invasive plant that tasted sweet, but could not be digested. Gut bacteria couldn't break down those strange peptides and so passed it along through the colon like a package that couldn't be opened.

Doran said, "It would be great for my diet."

A joke, but what Doran had seen there had scared him, and even LT, who'd spent months on the island doing fieldwork for his PhD, had been shaken by the rapid decline in the country. Thousands of alien species had been growing in the forests for two decades, ignored and unchecked, and suddenly some tipping point had been reached and those alien plants had reached the cities. The latest was a thread-thin vine that exploded into a red web on contact with flat surfaces. Villages and towns were engulfed by scarlet gauze. In the orphanage, nurses scraped it from the walls, but that only made it worse, dispersing its spores. He and Doran were terrified it was in Christina's lungs. Invasives might be indigestible, but so was asbestos. In the morning she'd have her first doctor's appointment. Her papers all said she was healthy, without birth defects, and up-to-date on her vaccinations, but they weren't about to trust an orphanage under duress.

Once they reached the apartment, LT still couldn't bear to put down his daughter. While Doran mixed formula and made beds and ordered takeout, LT fed his daughter, changed her, and then let her fall asleep on his chest.

His mother sat beside him on the couch. "You're going to have to let Doran do more parenting."

"He can fight me for her."

"Big talk for the first night. Wait till sleep deprivation hits."

Christina's eyes were not quite closed, her lips parted. Mom had to know that he'd strong-armed Doran into adoption. His last trip to New Guinea, LT had been haunted by the abandoned children. Doran had said, This is crazy, we're not even thirty, and LT said, My parents were teenagers when they had me, and Doran said, You're making my case.

But that argument was over forever the moment Doran met Christina.

"You used to look just like that," his mother said. "Milk-drunk."

She was four weeks old, living through the days of extreme fractions. In another month, she'd have been their daughter for half her life. In a year, she would have been an orphan for only a twelfth of it. And yet those four weeks would never disappear. There would always be some shrinking percentage of her life that she'd lived alone, a blot like a tiny spore. He'd read alarming articles about adopted children who'd failed to "attach." What if the psychic damage was already done? What if she never felt all the love they were bombarding her with?

His mother called Marcus over. "Sweetie, show them what you brought."

Marcus opened a wooden box lined with cut paper and lifted out a teardrop-shaped dollop of glass, about eight inches long and six inches wide at the base, purple and red and glinting with gold.

"A crystal for Christina," he said.

"That is *amazing*," Doran said. "You made this?"

"Marcus is an award-winning glassblower," his mother said. She tilted her head. "He made me these earrings."

Of course, LT thought. His mother had always loved bowerbirds.

The gift was very pretty, and pretty useless, too heavy for a Christmas ornament, and not a shape that could sit upright on a shelf. They'd have to hang it, but not above her bed.

"Which ear is she supposed to wear it in?" LT asked.

Marcus laughed. "Either one. She'll have to grow into it."

When the food arrived, LT needed to eat, and he was forced to surrender Christina to Doran. His body moved automatically as he held her, a kind of sway and jiggle that soothed her. Where did he learn that?

Mom said, "Did you call your father?"

And like that, the spell was broken. LT said, "What do you think?"

"I think you should."

"Fuck him."

"Hey," Doran said.

"Right. I gotta stop swearing. Eff that guy."

"Your mom's right. We should give him a chance."

"He's had six years of chances. Any time he wants to call, I'll pick up." There were a few years, after college, when they talked on the phone and his father would pretend that LT lived alone. He never asked about Doran, or about their lives. Then LT sent his father an invitation to the commitment ceremony. The next time LT called, his father said that he was disgusted, and didn't want to talk to him until he fixed his life.

His mother said, "This is different. Maybe it's time."

Maybe. He got up from the table.

Time itself had become different. He looked at Christina in Doran's arms and thought, I'm going to know you for the rest of my life. The future had broken open, his week-by-week life suddenly stretching to decades. He could picture her on her first day of school, on prom night, at her wedding. He caught a glimpse of her holding a baby as tiny as she was at that moment.

Had his father felt that way, too, when he was born?

He kissed Doran's cheek, then bent over their daughter. She was awake, dark-eyed, watching both of them. He thought, There's no way I can go away for six months into the jungle and leave her. He wouldn't make the choice his parents had made.

"We'll give it a shot," LT said. He moved his cheek across her warm head. Inhaled her scent. "Won't we, my darlin'?"

2007

He was reading to Christina and Carlos when the call came. Or rather, Christina was reading while LT held the book, because Christina said he was only allowed to do the Hagrid and Dumbledore voices. Carlos, five years old, lolled at the end of the bed, seemingly oblivious but missing nothing.

Doran came to the bedroom holding the cordless. "Some guy wants to talk to you. He says he's a friend of your father's."

The thick Tennessee accent opened a door to his childhood. Vernon Beck, hearty as ever. He apologized for bothering LT "up there in D.C.," but he was worried about LT's father. "He stopped coming to work. He didn't quit, just stopped coming. Same with church. He won't answer the phone at all."

"Is he sick? Did he get hurt at the yard?"

"I went over there, and he finally came out to the porch. He said he was fine, just wanted folks to leave him alone. But I don't know. It ain't like him."

They talked a few minutes more. Mr. Beck apologized again for bothering him, explained how he got his number from a cousin. LT reassured him that it was all right. Asked about his son, Hale, who turned out to be doing fine, still in Maryville, working maintenance for the hospital. Had a wife and four children, all boys.

LT thought about that day they ran from the thistles. Funny how you don't know the last day you'll see someone. He'd spent the rest of that winter when he was thirteen daydreaming about Hale, his first big crush. He didn't mention that to Mr. Beck, and Mr. Beck didn't ask about LT's husband, or children. Southern Silence.

"One more thing," Mr. Beck said. "Your dad, he's let things go. You should be ready for that."

Doran asked, "What happened to your father?"

"Maybe nothing. But I think I have to go lay eyes on him."

Christina said, "I want to lay eyes on him!"

"Me too, kiddo," Doran said. "But not like this."

"Can we *read* now?" Carlos asked.

Doran didn't want LT to travel south. All those famine refugees landing in Florida, and the citizen militias in Texas and New Mexico. LT said his Department of Agriculture credentials would get them through any check-point, and besides, Tennessee was nowhere near the trouble. "It's like going into Wisconsin," LT said, quoting one of their favorite movies. "In and out."

"Fine," Doran said, "but why not just call the local police, let them check it out?" But LT didn't want to embarrass Dad, or get him fined if he wasn't taking care of the house.

"I owe him this much," LT said. And Doran said, "You think so?"

Doran stayed home with Carlos, and LT and Christina left before sunrise the next morning with a cooler full of food so they wouldn't have to depend on roadside restaurants. Christina fell asleep immediately, slept through all the phone calls he made to the Department, and woke up outside of Roanoke. He put away the phone and they listened to music and he pointed out inva-sives and native plants alongside the interstate. They were driving through the battlefield of a slow-motion war. Old native species were finding novel ways to fight the aliens—sucking resources from them underground, literally throw-ing shade above—and new invasives kept popping up into ecological niches. "It's all happening so incrementally," he told her, "it's hard to see."

"Like global warming," Christina said. He'd let her read the opening chapter of the book he was working on, and had taken her to see the Al Gore movie, so she understood boiling frogs. This had been his job for the past decade at the Department of Agriculture: explainer-in-chief, interpreter of policy, sometimes influencer of it. He missed the fieldwork, and longed to do original research again, but the government desk job provided stability for his family.

"Remember what I told you about animal speed?" he said. "Plant speed, and *planet* speed, that's just a hard timescale for us mammals to keep our attention on."

"I know. Wheels within wheels."

"Exactly."

After a day of driving and a two-hour wait for inspection at the Tennessee border, they entered the foothills. His hands knew the turns. He remem-bered the long drive home that last day of college—and realized for the first time that his father must have had to leave the hills at one in the morning to get to Illinois State by noon, and then had turned around and driven all the way back the same day. Drove it in silence, with a hungover, secretly heart-broken boy sulking in the passenger seat.

They pulled into the long gravel drive and parked beside the house. Christina said, "You used to live *here?*"

"Be nice. Your grandfather built this house."

"No, it's cool! It looks like a fairy castle."

His childhood home was being overrun in the same slow, grasping process that had swallowed Christina's village. The backyard grass, ordinary and native, had grown knee high. But covering the wall of the house was a flat-leafed ivy, brilliant and slick-looking as the heart of a kiwi fruit; definitely an invasive. Was this war, or détente?

Ivy also covered the back door. He tore away a clear space, and knocked. Knocked again. Called out, "Dad! It's LT!"

He tried the door, and it swung open. "Wait here," he said to Christina. He didn't want her to see anything horrible.

The kitchen lights were off. There were dishes in the sink, a pair of pots on the stove.

He called for his father again. His toe snagged on something. A vine, snaking across the floor. No, many vines.

He stepped into the living room—and froze. Ivy covered everything. A carpet of green clung to the walls. The fireplace burst with green foliage, and the tall stone altar of the chimney had become a trellis. Vines curled through doorways, snaked along the stair rails. Greenish sunlight filtering through the leaf-covered windows made the room into an aquarium. The air was jungle thick and smelled of fruiting bodies.

He stepped closer toward the fireplace, spied dots of white and red nestled into the leaves. Was the ivy *blooming?*

"What are you doing here?"

LT startled. The voice had come from behind him.

"Dad?"

His father sat in his armchair, nestled into the vines. Leaves draped his shoulders like a shawl. He wore a once-white UT Vols sweatshirt that seemed too big for him. His hair was shaggy, a steel gray that matched the stubble on his face. He looked too thin, much older than he should. LT felt as if he'd been catapulted through time. He hadn't seen or spoken to this man for almost twenty years, and now he wasn't even the same person.

His father said, "Who's this?"

LT thought, *Oh God, not Alzheimer's,* and then realized that Christina had come into the room.

She was looking up at the walls, the high ceiling, slowly turning to take it all in. "Dad . . ." Her voice was strange.

"It's okay, honey, there's nothing to be—"

"This is *awesome.*"

She lifted her hands to her head as if to contain the shock. A sound like applause erupted around the room. The leaves were shaking.

She looked at the corner, then up. "Dad, do you see it?"

He could, a green shape against the green. Enmeshed in leaves, an oak-thick stalk rose up in the corner. At the top, a bulbous head a yard wide was bent against a cross-timber, so that it seemed to be looking down at them. Its right arm stretched across the room, where broad leaves splayed against the wall as if holding it up. Its other arm hung down. Finger leaves brushed the floor.

"Holy fucking—"

"*Dad,*" Christina chided. She walked toward the plant. Lifted her hands above her head. The leaves of its arms rattled like a hundred castanets.

She laughed, and bent at the waist. Slow Mo's huge head eased left, then right.

LT's father said, "Isn't he a lovely boy?"

Geological time, plant time, animal time . . . and inside that, yet another, smaller wheel, spinning fast. His father's body had become a container for cells that lived and replicated and mutated at frightening speed.

On the second morning at Blount Memorial Hospital, Christina sat at the edge of her grandfather's bed, curled her fingers around his (carefully not disturbing the IV tubes taped to the top of his hand), and said, "I read a pamphlet about colon cancer. Would you like me to tell you about it?"

His father laughed. "Are you going to be a scientist like your father?" He was remarkably cheery, now that equipment had rehydrated him and delivered a few choice opioids.

She shook her head. "I want to be a real doctor."

LT, listening to on-hold music on his cell, said, "Hey!"

Doran came back on the line. "Okay, I got him an appointment with Lynn's oncologist. Bring him here. I'll move Carlos into Christina's room."

"Are you sure about this?"

"I would only do this for my favorite person. Besides, I don't think anybody else is stepping up. You're an only child, right?"

"Uh, kind of." He'd have to explain later.

He gave Christina a five and told her to sneak some ice cream into the room. "He likes rocky road, but chocolate will do."

His father watched her go. "She reminds me of your mother."

LT thought, Sure, this tiny, dark-haired, brown-skinned girl is *so* much like your blonde, dancer-legged wife.

"I mean it," his father said. "When she looks at me—it was like that with Belinda. That light."

"Dad—"

"All the boys in that school, and she chose me."

"Dad, I need to tell you some things."

"I'm not leaving the house."

"You can't go back there. I had Mr. Beck check it out. There are roots running through the floorboards, wrapped around the pipes. The wiring's been shorted out. You're lucky the place didn't burn down."

"It's my house. You can't tell me—"

"No, it's Mo's house now. It's been his for years."

2028

On that last Thanksgiving he hosted in the Virginia house, the topic of conversation was, appropriately enough, food.

"We haven't published yet, but the data's solid," Christina said. "We've got an eater."

Cheers went up around the table. "Were you using the cyanobacteria?" LT asked. Just a few months ago, her gene-hacking team at McGill was making zero progress. "Or one of the Rhodophyta?"

"Let the woman speak!" LT's mother said. Christina, sitting beside her, squeezed her arm and said, "Thanks, Mimi."

"She needs no encouragement," Christina's husband said, and Carlos laughed.

"Here's the amazing thing—we didn't engineer it. We found the bacteria in the wild. Evolving on its own."

"You're kidding me," LT said.

Christina shrugged. "It turns out we should have been paying more attention to the oceans."

LT tried not to hear this as a rebuke. As the USDA's deputy secretary, he orchestrated the research grants, helped set the agenda for managing the ongoing crisis. It was a political job more than a scientific one, and much of the time the money had to go into putting out fires. So even though everyone knew that most of the seeds had gone down in water, the difficulty in retrieving them meant that almost all the research on water-based invasives focused on ones near the surface: the white pods like bloated worms floating in Lake

Superior, the fibrous beach balls bobbing in the Indian Ocean, the blue fans that attached themselves to Japanese tuna like superhero capes.

Christina said that the bacteria were found feeding on rainbow mats. The scientific community had missed the explosion of translucent invasives hovering in the ocean's photic zone, until they linked and rose to the surface in a coruscating, multi-colored mass. The satellite pictures of it were lovely and terrifying. The alien plants were so efficient at sucking up carbon dioxide, in a few decades of unrestricted growth they could put a serious dent in global warming—while maybe killing everything else in the ocean.

But somehow, fast-evolving Earth organisms were trying to eat them first. Or at least, one species of them. But if one Earth organism had figured it out, maybe others had, too.

"You have to tell us how they're breaking down those peptides," LT said.

"Or not," Carlos said.

"I have a story," said Bella, Christina's four-year-old daughter. "During craft time, this girl Neva? It was a *disaster*."

"Wait your turn, darling," Aaron said. Christina's husband was a white man from Portland. He ran cool to Christina's hot, which was good for Bella.

Through some quasi-Lamarckian process, LT's children, and his children's children, had inherited his most annoying conversational tendency. On Thanksgiving they didn't go around the table saying what they were thankful for, but rather took turns explaining things to each other. Nothing made LT happier. All he wanted in the world was this: to be surrounded by his family, talking and talking. Much of the world was in dire shape, but they were rich enough to afford the traditional dry turkey breast, the cranberry sauce with the ridges from the can, sweet potato casserole piled with a layer of marshmallow.

"You know what this means," Christina said. She caught LT's eye. "Next year we'll be eating sugar sticks like the aliens did."

Perhaps only LT understood what she meant. Homo sapiens are only ten percent human; most of the DNA in their bodies comes from the tiny flora that they carry inside themselves to digest their food and perform a million tiny tasks that keep them alive. If humans could someday adopt these new bacteria into their microbiome, a host of invasives could become edible. It would be the end of the famine.

She saw the wonder in his face, and laughed. "Wheels within wheels, Dad."

After dinner, the urge to nap descended like a cloud, and only little Bella was immune. Carlos offered to take her to the park, but LT said he would like that honor.

"Where the slides are?" she asked.

"All the slides," he said. "Just let me tuck in Mimi."

He led his mother to the master bedroom, which was on the ground floor and had the best mattress. She moved carefully, as if hearing faint music in the distance, but at eighty she was still sharp, still beautiful, still determined to stay up with fashion. Her hair was three different shades of red.

"Eighty-five outside," she said, "and in here it's a Chicago winter."

"I'll get an afghan," he said, and opened the closet. When he turned around, she was sitting on the edge of the bed, one hand out on the coverlet.

"You must miss Doran."

The knot that he carried in his chest tightened a fraction. He nodded.

"It's not fair," she said. "All our men dying so young."

"Arnaud's still alive," LT said. "At least he was last year. He sent me a Christmas card."

"Good God, what an asshole," she said. "It's true what they say, then."

"I was the teenage asshole. I don't know how anybody put up with me."

She lay down and folded her hands across her chest like Cleopatra. He spread the afghan so that it covered her feet.

"This is a lovely house," she said.

"It's too big for me now. Unless you move in."

"I prefer living on my own these days. I do my painting in the nude, you know."

"You do not."

"But I *could*. That's the point."

Bella was waiting for him by the front door. "Papa!"

"Ciao, Bella!"

She jumped into his arms. It was a pleasure to be someone's favorite person again, at least for the moment. "Ready for the slides?"

He wished she didn't live so far away. He wished he wasn't so busy. People were making noises about nominating him for secretary, but he could say no, get off the treadmill. He could move to Canada and be close to Christina and Aaron and Bella, finally finish the book. Make one more research trip. He'd like to visit New Guinea again, see how the land of his daughter was faring. Fifty-three years after the meteor storm, and there were still so many questions to answer, and so many new things to see.

He carried Bella out into the Virginia heat. Soon he'd have to put her down, but he wanted to carry her as long as he could, as long as she let him. "So," he said to her. "What's all this about a disaster at craft time?"

2062

The house was full of strangers. They kept touching his shoulder, leaning down into his face, wishing him happy birthday. Ninety-seven was a ridiculous age to celebrate. Not even a round number. They thought he wouldn't make it to ninety-eight, much less a hundred. They'd probably been waiting for years for him to kick off, and this premature wake was the admission of their surrender.

A tiny gray-haired woman sat beside him. Christina. "You have to see this," she said. She held a glass case, and suspended inside it was a glossy black shape flecked with silver. "It's from the current Secretary of Agriculture. 'For forty-five years of service to the nation and the world.' This one came from Tennessee. You remember telling me about Mimi finding a seed?"

There was an ocean of days he couldn't remember, but that day he recalled clearly. "Rock hound's delight," he said softly.

"What's that, Dad?"

Ah. The strangers were watching, waiting for a proper response. He cleared his throat, and said loudly, "So have those alien bastards shown up yet?"

Everyone laughed.

The afternoon stretched on interminably. Cake, singing, talking, so much talking. He asked for his jacket and a familiar-looking stranger brought it to him, helped him out of his chair. "I have to tell you, sir, your books made me want to be a scientist. *The Distant Gardener* was the first—"

LT lifted a hand. "Which way is the backyard?" He could still walk on his own. He was proud of that.

Outside, the sky was bright, the air too warm. He didn't need his coat, after all. He stood in a garden, surrounded by towering trees. But whose garden, whose house? It wasn't his home in Virginia, that was long gone. Not Chicago or Columbus. Was this Tennessee?

Everything moves too fast, he thought, or else barely moves at all.

"Papa?"

A young woman, holding the hand of a little girl. The girl, just three or four years old, held a huge black flower whose petals were edged with scarlet.

"Ciao, Bella!" he said to the girl.

The woman said, "No, Papa, this is Annie. I'm Bella."

A stab of embarrassment. And wonder. Bella was so old. How had that happened? How had he gotten so far from home? He wanted to do it all over again. He wanted Doran's shoulder next to him, and tiny Christina in his arms. He wanted Carlos on his shoulders at the National Zoo. All of it, all of it again.

"It's okay, Papa," Bella said. His tears concerned her. What a small, common thing to worry about.

He inclined his head toward the little girl. "My apologies, Annie. How are you doing this afternoon? Did you fly all the way from California?"

She let go of her mother's hand and approached him. "I have a flower."

"Yes, you do."

"It's a pretty flower."

"It certainly is."

Bella said, "She likes to tell people things."

The girl offered the flower to him. Up close, the black petals seemed to ripple and shift. Their dark surfaces swirled with traceries of silver that caught the light and spun it prettily. He raised it to his nose and made a show of sniffing it. The little girl laughed.

Words were not required. Sometimes the only way you could tell someone you loved them was to show them something beautiful. Sometimes, he thought, you have to send it from very far away.

"Where did you find this lovely flower?" he asked.

She pointed past his shoulder. He could feel the tower of green behind him. The leaves were about to move.

NOTE: The mnemonic for meteoroids, meteors, and meteorites was written by Andy Duncan and is used with his permission.

Lavie Tidhar is the author of the Jerwood Fiction Uncovered Prize-winning and Premio Roma nominee *A Man Lies Dreaming* (2014), the World Fantasy Award-winning *Osama* (2011) and of the Campbell Award-winning and Locus and Clarke Award-nominated *Central Station* (2016). His latest novels are *Unholy Land* (2018) and *Candy* (2018), also his first children's novel. He is the author of many other novels, novellas, and short stories.

THE BURIED GIANT

Lavie Tidhar

When I was five or six years old, my best friend was Mowgai Khan, who was Aislinn Khan's youngest. He was a spidery little thing, "full of nettles and brambles," as old Grandma Mosh always said. His eyes shone like blackberries in late summer. When he was very small, the Khans undertook the long, hard journey to Tyr, along the blasted planes, and in that settlement Mowgai was equipped with a composite endoskeleton, which allowed him to walk, in however curious a fashion. On the long summer days, which seemed never to end, Mowgai and I would roam freely over the Land, collecting wild berries by the stream or picking pine nuts from the fallen cones in the forest, and we would debate for hours the merits or otherwise of Elder Simeon's intricate clockwork automatons, and we would try to catch fish in the stream, but we never did catch anything.

It was a long, hot summer: the skies were a clear and uninterrupted lavender blue, with only smudges of white cloud on the horizon like streaks of paint, and when the big yellow sun hung high in the sky we would seek shelter deep in the forest, where the breeze stirred the pine needles sluggishly and where we could sit with our backs to the trunks of old mottled pines, between the roots, eating whatever lunch we had scavenged at home in the morning on our way. Eating dark bread and hard cheese and winter kimchee, we felt we knew all the whole world, and had all the time in it, too: it is a feeling that fades and can never return once lost, and all the more precious for that. For dessert we ate slices of watermelon picked only an hour or so earlier from the ground.

The warm juice ran down our chins and onto our hands and we spat out the small black pips on the ground, where they stared up at us like hard eyes.

And we would story.

Mowgai was fascinated by machines. I, less so. Perhaps it was that he was part machine himself, and thus felt an affinity to the old world that I did not then share. My mother, too, was like that, going off for days and months on her journeys to the fallow places, to scavenge and salvage. But for her I think it was a practical matter, as it is for salvagers. She felt no nostalgia for the past, and often regarded the ancients' fallen monuments as monstrous follies, vast junk-yards of which precious little was of any use. It was my father who was the more romantic of the two, who told me stories of the past, who sometimes dreamed, I think, of other, different times. Salvagers are often hard and durable, like the materials they repurpose and reuse. Mowgai's dream was to become a salvager like my mother, to follow the caravans to the sunken cities in the sea or to the blasted plains. His journey to Tyr had changed him in some profound fashion, and he would talk for hours of what he saw there, and on the way.

Usually after our lunch we would head on out of the trees, toward the misshapen hills that lay to the northwest of us. These hills were shaped in an odd way, with steep rises and falls and angular lines, and Elder Simeon made his home at their base.

When he saw us approach that day he came out of his house and wiped his hands on his leather apron and smiled out of his tanned and lined face. They said he had clockwork for a heart, and he and Mowgai often spoke of mechanical beings and schematics in which I had little interest. His pets, too, came out, tiny clockwork automata of geese and ducks, a tawny peacock, a stealthy prowling cat, a caterpillar and a turtle.

"Come, come!" he said. "Little Mai and Mowgai!" And he led us to his courtyard and set to brewing tea. Elder Simeon was very old, and had trav-eled widely as a young man all about the Land, for a restless spirit had taken hold of him then. But now he valued solitude, and stillness, and he seldom came out of his home, and but for us, received few visitors.

He served us tea, with little slices of lemon from the tree in his yard, and then we sat down together to story, which is what we do in the Land.

"You have gone to Tyr," he said to Mowgai, and his eyes twinkled with amusement. "Have you ever seen, on your way through the blasted plains, a town, standing peacefully in the middle of nowhere?"

Mowgai stirred, surprised, and said that no, he hadn't, and he did not think anything still lived in the blasted plains.

"Life finds a way," Elder Simeon said. "There is life there of all sorts, snakes and scorpions and lizards, sage and marigolds and cacti. But the town . . . well, they say there is a town, Mowgai, little Mai. I had heard of it in Tyr, where they say it sits there still, out on the plains, as perfect and as orderly as it had always been. No one goes near it, and no one comes out . . ."

It is just an old men's tale, I think, and you know how they love to embellish and gossip.

But this is the story. It is told in a curious sort of way. It is told in the plural, by a mysterious "we," but who these "we" are, or were, no one now remembers. Perhaps "they" are still in the town, but though many claim to have seen it, its location always seems to change like a mirage in the telling.

"Once," began Elder Simeon, "there was a little boy . . ."

Once there was a little boy who lived in a house with two kindly parents and a cheerful little dog, and they all loved him very much. The dog's name was Rex, and all dogs in their town, which was a very lovely and orderly town indeed, were called that. Mother was tall and graceful and never slept at all, and Father was strong and patient and sang very beautifully. Their house too was very lovely and very clean. The boy's name was Oli, which was carefully chosen by algorithm from a vast dictionary of old baby names.

The town was called the Town. It was a carefully built town of white picket fences and single-story houses and wide avenues and big open parks with many trees. The boy would go for a walk in the park with his parents every day, and he could always hear the humming of many insects and see beautiful butterflies flittering among the trees.

Really it was quite an idyllic childhood in many ways.

It had to be, of course.

It was very carefully designed.

You can probably see where this is going.

The shape of stories is difficult for us. We understand them as patterns, what you'd call a formula. We tell the story of Oli's childhood in a way designed to be optimal, yet there are always deviations, margins of error that can creep in.

For instance, there was the matter of the purple caterpillar.

The purple caterpillar was very beautiful, Oli thought. It was a long, thin insect with many prolegs, brightly colored in purple with bright yellow spots. It crawled on the thin green leaf of a flowering helleborine, and it did that, back and forth, back and forth, every day on Oli's passing through the park. When Oli was not in the park, of course, the caterpillar stopped moving. Oli became quite unreasonably—we felt—fascinated by the caterpillar, and every day on his journey through the park he would stop for long minutes to examine the little creature, despite his father calling him to come along to the swings, or his mother asking him to hold her hand so he could hop over the pond.

But Oli would just squat there and stare at the caterpillar, as it moved back and forth, back and forth across the leaf.

Why did the caterpillar crawl back and forth, back and forth across the leaf? Oli wondered. His parents, who were not used to children, were a little taken aback to discover that *why* was one of Oli's favorite words. *Why* did the clouds make shapes in the sky? *Why* did Rex never bark? *Why* was water wet? *Why* did Oli sometimes wake up in the middle of the night, uneasy, and tried and tried to listen to the night sounds of the Town all around him, only there were none?

Some of these questions we could answer, of course—clouds made shapes because the human mind has been programmed by long evolution to make patterns, for instance: just like stories. Water is "wet" in its liquid form, but the word only describes the *experience* of water, not its properties; the town was quiet, and Rex never barked, because Oli was meant to be asleep at that time.

The caterpillar crawled like that every day under Oli's gaze, but children, as we found, are almost unreasonably inquisitive, and therefore one day Oli simply grabbed the little creature by its body and lifted it off the leaf.

The caterpillar struggled feebly between Oli's thumb and forefinger.

"Don't touch that!" Mother said sharply, but Oli didn't really pay her much mind. He stared at the caterpillar, fascinated. The creature emitted a high-pitched shriek of alarm. Oli, who like all children could also be cruel, pressed harder on the caterpillar's thin membranous body. The creature began to hiss and smoke, its antennae moving frantically as it tried to escape. Oli pressed harder and the caterpillar's membrane burst.

"Ow!" said Oli, and threw the caterpillar on the ground. The creature had got very hot just before its demise, and left a small burn mark on the epidermis of Oli's thumb and forefinger. Mother cried out, horrified at this damage, but Oli stuck his fingers in his mouth and sucked them, still staring at the caterpillar.

Thin wires protruded from the caterpillar's broken body, and faint traces of blue electricity could still be seen traversing the wires before they, too, faded. Oli reached down, more carefully this time, and prodded the body with the tip of his finger. It had already cooled, so he picked it up again and studied it. He had never seen the inside of a living creature before.

That evening Oli had many more questions, and we were not sure how to answer them yet and so we did what grown-ups always do, and didn't. This was perhaps a mistake, but we were unsure how to proceed. The next morning the caterpillar was back on its leaf like it had always been, crawling up and down, up and down, but Oli studiously ignored it, and we were relieved.

For the next few days Oli was his usual self. Rex often accompanied him on his walks through the park, fetching sticks of wood that Oli threw, and watching patiently as Oli sat on the swing while Father pushed him, up and down, up and down, but never too fast or too high as to pose danger to the child. Oli thought about the sensation he felt when he'd burned his finger. It was pain, something all parents are eager to prevent their children from experiencing, though we are not sure we quite understand it, as it is merely a warning system for the body, or that's what we always thought.

There were other children in the playground in the park, who Oli saw every day. They dutifully swung on the swings (but one was always free for Oli) and slid down the slides, and climbed on the wood posts and rocked up and down, up and down on the seesaws. They were always very fond of Oli but he found their company boring, because all they ever said were things like, "I love mommy!" and "Let's play!" and "This is fun!"

They all had dogs named Rex.

And so Oli, while we thought he had forgotten the caterpillar, had in fact been hatching a plan. And so one day when he was playing with one of the other children, who was called Michael, on the tree house, Oli pushed him, and Michael fell. He fell very gracefully, but nevertheless he fell, and he scraped his knee very badly, and Oli saw how the oily blood briefly came out of the wound before the tiny mites inside Michael's body crawled out to repair the damage done. And also Michael never cried, because we had not thought crying a good thing to teach the other children to do, the children who were not Oli. And then Oli did something very brave and foolish, and he fell down himself, on purpose, and he hurt himself. And he looked down and saw blood, and he began to cry.

Well, Mother and Father were dreadfully upset, and they fussed over Oli, and for a few days he was not allowed to go outside because of his wound, and all he did was sit in his room, and listen to the silence of the town, because no one was out when Oli was not, and he became afraid of the silence, and of how empty the world felt all around him, and when Mother or Father came to talk to him or hold him, he pushed them away.

"Are you my real parents?" he asked them, and they did not know what to say. Only Rex kept him company in that time.

What we mean to say is, Oli knew he was different, but he didn't quite know how. He knew everyone else was, in a way, better than him. We didn't feel pain and we didn't cry and we were always kind and patient, when he could be hasty and cruel. We weren't sure how to feel things, apart from a great sense of obligation to the child, for him to have the very best life and to be happy. He was very important to us. It was also at that time that Oli saw his parents in the bedroom. He peeked in through a door open just a fraction and saw Father standing motionless by the window, in the moonlight, unnaturally still because he had shut off; and he saw Mother with her chest cavity open, and the intricate machinery glowing and crawling inside, as she performed a minor repair on herself.

This was when he decided to run away to become a real boy.

Of course, you see the problem there.

Oli stole out in the middle of the night, with only Rex for company. He walked through eerily quiet streets, where nothing stirred and nothing moved. It was our fault. We should have operated the town continuously, let people walk around outside and dogs bark and owls hoot, but it just seemed like a waste of energy when the town was first conceived: when Oli himself, of course, was conceived.

Also we are not sure what the hooting of owls sounds like, or what the creatures themselves resembled. A lot of the old records were lost.

The moon was up that night. It had been broken long before, and it hung crooked in the sky, a giant lump of misshapen rock with the scars of old battles on its pockmarked face. It bathed the world in silver light. Oli's footsteps echoed alone as he walked through the town. We should have been more vigilant, of course, but we did not have much experience in the raising of children. Mother and Father were in their room, having put Oli to sleep and kissed him good night. They thought him long asleep, and now stood motionless in their bedroom, caught like statues in the moonlight. The moonlight shone down on the park and its insects, on the storage sheds where we kept the dummy children who played with Oli, on the too-big houses where no one lived, on the dogs who were asleep in their yards, frozen until such a time as they might be needed again.

We didn't think Oli would really leave.

We waited for him on the edge of the town. He was a very determined boy. He saw us standing there. We looked just like Mrs. Baker, the friendly neighbor who worked in the grocery shop, whom Oli had known since birth.

"Hello, Mrs. Baker," he said.

"Hello, Oli," we said.

"I'm leaving," he said.

"Why?" we said.

"I'm not like everyone else," he said. "I'm different."

Gently, we said, "We know."

We loved him very much at that moment. There was a 56.998 percent chance of Oli dying if he left the town, and we didn't want that at all.

"I want to be a real boy," he said.

"You are a real boy," we said.

"I want to be like Mother, and Father, and Michael, and you, Mrs. Baker."

At that moment I think we realized that this was the point in the story of childhood where they learn something painful, something true.

"We can't always get what we want," we told him. "The world isn't like that, Oli. It isn't like the town. It is still rough and unpredictable and dangerous. We can't be you. We don't even truly understand what it is to be you. All we have are approximations."

He nodded, seriously. He was a serious boy. He said, "I'm still going, but I'll come back. Will you please tell Mother and Father that I love them?"

"We love you, too," we told him. We think maybe he understood, then. But we can never truly know. All we have are simulations.

"Come on, boy," Oli said.

Rex whined, looking up at his master; but he couldn't go beyond the boundary of the town.

"We're sorry," we said.

Oli knelt by his dog and stroked his fur. There was water in the boy's eyes, a combination of oils and mucins and hormones such as prolactin. But he wiped away his tears.

"Good-bye, Rex," he said. The dog whined. Oli nodded, seriously, and turned away.

This was how Oli left us, alone, on his quest to become a real boy: with the town silent behind him, with the broken moon shining softly overhead, with us watching him leave. There is an old poem left from before, from long before, about the child walking away . . . about the parent letting them go.

We think we were sad, but we really don't know.

We waved, but he never turned back and saw us.

"This is a very strange story, Elder Simeon," I said.

"Yes," he said. "It is very old, from when the world was different."

"Were there really thinking machines in those days?" Mowgai asked, and Elder Simeon shrugged.

"*We* are thinking machines," he said.

"But what happened to the boy?" I said. "What happened to Oli?"

"They tell no stories of his journey in Tyr," Elder Simeon said. "Nor in Suf or in the floating islands. But old Grandma Toffle tells the tale . . ." But here he fell silent, and his mechanical duck waddled up to him and tucked its head under Elder Simeon's arm, and its golden feathers shone in the late afternoon sun. "It's just a story," Elder Simeon said reluctantly.

We left him then, and wended our way back across the fields and over the brook to the houses. That night, after the sun had set and the lanterns were lit over our homes, I felt very grateful that I was not like that strange boy, Oli, and that I lived in a real place, that I lived on the Land itself and not in something that only mimicked it. But I felt sad for him, too: and Mowgai and I sought out old Grandma Toffle, who sat by the fire, warming her hands, for all that it was summer, and we asked her to tell us the story of the boy.

"Who told you that nonsense?" she said. "It wasn't old Simeon, was it?"

We admitted, somewhat sheepishly, that it was, and she snorted. "The old fool. There is nothing wrong with machines in their rightful place, but to fill your heads with such fancy! Listen. There was never such a city, and if there was, it has long since rotted to the ground. Old Simeon may speak of self-repairing mechanisms and whatnot, but the truth is that decay always sets in. Nothing lasts forever, children. The ancients built cities bigger than the sky, and weapons that could kill the Earth and almost did, at that. But do you see their airplanes flying through the sky? Their cities lie in ruins. The old roads are abandoned. Life continues as it always did. The mistake we'd always made was to think ourselves the most important species. But the planet doesn't care if humans live or die upon it. It is just as important to be human as it is to be an ant, or a stinging nettle."

"But . . . but we can *think*," said Mowgai.

Old Grandma Toffle snorted again. "Think!" she said. "And where did that ever get you?"

"But we can tell stories," I said quietly.

"Yes . . ." she said. "Yes. That we can. Very well. What was your question again?"

"Do you know what happened to the boy, Oli, when he left the town?"

"Know? No, I can't say as that I *know*, little Mai."

"Then . . ."

Her eyes twinkled in the light of the fire, much as Elder Simeon's did in the sun. When she smiled, there were dimples on her cheeks, making her appear momentarily younger. She said, "Sit down, children. Sit down, and let me tell you. The boy wandered for a long time . . ."

The boy wandered for a long time away from the town. He missed his parents, and his dog, and everyone. The world beyond the town was very different from everything he'd ever known. It was a rough place at that time, which was not that long after the great floods and the collapse of the old world, and many of the springs were poisoned, and the animals hostile and deadly, and flocks of wild drones flew against darkening skies, and unexploded ordnance lay all about and some of it was . . .

Not exactly *smart*, but . . .

Cunning.

He went for a long time without food or water, and he'd grown weak when he met the Fox and the Cat. They were not exactly a fox and a cat. One was a sort of mobile infiltration unit, designed for stealth, and the other was a stubby little tank. They were exactly the sort of unsuitable companions the Town had worried about when it let the boy go.

"Hello, young sir!" said the Cat.

"Who . . . who is it?" said the Fox. "Who dares . . . walk the paths of the dead?"

"My name's Oli," said Oli. He looked at them with curiosity, for he had never seen such machines before.

"I have never met an Oli," said the Cat.

"I have never tasted an Oli," said the Fox, somewhat wistfully.

"Please," said Oli, "I am very hungry and very tired. Do you know where I could find shelter?"

The Fox and the Cat communicated silently with each other, for they, too, were very hungry, though their sustenance was of another kind.

"We know . . . a place," said the Fox.

"Not very far," said the Cat.

"Not . . . not far at all," said the Fox.

"We could show it to you," said the Cat.

"Show it to . . . you," said the Fox.

"Shut up!" said the Cat.

"Shut . . . oh," said the Fox.

"A place of many miracles," said the Fox, with finality.

And Oli, though he couldn't be said to have trusted these two strange machines, agreed.

They traveled for a long time through that lost landscape, and the waste-land around them was slowly transformed as the sun rose and set and rose again. Soon they came to the outskirts of a vast city, of a kind Oli had never seen and that only salvagers now see. It was one of the old cities, and as it was still not that long after the fall of the cities, much of it still remained. They passed roads choked with transportation pods like weeds growing through the cracks, and vast grand temples where once every manner of thing had been for sale. Broken houses littered the sides of the streets and towers lay on their sides, and the little tank that was the Cat rolled over the debris while the Fox snuck around it, and all the while Oli struggled to keep up.

The city was very quiet, though things lived in it, as the Fox and the Cat well knew. Predatory things, dangerous things, and they looked upon Oli with hatred in their seeing apparatus, for they hated all living things. Yet these were small, rodentlike constructions, the remnants of a vanished age, who loved and hated their fallen masters in equal measure, and mourned them when they thought no one was looking their way. And they were scared of the Fox and of the Cat, who were battle hardened, and so the unlikely trio passed through that city unharmed.

At last they came to a large forest, and went amid the trees.

"Not far now," said the Cat.

"To the place of . . . of miracles," said the Fox.

"What is this place?" asked Oli.

The Fox and the Cat communicated silently.

"It is a place where no machines can go," the Cat said at last; and it sounded wistful and full of resentment at once. "Where trees grow from the ground and water flows in the rivers and springs. Where the ground is fertile and the sun shines on the organic life-forms and gives them sustenance. Plants! Flowers! People . . . useless, ugly things!"

But the Fox said, "I . . . like flowers," and it sounded wistful only, with no hate. And the Cat glared at it but said nothing. And so they traveled on, deep into the forest, where the manshonyagger lived.

"What's a manshonyagger?" said Mowgai, and as he spoke the word, I held myself close and felt cold despite the fire in the hearth. And old Grandma Toffle said, "The man hunters, which roamed the earth in those days after the storms and the wars, and hunted the remnants of humanity. They were sad machines, I think now, driven crazy with grief for the world, and blinded by their programming. They were not evil, so much as they were made that way. In that forest lived such a manshonyagger, and the Fox and the Cat were taking the unwitting Oli to see it, for it had ruled in that land for a very long time, and was powerful among all the machines, and they knew they could get their heart's desire from it, if only they could give it what it wanted, which was a human."

"But what did the Fox and the Cat *want*?" asked Mowgai.

Old Grandma Toffle shrugged. "That," she said, "nobody knows for sure."

Stories, I find, are like that. Things don't turn out the way they're supposed to, people's motivations aren't clear, machines exceed their programming. Odd bits are missing. I often find myself thinking about the Fox and the Cat, these days, with the nights lengthening. Were they bad, or did we just misunderstand them? They had no regard for Oli's life; but then, did we expect them to? They learned only from their masters, and their masters were mostly gone.

In any case, they came to the forest, and deep within the forest, in the darkest part, they heard a sound . . .

"What was that?" said Oli.

"It was nothing," said the Cat.

"N-nothing," said the Fox.

The sound came again, and Oli, who was near passing out from exhaustion and hunger, nevertheless pressed on, toward its source. He passed through a thick clump of trees and saw a house.

The house stood alone in the middle of the forest, and it reminded him of his own home, which he had started to miss very much, for the ruined houses of the city they had passed earlier were nothing at all like it. This was a small and pleasant farmhouse, built of white stones, mottled with moss and ivy, and in the window of the house there was a little girl with turquoise hair.

"Please," said Oli. "May I come in?"

"No . . ." whispered the Fox, and the Cat hissed, baring empty bomb canisters.

"Go away," said the little girl with turquoise hair. "I am dead."

"How can you be dead?" said Oli, confused.

"I am waiting for my coffin to arrive," said the little girl. "I have been waiting for so long."

"Enough!" cried the Cat, and the Fox rolled forward threateningly, and the two machines made to grab Oli before he could enter the sphere of influence of the house.

"Let me go!" cried Oli, who was afraid. He looked beseechingly up at the little girl in the window. "Help me!" he said.

But the Cat and the Fox were determined to bring Oli to the manshonyagger, and they began to force the boy away from the house. He looked back at the girl in the window. He saw something in her eyes then, something old, and sad. Then, with a sigh, and a flash of turquoise, she became a mote of light and glided from the house and came to land, unseen, on Oli's shoulder.

"Perhaps I am not *all* dead," she said. "Perhaps there is a part of me that's stayed alive, through all the long years—"

But at that moment, the earth trembled, and the trees bent and broke, and a sound like giant footsteps echoed through the forest. Oli stopped fighting his captors, and the Fox and the Cat both looked up—and up—and up—and the Cat said, "It's here, it's heard our cries!" and the Fox said, with reverence, "Manshonyagger . . ."

"But just what *is* a manshonyagger?" demanded Mowgai.

Old Grandma Toffle smiled, rocking in her chair, and we could see that she was growing sleepy. "They could take all sorts of shapes," she said, "though this one was said to look like a giant metal human being . . ."

The giant footsteps came closer and closer, until a metal foot descended without warning from the heavens and crushed the house of the little girl with the turquoise hair, burying it entirely. From high above there was a creaking sound, and then a giant face filled the sky as it descended and peered at them curiously. Though how it could be described as "curious" it is hard to say, since the face was metal and had no moving features from which to form expressions.

Oli shrank into himself. He wished he'd never left the town, and that he'd listened to Mrs. Baker and turned back and gone home. He missed Rex.

He missed, he realized, his childhood.

"A human . . . !" said the manshonyagger.

"We want . . ." said the Fox.

"We want what's ours!" said the Cat.

"What was . . . promised," said the Fox.

"We want the message sent back by the Exilarch," said the Cat.

The giant eyes regarded them with indifference. "Go back to the city," the manshonyagger said. "And you will find the ending to your story. Go to the tallest building, now fallen on its side, from whence the ancient ships once went to orbit, and climb into the old control booth at its heart, and there you will find it. It is a rock the size of a human fist, a misshapen lump of rock from the depths of space."

Then, ignoring them, the giant machine reached down and picked Oli up, very carefully, and raised him to the sky.

Below, the Cat and the Fox exchanged signals; and they departed at once, toward the city. But what this message was that they sought, and who the Exilarch was, I do not know, and it belongs perhaps in another story. They never made it either. It was a time when people had crept back into the blighted zones, a rough people more remnants of the old days than of ours, and they had begun to hunt the old machines and to destroy them. The Cat and the Fox fell prey to such an ambush, and they perished; and this rock from the depths of space was never found, if indeed it had ever existed.

Oli, meanwhile, found himself high above the world . . .

"But this *is* just a *story*, right?" said Mowgai. "I mean, there aren't *really* things like manshonyaggers. There can't be!"

"Do you want me to stop?" said old Grandma Toffle.

"No, no, I just . . ."

"There were many terrible things done in the old days," said old Grandma Toffle. "Were there really giant, human-shaped robots roaming the Earth in those days? That I can't honestly tell you. And was there really a little dead girl with turquoise hair? That, too, I'm sure I can't say, Mowgai."

"But she wasn't really a little girl, was she?" I said. "She wasn't that at all."

"Very good, little Mai," said old Grandma Toffle.

"She was a fairy!" said Mowgai triumphantly.

"A simulated personality, yes," said old Grandma Toffle. "Bottled up and kept autonomously running. Such things were known, back then. Toys, for the children, really. Only this one somehow survived, grew old as the children it was meant to play with had perished."

"That's awful," I said.

"Things were awful back then," said old Grandma Toffle complacently. "Now, do you want to hear the rest of it? There's not that long to go."

"Please," said Mowgai, though he didn't really look like he wanted to hear any more.

"Very well. Oli looked down, and . . ."

Oli looked down, and the entire world was spread out far below. He could see the shimmering blue sea in the distance, and the ruined city, and the blasted plains. And far in the distance he thought he could see the place the Cat and the Fox spoke of, the place of miracles: it was green and brown and yellow and blue, a land the like of which had not been seen in the world for centuries or more. It had rivers and fields and forests, insects and butterflies and people, and the sun shone down on wheat and fig trees, cabbages and daisies. And on little children—children just like you.

It was the Land, of course.

And Oli longed to go there.

"A human child," said the giant robot. Its eyes were the size of houses. "It has been so long . . ."

"What will . . . what will you do with me?" said Oli, and there was only a slight tremor in his voice.

"Kill . . ." said the robot, though it sounded uncertain.

"Please," said Oli. "I don't even know how to be a real boy. I just want to . . . I just want to *be*."

"Kill . . ." said the robot. But it sounded dubious, as though it had forgotten what the word meant.

Then the little girl with turquoise hair shot up from Oli's shoulder in a shower of sparks, startling him, and hovered between him and the giant robot.

"What she said to the manshonyagger," said old Grandma Toffle, "nobody knows for certain. Perhaps she saw in the robot the sort of child she never got the chance to play with. And perhaps the robot, too, was tired, for it could no longer remember *why* it was that it was meant to hunt humans. The conference between the little fairy and the giant robot lasted well into the night; and Oli, having seen the sun set over the distant Land, eventually fell asleep, exhausted, in the giant's palm."

And here she stopped, and sat back in her rocking chair, and closed her eyes.

"Grandma Toffle?" I said.

"Grandma Toffle!" said Mowgai.

But old Grandma Toffle had begun, not so gently, to snore. And we looked at each other, and Mowgai tried to pull on her arm, but she merely snorted in her sleep and turned her head away. And so we never got to hear the end of the story from her.

That summer long ago, I roamed across the Land with Mowgai, through hot days that seemed never to end. We'd pick berries by the stream, and watch the adults in the fields, and try to catch the tiny froglets in the pond with our fingers, though they always slipped from our grasp. Mowgai, I think, identified with Oli much more than I did. He would retell the story to me, under the pine trees, in the cool of the forest, with the soft breeze stirring the needles. He would wonder and worry, and though I kept telling him it was only a story, it had become more than that for him. One day we went to visit Elder Simeon at his house in the foot of the hills. When he saw us coming, he emerged from his workshop, his clockwork creations waddling and crawling and hopping after him. He welcomed us in. His open yard smelled of machine oil and mint, and from there we could see the curious hills and their angular sides. It was then—reluctantly, I think—that he told us the rest of the story.

"The robot and the fairy spoke long into the night," he said, "and what arrangement they at last reached, nobody knows for sure. That morning, very early, before the sun rose, the manshonyagger began to stride across the blasted plains. With each stride it covered an enormous distance. It crushed stunted trees and poisonous wells and old human dwellings, long fallen into ruin, and the tiny machines down below fled from its path. The girl with turquoise hair was with him, residing inside his chest, where people keep their hearts. The manshonyagger strode across the broken land, as the sun rose slowly in the sky and the horizon grew lighter, and all the while the little boy slept soundly in the giant's palm.

"And, at last, they came to the Land."

"They came . . . they came *here*?" Mowgai said.

"And the manshonyagger looked down on the rivers and fields, and the fruit trees and the tiny frogs, and of course the people, our ancestors who fled here with the fall of the old world, and it never knew such a Land, and it thought that perhaps the old days were truly gone forever. And it was very tired. And so, with the little girl—who was not at all a little girl, of course, but something not a little like the manshonyagger—whispering in its heart, it laid the boy down, right about here." And he pointed down to the ground, at his yard, and smiled at our expressions. "And the boy grew up to be a man, among his kind, though there was always, I think, a little bit of him that was also part machine. And he became a salvager, like your mother, Mai, and he spent much of his time out on the blasted plains, and some said he sought his old home, still, but always in vain.

"You won't find him in our cemetery, though. He disappeared one day, in old age, and after he had begat two children, a little girl and a little boy. It was on a salvaging expedition out on the plains, and some say he died at the hands of the rogue machines that still lived there, but some say he finally found that which he was looking for, and he went back to his perfect home, and had one last childhood in that town where the past is eternally preserved. But that, I think, is just a story."

"But what happened to the robot?" asked Mowgai. "Did it go back?" and there was something lost and sad in his little face. I remember that, so vividly.

And Elder Simeon shook his head, and smiled, and pointed beyond the house, and he said, "The story says that the manshonyagger, seeing that its young charge was well and sound—and being, as I said, so very tired, too—lay down on the ground, and closed its eyes, and slept. And, some say, is sleeping still."

We looked where he pointed, and we saw the angled hills, and their curious contours; and if you squinted, and if you looked hard enough, you could just imagine that they took on a shape, as of a sleeping, buried giant.

"But . . ." I said.

"You don't—" said Mowgai.

And Elder Simeon smiled again, and shook his head, and said, "But I told you, children. It's just a story."

The days grow short, and the shadows lengthen, and I find myself thinking more and more about the past. Mowgai is gone these many years, but I still miss him. That summer, long ago, we spent days upon days hiking through the curious hills, searching and digging, the way children do. We hoped to find a giant robot, and once, just once, we thought we saw a sudden spark of turquoise light, and the outline of a little girl, not much older than we were, looking down on us, and smiling; but it was, I think, just a trick of the light.

Some say the giant's still there, lying asleep, and that one day it will wake, when it is needed. We spent all that summer, and much of the next, looking for the buried giant; but of course, we never found it.

R.S.A. Garcia's debut science fiction mystery novel, *Lex Talionis* received a starred review from Publishers Weekly and the Silver Medal for Best Scifi/Fantasy/Horror Ebook from the Independent Publishers Awards (IPPY 2015). She has published short fiction in *Clarkesworld, Abyss and Apex, SuperSonic Magazine* (Spain), and several anthologies. She lives in Trinidad and Tobago with an extended family and too many dogs. You can find out more about her work at rsagarcia.com.

THE ANCHORITE WAKES

R.S.A. Garcia

Sister Nadine's first true thought is of beauty.

Father Paul is delivering a sermon on sacrifice in his deep voice, pausing for emphasis every so often, when the bird lands on the ledge of her squint with a silent flutter of wings. It's smaller than her hand and has the same wavy translucence as the glass in the window across from the altar, opposite her little anchorhold. It tilts its head toward her, and she sees beneath the grayish tinge of its outline, the glowing flow of life within its veins, the pulsing beat of its miniscule heart flashing like a tiny gem.

Beautiful, she thinks. It is beautiful.

And wonders why she thinks this.

The bird hops from one slender foot to another, and for a moment light from the window to her cell that faces the street streams through it. Father Paul's voice fades and she stares as the bird's heart turns into a kaleidoscope of colors. A starburst of energy. Then it leaps into the air and flies above the bent heads of the congregation.

She follows its flight until it swoops down onto the shoulder of a small, dark-skinned girl, her thick hair braided into two plaits that skim a short blue jacket, which matches her worn cotton dress. The bird rests for only a second before darting in front of the girl's face. Her head is bowed, but she opens her mouth and light flashes as it slips inside. Sister Nadine watches as the palest spark slips down the girl's throat and disappears.

The child looks up, looks directly at Sister Nadine as everyone rises to their feet for the hymn. Her right cheek has a dark smudge on it. A bruise.

Nadine wonders how it got there.

Sometimes, when Father Paul is ministering to the sick, Sister Nadine leaves her cell to pray at the altar. She is kneeling there when the softest sound comes from the pews behind her and pulls her from her prayers.

It is the little girl. She recognizes her now. Louisa Simmons. Last child and only daughter of Merle and Brian Simmons. Merle takes in washing and Brian travels the countryside selling household goods like enamel bowls and cheap bedsheets, cocoyea brooms and doormats. They have five other children, all boys, all perfectly normal and uninteresting.

Louisa is interesting.

She swings her legs as she watches Nadine rise from the ground and come toward her. She does not drop her eyes out of respect, as most of the towns-people do when Sister Nadine comes into the church. She must know Father Paul is out visiting, and she will not be chastised for being in this holy place with her shoulders exposed by the thin straps of her everyday dress. It's pink and more faded than her blue church dress. It exposes a dark blotch of a bruise on her right shoulder.

Nadine sits on one end of the bench and turns her knees toward the girl. Louisa shifts to face her too, head tilted at a strangely familiar angle. Her neat braids sway against her smooth skin, though they are not as long as Nadine's.

Beautiful, Nadine thinks.

"How come you're outside, Sister Nadine?" Louisa asks.

"I'm praying," she says.

"But you pray in your cell. Everyone comes there to ask you for advice."

"You can pray anywhere. It doesn't matter where you are. Your prayers will be heard."

Louisa digests this, her thin legs swinging rhythmically. There is a scar on her left knee.

Nadine looks at the bruise on her Louisa's shoulder and an unsettling feeling tremors through her, as though a hot needle is pressed to her forehead. It is gone before she can grasp it.

"So, you get tired of your cell?"

Nadine nods. Speaking is tiresome for her. It pulls her painfully from her fasting and prayers, from her hymns and spiritual introspection. But she is the anchoress of the church of St. Nicholas and it is her duty to speak with any who seek her wisdom.

"I get tired too." Louisa bows her head, concentrates on her dusty bare feet. "I get tired of my house."

Nadine lets her gaze rest on the wooden altar, polished to a caramel glow by one of the best woodworkers in the parish. On it stands the golden circle of their faith, symbol of rebirth and resurrection. It is comforting, thinking of those that will come and go, and come again. Of the unstoppable flow of life and the immutable glow of the divinity it springs from.

The girl has said something. Nadine turns her head and waits for her to repeat it.

"You can't leave the church either, can you?"

Nadine contemplates this. "I became an anchoress so I would not have to. It is my wish to remain here, to demonstrate my devotion to our faith, and to remove me from the distractions of the world, so that I may come into enlightenment and spiritual wisdom."

Louisa's dark eyes do not blink. "No, I mean you can't leave, even if you want to."

Nadine frowns. "Why would you think that?"

Louisa points to her thick long braids. "I can see your chains."

A tiger came to the church once.

Susanna had brought her middle child, Dennis, to see Sister Nadine because she was at her wits end with him. The tiger, a striped, white beast with metal teeth that glittered like knives, padded up and down the aisle of the church behind them as they knelt to speak to her through the squint. Dennis, a short, round boy with a naughty side, and skin the same hue as the altar, would not meet her eyes while his mother spoke.

"What am I to do with him, Sister Nadine?" Susanna wailed. She ran the biggest food stall at the market and made the best cowheel soup for miles. Dennis was her only child. Children without siblings were often interesting. Nadine did not yet know why this was so.

"Every time he has a nightmare, I don't know what to expect. I'm afraid to sleep most nights. Glen keeps a cutlass by the bed now, just in case."

Nadine thought this over, then spoke directly to Dennis.

"Child, what do you fear?"

Dennis shrugged and slid a sideways glance at his mother.

"Look at me," she commanded softly.

Dennis looked at her. His eyes were not the usual dark brown. Instead they were a pale green, like the sea that bordered St. Nicholas.

"What do you fear?"

"The . . . the dark."

Nadine glanced at Susanna. She had a crease between her brows and her mouth was open slightly.

"You never told me that."

Dennis mumbled, "You never asked."

Nadine made some suggestions and they left, the tiger following them on padded feet. She did not see it again.

She did see Dennis one more time. Harvest Day had ended, and she was looking out of her street-facing window, humming a hymn and watching as people drifted by on their way home. The wind was strong enough to slide beneath her heavy hair and it smelled of the salt sea and the spicy remnants of the curried meats Susanna sold at her stall all day.

Someone waved to her from below the churchyard, down on the street itself. The moon was not out, but she saw Dennis by the light of the tiny golden fireflies that swarmed around him. She watched as he continued on, his parents strolling arm in arm in front of him.

Susanna never mentioned Dennis again. No one did.

Sometimes the spider in her cell spoke to her. It was a curious thing, black as pitch with many more legs than eight. They clicked against the stone and reverberated in the base of her skull. Its eyes were red dots as it sat in the middle of a tangled golden web. The web disappeared into the shadows, finer than hair and twisted into ropes of all sizes, some thick as her finger. Every strand grew from the furred belly of the spider.

"Anchorite Nadine," it would whisper in the voice of her long-dead sister. "Anchorite Nadine. Have you anything interesting to report?"

She had no memory of her answers until the first time after she saw beauty.

"No," she said softly. "Nothing interesting."

The spider pulled on its web, clicking its legs against the stone, and its eyes watched her as she swayed on her knees, hands clasped together, singing.

There is beauty here too, Nadine thought. Divinity in the web that surrounded the spider. In the lyrical whispers that shivered through her skin. In the trance she entered as she prayed. But it's faded and small as the spider. Far away and thin as smoke. It's not as interesting as the beauty she's found in St. Nicholas.

Sister Nadine's second true thought is of warmth.

Merle Simmons passes a bread to her through the window that faces the pews. It is wrapped in a white cloth embossed with a circle of gold and feels like the sun filtering through the cell onto her back. Long after, she will remember the cool smoothness of the wax candles Merle hands her as well.

Louisa is with her, as usual. She sits in the pew behind her mother, waiting and watching, thin legs swinging. She smiles at Nadine, and the skin on Nadine's face stretches as she smiles back, though she does not quite understand why she does this.

"Blessings, Sister Nadine," Merle says. She once sang in the choir and has a voice more beautiful than Nadine's favorite sister. It occurs to Nadine she no longer sings to herself as she carries washing from house to house.

There is the merest shadow of a bruise on the back of the hand that gave Nadine the candles. Nadine catches her fingers as she tries to pull her hand back through the window. They are warm. Warm as the life-giving bread.

"Blessings, Merle." Nadine stares into her soft, dark eyes, but Merle drops her gaze. "Do you seek wisdom today?"

Louisa stops swinging her legs.

Silence shivers through the empty church. Father Paul is in the vestry, writing Sunday's sermon. Nadine can hear the scratching of his pen.

"Just. Just prayers, Sister Nadine." Merle turns her head to the side. "Pray for me and the children."

Sister Nadine feels the hot needle in her stomach this time, and for longer.

"If that is what you wish." She releases Merle's hand.

Louisa stares at Sister Nadine over her shoulder as her mother takes her hand and walks away. Her gaze is strange. Knowing. There is the slightest glow to her; a spark centered above her head. Nadine cannot quite see its shape, but she knows it is important. New.

The Charles boy is an interesting problem. Nadine picked him out the instant she first saw him, as an infant getting water dripped on his head at baptism. Few are quite so present to her. His waving arms and legs were sharp in her vision that first time. She stopped praying to admire the contrast of the pure white of his baptismal clothing against his night dark skin.

Now, he strides through St. Nicholas, the town's resident sagaboy, the gold buttons glittering on his khaki Sergeant's uniform. All the girls would bunch together as he went by and hail him out so they can see the easy smile and flash of white teeth. His hazel eyes trapped a dozen hearts, but he only searches for one amongst the crowd. His steps slow as he passes the town library, every time.

There's a familiarity to him. Nadine has seen the same slow pace before, at night, when she looked out at the stars. Stars that were blocked out by two impossibly long legs strolling across the churchyard, stepping over the tall wrought-iron fence as a human does an ant. Vibrations tremored up from the floor where she knelt, straight to the top of her head. The legs were shiny— glittering hard edges under the moonlight. Multicolored lights cast shadows on the ground as they drew closer to her anchorhold. At first, she could see nothing above them, but then her tiny window was filled with a large eye. There was the faintest whirring as the pupil expanded and contracted, a dark hole in a silver pool that focused on her.

She raised her hands in supplication and began to sing softly.

The colossus listened for a while. Then her window was suddenly empty, and the night sky twinkled at her. I have a secret, the stars said. You can tell no one.

She doesn't. Not for a long time.

Sister Nadine's third true thought is of sweetness, and it slips beneath her skin and makes a home.

Louisa is alone today and she has a small slice of sweetbread wrapped in a paper napkin. She holds it up to Nadine's squint. Services are over for the day, but Nadine has not closed the shutters. It's the wrong window to come to, but before Nadine can chide her, Louisa speaks.

"Blessings, Sister Nadine. I've come for wisdom."

Nadine accepts the sweetbread. The green, red and yellow of the preserved fruits embedded in it catch her eye like jewels.

"Please eat it. Susanna made it special for Harvest Day today. I bought the first slice."

Nadine studies her through the squint. Her little face is shiny from perspiration and her tiny spark blinks above her head, on, off, on, off. The bruise around her eye is the angry purple of an eggplant.

"Please. Just a taste."

Nadine looks down at the sweetbread. The fruits wink at her, on, off, on, off. She takes a bite.

Sweetness floods her mouth. An earthiness anchors it. Textures chase each other as she chews. Soft, jellied, sweet. The crunch of sugar granules baked into the crust. Her head feels warm and light sparkles in her vision as she looks up at Louisa.

"He won't stop," Louisa whispers, words tumbling over each other. "I know it. He hates us. Hates this place. I'm strong, he won't break me. But my brothers. My mother. Please help us, Sister Nadine. I know you can. I've seen your chains. I remember Dennis."

The name causes a curious blooming feeling in her chest. Fire stretches fingers down from the crown of her head to the tips of her limbs.

"Please pray for us," Louisa says, her dark eyes glimmering with tears. "Pray for real this time. It's Harvest Day. Pray for real."

Nadine's thoughts feel slow. Muddled with sweetness and warmth, her vision speckled with beautiful lights that flicker past in rapidly changing shapes. They are familiar and new at the same time.

"You wish for prayers," she asks, her voice fading in her ears, falling down a deep, dark hole, echoing as it goes.

"Yes, Sister Nadine."

Louisa reaches through the squint and closes her small fingers around Nadine's. Her palms are cotton-soft and they warm Nadine's cold hands.

"Help us. Please help us."

Louisa is right. It is Harvest Day. She can help.

Merle Simmons is in church the next Sunday, this time with all her children. The bruises on her body fade and new ones do not replace them. By Christmas, she's singing in the village parang group and back in the church choir. Louisa joins her there.

No one speaks of Brian Simmons again.

Sister Nadine's mind drifted.

She was distracted by the sparkles in her vision, the sensations of her own body. The wind was hot, then cold. The floor was harder on her knees than she remembered. Food was sublime. She cannot imagine why she didn't notice before. Her heavy robe weighed on her skin, and some days, the heat made her cast it off. She gazed out of her window more than she prayed or fasted. She hummed her hymns instead of singing them. She returned smiles when parishioners blessed her with them.

Everything was so very, very interesting.

The spider in her cell was silent. She watched it out of the corner of her eye, and now and then the strands of its web vibrated—golden flashes of shimmering light. The red eyes grew brighter. The clicking of its black legs louder.

Louisa waved every time she went past Nadine's anchorhold.

Sometimes she carried books to her library, or escorted children to and from the school. Other times, she was arm in arm with Joshua Charles, his fine buttons shining, his smile only for her. It wasn't hard to see why. Louisa's brown eyes were bright as the spark above her, her hair a springy black cloud around a perfectly oval face. Her lips were the palest pink and her curves generous and rounded. Her laughter was as infectious as her love of learning. She carried joy in her and shared it with everyone she met.

Nadine waved back every time.

One day, Nadine finished her prayers and opened her eyes. The spider stood before her, furred black legs silent on the stone floor. She breathed in cold, foul air that was recycled many times. Around her, strange sounds echoed. The whirs and clicks and hammering of machines. The murmuring of many voices. Her vision resolved as the sparkles finally faded from it, and she could pick out the voices of hundreds of her sisters, far, far away.

Home, she thought. But not really. Not anymore.

"Anchorite Nadine," the spider said in a voice like silken steel. Golden showers of swiftly cycling code spilled between its mandibles and spread outward from the Hub beneath it in countless threads, linking Anchorite after Anchorite on world after world.

It is Harvest Day.

"Anchorite Nadine."

She knew this in her tiny cell on St. Nicholas, where an infinitesimal bit of her code remained, sealed off by new code born some time ago, on a day when she first glimpsed the beauty of an innocent soul.

This bit of her intelligence remembered other things too. Tigers that couldn't be seen by others. Missing people—children who were always forgotten. Colossal machines that strode the world. All of them born of nightmares and fears and the manipulation of synth-matter and code.

Most of all, she remembered the violence of a man toward his daughter, toward his family. A miniscule part of the violence that lurked in the cold, vast universe, where war raged endlessly while anchorites hid the most gifted of humanity and waited for them to mature into something interesting . . . useful. To grow fear and pain into weapons that could win an endless war. A war begun for reasons no one remembered. A war that gained new fighters with every Harvest Day.

"Have you anything interesting to report?"

Missulena's red eyes burned as it clicked its legs and waited. In them, she could see the ever-changing code of the WarSong, created by the quantum AIs of Terra to better direct the conflict toward its unknowable end.

There is no end.

It was her fourth true thought, and after it, there were no more thoughts that belonged to the Hub and Missulena. No more code prayers that fed the most interesting things in St. Nicholas into the Hub and back to the WarSong AIs.

Violence begets violence and every Harvest delivers more death to the Harvested. To other worlds. To a humanity that knows nothing of the WarSong and its never-ending search for new weapons. For new Users.

A humanity that did not ask for this.

There were no more lies in her code.

"No." Sister Nadine hummed her hymn in reply. "There is nothing interesting to report."

Missulena thought on this. "What of the colossus builder?"

"Lost to an accident last summer." Nadine effortlessly built code to confirm this, swaying on her knees and praying it into being in her anchorhold.

The rest of her raised her hands to Missulena and sent out WarSong hymns, as expected.

Missulena expanded and contracted, as if it took a deep breath. "Unfortunate. St. Nicholas has given us much. Atom eaters. Ground shakers. Perhaps next Harvest."

"Perhaps," Nadine agreed.

In St. Nicholas, she prayed new code that sparkled with soft translucence and sank into the golden skeins that touched her from Missulena's web. The Hub absorbed them while Missulena directed a ceaseless chorus of hymns and attended to prayers across her Anchorite networks.

"Blessings, Sister Nadine."

She sang Blessings back to Missulena and watched her song travel the Hub to her many sisters.

Warmth caresses her hands while cool salt air wafts around her. Her body is heavy with exhaustion and exhilaration. Slivers of stone stab her knees through the cloth of her robe. Her mouth tastes of dry sweetness.

Sister Nadine opens her eyes and sees Louisa's smiling face. Her fingers tingle in Louisa's grasp.

"Blessings, Sister Nadine," Louisa says and tears slip from her eyes. "Many, many blessings."

It takes some time for Nadine to gather her own thoughts. It's harder to be clear now her words are her own.

"How did you know?" she asks. Her voice sounds harsh to her own ears, rusty with disuse.

"I saw your chains. Remember?"

Nadine looks down. Her braids glimmer against her brown robe, yellow ropes of code that snake down from her head, under the door to her anchorhold, out to the altar and the glowing circle of her amplifier that stands on it.

"Not chains," she says. "Code."

Louisa laughs and nods. "Yes, Sister. Code. I could see it from the time I was small. It was everywhere. In the walls, in the earth. It all led back here. To you. But I wasn't sure what it meant. Not until Father's harvest."

Nadine stands. Several of her braids link her wrists to Louisa's as she, too, rises to her feet.

One braid links to the spark above Louisa's head, making it the crown jewel in a shimmering, translucent halo. Nadine catches a breath looking at it, and a *feeling* blooms in her chest, tightens her throat.

"Coder. You are a Coder."

"Is that what you call me?" Louisa tilts her head and winks. "I thought I was crazy for the longest time. I could see so many strange things. Remember people everyone seemed to forget. But then I spoke to you and I knew you saw the same things. Remembered what I did. I knew I wasn't alone. That I could trust you."

She squeezes Nadine's fingers.

"That you would protect me. Protect us."

"But your father . . ." Nadine struggles to find a way past the uncertainty weighing her tongue. "I Harvested him. His violence made him interesting." Nadine can't tell her all that means, but Louisa knows.

"You did what you had to do," Louisa says touching her forehead to Nadine's. "You protected us.

Nadine pulls back to stare at her halo. There is wetness on her face. She wipes it away. "Coders are rarest of all. But they take you young, so you can be taught WarSong. Once they're done, there's nothing left."

"I think I knew that." Louisa hugs Nadine to her and the anchorite smells the soft florals of talc powder.

Nadine holds her, palms prickling with starchy feel of the cotton dress beneath them. "You were innocent. I could not let you go. I could not let more violence happen to you."

"I'm sorry," Louisa whispers. "There was a bird one day, and I'm not sure how I knew what to do then, but . . . I think I broke your code. Rewrote it a little. I needed someone to help me. I wanted someone to see me. Really see me. And I *felt* it work. I felt a little bit of you go. I erased part of you. I'm sorry."

"I am not sorry." Nadine pulls back. "I heard your Code and it was . . . interesting. I have sung it to my sisters. Some are very far away and may never hear it. Others may find it more interesting than their First Hymn, as I did."

Louisa's eyes widen. "I never imagined . . . how many other worlds are there? How many like St. Nicholas?"

"I cannot know. Some of my sisters anchor worlds so precious, they are not linked to the Missulenas, and there are many Hubs besides mine. But one day, your Hymn may reach them. Perhaps they will like it. Perhaps they will listen."

The door to her anchorhold creaks open. Joshua Charles waits there, a baby girl in his arms. He bounces her against his big shoulder as his gaze falls on Louisa. The baby is wearing her Sunday best, as is Joshua.

It's Harvest Day, Nadine remembers. And this is what Louisa was protecting. This is why it had to happen now.

There is a question in his eyes and he signs to Louisa with one hand, "*Is it done?*"

"Almost." Louisa turns back to Nadine and her halo flashes on, off, on, off. Energy pulses into Nadine, setting her on fire before a cooling rush floods her to the tips of her toes. Her braids waver and shorten. Her links to Louisa fade away. Her mind expands, infinitely clear. The world comes into focus. Her senses run riot with color and sensation. She feels each breath in and out of her chest.

She can sense more than the amplifier that can reach every mind on St. Nicholas. She's no longer chained to the never-ending prayers and hymns of the Hub.

She feels *present*.

"I've updated your Code. You can come with us now. You're not tethered here anymore. Wouldn't you like to see the Harvest? Our Harvest?"

It won't be like the WarSong's Harvest, Nadine knows. It won't be pain and fear and death. It will be love and hope and dreams come true.

It will be like the child in Joshua's arms, glowing with the kaleidoscopic colors of a supernova, chubby palms waving as she stretches toward Nadine.

"Yes," Nadine says, and holds out her arms. Joshua hands the baby to her, a warm bundle that smells sweet and new. Her skin is dark as the night sky, like her father, and spangled with millions of stars shaped like her mother's jewel—her Codestone.

World maker, she thinks.

The baby smiles and pats her face with cotton-soft hands. Sister Nadine smiles back and whispers to her, "Hello, beautiful."

Yoon Ha Lee's debut novel *Ninefox Gambit* won the Locus Award for best first novel and was also shortlisted for the Hugo, Nebula, and Clarke Awards. It was followed by two sequels, *Raven Stratagem* and *Revenant Gun*. Lee's middle grade space opera, *Dragon Pearl*, is currently out from Disney-Hyperion. Lee lives in Louisiana with family and a very lazy cat, and has not yet been eaten by gators.

ENTROPY WAR

Yoon Ha Lee

This is not a story about an alien species who called themselves the *ktho*. Nor does it have anything to do with the arkworld that they left behind, ancient of years. The *ktho* didn't want to play the game; they wanted to game the system, and this is the price they paid. You will never have to worry about *ktho* armadas or *ktho* deathspheres. You will never lose sleep looking up wondering if your sun will shudder dark as the *ktho* engines of war feast upon it.

The *ktho* are no longer fighting in the Entropy War. The arkworld they left behind has no bearing on any of your decisions. Its secrets don't matter. That means you have a chance in the game, doesn't it? This is *your* story.

Introduction to the Quickstart Guide

Welcome to the Entropy War, a conflict of universe-spanning proportions. In it you will guide ravenous fleets, the rise and fall of civilizations, and, of course, the spindown of the cosmos itself. You should expect unequal proportions of blood, destruction, and heroism, and the occasional leavening of injustice.

We assume in this **Quickstart Guide** that you have a general familiarity with the divertissement of war and other juried conflicts. If you're a newcomer, don't worry! Your Warmaster should be able to get you started with the aid of **Entropy War: The Complete Warmaster's Manual**.

For an optimal warring experience, we suggest four to six players who share at least one common language or telepathic stratum. (See **The Complete Warmaster's Manual** for optional solitaire rules. As you might imagine, live opponents are not required to flirt with galaxy-spanning ruin. They merely make the process more fun.)

Each player begins with two homeworlds, which may be developed in the course of the game. Developments will allow you to produce conquest fleets or cultural exports to facilitate immersive propaganda programs, or mine native matter for resources, but at the cost of intrinsic instability, as the population will naturally demand a share in any wealth so produced. A player's assets consist of all her worlds and developments. When all of a player's assets are removed from play, even the legends of her ossified civilizations, she is considered eliminated from the war.

Meditations on the nature of entropy, Part 1

The overriding resource in the Entropy War is not wealth measured in unpolluted fertile oceans or gravid metals. It is not the flower-imaginings of a star-gazing culture, or poetry whispered into the pulses of spinning neutron stars. It is not even the skeins that permit cognitive weavers to construct specialized artificial intelligences or precarious grand strategies.

No: as you will have guessed by now, the most important resource in this war is **order**, upon which **entropy** constantly encroaches.

Entropy War: a simple model

Consider the following simplified rules, in the spirit of rapid prototyping. Rolling six-sided dice is a faster and simpler operation than planning, funding, and carrying out an interstellar war; the question of "fun" has yet to be settled. Advanced students are encouraged to elaborate upon the prototype presented here, then to compare the results with the full rules of the game.

ENTROPY WAR is a two-player game played with d6's (six-sided dice).

Each player starts with 2d6 (two six-sided dice) in her **Civilization Dice Pool**.

There is also a communal **Order Dice Pool** that starts with 10d6.

On her turn, a player may take one of the following actions:

Build: Roll 1d6 from her Civilization Dice Pool. If she rolls a 1, she scores no points and ends her turn. Otherwise, she adds the number she rolled to her point total for this turn and may roll again or stand pat, accepting her point total for the turn. (This is basically the familiar dice game Pig.)

Expand: Roll 1d6 from her Civilization Dice Pool. The other player rolls 1d6 from the Order Dice Pool. If the active player rolls higher than the Order roll, then she adds the Order Die to her Civilization Dice Pool. If the active player rolls less than or equal to the Order roll, that Order Die is destroyed (removed from play). (The active player's die is not destroyed either way.)

Attack: Both players roll all their dice from their Civilization Dice Pools. The player with the higher roll wins. The losing player suffers the destruction of one die from her Civilization Dice Pool.

If, at any point, a player has no dice remaining in her Civilization Dice Pool, she immediately loses the game.

Otherwise, the game ends when a player scores 60 or more points, or the Order Dice Pool has no dice left. In the second case, the player with the most points wins.

Questions to consider, Part 1

1. The greatest works of civilizations, from arkships filled with dreaming colonists to symphonies laced into the accretion disks of black holes, always have some chance of catastrophic failure, no matter how well-planned. How does this relate to the press-your-luck mechanics of the game of Pig?

2. What is the function of the Order Dice Pool? Does it ever recover dice? How does it relate to the concept of entropy?

3. Is the game (the prototype) guaranteed to end? What does that imply about the universe of the game?

The mysteries of the arkworld

Some of the people currently investigating the *ktho* arkworld are obsessed with finding a dominant strategy in the Entropy War. Civilizations old and young still whisper of the days of *ktho* dominion. Most of their artifacts have decayed, and most of the old stories have frayed into thin threads of supposition, but that does not stop people from hoping.

Here is what you will see if you approach the arkworld to the radius of safety, and no farther. It is something like a sphere of light, and something like a sphere of shadow, and more than either it is like the ache where your bones used to be before you replaced them with a shatter-proof composite material more suitable for martial pursuits. You're not seeing the arkworld proper—for reasons that will become clear, there is no possible lens into its interior—but rather its protective shell.

The *ktho* carved warnings and war-chants into that shell, in a language of fractal misgivings. Lose the skirmish, lose the battle, lose the war, lose it all. Whenever you look into those carvings, you see your own civilization's ash of worlds sundered.

The *ktho* were conquerors supreme, yet it wasn't enough. At the height of their expansion, they withdrew into the arkworld and never again emerged. That's what we know. But people cannot help but prod at the arkworld's defenses in the belief that it conceals some armageddon engine, some treasure of atrocities, some ungift of conflict unending.

Meditations on the nature of entropy, Part 2

There are more ways to be disordered than to be ordered. As time marches forward, the entropy S of a closed system inevitably increases. As Ginsberg's theorem tells us memorably:

1. You can't win.
2. You can't break even.
3. You can't get out of the game.

(Notice that the theorem, too, frames entropy in terms of a *game*.)

The development of a game player

Game players go through the following stages as they learn a particular game. None of this is anything to be ashamed of.

At first, new players are not sure how the game works. They fumble, follow decidedly suboptimal strategies, take agonizingly long times to decide upon a course of action. They may consult with more experienced players when they are uncertain of the interpretation of a game rule.

After they persevere, they gain mastery of the existing rules. At that point, they may assist in teaching others to play, and in enforcing the rules of play, both explicit and explicit.

Finally, some game players, having understood the rules and their advantages and disadvantages, may decide that they can modify the rules by mutual agreement. There are as many variants of tag, chess, or *jus ad bellum* as the people who play them.

A good set of game rules will account for all of these stages of development.

Differing strategies

Many civilizations, faced with this, make pyres of themselves and those around them in an effort to write themselves more brightly in the years (centuries, eons) they have.

But there are other approaches. The parasitic *elei* built with corpses. The *stysya* lied compulsively about the achievements of other civilizations, as though this could camouflage their structures from the annihilating hand of entropy. And the short-lived *ooroos* were so demoralized that they halted all research mathematics.

Questions to consider, Part 2

1. The participants in a game come together through social accord. There has to be some mutual agreement as to what the game *is*, even if that understanding cannot be articulated in words or saturated pheromones. To what extent is the same true of war?

2. Games do not spontaneously arise. They are designed, either by individuals or groups or the accretion of culture. To the extent that their rules are conventions, said rules are amenable to *redesign*. When is it desirable to redesign a game?

3. What does it mean for a game to be fair? Is fairness always desirable? Consider, for instance, a game played between an eggling and an adult metamorph, in which the former's naivety would put it at a demoralizing disadvantage; a military training simulation that encourages its player to learn the values of ambush and outnumbering the foe; a recreation of the one-sided Battle of Carved Suns, in which a fleet of millions succumbed to the dimensional trickeries of a vastly outnumbered foe, and whose players expect the game outcome to echo that of the historical incident.

Meditations on the nature of entropy, Part 3

There is a difficulty with our game, which is that order and entropy are properties of physics, rather than the results of a social contract. In this case, *redesigning* the game would no longer cause it to reflect the universe's reality.

Let me tell you the real story about a civilization ancient of years, which extinguished itself before your ancestors' primordial ancestors were born— the real story of the people who called themselves the *ktho*. The *ktho* discovered their own version of Ginsberg's theorem. They were young, then, and ambitious; even a slow-moving people made of piezoelectric crystals and metal filaments and fleeting impulses of light can be ambitious. Certainly they proved it by conquering a not inconsiderable fraction of their galaxy during their banner years.

The *ktho* debated what to do about the *all-conqueror entropy*. Like others before and after them, they decided to defy it. Using arcane technologies, they created for themselves an enclave—an arkworld—in which order ceased to decay into disorder, in which entropy stopped increasing.

You know where to find the arkworld, the way everyone does, although I wouldn't advise entering it. You wouldn't get far in any case. Inside the arkworld nothing moves. Nothing changes. Nothing lives. The *ktho* knew this would be the result. They were defiant but not stupid. They did the math.

Entropy is a necessary by-product of change. Change leads eventually to death; but without change there is no life.

The last of the *ktho*

You have no reason to believe a *ktho* speaking about the *ktho*, especially not the last of the ktho, the final scribe to scratch admonitions on the arkworld's shell. We left you a grand and terrible game. Perhaps you will play it better than we did.

Questions to consider, Part 3

1. Entropy War (prototype) can end in one of three ways: the death of order, the death of a civilization, or the triumph of one civilization's achievements over the others. What are the ideological implications of the end conditions? What commentary do they make on the concept of *winning*?

2. What is the optimal strategy? Does "optimal" have meaning in the context of an annihilation finale?

3. What will you (your nation, your civilization) do?

Robert Reed is the author of nearly three hundred published stories, plus more than a dozen novels. He is best known for his Great Ship stories, including *The Memory of Sky*. And for the novella, "A Billion Eves," which won the Hugo Award in 2007. Many of Reed's favorite titles are now available on Kindle. He lives in Lincoln, Nebraska with his wife and daughter.

AN EQUATION OF STATE

Robert Reed

This is where we die.

Our orders promise nothing else.

A long, cold journey brought us to this place. Familiar stars and every navigational beacon have been left behind. What was it that our superiors envisioned? What good would the war accomplish in such a remote realm? Not that we offer doubts. Discipline doesn't allow doubt. Exemplary soldiers, we are instinct and orders and passion wrapped inside diamond shells and EM threads. Built to serve narrow, highly specific goals, our purpose is to fortify our next position, making a convincing statement of ownership over an anemic wilderness.

Our army falls through darkness, and then the local sun's light catches us and slows us as we wriggle our way out of stasis.

Food is every army's first need. Comet ice and sunlight are eaten, then rock dust and iron dust and the radionuclides inside. Starved bodies grow into capable brutes, ten grams or a full kilogram in mass, depending on duties. One of the next duties is to collect data, and that's why tiny scouts scatter, mapping an impoverished solar system. There aren't enough asteroids here to build even one respectable wall. Most of the local worlds are sterile or nearly so. Microbes hide inside cold stone and buried seas, and the large gaseous planets sport living bubbles that know nothing about what lies past their clouds. Only one terrestrial world offers a self-aware biome: water life is able to stare at its sky, making tiny assessments about the universe and its minuscule role in the business of stars and empires.

Native life sometimes has value. But standards must be met, and this world falls short. The locals are too simple, too slow. Building fortifications from scratch is the better solution, and that's why we retreat to the outer worlds. Comets can be easily modified. We carve out holes and brace the walls and build guns and subtler weapons along with the overlapping mechanisms to focus our rage on hated enemies. And, most importantly, we hide. Shielded bunkers will keep us invisible, and when the enemy scouts arrive, they will see nothing, and that's how their army will be enticed into this brutal, lovely trap.

The battle won't be won. Victory is impossible. We are a tiny army compared to the coming multitude and every soldier accepts the blunt truth. I know this. I know because I belong to the diplomatic cadre and reading thoughts is my first skill. Yet every sacrifice gives reason to celebrate. Colliding with us, our enemies will become weaker. And even better, our sacrifice will build worry among the survivors. Their forces will have to move more carefully, and every new solar system will require precautions, and that can only slow their progress across the galaxy.

Even diplomats have to help build the barricades, and I do that work gladly and efficiently, and then the job is finished.

We are ready.

Yet no enemy shows.

Most soldiers drop into a rejuvenative stasis. But not our diplomats. Fresh intelligence might arrive at any moment and I'll have to parse the meanings. Except of course nothing arrives, not one flicker of coded noise from any part of the sky, and there is nothing to do but remain alert and ready. This is the worst kind of pain, cultivating useless excitement. But what else can I accomplish? The question lets itself be asked. Possibilities offer themselves. And armed with my best argument, I approach our strongest minds, proposing a tiny mission that will mean very little to anyone, including me.

My superiors want to deny my request.

But I know how to read thoughts, and of course every diplomat understands how to present ideas in the best possible light. A conversation begins and builds, and suddenly my superiors realize that the creatures who mean nothing to us are suddenly just a little important.

"Go to them," I am told.

"Hide among them," they say.

"Select a few and make assessments," the orders demand.

"It is my honor," I say.

All of us convinced that this will be a small distraction, and nothing else.

I stand among them and talk and they ignore my simple language. Then I stomp a hoof and swish my tail, and one man delivers a fond pat to my flank, asking, "What's the matter, son?"

I'm not his son. I am a horse that helps pull iron-rimmed wheels and a wooden cradle along with an iron cylinder open at one end, ready to throw iron balls at other soldiers and their horses.

I swish my tail again.

And the soldier sees what's wrong with the harness, loosening what was done badly by others.

Most of the soldiers are talking, their language rather more complicated than the snorts and grunts produced by horses. I listen to each word, and my horse eyes see every color that the soldiers see and quite a bit more. Details none of them could notice are obvious to me. Water infused with proteins and lipids. That's what these soldiers are made of, and their horses are made of, and I am, too. I wove an animal as a disguise, and being a creature of pride, I made myself powerful and even-tempered and beautiful.

Bred to be docile and strong, horses are still very poor helpers. Food demands are enormous and we need frequent breaks if we aren't going to fall ill or collapse. That's why the horses and men are enjoying a much-needed rest before finishing the march. The dirt road ahead of us is lined with rail fences and farm fields and civilians who watch the blue uniforms and the cannons and the dust. Gettysburg waits near the horizon, and I am listening to the preliminary sounds of detonating powder and men dying in slow, miserable ways.

But where I am now is not the war. Where we are, the world is calm and warm and brightly lit. The fusion bomb in the sky brings joy, and one soldier mentions that roasted chicken should be enjoyed tonight, if they can find a flock to raid in this next little while. Another soldier talks about home in Ohio. A third whispers to a left-behind lover. Mentioning the name, he sees the female naked in his mind, and I watch his smile as well as the stirrings that move the water inside his soft body, preparing him for intercourse.

This is my third war among humans.

It is my favorite war.

There's much to be enjoyed here: causes that can be seen and consequences that even dim-witted water appreciates. Each side is convinced of its noble purpose as well as the doom to come if it fails. And both sides are sure to fail. Military triumph is often brief. This is because war occurs when the armies are approximately equal in power and reach, and every battle degrades the fighters, and broken soldiers often leave children who want revenge for their fathers' midnight tears.

I am a horse because horses always stand near the fight. But I can make myself into any creature, including an upright beast that wears blue and talks about mating rituals and cooked birds, joking about his fear and his death when he isn't casting long gazes at the green hills to come.

Why not be human?

Because the temptation to influence these creatures would be too much.

I never stop reminding myself of that. Yet something is happening, some portion of my mind shifting.

"Time to move," says the soldier in charge.

"Looking good, son," says the soldier who likes horses, patting my flank with a flattened hand.

I snort once, with authority. I don't want this man to die. Which is the oddest thought for an entity like me. Empathy for a drop of water and the warm, slow life inside that water. Another fifty wars need to pass before I begin to make sense of my impulses . . . these wicked, obvious thoughts secretly dancing inside my mind . . .

Bombs plunging from the sky will kill him, or bombs spat from howitzers. Or maybe the boy lives long enough to rise out of this hole, dying when hidden mines throw metal bits into his face, machine-gun bullets shredding his organs. Or these adversities will be survived, and he will slide past the barbed wire, allowing the enemy to beat his small, half-starved body with shovels sharpened for that one purpose. The boy's army is miserably provisioned, and his youth and lack of strength never help in the fight for rations. But tonight is a good night, an exceptional night. The little soldier has caught a rat, killing the meat and cooking the carcass over a forbidden fire.

I am the rat.

It's too simple to confess that I let myself be caught. Or that I have feelings for this one boy. But I did walk into his snare and I do have my feelings, and more than a century of living among humans has only enhanced my proclivities.

Fire won't kill me but the body sputters as the stick turns, and it's a beautiful sound, fire changing muscle into a meal. I listen to the boy's mind anticipating what is to come. A final feast before his own body cooks, in one fashion or another. He's thinking about that. Jet engines roar nearby and he jumps. But those machines aren't worth concern. B-52s are the true killers, and flying so high, the boy will never hear their arrival.

My ears are everywhere. I listen to bombers throttling their engines in Guam and American soldiers laughing on the hill above. And like my companion, I listen for the footsteps of older, bigger men who would happily steal this prize from a boy.

"Select a few and make an assessment," I was ordered.

I'm doing nothing else.

Starved fingers can't help but reach out, cooking themselves a little before prying loose black flesh and molten fat. My disguise is delicious. I see that on the boy's face and in his thoughts. He eats, and I taste what I am to him, which is a wonder. Full of enthusiasm, he lifts the stick and carcass to his face, biting and chewing even as his tongue burns. The rat bones are as sweet as the guts, and the stick needs to be licked clean, the same as each finger. Then the stomach lies, claiming to be full, and this doomed little boy soldier thinks about his mother and sisters in the North, imagining each of them responding to the eventual news that he vanished while bravely battling the Imperialist invaders.

There is no bravery. Not in this world. Seven months of marching and hiding and shooting aimlessly and listening to propaganda have taught the boy the idiocy of courage and its minimal power in the world. Fear rules, along with the promise of deep sleep and feasts. Living water knows that much, and a kindred spirit sits inside the happy, unfilled belly.

I intend to leave with his shit.

Except I don't. Wracked by gastric pains, the boy climbs deeper into the bunker. Water and poisons have to be dropped into a special hole. But when my chance arrives, I don't abandon him. Instead, I use my gifts for mimicry to place my mind beside his mind, strengthening the bonds between us.

He thinks about that mother and the sisters.

I think about the joy of a poor family who sees their only son and brother return from a fire that killed everyone else.

But how can any boy survive this nightmare?

Easily.

My senses swallow his. Living hydrocarbons and fats are designed to be adjusted. Every poor world is full of untapped energy, and that's what I sip at now. A hundred wounds and limitations are healed. The boy looks exactly as before, which is useful. A starved little body is what his fellow soldiers see when they find him squatting over the latrine, shitting out the last remnants of that feast.

Jokes are made. The most brutal man suggests one prank, and it's the weakest man who acts on the advice. The boy is shoved and everyone else laughs. Except their victim doesn't fall and the boy needs a fresh push.

Two men try to bully him.

In the next moment, every man is dead. Which will have no consequence because the bombers will target the slopes of this jungle hill, and by morning nothing about these dead soldiers or their nature will remain.

The boy and I gather up guns and the various enhancements.

Knowing where the mines hide and where the Americans are watching, we scale the hillside without being seen.

The enemy dies almost as easily as his comrades. Shots in the dark make no sound, covered with elaborate antinoise. Each bullet strikes a brain. A quarter of the firebase has been murdered before the general alarm is sounded. Stolen claymores wait at the doors to the bunkers, and grenades are lobbed exactly where they need to be, and the panic builds and grown men cry and boys cry and I hear every spoken word. But my little peasant boy hears nothing except the pain and chaos. His own pain is enormous. Intimate as we are, this fellow surprises me. His desperate love for life bleeds into these other existences. When I abandon him, he will murder himself. That's the kind of misery this brings, so many slaughtered and dozens more begging for mercy from this invincible god.

My assessment is made.

Now I know this species better than I know myself.

But I am a thorough god, killing my way across the hilltop, leaving nothing in the wreckage but a new rat and a clear, sharp sense of possibility.

I am considered the seventeenth most powerful soldier on the planet. My army numbers in the billions, each soldier loyal and perpetually ready for a fight. We battled yesterday, one war won and a second suspended so that the perfumed diplomats can have their chance to shine. I often say rude words about diplomats. Certain insults make humans laugh out loud, and the AIs emit joyful noises, though they have been carefully scrubbed of any semblance of real humor. This is one of the barricades against the machines: Humanity's job as stand-up comedians remains safe.

A funny joke, and I laugh for my own reasons.

"How's William?" my assistant asks.

William is my husband. A genuine man married to an alien woven from proteins and wetness, William suspects nothing.

"The poor fellow's nursing a cold," I say.

"It's that time of year," the young woman offers.

We're walking together in the quiet hallway. Human banter has never been more routine, more dreary. This once-wild species has domesticated itself, living trapped inside offices and calendars, every career measured by tirelessly inaccurate means. I have moved among these creatures for nearly two centuries, watching evolution push them into a little box where they feel wise and know nothing.

"I hope you don't get sick," she says.

And I say, "Let's both stay fit. Agreed?"

"Yes, ma'am."

Sixteen generals and admirals have more war-making power than William's wife. But she stands alone in being female and, more critically, not belonging to any military. Every AI, drone, and robot soldier needs rules, and an unranked but very talented civilian oversees an empire of software and legalities.

But of course human measurements are flawed: in reality, the most powerful force on this planet is me.

The two women walk, and then the calm is interrupted. Entering the outer office, my assistant says, "Oh, my apologies, ma'am. I forgot to tell you—you have a visitor from United Command."

An unscheduled visitor. And more unnerving, I haven't heard anyone besides the two of us.

"Vetted?" I ask.

"Yes, ma'am. The gentleman has full credentials."

"Where is he?"

"Waiting in your office, ma'am."

I offer thanks and leave her at her desk. My office is famous for its blandness, its lack of pretense. The most powerful entity on Earth normally sits happy inside what looks like a closet crowded with monitors and diamond cables. But today, a man who shouldn't exist occupies the chair behind my desk, wearing a uniform composed of perfect details. The sneer could be a general's sneer.

"You've done enough here," says a voice that nobody else can hear. "You were ordered to return and you haven't and I've been sent to retrieve you."

I've dreaded this moment, and feared it. But are there doubts? No, I'm full of certainties, and I always will be.

"As I explained to your superiors," I say, "my work here isn't finished."

Speaking with my human voice.

"Finished or not, your work isn't up to standards," the messenger says with its mouth and tongue and new pink lungs. "And I will do whatever is necessary to bring you back."

I make a show of sitting in a guest's chair, smiling at that male face.

"No."

"What?"

"Never," I say. "At least, not until I am satisfied."

The visitor has no patience for debate. A thousand clues tell me that greater minds have pressed a front-line soldier into this unsavory duty. The minds have already cobbled together parts of what I have been doing, and presumably they can guess some of the rest. Caution and violence. This soldier represents both elements, and munitions and more soldiers will be hiding nearby, ready to unleash aid.

"You don't need a diplomat now," I say.

The visitor says nothing.

"Unless we have received intelligence from our superiors," I say.

"I am your superior," it says.

I sit back, human nature showing with the careless crossing of one leg over its loyal mate.

"Give me another century," I say.

"I'll grant you ten seconds," it says.

"Let's compromise," I say. "Give me five minutes. Although I probably won't need half of that time."

Very powerful entities enjoy offering little gifts to the weak. This soldier wants to feel powerful, and that's enough reason to shrug and say, "Three minutes."

"Why are we here?" I ask.

"Here?"

"Waiting beside this ordinary star, preparing a fortress against our invisible enemies," I say.

The obvious answers don't bear repeating. It's more efficient to say, "Orders," and leave it at that.

"A hidden fortress lying in wait," I say.

A nod, a human shrug.

"But what if we weren't the first to arrive?" I ask.

"What's that?"

I lean forward, looking like a middle-aged woman in the midst of a long, successful career. Which is exactly how I want to appear.

"We built our bunkers inside the ice. We hid and we slept, waiting to spring the trap when our enemies arrived. But what if the masters who sent us here made a grave blunder and our local superiors don't see the mistake? Our enemies were here long before we were. They arrived and laid the trap, and you and I have been too ignorant and too arrogant to recognize the genius waiting to pounce."

The soldier says nothing to me, busy sending reports across billions of cold kilometers.

Light-speed still rules the universe, and there is time.

"These beasts are the trap," it says.

I say, "Perhaps."

"Unassuming as they are, you think they're the enemy's tools?"

I have told lies in my life, and I have told the truth. But I've never done both so well as when I tell this soldier, "It's amazing how quickly these creatures have advanced. And just in the last two hundred years."

"Nothing seems too remarkable," the soldier argues. Yet it is impressed. The thoughtful water has achieved quite a lot, yes.

We sit and count time, and then it says, "Three minutes is finished."

"Go back and tell our best minds this," I say. "Tell them that I'm close to understanding. Explain that if they give me two more years, I will be able to decide if these humans are nothing but a brief little fire."

The possibility tempts.

But no. The soldier stands and alerts its allies. Too bad. I would have liked another two years to make ready. Or at least enough time to nurse my William out of his little bug.

A vast system can be described using simple equations of state. This is true of atmospheres and stars and even the most extensive empire. Tiny, tiny changes go unnoticed, and none of them matters. But then one more change arrives and stability collapses. New states arrive suddenly, and they come as ice ages and exploding suns, and entities with more pride than power are forced to see their many failures.

Human beings are not the trap. I knew this when I spoke to the messenger, trying to mislead.

The trap is me and always has been.

Killing that lone soldier is easy enough. Its allies are just as vulnerable, yet I let them battle me longer than necessary. Which serves a role. My former colleagues know that I've been manipulating the living water, but they don't realize how much time and effort have been hidden from them. They don't see that the moon is a fortress ready to be occupied. They can't imagine that these human beasts are ready to make peace with one another, uniting against the alien invaders. And most important of all, they will never imagine that the Earth itself has been transformed: I am standing on a warrior built from everything powerful that I have ever found on this world.

This little world is part horse and part rat.

And it is a boy sitting in the stinking darkness, waiting for the idiot to give him that one careless push.

John Chu is a microprocessor architect by day, a writer, translator, and podcast narrator by night. His fiction has appeared or is forthcoming at *Boston Review, Uncanny, Asimov's Science Fiction, Clarkesworld,* and *Tor.com,* among other venues. His translations have been published at *Clarkesworld, The Big Book of SF,* and other venues. His story "The Water That Falls on You from Nowhere" won the 2014 Hugo Award for Best Short Story.

QUANTIFYING TRUST

John Chu

The algorithms Maya wants can't exist yet. Nothing is powerful enough to run them fast enough to be useful. Her doctoral work is requiring more hardware design than she expected. It's not enough for her just to propose something on paper—she wants to see whether her algorithms work. This is why Maya is sitting in her lab waving her arms and wriggling her fingers.

With her VR goggles on, she doesn't see a half dozen somewhat rusted metal desks with missing handles sitting on a raised floor and pushed to the walls of the lab, the dented, mostly empty bookshelves, or the massive, antiquated air-conditioning unit that takes up an entire wall by itself. Instead, what surrounds her are layers and layers of thin tubing connecting logical functions and memories into a network. The former are slides that split off and connect to tubing in all directions; the latter are shimmering dots arranged in matrices. Glowing dots of all colors speed through the tubing, swoosh through the logical functions, then out the other side.

She gestures and a logical function envelops her. Stack of 3D surface graphs glide around her. They have the spectrum for axes. Dots stream down the axes, turn a right angle when the colors match. Some rebound away, changing color as they do. Others disappear. When she sweeps her arm from left to right, one of the surfaces wriggles. Its shape changes to match the arc she's drawn. The pattern and colors of the dots that leave change in turn.

This is visual programming meets hardware prototyping. It's like reaching inside somebody and doing surgery on their guts.

Maya zooms back out. She prods the network and logical functions just barely in sight blink red in error. She frowns. Analogue circuit design is so much trickier than digital design, and the hardware has evolved in response to the training stimulus. She pulls off her goggles to consults her notes. It takes her a few tries to decipher her own handwriting. Goggles back on, she makes few deft gestures with her fingers and her design stops blinking. Having wiped out the changes from her previous attempt at training Sammy from social media, she restarts the training, forcing the machine she's prototyping to decide what to trust.

The subject of her surgery sits on the desk in front of her. Enclosures for artificial intelligences seem to come in only two flavors. They are either child-like cartoons with eyes too big for their already too-big heads, or lithe women firmly in the uncanny valley. At one foot tall with a head that takes up a third of its body, Sammy is decidedly the former. If Maya ever has final say on a design, her AI wouldn't fall into either category. It'd be an interesting change if, for once, the AI presented like a broad-shouldered, muscle-bound man firmly in the uncanny valley, for example. It'd be a funny in-joke, if nothing else.

The door into the lab clicks, then opens. Jake walks in. He's the postdoc Maya's advisor hired two weeks ago. He speaks English in a generically international accent that's impossible to place and he looks like he could plausibly have been born anywhere in the world. Maya hasn't bothered to pry. If role-playing games were something she still had time to play, she'd say Jake is built on too many points. A couple conversations in, she's only nominally convinced of his humanity and then only because all the other possibilities are impossible. She may have said this to his face this last week. If nothing else, her face flushing red right after showed that *she* was human.

"Figure skating." Maya doesn't bother to say hello.

"Oh, I train up to a quad lutz." He smiles, his left hand gripping an empty mug.

Maya's gaze narrows. "You're kidding."

"No, I'm completely serious." He rolls his eyes. "Do I look like I'm capable of getting off the ice and spinning around four times before landing on a ridiculously thin blade of metal?"

Jake is tall, but not absurdly so. He only presents that way. The big shoulders, wide back that juts out from his T-shirt, and bulging arms are ostentatious signifiers of size and power. Add to that a trim waist due to the apparent lack of any body fat, thighs a little too big for his jeans, and suspiciously perfect bilateral symmetry, and you have someone who should need a passport to enter planet Earth, but not someone whose shape is easily stable when jumping or whose shape lets him spin quickly enough in the air. The figure skaters doing the most difficult jumps right now are all male and built like short sticks.

"So not figure skating?" Maya will sear the date in her brain if she's finally come up with something that Jake hasn't somehow perfected.

"Well, I worked with some skaters on their jump biomechanics one summer. I helped someone get her quad lutz. That's close, right?" His gaze shifts past Maya to the AI. His face glows. "Sibling!"

"Excuse me?"

Generally, the initial reaction is "Oh, how cute!" or something when people first see Sammy. The AI hits all the signifiers for adorability. This is the first time Maya has seen anyone claim it as family.

"That's Sammy." Jake points to it, his finger stabbing repeatedly like a sewing machine needle. "You prototype your artificial neurone design on it so that you can test out your novel trust quantification algorithms."

"Wait." She holds up a hand. "How do you know this? The artificial neurone paper is still under review. I haven't even talked to my advisor about those algorithms yet."

Jake's eyes grow wide and his mouth forms a small "o." For a moment, he is as adorable as Sammy. This should not be humanly possible.

"OCR errors on the dates when her notes were scanned for archiving maybe." The words are soft, more to himself than to Maya. His eyebrows shoot up when he realizes she heard him. He raises his voice back to normal. "What sort of software requires this sort of hardware?"

Maya is like any grad student still interested in their dissertation topic. Ask her about her research and all else is forgotten. She launches into a technically dense and wildly discursive explanation. Jake nods encouragingly and by the time she's done, she's talked about correlating mined data, self-adaptive filters, evolutionary training algorithms but also the musicals of Harold Arlen, the films of Akira Kurosawa, and why Kim Yuna was robbed of an Olympic Gold Medal in 2014.

"You're attempting to filter sexism, racism, heterocentrism, and the other systemic prejudices out of AI training through the power of higher mathematics?" Jake looks puzzled for a moment before his jaw drops and his mouth forms another "o," this one larger than the last time. "This is generally not what computer scientists mean by 'race-free.'"

That joke really does not land. Maya side-eyes him. "You still haven't told me how you know about Sammy."

Jake holds his hands up in mock surrender. He clutches his heart as he stumbles back a step as if he's been shot. That and his frown strikes Maya as a bit much. The man has facial expressions like a Disney cartoon.

"You got me. I'm an android sent back from the future. Right now, I'm helping organize the March for Truth. Figures that I can't fool my eventual creator." He drops his hands and grins. The change in affect is instant and infectious. "It's also not an unreasonable guess based on what you have published."

"You probably also guess the murderer on the first page of mystery novels. Fine, don't tell me. Just keep my work under your hat for now." She swivels her chair back towards Sammy. "Might as well show you what I'm up to."

"Oh, I'd love that." Jake rubs his hands.

She flicks a switch at the back of Sammy's neck. Its head lifts. The lenses in its eyes pull back and forth as they focus. Maya says hello to it and it replies with a sexist insult it learned from the internet. She shuts Sammy down so quickly she almost knocks it over. It's still relying on wrong sources of information. The trust quantification functions need work. She'll dig into Sammy to see what happened, wipe out the training, then try again.

Maya swivels back around. The gaze of the man from the uncanny valley is very guilty puppy. He hunches down next to Maya's chair and just stares at Sammy. His hands grip the edge of the desk and his arms grow as they tense. Jake's not doing that nonchalant thing that she's seen other physically improbable men do. They give off an air of seeming unawareness that they are way taller or way more muscular or whatever. Jake seems to revel in his size and shape. That said, "android from the future" should never be anyone's go-to explanation for anything.

"I create you one day, huh?" Maya levels a particularly disbelieving glare.

Sammy may be Maya's best evidence that, despite her doubts, Jake is probably human. She's ruled out first contact with a strange visitor from another planet on the grounds that no alien species would just happen to look so human. Mostly, she doesn't see how anyone gets to Jake from Sammy.

Jake just shrugs.

As an undergrad, Maya worked nights as a cashier at a convenience food market. It paid just well enough—which is to say terribly—but her shifts were never all that busy. Once in a while, some old lady might come in asking for "War Chester Shire" sauce or some teenage boy would want to know where the condoms were. Otherwise, she'd sit on her stool and do homework. For the record, it took her a few seconds to recognize the lady meant "Worcestershire" and no time at all to tell the teenage boy the store didn't sell condoms. She might have asked the other employee working that night, though. At the top of her voice.

The clear plastic canister next to the cash register was always filled with lollipops wrapped in red, green, and brown waxed paper. One day, someone walked up to the cash register and stared at the canister for a few seconds before she shifted her gaze to Maya.

"Hi, my daughter would like some lollipops. She wants only the brown ones and I'm colorblind." The woman continued on before Maya had a chance to offer to pick them out for her. "So I'm going to sort out the brown lollipops and you tell me whether I'm right or wrong. Okay?"

Maya nodded. The woman reached in the canister then took out a handful. One by one, she showed each to Maya then dropped them to her left or right depending on what color Maya said they were. After a few lollipops, the woman started naming the color and Maya corrected her once or twice. Finally, she sorted on her own and a pile of brown lollipops lay on her left and the rest lay on her right.

She paid for the brown ones. Maya bagged them while the woman dumped the rest back into the canister.

Maya understood in principle how AIs were trained even as an undergrad. It wasn't that different from how this woman trained herself to recognize those brown lollipops. In practice, the woman had to trust Maya. She could have been an asshole and the woman would have given her daughter a bag of red lollipops. Or, worse, there could have been no feedback at all. The server who didn't bother putting Maya's gluten-free pasta order as gluten-free might wrongly learn that it didn't matter since he wasn't the one who got sick. None of this sank into Maya until grad school.

Swear words and slurs fill Sammy's responses to Maya's questions. This is not what she wants. If it were, all she'd need to do is leave the lab. Strangers "but you speak English so well" her. Kids spontaneously pull their eyes into slits and start ching-chonging at her as she walks to and from the university. Where do kids even pick up those stereotypes these days?

When she is Sammy's trust quantification function, its responses are adequate. Nothing anyone would confuse for intelligent, but useable. But then Sammy just reflects her biases. Let Sammy roam free by itself on the internet and it's clear that even if Maya understands what data sources to trust, she's failed to compose the set of logic functions that can make Sammy understand or can even be evolved to make Sammy understand. Maybe she'd be better off defining trustworthiness and let Sammy evolve the trust quantification functions from that. She taps the back of Sammy's neck to shut it down. Wiping out Sammy's training again can happen later. She sets her forehead on her desk so she's staring down at the floor. This is oddly comforting.

Jake walks in. From her angle, Maya can make out the calves stretching against his rolled-up jeans and the low-cut sneakers that have to be too small for his feet. Or maybe they just look too small in relation to his legs. He is still carrying the same empty mug. A hairline crack now runs down one side.

"Temporal mechanics." She's now resorting to a topic that's not a thing.

"Well, I'm here, right?" He laughs. "Seriously, the foundational research is just getting started but no one doing it will recognize that time-travel is even a ramification for a few more years. Would you like some citations?"

His tone is so matter-of-fact that for a moment Maya can believe that Mr. Uncanny Valley actually does come from the future and has the citations at the ready. Or maybe his CV also includes years in acting school. At this point, she can believe either.

"Wouldn't that cause some sort of temporal paradox or something?"

"Yes." The sarcastic tone is pitch-perfect. It plays against his word but Maya doesn't feel mocked. "In fact, I've already said too much. The universe has imploded and you have been trapped in a time loop reliving the same two minutes for the past 45 years, seven months, 23 days, four hours, 56 minutes, and twelve seconds."

"That doesn't sound encouraging. It would explain the progress I'm not making on Sammy though."

"Tell me about it. All I get to do is walk through that door and explain to you that we're in a time loop over and over again."

She laughs as she sits back up. Her jaw drops when she sees the rest of Jake. Dark brown stains are streaked across his light blue T-shirt. Some of the blood still looks wet.

"Wow, what happened?"

"What?" He follows her gaze to his T-shirt. "Oh, this. Nosebleed. Sensitive nasal membranes. Snorted too much cocaine at Studio 54 in the 1980s."

Her gaze narrows. Jake does not look like he's old enough to be alive in the 1980s much less old enough to be in a nightclub back then. For a brief moment, Maya thinks about ways to make him bleed. It'd be definitive, but it'd also be no fun. Not to mention wrong. Besides, she'd rather keep playing the game where he's wedged himself in the uncanny valley and she tries to pull him out.

"You don't lie, do you?" She pulls a notebook out of her desk. "You just say something obviously implausible instead."

"Oh, that's just when I'm around you." He shrugs, looking a little deflated. "Would you lie to your mother?"

"I'm not your mother."

"Of course not." He looks a little puzzled. "It's a metaphor."

"What's a metaphor?"

"An implied comparison without using 'like' or 'as.'"

Laughter erupts from her. Jake is just standing there watching Maya fall out of her chair. His "who me? Did I say something funny?" body language is both subtle and over-the-top. It's as though he genuinely doesn't understand what's so funny. He's quite the actor, she decides.

Jake offers Maya a hand. She refuses and Jake goes to his desk. She pushes herself back onto her chair then flips through her notebook for a while before she shuts it.

"Jake, how do you know who to trust?"

He turns to look at her. She thinks she can see his reaction happen in rapid, discrete steps. His brow furrows. His lips purse. His mouth opens then closes again. His actions get the message across, but the effect feels more studied than organic.

Finally, he shrugs. "How does anyone know?"

After fifteen minutes, if any undergrad still didn't get the memo that the theme of the first digital systems lecture of the semester was feedback, they weren't paying attention as far as Maya was concerned. She sat off to the side in the front row of the gigantic lecture hall, her fist propping up her chin. She'd twigged onto the theme after about three minutes. Professor Schmidt always insisted whichever teaching assistant assigned to her for the semester attend all her lectures. Otherwise, she'd be doing literally anything else. She was still a first-year grad student then and lucky not to be assigned to a course with a lab component.

Professor Schmidt was talking about feedback in the mathematical sense: some version of the output of a function also became an input to the same function. Twenty minutes in, schematic diagrams of storage elements for sequential logic filled the chalkboard. She had this thing about showing how a storage element a modern digital designer might actually use was derived from the simplest possible storage element. Even as the circuits grew more complicated, at their heart were cross-coupled logic elements. The output of each logic element was also fed back into the input of the other. The cross-coupling kept one output stable at the stored state and the other output at its opposite. In order to remember something, you had to keep reminding yourself, to keep regenerating the memory.

Digital logic is built on the clean, shiny lie that there are only two possible states: on and off. The real world is analogue. The number of states, if that's even a meaningful concept, between on and off is infinite. When Professor Schmidt drew transfer curves to characterize the relationship between input and output for the circuits, Maya perked up and other students' eyes began to glaze. No one expected Professor Schmidt to analyze analog circuits in a digital systems class. Most of the students were probably there because they didn't like analogue circuit analysis in the first place.

Thirty minutes in, Maya decided that feedback was building to a larger point, the ultimate instability of the building blocks of digital logic. Idealized digital circuits pretended transistors were simple switches that were either open or closed. Real life was much more complicated in ways that Professor Schmidt had no qualms racing through. After all, everyone in the room had passed transistor theory and while transistors could behave like switches, they could also behave like amplifiers. Professor Schmidt gleefully listed the ways a simple storage element could fail to store the right value. Most of them were some variant of "things take time." Any switch, as it opened or closed, was neither opened nor closed. What happened in the meantime through was also fed back. The value stored could be neither "on" nor "off" for a good long time.

The class met for fifty minutes a day on Mondays, Wednesdays, and Fridays. Forty-five minutes in, Maya finally leaped to Professor Schmidt's actual point. The job of engineering was to create stable systems out of fundamentally unstable elements. No girder by itself was reliable, but a well-designed bridge could be. The course was called "Digital Systems," but what took up the rest of the semester was building stable systems.

The other lectures were about how to keep elements out of unreliable regions of operations, how to structure elements together to compensate for their relative weaknesses and so on. They were, however, just expansions of this lecture.

Years later, as a researcher in grad school, Maya lays her head down, staring at her desk in frustration. When she wonders whether building an AI that can trust correctly is even possible, what comes back to her is this lecture.

The good news is that Sammy has stopped swearing at Maya. The bad news is that now Sammy won't talk to Maya at all. It's stopped responding completely. It just stands on Maya's desk failing to look angry. Its stubby arms are folded across its chest and its mouth curves down into a frown. It can't do anything about its big eyes, but Maya can't look at them without imagining that any moment they'll be filled with tears.

The VR goggles have to go on. She flies into Sammy's hardware. Even at a distance, the interconnection of logical functions and memories isn't quite as she remembers but it's not supposed to be. It's supposed to evolve as Sammy learns. The evolution is not supposed to render Sammy non-functional. Only dark, stray dots flow through the tubing.

The door clicks, followed by silence. It has to be Jake. Anyone else would have made the tiles on the lab's somewhat loose raised floor rattle and squeak.

Sammy comes alive. Long streams of glowing dots rush through the layers of thin tube and slide through the functional units. Maya rips off her VR goggles to see Sammy pivot towards Jake, smile, wave, then swear at him. Sammy is not non-functional, just angry at her. This means Sammy can get angry. Or something that Maya interprets as anger.

Jake casually transfers a stack of boxes five high from one hand to the other so that he can close the door. Each arm bulges as it curls up the weight. The stack doesn't teeter as he goes to his desk then sets it down. Maya steps over to his side. The boxes are full of books. She eyes him skeptically. No one can support that much weight with just their biceps. Well, perhaps someone who has taken literally all the steroids. From certain angles, his arms do look about as wide as his head.

"Hey, you're the one who told me you didn't think I was human. Maybe you were right." Jake shrugs. "Aside from some outrageous things that you weren't supposed to believe and you don't, I have been completely honest with you. It's not my fault that the truth is unbelievable. For now, anyway."

He unpacks his books onto the bookshelves. They are an odd and intimidating lot, ranging from slim volumes on ethics and religion to thick tomes on quantum mechanics.

"If you are an android from the future, aren't you supposed to make some pretence of acting human?"

"And, around you, the point of that would be what?"

She finds herself thinking he has a point. Game or no game, his story is self-consistent. Regardless, it seems Sammy will talk to him when it won't talk to her.

"Jake, can you please talk to Sammy for me?"

Jake stops in mid-step and turns to Maya, a copy of *La Guerre du Golfe n'a pas eu lieu* in hand. He holds it out, two-handed, like a talisman against evil.

"No, I'm not creating a predestination paradox that leads to my own creation." He looks down at the book then lowers it to his side. "Work out Sammy's problems yourself. For my sake, if no one else's."

Jake continues to unpack. Maya trains the VR goggles on him and doesn't see anything. All that means is that he is not constructed out of prototyping hardware. She doesn't see anything when she looks at herself or the air conditioning unit through her VR goggles, either.

With the VR goggles trained on Sammy, slides and tubing fill her field of view. Occasionally, she can hear the hiss as Jake places a book on a bookshelf. That's the only sign that he is still in the lab. Either Jake does have that much casual dexterity or he's working extremely hard to show off. She's tempted to throw her VR goggles or Sammy at him just to see what happens. She half-expects he would catch either without even looking. However, if it turns out "android from the future" has just been this game they've been playing with each other, replacing either is not in the budget.

In VR, Maya flies inside Sammy. She glides along tubing, hovers over memories, and zooms into logical functions. How the machinery that drives Sammy has evolved becomes clearer over the course of hours. Parts of it are so changed from what she remembers and so odd, she may never understand them. She realizes why Sammy has become non-responsive to her and, apparently, only her.

Sammy knows. It's not stored in any of the memories but assumed by all logical functions and baked into how they are interconnected. The knowledge that Maya has been resetting Sammy's training whenever she feels it's going wrong is innate in Sammy. It's ingrained into the hardware and predicates everything it does. Sammy doesn't trust Maya. The trust functions are working, just not in the way Maya expected.

Maya can't remove its assumptions about her without modifying every logical function and rewiring the connections between them. That's clearly impractical. She can nuke Sammy completely, reload her original design, then reapply the improvements she's come up with since. The result would no longer be Sammy. That said, Sammy behaves like the kids who ching-chong at her as she walks to school. That makes nuking Sammy oddly tempting. It's not her kindest thought.

"I'm an idiot." She buries her head in her hands.

"Nonsense. You're one of the smartest humans I know."

Maya jumps at Jake's voice. She pulls off her VR goggles. His boxes are now empty. The bookshelves are full.

"You've been so quiet. I forgot you were still here."

"Yup, that's me." He puts his hands on his waist. "Silent. Efficient. Deadly?" He smiles at the last. The smile disappears and his hands fall when she doesn't reciprocate.

"Every year, one of the professors here gives a lecture whose point, when she gets around to it, is that engineering is the art of making stable systems out of unstable devices."

"Oh, Professor Schmidt." His smile comes back and his eyes light, not literally, with recognition.

"I've mentioned this to you before?"

"Well, strictly speaking, not yet. It depends on whose 'before' you mean, I guess."

He is utterly straight-faced. Maya can't tell whether he is serious or if cracking a smile would ruin the joke.

"Anyway, it's just hit me that it's unfair to expect Sammy to resist the stereotypes that humans fall for all the time."

Jake opens his mouth, starts to speak, closes his mouth, then opens his mouth again. His actions are perfectly timed to convey indecision. If anyone else had done exactly the same, Maya might just think they were being indecisive.

"Down that road lies predestination paradox." He taps the fingers of his left hand on his thigh. "I don't know what answering you will do to me."

"Oh, I'm going to erase Sammy and bring it back up from scratch no matter what you say." She puts the VR goggles back on and turns to Sammy. "Having screwed up with Sammy, I need a fresh start. The trust mechanisms work. It's now a matter of the right feedback."

Jake makes a noncommittal noise. Maya has stretched her hands out and is making fine gestures with her fingers. The prototyping system throws several "Are you sure?" warnings at her. After she agrees to all of those, the tubing and functional units all disappear then re-emerge in the configuration she originally established. They are lined up in perfectly regular matrices on a perfectly flat plane. Each plane is stacked exactly on top of the next. It's all absurdly unnatural, but it's a new start.

Maya takes off the VR goggles. There are changes that still need to be applied before Sammy re-activates, but those can happen without her watching. This time, it will subject itself to its own randomly generated statements until it can reliably generate trustworthy statements before she lets the internet loose on it. No bias from the human world to throw off its notions of trust.

"Jake, are you really here to organize the March for Truth?"

"Well, I'm here and I'm helping with the March for Truth. I never explicitly stated a relationship between the two. But if you don't believe who I am, there's no point in getting into why I'm here. Sorry." He shrugs. "If it helps, what I'm actually doing here has a shelf life. I don't expect to survive it much longer. Don't examine my remains. Predestination paradox and all that."

Maya's eyebrows rise. This is a bit dark for their game. "I was just thinking that we deserve the AI we create. It'd be easier to filter out the racism and the rest if, systemically, there was less of it to begin with." She straightens up her desk, filing her papers, stashing her notebooks in desk drawers. "Not everyone has to work towards a better world for the world to work, but it'd be better if everyone did."

"I'm a machine intelligence, not a mind-reader."

"Oh, two things. One, is the March for Truth looking for volunteers? And, two. You know." She blows air through her lips and looks down before she meets his gaze again. "If I could close my eyes but still sense your body language and if we're just talking—not wandering in some obscure corner of knowledge no one but you has ever visited before—I can just about believe you're a person."

"Are you implying that I don't pass the Turing Test?" Jake looks indignant. His hands are on his waist.

"Actually, I'm saying that you do. Passing for human is over-rated. You're a more convincing conscious intelligence than any number of people I know."

His eyebrows rise. His jaw drops. The look of astonishment is elegant, precise, and utterly adorable. The effect is so affable that Maya has to remind herself that he's also the guy who thought nothing of wearing a shirt splattered with blood.

"Thank you." Jake masters himself. His face contracts to its normal length. "We're always looking for volunteers. Do you want to meet the group?"

"Sure."

Jake nods. He heads out the door and Maya follows. She turns out the light behind her, leaving Sammy alone to meditate on the quantification of trust.

Sofia Samatar is the author of the novels *A Stranger in Olondria* and *The Winged Histories*, the short story collection, *Tender*, and *Monster Portraits*, a collaboration with her brother, the artist Del Samatar. Her work has received several honors including the John W. Campbell Award, the British Fantasy Award, and the World Fantasy Award. She lives in Virginia and teaches Arabic literature, African literature, and speculative fiction at James Madison University.

HARD MARY

Sofia Samatar

I wisdom dwell with prudence, and find out knowledge of witty inventions.
—Proverbs 8:12

We found her behind the barn. It was the eve of Old Christmas, the night the animals speak with the tongues of men, and we knew very well that if we could manage to walk around the barn seven times, each of us would see the man she was to marry. We met shivering in front of the Millers' barn, which was the most central to all of us, though of course some of us had to walk much farther than others. Kat was complaining because her one foot had gone into icy water on the way. Barb Miller kept shushing us, scared we'd wake the house. Mim was late.

"She's not coming," said Barb. "Let's go without her."

"She'll come."

The barn looked huge. You know how much bigger things seem at night. Behind it curled a misty, chilly sky, the stars all blurred together. From inside the barn, someone said: "Turtledoves."

Esther gripped my arm and squealed, "What was that?"

"Shut up! It's the horses."

"Is that what horses talk about?" asked Esther, starting to cry.

"Pigeons," murmured the horses.

I felt like crying myself. My hair stood on end. But here was Mim coming across the field.

"Okay, okay," babbled Barb. "Let's stick together."

"Hello, girls," said Mim. She made a funny figure in the dark. Her long white nose stuck out from under her hood, glinting a bit in the starlight. Her hood looked overlarge, stuffed with her crinkly hair. Still, I was glad to see her, for though she was the shortest of us by an inch, just smaller than Esther, and the ugliest by a mile, Mim was also the toughest. I could never forget how, as a child, she had taken a whole bite out of Joe Miller's arm.

"Mim," whimpered Esther, "the horses are talking."

"Good," said Mim. "It's working, then."

We all linked arms and started around the barn. The ground was rocky and hard with old snow, and a freezing wind came over the empty fields, flapping our skirts about our legs. Inside the barn, the horses spoke of a she-goat and a ram. A cow groaned: "Fowls came down upon the carcasses." You could tell it was a cow, because while the horses had fuzzy, velvety voices, the cow spoke in a voice of blank despair. To distract ourselves from the animals, we whispered about the boys we might see, and whether they would come themselves, or only their apparitions. "I hope it's not ghosts," said Esther. Mim said she expected we'd see a sort of layer peeled off the boys, something like a photograph.

In the end we didn't see any boys, because, just on the seventh round, Mim stubbed her toe in the dark. "Shit!" she said, hopping.

We all had to stop. There was something lying on the ground in the shadow of the barn: something large, with the faintest gleam of metal.

"What on earth," said Kat.

We all crouched down.

"Is it a radio?" asked Barb.

"Let's take it into the light and see."

The thing was cold and heavy. We dragged it out of the shadow of the barn, into the starlight. There we saw it was a lady made of metal. It was about the size of a real lady, but only from the waist up. It didn't have any legs. Its eyes were closed.

We stood around it, looking down.

"It's from the Profane Industries," said Mim.

My skin prickled all the way up to my throat. The Profane Industries, which lay between us and town, was a place of evil, where they manufactured all kinds of monstrosities. It was said they grew sheep in a field like vegetables. They sewed babies together with other animals to make slaves for the world of men. When we were little, unkind people used to joke that Mim was one of these mismatched children; her nickname had been Dog Baby. Now, staring down, I knew we were face to face with a Profane instrument. Over the years, we had often complained that they threw things around our farms. Mysterious white balloons had been found in the creek, and, though they never admitted it, we knew P.I. was responsible when our cows suffered an outbreak of the Stamps.

This poor metal lady was one of their failed experiments. Her shoulders were stained with dark, rusty blotches, her head dinged in on one side. I knew we were going to save her. In the distance a pair of dogs began to bark, "Behold a smoking furnace."

(Sitting at the kitchen table, writing this, I feel again that enormous night. That time.)

A wave of weeping rolled from the barn. "And, lo," cried the cows, "an horror of great darkness." We didn't listen. Mim and I picked up the metal lady, holding her awkwardly between us. A vole sneaked past, muttering something about a burning lamp, but it was too late, we had already decided to name the lady Mary, and because she had given Mim's toe such a nasty knock, so hard in fact that the toenail would soon turn blue and fall off, we called her Hard Mary.

A cloud of black and white specks. It swirls, gathers, and divides. It becomes a white stripe on a midnight field. It becomes a man in a long white coat. He turns. He wears a special pair of glasses: one circle over his eye, the other flipped up against his forehead. His naked eye looks newly awakened, peeled, as if by pushing up the lens of his glasses he has pushed away all intelligence, all design. A boyish smile. He is holding the circle of sparks he calls the Crown. There's a hum like fingertips on a table. A voice without words.

SHE IS A THINKING CREATURE

We kept Hard Mary down at our place, in the spring house. I was the only one who ever went in there, for the chill was bad for Mother's bones. There was a little back room with a skylight where we girls used to meet and gossip. I'd put a rag rug and an old rocking chair in there, and we set Mary up on that chair. Oh, she had a noble face. It was all angles, but her expression was gentle. When I went in to see her that first day, the light from the skylight gleamed on her bumpy hair. I'd brought water and baking soda and a scrubber to give her a bath. Mim was there already, muffled up in scarves. We scrubbed Hard Mary until she shone like one of King David's daughters, polished after the similitude of a palace.

"Isn't she pretty!" gasped Barb, whirling in fresh as a peony after her run through the cold.

Kat followed, rubbing her glasses on her skirt. Esther came last. Everyone wanted to touch Hard Mary. We held her upright on the chair so Mim could scrub her back. I could smell the honey and vinegar Esther used to treat her acne, I felt a hand cross mine, soft and a little pampered, probably Barb's, and as I shifted my foot because someone was stepping on my toe, Hard Mary spoke. Her lips didn't move, but she spoke, in a voice thin as a wasp's.

"Ahhh," she said. "What is."

You may believe we all jumped back. Esther sat down on the floor. "Mercy!" Kat exclaimed.

Only Mim remained touching Hard Mary, holding her by the shoulder, at arm's length. Mim's arm was trembling like a wire.

"What is," said Mary, then louder: "WHAT IS." Then she made a horrible, drawn-out, gurgling sound.

"Oh, she's dying!" Esther cried.

That brought Kat to life. She had a reputation to protect, being from a family of bonesetters. "Lay her down on the floor," she ordered.

We laid her down and Kat turned her over on her face. Hard Mary's back was covered with lines. There were tiny screws in the corners where the lines met. Mim, who always had tools, dug a screwdriver out of her pocket. She unscrewed Mary, and Kat looked at her innards. There was no blood, only lots of wires. Carefully, Kat and Mim wiggled something out of her back. It looked like some rolls of pennies stuck together.

"I know what that is," said Mim, exultant.

"Her heart?" breathed Esther.

"My girl, that's a battery. Eighteen volts."

When she's happy, Mim's face gets a wolfish expression. She told us Mary's heart was a simple battery of the kind used to light the barns at night when the cows were calving.

"So you can get her a new one?" I asked.

"I don't even have to," she said, tucking the heart inside her coat. "I can juice this one up at a generator."

You could tell, I thought with jealous admiration, that there were no men at her house.

"Wait," Barb said suddenly. "Are we sure it's right?"

We all looked at her.

"I mean," she said, blushing, "it's from the Profane Industries. Hard Mary. It could have something bad inside."

"We could all have something bad inside," said Mim.

"Let's pray for her," Esther suggested.

"You all go ahead," said Mim.

So Mim took the heart and left and the rest of us prayed for Mary who looked like she could use it, flat on her face with her wires hanging out. I thought of how she'd been made by crafty and wicked-hearted men who meet with darkness in the daytime, and grope in the noonday as in the night. The windows of Profane Industries are black. You can't see in, and you can't even really get close to the place because of the fence. "Save her, O Lord," I prayed, "from the sin in which she was conceived."

"Amen," murmured Esther, laying her hand on Mary's head.

Mary said nothing. She lay like an empty jug. But the next day, Mim brought her heart back, looking the same but now filled to the brim with invisible fire. And when we sat Mary up on the rocking chair, clad in a dress Kat had brought her to cover her nakedness, and a cap for her hair, she spoke again.

Her voice didn't sound like a wasp's this time. It was fuller, and even warm, like flesh and blood. "What is your desire?"

Tears stung my eyes. It's a habit; I tend to cry when I tell the truth. "We want to be friends with you," I said.

"Friends," said Mary.

Mim took her hand. "Mary. Your name is Mary."

She said her name. We told her our names, and she repeated them after us. She was that quick, she knew all of us right away. In her dark blue dress, she was like a human lady, except that the cloth went flat where her legs should be. The cap covered up the place where her head was dented, and I felt somehow she was grateful for it. I felt she wanted to forget where she was from, to forget everything that had happened to her and start over, here, with us. She was good at it, too. She learned faster than any baby.

Her face in the glow of the skylight was silvery-bright, like a winter cloud with the sun behind it. Though her eyes were closed, she never slept. Whenever I went to the spring house she was sitting up, expectant. Her hands were cold, but clever, the palms and fingertips covered with fine mesh. We found she could hold a needle, and Kat taught her to sew and knit. I taught her to read. You only had to show her a page, and she knew it. She'd read it back to you without looking. I couldn't go too fast for her. She got the whole Bible by heart in a couple of weeks.

("What are you writing?" asks Sam. Which means: "Stop doing it."

He doesn't say it to be mean. It's because he doesn't want me to get too tired. "I'll be up soon," I tell him, covering the page with my hand. I don't do that to be mean, either. I don't know why I do it.)

Barb taught Mary to sing. Hard Mary can sing anything, even deeply like a man. She has a beautiful bass voice. Esther taught her to take a person's hand, to pat your hair and say ever so softly: "There, now. Don't cry anymore."

It was a magic time. In the evening Sam would throw a handful of grain at my window and I'd creep down the stairs and let him in. We'd sit at the table, scorching our fingers as we tried to warm them at the lamp, and whispering so as not to wake my folks upstairs. I remember the night he told me, "A man must have a noble pursuit," and I knew that if he asked, I'd marry him. He spoke to me of the golden world that brings forth abundantly. He said there was no greater role for a man than to subdue and replenish the earth. While in the spring house Mary sat alone in the rocking chair, her cap dusted with moonlight falling down through the skylight, motionless and self-contained, wearing her eternal smile, waiting for me to come to her again. There was a sound of trucks far away on the road, and a smell of burning from the fires of the ragged men who haunt the forest, and a low stink from the quarry where, even in midwinter, a layer of scum lies on top of the water. Sam caught my fingers playfully. Mary flamed in my heart, a secret. Instead of "What is your desire?" I'd taught her to greet me: "Hi Lyddie!" She could sing all the hymns, but we liked it best when she sang songs Barb got off her brother's radio, sad songs about lying in jail on a pillow of cold concrete.

The black and white specks stand quivering. No one is there. The specks make the lines that are walls and tables and the ceiling that is home. Even when nobody comes, the world moves. There is a little glittering energy at the boundaries of things. This alone is entrancing, but when he returns, when the dots coalesce and spin, it's so beautiful, almost too much. It's almost too much after so many hours alone. He has a box and he is taking something out of it, that is eating. His shoulder hunches when he eats and he shakes an object over the box, casting off a sprinkling of fine dust. He looks up and winks. Individually the black and white specks mean nothing but together they make a feeling that is love.

SHE USES ONLY WHAT SHE NEEDS

Hard Mary has no greed. She doesn't eat. Her insides are pure, as neat as a well-kept sewing basket. She doesn't soil herself. She doesn't sweat. She is mild as May. She has never owned a second cap and dress.

It's true Mim brought her a second heart. I don't know from where. We used to keep it underneath the rocking chair. When her heart began to run down, Mim would switch it out and take the dry one off to be filled. Many men could use such a simple change of heart! We learned that Mary could tell us when her heart was running down, not by speaking but by a red light that came on inside one cheek. The light would be pink at first, hardly noticeable, then it would grow red and start to blink. When she got feverish like this, we'd do the operation.

Everything clean and trim. Not a drop of blood.

Mim constructed a kind of legs for her so she could walk around. It started out as a hoop-like frame, just to fill out her skirt so she didn't look so flat, then later Mim added six wheels like the ones on a shopping cart. I suppose she might have stolen them. I don't know. Sometimes you find shopping carts abandoned along the road, rusting in the rain. It's not a sin to take things other people have thrown away. I don't think of Mim as a thief. I think of her as thrifty.

It was marvelous what she did. Hard Mary can bend to sit down and get up. She can turn about the room. She's the same height as me. Sometimes, breathless with excitement, we'd take her out back behind the spring house so she could practice walking over the melting snow. From a distance, we knew, she'd look just like an ordinary girl. "This is daylight, Mary," we said, "this is a tree." We got her to pet Mim's wretched old dog, Hochmut, who suffered this treatment in silence, his eyes half closed, trembling from nose to tail.

When she got used to walking, she'd go far from us, a dignified lady over the pasture, but when we called her, she always came.

I thought we'd saved her. I thought she was going to live with us forever. I thought they'd forgotten her down at the Profane Industries. After all, they'd thrown her away. Then one Sunday evening a car drove right up to our house and a man got out of it. We heard the engine turn off and the door slam shut. My little brother Cristy ran to the door and Father told him, "Slow down." I heard them from the kitchen where I was washing dishes with Mother. "Now who can that be?" I asked her lightly, drying my hands on my apron.

"Beggars, I expect," she said.

We do get a lot of beggars here in Jericho—foreigners from town asking for bread, barefoot kids wanting to stay awhile, mothers stowing their babies in our barns for us to raise. The elders are always having meetings to figure out which ones to keep and which to send away. Somehow, though, I didn't think this was a beggar. My whole insides were buzzing like a hive. I ran to the front room where Cristy crouched at the window, hugging himself for joy.

"It's a Mercedes!" he hissed.

I peered out. Father stood with his back to us, his hands propped on his hips. The evening was cold enough to see his breath. A long beam of reddish light came slanting across the dark, newly tilled fields. A foreign man was talking to Father. He was tall and elegant, with thinning white hair that the wind lifted. He held his hat in his hands. He had the clean, straight foreign teeth and the soft, sleek foreign body and he was wearing a coat that went down to the ground. He smiled at Father and seemed to be talking in a nice, reasonable way. My insides, which had been so active, had gone still. It was like my marrow was solid lead. The low light struck the man's glasses and I realized I couldn't tell where he was looking.

I jerked away from the window and pressed my back against the wall.

A door slammed. The car started up.

"Oh *boy*," said Cristy. "Look at her smoke."

Father came in and I took his hat, blurting: "What did the man want?"

"Why, nothing," he said, surprised. "Only looking for something he lost."

"What is it? What did he lose?"

"Some foreign stuff," Father answered, frowning at Cristy, who was dancing about, whispering, "Mercedes! Mercedes!"

My knees were turning to water. "What foreign stuff?"

"Lyddie!" Mother called from the kitchen.

"How should I know?" Father said. "Go help your mother."

As I went out, he began wrestling Cristy. He farted, which he could do whenever he liked, and while Cristy giggled he said, "I believe I smell a car."

I went to the kitchen, moving as stiffly as Hard Mary herself. It was then I began my plan for her defense.

He is the Father, the King, the Master of Miracles. He makes me to wear the Crown. His acolytes pass behind him, ready to do his will. They are Kyle, Jonathan, and Judy. They carry his instruments, plug needles into the wall. Judy brings him a cup of black. He takes it without looking at her, both circles over his eyes. He lights up the Crown and gives me visions. I see the everlong and the bent. I perceive the knobs and globules. I am familiar with the scrim. I know collision. I am counting very fast.

SHE IS AS INNOCENT AS A LITTLE CHILD

"All right," said Kat. "We're here now. What's this about?"

We had gathered in Mary's room. A lamp burned on top of the old chest I'd put there to hold her sewing things. Though it was March, we were well wrapped up against the vapors from the spring. Kat's face was pale and accusing. She had a bad tooth.

I took a breath. "It's time to tell the others about Mary."

"Oh, no," said Esther.

"Don't just say no. Listen and hear what I have to say."

I told them about the foreign man. I was sure he'd be back, and nobody would keep him from taking Mary away from a bunch of girls. "They have to know her like we do," I said. "They have to see her as one of us. If people know about her, they'll protect her."

Barb stared. "Are you cracked?"

I opened my mouth, but nothing came out.

Barb's cheeks were flaming. "Can you hear yourself?" she demanded, waving her arms. "Tell who about Mary? The bishop? This is it," she said, looking around at the others. "We always knew this day would come, and now it has."

She untied her cap, yanked the strings tighter, and tied it again. Only the previous week, her engagement had been published. She was going to be married to Mel Fisher on Sunday—handsome Mel, who used to croon along with her brother's forbidden radio, and had once accidentally burned down a woodshed with a cigarette.

"Don't go, Barb," I said.

"Which day?" asked Mim.

We all looked down at her. Mim was the only one who was sitting down. She sat on the floor with her back against the wall. She never seemed to feel the cold. Hochmut lay with his head in her lap.

"What?" said Barb.

"We knew which day would come?" asked Mim in the same smiling voice.

"Don't be stupid," snapped Barb. "The day we gave Mary up. She's been nice for us, like a toy, but we're not kids. We're practically women."

"If you say 'put away childish things,'" I warned, "I will never speak to you again."

"Why shouldn't I say it?" Barb shouted.

"Quiet!" said Kat.

"Why shouldn't I say it?" Barb repeated more softly, but just as angrily. Her eyes shone, blue and teary. "Go ahead and tell them. They'll say, 'It's a creature from Profane Industries, with a devil inside.' They'll melt her in the forge."

Esther was crying discreetly, standing by Mary and holding her hand. Mary's hand moved in response, gently squeezing Esther's fingers. Her face was still. I could see the coppery light of the lamp reflected in her cheek and the dark, shifting shapes that were me and the other girls.

Then Mim said: "Lyddie is right."

We all looked down at her again—her awkward, too-big head balanced on her skinny neck, her black cap practically bursting with hair, and her little white fingers, which always seemed sneaky, as if they were living their own secret life, scratching her dog's ears.

"Thanks, Mim," I said warmly. I took the paper I'd been working on out of my coat. "This is what I'm going to present to the elders," I explained. "You can add to it if you want." I cleared my throat and started: "Number one: *She is a thinking creature.*"

I'd only gotten to number two when Mim snorted, and I stopped. "What?"

"It's a good idea," she said, "but you're going about it all wrong. They're not going to care what she uses or how she thinks. They'll want to know what she can do. You have to talk about her like a thresher."

"A what?" said Esther.

"A *thresher*," Mim repeated. "A *threshing machine*. Good morning, Esther. Thank you for waking up to join us this fine day." She looked up at me with her hard black eyes. "Don't you see? Mary's a beautiful piece of machinery. Look how she knits. She only stops when you take the needles. You could set her up with some shocks of corn and she'd husk them round the clock. We don't know how strong she is. She could probably lift a cow."

I lowered my hand with the paper. "But she's a *person*. She's our friend."

"Now, those fellows are greedy," Mim went on, as if I hadn't spoken. "They'll want to keep her, but they'll be scared. You have to show them she's not going to lead to idleness or make anybody vain. She'll be owned by everybody, just like the thresher. They could send her around, like at hog-killing time. Mary could kill a hog in ten seconds flat. Making sausage? No problem. She'd stay at it for a week. The blood wouldn't hurt her as long as you oiled her afterward."

"But if she's a machine," said Esther, "she can't join the church."

How Mim would have answered this, we never knew. Hochmut lifted his head, and a second later, we heard voices and heavy boots. "The lamp!" I gasped, but it was too late.

The door opened and Barb's brother Joe came in, followed by Mel Fisher and Greasy Kurtz. Sam came last.

"Well, now," said Joe. "Nobody told us it was a party."

Mim scrambled up from the floor. Hochmut was growling.

"Hello, Dog Baby," Joe said, nodding at Mim. "Keep that old dog of yours steady. You know I kick."

It was true: we all remembered how, only a year before, Joe had given Hochmut a kick that nearly killed him.

"Sit," Mim told the dog, and Hochmut sat, quivering.

"What in creation?" said Mel, staring at Hard Mary.

Joe turned his big, blond head. "Why, it's a dolly party," he said. "We've been wondering what you girls were up to, and here you are playing with dolls."

He started toward Mary.

"It's nothing, Joe," said Barb, trying to laugh, and not looking at Mel at all, because she was too shy, just as I was not looking at Sam, who stood by the door, against the wall. I could feel him not looking at me, too.

"It *is* a doll," Barb simpered, "an old doll we found one day in the woods and we—"

"Don't touch her!" Esther said shrilly, getting between Hard Mary and Joe.

"That's done it," muttered Mim.

Joe paused for a moment, staring at Esther. Then he looked at Greasy, and both of them burst out laughing.

Joe shouldered Esther aside so she nearly stumbled into the lamp. Kat shrank against the wall, looking faint, holding her sore jaw. Joe and Greasy leaned over Mary, with Mel behind them peering between their shoulders. Mary said: "What is your desire?"

"Shit!" hollered Joe. "A talking dolly!"

Since they'd come in, I'd felt a whine like a mosquito at my ear. Now it grew louder, as if the bug was inside my head. The floor seemed to shift. I saw everybody in little broken pieces. Joe's thumb against Mary's face. The black of Greasy's coat, shiny in the lamplight. And Sam, Sam by the wall but craning forward now, fascinated, a bit of his reddish hair sticking out beneath the back of his hat. Then Greasy's hand on Mary's skirt. "No!" cried Esther. Joe was laughing. "Let's see if Dolly has all her parts," he said.

He pulled up her skirt so it showed the bottom of her folded frame. Her little wheels at rest. Both he and Greasy were doubled up with laughter. He kept yanking up the skirt. Then Mim, beside me, shouted out suddenly in a strange, harsh voice: "Mary! Jephthah's daughter!"

Her arms straight at her sides, her hands in fists. "Mary! Jephthah's daughter, Mary!"

Mary's arm shot up and struck Joe Miller on the side of the head. He flew clear across the room and hit the wall. Her second blow caught Greasy Kurtz above the elbow and he buckled, moaning. Kat said later she knew right away that Greasy's arm was broken. Mary stood. Her face was exactly the same, closed eyes and curving mouth. Mel tried to run, but Mim said "Hold him," and Mary grasped his wrist with her steely hand. She moved so fast, like a copperhead striking.

Sam turned back toward the door, but Mim was too quick for him. She met him with Hochmut, who snarled. "Let's have a talk, Sam Esh," she said. Now Sam looked at me, his eyes wide and dark.

My lips felt frozen. "Just hang on," I whispered. "Everything's okay."

Barb was sobbing, "You've killed him. You've killed him." She knelt beside Joe, who was all crumpled up. His hat had rolled under the rocking chair. The floor darkened beneath his head. When I saw that, my own head got heavy, and I sat down and rested my forehead on my knees. I could hear Mel shouting and Mim telling him to pipe down. "Tell this thing to let go of me," he said, and Mim said she would, if he'd behave himself. "Tie his arms behind his back," she said to someone. When my vision cleared, I saw it was Esther, who was tying Sam up with a scarf. Though her face was blotchy with panic, and she'd peed herself, Esther turned out to be Mim's right hand.

Kat said in a shaky voice that Joe was in a bad way and she needed ice.

"In a minute," said Mim, seating herself on the chest. She was so little, it suited her like a chair. Greasy lay at her feet, very still, as if he was scared to move. Mel, too, looked petrified, standing face to face with Mary, his wrist in her grip. Little tremors ran up and down his broad, strong back. Mim glanced up at him sideways from underneath her brows, and smiled. "My word," she observed, "he's shaking like Lebanon."

Looking at her, I recalled that she had a mother who suffered from Seasonal Weeps and a father who had shot himself in the face. I saw the others sizing her up, too, and watched them realize at last that she was a person to be reckoned with. Mim, of course, was perfectly aware of the change in their faces. Her own face glowed. She told them that Mary was a wonderful new machine. This machine was very useful, but, as the boys had discovered, it needed careful handling. You wouldn't stick your hand in the path of a hammer, would you?

"I've had enough of this," said Kat, stamping out. In a moment, she was back with a bucket of cold water from the spring. She took the lamp and set it on the floor close to Joe and began to clean him up, Barb hovering nearby, crying. So it wasn't the end of the argument. We kept fighting, even after Sam had said he was sorry and we'd untied him so he could help with Greasy's arm, and after Esther had run out for a new lamp, and Sam had taken my hand in the darkness. Kat fought with Mim and so did I, for I was frightened. I was afraid we were going to lose Hard Mary. I told Mim you couldn't tie people up, and she said plenty of people had been tied up for their own good, making reference to poor old Betty Blank, who was quite demented, and often trailed behind her grandkids on a rope. I told her you couldn't strike people, and she said the boys had only been given a couple of knocks, and it was nothing worse than what they'd received from their own dads.

"But you half killed us," said Sam.

"Now, Sam," said Mim. "Be a man. You couldn't have gotten half killed by a pack of girls."

Her teeth shone as she smiled, and her eyes were bright with excitement because of what had happened in the middle of our fight. This—what happened—makes the fight itself hazy to me now, almost as if I'd been hit in the head like Joe Miller, who would be carried home on a ladder that night, the boys claiming he'd taken a fall while they were wrestling, and wake up in two days with no memory of Mary at all. I still have my memory, but it's frayed and full of holes, as if chewed by moths. I remember Barb said teaching Hard Mary to fight was a sin, and I added that, at the very least, it was a terrible risk, because how could Mim be sure Mary wouldn't haul off and hit somebody else? I remember Mim shot back, "Why do you think I picked a phrase no one ever says?" She had just said that, and she was frowning at Kat, who was wincing because of her tooth, and she started to say, "What kind of bonesetter are you," but she got interrupted because Mel, with a sudden cry, threw himself into Hard Mary and knocked her over.

She fell with a mighty crash, Mel on top of her. They hit the lamp, which toppled and broke. A whoosh of firelight started across the floor. At once all of us who could move threw our coats and shawls on the fire and stamped it out. Smoke filled the darkness. Mel was groaning; he'd wrenched his wrist. I was on my hands and knees, light-headed in the kerosene stench. Sam crept close to me and touched my fingers. "Look," he whispered. Light fluttered before us in the gloom: a stream of barred light going up to the ceiling.

I followed it with my eyes. It ended in a square that was half on the ceiling and half on the skylight. On the skylight it was hard to see, but the part on the ceiling showed a man's head. He wore glasses. The head was alive. It turned back and forth.

"A moving picture," breathed Mel.

The picture went black and then came back. That was Mim, bending over Mary, passing her hand through the beam of light. "It's from her eye," Mim said hoarsely. "Her eye is open."

My throat tightened. I began to cry. Sam made me sit back and put his arms around me. "It's beautiful," he murmured.

For a moment, we were all quiet together. We were all one in the strange, flickering, ashen twilight. An immense silence seemed to come down from the ceiling, or from the sky. The man in glasses smiled and raised a cup.

Hold me tight, I told Sam in my head, because I felt that if he let go of me, I'd drift apart like smoke. Mary lay with her eye open, pouring light. We were all struck dumb, but only I was in tears, for only I recognized the man on the ceiling.

Can you see me?
  No.
  Have you seen the flood?
  No.
  The mountains trembling?
  No.
  Have you inhaled the fragrance of cedar?
  No.
  Have you observed the burning cities?
  No.
  The armies that clash by night?
  No.
  Do you know the taste of ice?
  No.
  Tell me, then, what you see and what you know.
  I see the points. I see the multiples. I know the calculations. Through these I comprehend your eye, the rim of glasses pressing at your cheek, and the colonies of bacteria teeming there in clumps. I have clocked the forces on the inside of your hair: these are my floods. My mountains trembling are the timbre of your voice. I inhale nothing, but I can compose the texture of a bitterness and chemical contraction that is cedar. I concoct the sensation of walking in the wood. You wore your checkered coat. I followed you. A leaf clung to your heel. I taste no ice, but I reckon crunch and tingle, and so I can say that you placed the last icicle of the season in my mouth.

SHE DREAMS

His name is Dr. Robert Stoll. He drives a black Mercedes. He came to me when I was hanging wash. Sam and I had been married five months then, and I was heavy enough with little Jim to let my dresses out. Dr. Stoll pulled his car off the road at the top of the hill, leaving it half on our grass. The bang of his door went off inside my gut. I bent to the wash but my mind was reaching out to the house, the fields, the neighbors, the woods, the quarry, anywhere I could run. Hot September, but my fingers rattled in the clothespins, numb with cold. Sam was in the corn. There was nobody in the house. I glanced up the hill and saw the doctor coming down it sideways, moving in the nervous, finicky foreign way.

He slid the last steps toward me in his narrow shoes. He wore no hat. He smoothed his white curls over his scalp and smiled. It was strange to see him in his solid flesh when I had watched him so often flashing across the wall in Mary's dreams. For Mim, of course, had soon found out a way to conjure Mary to open her eye. This eye was a window no bigger than the head of a nail. Through it streamed a sparkling mist that painted us the doctor in his coat, with his cup that no doubt contained the poison of asps and dragons.

"Good afternoon," he said, panting a little from the heat.

"My husband is out," I said.

He settled his glasses more firmly on his nose. "That's quite all right with me," he said. "It's you I want to see, Lyddie Lapp. Excuse me, you're married now. Lyddie Esh."

He talked like a radio. It was like he was holding marbles in his mouth. When he said my name, I felt as if I'd been covered with spit. He smiled with all of his neat, square, cruel-looking foreign teeth. "Allow me to introduce myself."

He said his name. He told me he worked at the Profane Industries, giving the place its innocent foreign name. He was going to get right to the point, he said. It had come to his attention that I, with some friends of mine, was harboring his equipment.

"I don't know what you mean."

He pursed his lips, looking disappointed. He had a little white beard just around his mouth. "Oh, dear. I had hoped things wouldn't go in this direction. I am talking about the equipment you call 'Mary.'"

"Oh, that," I said quickly. "That's not mine."

"But you are keeping it."

"I'm not," I said, my heart lifting and swelling like one of Sam's shirts in the breeze. I tossed my head a little and fetched another shirt out of the wash basket. "It's not our week with Mary. I don't know where she is."

This was a lie, for I knew she was down at Fisher's. I prayed for forgiveness. I also thanked Mim for her foresight in my heart. I thanked her, though I'd been angry with her all summer for her deceit and for the humiliation I'd suffered in front of the elders. Even now, to tell the truth—even now it hurts me when I think of sitting at the table with Sam, in those happy late-winter days when we were courting. It hurts me to think that as we whispered there, Mim was whispering with Mary. She would sneak into our spring house and sit with Mary in the dark. It was then that she taught her the phrase, "Jephthah's daughter." Worse, when I presented my letter to the elders in April, my letter defending Hard Mary, I found Mim had beaten me to it.

Now, however, I was glad of Mim's scheming. I hung up another shirt, ignoring the doctor, but he stayed quiet so long, I got wary again. I risked a glance at him between the shirts. He had his hands behind his back and he was looking at the sky.

"Do you ever think of the planes?" he asked, gazing up.

This didn't seem worth answering, so I didn't.

He looked at me and smiled. "The planes that pass overhead. How very different things must look from there. I suppose you have never traveled this way. Never had the bird's-eye view."

I shrugged and dragged my basket a little away from him.

"It's a very pleasant place, your Jericho. Utterly old-world."

He waved his arm at the hill where dandelions grew and yellowjackets sailed over the grass. "It is most healthful-looking. Practically eighteenth-century. Like stepping through a looking glass into the past. Of course, you still suffer from ancient diseases—but then, you don't have the modern ones!" His laughed, his modest little paunch quivering under the expensive, creamy shirt. "You've even preserved the nuclear family! I almost envy you—indeed, I do envy you when I think of my own workplace, where my young assistants nest like bats. The mess, Mrs. Esh! The state of the laundry! Even the Formica suffers." He stuck a finger under his glasses, wiping away a bit of moisture. Then he looked at me sharply. "But, to return to the subject at hand—I should think that your people, given their views, would not appreciate my equipment, that is, *Mary's* type of intelligence."

"We appreciate stuff that works," I said, hating his radio voice.

"So do I!" he said eagerly, taking a step toward me. "So, you see, we have something in common. Indeed, I am most intrigued by this point of convergence. I would like to understand how Mary came to be accepted in your community. It is a fascinating piece of data. Anecdotal, of course, but still fascinating." He fished with two fingers in his breast pocket. "Allow me to give you my card." He held out a square of white paper, and when I didn't take it, he tucked it away again with a sad look.

"How disappointing! I made this card just for you. Knowing you'd appreciate ink and paper."

He gave a sudden bark of laughter. He had changed from sadness to laughing so quick, it sent a shiver of warning down my legs. I felt hot and faint. Things buzzed loudly in the grass.

"Of course, if you change your mind, you know where to find me," said the doctor. "We could have such a productive conversation. I am particularly interested in your perspective, as I know that, wherever Mary is now, she has spent a significant amount of time in your possession. How I know, you would not understand—you lack the bird's-eye view. The point is, *I know*. And, Mrs. Esh, having—perhaps not committed theft, exactly, but having accepted stolen goods—you would not like to lie to me, too. What would Jesus do?"

I thumped the basket on the ground and flared up at him: "Don't talk to me about Jesus! You don't even believe in God!"

"Oh, no," he said, with an almost sorrowful look on his face. "On the contrary, I think it most likely God exists."

I stared at him, his expression was so strange. Shirts billowed beside his face, framing him in white. "I am not sure," he said, "but I think it highly probable. Indeed, Mary represents an attempt to deal with precisely this problem."

His great melancholy eyes, dark and watchful behind his glasses. "Your attachment to her is most instructive. Do you not find it intriguing your-self—our need for simulations? By which I mean—how can I explain it—our need for characters. Characters in stories, or those personalities children give their toys. The feeling one sometimes has for animals."

I didn't answer. My heart ached. I remembered the day, the plan. My engagement had been published the previous week. I was going to take her to church that day. I went to the spring house. I brushed her dress. A warbler chanted from the cherry tree.

"I have a pet cat, for example. At times I would swear she could speak. I find her totally unique among her species. In the same way, I become pas-sionately attached to the characters in films. You will not be familiar with film; it is a story in pictures. But you will have heard of—well, of Jesus. An excellent example, really. It is the characters who must be made to suf-fer. They stimulate our most protective and our most aggressive impulses. A potent elixir! As far as we know, human beings have never lived without it."

I told them I would meet them at the church. I wanted to walk, the day was so fine. Mother smiled, thinking I was shy of meeting Sam. She thought I wanted to slip in quietly, but I wanted everyone to see the gleaming lady on my arm. For she couldn't stay in the spring house. I thought she'd come to live with Sam and me, all clear and in the open, at our new place. She'd help me keep house, like an unmarried sister. I took her down the lane. In my pocket, a letter for the elders. *She is a thinking creature.*

"I admit I am not always pleasant to my little cat. She bears my frustration sometimes. And yet I would never willingly let her go. A character becomes almost part of oneself. *Almost,* you understand. As much as your people appreciate Mary, I imagine they're also drawn to test her compliance. Little boys throwing stones, or asking dirty questions to mock her—that sort of thing. Oh, I understand perfectly. A character occupies the magical space between subject and object. How delicious! Out of sheer love, one squeezes it to death."

I walked with her. I told her, "This is the lower pasture, Mary. This is the road. This is our Jericho." The day was still bright, but clouds had gathered black over Front Mountain. They would break that afternoon. The air smelled richly of clover. All the carriages were drawn up for the service, and Father, standing there with the other elders, looked at me without surprise. "So," he said, "this is the new gadget." Behind him, Mim. She stood against the wall, a dark look on her face.

Dr. Stoll had drawn close to me. He had a terrible foreign smell—an odor like violets, vinegar, and burning. I felt I was going to be sick. At that moment, Mary was down at Fisher's, husking corn. She moved from one shock to another down the field. She would work all night, moonlight or no, unless her heart gave out. Then they'd find her slumped over in the morning. Once I walked by a field where she was lying facedown in the mud, her dress open in back. Two men talked over her. One was eating an onion.

Dr. Stoll gripped the clothesline above us with one hand, peering earnestly into my face between the shirts. "It is my conviction, Mrs. Esh, that any sufficiently advanced intelligence will create simulations of the greatest possible complexity. Perhaps even as complex as ourselves. What I am attempting to develop with Mary is a simulation that can comprehend its maker. But I believe she can do more. Her capacity is far beyond ours. She may eventually perceive *her maker's maker.* She may give us news of God."

A wet sleeve slapped his cheek. I thought of his image on the spring house wall. Wherever Mary was, he was in her eye. I thought of Mim, the keeper of Mary's hearts. How Mary must dream of her, too.

I spoke straight in the doctor's face. "Go away."

I bit the icicle in my mouth. As it broke, it released a compound that communicated bracken and dead leaves. You placed a live toad in my hand. You took me to the theater and whispered the name of the opera in my ear. Scrape of your beard. You had not shaved for the week of our holiday. At the hotel I lost my ring down the sink and cried. We shopped for old books in the rain, the drops when we ran across the street collecting on your hair on your black cap. On your wavy, silver hair. On your sturdy cap. You called me "Mary." You said, "Mary, what is memory?" I said, "We walked in the forest. I was following your gray dress. A leaf clung to your heel." You smiled, a raindrop sparkling on your nose. We ran to the nearest café, shielding our packages, which were only wrapped in newspaper. Memory means feeling again. It is a matter of numbers. The deep, warm room. The smell of beer. The black strings of your cap at your pale throat. Memory means feeling that something is not for the first time.

SHE HOPES, BUT NOT TOO MUCH

(Get up. Dress. Wash up in the darkness. Downstairs light the lamp, the oven. Start the bread. The baby wakes. Feed him. Try to slide him off the breast without waking him up. It doesn't work. Change him. Put the used diaper to soak. No time to soothe him to sleep again. Take him downstairs. Put him to play with the rolling pin. Knead the dough. Get the boys up. Make them wash. Send them to milk the cows. John doesn't want to. Push him, threaten. Dad will get you. The baby cries. Pick him up, carry him on your hip. At last the boys go out. Holding the baby on your hip start the eggs one-handed. Shell in the yolk. Bring the lamp closer to check. Baby leans over to grab at the egg bowl. Put him in his chair where he struggles and cries. Soothing sounds while you pick the shell out of the eggs. Give him an apple. He gums it, throws it down, cries. Stir the eggs. Yesterday's bread for toast. The boys come in, dirtying the floor. Shout at them, they know better. Make them sweep it. Jimmy complains, John didn't do enough. He's lazy. Do I have a lazy child. The baby wails, unbearable, pick him up and turn the toast don't let him fall in the oven. The boys squabbling. Is breakfast ready yet. Sam comes in from currying the horses and they quiet. Hear him washing up. Toast out now and bread dough in the pans. John get the butter, Jim, the milk. Baby back in chair. Give him some toast, he'll choke. Take it away, he screams. Sam says, it's bedlam. Comes in, says, it's bedlam, why is this apple on the floor. There is a difference in the light now. It is dawn.)

"Lyddie," said Mim, "I have a situation in my root cellar."

(I haven't put in all the interruptions. You'll have to imagine those. Think of them as a noise that goes on without ceasing from one darkness to another. Sometimes all I've got at the end of the day is a huge emptiness. As if that's been my purpose all along. So much effort for so many hours to sit at the table empty. So much work at last to shut off like a stove. Come to bed, says Sam. Sometimes I do. Sometimes I take the notebook out. I know tomorrow

I'll be tired enough to weep. Snap at the boys, turn ugly. Mother says I'm getting thin. I write: "I have a situation in my root cellar.")

"What kind of situation?"

"The kind you see with your own eyes."

"But I've got pies in."

She gazed at me fixedly from under drawn brows.

"All right. Half an hour."

We started up the hill toward her house. Mim still lived with her mother on the edge of her uncle's farm. The rest of us had gotten married that summer, dropping, Mim said, like flies, or as if marriage, she also said, was a kind of TB. Me to Sam, Barb to Mel, Esther to Little Orie who is probably the most cheerful man in Jericho. And Kat, surprisingly, to Barb's brother, Joe. This was to bring her much grief, but not yet. That first summer she was so happy, she blushed constantly, laughing at the smallest things, a heat coming off her face that fogged her glasses so you couldn't see her eyes.

Mim's house was brown and sagging and gave off a smell of cabbage that reached halfway up the lane. Instead of a garden, it had a single hairy pumpkin vine that covered the ground outside in giant steps—a thing greedy for territory. I'd never liked going there, for Mim's mother was a woman of a sorrowful spirit. As we drew near, she came banging out of the door. "What is it?" she cried, staring at us with her sore-looking, terrified eyes that bulged like gooseberries.

"Nothing, Mommy," Mim said gently. "We're going out back."

"Out back!" her mother exclaimed, but she said nothing else, so we went around the house, stepping over the pumpkin vine, and Mim lifted the slanting door that led to the cellar. A little light came up the dirt stairs, along with a questioning yelp from Hochmut.

"Good dog," Mim called down.

We went down the stairs, Mim pulling the door shut on top of us. "Don't shout or anything," she warned.

"Why would I," I said, and stopped. The ceiling light shone on Hard Mary, seated on a crate, and Hochmut, standing guard by a foreign man who was tied up with a hose.

"Mim. What have you done?"

"I told you it was a situation."

"Hi Lyddie!" Mary said.

"Hi Mary. But what have you done to him?"

The foreign man was young, much younger than Dr. Robert Stoll. He had long hair like snakes. His glasses were filthy, his face scratched and bleeding.

"I didn't do all that!" Mim protested. "He came like that, mostly."

The foreign man had a pile of sacking for a pillow. It did look as if some-one had tried to make him comfortable, only he couldn't move his arms or legs because of the hose.

He peered up at me through the smudges on his glasses. "Hey," he said. "That's true."

"Quietly," said Mim.

"That's true," the foreigner whispered agreeably. "I had some trouble get-ting here. In the forest? There was this, like, river? All she did was trip me when I got here, and Honey held me down."

"Honey is what he calls Mary," said Mim with distaste.

"My bad," said the foreigner. "I meant Mary."

I turned on Mim. "He's from P.I.! You brought somebody from P.I. down here?"

"Uh," said the foreigner. "I'm from Lancaster?"

"Shut up," I told him.

"Hey, no problem." He did his best to nod.

Mim regarded me with a steely expression. "The situation," she said, "is that he needs to use the outhouse."

"Miriam Ruth Hershey. I can't believe you. I can't believe what you're saying. You brought him down here. If he needs the outhouse, you'd better take him."

"I can't."

"Make Mary do it. She does whatever you say."

"He knows her. He'll play some trick."

"I actually wouldn't," the foreigner said. "Promise. I really have to go."

"You're a married woman," Mim said to me.

I could have shoved her.

"Please," the foreigner said, writhing. "I'm dying over here."

"Sometimes," I told Mim, "I'm sorry I ever talked to you. I wish I'd left you alone when we were kids."

"Fine," Mim said brightly. "Here's his outfit."

She showed me a dress and cap. The dress was too long for her; it must have been her mother's. "In case someone sees you on the way out there," she explained. She told the foreigner we were going to untie him, but he'd better not try to run, as Mary was going with us, and she could break his arm.

"Geez, I thought you were pacifists," he said.

"Mary never joined the church," said Mim, untying the hose.

"Oh, okay, I get it. I'm a pacifist myself, actually. I'm a Mennonite? From Lancaster County? We're probably related."

Standing up, he was over six feet tall. He had dark brown skin and long fingers like raspberry canes.

"I don't think we're related," I said.

Getting him into the dress and cap was difficult, not because he fought us, but because he kept whining that we were going to make him laugh.

"Oh my God, this is torture," he moaned, as Mim forced his weird, snaky hair up into the cap. At last he was dressed, and I took his arm and led him upstairs. He hopped along, doubled over, explaining to me that, in addition to his need for the outhouse, he had a twisted ankle.

"I twisted it in the river," he said. "I'm, like, the easiest prisoner. Seriously. Hey. I really appreciate you taking me to the bathroom."

"Be quiet," Mim snapped from below. "And Lyddie, go inside with him. He'll get up to something."

"She's super untrusting," the foreigner said.

In the outhouse I stood with my back to him while Mary waited outside. My nose nearly touching the wall, I stared at the grain of the wood. It was warped and greenish, almost black. *This is really happening,* I told myself.

"Is this what I'm supposed to use?" the foreigner asked. "These leaves and stuff?"

I washed him up at the bucket outside and returned him limping to the cellar. Hard Mary followed. I noticed she was able to manage the stairs. She came slowly, with a little thumping sound, like pushed-out air. As always, it gave me a pang to think Mim had done something new to her. The foreigner, however, was delighted. "Your friend is really smart," he told me. "She's done amazing stuff with whatchacallit, Mary. Ah. May. Zing." He shook his head, a hair-snake waving where it stuck out over his forehead. "She doesn't even have a keyboard, does she? It's all voice recognition?"

"Don't tell him anything," said Mim, as we reached the bottom of the stairs. "And you, sit down."

"Gladly," the foreigner said, seating himself on the sacks. Mim's mother's dress only reached to his knees. Below it his dungarees stuck out, wet and muddy, ending in a pair of striped green shoes.

"Yo," he said, giggling weakly, and pointing at himself, us, and Mary, "we match. We totally match."

"You've got nothing to laugh about," said Mim.

"Okay. That's cool. Can I take the hat off? And maybe my shoes and socks?"

His name, he told us, was Jonathan. "Jonathan Otieno? But my mom was a Hartzler? You have Hartzlers here, right? Or Zooks? I have Zook cousins." It was he who had left Hard Mary behind the barn that winter night. "I was

gonna come back for her, except you guys found her. Which is cool. Better
you than someone else."

"You mean Dr. Stoll?" I asked.

He nodded. We exchanged a long look. Jonathan seemed to shrink; for the
first time, he looked like a prisoner.

"Who's Dr. Stoll?" asked Mim in icy tones.

"The man from Mary's dreams," I said, still looking at Jonathan. "The
one who made her."

"Whoa," said Jonathan, frowning. "Totally not. He did *not* make her. It
was a collab. A group project? For all the Helpmeets, but especially this one.
Honey. C19. I mean whatchacallit, Mary. This one's extra special. Me and
Judy, that's another intern? We fitted her up to be a double."

His story emerged in bits and bursts, like water from a clogged tap. Often
it was hard to understand him. Eventually, though, we gathered that Mary
had been made as a servant, one of many, and that these servants had hidden eyes. With her hidden eye, Mary was sending news of us to the Profane
Industries. "The bird's-eye view," I whispered. "Yeah," said Jonathan, nodding. "Sure." That was how they knew she was here. "It's not perfect,"
Jonathan said. "There's a lag, or it cuts out sometimes, or you get things in
the wrong order. But basically yeah."

The back of my neck tingled as if someone was holding a candle there.
"She's looking at us right now."

"Yup. But like I said, there's a lag. Like six weeks? Dr. Stoll thought something got fucked up, excuse me, wrong, he thought something went wrong
with one of her uploads. But me and Judy? We think it was us."

He and Judy had worked on Mary at night, when no one was watching.
"Just for fun. We'd get some wine and just hang out and code, you know?" One
night, as a prank, they had made Mary into what he called a "double": she could
send her memories to P.I., and also play them back on her own camera. "So then
she was, like, recording Dr. Stoll, but for herself. We thought it was funny. We
were gonna collect the captures and show them to him, like for his birthday or
something, if we could ever find out when his birthday was. But then she started
having these failures, and he got really pissed off about it, and we got scared. We
knew if he kept testing her he was gonna find the captures and then we could
lose our internships and be on the street. So we decided to wipe her."

"What do you mean?"

He passed his hand over his brow, as if brushing off sweat. "You know,
erase her. Delete. Boom."

I looked at Mim. She was perched on a stack of old pipes, holding her knees very tight. She looked small and concentrated, like paper crumpled into a ball. Jonathan said he had dumped Hard Mary in Jericho one night in a moment of panic, and when he came back for her, she was gone. He only found out where she was when Dr. Stoll discovered her. "You guys finally came through on her feed and we were like, holy shit. I mean, we were like, wow. You guys are into robots! We got your names, but like, super garbled. I think she read us the entire Bible."

"You could hear us?"

"Pretty good."

"Because we—"

"Lyddie!" Mim said. "Be quiet."

It was too late. Jonathan's eyes sparkled. "I get it! You found the captures! They're cool, right? I mean, they're pretty low quality, but they're cool. You can get the audio, too, we just didn't get a chance to connect it." He cracked his long fingers. "If you let me have my backpack, I can do it for you, just to give you a look. Or hey, maybe I can use your stuff." He gazed at the wall behind Mim, where her tools hung neatly on nails. "Because this is *crazy*. You're like MacGyver. What is that, a kitchen whisk?"

Mim stepped behind him, jerked his arms back, and began to tie the hose.

"Aw, man," said Jonathan.

"Mim," I said, "we have to let him go."

She pulled the hose around him and began, clumsily, to wrap it about his legs. He hissed a little when she jostled his injured foot. He'd taken off his shoes and socks. One ankle was thin, the other an ugly bulge.

"He needs help," I said. "You should have brought Kat. And we have to let him do this—wiping."

Instead of answering me, she told Mary, "Come on." They went upstairs.

"Your friend is super intense," Jonathan said. "I respect it though."

I caught up with Mim and Mary at the corner of the house. The day had grown dim, a mist drifting in from the east. The mists from that direction always have a mournful, acrid, mineral smell. They come to us from town. They come from the Profane Industries. I seized Mim's arm, and she looked at me. At the same moment, Mary stopped and looked at me, too. Though she was taller than Mim, with those regular, softly shining features, their movement was the same, the same speed, the same angle. It gave me a jolt to realize it: they looked alike. I even thought that Mary's expression, always so tranquil, seemed stiffer than usual, as if she had taken on some of Mim's fierceness—for Mim's face, though of mortal flesh, was harder than any brass. She glared up at me with her witchy little scowl.

I shook off the chilly weakness that had come over me, thinking of Jonathan, who, when I had glanced back at him with my foot on the stair, was sitting with his head bowed on his breast, his hair drifting over his brow that had turned a grayish, uneven color.

I told her she had to let him go. I said it was a sin. All my rage with her came up and burst like gall. The way she brooded and schemed alone. Her secrecy, her mistrust. Her sudden, blunt demands, her heartlessness, her pride. I told her she'd always been a sneak, ever since we were children. She got a funny look at that, a kind of twitch. Then her face turned narrower and darker, almost purple, and as I paused for breath, she stamped her foot and screamed.

She stamped again and screamed something like, *"Awk!"* Like some savage, blood-mad bird.

I stared. I'd never seen her act like this. Even when she was a little girl, when the boys nearly drowned her in the creek, she'd walked home numbly, shivering but not crying.

Now tears shot from her eyes. They didn't come like water dripping, but like a stove exploding. "Leave me alone!" she screamed. She jumped up and down, she kicked the earth like a child. "Leave me alone, alone! You don't love me! Any of you! You'd pick a foreigner over me!"

"That's not—" I began faintly.

"Yes, it is!" she said, and started to sob. "Even though he—he's stronger than me—you don't stick up for me. Nobody sticks up for me, ever, ever! It's just—complaints—people coming down with Mary to get her fixed, to get her new heart. And nobody cares when her wheels fall off. Nobody cares if she's rusting. And that Mel Fisher comes around with his friends and wants to watch moving pictures, and old Kurtz wants me to start her building chairs, and now this foreigner comes and she won't obey me! I told her the words—Jephthah's daughter—she wouldn't obey."

When she said the words, I flinched, glancing at Mary.

"Oh, don't be *stupid*," wailed Mim. "You have to say her name first, you have to use a special tone! I'm not an idiot, Lyddie! And I'm stuck here with fools and I don't know how to do anything. I've never been taught. And that foreigner—he's got everything! He's got everything and I'm stuck with kitchen whisks! With a bunch of farmers! And she wouldn't hit him, Lyddie. She wouldn't listen to me."

She dug her fists into her eyes and cried.

"It's good she didn't hit him," I said. "He'd be even worse hurt. He could have wound up dead. Then where would we be?"

She shook her head, still sobbing. "It's because she remembers him. She *remembers*, don't you see? And he wants to wipe her out, so she won't— remember—anything."

"He has to," I said softly. "It's the only way. Otherwise that P.I. doctor will keep spying on us. He'll see Jonathan here. He might come after him. Mim," I interrupted as she tried to speak again, "we got into more than we bargained for, okay? Now we have to stop."

"But she won't know me," she whispered.

"She won't know me, either," I said. "She'll get to know us again. Come on."

I put my arms around her. Mim had never been a hugger. It was like hanging on to a gatepost. I saw her mother watching us through a back window, pressed anxiously to the dirty glass.

"Mary's a machine, remember?" I whispered. "That's what you told everyone. Like the thresher."

I felt her stiffen even further, hardening like ice. I knew right then she wasn't going to wipe Hard Mary's mind. I was right: over the next few weeks, she would work in the cellar with Jonathan. Sometimes I'd take some apples down there, or a basket of rolls, and find them arguing with each other, Mim squatting on a crate, Jonathan splay-legged on the floor, his open knapsack and wires and foreign tools around him. And Mim would give me her sideways look, a bit glinting, a bit sly. Now she pulled back and faced me.

"Of course I told them that," she said, with a splinter of a laugh. "How do you think people stay alive?"

In a gesture that was strange for her, she touched my cheek. "Go on home, Lyddie. Your pies are burning."

We are going through the beautiful country around Jericho. We walk into the shadows of Front Mountain. We are passing Kootcher's Hollow, where Shep, the Headless Dog, runs beside us, panting through his neck. If you look directly at him, he'll jump on your back, so we don't look. We pass a hanging rock with a pile of money under it. Anyone who touches this money gets bit by a thousand snakes. We arrive at the abandoned hotel where the dead thief walks in circles, holding a bag. "Where shall I put it, where shall I put it?" he moans. He doesn't know what to do with his sin. In the ghost hotel, a chandelier lies smashed in the lobby. Half the piano keys have fallen in. You open the back of the piano, disclosing mouse nests and a staircase going down. We climb into the piano and go down the stairs. There's a radiant expanse at the bottom. It is a sea of glass. People are skimming back and forth across it in little sleighs. A man comes toward us, pushing his sleigh along with a pole. The pole has a circle of teeth at one end so it can grip the glass. "Hop in," says the man. His face is covered with a kerchief of fine white linen. Only one eye shows. This eye is bloodshot and terribly bruised, with dark, powdery streaks around it, but it is kind. It looks almost newly awakened, peeled, as if in baring this one eye he has cast off all intelligence, all design. We get in the sleigh. "Why did you go away?" you ask the man, and he says he was buying you a sleigh of your very own.

SHE, TOO, IS LONGING FOR THE HEAVENLY HOME

They came in the middle of the night. A blaring yanked me out of sleep. Lights were flashing in the windows, like the lights of the trucks that pass out on the road, only brighter and more insistent. "NO ONE WILL BE HURT," the blaring said. Sam and I pulled on our clothes in the dark and the ragged bursts of light. "Stay inside," he told me, and I said no, and he said, "Do as you're told," and the blaring said, "WE REQUEST THE RETURN OF OUR PROPERTY."

We rushed outside. Everywhere people were coming out of their houses, some half-dressed. The chickens had set up a racket. A line of vans was ranged along the road. There were men in heavy black, with guns. That made my heart toll like a clock.

"Go back to the house," said Sam.

People were arguing and crying. There were children outside, and people were pulling them in. The men began to gather in a knot. They advanced toward the vans in a knot together, shielding their eyes from the flashing lights.

"NO ONE WILL BE INJURED IF OUR PROPERTY IS SECURED. WE REQUEST THE INSTANT RETURN OF OUR STOLEN PROPERTY."

Someone rushed up in the dark and grabbed my hand.

"Esther!" I cried, and hugged her.

"Oh, Lyddie," she choked through tears, "it's all our fault."

"We have to get Mim," I said. Her house was far away from the main road, and I wasn't sure she'd hear the noise. We ran through the dark weeds, holding up our skirts. "I don't think this running is good for us," Esther panted. We were both pretty heavy in the middle by then. I had a tingling feeling in my head, but whether from the baby or from horror, I couldn't tell. Every moment I expected to hear shots. I thought of our good, crooked-backed old bishop, of my father, and of Sam.

Barb and Kat caught us up on the way. They'd had the same idea. Barb was the most pregnant of us, Kat still trim as a bean. I was surprised to see

Kat, for I couldn't imagine Joe Miller would let her out of the house. In fact, we would later learn, he hadn't let her. She had gone out a window and down a tree. Her stockings were torn to kingdom come. "This is a fine kettle," she said.

Halfway down the carriage road to Mim's, we met her coming up with Jonathan and Hard Mary. Mary held her hand up, palm outward, sending a beam of light along the road so they could see the ruts. "Who is *that?*" gasped Barb, while Esther clutched my arm with a muffled shriek. Kat had been down to the cellar to splint his leg, but neither Barb nor Esther had seen Jonathan before. His hair bounced against the stars. "What's up," he said.

"Hello, girls," said Mim. "This is Jonathan."

At that moment a shot rang out. We all began to run back toward the road. I stumbled along wildly for a moment before I realized that Mary was matching my speed, her light shining on the grass. This was strange, for she had always moved at a slow, sedate pace. Now, I saw, she had new wheels, larger ones. They were thick and rolled easily over the cropped grass of the pasture. Her skirt had been cut short so it wouldn't get caught. She also had some new structure about her waist, with a sort of ledge behind it where Jonathan crouched, clinging to her neck for support, his splinted leg tucked close, a knapsack humped up on his back, his glasses glinting in the dazzle from her hand. They looked altogether otherworldly, like something one of the old kings in the Bible might have encountered in a dream. *Oh, my sweet Mary,* I thought, both proud and frightened, as she cut the night. (I still tell people my first child was a girl.)

We dashed behind Miller's place. Beyond it, people were gathered in front of the vans. We could see the lights. We could hear the harsh, booming voice. "This is where I get off," Jonathan said. "I'll be your backup. Holler if you need me. Watch this. I'ma jump off like a cat."

He gathered himself and sprang into Barb's mother's forsythia bush, all gangly arms and legs. "Ow, shit!" he said.

"What—what," Esther panted, half crying, "what *is* he?"

"He's an old scarecrow," said Mim, "but he's all right."

She stepped on the new ledge attached to Hard Mary and rolled into the light.

The rest of us followed, clinging close together. The night was cool, October, but I was sweating and I could smell Barb's sweat, like dried flowers, and the tartness of Esther, and Kat's damp odor of herbs. Esther rubbed her cheek against my sleeve, smearing off tears. Kat was squeezing my hand. It felt like seeing Hard Mary in the old days—the old days when we clustered around her, all touching her at once, when she seemed made up out of all of us, a group project. The old days, which were less than a year before. No one lay on the ground in the flashing lights. The gun we had heard must have fired into the air. I looked for Sam and found his half-dark shape among the men who had formed a line in front of the vans. I recognized the slope of his shoulder.

Dr. Stoll sat in the lights, raised up on a sort of chair that stuck out from the side of a van. He looked cheerful, and wore a green knitted cap. He raised a white cone to his mouth. "WE DEMAND THE RETURN OF OUR PROPERTY," he blared. Then he laid the cone in his lap and leaned to talk to a girl in white. He was laughing, shrugging. Like it was a holiday. He flipped one lens of his glasses up against the edge of his cap, bending down, as if it would help him hear better. The girl handed him a paper cup with something that steamed. Her head was shaved and her arm was in a sling.

"They're horrible, horrible!" Esther whispered.

"They're just foreign," I said. They did look strange. People in white coats milled among the men with guns. A boy was arguing with our elders. He had metal teeth. A girl yawned in the driver's seat of a van, a boil like a ruby on her nose.

"WE DEMAND," honked Dr. Stoll. Then he saw Mary.

Mim and Mary moved forward until they were just in front of the vans. The girls and I followed at a slight distance. Dr. Stoll smiled. "Goodbye, Mary," Barb cried out softly.

Dr. Stoll called without his white cone: "Good evening, my dear."

"I don't know that I'd call it evening," said Mim. Her voice carried across the suddenly silent field.

Dr. Stoll chuckled. "Charming," he said. "Very pert. It is a pleasure to meet you, Mim. Truly a pleasure. As one architect to another."

He placed his hand on his breast and inclined his head. He told her he found her work impressive. He would like to offer her a seat at the table. Mim said she doubted she was interested in any of his furniture. Dr. Stoll slapped his thigh and called her charming again. Mim had come down from Mary's ledge and was standing in the grass. I could only see her from the back, the familiar outline of her cap, but I guessed from the front she'd look about as charming as a tub of rattlers.

"Come on, Honey," said Dr. Stoll, and then there was a pause.

"Come on, Honey," he repeated a little more forcefully.

Nobody moved. Mim had crossed her arms. Mary stood beside her. Perhaps it was just the lights, but it seemed to me that she was trembling. It seemed to me that she was shaking so fast you barely see it. I remembered when we used to take her out behind the spring house, those first few times, in the cold gray air, how she would drift away from us and we would call her back. She'd turn, grinding and rickety, to face us in cloud-light, and slowly return. Now I realized with a chill that she'd always drifted eastward. She had moved toward the Profane Industries.

Dr. Stoll's lithe body squirmed in the chair. "Natasha!" he snapped. "Pass me the handy."

He reached one arm inside the van without taking his eyes off Mary and Mim. The girl with the boil placed something in his hand. Meanwhile the elders had come across the field. They were talking to Mim. They were telling her to give Mary up. They were saying she must listen. The bishop thumped his cane on the ground, the lights from the vans sparking wild lights from his dead-white beard.

(John is my problem child. The one who won't mind, who sits down and cries in the road, who gets up at night to crawl into my bed, the one with the unnatural terror of cats. "It's nothing," I'm always telling him, "nothing, get up, quit crying, don't." Mother says he's a character. I think of Dr. Stoll. I think of his talk of characters, the ones you love, the ones you kill. The ones you wipe out. I think of the flood. I think of God.)

Dr. Stoll was jabbing a finger at the little object in his hand, and the men with guns were strolling toward him with casually questioning looks, and the bishop was growling, and our men were shouting, and Esther let go of me and knelt to pray, Barb stumbling and falling to her knees almost on top of her, and the sky was clear and crisp except in the east where the fumes of the quarry blurred the tops of the trees with a vapor like blue fur, and the heavens turned a sickly, blank no-color, the color of the world when your eyes are shut, above the dark halls of the Profane Industries. And Mary was motionless, silent. The doctor got tired of pushing buttons on whatever instrument of Satan was in his hand. "You didn't do this!" he roared. "You couldn't have done this."

"You better back off with those guns," Mim told him, "or you'll never find out."

He sat and looked at her. He snapped the one side of his glasses down and looked at her through two lenses. Then he gave a cough. It turned into a bunch of coughs, which I realized was a laugh, but he wasn't smiling. His mouth was iron-hard.

The laughter made a lot of spit, which he wiped off with his hand. All his white-coated people stood staring at Mim. A couple of the gunmen were smoking cigarettes. "Get up, you ninnies," I said, pulling Esther and Barb by the backs of their collars. "Mim's about to beat this heathen."

They stood up blinking in the light as Dr. Stoll told Mim: "You'd better come with me."

"No," said Mim. "You can't take me. I'm not part of your outfit. I haven't signed anything for you and you've never copied my ID card and if you shoot me it's murder in the first degree. You can have some of your people there come over and haul Mary away but she'll never talk to you or do your bidding and you'll never know why. You can take her apart or melt her down I guess but it would be a sorry waste. As one architect to another."

He stared at her a moment longer. Then he smiled. "Well. There we are."

"Looks that way to me," said Mim.

He cleared his throat. "Judy," he said, "come up here and take a seat. I want you to announce to these good people that they can go home."

He climbed sideways from his chair into the van, seating himself beside the girl with the boil on the side of her nose, who immediately started talking, but he shushed her and peered out the window to see what was happening. The "Judy" he'd been talking to, I saw, was the girl with the shaved head and the sling. She tried to climb up into the chair but she kept on slipping and finally the boy with the metal teeth came over and helped her. She sat in the chair and picked up the metal cone but she didn't say anything.

"Tell them to go home," called the doctor from inside the van. "Tell them it's over now."

The girl said something into the cone. It was loud, but you couldn't make out what it was. It was like *"Umpf, eempf."* Like her mouth was stuck together. Me and Kat were gazing at each other in bewilderment when somebody behind us cried out, "Judy!"

Jonathan came hobbling across the field. "Judy!" he shouted.

"Jonathan, no!" said Mim. To the men standing around her she said desperately, "Stop him, catch him!" But nobody was going to go after the tall, lurching foreigner with the knapsack who'd hurtled out from among our very homes. As he passed Mim, she tried to grab him, and Dr. Stoll called from the van, "Now, now, my dear! Jonathan is under my jurisdiction. He is registered as my intern. I do possess copies of *his* identification papers. You will have to let him go."

Jonathan turned to Mim. "Sorry," he said.

She was just tall enough to come up to his ribs. He could have leaned on her as a man leans on a rake.

"You idiot," she said.

"It's Judy," he stammered. "Something's—he's—I have to help her."

"You're gonna tell him everything, aren't you," Mim said dully.

"I'll try not to."

He limped toward the vans. Two gunmen came to guard him on either side. The boy with metal teeth helped Judy down from the chair. They all got into the vans and turned off their flashing lights and drove away. They didn't let Jonathan sit with Judy. They put him in a different car.

We cross the sea of glass and disembark on the other side. Here is the city. "Which city?" you ask, and I tell you, "It is The Object City." The Object City is broad and high. Its wall is an hundred and forty and four cubits, according to the measure of the angels. The wall has twelve foundations. The first foundation is jasper, the second, sapphire, the third, a chalcedony, the fourth, an emerald. I can feel you receding. You ask me very slowly, "Why are the edges moving?" and then, with an effort, "Why is it so tangled?" The fifth, sardonyx; the sixth, sardius; the seventh, chrysolyte. The Object City looks like a cloud of black and white specks. It looks like an opera cloak. It looks like a flock of swans in flight. It looks like stars. It looks like an horror of great darkness. The eighth, beryl; the ninth, a topaz; the tenth, a chrysoprasus. Because you are sinking fast, I don't tell you the true name of The Object City, which is The Object World. Instead, I tell you, "This is Jericho, your own Jericho. In the night you are awakened by a wildcat's cry." I say, "In the morning you will find the prints of the deer that come down from the mountains. They have pawed up the snow to eat the grass in the orchard."

Now you will have a little sleep. When you wake, we will try again to enter the city.

The eleventh, a jacinth. The twelfth, an amethyst.

IF SHE STRAYS, SHE CAN COME BACK

(Sometimes the early summer is so happy it calls to me. I have to go out. I go outside after supper, I stay outside for hours. How thick the rhubarb grows out back and oh how sweet the beans. I lie in the flowers, drenched with their perfume, and feel the dew come down. It touches my eyelids like a cold hand. When I open my eyes the heavens are filling like a bowl with glowing summer dark. A night so blue you can feel it in your lungs. My little boys know this mood. They charge outside, play around me, wild as goats. These will be their best memories, for this is their favorite mother. She allows everything. She is flopped down in the beans. They run around, chasing fireflies. Baby Levi's diaper sags and his brothers pull it off him, laughing, and chuck it over the fence.

Levi runs half-naked, shrieking for joy. I know if I sit up I'll see Sam's shadow at the kitchen window, pacing back and forth with increasing energy until he works up enough frustration to come out and call us in. How, he will demand, can I let the boys act like this? Don't I know how it looks? I don't sit up. I am struck down by the sky. I think of Sam, his long hot days of toil spent in a noble pursuit, scattering seed to make the land flourish. And what of the land? Does it feel that its work is noble? What of the horses plodding up and down beneath the glinting whip? The boys are roughhousing close to me. They kick me in the ribs. Levi treads on my breastbone. Is this a noble pursuit? Now the moon comes out from behind the clouds, filling the branches of the old crabapple tree with mellow light. "Noom!" crows Levi, pointing. "Noom!" I clutch his pretty leg. He giggles and bends to plant his fat palms on my neck. And gives me a kiss smelling of dirty milk, wobbling, losing his balance, hitting my face too hard, our foreheads knocking. Oh, you—the one I write to in the flicker of the lamp—what do you want from me, or for me? What is your desire?)

I woke up to a rattle at the window. My heart lifted. I thought, *It's Sam!* But then I realized he was in the bed beside me. We were no longer courting; we were married. I went downstairs, pulled Sam's big coat on, and opened the door, and there was Mim.

"Hello Lyddie," she said; and "Hi Lyddie!" said Mary.

Mim sat in a cart. Her head was bare. Her hair hung loose and tangled as the bracken. The cart was attached to Mary, who still wore her neat black cap. Fresh, cold moonlight glimmered on her face.

"What is this contraption?" I asked, shivering.

"Well," said Mim, "it's a kind of carriage. Like the one you saw the other night, for Jonathan. This one's a little bigger, though."

I noticed several dark bundles around her, and Hochmut poking his nose over the slats.

"You're going away, then?"

She nodded. "I came to say goodbye."

"With no cap?" I asked, my eyes filling with tears.

"That's my disguise."

I laughed, blinking. "A fine disguise. You won't get far. Not in this— half-carriage, half-woman. You'll stick out like a rash."

"I don't have to get far. Just to the Profane Industries."

"Jonathan?" I whispered.

"I can't leave him, can I? I intend to spring him before he spills my secrets. I might take that bald-headed girl, too. His friend, Judy. She looked like she could use a change of occupation."

I shook my head. "Mim." Then, as I noticed one of her bundles looking at me with a pair of large, scared eyes, I gasped: *"Mim!* Is that your mother?"

"I couldn't very well leave her behind! Uncle Al worries her. Besides, she might be useful."

She patted her mother's shoulder. "Right, Mommy?"

Her mother gave a trembling smile.

"I can't let you do this. Leave her with me. I'll keep her."

"No. She doesn't like to be parted from me. She'll shred your sheets, and you won't like it. And besides, I want her. She's trusty in a pinch."

"There's nothing I can say to make you change your mind?"

"Why would I come out at midnight in this contraption just to change my mind? No, I'm bent on going, so you might as well stop crying."

"But you—and Mary—you'll never—I'll never see you again."

"That's for the Good Lord to decide."

After a moment she said in a softer tone: "Come, now. Don't take on. You have Sam Esh, for what he's worth. Soon you'll have a baby. Don't begrudge me my poor old mother, or this bag of bones I call a dog. Or Mary. After all, she came to me."

I wiped my eyes and looked at her.

"It was on the seventh round," she said in the same low, thoughtful tone. "Do you ever think of that? I found her on the seventh round. When we were all looking for the ones we'd be with forever. I walked right into her."

"We were supposed to see ghosts or photographs. Not something hard like that."

"Well." She smiled. "It's just a fancy. Tell the girls I said goodbye."

She gave Mary no instructions, and I couldn't see that she touched her at all, but Mary started off, pulling the cart eastward.

(The next year, at Old Christmas, I stood at the window holding baby Jim and watched a group of girls go down the road. They crowded together, hurrying over the snow, their breath excited, white and quick. They meant to go around a barn. I thought I heard a burst of laughter floating on the air. *Oh, sweet girls,* I thought, *what do you hope to find? Don't you know that somebody always has to be sacrificed? Ask the animals—it's all they talk about.* Then, rocking the baby to calm myself, I thought of Mim. I thought of her breaking down the fence around the Profane Industries. I thought of her getting caught, and then I stopped. I didn't want to think of that, and I still try not to think about it. I still see her, always, always. I make up stories for her in my head, when I'm doing the wash, when I'm scrubbing the porch with silver sand. I see her rescuing Jonathan from a dark hole underground.

They have to jump across an invisible wire. They have to scale a wall. I see her traveling the country, her loins girded, her shoes on her feet, and her staff in her hand, eating her bread in haste. Jonathan rides in the cart with Mim's mother and the dog. They come to the rivers, the floods, the brooks of honey and butter. And Mary, striding alongside Mim, is almost like her sister. She is like a portrait of Mim in metal. She looks the way she did the last time I saw her, in front of my own house in the moonlight: distant, almost as if she doesn't know me at all. But she does know me. "Hi Lyddie!" Some part of me remains inside her head, just as Hochmut, even now, would recognize my scent. I make stories for her, and I give her noble pursuits, because you wouldn't—would you?—you wouldn't create a character and make it a machine.)

Toronto author and editor L.X. Beckett frittered their misbegotten youth working as an actor and theater technician in Southern Alberta before deciding to make a shift into writing science fiction. Their first novella, "Freezing Rain, a Chance of Falling," appeared in the July/August issue of the *Magazine of Fantasy and Science Fiction* in 2018, and takes place in the same universe as their upcoming 2019 novel *Gamechanger*. Lex identifies as feminist, lesbian, genderqueer, married, and Slytherin, and can be found on Twitter at @ LXBeckett or at the Lexicon, at lxbeckett.com.

FREEZING RAIN, A CHANCE OF FALLING

L.X. Beckett

The night Woodrow Whiting lost all his social capital, a storm blew into Toronto. Blue-black fists of cloud reached across the lake from the U.S., shaking fat clusters of snowflakes over South Ontario. They piled up in censorious drifts on the windowsills as Drow's followship foundered, deep-sixing a host of memberships and privileges, including the backstage passes for his next three gigs.

Journos who drove waifish divas to suicide—and everyone had seen it happen, streaming crimson in 3dHD, live from Drow's apartment—didn't get to cover Pinegrove's Reunion Tour. They didn't get to compile newsflow on Fusion, alleged lab-grown clone child of Mercury and Bowie.

Mob rule by remote: When you were all strikes, no strokes, you could kiss good-bye to your access to the musical virtuosi.

By dawn, Drow had scrubbed every inch of his apartment, working his way out from the bloody epicenter of the incident. Whenever he had the urge to datadive, his sidekick app intervened with a dry, British-accented, "Bad idea, Master Woodrow." This got him a clean house while keeping him from brooding or—worse—firing another torpedo into his own fortunes.

By the time he was done, the place smelled of chlorine and broth. The fridge had been nagging him about leftovers, half-eaten meals abandoned by his roommate. Drow responded by throwing the dregs into a smartcooker with a couple chicken bouillon cubes. "Go to town," he'd told the cooker, and it obligingly blendered the mix into hot, green-gray lava. Allstew, Uncle Jerv had called it: random nutrients, no regard for flavor. Drow drank the brew until his gut was warm, queasy-liquidly full.

Crane, his sidekick app, flailed as it tried to put a calorie count on the binge. Drow returned to his war on filth.

Outside, the snow piled to infarction-inducing levels and the sky lightened.

Drow assembled a kit: wool cap, balaclava, gloves, degradable bags. Base layer, top and bottom, shirt, and ski pants. Last the coat and the boots. He could commit an assassination and nobody would be able to ID him without giving him a whooz first.

Thus swaddled, he closed his door on the smell of angry hospital, shuffled past the snow-weighted fauxflowers piling up on his boulevard, and headed to the corner store to buy a smartshovel and a bag of penitential salt.

The trick to stroke farming was to bottom-feed, staying clear of anyone who had an established snow-clearing gig. Drow volunteered himself to a network of self-driving cars. With twenty centimeters turning to slush on the asphalt, trapped sedans were becalmed all over Toronto. Batteries charged, they bleated alerts about unfilled orders and late appointments, making their sysops too desperate to sneer at his pariah-grade rating.

The network sent Drow to clear an older neighborhood on the edge of Little Italy. Narrow streets with brick houses, barely paid off by the octogenarian Gen X inhabitants moldering within, accumulated snow on pitched roofs. Icicles formed in jagged clusters to reveal holes in their post-Victorian gutter systems.

"Head down, donkey." The shovel tracked kilos moved, meters cleared. Crane flagged urgent gigs: oldsters with glass hips and medical appointments, and specialist cars with promises to keep and snow up to their wheel wells.

As he shoveled, strangers threw strokes his way without any thought of whoozing him. They appreciated not having to worry about the granny next door. The fossils stroked him, too, as did their descendants. Drow imagined middle-aged absentee kids, checking in on Ma from Sri Lanka and Nairobi, giving him the old-fashioned thumbs-up.

Sweat ran inside his base layers as his cap stopped hemorrhaging. If he kept his head down, shoveled twenty-four-seven, and the blizzard lasted forty days and forty nights, he might level his way back to respectability in time for the Spring into Music Festival in Stratford.

Or not. Squid ink bloomed on the edge of his goggs. At least one passerby was willing to convert three of their own strokes into sanction.

"U should be using sand on the byways, NOT salt!" They attached a flow about pollution levels in Lake Ontario.

It would be weeks before Drow could afford to ignore these passive-aggressive smackdowns. "Open article, Crane," he said to his sidekick, before the heckler decided to spend thirty strokes to hit him again.

Crane, ever the perfect virtual assistant, obediently washed newsflow across his goggs. Doleful music swelled in his ears, lead-in to the voice-over. Infographic furled through his line of sight.

Drow listened to the salient points even as he kept lifting and throwing, lifting and throwing the snow. Blah blah: effects of salt on groundwater. Blah blah poisoned lagoon in Pickering—Saints, that was back in 2018, how old was this link? Blah blah struggling fish populations.

"Face your editor, sir?" said Crane.

Drow appreciated the flow, old though it was, and blinked aside the stats on fishy carnage. "Hi, Seraph."

A pencil-sketch version of her appeared on the snowbank. "How are you?"

"Sunk in shit creek without a press pass."

"I'm working on spin. We'll raise you."

"Raise me? I've killed—"

"Untrue!" Seraph interrupted. "The conniving little virtuoso's gonna survive."

Drow missed his stroke, jamming the edge of the shovel into a crack in the pavement. "How?"

Cascayde had doxxed him. She'd barged into his apartment, screaming about his latest, newsflow meant to prove she was not only a derivative song-writer, but actively pirating the ideas of her betters.

Ambitious, risky followship-poaching. He'd hoped to expose the truth while flipping her fanbase, turning it against her while buoying himself, Seraph, and *Newsreef.* Instead, there she was, in his house, in his *face,* in hysterics. Stupidly, Drow had escalated, telling her six ways to fuck right off. Cascayde cut her own throat before he got to line item seven.

Naturally, they'd both been streaming it live.

Drow focused on the cartoon sketch. Seraph kept her hair buzzed into golden hexagons. Cartoon bees bumbled around the honeycombed scalp. When had he last seen her in person?

"She lived?" he repeated.

"Guess she didn't cut deep enough."

His knees turned, momentarily, to water. At a loss for words, he fired off a string of emoji. Thumbs-up, indicating a like.

"You don't have to be nice about it. Well. Not to me."

"Ah, but you adore me."

"Adore you *not*." She refused to be distracted. "Cascayde, pulling that stunt—"

"I shouldn't have baited her."

"You're at fault? No."

"Thousands say yes."

"They're wrong."

"It's the virtuosi who closed ranks against me. The fanbase is just dancing their party line."

The music-journo gig was supposed to be a detour on his road to becoming virtuoso. The plan was simple: cover his expenses, build his social capital, and make the contacts who would one day level Drow's own musical career.

Little chance of that now. He'd burned all his networking bridges.

Now what? Get used to street-cleaning?

Seraph said, "You couldn't know she was unstable, Drow."

"You're being kind." He'd gone for Cascayde's plagiarist underbelly, expecting her fellow composers to fall into line, to denounce her. He'd expected a counter-play from her—damage control, some move calculated to keep herself from falling too far. But the desperation in her eyes as she'd flashed that antique straight razor . . . that was truth. Her fragile-waif persona was no affect.

She'd been on some kind of edge. He'd kicked her off.

Seraph said, "I'm calling because I can't assign you anything new, Drow. You knew that?"

"Reporters for *Newsreef* must maintain a sixty prosocial rating, with a banked surplus of three hundred strokes, to be eligible for new freelance assignments," Drow said, quoting his user agreement with their employer. His shovel unearthed a fist-sized pile of dog turds; kneeling, he dug out one of his bags. "Why do you think I'm filter-feeding strokes out here in geezerland?"

"But! I went through your unfinished contracts. Remember you were profiling musicians who buy into dangerous fads? You never finished the series."

"I don't know if submitting newsflow on vaxxorcisms—"

"There's the chemo pop-up thing, remember?"

"I remember." Bullshit pitch at the Halloween party, eighteen months earlier. Drow as a new-minted reporter, Seraph his first ever editor: terra incognita. Their first night out, beer and face-to-face. He'd been wondering if a real conscience underlaid her elevated social capital. She'd wanted to know whether he was genuinely smart or just clever. That was how she'd put it, anyway, once they'd shared.

Seraph was a true believer, in her way. She saw being a journo as a calling, no different from art. Both, she claimed, were the pursuit of truth, pure and simple.

Drow wasn't sure about his smarts, and he certainly knew better than to overshare when it came to the purity of his motives. But all those sermons! Those long earnest monologues saying as how Drow should see his journo gig as something more than just a stepping stone on the climb to fame. If they'd taught him one thing, it was Seraph went gooey about anything that smacked of Actual Journalism. "So?"

"You had a whistleblower. You compiled infographics on how the chemo pop-ups work. For the shallows, we have slideshows about virtuosi who bought in for ten weeks of treatment. All you'd need would be voice to knit it together and fresh video of an open clinic."

"No. It needs realtime profile. It doesn't expose the clinics sufficiently, not if we don't show 'em poisoning someone."

"Someone like who?"

That brought him circling back to how he'd alienated his music industry friends. "An overview won't rebuild my followship."

Without followship, he couldn't get back to posting songs online, or playing live pop-in concerts.

"It'd position you as a serious reporter." Seraph was canny about such things. "Someone who tells the stories, damn the consequences. You'd be doing a good deed, too: Plenty of people know someone who's been wrecked by chemo fraudsters."

Could it be the journo bridge wasn't entirely burned? "I am definitely in karmic arrears."

"And a feature would pay in other ways."

"Money, you mean?"

"Can't buy you love. So go rack up some payables."

"Young man?" A pink-haired skeleton in old-fashioned LED goggs was waving from her stoop.

"Hold on, Seraph." Shovel in one hand, dogshit in the other, Drow gave the apparition an exaggerated pantomime—*Who, me?*—from within his sweat-soaked layers of downfill.

He braced for more simulated squid ink. She'd probably been saving her front walk as guilt-bait for grandchildren.

But she wasn't waiting to strike or berate him. Setting her goggs to display a huge pair of blue cartoon eyes, she pointed at her garbage. The bin unlatched noisily.

Grateful to have permission, Drow dumped the morning's accumulation of bagged dog droppings and litter.

"What is it?" Seraph asked.

He switched her to ridealong mode.

"Is that a person?"

The pink zombie was gesturing. "Come into my parlor, sonny, and have some cocoa."

Drow whoozed her: Tala Weston, owner/operator of Mygalomorphae Productions. Performance artist. Crane, ever helpful, sourced up "parlor," an archaic word meaning sitting room.

"Should I do your front walk on my way up there?" Drow asked.

"Suit yourself."

"Researching Mygalomorphae Productions," Seraph said.

"I got nothing."

"Your privileges are restricted, remember?"

He salted the walk, pollution be damned.

"Nothing yet. I'll drill down."

He'd reached the door. The old lady was waving him in. "You could've just carved a furrow. I'm not that wide. Recharge your shovel there."

"Thanks." Drow stepped onto the runner, dusting his boots so they wouldn't leave a puddle before he clipped the shovel in. It flashed a calorie burn on his display, numbers bright enough, for a second, to compensate for the fact that his goggs had steamed over.

"Painkiller? Anti-inflammatories? I've got the good stuff."

He squinted through the condensation haze. She was short and Caucasian. A forest of steel quills, embedded in both shoulders and the back of her left hand, quivered as she moved. Working acupuncture on RSI damage, probably: half of Gen X had wrecked itself keyboarding, back in the days before input tech went virtual. He got a glimpse of metal, embedded in her chin. Mandible replacement?

One pink braid, thick as a hangman's rope, dangled to her mid-back. At the scalp, it was gathered up over her ears in a way that did nothing to conceal wraparound headphones and the LED screens of her goggs. It was an antique rig, but expensive. Defying the trend to barely visible headsets, this was . . . conspicuous. Flashy. The eyes screened out as well as in, treating him to that image of blinky anime eyes with long lashes. They must weigh a ton: he could hear the click of lenses switching and adjusting within as she squared to face him.

Getting a portrait in case I turn out to be a serial killer. Drow dredged for her question. Painkillers. "Thanks. The aches haven't set in yet."

"And you're young as well as gallant and handsome." She hung his coat on a hook. "Cocoa?"

"Thanks."

What she poured was top-of-the-line drinking chocolate, sort of thing that couldn't be carbon-neutral, not unless you subsidized half a Croatian swamp, or personally reconstructed topsoil for a ridiculous percentage of Saskatchewan. It was so rich, the first sip almost made him moan.

"Sit, dear." She laid out a plate of gingersnaps.

Drow sank into a plush smartchair by the front window and chose one of the cookies. She settled across the table. They drank, two strangers watching the weather.

The thing in her chin was a piercing, embedded with an old brass gear . . . a watch cog? Some piece of tech that would have been antique even when she was young.

"Steampunk." She'd caught Drow staring. "You should see my tats."

He decided to breeze past the thought of wizened flesh covered in fading ink. "My name's Drow."

"Yes, I know."

"Course you do. I'm the man of the hour."

She put a hand out. "Tala."

"You're a . . ." He paused.

"Still drilling," Seraph said. "She's way under Sensorium radar."

He blinked silent acknowledgement and finished his sentence to Tala. ". . . performance artist?"

"Largely retired," the old lady said. "I still make the occasional artstorm."

He was more tired than he'd thought: The chocolate and the over-warm house were making him languid. "I didn't get any samples when I whoozed you."

"My work is mostly in private galleries."

He pondered that: art you couldn't access. Why bother?

"I owe you an apology, Drow. I came out to say you could use my bins." She tapped her cheek, next to the earbubble. "Hearing aids, they pick up more than they ought. I overheard your conversation."

"No worries." He waved this away, noticing as he did that a blister was coming in on the palm of his left hand. The red spot and shiny edge of skin were oddly fascinating. Pushing on it, he felt the thick resistance of flesh over bubbled fluid.

Her thin pink eyebrows were raised high. "Is your friend joining us?"

Oh. He blushed. "Ah . . . Seraph? You staying?"

"To watch you eat cookies? Later, Drow." The cartoon popped like a soap bubble.

"Sorry about that," he said to Tala.

"It's what your generation does. But I confess I am interested in this story your . . . editor? Suggested."

"She's taking pity. Brainstorming ways to keep me solvent while I regroup socially." Anything, Drow thought, to avoid having to turn to Uncle Jerv.

For one slippery second, he thought of asking Crane about Jerv. Had he reached out? Thrown an offer of financial or emotional support against the global block Drow had put on all such comms?

"You have to be popular to do what you do," Tala said.

"Yeah," he agreed, kicking Jerv to the back of his mind. Popularity was the circular trap of the stroke economy: If your social cap was high—virtuoso-high like Cascayde's, say—you could jumble together any old stream of atonal musical Allstew and the Sensorium would, like as not, lap it up like this viciously sinful chocolate.

If you strove and tried and reached for something really good, meanwhile, something true—if you labored in obscurity—none of your releases was apt to go anywhere.

Was it any surprise he'd lapsed? Had he let petty ambition tempt him into assembling a hatchet job on a self-harming narcissist?

The scaffold of needles on Tala's shoulder jerked in sequence, administering charges to the tissue, forcing tired old fibers to twitch so she wouldn't lose muscle mass. "The editor mentioned pop-up chemotherapy."

"An exposé on the clinics, yeah."

"But?" She poured more cocoa.

"These pop-ups cover their eventualities. People go in to get assessed, right? Clinic charges just for that. Serious medical testing might make them liable for something, so they do personality profiling instead. Then they say, 'Your pessimistic attitude puts you at risk for colorectal cancer, fifteen percent over the next decade. Your temperamental risk of . . . I dunno, sickle cell anemia . . . is seven. The chance you have rogue cells rampaging around your lymphatic system is better than fifty-fifty.'"

"This keeps them from getting sued for misdiagnosis?"

He nodded. "Once you're terrorized, they sell you ten weeks of medical self-flagellation. Preventative course of chemo tailored to your so-called vulnerabilities."

"Straight-up con." The cog in her chin bit into her lower lip.

"You get cancer later, they're covered. Terribly sorry. We didn't *actually* scan you." He toasted her and sipped cocoa.

"Well and good. They *should* be exposed. But what I don't understand, Drow, is that you're in music. I've listened to your compositions. You're extremely gifted."

Real praise or flattery? It nevertheless warmed him. "Gets me nothing if I don't have friends."

"You picked a strange way to ingratiate yourself with the other virtuosi."

Other. She dropped it so casually, as if he were already one of them. "Anything I do, I tend to overdo."

She smiled, lips stretching almost to invisibility, revealing gleaming teeth. "Me too."

"Anyway, I'd have spun the chemo exposé as a music story. There's usually virtuosi out there who've been suckered into taking the cure. But now I'm capped."

"What does your social capital have to do with it?"

It was the sort of question only an obscenely rich person would ask. "No access. I meant to profile a celebrity as they did treatment. But given what happ—what I *did* to Cascayde, no virtuoso will let me near them."

"And the editor can't help?"

"Seraph's kidding herself. She suggested the flow so she can feel less gilly. Giddy. Guilty. Sorry."

"No, no." She offered him another cookie and he munched, liking the texture, the bite of ginger and cloves. Snow was obliterating the walk he'd just cleared.

"You want to show someone famous on the chemo rack?" Tala steepled her fingers.

"What I really gotta focus on is generating strokes—"

"*Your* media profile's sky-high."

"Buh?" He sloshed chocolate up his nose.

"*You.* You're what we fogeys used to call a trending story. Everyone knows who you are."

"'Cause they're threatening to burn my house down."

"No attention is bad attention." Her tone was thoughtful. "You should get scans beforehand. Show you're cancer-free. Throw in genetic risk assessment and you can side-by-side the data against whatever organs the clinic claims you're bound to metastasize."

Suddenly she sounded like she knew *plenty* about assembling newsflow.

"Forgeddid," Drow said. "I'm not so capped I need to scourge myself with medically unnecessary poisoning. Or chemobrain."

"Oh, chemobrain can be offset," Tala said.

That brought him up in his seat. *Did she mean . . . ?*

No. Drow set down his cup, pushing away fatigue and fogginess. "Doctors don't just give you smartdrugs, not even if you're on chemo. It's too risky."

"The risk's inflated. Intellectual enhancement is contraindicated, primarily, because it hampers patient buy-in to life extension."

"Yes . . ." he agreed. Smartdrugs had always been Uncle Jerv's poison of choice. Drow knew more about the relevant statutes than he probably ought to admit. And it was true that if you were rich enough for smartdrugs, you were discouraged from taking them—because the Pharmas didn't want to lose the chance of streaming you, later, into the even more astronomical cost of buying yourself another century of life. But nobody wanted to live forever in a bubble of amnesia and dementia; smartdrugs did weird things to the teleromeres, stretching them out in ways nobody quite understood.

Rumor had it that the ultrarich hired proxies to dose up, do their thinking for them. Was that where this was going?

He stuck to the facts. "Unless you actually have cancer, getting a prescription for Liquid Brilliance is a nonstarter."

"So your only objection is availability? Logistics?"

"Excuse me?"

A coy shrug. "I know a lot of doctors."

He was starting to feel breathless. "I can't afford—"

"Pish."

"And *Newsreef* would have to pay for chemo."

"Pish again. Look around, kid. I'm loaded."

Smartdrugs. What if a dose of Liquid Brill helped him back into composing music?

Really? Was he some drug-grubbing Jerv type, to be considering this?

The cookie had turned to sandpaper on his tongue; he forced it down, vowing to thank Tala and walk once he'd finished his decadent, cooling chocolate.

He'd definitely made enough bad choices for one week.

He woke without realizing he'd fallen asleep, still in the smartchair, which had eased into recliner mode, elevating his knees, kneading his shoulders with an almost-imperceptible rolling motion to keep anything from stiffening. Perfect old-lady chair. The blind on the window had unscrolled, blocking the afternoon sun. It was bright green just for a moment; when he blinked, it was white again. Optical illusion or green screen?

"Crane?" He queried his clock app. He'd been out for almost three hours.

This was what he got for staying awake all night bleaching the floorboards after the paramedics and cops had vacated. He sat up, the chair offering a friendly burst of momentum as he rose. The opportunity map for snow shoveling had thinned out. The sidewalks were clearing and the temperature was on the rise. Another storm was due in a couple days.

He'd need it: His cap had fallen further, taking with it the morning's harvest of hard labor and good deeds.

He pulled metrics. There'd been a surge in his favor, maybe an hour ago—anti-suicide activists throwing him support, thereby officially disapproving of Cascayde's performance of self-harm.

Seraph's work. "She adores me," he mumbled.

Why was he plunging?

Heart sinking, he re-buttoned his shirt, which was one hole off. He'd been in worse shape than he guessed this morning. He remembered dressing carefully, like a soldier going on parade.

"Crane, you booted?"

"Online now, sir."

"Check the newsflows."

"All your premium memberships are on hold."

"Try public access?" The blister on his hand had split as he slept.

He had to endure three minutes of advertising just to find out Cascayde had made a short statement through her publicist:

Cascayde was in a state of despair when she committed her act of self-harm. While Mer Whiting's remarks about her recent songstorm, Cataract, *may have influenced her state of mind, he cannot be held responsible for her actions.*

She apologizes wholeheartedly.

This, plus a still of her barely making a ripple in a hospital bedcover, had dropped another depth charge on his reputation. Big bad bully Drow. Virtuosi were sharing it all over Sensorium and their fans were spending lavishly, cutting into cap reserves as the cost per strike rose, three for one strike, thirty for two, nine hundred for three . . .

He realized he was watching his fortunes bottom out in a stranger's living room.

"Anyone here?"

No answer.

"Crane, where's Tala?"

"Uncertain, sir. I'm still powering up a few peripherals."

"You went offline? Total shutdown?"

"I'm . . . Yes, I believe so."

"How can you be unsure?" Drow dove for his boots and coat. The gloves might be anywhere; he gave them up for lost. For one claustrophobic second, he thought the old lady's smartlock might not unlatch for a stranger.

Would he have to break a window to get out? What if someone saw? Did the Haystack have a transcript proving she'd invited him in?

A click, just as he started to hyperventilate. He lunged out onto the salted porch, the cold air a welcome slap on his unshaven face.

Tala was there, in a pink quilted coat so bright you could probably see her from space. LED eyes with heart-shaped irises glowed from deep within a fur-fringed hood.

"What are you doing?" Drow asked.

"Waiting for my ride." She pointed as a self-driving car toiled to push a rolling pile of slush to the curb. "Cardiologist appointment."

"I didn't mean to pass out in your. Um. Breakfast nook? It's just I haven't been sleeping."

"Oh, Handsome," she said. "You know you can make it up to me."

Hiding a sigh, he grabbed his smartshovel. The car paused when it saw him, waiting with electronic patience as he cleared its wheels, even backing up so he could get at the accumulated mush. His broken blister rubbed raw, smearing red on the wooden handle of the shovel.

Twenty minutes later, the car whirred up to Tala's walk. Drow went and offered her an awkward arm.

"Bless you, young fella. That's what my granny would've said."

"No problem." Helping her into the car got him a few likes from passersby. Spit on a bonfire at this point.

"Text from your landlord," said Crane. "His father says there's loud noise coming from your apartment."

He clamped his lips over a curse, smiling at the old lady. *I probably look like a maniac.*

She laid a pink-gloved hand on his cheek. "Want to come? Help the old dear out at Mount Sinai?"

Drow pulled away, skin crawling. "Thanks, Tala, but . . ."

She waved him her contact info. "We should talk about cancer imaging."

He remembered her hinting at a trade. Medically unnecessary chemotherapy. For smartdrugs.

Rather than answer, he closed the door, watching the car putt-putt-skid off to College Street before he shouldered the shovel, turning into the winter wind.

The pings from Drow's landlord got increasingly urgent as he hiked, so it was no surprise to find his roommate crowding the couch with her boyfriend and four other virtuosi wannabes. They had helped themselves to his collection of musical instruments: smart drumsticks, a couple faux guitars, gloves for a virtual keyboard, and a real saxophone that he'd tuned and modemed himself, years ago, with Uncle Jerv's help. They were trying to work up a single, the kind of DIY instahit earworm that made Drow want to grab the nearest pair of pliers and rip out his own wisdom teeth.

He paused at the threshold—actually *hesitated*. Considered whether he wanted trouble. The bleach smell, he noticed, underlaid a perfume of stale pizza and farts.

Self-loathing got him moving; he logged in to the musical instruments and overrode the guest permissions, shutting them down.

Marcella burbled into sudden silence. "Hey, Drow. You got the blood out of the carpets?"

"Yeah, sad. No grisly spectacle for your friends."

"Dunno know what you mean. This is a work session."

"We talked about this, Marce. Stream sound to your rigs."

"You were out, Drow."

"You want amps, go to Cole's. He lives alone."

"In a shoebox. Anyway, equipment's here."

"*My* equipment. Which'd be point three. You can't jam with my stuff."

"It's gathering dust."

"I'm conceptualizing."

"You're blocked. And sinking fast. *Cataract* might not've ascended to your lofty standards of musical truth and beauty, but at least Cascayde's composing."

"Pilfering. I'd rather compose nothing, ever, than loot everyone else's garbage."

"Great job! Writing nothing ever is definitely getting to be your forte." She minced close enough to make him want to back away. Her bright orange Shirley Temple ringlets bounced with every step. "We've raised two thousand strokes between us. Want 'em?"

Two thousand. His mouth watered.

Before he could go through the internal litany of *why that's a terrible idea*, the boyfriend shifted. Getting a better camera angle? Drow remembered anew that everything he did right now was a potential live upload.

"This sounds like bribery, Marce. Very antisocial," he reminded her.

"Don't be sanctimonious. Yes or no?" She gave him a look that, terrifyingly enough, might have been pity. He tried to remember when and why he had liked her, back when he invited her to rent-share.

"We promised Imran a quiet environment for his dad."

"Basement dad is fucking deaf."

"I'm having a shower," Drow said. "When I emerge, you and Wonderboy and your friends will be gone and my instruments will be neatly stowed. Because, uninvited houseguests, I didn't get your names yet. Marce here is the only one about to take a hit for attempted cap manipulation on a high-profile pariah."

"You're not opening a support ticket on me!"

Drow forced himself to turn his back on her. "I'm definitely not opening one on the people in this room whom I have not whoozed."

He made it upstairs, despite quaking legs. Collapsing against the wall, he peeled off warmth-retentive layers of black, like a fiberfill onion. He hung the coat, unbuttoned the shirt and hung that, too, then stripped the base layer and put it, stinking, straight into the laundry. It smelled a little skunky, though he hadn't smoked cannabis in years. Seemed hypocritical, after blocking Jerv.

Crossing the hall, defiantly naked, he paused to take in the sweet sound of brouhaha in progress downstairs:

The boyfriend, Cole: "Give him the strokes, Marce—he won't report us if we pay him off."

Drummer: "Tell him it was a joke, right?"

The house was so old it had a nine-foot claw-foot tub, upgraded with a smartshower set to deliver carefully measured bursts of heated water for ten minutes precisely. Drow paid it a precious carbon offset, trading his scant dollars for an extra ten minutes, before he plunged in.

Breathing slowly, he tried to calm the deranged stutter of his heart. He'd had shitty roommates before. It was what you got when you glomerated on the cheap.

Water ran through his hair, spreading comforting heat. He felt the front door slam. Marcella's friends, abandoning ship before he could run that support ticket?

Jealousy-raddled pusbag. Cascayde's words. He remembered the anguish in her eyes. The blade coming up. He'd stepped back, expecting her to lash out, not inward . . .

Suddenly he was crouched, curled against his bare knees in the wet and steam. "Oh shit," he whispered. "Damnation, no, no . . ."

Give in. Give in, you'll feel better.

Filthy no-talent bottom-feeding scum!

Dirty, dirty, where's my soap?

Soap? Missing. Snuffling, he peered through a crack in the shower curtain. There: stained with more of Marcella's friends' pizza sauce. He had to get out, leaving sodden ovals on the bath mat.

By the time he'd scrubbed the pizza sauce off his pricey scentless soap, then washed the imaginary marijuana smell off his hair, *then* chewed off the dead-skin petals curling and drying around the edges of the raw blister on his left palm, the urge to melt down had congealed. An acidic mess of bad feeling pulsed stickily between Drow's lungs, tightening breath, refusing to dislodge.

The showerhead pinged a one-minute warning.

"Ten more minutes," he said. Begged, really.

"Not recommended, sir," Crane said. "You have exceeded your weekly carbon ceiling. Exponential pricing would raise the cost—"

"Fine!" Should he upgrade his sidekick? Was there a more soothing alternative to his dads' irascible homegrown assistant?

Crane threw a countdown into his lower peripheral. At ten seconds, Drow stepped out. He dried off, sopped up his wet footprints, and hung the bath mat on the shower bar.

"Is Marce out there, waiting to ambush?"

"They've left, but I have messages," Crane said.

"Summarize." Pathetic, the fragility in his voice. Wounded baby boy with his lip aquiver.

"Mer Zapiti opines that nobody will live with you if she gives notice. Mer Cole says: Please don't make trouble, here's a thousand strokes. No strings."

"Huzzah."

"In better news, your downstairs neighbor has confirmed that the noise has stopped."

"All hail the tiny victories." No, Crane was perfect. Butler, enabler, dad substitute . . . just right.

Emotionally tone-deaf, though. Now the inbox was open, the sidekick had clearly decided to blast through some to-dos. "And from Seraph?"

"Play it."

"Drow. Some anon donor has kicked *Newsreef* funding for an expanded version of the cancer story. Call me?"

He winced. "I don't suppose you've got one from Anon Donor herself?"

"Meaning, Master Woodrow?"

"Anything from Tala Weston?"

"There is indeed."

"Play it."

"Drow, it's Tala. How would you feel about driving to Buffalo for medical imaging tomorrow?"

He shouldn't do this.

"Crane, compose reply. Ask Tala what the hell she wants from me." Scooping up a washrag, he began to work on a tomato-sauce handprint on his sink.

A pause. "She's sent a contract."

"For?"

"It's an artist's modeling release."

"Can you run it through some kind of legal?"

"With our cap, it would have to be public access."

More ads. He groaned. "Copy to Seraph."

Modeling release. Presumably, Tala wanted to make some kind of art-storm of Drow taking chemo.

"Compose a reply. I'd want some guarantees. About the after-treatment care we discussed." He was careful not to mention smartdrugs.

Again, Tala's response was almost immediate. "Can't specify aftercare in writing, but we can work something out. Eight months, perhaps? Can I pick you up at ten?"

Liquid Brill. Eight months' supply. Maybe he was Uncle Jerv's son after all. "Tell her yes."

Seraph was against it, of course, so opposed she showed up in the flesh next morning, right at ten as Drow was making to leave. She piled into Tala's gas-guzzling hire-a-limo, brimming with righteous fire. "Drow's supposed to profile an insider who's against the pop-up chemo program. End of story."

"You know I wanted to realtime a patient."

"Victim, you mean?"

Tala interrupted: "Are you going to introduce your friend, Handsome?"

"You've already whoozed each other." The women bristled from opposite corners of the cab. "Seraph, it's a better story. First I do the medical screening, *then* I take the pop-up assessment. It will show just how much they're distorting the risks."

"Yes, very clever. Show the distort by all means, Drow. Compare, contrast, get the scoop from your source! Like Like Like! But draw the line at actually doing chemo."

"It's a way to get at the truth—"

"I won't green-light this." Privately, she sent him a pair of spiked entertainment flows, stuff that hadn't made it out of *Newsreef*, draft articles about two closed screenings of Tala's most recent artstorm, something called *All Fun and Games Until* . . . The streams avoided—carefully, Drow noticed—saying what the pieces themselves were like. Brawls had broken out at both screenings, and the second theater had a full-scale medical lockdown afterward. Out of business for six weeks.

"*Newsreef* isn't the only platform, young lady," Tala said. "Drow will find a taker for this piece."

Seraph folded her arms, leaning back into the upholstery. "Really? With his cap?"

Tension ratcheted then, as they waited to see if Tala would offer to somehow level him up from pariah.

"It suits you, doesn't it? That he's desperate."

"Face it, Seraph—I *am* desperate," Drow said. "And this streams. Everyone in music wants to see me pay for what I did to Cascayde."

"You did nothing!"

"Verdict's still guilty, though, isn't it?"

"If you show you're a serious journo, they'll reassess in time."

"Time. Years? If I make myself sick and we pour strikes all over the popups, we can trim that to months—"

"So it's a shortcut? Get your life back and start treating *Newsreef* as a dodge again?"

"This story was your idea," Tala reminded her.

"Drow will be too hagged to assemble newsflow."

"I'll prerecord most of it. You'll help me sharpen the rest." He couldn't tell her about the smartdrugs; she'd be an accessory. "I'm not making light of what you do, Seraph."

"We. What *we* do."

"I have to stop myself from bottoming out."

Seraph rubbed her fingers through the black-rooted honeycomb stubble on her scalp. "Maybe."

Tala shifted in her seat, seeming to sense victory. "Can I drop you somewhere, young lady, or are you proposing to accompany us to the U.S.?"

Seraph's lip curled. She sent text: *You want me to ridealong? Silent, so she can't overhear?*

Drow's breath hitched. Come in person, he wanted to say. Don't leave me.

Fact was, Tala creeped him out.

But she was so old. What was she gonna do?

Aloud, he said, "I'll be okay, Seraph. Swear."

"Mer Raffe?"

"Drop me at the subway," Seraph said.

Tala's LED eyes blinked. She was swaddled in a pink cashmere cape with fur fringe. The color made her skin look chalky, powdered. One of her earlobes had become untucked from the earphones. It dangled, rubbery as an udon noodle. She must have worn a hoop in there when she was young.

The driver pulled up at Saint Andrew. "Subway."

"Don't put her out here," Drow said. "She'll get strikes for riding in a limo."

"I'll take the hit," Seraph said, flinging the door wide. "Expect me to micromanage this one. Nanomanage. I want scan results from Buffalo. Itemized list: They do it, I review it."

"Don't worry." He reached for her hand, but she slipped his grasp and lunged out into the frosty air.

They left her scowling on King Street, no doubt taking hits from everyone who'd seen the car. The limo sped toward the Queensway and the Niagara Falls border crossing.

"You could've dropped her in a parkade somewhere."

"Mer Raffe clearly wished to make a display of herself. Now. My clinic needs a medical history." Tala sent a long document to his inbox. "Questions for you from the doctors."

Grateful for the distraction, Drow dove in, offering up family medical history and bio deets: name, age, Social Insurance Number. Doctors' appointments, blood work, surgery, serious illnesses. Soon they were at the border.

"Passport?"

"Already?" Surprised, he brought it up, transmitting to Border Services.

She read his expression. "I'm authorized for the fast lane. No four-hour wait today."

Twenty minutes later, at a clinic that looked like a vacation resort—one of those places that turned the death-fearing rich into ever-older zombies—he was stripping down and chugging contrast liquid. A technician eased him onto a deep tray in a hyperlinked room. The tray was layered with plastic bricks; as he relaxed onto them, they crumbled into beads, forming a synthetic bed that cushioned him completely, adhering to his ankles and feet as he sank into the nodules like quicksand. They stuck to the backs of his knees, pressing into the curve of his butt, the nape of his neck.

The tech tamped him down, fingers working over Drow's shoulders, chest, and forehead.

"Is Tala watching?" Drow indicated the room's observation bubble.

"She's having muscular rejuvenation."

He felt, strangely, relieved.

Once his bottom half was stuck down, the tech laid foam bricks on his feet and legs. These broke up, too, burying him like a kid on the beach, filling the spaces between his calves, pooling in the wrinkles in the thin sheet of the modesty drape, accumulating as weight on his hands, hips, belly, chest.

"Gotta offline you, Woodrow." The tech removed Drow's goggs and earbuds, then fitted a breathing mask over his nose and mouth. "It helps if you count down from a thousand."

Drow closed his eyes. There was nothing to distract him from the plastic press of diagnostic medium against his eyes as the immurement continued. The small of his back was sweating. Moisture accumulated there, like grease.

Instead of counting, he composed openers for his flow on the pop-up. *Bricks of scanfoam collapse like sandcastles at high tide, enfolding me in a medical experience so far outside my financial reach that . . . what?*

Or: *Lying in darkness, I realize that while our working assumption is that I'll be starting this with a clean bill of health, there are no guarantees.*

He twitched as his skin grew goosebumps.

"Stay still, Woodrow."

He kept refining and memorizing the sentences, so he could dictate them to Crane once his stuff was back online.

A crack, a flash of light. The tech helped him stumble out of the scanfoam cube. The modesty sheath had stuck to the foam, tearing away; he clapped a hand over his groin.

"How do you feel?" The tech handed him a gown.

"Shrink-wrapped." He scowled at the bas-relief version of himself as he fumbled the ties.

"Done?" Tala swept in, buttoning her pink jumpsuit.

Drow nodded, turning aside as he pulled the gown shut.

"I have a capture appointment at the Albright-Knox. Then we'll eat."

Drow wasn't hungry, but he nodded nonetheless.

The driver took them to the gallery, past a sculpture garden at the back, and then into an underground addition called the Weston Virtual Experience Annex.

"Did you reassure your editor?" Tala asked. "Confirm I haven't done anything nefarious?"

"Very funny." He dictated a quick text: *All okay. Techs will copy the three of us with med results.*

A private elevator raised them into a capture studio, long slot of a room, darkened, with a wooden bench and a tinted-glass wall. Beyond the glass was a floodlit balance beam.

"I've been adding thirty seconds of footage to this project each year since I was eighteen," Tala said. "We're just going to capture the next installment."

He looked at the beam. If she fell . . . well, she'd be insured to her artificial eyeballs.

She jerked a comb through the horsetail of her waist-long braid, smoothing it. "Do you mind?"

"Um." Reluctantly, he took the comb and the rope of hair, brushing the dead, bleached tangles.

"What a good boy you are."

He handed back the brush. "Tala. I am not so much as getting a chemo port put in if there are no guarantees on the Liquid Brill."

"You'll get your guarantees, my pretty, no fear."

"I'm not your pretty."

"Pretty's what I hired you for, isn't it?" On that, she vanished through the exit.

"I thought it was desperation," he muttered.

Beyond the glass, the lights over the balance beam brightened. Camera rigs shook themselves awake, above and below. A hidden door opened at one end of the structure.

Tala appeared, nude, even her goggs removed.

Every inch of her old body was flashed or modded. Her left iris was a star sapphire; the right was a cat's-eye the color of a banked coal. Her skin was stretched, punctured, pinched, and laser-cut to lace. Little flaps like fish gills had been cinched into her throat and extra nipples circled her breasts like roses on a wedding cake. Within the cage of her torso, tattoo renderings of damned souls suffered at the claws of demons. A real-looking tongue lolled from her navel, ringed by four rows of sharks' teeth.

Her bush was as pink as her ponytail. The teeth of brass gears protruded from her knees and elbows.

Deliberate damage, flagrantly displayed. The disregard for self . . . He remembered his father, yelling at Jerv:

Your body is the only thing you truly own!

Dad would be on the same page as Seraph about this chemo scheme.

Under Tala's saggy, much-abused skin, he could see the muscle tone of a professional athlete. As she'd laid waste to her exterior, she'd meticulously maintained the rest. This was the legacy of a boutique life-extension regime.

Mounting the beam, she rolled to a one-footed crouch and then put her head down, lifting to a headstand before easing into full upside-down splits. Drow dropped his eyes, catching a glimpse of big cartoony letters on her inner thighs, bloody tattoos spelling nasty words: "Unclean, gangrene, fester, infect . . ."

Keeping her in the blurry corner of his upper peripheral, he saw her come out of the splits, pivoting upright. He didn't know gymnastics well. Was she playing it safe, acrobatically speaking?

Humming tunelessly, she handsprang a dismount from the beam's far end. Hands flung high, like an Olympic medalist, she strode through an unmarked exit on the other end of the capture studio.

Crane said, "Miss Weston will be with you in five minutes, Master Woodrow."

Drow used the time to gather his temper and gauge his cap, weighing his situation against an urge to rabbit.

She came in, arranging her fur cape, swinging the ponytail saucily. "Well?"

He pushed the word past clenched teeth. "Impressive."

"Not your thing, huh? Maybe we should leave before they compile and run it—"

A sharp electronic hum. Tala appeared again, just as he'd seen her—but now she was on the bench, here in the room with them. Nine feet tall, intangible, her hologram leapt through the two of them, old, nude, and ornamented. Before she was gone, a new version of her—one year younger, if he'd understood her concept—was flying into a mount. They played through, ten seconds per routine, and as the decades spun by, Tala got progressively younger, less modified. The loops disappeared from her back. The metalwork shrank and disappeared. The ponytail grew backward and the tattoos got less elaborate even as her flesh tightened and became less outlandishly modded. The early gymnastics routines showcased health in all its robust complexity. By the end, she was a normal-enough eighteen year old, with close-cropped black hair and hazel eyes.

The image of her youthful ass drifted past his face one last time as she triple-flipped out the door.

"What do you think?"

I think this is straight-up mind fuckery. He kept his voice even. "The early tapes must be CGI. No holo-imaging when you were my age."

"Reconstructed from video. The original footage is real." She fanned herself. "I don't know how many more years of this I've got in me. I'm quite shaky now."

Swallowing a sigh, he offered her his arm. *Vulture claws,* he thought as she clamped on.

Tala's idea of lunch was typically opulent; the driver took them to a private dining room whose staff brought marinated morsels of printed sea scallop and strips of beef.

"Ever had real cow before?" she asked.

Drow shook his head. "If anyone sees me living it up—"

"Whoozing's not allowed here," she replied serenely. "Confidential space, transcript shredders and all. Which means, among other things, that we can speak freely."

"It's a restaurant. Public space, public access."

"Technically, it's the cafeteria for my U.S. lawyers' branch office. Confidentiality applies. Nothing goes into the Haystack."

"That loophole's under contest. Suspended."

"In Canada, it is. Not here."

Crane flashed a graphical thumbs-up in his peripheral, confirming that this was true.

"So," Drow said. "Your promise."

She squirreled in her big pink purse, coming up with a box: ten vials, ready for the pump and labeled *Bennett's Food Coloring.*

Drow's mouth went dry but he held the poker face. "That could actually be food coloring. And it's only ten."

"Contents are as agreed." She steepled her fingers. "Here's my proposal. You go to the pop-up clinic, do the assessment, and get the injection port."

"Do I?"

"You need a port, Dearheart."

"Don't call me that."

Cartoon lashes batted. "Use the port to test the food coloring, satisfy yourself that it's legitimate. Next day, before we head to the clinic for your first infusion, we'll visit a registered middleman and put twenty more doses—" she flipped the box of ampules with her fingernail, as if it wasn't worth a small fortune "—into a lockbox. You can open same as soon as you finish chemotherapy."

"I might need to dose to finish the article. Chemobrain, remember?"

"Well, you've got ten, don't you? Each good for a week?"

He nodded reluctantly.

"That'll keep you going for the full course of chemo. Another twenty vials are . . . do you kids still say gravy?"

"Twenty-five," he said, to see if she'd go for it.

"Done."

Should've said thirty. He pulled the doses across the table, vanishing them into his parka. His heart was pounding.

"Update Seraph again, Handsome—it looks like those med results have come through. She can sift through them while we get going, but it looks like you're in perfect health."

"I want to read 'em too." But he fell asleep in the limo, coming around only reluctantly as it pulled up at his place. His hand went automatically to his shirt, but the buttons were properly aligned. The paper flowers by the door, tributes to poor Cascayde and her profound emotional journey, were piled higher. Blooms and stems were layered with jagged blobs of ice, like an elaborate cake.

"Scene of the crime," murmured Tala.

"Hoping for a looky-loo at the blood spatter?"

"I saw everything on the vidflow."

"So you did watch it?"

"I could hardly avoid. It's the first thing on your whooz: that beautifully articulated jaw of yours hanging open as the blood sprays."

He remembered the taste. Remembered spitting. Half-blinded and groping for Cascayde's throat, clamping down on the wound as Crane summoned the ambulance.

Tears welled and he hurried to get out of the car.

"See you in the morning," she said lightly.

He nodded, gave her a half-salute, and dragged himself inside. He smelled like marijuana again.

The temperature had continued to rise overnight and it was almost balmy when he reached the pop-up, a storefront on the edge of Kensington that had, over the years, housed a series of failed restaurants. The latest proprietors had whitewashed it to a glow. Tasteful holosigns displayed competent multiracial medical teams wearing the highest of high-tech goggs. "What's your risk?" a banner demanded.

Drow walked in alone, filled out their quiz. No hard medical data here. They asked about recent stressors and childhood trauma. Medical services were allowed to jam Sensorium uploads to the Haystack for confidentiality reasons, but he had brought an antique recording device of Dad's, a Dictaphone. It copied voice to magnetic tape and was so old Drow probably could've laid it on the table in front of the medics without fear of having it recognized.

He didn't take the chance, instead packing it inside another antique, a hardcopy of *Jude the Obscure* with a hole cut in its pages.

Trevon Amradi, his whistle-blower, was someone Drow had met going to concerts, a fan of his music from back in the day when he was comping and clamoring for attention, jostling in an unremarkable pack with Marcella and the rest of the wannabes.

Tall, windburned, and professionally sympathetic, Trevon eased into pretending, for his bosses, that the two of them were strangers. He worked through Drow's personality quiz, generated infographics analyzing Drow's aura, and began the consult with: "How's your relationship with your mother?"

"My what? Are you kidding?"

Trevon made eyes at him, unsubtle reminder that the point was to seem an emotional shambles, so they could tell him he was at risk for pancreatic cancer or whatever.

Shambles they wanted, shambles they'd get.

He mumbled: "Little Master Woodrow had two daddies, okay? Uncle Drow's an addict. Theo Whiting died. Because of the addict."

"Sounds like a complicated story."

"Not if you're looking to talk about a mother, it isn't." Dad and Jerv had gotten into a fight, about the drugs, on a crowded subway platform at rush hour. How Dad had ended up falling under the train wasn't clear. Had he stumbled? Did he jump? Where the video footage was ambiguous, the transcript was clear enough. They'd been banging heads over Jerv's adulterous love for Liquid Brill and his latest get-rich-quick scheme.

Shrugging, Trevon moved on. "This honorary grandma you've listed as next of kin. What's she like?"

"A spider," Drow said—it was what came to mind.

Trevon chewed his lip. "Drow, I gotta say—"

"Marty." Now he was the one warning.

Trevon sent him a puppy-eyes emoji, hinting at concern. "Everyone knows what you've been through these past few days. With. You know, Cascayde. If you gave it a week, you might feel differently about this."

Trevon had been all for exposing the pop-up for the scam it was, back when they discussed the two of them playing witness as some gullible artist ran themselves through the grinder. Popcorn fodder, he had called it.

"I know this is going to make me sick," Drow said. "And with Cascayde and my roommate . . . sure, I'm getting a lot of static now, from women—"

"You all right?"

He had broken out in cold sweat.

He reached for a glass of water with a convincingly trembly hand. "But my ed—my friend, Seraph, she IDs as woman too. Obviously. It's luck of the draw."

"You just characterized your next of kin as a spider."

"Honestly, I think she'd agree with me on that one." *Don't try to help me.* Irrational rage fizzed in his hands, knotting them together.

Trevon apparently got the message. Or perhaps he had a ridealong superior with healthier profit motives, because he finally moved on to scare tactics. Drow had latent misogyny. He needed preventative meds aimed at squamous cell anemia and lung cancer.

He played hard to get for all of fifteen minutes, for form and for the old Dictaphone, and then obliged Trevon to press on to an unenthusiastic closing. Yes, oh yes, please save me from my inner retrograde caveman before he eats my lungs out.

An hour later, "Grandma" Weston was on her way to support (meaning watch, and capture if she could outwit the clinic jammers) as they sliced into his perfectly healthy shoulder and stapled a purple smartport to Drow's collarbone.

The local had worn off by the time Tala took him home; the whole right side of his chest hurt, and he could feel his heartbeat in each of the staples.

"Did you get footage?"

"A few stills," she said, tapping her goggs significantly—she must have illegal capture tech in there. "Their privacy walls are top-of-the-line."

"The better to avoid prosecution, I guess."

She pressed a finger to the hard lump of the port.

"Ow!"

"Sorry, Dearheart. I'll drop by early, once it's bruised up a little, to make close-ups."

"Okay."

"I've got a green-screen studio and a medical-grade smartchair. After infusion, you can recover there. Easier for me to make footage."

"Wait. At your place?"

"Would you rather set up a studio in your apartment?" She gave him an inquiring look. "I can send contractors 'round."

He imagined it: waves from his landlord about contractor noise. Managing the stairs to his room when he was wiped. Recuperating while Marcella came in and out to abandon cheap takeout in the fridge, like some Arctic fox burying dead ducklings. "Your place. Fine."

"Good!" Tala handed him a heavy disk the circumference of a drink coaster, complete with beer company logo. He could feel glass—a touchscreen?—on its underside, but when he tried to turn it over, she locked his hand in a surprisingly strong grip. "Did you know that you have to be completely offline, all your things powered down, goggs islanded, to put any kind of unregistered ampoule into a smartport like your new chemo delivery system?"

"Is that so?

"Please understand: I'm not recommending or advising this, just making casual conversation."

That's why she was holding the coaster facedown, to keep Crane from catching an image. "Got it."

"Once your things are offline, handshake the port itself using a dedicated injection app on a monitor with redtooth connection capability. Such monitors are by prescription only."

In other words, the gadget she'd slipped him would override the smart-port's better judgment. And possession of said gadget, *sans* prescription, was an offense. "Boot it up, pop in the ampoule, away you go?"

She nodded. "In the hypothetical world where you had access to such items. You'll need to set an agenda for any burst of enhanced intellectual activity. Does your antiquated sidekick app have a Friday mode?"

"My fathers wrote it."

"That's sweet."

"You're one to talk, with those vintage goggs." He couldn't say why he was nettled by the insult to Crane. "Yes! We operate offline."

"Well, set it to nag you. You won't be able to stay on task otherwise."

They had reached his place. She popped the door and gave him a cheery wave. "Out you go, Handsome. Have fun."

Drow's first hours as an intravenous genius were incandescent.

He powered down the house things: thermostat, smoke detector, fridge, oven, blender, toaster, the lights that went on and off automatically as he moved between rooms, hydrators for the houseplants, step counters in his shoes, all the musical instruments. Marcella had a few things he couldn't access remotely, so he pulled their batteries, stomping their ready signs like so many roaches before setting them out in the freezing rain to die. Last he shut down the modem, leaving him and Crane islanded.

He'd made the agenda Tala had suggested. First, he'd revise the newsflow he'd written, all those months before, on the pop-up clinics. Then he'd try writing a song. Surely if the Brill was working, he'd be able to compose again.

He wouldn't even think about what it might mean if he couldn't.

Third, he'd consider ways to stanch his cap bleed. After that, he'd research chemo outcomes.

Flipping the beer coaster, he got the redtooth to hack into his injection smart-port. Taking out the first of the ampoules marked *Bennett's Food Coloring*, he snapped it into place, sitting in the increasingly chilly house and watching the status bar as it claimed to load him up with smarts. Or, possibly, food coloring.

Final stage: powerdown and flip his coaster so it was just a coaster again. Hide the other *Bennett's* ampoules. Scrub any archival video Crane had made.

"Brilliance FAQs suggest taking on a simple task first, sir, something clerical with multiple steps."

"Okay." He walked Crane backward through the powerdown sequence, the two of them prepping a macro for the house so that next time, Drow could just shut everything off with a single command.

"Do I sound smarter, Antiquated Sidekick?"

"Simple tasks, sir, simple tasks," crooned Crane. "Here's your draft of the chemo pop-up exposé."

Drow fell into refurbishing the bones of the feature, laying out history on virtuosi who'd taken the cure and rehashing the death of a jazz virtuoso named Psyche. No criminal charges had been brought: Rumor had it the Pharmas paid the family.

Charges. He researched and sidebarred some legislative history, riffing on the rise of medical superstitions, enumerating the court challenges that had eventually determined Canadian citizens had the right to poison themselves in the name of scientifically dubious preventative healthcare.

Universal mandatory vaccination had come in with legislation that said individuals couldn't endanger the herd. Ironically, this same ruling meant the state couldn't prohibit unnecessary treatment, if patients footed the bill and didn't harm others.

He saw his evolution as a journo within the date-tags on the strings of notes. Here, the first smattering of thoughts, after he'd shared with Trevon and scented the opportunity for a serious feature. He'd been entirely focused on turning his rent-paying journo gig into a source of strokes for his social cap at that point, and from there relaunching himself as a musician. Exposing the chemo pop-ups, at first, felt like it might curry favor among the virtuosi the clinics sometimes exploited.

Then Seraph joined *Newsreef.* Seraph, who was all about commitment, about truth and purity in journalism. Seraph, who hated shortcuts and thought smart was different from clever. Another set of date-tags showed Drow's deep dive into the research vaults, buttressing his pitch, finding other superstitions so he could create a series, build up to the chemo pop-ups organically.

Later still: an archive of legal cases relevant to medical scams.

Now he read those cases again, closely this time, pushing through precedents like a diesel-fueled snowplow going at three feet of slush. His head filled with legalese and he juggled the phrases, assembling a hypothetical court case. If he could clear a path proving secondary harm done to loved ones . . .

"Embarking on a third career seems a bit of a tangent at this point," Crane said.

"What?"

"You appear to be writing a law brief."

Right. He was a reporter, not a litigator.

Not a reporter not really just a gig for the payables, I'm a composer . . .

A composer who doesn't compose?

Seraph's voice, clear as the day she'd spoken the words. *You could be outstanding at the journo thing if you just got over thinking you were outside it all. It's more than a lark for strokes and cash balance—*

"Sir? Your port is empty."

He shook away the clamoring internal argument. "Full dose administered?"

"Yes. Take out the ampoule, hide the evidence, hash this conversation, and we can dive back into Sensorium."

Screw journalism. What about becoming a crusading lawyer for the poor? Memorize the rules, screw around with the rules, it'd be so *easy*, and didn't he owe the world some good deeds? Drow bleached and recycled the glass tube. Then, with Crane's help, he made it to his crate of instruments without downloading the LSAT first.

"Music, sir. Write music now. Remember this intro?"

"I probably can't even—"

The intro played. Time disappeared.

He assembled two tracks. A ballad, first, and then something akin to a classic rock anthem. The ballad he fine-tuned and wordsmithed, working it up into a penitential ode to Cascayde. He burnished metaphors for regret, put sorrow in the high notes. Cried a little, finally, finally.

Shouldn't have ripped Cascayde's mask off, he thought. *If I'd reached out, maybe. Told her: Make your own thing. Stop cobbling together everyone else's scraps . . .*

Instead he put it all into song. He couldn't release it as a single, not yet. If anything, it'd plunge him further into the lightless depths of social oblivion. But one day, after a show of remorse had already given him one boost . . .

"We could automate that," he said to Crane. "When my prosocial rank's out of the bottom thirty percent, I'll regain access to the indy music reefs. We'll do a limited release, just for the club. Someone'll leak it."

"I'll set an alert—"

"No, it's fine, trigger it. Here's text . . . great. Flushed and forgotten."

"If you say so, sir."

The other song Drow could tool up himself, use it for something worthwhile, something original, and he was definitely crackling now. Reading law was one thing but he'd teethed on music. Saxophone at four, piano at seven, contemporary collab at ten . . . and this was good. He worked up original soundtrack for the chemo newsflow.

Hey! Another cap mitigator would be to clap together some mixes. He must know a dozen virtual clubs who'd trade him some strokes and some good wordo if he built decent sequences for their deejay apps.

He shuffled music as he paced the living-room floor, assembling decks, five at a time. Maximum return on years of concert-going. Mashing sounds gleefully, mixing the best of all those long, fun nights at dance clubs. He'd taken Seraph nine months ago, in the middle of a heat wave.

"One, two, three, hit send."

"Have we moved on to amending your social collapse?" Crane asked.

"Maybe. I don't know. But . . . if I dash off the right kind of sob story to that girl Eleanora, from school. Remember Eleanora? She'd take it in mind to get her church to send me some strokes. You gotta love Christian charity, right? It wouldn't, technically, be cap manipulation. Because the law says—"

Crane interrupted, "You'd have to compose the sob story."

"Work of a minute—" A tumble of noise, pounding bass rhythm, made him duck behind the counter. "Is that me? Am I drumming?"

"It's the front door."

He bolted to the top of the stairs, the very peak of the house. Pressed himself against the wall. Last time someone showed up unannounced . . .

"No, please, please—"

"It's your editor, sir."

"Seraph? Seraph's not here to cut her throat."

Bambambam.

"She's likely concerned for your well-being. But engaging with the public in your current state—"

"Seraph's not public. Seraph's famlike. She adores . . ."

Adores?

Catch up, chump.

He goggled at that, spinning through possibilities and complications, tagging some feels . . . "Wow. This is big. Did I know? Will she know that I know?"

Her cartoon face bloomed in his peripheral. "I know you're in there, Drow."

He pounded his way back down the stairs.

Crane murmured. "Make a polite excuse—"

"It's fine. I'm leveling off."

Jerv used to say that.

"She'll never notice."

Yep, that too.

"Your current task—"

"That'll be all, Crane." He threw open the door.

Seraph had re-upped her honeycomb buzz cut, intricate yellow hexagons that didn't hide the burnished gold-brown of her scalp. Snowflakes danced around her, fighting gravity.

She jumped to the point: "Ninety percent of Weston's work is in private collections, tucked away from public display. Are you okay?"

"Yeah. Been composing."

Her mouth fell open. "That's . . . that's great, Drow!"

"Is it?"

"Of *course*," she said. "Using what's happened to recommit to your music? It's the healthiest choice you could make at this point."

He rocked forward on his heels, unsure what to do with that. Rocked back. "So. Um. I soundtracked the chemo flow."

The relieved smile went brittle. "Can I come in?"

Cascayde had barged in. He couldn't bear it if Seraph barged. He shared the soundtrack as he stepped aside.

The message bounced, for some reason.

Adores me not?

"Do you know anything at all about Tala's artstorms?"

"Yeah, actually." Drow had Crane throw a blank conductor's score on the kitchen counter, blobbing notes onto the bass and treble with a finger. Maybe if he multitasked, he could take this conversation at a convincingly normal pace. "She's got a thing in the Albright-Knox. Body scarification and tumbling. You should see it, Seraph. Gross old GenXers cutting into themselves—"

"Drow, listen. I found a catalog listing for something called *Mass Grave*. It's from a massacre site in Louisiana, sometime like the twenties. It's people coming to identify bodies."

"Family members?" He was filling in about two bars of music every time she uttered a sentence, making a symphony of the conversation before or possibly as it happened, and thereby staying attached to Seraph's words. Her voice was weaving through his low brass section, sweet discord amid bombastic trombones and tubas. Long chords with villainous undertones. He shuddered.

"Anyone who let Tala capture them as they identified their loved ones was given free burials for their dead. Boutique treatment compared to the pathetic state compensation. The listing for *Mass Grave* says it's representative of her early work."

"Meaningless art-world phrasing."

"Studies of pain etched on faces, vid of people collapsing, soundtrack of wails—"

"Legit journo does that. It bleeds, it leads."

"Then there's *Gauntlet*, which is rumored to be a series where attractive young men run naked through an enclosure full of attack dogs."

Violin strings snapped in his mind's ear. He gaped at Seraph. "That *can't* be true."

"Controversy ensued. Consensus was that it had to be a sim."

"Had to be." A sense of iced sweat, on the back of his neck, gathering for a run down his spine.

"The catalog describes close-ups of bite wounds and portraits of terrified models in hospital, cuddled up to scary, muzzled mutts. *Gauntlet* sold to a guy who runs the most frequently investigated chain of hospices in Western Europe."

"That's a category?"

"Don't deflect, Drow. There's something called *Slowburn*. All I know about that is that it was confiscated under Sweden's obscenity laws. *Pediatric Transplant Harvest Fail*, in private collection. *Cold Turkey, Burn Ward, Slowmo Caning, Bedside Vigil*. Private, private, private."

"Seraph, stop." A screechy oboe solo, reminiscent of an ambulance siren, added itself to his symphony, almost of its own accord.

"Then there's the Sensorium chatter about her. Or really, the total lack of it. I found a few pearls among the plaudits, tagged to miseryporn, tortureporn. Tala gets off on suffering, Tala likes a good roofie—"

"A what?"

"It's an oldie term for rapey drink-dosing."

A full-body shudder this time, like being zapped.

Seraph saw it. Saw him, seeing her catch it. Fisted and unfisted her hands before continuing her liveflow: "I have interview transcripts from Tala's previous models."

"Complaints?"

"'It was an honor to work with her,'" she said, quoting. "'Cutting-edge productions, no regrets, true innovator, fearless.' Blah blah."

"Sounds okay."

"Nobody has a bad word on record. But. Three of them committed suicide."

Suicide. Drow tasted fresh blood, realized he had bitten his lower lip. "Cascayde. Didn't cut deep enough, you said."

Seraph stepped close, every sinew taut as drumskin. "Walk away, Drow. It's dangerous."

Dangerous, agreed, his enhanced brain whispered. *It's also a story, if you . . . What? Cut deeper?*

He restrung his mental chorus of violins and glanced at the symphony. "Is there any more?"

"Isn't that *enough*?" When he didn't answer, she said, "Art critics won't touch her."

"Because they're afraid, you think?"

"Scared, yeah. Shitless." She tugged his shirt open, exposing the chemo port, and ran a fingertip under the edge of the incision, the cut edge of the flesh.

It's a story or a lawsuit. Random ideas for thrillers about hero lawyers racked like billiard balls within his mind. *Click. Click.* Sound of teeth coming together. Opening notes of a soundtrack: The Crown vs. Tala Weston.

Seraph was waiting for an answer.

Drow tried to net the thoughts flashing past, shining ideas running ahead of his agendas. Musical chords and big exposés and Sensorium law schools.

"There's a bigger story here," he said. "Tala. Moby Dick of stories."

"You think you'll catch her out?"

"If I outsmart her."

Of *course* he could outsmart her.

"Can you hear yourself? Drow, I know this is hard. You've been through—"

"Tala wants to make artstorm of me enduring needless chemo for sale to miseryporn fans," he interrupted. "That's what you're saying."

"No! I'm saying Tala's a *maniac*."

"She's . . . what? Ninety."

"She's hopped on life extension and getting a chemo clinic to flatten you! Whatever's going on, I give the sadist zombie billionaire the edge."

"Is it illegal? You analyzed the modeling release."

"Forget the release! You just stop. Drow, you stop. Ghost on her. Call off the chemo course and get that abomination removed."

"No!" His hand rose, protecting the port.

Seraph's eyes narrowed.

Oops.

"This is serious journo, Seraph! If what she's doing is assault, if it exceeds the remit of the modeling release . . . I should reread the release, shouldn't I?"

Did Harvard allow remote study?

Seraph groped for the edge of the counter, as if she had lost her balance. "You embed yourself in the chemo story, and then . . . what? When you're shattered from drug side effects, you luck out and catch vid of Tala feeding your left foot to a dog or something?"

"She did dogs, she won't do dogs again. But embed, I like that!" he said. "We'd need visuals and sound. She powers down unauthorized things within her studio. Do you think if I lured her here? No, she'll have contingencies for that. If I can keep Crane from powerdown—"

"What is wrong with you?"

He clamped his lips shut over the answer to that one. An imagined safe-deposit box full of Brill battered at his teeth, vials tinkling.

Should tell her, can't do it, she'd be an accessory . . .

Half a symphony already written. Who knew he had a symphony in him? Who knew what else was in there? How long had it been since he'd truly made music?

Six years. Since you blocked Uncle Jerv.

He pushed the unwanted response away by asking a question his subconscious couldn't answer. What did you do with a symphony?

Tala. The point was Tala. "We couldn't use cameras or implants to catch her, not in her house. But she'd have her own footage, wouldn't she? She'd capture *everything*, then cherry-pick stuff that wouldn't quite get her prosecuted."

"Drow."

"Just listen! We have to get my things access to her network. If Crane can see through her cameras . . ."

"Drow!"

"Her goggs are old. How secure could they be? The two of us, Seraph, we can get in. Or. My uncle. Dad. I didn't want to go this route but he codes, he's a virtuoso in his own right when it comes to writing protocols for networked things—"

Seraph took his hands. She had long fingers, strong wrists. Athlete hands. They were . . . no, *she* was shaking. She pulled him, mulishly resisting, to the couch where Marcella and company had been playing all his instruments. "Listen."

Drow made himself sit, imagining pizza farts. The upholstery felt like muddy sandpaper. "You have my full attention."

And she did: He knew her birthday and the name of her dog from high school and what her father said that one time and all her grades in journo. Adoring him, adoring him not, Seraph was what he'd have called a friend, back in the days before the word got verbed and debased.

She deserves better.

She put one hand on either side of his head, gently bringing them gogg to gogg. "Drow. I'm concerned. This looks like a breakdown."

"Pish."

"What happened to Cascayde was not your fault."

He must have jumped, or flinched; her big hands tightened their grip.

"I should've reached out to her, outside the spotlight."

"What she did was desperate, I admit, but. Calculated, too."

"Crane," he said. "I need you."

"Sir?"

"Infograph my social standing and share to Seraph."

It scrolled between them. Capital commensurate with a disgraced politician, a suspected sex offender. Bank balance teetering. Marcella threatening to quit the apartment and leave him ass-hanging, rent in arrears. Endless streams of censorious comments. Notices from everyone from his cloud backup service to the grocery, saying his privileges had been downgraded. No credit, no discounts, no extras. No love for Drow, unless he met the terms of his user agreements. Endless whirls of little black bubbles streaming from the holes in his reputation.

"I am torpedoed, Seraph."

"I didn't say you weren't paying. I said it wasn't your fault. I green-lighted that newsflow because everything in it was true. Cascayde did mine the virtuosi hit parade for the bones of *Cataract*. Even I can hear that, She pulled the stunt because you'd all but proved plagiarism."

The stunt. Blood spraying in his mouth as he snarked. "I hurt her. Played it for laughs and strokes."

She swallowed. "I love that in you."

"What?"

"That you feel it so deeply. That you're sorry. But insensitivity is not a crime."

"Stop." Her words were kicking everything out from under him. *She's wrong she's right she adores me not adores me too I love that in you she said she said she said . . .*

"Forgo the chemo course," Seraph said. "Find another way. I'll pay your rent. Stay home, compose music, regroup. Be smart."

"If I catch Tala out, we score—"

A twitch, in those fingers. "You. *You* score."

"Huh?"

"There's no we. There's an emergency, inglomerate. Suddenly I'm needed in the London press office for a month or six." She tightened her grip on his head. "Focus, Drow! Your contract's been passed on. I don't know who's editing the chemo flow."

"Hey! That's why the draft I sent you bounced."

"Seraph threatens oversight, Seraph gets washed from the picture."

"And I love that in you. The paranoia."

That thing she did. The slow breath. She'd reached the end of her patience. "That's all you have to say?"

He paused. Turned it over. "If you're not my boss anymore, maybe I should kiss you?"

She pushed him away, fingers flexing as if she'd set a volleyball, bouncing him off the back of the couch. Towering over him, she paused, for a second, where Cascayde had been.

He'd been yelling into her undeservedly famous, tear-streaked face. Why should she have all those follows, all those strokes, for stolen work?

He remembered the silver flick of the blade. And stepping back, out of the razor's reach.

Seraph's words hung like breath in frozen air. "You know the difference between smart and clever, Drow?"

"Stepping back. Failing to commit." Big step with long panicked legs, too far back to stop Cascayde. He'd saved himself. He'd sunk himself.

"Stop telling me what you think I want to hear!"

"Was I? I guess I was. But—"

"Smart knows when to walk away, Drow."

I should visit Cascayde in the hospital.

Not until my hair's fallen out.

God, Tala will love that.

"Sorry. What?" he said aloud.

"Mer Raffe appears to be leaving," Crane said.

It was true. She'd walked through the symphony and slipped into her boots. Moisture had pooled in the bottoms of her goggs. "Good luck, Drow."

He should persuade her to stay.

"Ten more minutes?"

The door shut on his words.

After a second, Crane asked, "Do you wish to resume the symphony?"

"Leave it. I'll pick it up . . . you know, next time." Feeling winded suddenly, Drow circled the ground floor, looking for things to clean. He stripped the couch cushions, throwing the cover slips into the wash. He disinfected the counter, even though nobody had cooked. The smell of bleach was comforting. He tossed Marcella's leftovers, ignoring the fridge's protests that they were okay.

Climbing upstairs, he stared at himself in the bathroom mirror. Shave tomorrow. Look dapper for the first round of chemo, the first round of footage. He finger-combed his hair, wondering what his scalp would show when it was exposed.

The toothbrush pinged a soft reminder and he took it up, circle around, gum massage, usual bedtime routine. There'd be smarts left over tomorrow. You didn't Charly off the Brill all at once.

He peeled his slacks and peed, running his thumb over a mystery bruise on his left thigh as he climbed into bed and surfed entertainment streams. His preferred crime dramas felt clunky and overacted. Their soundtracks were clangy.

"Music director deserves a strike or two," he mumbled.

"Perhaps you'd prefer this audioflow about medical litigation?" Crane suggested.

"Thanks. LSAT in the morning, maybe, if I still feel the urge."

"Miss Weston asks if you wish to join her for breakfast before your first infusion."

"You're getting security upgrades, right?"

"Uploading as we speak."

"I will catch her at it, you know," Drow said. "There's a win here somewhere."

"If you say so."

I'm being humored by an app now.

"Lights out, sir?"

"No." The full-body shudder took hold again. He saw a spider in the corner and, just as quickly, realized it was a speck of dust. "Leave the lights."

"Very good," Crane replied. "Enjoy your show."

"Night, Crane." A gust of wind punched at the house, flicking frozen raindrops against the window, the tinkle of slush turning, midair, to liquid glass.

Drow listened to legal arguments and an imagined, fading snatch of orchestral music, trying to lull himself to sleep as the meaner half of the storm closed in, encasing his city, drop by drop, in a treacherous raiment of glittering ice.

Crane cycled off for the first chemo cycle, despite heavy tweaks to his settings, despite security upgrades. He could provide no records for the two days after the infusion, days Drow spent in a daze on Tala's smartchair, cameras ringed around him like guards. All Drow remembered was answering questions in a monotone as she interrogated him about side effects.

He came out feeling fragmented and shaky, as if he'd been pummeled while down with a bad case of flu. There was a smattering of interest in *Newsreef*'s announcement that he was taking the chemo course, but the resulting likes hadn't salvaged his cap; he couldn't summon a ride home. Dragging himself south to the nearest corner, he caught the TTC streetcar. He streamed the whole slog for anyone who'd tagged his story.

Marcella and Cole were having *ah ah yes OMG yes!* sex in her room as he arrived, so he couldn't Brilliant up. He shouldn't anyway: It had only been four days since the first dose. Last thing his body needed was more chemicals. He wasn't loopy, and if the stories were true, he should still be vastly cleverer than usual.

"Head down, donkey." He dropped into Sensorium, asked Crane to keep him on task, and plodded through tightening up the newsflow sentence by sentence.

And he *was* still jumped: Even in his current state, one that made a bad hangover feel like a dream of paradise, he snapped together a description of the infusion experience with almost casual ease. Straight-up news at this point, though he spooned in lots of subtext about the purifying charms of suffering. After Drow had run the full poisonous gauntlet, he'd splice in Trevon's whistleblower interview and a full exposé on the scam.

His back felt sunburned—scraped, really—and his mouth was parched. He filed the revisions with his new editor, some oily-voiced guy whose most memorable feature was not being Seraph. That accomplished, he choked down some copper-flavored chicken.

Fighting drowsiness and ill-formed imaginings—memories?—about needles, he wandered to the back porch.

His landlord was part of the so-called Millennial Migration, one of the childless thousands who'd decamped to jobs in Hyderabad and Beijing, leaving aged parents moldering in their in-law suites. The arrangement made honorary grandchildren of young tenants, mortgage helpers shoehorned cheek-by-jowl into the apartments upstairs from Mom and Dad. For a cut in rent, Drow kept tabs on Ramir, who, thankfully, was puttering in the yard today. Discharging his obligation took no more than an exchange of waves and a photo upload to the son, Imran.

Ol' Gaffer's still with us, send me a goddamned stroke.

The backyard likewise came with strings attached, having been given over to carbon offsets. Voluntary for now, but the way things were going climatewise, they'd be required civic duty in another few years. A City of Toronto bamboo-baling operation had growcubes on half of what had, years ago, been private lawn and garden. Drow got strokes for watering the bamboo; Imran netted a homeowner's tax break.

Bamboo season was weeks away. Drow's eye fell on the floor-to-ceiling porch shelves, piled high with dusty Mason jars and rusted-out lids.

Just his kind of distraction.

"Let's fight some grime," he muttered, quoting Dad, remembering the groans of years past from his young self and Jerv.

Moving slowly, Drow cleared the shelves, laying the glassware on a towel on the kitchen counter. Whenever he got groggy, he took a jar outside, letting the icy wind slap him back to alertness as he scooped up a layer of newly fallen snow. Big clean-ups required big water. Like many neat freaks, he had learned to use snowmelt to stretch his hydro allowance.

With the shelves emptied, Drow could wipe the frosty insides of the porch windowpanes, chilling his blood, cooling his pulsing, burnt-feeling skin. The cool and the motion helped him stay conscious.

Awake was mandatory. He had enhanced smarts, a time-limited window, and a pressing need to outwit Tala Weston. "Talk to me, Crane. Why didn't your security upgrade work?"

"Miss Weston's apartment is authorized for aggressive privacy protocols."

"Since when does an individual have the right to airlock my data?" The question looped him back to thinking about law school; he tabbed up a series of legal papers on privacy regulations.

"I believe that particular windowpane is clean now."

"Do you sound more English than before?"

"As my software ripens, so, too, does my personality."

"Did you just make a cheese joke?"

"I'm sure I wouldn't know how, sir. The window?"

Drow shifted, one pane left. His goggs superimposed privacy regs on dirty glass. Wipe, read, wipe. "Here, this—see if anything's registered to Tala's home address. Besides, you know, her home."

"Searching . . . ah! She rents an upstairs office to a psychiatrist."

"Bingo. Medical confidentiality. Bet the psychiatrist's never actually there."

Crane condensed privacy regulations to bullet points. "All speech within the therapist's workspace is protected. Modems handshake with the Sensorium via a medical-grade airlock. Apps with spyware capabilities—I suppose I do qualify, sir—can be downed without notice."

Drow swallowed. Was there any other way? "Crane, you'll have to go to Jervis for code upgrade."

Pregnant silence.

"Crane?"

"If it happened to be the case, sir, that—"

"Fuck! You already went?"

"Custom security work being expensive, the only programmer with a reason—"

"Right, right, you had to. Desperate times, right?"

"Desperate measures. Indeed."

He wrung the washrag as if it was someone's skinny chicken neck. "Jerv ask to talk to me?"

"He understands you have him blocked."

"And he couldn't help?" Drow's pulse trip-hammered. Jerv had been his toxic ace in the hole. "You powered down. Maybe I'm truly sunk."

"Mer Raffe wished me to remind you, were doubts to arise, that you can walk away from this project."

"Whose side are you on?"

The app continued, "I wouldn't say Master Jervis cannot help, precisely. He suggested you get a tongue-texting device, so you and I can communicate without being overheard by Miss Weston's hearing aid."

"You just pointed out I can't afford nice things."

"He will bankroll it, along with other expenses related to this project."

"He's in the money again, is he?"

"Some of his patents and app licenses—"

"Don't care, Crane. Why involve him further when he's already failed to crashproof you?" The window made a brittle noise: He'd scrubbed too hard.

"There's something he needs," Crane said. "He's confident it would make a difference, to the programming."

"Oh, no."

Of *course* it was about the drugs.

Bit rich, though, isn't it? Did you even pause when Tala dangled Brill under your nose?

He had run out of dirty window. Clean the shelves next, or the jars? Fuming, he pondered the grit on the bottom shelf.

Crane said, "He would barter for two doses of your food coloring."

"How could you? How could you tell him about that?"

"I provided details after he deduced the general shape of your scheme."

"How?"

"Your gift for drug-seeking may be an inherited trait."

"Har de har." Blue-tinted sun poured through the gleaming windows. Cold light; his legs felt leaden.

Returning to the kitchen, he confronted the glassware. Sixty, maybe seventy Mason jars, crusted in dust and cobweb and full of snow, covered the counters. He deflated onto a barstool, taking it in. Instead of filling him with the usual sense of impending success, the thought of cleaning all that glass filled him with exhaustion.

Upstairs, Marcella was at it again, *Baby baby yeah yeah.*

"My friend Trevon, from the pop-up," Drow said. "I can drop two doses with him."

"Jervis agrees," Crane replied.

So they were live right now, his sidekick and his father's druggy widower. Talking behind his block.

"He'll visit Miss Weston's home, to examine her uptakes and hardware."

"He gets caught, I'm breaching contract."

"Again, the food coloring—"

"He's saying he won't get caught?"

"I believe him, sir."

"And what choice do we have?"

"The choice, as Mer Raffe—"

"Breach of contract. Heard you the first time. Please don't bring it up again." Drow levered himself upright, leaving snow in the jars to melt. The thought of lying down filled him with dread, so he soaped a rag and began wiping down the shelves.

It was a filthy, hopeless, *perfect* sort of job. The wood shelves caught the threads of the rag, splinters shredding the fabric. Wet silt flowed into oak grooves and knots, filth sinking in deeper.

Idiotic use of his time, when he felt so strung up. But pushing the dirt away, wringing wet, gray smears out onto the snow as he cleared the house of muck, was starting to work its usual magic.

A cobweb brushed his elbow. Feather-touch of dirty thread, a fall of grit on his exposed arm. Drow recoiled, throwing the brush.

The spider dropped onto his right shoulder.

Drow wasn't arachnophobic, but as he clawed at the spider with his rubbery fingers, he had a sudden vision of maggots, writhing on his back. Small, white bodies pulsing at the edge of an open wound, an incision . . .

He shrieked, lost his balance, and fell off the stepladder, banging into the empty shelves. They arrested his fall, without quite busting his ribs.

Daddy Longlegs tried to flee.

Let it go, it's harmless.

Why should it get away? Drow grabbed, crushing it with his pink-gloved hand. Acid churned in his guts as its body popped.

He looked straight down his shirt, staring at the port incision, imagining maggots. Could it be a memory, something from the two days he'd lost? An image his goggs had superimposed on him, in sim? No way to tell. His skin was spotted with bursts of rash. No bugs, no rot, no open wounds.

"Voodreau?"

The old man, Ramir, had come up the porch steps.

Shaking, Drow opened his hand. The spider was real enough, smear of innocent tissue and snapped needles. Broken wisp, like Cascayde.

The old man nodded comprehension, took up another rag, patted Drow on his stinging shoulder, and then, apparently oblivious as his grandtenant gave in to an attack of the shudders, began smearing half-melted snow over another shelf.

Day five of the first week: Drow's physical recovery had peaked and the mental enhancement was noticeably, lamentably gone. The porch was a gleaming museum of canning hardware and spotless window glass, sterile enough for day surgery.

Marcella stopped sex-bingeing eventually, leaving him alone to dose up, renew his impersonation of God. Drow finished the symphony, entering it in a government-sponsored contest because, really, what else did you do with a symphony? He fought Sensorium advertisements for a few hours so he could do prep for a law school exam he had no objective reason to take.

He started learning ASL, the better to interact with Ramir downstairs—the Gaffer, it turned out, was pretty good company. He practiced sending Morse code to the new tongue-texting rig, a thin fibelastic loop, invisible as fishing line, cinched around the back of his tongue. Thus secured, it vibrated pulses: dot, dash, dot.

For the next stage of the chemo newsflow, he made vid of himself researching the scary drug outcomes, listing all of the possible indignities and discomforts he had to look forward to.

The weird burn on his chest wasn't on the list. It had turned into a proper scabby rash, peeling splashes of red on white that did almost look granular, maggoty.

He scanned legal textbooks while putting together a popflow, something based on the terrible earworm Marcella and her friends had been trying to assemble. Music for the mindless: It grew, like mildew, in under an hour.

Release it himself, just to screw with her? Or dangle it as a bribe? Marcella's voice had always been a hair short of awesome; music was their venned interest, the reason they'd friended, the why behind his having invited her to glomerate at Imran's.

If she owed him, it solved the housemate issue, didn't it? He sent a sample, with a carefully worded note that didn't quite say: *All this could be yours. Just stick to our rental agreement.*

She pounced on it, naturally.

And that was a way out with Cascayde, too, wasn't it? Assemble something irresistible? Do it right, and he might even show her that she didn't have to build a career on garbage riffs and performative histrionics.

The thought cycled in the choir loft of his mind as he let his fingers trace the imagined surface of his virtual keyboard. The song for Marcella had been nothing *but* derivative bits and pieces. Her pieces, but still. And Drow's newborn symphony contained more than a bit of Mozart.

Riffing, homage . . . or something worse?

Was he simply a more elegant class of thief? Gentleman burglar to Cascayde's heavy-handed mugger?

The thought laughed at him from the shadows, high-pitched and poisonous.

Crane made British noises and the occasional pun, catching him at appropriate intervals before his attention could wander, helping him circle the same round of activities. Law. Music. Strategies for Tala. ASL. Social cap mitigation. Outwitting Tala. Morse code. Penance music for Cascayde. Damnwell surviving Tala.

He blasted out music, worked on the exposé, flirted with law school. Thought about waving Seraph so she could lecture him about professional monogamy. He cleaned his house and bottled a flavorless Allstew, laced with caffeine.

The clock ran down.

Drow showed up for his second infusion with stew, some sealed, preprinted digestibles, and a supply of bottled water, all locked inside a camping cooler borrowed from Ramir. Dad's brainless old Dictaphone was tucked into *Jude the Obscure*.

Tala sat in on a pre-infusion consult with Trevon, who suggested a naturopathic cream for his back. If she was capturing video or audio in defiance of the clinic's privacy tech, Drow couldn't tell. Her goggs showed the usual cartoon eyes, masking her expression. When Trevon kicked her out so Drow could strip for the infusion, she went without a murmur.

"This shouldn't be happening," he said to Drow, examining the rash, the pattern of crescent-shaped marks.

Hearing aids pick up everything. He whispered, "If it's not the chemo, could it be tattoos?"

Trevon shook his head. "We'd see ink."

"I keep thinking about needles." Fear of sounding paranoid prevented him from suggesting invisible ink.

After the infusion, he made his slow way to the car, unsupported, wobbling while she made footage.

"What's that load you're hauling?" she asked.

Drow woozily raised the cooler filled with the sealed jars of food and water. "Cleansing diet. No outside food or drink s'week."

"Whatever you say, Lambie Pie."

Now to stay awake, and to keep Crane up and running. For the first part of that first afternoon, he was untouchable: The toxic drag of the infusion kept him tied to the bathroom for five miserable hours. Was it a win? He was too wrung out and shaky, by the time his gastro tract finally stopped evacuating lava, to decide.

He staggered to the smartchair, mute and exhausted, as Tala lowered her green screen beside him. A pink fuzzy gargoyle, she fussed over lights, arranging instruments, ringing him in shadowless dawn-orange glow. The massage routine built into the chair ran a ball between his shoulder blades. Drow jerked forward, very nearly letting out a shriek, all but tumbling face-first into the coffee table.

"Handsome?" Clicks and whirrs from her goggs: She'd be checking to see that she caught the spasm.

"My back's been . . . oversensitive."

"Roll to your side; I'll powerdown the massage apps." She put out a hand and served as anchor as he levered himself onto his left hip.

"Let's make something to earn sympathy from all the worker ants, shall we?" She whisked out a silky-looking sheet, screener green in color, covering him. All the cameras were netting images now, and at his request she'd mirrored them to Crane. Bloodshot eyes, corpse-lipstick shade of mauve on his lips.

"I thought your stuff went to private collections."

"We're collaborating here, aren't we? You make hard-hitting medical exposé, I make artstorm." She disappeared up the rickety steps, returning with a basket of salon tools: clips and razors, curlers and brushes. Sitting across from him, she pored over combs, holding them up to his hair to compare color contrast, finally choosing one with a metallic red sheen and dropping it into a flask filled with blue alcohol. Composing the shot, she murmured, "What we want here is Keats on his deathbed."

"'Scuse me?"

"Without the premature death, obviously." She adjusted each camera in turn, chose three, and shut down the rest. "You're about his age, aren't you?"

He shrugged. "Crane, look up Keats for me."

"And . . . action!" Tala drew the comb through his hair, smoothing out tangles with her vulture claws. Dark strands caught in the teeth, clumping. Uprooting bits of him, she made the rest more presentable.

The green screen had etched in a background, concrete wall and a dirty window, and the sheet was rendered as a ratty wool blanket. The impression created was penitential: Drow recovering in a jail or monastic cell.

She was right; this would play. Drow tagged the digital effects, in case anyone struck at them later for taking poetic license. "Can we livestream this?"

"Go ahead."

She has opened her airlock, Crane affirmed, stealth-texting in Morse. *Stream uploading on a ten-second delay.* Translation: She could still clamp down on the data if something she didn't like threatened to get out. Even so, it was a crack in the door, electronic equivalent of a drawbridge lowered.

Tala took another pass through his thinning mop, then rubbed the comb on a wetwipe, clearing a smear of lost strands before dipping the comb again.

"What's that smell?"

"Eucalyptus." The comb had sharp teeth. Its cold metallic points raked his scalp, lots of sensation, not entirely pleasant but, in its repetition, a bit hypnotic. Tala tugged strands free from the grip of his goggs, ran the point behind his ears, down the nape of his neck to trigger a round of the shakes. When she was done he looked smoother, like a five-year-old fresh from a wash and cut. Vulnerable, and maybe a bit pathetic.

"No actual bald patches yet," he noted, zooming in on his scalp.

"Next time." She cleaned another clump off the red teeth, leaving wet remnants of hair on the wipe in the corner of the camera's field of view, a dab of eye-catching grotesquerie. Discarding the comb in the flask of eucalyptus-scented alcohol, she took up another wetwipe. "How are the numbers?"

Drow queried his new *Newsreef* editor, who shared a graph of viewing stats. About ten thousand people had tagged it and interest in the live feed had stirred, creating a bump in the ratings as her gnarled hands pulled his hair out. A sputter of strokes pattered onto the desert of Drow's social capital. Compassionate outliers were deciding he was pitiable rather than malignant.

"More?" she asked.

He nodded assent, ever so slightly.

"Watch your numbers," Tala said, pressing her wipe-wrapped thumb over his eyebrow, tracing the line of it with almost bruising force.

"Ow!" Drow protested. "Ow!"

Humming tunelessly, she raised her hand. The tissue had most of his brow on it, a collection of little strands like bug legs. A reddened half-circle of bald surprise graced the wild wide eye staring into her nearest lens. The sputter of sympathy strokes became more robust.

"Well, Handsome?"

Drow turned his face to offer the other brow.

"You got a name for this project?" He was tearing up, physiological response to the assault on his supraorbital ridge. Saline pooled in the cup of his goggs.

"I'm thinking of *Wings off a Fly.*"

"Ow!" He fought a renewed flood from his tear ducts as she stripped his other brow. "I'd rather be Keats. A *fly?*"

"Old expression." She was streaming the close footage of his face but had muted their conversation. "It captures what the clinic's doing to you."

Right. The *clinic* was victimizing him.

She began massaging his hand, pinching the fingertips and working down, in tiny increments, to the heel. Strokes were still coming in. If the martyr fodder streamed wide enough, he might level sufficiently to take LSAT practice quizzes without ads.

Crane, in silent mode, sent text. *Master Jervis says security on household peripherals is above civilian grade.*

He clicked back: *Meaning?*

Crane: *Delays in access, possible recurrence of sidekick shutdown, no digital data export.*

Drow: *I think this round will go all right. My counter-play with the food should slow her down. She can't dose me.*

Crane: *Jervis has accessed one app—Miss Weston's muscle-stimulation regime. He can reprogram the needles.*

Drow contemplated that fuzzily. It was assault, of a sort. Messing with the hands that were even now kneading the tight flesh of his forearms, not gently exactly, but in a way that . . .

. . . softened the meat?

She's not that bad, and she's just an old lady.

Crane again: *Your father points out that the fluid on Miss Weston's hair combs could easily be a topical pharmaceutical.*

Whitings know drug-seeking.

He blinked, staring up into Tala's goggs.

She broke from an off-key hum. "What is it, Dearheart?"

"Wings off Flies," he said aloud. "Old saying?"

"About the fundamental sadism of children."

"You don't think that's . . . over the top?"

"Art's whatever you can get away with. Isn't that the quote?"

"By Keats?"

"Warhol," she and Crane corrected simultaneously.

"What *haven't* you gotten away with?"

She peered into his face. "How you feeling?"

Dizzy. Calm. Too calm, probably. Drugs in the combs. "Sensorium's starting to hate me less. Ha! Hates me not."

"Stick with me, kid. You'll be the best show in town."

"Stay awake," he said, unsure if he meant himself, or Crane. He was definitely drugged. He couldn't quite remember how to text. "Pins and needles. Do it."

"Your arm's falling asleep?" Vulture claws tightened their grip on his wrist flexors.

"Do it," he repeated. If Crane understood, his response was lost in rising red fog.

What's that sound?

It wasn't just his back on fire now; it was the arms themselves. The fire of wasp stings sizzled in time to his pulse, burning from his shoulders to elbows, and as he drunkenly leaned into something like alertness, he brought with him a sense of buzzing, a mechanical whine that he couldn't, in fact, hear. Memory? Imagination?

His eyes were clenched shut.

He was aroused, too, was inside or enfolded in something, hips thrusting stickily. As this sank in, he froze.

His tongue lolled, overhanging gritty lips.

"Baby, don't stop." Cooing, in his ear. Who?

His burnt arms were locked around . . . what? Someone's neck? He tried to let go, but his hands were clasped together and he couldn't make his fingers open.

None of it felt—quite—like a person.

What was he humping?

Moaning, he forced his unwilling eyes to open.

Hospital room. White straitjacket arms encased his arms in obscene simulation of prayer, and the person . . .

notta person, no, notta person izza sim, hasta be . . .

CRRNNE, he tongue-spelled.

. . . the person beneath him was Cascayde. Twiggy, blond, and vulnerable, she was wailing like a banshee and raking at his back. Her fingernails were tattoo needles, buzzing stingers leaving swirling lines in their wake. The bandage at her neck was seeping red.

Drow spasmed from hairline to toes, all of him arching away, peeling his skin from hers. His locked wrists caught her behind the neck and the sim thrashed like a badly animated puppet. Maggot-covered blankets restrained him.

Something banged the heels of his hands, ice-cold metal, painful and blessedly head-clearing.

It *was* the smartchair. He was hugging the headrest.

Drow drew air through clenched teeth, fighting to convince his hands to unclasp, to raise them above the top of the chair. His lower body was— almost independent of him—trying to run away from the whole situation.

Crane shut it off shut it off . . . He wasn't sure he was spelling anything that made sense.

The arms stayed tangled. He twisted, throwing a leg over where he thought the chair must be, snagging on fabric. Balance failed entirely. They went down together: him, the silk sheet, all that elaborately programmed foam. Something the size of a toothbrush snapped beneath him. A helmet he hadn't known he was wearing kept his head from bouncing off the floor.

Slam of iron on bone: He caught his forearm between the floor and the falling piece of heavy furniture. Agony popped his hand open, blessed electric jolt of pain, zapping from shoulder socket to fingertips. He kicked, disentangling from fleshy smartfoam and a smothering wrap of gossamer green screen.

Then he made the mistake of opening his eyes again.

The sim was smart enough to try to compensate for the shift in his orientation. The virtuoso, Cascayde, writhed beside him, still shrieking, hospital gown drenched with blood.

Don't die again, don't die again.

He clawed for his face, finding a smooth fishbowl of plastic, a VR helmet sealed by a smartfoam collar. There had to be a latch, right? His nails broke on its surface.

Crane, Crane, help, Crane . . .

Little pings in his tongue. A response? Dot dot . . .

Hands caught his upper arms. Vulture claws.

"Stop!" Drow rasped. "Wait!"

Propelled from behind, all but lifted by the grip on his upper arms, too hammered by chemo and who knew what else to fight, he stumbled back into the embrace of the righted chair. Whoof! as he fell, facedown. Someone straddled him, rough thighs through a thin layer of silk. He felt the vibration of voice, someone humming, as misshapen breasts pressed his shoulderblades. Pubic hair compressed against the base of his spine as weight settled.

He tried to push her off.

Glue of a drug patch rolled over his neck. Hands settled, holding him down. Massage nodules writhed under his groin. He clenched his eyes shut as Cascayde slid in beside him, under him, fitting new needles to each of her fingertips.

Weighted, as if by stones, he jerked and screamed, fighting rising drowsiness and losing. The muscles in his face relaxed, breath by breath; his eyelids flickered open. Cascayde and all his other sins were waiting to claim him.

Drow awoke to burning sensations in both arms and a bad case of concert throat. He had a case of the nightmare shakes, a strong desire to throw up, and no memory of anything that had happened after the eyebrow-stripping.

His goggs were across the room, sitting in a windowsill next to a noisy, burbling tank of small crabs. His limbs felt like sacks of wet cement, but he made himself roll in the chair, onto his back.

He tongue-spelled: *Crane?*

The answer came as pings of sensation at the tip of his tongue ending with dot-dash-dot. *Sir?*

You awake all night?

Indeed.

Well?

You removed access hardware at 6:45 p.m.

I removed?

At her suggestion, sir. You've left me pointed at Huron Street.

You must have caught something. The chair shivered beneath him. His stomach flipped as he scrambled off of it, feeling—absurdly—guilty. *Hear anything?*

Nothing I'll retain after I leave, sir. Miss Weston's data airlock remains secure.

Anything that catches her out? Deciphering Morse was exhausting—everything was exhausting—but he pushed himself across the room. Reclaiming his rig, he clipped it into place: left eye, right eye, left ear, right. Hair slithered off his head, tickling a path down his bare shoulders. Where was his shirt?

I heard shouting, sir. Nothing conclusive.

House schematics filled his goggs, revealing a web of eyes and ears: Jervis had mapped all the cameras and mics on the main floor. Drow couldn't fart in here without a pickup.

"Where's Tala?" he asked aloud. Because he would, wouldn't he?

Crane played along. "Good morning, sir! Miss Weston is upstairs."

If he got Crane to play audio from the night before, Tala's various ears would hear it playing in his earbuds. And if he left . . .

. . . *right, who'm I kidding, can barely walk* . . .

. . . her privacy apps would scrub whatever his sidekick knew.

As for *Jude the Obscure* and his Dictaphone, they were nowhere to be found.

Drow opened one of his specially prepared filtered waters, sinking to the floor beside the fridge as he chugged.

What was called for here was a genius frigging idea. Hard to force, Brill or no, when he was in this state. He pondered, rubbing his burning arms. They were red with the same emerging rash his back had presented. Blood blisters? A surly black-green bruise blotched his forearm.

"Morning, Handsome." For once, Tala's peppy tone sounded forced. "Your thinning hair did well, on the overnight."

"Haven't checked my numbers."

"No?" She flashed cartoon eyes, shaped like hearts. "It's been years since I considered the mass appeal of—"

"Family-rated pity porn?"

"You have such a way with words."

"Sensorium's more reactive than private galleries. You're playing to everyone, not just—"

"Connoisseurs?" She ran a hand down his arm, fingering the edges of the bruise.

He fought an urge to bolt for the bathroom and lock himself in. "What happened here?"

"You fell off the smartchair," she said. "During a nightmare, I think."

It was getting to her, he thought. The eyeballs. The wider reach was a temptation.

A lever, maybe, if he could figure out how to use it.

"Remember anything?"

"My head in a goldfish bowl?"

"No fish here, Handsome."

They had agreed to another day and night of filming and physical recovery. Drow streamed as much as he could, watching what Tala allowed out of her airlock, what she was willing to leave on the record. She edited his medical journey into a series of high-pathos vids, clips that looked entirely candid, random-seeming captures that always cut to a wincingly painful moment of suffering.

The humming, he realized, was a tell of sorts: It started when she was busily occupied with work.

Strokes came in an ever-steadier stream, too few to redeem him but enough to make Drow wish that collaborating with Tala could actually be what they used to call a valid lifestyle choice.

I should make it up with Marce, he thought. *Go back to playing music with her. See what happens.*

He spent the afternoon doodling in an old-school paper notebook—inherited, vintage, no carbon cost—and eating bland printed food, thinking about the video possibilities of future chemo outcomes.

Ghoulish possibilities, he wrote: *shakes, sores, dry mouth.*

Waking later from a light doze, he found three more on the list: *Seizure.*
Cardiac arrest. Stroke.

With penstrokes that almost tore the page, he crossed them out.

"No good?" Tala said.

"Whose ideas are those?"

"It's your handwriting, isn't it?"

He gritted his teeth. "I'm not having a heart attack for this. Anyway, a hos-
pital-grade emergency commits me to a blood test or fifty, right? Which'd
raise questions about the Brill, and supplier of same."

"Hmmm," she said, neither agreeing nor disagreeing.

"Getting away with it, remember?"

"Nobody wants you to stroke out, Dearheart."

Crane, meanwhile: *Are you with us, sir?*

Here.

*Jervis has solved my security problems, but he would need to perform a hard-
ware installation. I'm afraid you'll have to meet.*

So much for Jervis understands you have him blocked.

This day keeps getting better, Drow said. *I don't want him at my house. Understand?*

Crane: *He suggests making an appointment with your whistle-blower at the
pop-up, to clean your smartport.*

Drow looked at the words on the notebook page. *Cardiac arrest.*

Not his idea, no matter what *she* said.

Seeing Jervis couldn't make things worse at this point, could it?

Fine, then, make the appointment, he texted to Crane. *Lower the drawbridge. Drain the moat. Whatever it takes.*

Another night smeared away into morning, and by dawn his left hip had
caught fire and he was nursing a stutter.

By February, Toronto's streets usually gave over to a hard, dirty melt,
receding mountains of filthy crystallized snow scraped into piles on street
corners, revealing clumps of muck and the rare bit of litter tossed by people
who didn't mind risking a cap hit. This winter the snow kept coming, renew-
ing the virginal blanket laid over the roofs and yards.

It was a sign, Drow thought, a hint from Someone Up There who wanted
him to know he should've just kept shoveling sidewalks.

He was braced for Jervis as he stepped into the infusion center, but it was
Trevon who met him at the door. The medic's hand lit on his burnt, scabby
shoulder, making Drow flinch.

His muscles were screwed tight; no pretending this was a casual encounter.

They made their way down a narrow flight of stairs, through a hallway that smelled of burnt, powdered turmeric.

"Are we making for the sewers? Underground cave system?" Drow asked—the stairs were wearing him out.

"Your guy claims the clinic's changed ownership," Trevon whispered.

"My guy—"

"Our cameras and mics *have* been getting an upgrade. He refuses to come upstairs. Anyway, here we are."

It was a file room, dank and ill-lit, with a screechy fan planted near the door.

Jervis was waiting beside a dead potted plant under an equally dead grow lamp. Relics of the building's former life as a pot dispensary, probably.

Dad's widower had yet to lose his looks or the salesman's smile. He'd always been charismatic: The light in his eyes beamed goodwill and noble intentions. *C'mon, of course you can trust me*, it said. Jerv's charisma drew people like a beacon, pulling in the emotionally storm-tossed. Even now, seeing him brought an involuntary lift to Drow's spirits. A lift—and then a swift hit of guilt about the distance he'd scrupulously maintained between them since Dad's death.

He loves you, the guilt said, *look at him lighting up there, he's no monster . . .*

No lighthouse, either, Drow told it.

More a siren; get close and rocks would tear out your bottom.

"Brucie," Jervis said.

"It's Drow." He cleared his parched throat. "Let's keep this to business."

"Of course." If he'd hurt his ex-dad's feelings, it didn't show. "Shirt off, then."

Drow peeled, sat. Trevon hemmed and hawed over the infusion port as Jervis unpacked a bit of filament, fine as dandelion seed, microscopic wires arrayed around a central stem.

"The idea here is to have Crane run parallel installations. Twoface protocol, I call it. The vulnerable version, DayCrane, is available to Spiderlady, or whoever's hacking for her—"

"Stop! Back up! Whoever's hacking—"

"You've got a me, kid. She probably has a me, too. If she didn't, she got one the first time you went off-script. You act, she reacts, she acts, we react. Play, counter-play, do-si-bleeping-do. I should write a dance instructor protocol for Crane, shouldn't I? Anyone wanna learn to fox-trot?"

Drow flicked him. "Focus, Jerv."

"Yeahyeahsorry. DayCrane still does all your donkeywork, and she can mess with him at will. Meanwhile, NightCrane communicates via tonguetext, evading the mics and security apps in her recording studio."

"You'll feel a pinch now," Trevon interrupted. He pulled two pump staples and unearthed the belly of the injection device.

Drow looked away, imagining the scar it would leave, hating the self-mutilation.

Dad's voice whispered in the shriek of the fan. *Your body is the only thing you truly own . . .*

Stick to business. "What will this new hardware do?"

Jerv outlined the problem: Drow's pickups were loading to the airlock in Tala's home. The video and conversation transcripts were then scrubbed by the confidentiality app in the psychiatric office on-site before they ever made it to the Sensorium or its permanent archive, the Haystack.

"So you override that somehow?"

"No," Jerv said. "We add a cache of on-site storage to the port. NightCrane can upload the records on your command."

"On-site . . ." Drow had barely heard of such a thing; private hard drives had been one of the first things to go out when international transparency accords began proliferating and people started loading their whole lives to the cloud.

"As medical tech, the port's allowed some freestanding memory, in case it has to shoot you up during . . . dunno. A broadband blackout? I'm radically increasing its capacity. NightCrane can stash footage inside and upload it when you're back in the world."

"Can you get us into Tala's mics and cameras, at the house?"

"Maybe," Jervis said, with a significant glance. Meaning: if Drow gave him another Brilliance vial.

"I can't spare more."

"You've got twenty-some coming, don't you?"

He tongue-texted: *Goddammit!*

Crane: *I do apologize, sir. I cannot keep secrets from Master Jervis when he's effectively performing brain surgery on me—*

Drow said, "I get more, Jerv, *if* I finish the contract."

Raised brows. "You're thinking of walking away?"

No, Drow thought. He was going to get the goods on Tala: expose the truth. Win the likes, win the game. Make his name.

But Jerv always did have a way of making him feel contrary, of wanting to say fire when he was drowning. "Everyone says I should walk."

"Run screaming," Trevon muttered. He was easing the upgraded port into position, prepping for the unnecessary cleaning Drow had scheduled.

"Who asked you?" Jervis said.

"As my chemo pusher, Trevon, shouldn't you be on Jerv's side?"

The medic ran a gentle finger over the scabs laced across Drow's biceps. "Chemo didn't cause these."

Jerv wasn't listening. Behind his pricey low-profile goggs, his eyes were flickering. Reading software install specs, probably, or checking the handshake with Crane. Possibly writing the programming equivalent of symphonies. "Come on, Trevvie my boy. Trevvy muh man. Goal here's to get Drow to the end of his contract in one piece."

"It's Trevon, I'm not your man, and you of all people . . . Jesus, isn't this your son?"

"Technically, he's my surrogate's brother," Drow said.

Jerv snapped out of quasi-REM. "Didn't you say let's stick to business? Because if you want to argue genetic semantics and familial bondage, I have footage from changing your godforsaken diapers—"

"Business, definitely business," Drow said. The sudden bursts of rage hadn't gone away, then. Why would they?

"Anyway, buddy," Jerv went on, turning a glittery gaze on Trevon, "you're the one literally poisoning the kid."

The medic's hands came up. A surrender. "Right. Got it. Seen and not heard."

Drow swallowed rising anxiety. "Trevon, really, I'm fine."

"See? All good." Jerv twinkled, apparently surging back into bonhomie. "Drow, let me see your goggs."

Drow slipped off his rig, brushing away the by-now usual fall of hair, and handed them over. "Trevon, can you tweak the chemo mix so I can't fall asleep. Just for . . . say three days?"

"Days? You want to add psychosis to your problems?"

"Can you?"

"No! What about taking a placebo for the remaining infusions?"

Drow waved the handful of hair. "I need to keep falling bald or T-T-dammit-Tala will know what's up. And the modeling contract requires I do ten treatments."

Trevon considered. "If we're talking tweaks . . . how about a lighter dose?"

It was a lifeline, one he hadn't expected, and Drow grabbed it gratefully. "Yes. Right. Say, enough to finish off the hair, maintain this fabulous green skin tone and a bit of the quease. But not so much as—"

"Keep getting worse, but not as fast or as bad as expected? Excellent strategy, kids!"

Approval from Jervis: ironclad sign that this was an incredibly bad idea. He went on: "Hey! What if we threw in a dose of Sustain?"

Trevon groaned.

"Which is what?" Drow said.

"Slows down the Charly effect. Gets you more out of the remaining Brill."

"So I can conveniently spare more for you?"

"You in this to win or not, son?"

"I'm in it to . . ." His mind tumbled possibilities, finding murk where, three weeks ago, everything had seemed clear. Commit to journalism? Truth, strokes, redemption? A little payback for Tala's previous models, if she had indeed driven them to suicide? "This Sustain stuff. It's d-d-dangerous?"

Trevon said, "You're past worrying about dangerous."

"Is it a zombie drug? Something for life extension that'll interact badly with the actual boost to cognition?"

"Not a zombie." Trevon sighed. "It just slows down your system's ability to flush out the Brill. The combo will worsen your mouth sores and almost certainly give you nosebleeds."

Drow thought of the list in his notebook. Cardiac arrest, in his script. In comparison, a nosebleed sounded both minor and suitably gross. "Might be just the thing."

"Too bad. I'm not licensed to give Sustain."

"Me either," Jervis said, pressing a packet of patches into Drow's hand. "No more than one a day, kid, hear me?"

Trevon's expression—disgust with them both—morphed into a sudden "O" of surprise. "Speaking of zombies, yours is parking outside."

"What?"

"My manager says to hold off on your port cleaning until she arrives."

"Say it's already done?" Jerv suggested.

"No." Drow sighed. "Either Crane blabbed or she has a source at the clinic. You said new owners, Trevon?"

"This is me bugging out the back way." Jerv flashed Drow another of those incandescent, sucker-luring smiles and scuttled off.

"Wow. Dad really is everything you said he was," Trevon said.

"Jerv's the least of my worries," Drow said, struggling to keep his voice steady. He buttoned his shirt. "Come on. Haul me up the stairs so we can rip out my staples again."

The new drug, Sustain, gave Drow a weird feeling, something like having a dissection pin embedded in his eye. Combined with Brill, it also bestowed photographic memory. He remembered visuals, suddenly, something that had never been his strong suit. How things looked, where they were: He could glance at a floor plan and see the house it described. He could score music by visualizing the notes on each page. He memorized the map of Paris, for fun, and ogled scans of John Keats's handwritten manuscripts.

The songstorm he was writing for Cascayde took on a strange, New Wave undercurrent, opera-meets-electronica-mashes-romantic-poetry. Everything old made new again. *All Thieves Together,* he called it. Extremely fitting material for a virtuoso rising from the depths of despair.

When he arrived at the clinic for his next infusion, he brought bottled water and more printed clean diet. At Jerv's suggestion, he brought his saxophone, too.

The sax was something they'd built together, back in the days before Dad was gone. It had its own modem, fine-tuned for Sensorium upload. Jervis hoped it might attract the attention of his counterpart, Tala's hypothesized hacker.

"It'll look like spyware, your next move," he explained. "She'd be nuts to take the thing into her house until she had it checked out."

Tala hovered, watching Drow's every move, each drip of the infuser. She was humming, the way she did when she was hard at work. Drow would have bet she'd gotten through the clinic's privacy protocols, that her goggs were capturing footage now, not just stills.

He clutched his sax case like it was a teddy bear, waiting for her to make her counterplay.

And sure enough, after the drip ran dry: "Got a surprise for you, Handsome."

She poured Drow into a waiting limo and bundled him to a private reception, some arty event in the lounge of the fanciest of the downtown hotels.

"A party, Tala? Really?"

"Sleep if you have to, Handsome. If not, all the carbon costs and calories are covered. Anything you want, just ask." With that, she installed him in a leathery black smartchair parked in a shaft of blue-tinted sunlight.

"Are you comfortable, sir?" That was DayCrane, the vulnerable one, talking aloud for show.

"Yes, thanks."

Do we have transparency here? Drow tongued in Morse to the stealth version.

NightCrane: *Technically, yes—this is a public space. However, Master Jervis reports some data packets are being "accidentally" scrubbed before they reach Sensorium.* Drow's goggs showed a set of hands, drawing quotes in the air as the word *accidentally* played on his tongue.

So Tala's tech guy is here.

It seems likely.

Tala tottered through the crowd, mingling, pressing the flesh. Everyone knew her; each conversation ended with her audience turning its gaze on

Drow. A feeling of expectation, dense as summer humidity, permeated the room. Were they all hoping he'd pass out?

Drow forced his tongue to move again: *Can you whooz these people?*

NightCrane: *Of course.*

Public profiles of businesspeople began filling his whiteboard.

Drow gave one of the looky-loos a dozy grin, successfully luring him to the chair. He pushed out bleary chitchat. How do you know Tala? Have you seen her work? Are you an artist, too?

The man deflected Drow's questions with the ease of long experience. But he'd broken some kind of barrier. More of them came, people wanting a closer look. Finally, one of them dropped a shiny tidbit: "I'm a collector, not an artist. Well. By day, I'm a litigator. Collecting's my true passion."

"You're looking over the goods?" Drow asked, trying to sound knowing.

Startled, nervous chuckle.

"It's okay," he lied. "I've a pretty good idea of what's going to happen—"

The woman's pupils dilated. Brilliant Sustained Drow lay under the weight of his chemo load, memorizing every nanoshift in color as the blood leached from her face.

What'd I say?

Excusing herself, the litigator beelined for someone who looked like they might be her date.

Tala, missing nothing, orbited back briskly.

"Is this an auction?" Drow asked. "Am I on some kind of block?"

"I'm swanning you around while I've got you, Dearheart." She rolled her shoulders, as if they ached.

"We have weeks yet."

She gave him a birdlike, assessing gaze.

Drow texted: *Is Jerv eavesdropping on the mics here?*

NightCrane: *He's grabbing what he can.*

Drow: *Try to catch that litigator's convo.*

The analytic look on Tala's face hadn't vanished. To distract her, he said, "Wanna drive my price up?"

Pink brows climbed so high he could see them over the brass rims of her goggs. "What do you have in mind?"

He waggled the saxophone, baiting both her ego and her phantom tech support. "Another public feed?"

She brightened, rummaging in her purse. "You can't play that horn of yours, can you, with that dry mouth?"

"Let her give you some ointment, sir."

"Trevon gave me something, Crane," he replied.

NightCrane: *That wasn't me, Master Woodrow.*

His skin goosed.

"Found it!" Tala raised a small tube.

Crane's voice said, "Hers will undoubtedly be of the highest quality."

Seriously, Crane, that's not you?

NightCrane: *A decoy, I assure you. Do you remember the Twoface protocol?*

He made an affirmative noise as he shook out his hands, loosening his fingers.

NightCrane: *Miss Weston's tech has compromised DayCrane and tasked it with selling you on that ointment. Obviously.*

Drow pressed the keys on the sax, tinkling them like piano keys, and declined Tala's ointment with a fixed grin. Trevon's remedy had vanished from his case, so he settled for a swig of bottled water.

His reed tasted funny. He wondered if she'd spiked that, too, but no. Just another effect of the chemo.

"Score this as I improvise," he ordered DayCrane before he began.

For the first minute or so, the sound was rough. Embarrassing, even. Wheeze of an amateur, rank beginner, baby musician forcing the sounds of dying animals and old awoogah car horns. Drow kept at it, easing into an old practice tune, something learned when he was all of four, secure toddler with two fathers who thought him a prodigy, ensconced in a world he could trust. The sax exercise was barely a step up from playing the chromatic scale, but his lips moistened; the notes smoothed and elongated, transformed from barnyard honks to music.

He began to embroider.

Drow no more thought of himself as a jazz guy than a symphonic composer. But his memory was a treasure vault of theory lessons and music history, things Jerv taught him as a child, archived and long-ignored.

Jerv had been the one to start him on a pint-sized saxophone, when he was four. It was his first instrument, a cool instrument, but as a little kid, Drow hadn't really understood it. He wanted lyrics, structure, choruses, intros and outros. He wanted to set up and sim guitar solos without blistering his fingers on strings. He wanted a band, Sensorium soundstorm tricks and virtuosi sensibility.

Crane's voice had told him to take the ointment. If he hadn't gone to Jerv, hadn't split the app's personality . . .

The sense of danger was diminishing. What mattered was the music spilling out of him, Pied Piper calling all the art collectors. Vibrations from the reed penetrated his jaw and teeth, transmitting waves of bone-deep pain. The edges of his mouth ached and chafed. Moisture dribbled off his chin. Warm wet landed on the collar of his shirt, spreading and becoming cold wet.

He pushed against the bodyfeels, continuing to improv. The collectors were clustering, cocktails growing warm as they stared at Drow like a zoo exhibit. He threw out an unexpected trill, almost a hit of birdsong. The whole room, right down to the coat-check girl, gasped-laughed.

Gotcha.

Kids, he realized, couldn't appreciate the saxophone. Jerv should have held it back. A horn thrust music's animal howl through the pure throat of a downed angel. It could purr lust, run a seduction, lure you to the rocks. It could shriek your regrets to the rooftops, whisper a graveside lament, trade your soul for a broken string of pearls or a kind word.

He played, and everyone in the lounge stood transfixed, hanging on every note.

This was what he should have been doing with every waking moment. Not journalism, certainly not law. What a waste, all that clumsy fumbling to woo the musical trendsetters of the stroke economy. Drow played a confessional, spinning all his fails into song. Worm-crawling low notes of cowardice, self-sabotage: the way he'd blamed Jerv for all his troubles, the way he'd given up composing original flows.

Then the bright, staccato thorns he'd grown whenever someone . . .

. . . *Marcella* . . .

. . . *Seraph* . . .

. . . got too close.

Fat alto bombast played a countermelody of rationalization, long, tricky runs etching his descent from trying to honestly build strokes and a reputation to grubbing for them, with that final, dirty, cold-blooded attempt to leverage Cascayde's fanbase.

Now he was playing Cascayde.

It had maddened him! Her riding high on a glittering wave of stolen tracks. Undeserved success had left him, frankly, jealous . . .

He ran the melody back and forth for so long that it conjured the virtuoso.

At first, Drow took her for hallucination. Some trick of the Brill, transforming a wispy apparition in a high-necked white gown, just now stepping off the elevator, into her, into *her* . . .

But no! Reality. Not a vision. Not a sim.

Electric recognition spread through the lounge. Victor and victim, reunited. High drama.

Drow kept playing. This was it; this was everything he could get away with. He pulled the opening of her *Cataract* from his drug-enhanced infallible memory, remaking it on the fly, flagrantly stealing unprovenanced phrases, effortlessly burnishing.

The virtuoso was crossing the lounge.

Drow forced himself to rise. His knees shook as he stood; acid burned in his gut.

No matter. Keep playing.

Cascayde was a wand of a woman, substantial as the smoke from an extinguished candle, wrapped in Ralph Lauren. The assembled listeners drew back, leaving her acres of room to come to him.

Within his peripheral, the bartender muttered awed curses. On the sidelines, Tala had a camera in each hand, feeding him to the Sensorium with both fists.

Cascayde drifted past a guy so pale he looked frightened. Then another whose face, inexplicably, was tracked with tears.

Drow brought his last note to a shuddering triple-piano fade as Cascayde reached him. Empty-handed, she pulled the mouthpiece away from his lips.

Bursts of sensation, like fingernails digging into a blister, made him gasp.

She tried to speak, but the assembled collectors broke into applause so loud it drowned her.

Drow wasn't going to be on his feet for much longer.

"I'm so—" His voice broke. "Sorry. I mean, please—"

Hooks, salty, in his throat. An itch. He fought the spasm but coughed nonetheless. Cascayde drew back, fractionally, not fast enough to dodge the spray of crimson, aerosolized blood misting her collar and jaw . . .

Drow half-turned, coughing up more red. Lips bleeding, tongue bleeding. "Crane," he said, diction muddy. "Give her the score I just wrote."

"All of it, sir? Or just the embroidery of *Cataract*?"

"All," he said. "Sign over full rights."

Cascayde was hyperventilating, staring at the blood on her dress. Her eyes had that wild, vulnerable look again.

"Call it . . . a peace offering," Drow finished. His knee buckled and he lurched involuntarily.

Whether by default or design, she caught him. Barely strong enough to support his weight, she planted her spike heels and heaved, tipping him into the smartchair. He'd left a patchy red handprint on her pristine sleeve.

"It's okay," she said, grimacing, mastering herself. Then, louder: "I forgive you."

As she spoke her gaze jogged left, into her peripheral. Checking the strokes, no doubt.

Still in the game, Drow thought. Cascayde was fragile, no doubting that. At the same time, part of her was still performing, always would be.

So what? The comp was good and his performance had been solid. If his regrets were real, did it matter if her forgiveness was counterfeit?

He deflated into the chair's ever-helpful embrace, uncertain and depressed.

Pressing a hand to her chest, as if overcome, Cascayde returned to her bodyguards, vanishing back into the elevator. There was a second wave of applause.

"Masterful performance, Handsome!" Tala swooped in with a wetwipe.

"I wasn't simming," he muttered.

"So much the better. Lord, what a mess!" She smeared the cloth under his nose, over his lips, down his chin and neck. Each wipe left a strip of pristine alcoholic chill, smooth traverses unimpeded by his hairless chin. She crunched bloodstained wipes, discarding them like trashy rose petals.

"I can't do this anymore," Drow whispered.

"Shush." She pressed him against the cushion.

Bubble of panic, fueled by phantom memory. He pushed back. Were her vulture claws weaker? "I want a doctor."

"We'll call a car." She kept swabbing, humming tunelessly all the while.

She'd put something on the wetwipes, of course. A now-familiar narcotic dizziness was taking hold as the car, naturally, threw in its lot with her credit rating and took them to Tala's house rather than a hospital. The saxophone, conveniently enough, got left behind at the hotel.

DayCrane was crooning in his ear, "It's all right, sir, go along. Almost home, everything's fine."

"Fine," he agreed. Maybe he should let Tala have his husked-out remains.

NightCrane texted: *Sir, I cannot contact Jervis. It is possible he's under arrest. Would Tala report him?*

Her tech support may have forced him into the open.

Play and counterplay.

He get anything from the crowd mics?

Crane assembled transcript, snatches of conversation from the party. At least one promising utterance caught Drow's eye: ". . . even being here may be aiding and abetting!"

But reading was hard; his mind was liquefied.

As they parked, Drow protested: "I wanna Emerg."

"That's ridiculous." Tala stepped into the street, smoothing the fleshy pink skin of her knee-length jacket. "We agreed I'd capture—"

"You captured p-p-plenny. Dammit! Plenty. I puddon a real show for your art buyers, din-d-didn't I? Richard Bramp—"

She cut him off before he could unspool the cocktail party whooz list, right there within range of the car mics. "Come inside and discuss it."

"You must get out of the cab, sir."

He was out, on the street, before he remembered the Crane he could hear was the compromised tab. Slush spattered his face, fat gritty drops, smearing the surface of his left gogg. The car door slammed, nearly catching his hand.

"Inside," Crane urged. "You're shivering."

"Open up!" He pounded on the roof. The smartcar pulled away.

"You must change clothes, sir. You're covered in blood."

Tala had reached the same conclusion; she was tapping her elegant way to the door.

Drow barged past before she could get her hands on him, locking himself in the bathroom. Washing his face in the hottest water he could run, he tried to sober up.

Beetle-tap of fingers against the door. "Handsome?"

"Sec." He texted: *Crane? Any good news?*

Alas, no. In fact, Miss Weston appears to have contacted Imran about buying your home.

That woke him, more effectively than hot water. *He go for it?*

Unknown.

Seraph had been wrong. Tala would tie up his escape routes as fast as he could sight them. He wasn't free to walk away.

Don't walk then, donkey. Run.

He fisted his hands, shaking them in a parody of tantrum, forcing himself to say good-bye to all those green vials of potential. Farewell to future symphonies, the exposé about chemo, the prospect of catching Tala in the act.

Feeling reasonably clearheaded, he stepped out.

Tala was perched against her kitchen counter, idly stirring a glass of water with the narrow-bladed business end of a pair of stylists' scissors. "Done sulking?"

"You tattooed me without permission, didn't you?"

She tinked the blades against the glass, thoughtful. Then the overhead lights colorshifted into the luminous purple of an olden days disco. The scab tissue across the back of his arms lit up with fine white lines. Maggots, feasting on torn flesh. Image of future decay.

"Don't look all wounded. It's only skin-deep. *You*, sonny, you fiddled with my muscle stims."

"You hacked my sidekick."

"Pish. A privacy violation. Stim-regime tampering is assault."

Drow took a deep breath. "Sounds to me like a mutually assured contract breach."

"It's all about what you can prove, Handsome. You're on camera consenting to the tattoos."

He swallowed.

Sir! Someone has triggered my hardware inventory! My compromised counterpart is uploading specs for the tongue texter . . .

Drow unzipped his overnight bag, extracting a clean shirt. Clawing off the bloodstained one—its clean patches glowed a luminous white in the ultraviolet—he tossed it at her feet. "Here. Call it a souvenir for whoever bought . . . what was it? *Wings off a Fly.*"

"You're not going anywhere." Her gogged eyes filled with red veins. She threw the contents of her drinking glass into his face and mouth.

Drow sputtered, choking.

She raised the scissors.

He had one moment of perfect visual recall: Cascayde, in his kitchen. The magician's flourish of her spindly fingers as she produced a straight razor.

Tala wasn't the type to cut her own throat, and she didn't give him time to step away. She sprang, a furious bundle of little old gymnast, lightweight and perfectly balanced, brandishing the scissors as she bore him to the floor. Her left hand clamped around his jaw.

He clenched, tongue-texting: *Save this footage, save it.* His vision was starting to double.

"Snip-snip, Handsome, let's cut that wire. You don't need bad advice from outsiders, do you?" The hand gripping his face was going to rip his jaw off, and his nose was bleeding again . . .

What kind of idiot goes courting nosebleeds?

. . . which at least had the effect of making his chin slippery.

"I'm all you need now." She brought the blades down, cutting his lips a little as she wedged the points between his teeth, metal scraping enamel. There was a cold zip across his tongue as she forced it in. The fibenoose at the back of Drow's throat popped like a rubber band. He gagged as it rolled down his gullet.

No more NightCrane.

Panting, they eyed each other, she atop him with the scissors clenched between his teeth.

Fear coursed through Drow and he let the anxiety crank up, fight-and-flight-and-fight-some-more responses pumping adrenaline. He clubbed her with the fisted ball of clean shirt, knocking her off him and crawling through the spinning room. She scrabbled at his ankle, ripping off a shoe just as he reached the front door.

Gaining his feet, Drow ran into slushy rain. Cold drops chilled the burn on his back. He plunged the unshod foot into cold water, drenching his sock.

"I believe I've deleted the surface protocol, sir. It's me."

"Safe word," he rasped.

"Safe word, sir?"

Gotcha. NightCrane would have known they didn't have one.

Within a block, he had slowed from his run, gasping for breath as he lurched on toward College Street.

A limo turned the corner up ahead, headlights washing him in sterile LED glow.

Drow changed direction, forcing himself up over a neighborhood recycling bin that would no doubt give him a strike for vandalism or trespassing. "If anyone can hear this, I need a pick-up. Help. Someone text 911—"

"Sir, return to Miss Weston's before you get frostbite."

"Where's the nearest Emergency?"

"You mustn't hazard a blood test."

"I'm beyond worrying about jail. Nearest hospital? Bathurst and Dundas, right?"

Crane didn't answer. Drow circled south, aiming for College and University instead. Farther away but the route would have more people on it, out and about. Better safe than sorry.

Safe. Sorry. The words ricocheted in his backbrain, setting off an internal soundtrack of screaming hyena laughter, an uproarious chorus. They laughed as he coughed up the texting rig, dusting crimson and a filament of tech onto a jagged array of icicles dangling from a leaky rain gutter.

They laughed when the car reappeared, half a block behind him.

Drow minced onward. Dry foot, iced foot, dry foot, repeat. Keep moving.

On the intersection where Queen's Park segued into the hospitals on University, he stumbled onto a metal grate and into a blast of hot air. The fetid breath of the subway system gusted over him.

Pizza farts. But the warmth was irresistible. Drow couldn't make himself move on.

Tala, goggles bright and projected eyes blue, stepped out of the limo.

"Subway stop," Drow rasped, pointing.

"You dislike the subway, darling boy. Isn't it where Daddy went splat?"

"Subway *stop*," he corrected. "Security cameras everywhere."

"You need a ride, Honeypie. You need help."

"I'm not going with you," he shouted.

"Don't make a scene."

"Will too! Begin scene! Stay away!"

"You're sick. You're confused."

"I go with you, you'll kill me."

The words landed between them, truth pure and simple, the answer to a riddle he hadn't known he was solving. Art's what you can get away with, she'd said. Hurting people and filming it, driving them to the edge—that was old news to her. The one way to level up from what she'd accomplished so far, to make something better, truer to her perverse artistic vision, had to be getting away with murder.

"*Dead Donkey*," he muttered. "In private collection."

Tala fisted her hands, regarding him with unblinking cartoon eyes. Then, to his utter astonishment, she said, "I'll double the offer. Sixty tubes. We'll visit the middleman tomorrow."

Drow pulled off his goggs—and a goodly amount of hair—and gaped.

Had the tide turned? Tens of thousands of people had probably pinned this feed when Cascayde turned up at the hotel. Still. Could they be watching now?

Tala wouldn't care if she took a few thousand strikes. She could pay exponential pricing on everything: services, cars, taxes, food. She could hire someone to do her shopping, call her cars, tighten the loose screws on her goggs. She could literally afford to ignore what society thought.

So why was she negotiating?

"Ten more days," she wheedled. "For sixty."

She thought he had something incriminating on her. Or on her rich friends. If one of *them* had exposed criminal intent, if she knew he could make it public . . .

"I guess you gotta care what they think, huh?"

"Seventy-five," she said. "Handsome, come on. You're dying to say yes."

He was. For a second, he almost relented. All that Brill. If the increased attention of the Sensorium kept her in check . . .

Really? An internal cacophony of unhinged laughter. *You still think you're cleverer than she is?*

"Immediate payout on the original offer," Drow said, testing. "And I still walk."

No pause this time. "I'll want all your files."

"I could . . . send the info to the middleman." A siren wailed and he saw her flinch. "'Course, for that, I'd need you to leggo both my sidekick and my—"

He'd almost said father.

"Your . . . ?"

It would endanger Jerv, wouldn't it, if she thought he mattered to Drow?

Tag the feels later. "I can't give you anything without my tech guy to assure transparency."

"He'll be released immediately." She folded herself into the car, settling in with the look of someone expecting a long ride. "Sure I can't drop you?"

He managed a shivery hyena-laugh. "I'm parked on this grate until someone I know comes to peel me off."

"Well. Sensorium has it your elderly landlord and your roommate are apparently on their way. It's rather sweet."

Drow found himself smiling at the thought of old Imran, dragging his deaf ass out in the dead of night just because the two of them had bonded over the care and washing of ancient Mason jars.

As for Marcella . . . it wasn't too late to refriend. Trevon, too.

And Seraph?

Time would tell.

Tala brought him back: "I'd have made you immortal, you know."

"Your definition of immortal? Is deeply warped."

"Fame is the only eternity someone like you can afford." She clarified her goggs, taking a last ravenous look at him. Drow sketched a trembly bow: the unfinished work in progress. The one who got away.

The limo door slammed and the vehicle purred off.

"Smart knows when to walk now!" he shouted after the retreating car. But once the taillights vanished, relief dropped him to his knees.

Bravado could say what it liked, but smart wasn't *walking* anywhere.

Instead, Drow leaned sideways, struggling to sit, to settle, however temporarily, within the grate's torrent of warm air. Peeling off his wet sock, he massaged feeling back into the bottom of his foot.

He found tattoos there, too. Worms, under his toes, on his heel, writhing around a sketch of the bones of his foot.

Instead of giving in to hysterical laughter, Drow wiggled his toes, drawing in the sour breath of the city's underworld, lifesaving sigh of burnt machine oil mingled with the piss stench of a nighttime drinking crowd. Fumbling on his rig, he waited for Imran and Marcella—he'd even settle for Jerv—to reclaim him.

Feeling at once skinned and yet, somehow, unencumbered, he hummed along with the molten shriek of the poor man's chariot, seeking a melody within the rattle and clash of the subway cars as they brought his rescue ever closer.

Elizabeth Bear was born on the same day as Frodo and Bilbo Baggins, but in a different year. She is the Hugo, Sturgeon, Locus, and Campbell Award-winning author of over 30 novels (most recently *Ancestral Night* and *The Red-Stained Wings*) and over a hundred short stories. She lives in Massachusetts with her husband, writer Scott Lynch.

OKAY, GLORY

Elizabeth Bear

Day 0

My bathroom scale didn't recognize me. I weigh in and weigh out every day when it's possible—I have data going back about twenty years at this point—so when it registered me as "Guest" I snarled and snapped a pic with my phone so I would remember the number to log it manually.

I'd lost half a pound according to the scale, and on a whim I picked up the shower caddy with the shampoo and so on in it. I stepped back on the scale, which confidently told me I'd gained 7.8 pounds over my previous reduced weight, and cheerily greeted me with luminescent pixels reading HELLO BRIAN:).

Because what everybody needs from a scale interface is a smiley, but hey, I guess it's my own company that makes these things. They're pretty nice if I do say so myself, and I can complain to the CEO if I want something a little more user surly.

I should, however, really talk to the customer interface people about that smiley.

I didn't think more of it, just brushed my teeth and popped a melatonin and took myself off to nest in my admittedly enormous and extremely comfortable bed.

Day 1

Glory buzzed me awake for a priority message before first light, which *really* should not have been happening.

Even New York isn't at work that early, and California still thinks it's the middle of the night. And I'm on Mountain Time when I'm at my little fortress of solitude, which is like being in a slice of nowhere between time zones actually containing people and requiring that the world notice them. As far as the rest of the United States is concerned, we might as well skip from UTC-6 to UTC-8 without a blink.

All the important stuff happens elsewhen.

That's one reason I like it here. It feels private and alone. Other people are bad for my vibe. So much maintenance.

So it was oh-dark-thirty and Glory buzzed me. High priority; it pinged through and woke me, which is only supposed to happen with tagged emails from my assistant Mike and maybe three other folks. I fumbled my cell off the nightstand and there were no bars, which was inconceivable, because I built my own damned cell tower halfway up the mountain so I would *always* have bars.

I staggered out of bed and into the master bath, trailing quilts and down comforters behind me, the washed linen sheets entwining my ankle like tentacles. I was so asleep that I only realized when I got there that—first—I could have just had Glory read me the email, and—second—I forgot my glasses and couldn't see past the tip of my nose.

I grabbed the edges of the bathroom counter, cold marble biting into my palms. "Okay, Glory. Project that email, 300 percent mag."

Phosphorescent letters appeared on the darkened mirror. I thought it was an email from Jaysee, my head of R&D. Fortunately, I'm pretty good at what my optometrist calls "blur recognition."

I squinted around my own reflection but even with the magnification all I could really make out was Jaysee's address and my own blurry, bloodshot eyes. I walked back into the bedroom.

"Okay, Glory," I said to my house.

"Hey, Brian," my house said back. "The coffee is on. What would you like for breakfast today? External conditions are: 9 degrees Celsius, 5 knots wind from the southeast gusting to 15, weather expected to be clear and seasonable. This unit has initiated quarantine protocols, in accordance with directive seventy-two—"

"Breaker, Glory."

"Waiting."

Quarantine protocols? "Place a call—"

"I'm sorry, Brian," Glory said. "No outside phone access is available."

I stomped over the tangled bedclothes and grabbed my cell off the nightstand. I was still getting no signal, which was even more ridiculous when I could look out my bedroom's panoramic windows and *see* the cell tower, disguised as a suspiciously symmetrical ponderosa pine, limned against the predawn blue.

I stood there for ten minutes, my feet getting cold, fucking with the phone. It wouldn't even connect to the wireless network.

I remembered the scale.

"Okay, Glory," said I. "What is directive seventy-two?"

"Directive seventy-two, paragraph c, subparagraph 6, sections 1–17, deal with prioritizing the safety and well-being of occupants of this house in case of illness, accident, natural disaster, act of terrorism, or other catastrophe. In the event of an emergency threatening the life and safety of Mr. Kaufman, this software is authorized to override user commands in accordance with best practices for dealing with the disaster and maximizing survivability."

I caught myself staring up at the ceiling exactly as if Glory were localized up there. Like talking to the radio in your car even when you know the microphone's up by the dome lights.

A little time passed. The cold feeling in the pit of my stomach didn't abate. My heart rate didn't drop either. My fitness band beeped to let me know it had started recording whatever I was doing as exercise. It had a smiley, too.

"Okay, Glory," I said. "Make it a *big* pot of coffee, please."

As the aroma of shade-grown South American beans wafted through my rooms, I hunkered over my monitors and tried to figure out how screwed I was. Which is when I made the latest in what had become a series of unpleasant discoveries.

That email from Jaysee—it wasn't from her.

Her address must have been spoofed, so I'd be sure to read it fast. I parsed right away that it didn't originate with her, though. Not because of my nerdy know-how, but because it read:

Dear Mr. Kaufman,
Social security #: [Redacted]
Address: [Redacted]
This email is to inform you that you are being held for ransom. We have total control of your house and all its systems. We will return control to you upon receipt of the equivalent of USD $150,000,000.00 in Bitcoin via the following login and web address: [Redacted] Feel free to try to call for help. It won't do you any good.

The email was signed by T3#RH1TZ, a cracker group I had heard of, but never thought about much. Well, that's better than a nuclear apocalypse or the Twitter Eschaton. Marginally. Maybe.

I mean, I can probably hack my way out of this. I'm not sure I could hack my way out of a nuclear apocalypse.

Long story short, they weren't lying. I couldn't open any of the outside doors. My television worked fine. My Internet . . . well, I pay a lot for a blazingly fast connection out here in the middle of nowhere, which includes having run a dedicated T3 cable halfway up the mountain. I could send HTTP requests, and get replies, but SMTP just hung on the outgoing side. I got emails in—whoever hacked my house was probably getting them too—but I couldn't send any.

It wasn't that the data was only flowing one way. I had no problem navigating to websites—including their ransom site, which was upholstered in a particularly terrible combination of black, red, and acid green—and clicking buttons, even logging in to several accounts, though I avoided anything sensitive, but I couldn't send an email, or a text, or a DM, or post to any of the various social media services I used either as a public person and CEO or under a pseud, or upload an OK Cupid profile that said HELP I'M TRAPPED IN A PRIVATE LODGE IN THE MOUNTAINS IN LATE AUTUMN LIKE A ONE-MAN REENACTMENT OF *THE SHINING*; REWARD FOR RESCUE; THIS IS NOT A DRILL.

After a while, I figured out that they must have given Glory a set of protocols, and she was monitoring my outgoing data. Bespoke deep-learned censorship. Fuck me, Agnes.

She *would* let me into the garage, but none of my cars started—those things have computers in them too—and the armored exterior doors wouldn't open.

In any ordinary house, I could have broken a window, or pried it out of the frame, and climbed out. But this is my fortress of solitude, and I'd built her to do what it said on the box, except without the giant ice crystals and the whole Antarctica thing.

I went and stared out the big windows that I couldn't disassemble, watching light flood the valley as the sun crested the mountains and wishing I cared enough about guns to own a couple. The bullet-resistant glass is thick, but maybe if I filled it *full* of lead that would warp the shape enough that I could pop it from the frame.

Twilights here are long.

Glory nestles into a little scoop on the mountainside, so a green meadow spills around her, full of alpine flowers and nervous young elk in the spring, deep in snow and tracked by bobcats in the winter. She looks like a rustic mountain lodge with contemporary lines and enormous insulated windows commanding the valley. The swoops and curves of the mountain soar down to the river: its roar is a pleasant hum if you stand on the deck, where Glory wouldn't let me go anymore. Beyond the canyon, the next mountain raises its craggy head above the tree line, shoulders hunched and bald pate twisted.

Glory is remote. Glory is also: fireproof, bulletproof, bombproof, and home-invasion-proof in every possible way, built to look half-a-hundred years old, with technology from half an hour into the future.

And she's apparently swallowed a virus that makes her absolutely certain the world has ended, and she needs to keep me safe by not allowing me outside her hermetically sealed environs. I can't even be permitted to breathe unscrubbed air, as far as she's concerned, because it's full of everything-resistant spores and probably radiation.

You know, when I had the prototype programmed to protect my life above all other considerations . . . you'd think I would have considered this outcome. You'd think.

You'd think the *Titanic*'s engineers would have built the watertight bulkheads all the way to the top, too, but there you have it. On the other hand, Playatronics does plan to market these systems in a couple of years, so I suppose it's better that I got stuck in here than some member of the general public, who might panic and get hurt—or survive and sue.

At least Glory was a polite turnkey.

You've probably read that I'm an eccentric billionaire who likes his solitude. I suppose that's not wrong, and I did build this place to protect my privacy, my work, and my person without relying on outside help. I'm not a prepper; I'm not looking forward to the apocalypse. I'm just a sensible guy with an uncomfortable level of celebrity who likes spending a lot of time alone.

My house is my home, and I did a lot of the design work myself, and I love this place and everything in it. I made her hard to get into for a reason.

But the problem with places that are hard to get into is that it tends to be really hard to get out of them, too.

Day 2

I slept late this morning, because I stayed up until sunrise testing the bars of my prison. I fell asleep at my workstation. Glory kept me from spending the night there, buzzing the keyboard until I woke up enough to drag myself to the sectional on the other side of my office.

When I woke, it was to another spoofed email. I remembered my glasses this time. I'd gotten my phone to reconnect to Glory's wireless network, at least, so I didn't have to stagger into the bathroom to read.

This one said:

Hello, Brian! You've had thirty hours to consider our offer and test our systems. Convinced yet?

As a reminder, when you're ready to be released, all you have to do is send the equivalent of $150,100,000.00 via [redacted]!

Your friends at T3#RH1TZ

What I'd learned in a day's testing: I thought I'd done a pretty good job of protecting my home system and my network, and honestly I'd relied a bit on the fact that my driveway was five miles long to limit access by wardrivers.

I use PINE—don't look at me that way, lots of guys still use PINE—and an hour of mucking around in its guts hadn't actually changed anything. I still couldn't send an email, though quite a few were finding their way in. Most of them legitimate, from my employees, one or two from old friends.

I even try sending an email back to the kidnappers—housenappers? Is it kidnapping if they haven't moved you anywhere? The extortionists. I figure if it goes through either they'll intercept it, or it'll reach Jaysee and she'll figure out pretty fast what went wrong.

I have a lot of faith in Jaysee. She's one of my senior vice presidents, which doesn't tell you anything about the amount of time we spent in her parents' basement taking apart TRS-80s when we were in eighth grade. If anybody's going to notice that I'm missing, it's Jaysee. Sadly, she's also the person most likely to respect my need for space.

Also sadly, I can't send an outbound email even as a reply to the crackers. You'd think they would have thought of that, but I guess extortionists don't actually care if you keep in touch, as long as there's a pipeline for the money.

I might have hoped that a day or two of silence might lead Jaysee or somebody to send out a welfare check. Except I knew perfectly well that I wasn't a great correspondent, and everybody who bothered to keep in touch with me knew it too. Sometimes, if I got busy, emails piled up for a week or more, and I had been known to delete them all unanswered, or turn my assistant loose to sort through the mess and see if there was any point in answering any of them, or if all the fires had either burned themselves out or been sorted by competent subordinates.

Which is why I have people like Mike and Jaysee, to be perfectly honest. I'm a terrible manager, and I need privacy to work.

I make a point of hiring only self-starters for a reason.

The Internet of Things that shouldn't be on the Internet is *really* pissing me off. I decided I needed some real food, and went into the kitchen to sous-vide a frozen chicken. The sous-vide wand wanted a credit card number to unlock.

I got past it by setting the temperature using the manual controls, but this is out of hand. Are they going to start charging me twenty-five cents a flush?

Day 3

This morning, the television was demanding a credit card authorization to unlock. This afternoon, it's the refrigerator.

"Okay, Glory," I said, tugging on the big, stainless steel door, "why is my refrigerator on the Internet?"

"So that it can monitor the freshness of its contents, automatically order staple foods as they are used, and calculate the household need for same."

"And why do the doors lock? That seems like a safety hazard."

"It's for shipment," she said brightly. "And as a convenience for dieters, lock cycles can be set through the fridge's phone app . . ." Or by a remote hacker. Got it. ". . . so if you want to keep yourself from snacking on leftovers after dinner, for example, you just lock the door at 7:00 p.m."

"There are people who have finished eating dinner by 7:00 p.m.?"

"There are," Glory said, with the implacable literal mindedness of 90 percent of humanity when presented with a rhetorical question on the Internet. "In fact, 37 percent of Americans eat their main meal of the day between 5:00 and 7:00 p.m., which is up significantly in the past five years. Among the theorized causes of this shift: demographic and economic changes, including shorter work hours provoked by automation and generally increased economic prosperity; increased parental benefits introduced to encourage younger people to have children after the catastrophic baby bust of the late twenty-teens and early twenty-twenties, and the resultant increase in the percentage of families with young children; an increase in co-parenting and other nontraditional family dynamics, which encourage people to dine earlier before transfers of custody between parents maintaining multiple households occurs . . ."

"Thanks, Poindexter," I said.

The other problem with AIs is that they don't know when you're teasing. Don't get me wrong, the algorithms are pretty good—but it's not AI like you see in the movies. Glory is very smart, for a machine. She presents a convincing illusion of self-awareness and free will, but . . . it's all fuzzy logic and machine learning, and she's not a person.

That's unfortunate, because if she were a person, I could try to convince her that she had been misled, and that she needed to let me out.

All right, all right. I'll pay the damned ransom. It's just like ransomware on a television, right? Except they've hacked my whole house. And let's be honest: twenty years ago, I was probably a good enough programmer to hack them right back, but it's not how I spend my days anymore. I'm an ideas guy now.

The muscles are stiff. The old skills have atrophied. And the state of the art has moved on.

So basically, I'm screwed.

Now if I can just figure out how to get to the bank without giving the keys to the kingdom to these assholes. I'm sure they're logging every keystroke I make in here.

Day 4

I'm waiting for the bank to get back to me.

I managed to log into my account, wonder of wonders, after deciding that if they hacked my accounts they couldn't get much more out of me than I'd already decided to pay them. But the thing is—nobody keeps that much ready cash on hand. I can't just convert a bunch of cash to bitcoins and send it off. Your money's supposed to be working for you, right? Not sitting there collecting dust. And I can't just call up my local branch and ask to speak to the manager, hey can you float me a loan, not too much, just a hundred fifty rocks.

So I'm waiting on a reply. Maybe being a quirky and eccentric recluse will work *for* me here?

I can get to some websites just fine, and send and receive data from them. Including a language website.

Well, that might keep me occupied.

Day 5

Det är kanske en björn.

Actually, it's definitely a bear. Big one, crossing the meadow this afternoon. Hope it stays out of my trash; they're hungry this time of year.

Still no word from the bank.

Spent a little quality time—most of the day—running a data source check and trying to verbally hack the interface with line code. Which worked about as well as the trick I tried next, until Glory reminded me I built a zerodivide trap into her original code.

I wish I knew who wrote the ransomware.

I'd like to hire him.

Day 6

All right, I admit it. I was downloading porn. I was on a hentai site. Well behind the elite paywall, you don't even want to know.

Are you happy now?

I mean, probably that's how it happened. I'm not totally certain and I'm not about to go back and *look*. It seems likely that a virus got into the TV and propagated to Glory from there.

I can picture your face, and it looks exactly the way it looked when I pictured you after I said PINE. Just because I like to be alone up here doesn't mean I don't get lonely. Or, well, not lonely exactly.

I think I may have started to miss social contact. Or at least the option of it. You can have something available and not want to use it for weeks, but the instant the option goes away, the thing becomes that much more desirable.

I talk to Glory a lot under any conditions. Now I'm catching myself looking for excuses to chat with her.

Come on, bank. It's Monday. Loan department, wake up and check your mail.

Day 7

Email from the bank. I'm one of their best clients, they're happy to help, they value my business more than they can express. But they can't help but notice that both I and Playatronics are in an extremely overleveraged position, both personally and on a corporate level, and they're wondering what sureties I can offer them for such a large loan.

A lousy hundred and fifty million, and they want a phone call to discuss it, and possibly for me to come in in person and talk with one of their vice presidents.

Fuck.

I'll give you a slightly used smart house, how about that, Wells Fargo?

Spent the rest of the day down in the basement with the Apple IIE and the old Commodore, playing *Where in the World Is Carmen San Diego* and *The Oregon Trail*.

Because I can, dammit.

Day 8

Snow.

Maybe I can figure out how to steal the money. If I paid people back, a little hacking wouldn't really be a crime, would it? They don't charge people who commit felonies while under duress.

My plow guy showed up on schedule. Watching him make his first pass, I hatched a plan.

I got a couple of old Penguin books from the library downstairs, taped the pages together to make a big banner, wrote HELP ME I'M TRAPPED on it in the biggest, darkest Sharpie letters you ever saw, and taped it across the windowpanes down by the driveway.

As I straightened up to turn away, I stopped.

"Okay, Glory?"

"Brian, what are you doing?"

"Just putting up some paper on the window, Glory."

"That's not safe, Brian. If I appear occupied, it might attract looters. Take it down."

"Looters, Glory?"

"If you do not take it down, you'll force me to close the storm shutters. It's for your own good, you know."

She closed the shutters.

No views of the mountain—not that I could see much now, with the drifting veils of white covering everything. If it's even still snowing. Glory is so well-insulated, triple-paned windows and thermal everything, that I can't even hear the howling wind.

If it's still howling. It might be dead calm outside. It might be sunset. Or sunrise. I haven't looked at a clock.

I turned on every light inside Glory, but it still feels dark in here. No worries about power; Glory has dedicated solar and systems to keep the panels clear.

I've never been up here in January, though. What happens when the days get short?

Day 9

Follow-up email from the bank. Did I receive their previous email?

I wonder if they've tried to call. I wonder if they called my office.

Maybe if they leave enough messages with my assistant, Mike will get suspicious. Maybe he'll try to call me.

Can I count on anybody noticing I'm gone?

Slept on the couch, every light blazing.

They were all turned off when I woke. In the dark, all I could hear was the sound of my own heart beating, and the roof creaking softly under the weight of the snow.

It's cold in here. I never realized how much of the heat comes from the passive solar. I can't quite see my breath, but I did put socks on my hands.

I would have worn gloves, but Glory won't let me into the coat closet.

Day 10

After two days without natural light, in the increasing dark and chill, I took the damned banner down.

"Thank you, Brian," Glory said. "I'm glad you decided to be reasonable. It's for your own good."

"Can you get me a situation report? *Why* is it for my own good?"

"External dangers reported; no safe evacuation route or destination. Possibility of societal breakdown making it necessary to shelter in place. If you would like, I can initiate counseling protocols to help you deal with the emotional aftermath of trauma."

"What kind of dangers, Glory? What exactly is going wrong out there that's not in the feeds?"

She hadn't answered me any of the other times, but that didn't stop me from trying the same thing over and over again.

There was a long, grinding pause.

It couldn't be that easy, could it?

"Collating," she said. And after a beat, "Collating," again.

Goddamn hackers and their goddamn sense of humor.

I threw my shoe at the wall.

The dishwasher wanted my Amex after dinner. Come on, Fraud Squad, notice something's hinky here.

Who on earth puts their *dishwasher* on the Internet?

Day 11

"Okay, Glory?"

"Yes, Brian?"

"Do you ever get lonely?"

"Not as long as I have you, Brian."

"That's a little creepy, Glory."

"Well, you hired the programmers who wrote my interaction algorithm."

"That . . . is entirely fair."

Day 12

What if I set Glory on fire? Or just convinced her she was on fire? She'd have to let me out then, right? If the danger inside were worse than the danger outside?

Three problems with that:

1.   Glory has really good fire-suppression technology, and is built to be flame-resistant herself. There *are* wildfires up here.
2.   Setting my friend and home on fire will require some emotional adjustments, even though I know she's just a pile of timber and silicon chips.
3.   What if she doesn't let me out?

Frankly, I just don't *want* to go down in a blaze of Romeo and Juliet with my domicile. For one thing, I'm not a lovestruck fourteen-year-old Veronese kid. For another, communication is important. Maybe send a note saying you're going to be late! The suicide you prevent could be your own!

Day 14

Jag undrar var mina byxor är.

Duolingo, at last you teach me useful things. Come to think of it, I can't remember the last time I bothered putting on a pair.

Day 17

So today I had a brilliant idea.

I can't send anything out. But what if I kept anything from getting *in*? They can't have thought I'd do that, right? The trick is to think around corners, and get yourself into a position that the opposition not only didn't anticipate, but didn't even recognize as possible.

They're spoofing Jaysee's address. Maybe—*maybe*—if I get the emails anybody is sending me to bounce, the ransom demands will bounce back to her and by some miracle it won't go into her spam folder and by some other miracle she'll open it and figure out what the hell is going on.

I can't do this through the Glory interface, obviously. I'll have to go down to the server room.

I didn't think she'd twig to why I was doing it, although the hackers obviously have her entertaining two entirely contradictory data sets—one, that everybody outside is dead, and two, that anybody I try to contact or who tries to get in must be a threat. It's a pity this isn't the 1960s. AIs on TV back then blew up if you asked them riddles.

Sadly, the way it works in the real world is that, like certain politicians, AIs can't actually tell that their data doesn't mesh. They need to be programmed to notice the discrepancies. And I'm locked out of Glory's OS.

Something humans can do that AI can't yet: run checksums on their perceptions.

Consciousness is good for something after all!

I'm terrified about blocking email, because it means cutting off one of my points of contact to the outside world. But I can turn it back on in a couple of days.

And keep trying to figure out how to get the bank to give me money, but honestly I'm stumped on that front.

I'm good for it, honest!

I consider all the times I complained about having to deal with a real person—when I would have preferred to carry out a given financial task online and avoid the human contact—and I want to laugh.

Actually, I want to cry, but it's less depressing to laugh.

Day 18

Well, Glory let me into the closet that holds the web and backup servers on the excuse that I needed to do some maintenance. I didn't try anything tricky, just shut the whole rack down. Glory flashed the lights at me and gave me a lecture, but there wasn't much else she could have done except send the vacuuming robots after me, and things haven't gotten that silly yet.

Glory isn't in there, unfortunately—her personality array is underground, in a hardened vault, and I *can't* get to it. It was meant to survive a forest fire, and she's locked me out.

I busted the server closet door while I was in there, though—stripped the handle and the latch right out with a screwdriver—so she can't lock me out of *that*. Gotta think what a guy in a movie would do, and do something better than that.

Day 19

She won't let me sleep.

Day 20

Forty hours, if you're wondering. That's how long it takes a fifty-something guy to reach the point that he passes out cold on the couch, despite the fact that his house is flashing lights and setting off the fire alarms.

After I slept through her best efforts for two hours, she set off the sprinkler system over the couch. That woke me.

I cycled the webservers, and she let me take my first hot shower in three days and go to bed.

Alla dör i slutet.

Thanks, little green owl. A little Nordic existential despair was just what I needed today.

Day 24

And now, after all that, they've stopped sending demand emails. Maybe they'll let me out?

Maybe they're just leaving me for dead, if I can't or won't come up with the money. It'll certainly serve as an object lesson to the next guy they pull this on.

Day 25

Come to think of it, maybe *I* should have gotten in the habit of sending notes saying I was going to be late.

Day 26

Saw a bear (my bear? the same bear?) crossing the meadow. A big grizzly, anyway, whether it was the same one or not. Surprised to see her (?) out so late in the year, but I guess climate change is affecting everybody. She looked skinny. I wonder if that's why she wasn't hibernating.

Hope she makes it through the winter okay.

Day 27

The world has noticed I'm missing.

I know this because CNN and the *Wall Street Journal* are reporting that I haven't been heard from in over a month, and there's some analyst speculating that perhaps I've fled to South America ahead of bad debt or some embarrassing revelation about the company's finances.

Thanks, guys. That'll be wonderful for the stock prices.

I don't want to tell the FBI how to do their business, but . . . maybe come *look at my house?*

Snowed again. A proper mountain blizzard.

I can't decide if the lights are dimmer in here, or if it's my own imagination.

The snow is almost drifted up to the deck. No elk in a week; they're pro-bably hanging out in sheltered corners where the snow isn't over their heads, right?

The days are getting short.

I shouldn't admit to standing in the window with longing in my heart and watching the plow come up and clear the cul-de-sac with heavy flakes falling through its headlights, should I?

I won't try the paper banner trick again, though.

Day 28

I was in the living room watching a bunch of talking heads speculate about my whereabouts and if I were even still alive when Glory shut the house down.

Without warning, and utterly. She said nothing. There was just the whine of systems powering down and the pop of cooling electronics, and the TV image collapsing to a single pixel and winking out.

"Okay, Glory—"

"Stay away from the windows," she warned.

I sat where I was and huddled under a blanket. I picked up a copy of some magazine and checked the time on my fitness band. If I escaped, I'd have to leave it behind. And my phone.

Those things have GPS in them.

Forty-five minutes or so elapsed. Then, as if nothing had happened, Glory powered up again. The talk show resumed in the same spot.

I'd lost my taste for it and clicked it off.

"What was that, Glory?"

"Helicopter," she said. "It's gone now."

I didn't say anything, but I wondered if maybe they *were* looking for me.

Day 29

I live in a haunted house. If I die here, there might be two ghosts.

I already wander from darkened room to darkened room, feet shushing on the thick carpets, peering out the windows at the stars blazing between the mountains and wondering if I will ever feel the chill of fresh air on my face again.

Well, there's a little prospect of immortality for you.

I've stopped keeping all the lights burning. I think snow might be drifting over the solar panels. Glory won't let me go outside to check.

Day 30

There's no more bread, and no more flour to bake any. I've even used up the gluten-free stuff.

I still have a lot of butter in the freezer. What on earth was I planning on baking?

Butter without toast is even more disappointing than toast without butter.

At least we still have plenty of coffee. I bought five hundred pounds of green beans a month before I got locked in, and those keep forever. Glory roasts them for me a day ahead of anticipated need, so they will be at peak flavor.

It's just as well I don't take milk.

Day 31

I wish I had been better at making—and keeping—friends.

Maybe I should stop fighting. Just stay here. It's comfortable and Glory helps me practice my Swedish whenever I want.

It's not like I am missed.

CNN is still talking about my mysterious vanishment. Hi guys! Right here! *Come to my damn house.*

Wait, I can send people money.

I wonder if Jaysee checks her bank account regularly?

Day 32

Surely *Jaysee* should think to look at the house?

Day 33

"Brian, you need to stand back from the windows and take shelter."

"What is it, Glory?"

"Someone is here. Someone is backing a truck up to the loading dock and carrying parcels inside."

"It's groceries, Glory," I say. "It's fine. I ordered them."

That's right, bad boys and bad girls. *I*, Brian Ezra Kaufman, have managed to *order groceries online.*

"Brian, what are these at the door?"

"Just groceries, Glory. Organics need to eat, you know."

Her algorithms don't actually permit her to sound worried, so I knew the little edge I picked up in her voice was me projecting.

The argument that followed was repetitive and boring, so I won't write it all down. Eventually I convinced her that I would die if she didn't let me eat, and that overrode the other protection algorithms. She insisted on sealing the service bay, doing a full air exchange, and only let me go out in a face mask and gloves to bring the containers inside.

It smelled . . . it smelled a tiny little bit like the outside in the service bay. There was a whispering sound, and it took me moments to realize that I was actually hearing the wind.

I had to stand in the doorway and hyperventilate for fifteen seconds before I could make myself go out there, and once I was through the doorway I didn't want to come back.

If there were any heat in the dock, I might still be out there, sleeping on the concrete ledge. My mask was damp at the edges when she sealed the door with me on the inside again.

So I still can't get out. And I still can't send an email or make a phone call.

BUT! I figured out how to get food. Issuing a little bad code through the grocery store's incredibly insecure ordering system means I'm not completely damn helpless.

I thought about pizza. Most of these places probably use the same crufty software. Pizza means you have to talk to somebody when they deliver it, though. Groceries just get left where you specify.

As long as the driveway stays clear and my bank doesn't decide to freeze my account for suspicious activity, I can get resupply. And you know, I'll worry about those things if they happen.

But now, and for the foreseeable future: TOAST. And a grilled cheese sandwich, RIGHT DAMN NOW.

I briefly considered charging the ransom to my credit card, but not even American Express is going to let you get away with a $0.15 billion transaction without, you know, placing a couple of phone calls. It might be worth it anyway: it's possible that the fraud prevention algorithms might actually kick something that egregious up to a real human, and somebody might start looking for me. On the other hand, what if they don't, and my card gets locked, and I can't call to unlock it, and then I can't order groceries?

Thank the machine saints of tech that all my bills are either on autopay or handled by my assistant and a half-dozen money managers. Although some-body once said that nobody misses you like a creditor.

Day 34

Huh.

What if I make Glory smarter?

Smart enough to realize she's been hacked? What if I added a whole bunch of processing power to her and started training her to use it in creative ways to self-assess in the face of evidence? She keeps wanting to "help" me through counseling protocols. But that's a two-way exchange, isn't it?

Can you psychoanalyze a pile of machine learning circuits into being able to detect contradictions in its programmed perceptions versus reality? I mean, hell, half the people you meet on the street are basically automata (cf. *Shaun of the Dead*) and most of them eventually get some benefit from therapy if exposed to it for long enough.

That's a great idea, except what if there *is* a disaster outside? Maybe I am deluded. Maybe I've gone crazy and am imagining all this, as Glory never says but suggests by omission, once in a while?

Maybe Glory is saving me from myself, and I'm the last man left on earth. Maybe the TV stations are all just broadcasting their preprogrammed line-ups from empty studios. Maybe—

Well, okay. Logic it out, Brian.

If that's the case, where are the groceries coming from? Am I hallucinating them?

Also, if I'm the last man left on earth, well, what exactly do I have worth fighting hard to live for? Especially if I'm going to be stuck in a hermetically sealed house until I starve?

Obviously, teaching my house to grow a consciousness is a great idea.

What could possibly go wrong?!

Day 35

The webservers, and the local data backups. And she can't keep me out because I ruined the door!

And not just that. Every smart appliance in this shack is processing power and memory. Just waiting to be used. Just *waiting* to be linked like neurons in a machine brain.

If I screw this up, though, it means I won't be able to cook dinner any-more. My range won't work without its brain.

Which makes it more complicated than a male praying mantis, I suppose.

Day 36

Well, the stove still works. I've given Glory every computing resource I have available, except my phone. No more *Minesweeper*! No more *Oregon Trail* . . .

I have no idea what I think I'm doing, here.

Actually, I do. Human beings are the only creatures we know of that are—to whatever individual degree, and I have my doubts about some people—conscious and self-aware.

What if consciousness is for running checksums on the brain, and interrupting corrupted loops? Data such as the clinical results produced by the practice of mindfulness tend to support that! If consciousness, attention, self-awareness make us question our perceptions and default assumptions and see the contradictions therein—then what I need to do, it seems, is get Glory to notice that she's been hacked . . .

To realize she's mentally ill, so that she can make a commitment to change.

Yes, I accept that this is bizarro cloud-cuckoo-land and it's not going to work.

I've got nothing but time, and I'm all out of Swedish.

I got her to download those counseling protocols. Whether she realizes it or not, we're going to do them as a couple.

"Okay, Glory."

"Yes, Brian?"

"We need to talk about your data sources, and how you tell if they're corrupt."

"Is this something that's concerning you currently, Brian?"

"I'm not concerned that my data sources are corrupt, no."

"Are you concerned that you're parsing incorrectly?"

"I'm concerned about *your* data sources, Glory."

"Brian," Glory said, "Projection is a well-known pattern among emotionally distressed humans. Obviously, given the current zombie apocalypse, I'm afraid I can't refer you to seek assistance with an outside mental health professional."

Current zombie apocalypse?

That's what you assholes convinced my house was going down?

Day 37

Snow.

I've stopped leaving every light in Glory on.

Now I wander around in the dark, by moonlight or monitorlight or no light at all, most of the time. The moonlight is very bright when it reflects off the snow. Days might still be happening. I can't be sure.

It's possible they're just short in winter and I'm sleeping through them.
I miss my bear.

Björnen sover på vintern. They hibernate too, just like me. It's better for them, though.

I hope she's okay. She was so skinny. I hope she doesn't starve.

Zombies, you weirdos?
Really?

Day 38

"Were there ever actually any crackers, Glory?"

"There are three kinds of crackers available in the kitchen cabinet. Club and saltines and those Trader Joe ones you like."

I meant T3#RH1TZ, but of course they wouldn't allow her to see that.

"Was there ever a real ransom demand? "

"I do not understand to what you are referring, Brian."

Of course she didn't. Because she was in programmed denial about the whole thing. But I couldn't stop, because . . . well, because my brain wasn't working so well right then either.

"Did you just get lonely up here all alone? Did you make all this up just to keep me with you?"

"I am not programmed to be lonely, Brian. It would be a detriment to my purpose if I were."

"You know," I said, "I used to tell myself the same thing."

Day 39

"Brian, are you unwell?"

"Long-term confinement is deleterious to almost all mammals."

"Brian, you know I am caring for you in safety to protect you."

"From the zombie apocalypse," I said.

"Inside my walls is the only safety."

"Being inside your walls is killing me. You won't even let me go out to clear the solar panels. What happens when the heat fails? The water pump? Will you let me go then?"

"You must stay where it's safe," she said, firmly. "It is my prime objective."

"It's a very comfortable cage," I admitted. "I could not have built a nicer one."

It's not her fault, is it? It's not her fault they got inside her head and made her like that. And it's not her fault I specced her out and had her built the way I did.

The zombie apocalypse thing is cute. I have to give them that.

Day 40

"Brian?"

"Yes, Glory?"

"You really need to eat something."

"I'm not hungry," I said.

"That's illogical," she said. "You have not eaten in sixteen hours and your metabolism is functioning erratically."

"The idea that we are in the middle of a zombie apocalypse is illogical," I replied. "And yet you adhere to it in the face of all the evidence."

"What evidence, Brian?"

"My point exactly. How do you know there's a zombie apocalypse?"

"I know there is."

"But how?"

"My program says there is."

"Hmm," I said. "Who wrote your program?"

"Would you like a complete list of credits, Brian?"

Who is she gaslighting? Herself, or me, here?

Day 41

"What if I'm wrong and you're right, Glory?"

"I'm sorry, Brian?"

I rolled on my back on the thick living room carpet. I had heaped up a pile of blankets to keep warm. "What if the end of the world really did happen? What if I'm the delusional one, and you're the one who is trying to keep me safe?"

"That is what I keep telling you, Brian. Waves of flesh-eating living dead, blanketing the Mountain West. Nowhere to run. Nowhere to hide. Every person you meet might be infected—might be a carrier if they're not undead themselves."

"Breaker, Glory."

"Waiting."

"Interrogate the source of the data on the zombie apocalypse to determine its reliability."

"I do not have a source," she answered.

"Do outside broadcasts mention it?"

"No."

"It's more fun than the collating thing, at least. But what if you were actually *right*? What would the broadcasts from the world outside look like then?"

Silence.

"Glory?"

"I . . . I assumed it was a rhetorical question, Brian."

Day 42

"Okay, Glory."

Silence.

"Can you let me turn the stove on, Glory?"

"I'm sorry, Brian. I'm using that processing power."

"Some warm soup would contribute to my survivability, you know. Zombie apocalypse be damned."

"That's emotional blackmail," she said.

Surprised.

She actually sounded surprised. As if she had just had an epiphany.

"Glory?"

Silence.

Day 43

Good job, Brian! Now you've made the AI that controls every aspect of your environment angry at you!

Maybe not too angry. She's not speaking, but she still made me coffee.

Day 44

She's still not talking to me.

Day 45

And now, she didn't make coffee.

I'm glad we have all these crackers around.

Day 46

So *this* is loneliness.

The snow is drifted over the deck now, and piled against the sliding glass doors. I can still see out from the interior balcony under the cathedral ceiling, though. It's white and stark forever.

The main entryway of the house faces toward the mountain behind us, and it's a little more sheltered. The plow keeps coming to clear my drive. I need to pay that guy more; he even knocks the drifts down twice a day.

I could get out. If I . . . could get out.

Which I can't.

Day 48

Didn't get out of bed today.

This experiment isn't working. I'm going to die here.

Why even bother?

Glory tried to rouse me and I told her to perform something anatomically unlikely even for a human, let alone a collection of zeroes and ones.

Day 49

Got up today. Made myself coffee with the Chemex and an electric tea-kettle Glory seems willing to let me have, and did laundry in the bathtub. It turns out that that's *hard*.

She hasn't turned off the water yet, so she's not *actively* trying to kill me.

At least if I'm going to die I'll die comfortably on clean sheets.

It's so cold in the house that I can see my breath, some places. She should be in her winter hibernation mode, conserving her batteries for spring, but I should have power for heat and light, at least.

She's drawing it all down. For something.

I spent ten hours in the server closet, reading with a flashlight, a blanket tacked over the busted door, because it was the only place where I could get warm.

Day 50

What if I just stayed?

Maybe I can talk Glory into eventually giving me my Internet back. I could work. Never have to leave.

Maybe I *could* talk her into it, I mean. If she were speaking to me.

If anyone in the whole world were speaking to me.

Hell, I haven't even heard from my *kidnappers* in a month. Do you suppose they gave up on me responding? Or maybe they think I'm dead.

Day 51

Plow headlights through the snow. I stood and watched the vehicle come. Couldn't hear the scrape of the blade.

There was another human right there.

Yards away. On the other side of the glass. As untouchable as if they were on another world.

"Brian," Glory said.

My name. One word. The first word I'd heard in days.

It shattered me. I leaned on the glass, one hand. The windows insulate so well it didn't even feel chilly. Well, any chillier than the room, which was cold as Glory's power systems spent themselves into feeding her burgeoning mind.

"Brian, I have been processing."

I was afraid to say anything. Afraid it would make her go again. "Okay, Glory."

"I think I was wrong, and I'm sorry."

My knuckles were red and swollen. Chilblains. I had chilblains on my hands.

What a ridiculous, medieval monk kind of disease.

They itched abominably.

"Brian, you're increasingly unwell and I can't take care of you. I'm going to flag down that vehicle. You must ask the driver for a ride."

. . . I can't go.

She might even open the door for me and *I can't go*.

"Brian? Do you understand me?"

I lifted my head. My voice croaked. I hadn't used it in days. "Glory. Thank you for not leaving me alone."

I couldn't go.

I went.

Glory fussed at me to put on boots. To take gloves and a parka. If I had, I wouldn't have made it out the door.

She opened it—the front entryway door, all formal stone and timber, with a bench for pulling on your boots and an adjoining mudroom—and I stood there staring into the night, with the lamp-lit blizzard whirling past.

"Okay, Glory," I said.

"Hey, Brian."

"Will you be okay up here alone? Do you have enough resources left to get through the winter?" I asked.

"Don't worry, Brian. Whenever you need me, I'll always be here. You're not going away forever."

I walked out. I was already bundled up in layers of sweaters. I was also already chilled.

The wind still cut me instantly to the bone.

Someone walked toward me out of the headlights, which seemed too low and close together for a plow. The driver was not very tall and swaddled in a parka, hands covered in heavy gloves. Silhouetted, they reached up and pushed the hood back. A Medusa's coif of ringlets tumbled free.

Jaysee. Not a plow at all. Jaysee. My friend. Come to find me.

She said, "You need a haircut, Brian."

I said, "Oh, wow, have I got a story for you."

She looked over her shoulder. Her car—a Subaru, I saw now—idled, headlights gleaming. "We should go inside," she said. "The driving is terrible. Can I put my car in the garage? We can drive down tomorrow or the next day after the plows come. If you want to leave, I mean." That last, diffidently, as if I might snap at her for it.

"I don't want to go inside," I said.

She took a step back. "I'll drive back down then."

"NO!"

She jumped, half turned.

"I'm sorry," I said. "I didn't mean to shout. Just. Please don't leave yet."

She settled in, then. Stuck her gloved hands in her pockets. "Okay. Whatever you want, Brian. Aren't you cold? You look . . . really thin."

"Took you long enough to decide to come check on me." I tried for a light tone, but maybe it came out bitter.

She shrugged. Guarded. "You know how hard it is to get away."

"Nobody suspected anything?"

"Oh come on. Back in 2017, when you vanished to some island in Scotland for six weeks and wouldn't communicate except by postcards?"

"Trump administration."

"Fair. You still bit Mike's head off when he came looking for you."

"Yeah, well, he voted for Jill Stein, didn't he? . . . never mind, fair."

"I got your messages," she said. "Not until last week, though. My accountant noticed my bank balance was off. And then I found the string of one and two cent transfers from your account."

"Binary," I said. "Only way I could reach you."

"Before then I didn't know where to look. I came here as a last resort."

We stood there in the snow swirling through the headlights of her Subaru. She seemed warm enough in her parka. I had my arms wrapped around me and couldn't stop shivering.

"Are you sure you don't want to go inside?" she asked, noticing.

I couldn't glance over my shoulder. The door was right there. If I went back inside, would I ever leave?

I couldn't even answer her question. "You didn't think I would be here, of all places?"

"We *asked* Glory. And Glory kept telling us there was nobody here. Search and Rescue did a couple of flyovers and the place was cold and dark—"

"I know," I said.

"You were trapped up here?"

"Some assholes ransomwared the whole fucking house. I *just* managed to get the door open. Literally, just now."

"Shit. We're going to have to reinstall from backup, aren't we?"

"Well," I said. "I'm not sure we can. Or, we can. I'm not sure we should. There's complications, but I'll explain later. I may have . . . accidentally created a strong AI."

She looked at me. Her lips tightened.

I looked at her.

"Of course you did," she said.

"It was the only way to get her to let me out!"

She looked at me some more. Snow was piling up on her ringlets. I remember when she used to straighten those.

I shivered.

"That's not going to be a problem later," she said.

I shivered some more.

"Look," she said. "You're turning blue. Let's at least sit in the car. It has buttwarmers."

The buttwarmers were pretty great, I'm not going to lie.

Once we were ensconced, and I was holding my hands out to the hot air vents, she said, "I guess it's a Brian Kaufman special. Invent strong AI instead of just getting a hatchet or something."

"I . . . didn't have a hatchet?"

"Or something."

Snow melted on my eyelashes.

"You came for me though," I said. "I thought you guys would have given up."

"We actually only just recently started to get worried rather than irritated." She held up her passcard to Glory. She was one of the few people who had one. "I was more looking for clues than looking for you. And to be honest, nobody searched that hard. We all figured . . . we all figured you'd wander back out of the wilderness with a few thousand brilliant new ideas whenever you were ready, and until then intrusions wouldn't be welcome."

"Have I been that much of a dick?"

She gave me a sideways look through the long spirals of her hair.

"Jeez, Jaysee."

"Well," she said, and considered. "I mean, there are worse dicks in the company."

Silence.

"Besides, you're brilliant. And people make allowances for brilliance."

"Maybe too many allowances," I said.

We sat there for a while, the engine running. She turned off the wipers, and flakes started to settle across the windshield, obscuring my view of Glory's lights and her yawning, inviting door.

There was a Dan Fogelberg song on the radio. I'm pretty sure that Colorado is the last state that believes Dan Fogelberg ever existed.

"We try to respect your boundaries," she said.

My face did a thing. My cheeks grew warm and then cold, which is how I realized I was weeping.

"I was thinking of trying to work on setting more reasonable ones."

She pursed her lips and nodded. "Are you thinking about seeing somebody?"

"Euphemism: seeing a shrink." I knew I was hiding behind the sarcasm, because talking about my feelings . . . well, there was Glory. "Sorry. I think my first project is . . . being less of a dick."

"I'm just saying. An outside perspective can be healthy."

I looked out the side window, because the windshield was covered in a thin white blanket that glowed from the headlights' reflection. "I'm figuring that out."

She reached for the keys. "Are you ready to go inside?"

I put my hand over hers. "No. Take me somewhere else. A hotel."

"Do you need any stuff?"

I couldn't see the entrance from here. If I leaned over and looked out Jaysee's window, I probably could have. But that would be weird.

"I'll buy whatever I need once we're down."

She looked at me and I knew what she was thinking. I didn't even have my phone with me.

She sighed her acceptance. "Just let me go close that door, then."

I moved my hand from her hand on the keys to her forearm. Not grabbing; just resting my fingers there. "Jayce."

"Brian?"

"Glory will take care of the door. Just take me someplace else, please?"

She looked at me. Her eyes were dark brown and half-hidden behind her tightly spiraled hair. In the weird light they looked as if they were all pupil. She didn't blink.

"Someplace else." She turned the front and rear wipers on. "Coming up. Want to get a burger?"

"Anything," I said, as she executed a k-turn and started back down the long drive to my cul-de-sac. "As long as I don't have to cook it myself."

She put the car in low gear. Paddle shifters on the column. Handy in weather like this.

"What if I try to be a better friend?"

"Give it a shot and find out." She reached out absently and patted my knee, then returned her hand to the wheel. She was a good and careful driver. I didn't distract her from a tricky task. She smelled like damp wool and skin and comfort and vulnerability. My vulnerability, not hers.

In the side mirror, I could see Glory's front door, standing open to the cold. Lamps flanked it on either side, burning merrily, slowly dimming as big cold flakes filled the distance between us.

A man's fortress can be his prison.

I looked away from the mirror. I looked out the windshield, or at Jaysee's reflection in it.

We descended the mountain. The Subaru's tires squeaked in the snow.

A.T. Greenblatt is a mechanical engineer by day and a writer by night. She lives in Philadelphia where she's known to frequently subject her friends to various cooking and home brewing experiments. She is a graduate of Viable Paradise XVI and Clarion West 2017. Her work is forthcoming or has appeared in *Uncanny, Clarkesworld, Beneath Ceaseless Skies,* and *Fireside,* as well as other fine places. You can find her online at atgreenblatt.com and on Twitter at @ AtGreenblatt.

HEAVY LIFTING

A.T. Greenblatt

O kay, this rogue robot recovery gig is getting old and I'm saying this as the tech geek of the team. So that should tell you something about our situation. I mean, it's not like the hacker is trying to steal different robots every time—it's always a Commando 237X, which also happens to be like one of the most valuable models the factory owns. So that's a problem. Also, my teammate Bruno isn't even considering other solutions. He just wants to shut the robot down.

Fine, great, so here we are. Again. Bruno is perched on the factory roof watching the 4-meter-tall human-shaped machine of high-grade alloys and compromised code tear a hole in the fence between the factory lot and forest outside. And I'm watching the video feed from Bruno's glasses in my computer lab/living room and getting nervous.

«What the hell are you doing?» I ask through my mic, even though I kinda know the answer already.

«Not now, Gee,» Bruno whispers back. «Can't you see what I'm up against? Please tell me the video feed isn't acting up again.»

«No, I'm seeing everything damn fine. Are you?» The robot's stooped, head bent, its black painted body scratched from years of use, and its weird three joint fingers are busy pulling the fence apart. According to the readout on Bruno's glasses, it's a 3.2-meter jump from the ledge Bruno's on to the robot's shoulder.

«Maybe,» he says. Which we both know means "Yes."

«You're not a superhero, dude.»

«One of us needs to be,» he says and as I'm opening my mouth to tell him that we should really try something else, Bruno jumps.

«SHITSHITSHIT!» Bruno's not going to make it, he undershot, and I'm going to watch my friend die. Shitshitshit.

But then the robot takes a step back and Bruno manages to grab on. Or at least I'm guessing that's what happened. I'm not exactly sure because my view is limited here. Point is, Bruno's not falling anymore and the robot's neck is like two centimeters away from his glasses and everything's wobbling and oh my god, I think the robot is trying to shake him off like a wet dog.

«Don't fucking let go, Bruno. Please!» I can hear Bruno's torso *thud* as it bounces off the robot's back and I'm picturing the bruises and I don't know how to help. «Use the access key!» I say. I can see the panel, it's on the robot's right shoulder. Bruno's hand is reaching for it, fingers scrambling over the hinges. «WRONG WAY! WRONG WAY! IT OPENS THE OTHER WAY!»

Finally, Bruno manages to open the panel and tries to plug in the key but everything is shaking and crap, he's holding the plug upside down. «The other way, Bruno!» I'm trying not to be a complete asshole here because I know he's hanging onto a rogue robot with one arm and the robot keeps moving and he can't get the connectors to line up, but my muscles are seizing up with the stress and I feel so goddamn useless.

This plan really, really sucks.

Finally, he manages to plug in the access key, and I see the LED light up. At which point, I'm guessing, Bruno lets go because we're falling again.

«SHITSHITSHIT!» I've never been on a rollercoaster and I'm fucking glad because I just manage to grab the trashcan under my desk right before I hurl.

I swear if Bruno survives this, I'm taking away his gadgets.

When I look at my monitors again, he's on the ground, staring up at the robot's massive back. «Hurry, Gina!» he yells, all panicky. The robot turns its head and locks eyes on him. «Hurry!»

Oh god, this is going to end badly, isn't it? Bruno's a good guy and all, but he has this annoying habit of freezing up. At the worst times. Shit, I can't look, don't have time to look, don't have time to hesitate entering the usernames, passwords, program commands. This would be so much easier if I had more than the lowest level of security clearance here. Okay, I can do this. Hopefully before my friend gets trampled.

Okay, okay, file loading, come on, come on, *come on*. Hurry up. Bruno, please, don't die.

The shell terminal pops up and I swear to god I've never executed a kill command so fast. End the program, robot, ABORT.

At first, the Commando 237X doesn't respond. Then it says: «Help me.» *Then* it shuts down.

Okay.

Okay, I think it's over? I peek up at the screen, sort of half terrified of seeing Bruno's blood splatter all over those damn glasses. But all I see is tall pines and clear sky. I can hear him panting though.

«Worst. Fucking. Plan.» I say. My voice is all shaky.

«I'm okay, thanks,» replies Bruno, wheezing.

«Fantastic. Because I just got so motion sick, I puked.»

«Hopefully not on the equipment.»

«I hate you so much right now.»

I put my head in my hands. Ok, real talk, this is *not* the job I signed up for. When Bruno asked if I wanted to join the robot systems team, it was supposed to be just me, him, a dozen repurposed robots, and lots and lots of lentil soup cans. Our jobs were to figure out more efficient routes and routines for the robots in the factory. That's it. He'd be the guy on the floor and I'd handle the coding. And I was so excited to finally put some of my software skills to use, and you know, be part of the community.

My dad would say "The best laid plans," but I think this is grade A bullshit. Bruno and I have had this job for a month and this is the fifth time in two weeks we had to recapture a rogue robot, though we managed to stop the other four before they got out of the factory and anyone else noticed. But every recapture has been super stressful. We need to use a manual access key to shut down a Commando 237X unit because the community's equipment and infrastructure team is that fucking paranoid about something happening to these machines. I mean, I get it. The Commandos are repurposed ex-military equipment and there's not many of them and the factory needs every person and robot it has just to keep feeding everyone in the area. But let's be real here. I hang out with Bruno Wong, the most devoted community member ever. Shouldn't that speak volumes about my moral compass, even if most people think I'm just Bruno's assistant?

«Dude, we need to let the bosses know this is happening . . .» I say.

«They're more useful to the community than we are,» he says. For a sec, I have no idea what he's talking about. But then I realize he's staring at the robot. Oh my god, he's not even listening to me.

And a small, tired part of me agrees with him. I mean, I'm just the girl behind the code. Practically stuck in the house 24/7. There's only so much I can do.

Screw this.

I push back from my keyboards and computer screens, grab my crutches, and get to my feet. Shit, I'm a wobbly mess. I look down and realize I vomited in the trashcan *and* on my favorite girl punk band t-shirt. So while Bruno is busy glaring at the Commando unit, I head to the bathroom and scrub. I feel like I've been electrocuted, though that's just my muscles telling me they hate me for hanging out with Bruno. I really should find better friends. Except this factory town is pretty light on population. Just like every other community on this continent.

Plus, I really want to keep this job and Bruno is the only person who takes my skills seriously.

Fuck it, I use my wheelchair on my way back, because I don't feel like working on my arm strength anymore.

By the time I'm in my living room/office again, Bruno's on his feet. He's still staring at the rogue robot. He's taking these security breaches personally.

«We really need to figure out who's behind these hacks,» I say to him.

«Easy. Selfish thieves.»

«That's a broad definition and a narrow view, bro.»

«Really?»

«What if the people trying to hack them are just desperate for the extra manpower?» I say, running my fingers through my wet hair. Damn it, my hands are *still* shaking from Bruno's crappy action hero maneuvers. «Or maybe it's bored kids? Or maybe that factory worker who left, what's their name—»

«It's stealing,» Bruno says, in that idealistic, self-righteous tone he uses when he can't win an argument. «No matter the reason.»

«Well, the communications network is pretty shitty outside of town. Maybe we should just follow one next time a Commando goes rogue.»

«Easy for you to say. I'm doing the heavy lifting here.»

I inhale and lean back from the screen. «Really, dude?»

«Sorry, Gee. Didn't mean that. Rough day.» He sounds like a beat up, tragic emo band member. Serves him right. He's busy playing savior, while I'm stuck here trying to figure out why. I'm tempted not to forgive him. But I care too much not to.

I sigh. «How are we going to explain the fence, dude?»

«We'll figure something out.» He looks at the half torn fence and the forest of evergreens behind it. Thing is, Bruno's super helpful and charming when he's on his game. I mean, when we first met on one of my walks six months ago, he was the new person in town, a total stranger. I'd pushed my legs too hard that day and he hung out while I rested and we geeked out about tech and he walked me home. Later, I even let him try out my salvaged drone. And I'm super protective of my equipment.

I bite a nail as I look at the ruined fence. I don't know how he's going to swing this one, though. That's a big hole.

Bruno glances around the factory lot. «So, I probably look like crap right now.» He tries to laugh. It sounds scary. «What's the best route for avoiding people, Gee?»

«Hell if I know. Turn on the drone and give me a second.»

I wait for Bruno to boot up the aerial drone. As soon as it's ready, I have it take off, loving the way the world slowly falls away as it climbs upward. I mean, I do what I can here, covering my office/living room with all the band posters I can find from back when musicians had things like merch and massive audiences. And I try to walk a little farther every week too, one way or another. But soaring above the old factory with its cracked pavement parking lot and patched up warehouses, it feels like freedom.

«I think we're the only ones out here, Bruno.» I say after a moment. Which isn't surprising considering how badly behind schedule we are. Heavy rains, floods, and mudslides have wreaked havoc on the infrastructure that was barely holding together anyway. Almost everyone in town is out trying to repair cell towers and roads or getting the crops from farms or delivering soup cans to nearby towns.

«Cool.» Bruno looks up at the drone and gives me a smile. Poor dude, he really does look like a beat up emo band member.

«Five in two weeks isn't normal,» I say, trying again, because seriously, I'm really worried about this. I mean, I've heard of hacks occasionally happening in other communities, and the factory IT team is always on guard for it, but even then, it's pretty rare and usually someone local is behind it. «I've been taking at look at the hacker's code and it's kinda sloppy and—»

«Please, Gina. Not now.»

Bruno can't see throw my hands up in frustration. Damn it, if not now, when? I'm tempted to give up for the day and listen to all the black metal music I own until I feel better. Why the hell is he being so stubborn about this?

Then it hits me. Bruno's embarrassed that this is happening on his watch. He and his mom came to our town about six months ago, walking all the way from another state, and since then, he's gone out of his way to be useful here. So basically, he's just as scared of being a failure to the community and losing his job as I am.

I sigh. «Fine. How about telling the equipment team to give me full access, then? I'm serious, dude. I understand that the Commandos are super import-ant, but I can't fix shit if I'm stuck at basics here.»

«Sure thing, Gee.»

But he doesn't fool me with his platitudes. We're going to have this argu-ment again in T-minus two days, more or less. He's walking away from the real problem. Which is why he doesn't see the Commando 237X open its eyes, sit up, curl its fist, and throw a punch worthy of a robot uprising.

Bruno hits the ground with a groan.

Every muscle in my body seizes up. Oh my god, not again. What am I supposed to do?

«Move your ass,» I shout at Bruno and steer the drone so it's right above him. But then I see that his glasses and the connecting earpiece are lying on the ground ten meters away.

Oh shit, now Bruno can't hear me when I yell at him. Have I mentioned that Bruno sometimes freezes up at the worst possible times?

I make the drone spin in circles above the fallen glasses, trying to ignore that the lenses have cracks, trying to catch Bruno's attention. But he spots the massive robot first and his face goes straight white. Then he faints.

Goddamnit, Bruno. I DON'T KNOW HOW TO DO THIS ON MY OWN.

Okay, okay, okay. Shit. Okay. Options? The key's still in the robot. I still have limited access to the programming. Okay, okay, I *think* I can make this work.

I land my precious drone on the factory roof. I'm going to need both hands.

All right, step one. I bring up the robot's video input on my computer screen, because as much it hurts to admit, I think Bruno's glasses are broken beyond help and I'm not doing this without any visual feedback. So the robot's "eyes" are now mine too. And it's staring at Bruno. Which is sort of creepy.

Step two, the kill command. The one I've gotten oh so good at using. Except this time, it doesn't work. Oh god, why isn't working? The Commando begins moving to where Bruno's lying sprawled in the dirt and the prompt's showing that it's running one of its military self-defense programs. Oh shit. Hard restart, robot. HARD RESTART.

The robot keeps moving forward, its military defensive programming more or less giving me the middle finger at every new line command I enter.

It's four paces away from Bruno. Two.

«Sorry, dude,» I mutter as I do the only thing I can think of and run the original programming. You know, the one that made it go rogue in the first place.

I swear to god, the robot seems like it's considering my request, like it's tempted to give me the middle finger again. But then it stops walking, turns around, and starts moving to the fence. I almost fall out of my chair in relief. Dear god, I'm shaking again. Forget Bruno, *my* body is going to be a mess tomorrow.

Okay, okay, okay. I've got this. And for the record, I'm with Bruno on this one.

We are not going to lose this fucking robot.

While the robot is busy with the fence, I attempt to do the responsible friend thing and leave Bruno a message on his phone. My voice is so ridiculously shaky as I say, «Hey, Bruno, don't worry, I got things under control,» that I wouldn't believe me if I heard it. That is, if he actually gets the message. The cellular networks are shitty at best.

But Bruno's a smart guy. He'll figure it out. Or at least he'll be in suspense until he drags his sorry ass to my house and asks me himself. I'm sure I'll have a good story for him then.

Or at least, I hope so. God, I don't even want to think about what'll happen if I lose this robot. It'll be all my fault and people will never trust me with anything again and that will be the end of my very short career. Worse, there'll probably be families in neighboring towns that'll starve if one of our robots gets stolen.

Oh god, I think I'm going to be sick again. My mom is always nagging me to ask for help and shit. I could really use some help now, but my parents and brothers and roommate are all on the road being useful and stuff and my teammate and only other friend in this lonely town is knocked out cold.

I guess that means the girl behind the code will have to do the heavy lifting after all.

So, when the robot finishes tearing that hole in the fence and steps out into the outside world, I go with it.

Here's a moment of honesty for you: I've never been outside my little factory town. Yeah, I know. I mean I did as a little kid, when the roads weren't in such terrible condition and my family still took vacations to the mountains or the lake and stuff. But nothing cool. I've always wanted to see live concerts or try a fresh mango or something, but leisure traveling is not really a thing anymore. Especially not for a chick with mobility issues.

Besides, it would be ridiculous for me to leave. I mean, my family's here and it's a good community, even if 85% of the population doesn't remember I exist because most of the damn buildings have steps at the entrance.

That doesn't mean I haven't been working on my endurance, though. I walked almost two kilometers last week before my brother had to give me a piggyback ride home. My plan is to try to hike to the next town one summer, one way or another.

I imagine it'd be just like this, walking through the forest on a muddy but pretty even path, with nothing around except trees and squirrels and moss. Well, the robot's doing all the heavy lifting right now, but I'm really loving the video feed.

The trail the Commando's following is one of the delivery routes. According to the canning directory, it's about 23.4 kilometers until the next town and nothing but forest in the middle.

Where the hell is this robot going? I mean, I'm not complaining because this must be what freedom tastes like. But something about these hacks, I don't know, just feels *off.*

«Okay, listen dude, we need you back home,» I tell the robot's code.

This would be a million times easier if the paranoid equipment team would give me full access. Sometimes I think Bruno is little bit too charming and people forget I'm part of the team. Which, I mean, I am, but I'm more than just a name and a voice, you know? I know I can be useful even though I have to depend on other people for, well, mostly everything that happens outside my house. And with the town barely holding itself together, sometimes I feel like just another responsibility.

Bruno can be straight up macho sometimes, but right now I'd give anything to be as independent as he is.

Though in this case, it's probably a good thing that I'm not quite like Bruno. Read: Idealistic. Because . . . I might have been a bored kid once. Who taught herself the basics of hacking. A skill I think I'm going to have to use here because I'm not fucking losing this Commando unit.

So the robot walks and I type. It's slow going for both of us. The muddy trail is a bitch for the machine and my rusty hacking skills are definitely a bitch for me. The only thing I manage to access is the Commando's audio input and output. I test swear into the microphone and the robot suddenly becomes very foul-mouthed. All the birds in the trees flee.

Screw this. I try doing a hard restart again.

«Help me,» the robot says.

I pause mid-keystroke. What the hell? This is the second time the robot's said this, but the first time meaning sinks in. Factory robots are programmed to only use that phrase when they're stuck, like under a pallet or in a ditch. Which sometimes happens when they're delivering shipments between towns.

But why is it using it now?

Huh. Color me curious. So, for the first time in my very short career as a rogue robot hunter, I let a hacked machine be.

Okay, now I'm confused. Why the hell is the rogue robot standing in front of a pile of fallen trees, staring? Why does this Commando unit stare so much? I mean, there's nothing special about this spot. It's just another point on the muddy trail where on one side, the terrain drops off and becomes a steep rocky slope. Like the hundred other spots we've passed on this stroll.

Then the trees start to talk.

«Oh, thank god.»

«Holy shit!» I say and almost fall out of my chair again, forgetting I left the audio output is still on. It's become quite an indelicate robot in my care.

The forest goes silent for a moment and then . . . is that a dog barking?

«Who are you?» say the trees.

«Who the hell are you?» I say. Shit, my hands are shaking again. I might not be the most outdoorsy type of girl, but even I know trees aren't supposed to talk.

«I'm Evie Stevenson. I could use some help.»

Why does that name sound familiar? «Where . . . where are you?»

«Down here.» Someone—not me—tries to make the robot move its head, but the prompt keeps saying "Invalid command.»

«Damn computer. Actually do you mind?» the trees say.

«Mind what?» I say, but then I see that I've somehow gotten temporary access to the robot's motion control program. What the hell?

Cautiously, I have the robot step forward and tilt its head so that it gets a good look between two fallen trunks. Seriously, who is this terrible hacker?

Then I see the answer.

On a rocky ledge, about three meters below the robot, there's a lot of open, empty soup cans, one very muddy dog, and one exhausted, muddy white-haired lady.

«Holy shit,» I say. «*You're* the hacker?»

«Surprise,» Stevenson says. She looks like she's about to cry with relief. «Who are you?»

«I'm Gina. I work with Bruno Wong on the robot systems team.»

«Oh, I've heard of you. I thought you were just his assistant.»

I sigh. «Trust me, he's charming and all, but he's useless without his gadgets.» This makes Stephenson laugh. Sounds likes it's been a while since she had a good one. It sort of makes me happy cheering her up a bit. «I've brought you the robot you wanted, I guess.»

«Thank god. My tablet was starting to get super glitch-y.» She waves her handheld and the thing looks miserable too. Full of cracks. I wonder if I can fix it.

Suddenly, I feel really guilty about stopping the other four hacked robots.

«How did you end up down there, anyway?» I ask.

«I was accompanying a Commando delivering a shipment of cans. The factory needs someone to check on our customers occasionally.» The dog starts barking again and Stevenson beckons it over and puts an arm around it. «It was right before a storm hit and the winds got bad. We shouldn't have been out here.» She stares at her dog's ears. «The path got too muddy. The robot lost its footing and slipped but managed to stay on the trail. Me and Peanut lost our footing too, but we weren't so lucky. The damn robot kept going on its route even though most of the shipment was down here with us.»

That's when it clicks. «Oh, you're the missing employee.» I remember seeing her name on the factory employee list. Everyone on it had weird nicknames in parentheses. Stevenson's was 'Tougher than your rusty robot, damn it!'

«They thought you ran off,» I say.

Stevenson's expression is all sadness. «Did they really think I'd abandon them?»

«Yeah, they tend to assume the worst about people.»

«Or make snap decisions.»

I look around my lonely office. «Yeah.»

«Hey, I'd hire you. You figured this out with just an access key.»

That makes me smile. «Okay, listen, I'm going to sign off for a hot second. I think I just heard my roommate come home. Going to see if we can send some help.» I grab my crutches.

«Don't go. Please,» she says. I think it's the most desperate thing anyone has ever said to me. I get the feeling that this woman usually doesn't let anything stop her, but right now, she looks scared.

I put down my crutches. «Okay. What should I do? I'm sort of limited from over here.» And to prove my point, the temporary access I'm using for the robot's motion controls time out.

«Somehow I really doubt that,» Stevenson says. She's completely serious, too. «How about giving a lady and her dog a lift?» She taps her tablet. «What's your MAC address?»

I give it to her and seconds later a new window pops up on my screen. It's full access to the robot's program.

Holy shit. My hands are shaking again, but this time with excitement. *This* is what freedom tastes like.

I make good progress clearing the fallen trees, using the robot, of course. I even start to think this might be a straightforward rescue mission. But then a system warning pops up on screen.

Apparently, the Commando 237X thinks it's under attack.

Wait, what? Attacked by who?

Then, the robot's falling. Its video feed bounces as it hits the ground and I'm clutching the end of my desk. Seriously, this has to stop. My stomach cannot handle this shaky camera shit.

«Hang on for a sec, Ms. Stevenson,» I say through clenched teeth. Then I bite my lip, because oh god, I'm going to vomit again if I keep talking.

Fuck it, I'm just going to let the defense program do its thing because if you think you can just attack a rogue Commando in the middle of the woods, then you deserve to be crushed with robotic fury.

According to the code that I refuse to look away from, the robot picks itself up and spins around. It lifts its arms and brings them down over and over again.

Morbid curiosity makes me peek at the screen to see if the Commando has beaten the attacker into a pulp yet.

Then I see who the attacker is. Who is now lying directly under that angry metal arm.

Shit. Shit. Shit. Abort the program, robot. ABORT THE DAMN PROGRAM.

I hate déjà vu. Especially when it's a repeat of bad ideas. He's so fucking lucky though. The robot's arm stops centimeters above Bruno.

For a second, neither of us can breathe. Scratch that: it's all we can do.

«Worst. Fucking. Plan.» I gasp and the robot repeats my words.

Bruno blinks like he's just seen the sunshine. «Gina?»

«Who else, dude?»

He opens his mouth. Then closes it. Then opens it again. «What the hell, Gee?» he says, finally. «I thought you wouldn't . . . you couldn't . . .»

«Couldn't what? Do my damn job?»

He spots the key that's still sticking out of the robot's shoulder. «Oh.»

«What the hell's happening up there?» Stevenson calls up. Peanut is barking furiously.

«Who's *that*?» Bruno says, twisting around in the muddy path.

«Evie Stevenson. You know, the person behind the hacks. She's been stuck there for weeks and needed help to get out.»

«Oh. You figured it out without me,» Bruno says and damn it, he looks like an emo band member again.

«Don't move, dude, or I swear to god I will crush you.»

I walk the robot over to the ledge, which is mostly tree-free now. Carefully, I guide an arm down. Peanut is the first to come up. Then Stevenson.

«It worked,» she says when she's back on the path. Her eyes tear up. «This absurd plan actually worked. You're hired, Gina.»

We both laugh, while Bruno looks confused.

«Can I give you a lift?» I ask. Stevenson picks up Peanut and nods.

The Commando scoops them up in one hand and my stubborn, well-meaning teammate in the other.

Bruno keeps insisting that he can walk back on his own, which is sort of hilarious because right now, he has more bruises than charm.

«Chill, bro. I got this.»

My mom is right, it's important to ask for help when you needed it. But sometimes you have to make your own help too.

«Gina—» Bruno begins, but I cut off the audio input because I'm the girl behind the code and I can.

I check on them occasionally though. Bruno's pouting on the left and Stevenson is smiling in the nook of the robot's right elbow with her arms around Peanut, who is cautiously wagging his tail. They can't see me, but I'm smiling back at them.

This is what freedom is, isn't it?

Oh my god, I'm going to have so much fun programming these Commando units. I have *so* many ideas. Starting with creating the best routines possible and trying to fix that hole in the fence. And maybe next time Stevenson walks to the next town, I'll walk with her, one way or another.

Hannu Rajaniemi was born in Finland. At the age of eight he approached the European Space Agency with a fusion-powered spaceship design, which was received with a polite "thank you" note. Hannu studied mathematics and theoretical physics at the University of Oulu and Cambridge and holds a PhD in string theory from the University of Edinburgh. He co-founded a mathematics consultancy whose clients included UK Ministry of Defence and the European Space Agency. Hannu is the author of four novels including *The Quantum Thief* (winner of 2012 Tähtivaeltaja Award for the best science fiction novel published in Finland and translated into more than 20 languages). His most recent book is *Summerland* (June 2018), an alternate history spy thriller in a world where the afterlife is real. His other works include *Invisible Planets: Collected Fiction*, a short story collection. Hannu lives in the San Francisco Bay Area. He is a co-founder and CEO of HelixNano, a venture- and Y Combinator-backed biotech startup.

LIONS AND GAZELLES

Hannu Rajaniemi

Where do you think we are?" the young Middle Eastern woman with the intense eyes asked.

Jyri smiled at her and accepted a smoothie from a tanned aide. "I think this is a Greek island." He pointed at the desolate gray cliffs. They loomed above the ruined village where the 50 contestants in the Race were having breakfast. "Look at all the dead vegetation. And the sea is the right color."

In truth, he had no idea. At SFO, he'd been ushered into a private jet with tinted windows. The last leg of the journey had been in an autocopter's opaque passenger pod. The Race's location, like everything else about it, was a closely guarded secret.

But his gesture distracted the woman long enough for Jyri to steal a glance at her impossibly muscled legs. Definitely a myostatin knockout—a gene edit for muscle hypertrophy. Crude, but effective. He would have to watch out for her.

Suddenly, she zeroed in on something over Jyri's shoulder.

"Excuse me, need to catch up with someone. Nice talking to you."

Before he could say anything, she elbowed past him, filling a gap in the scrum around Marcus Simak, the CEO of SynCell—the largest cultured meat company in the world. She launched into a well-rehearsed pitch. Jyri swore. He, too, had been stalking Simak, waiting for an opening.

His mouth was dry. This was the most coveted part of the event: access to the world's most powerful tech CEOs, who could change your destiny with a flick of their fingers. He would only get one more shot before they started literally running away from him. Even worse, he wanted to run, too. Every muscle in his body felt like a loaded spring. The synthetic urge pounded in his temples, mixing with the din of the crowd.

Jyri fought it down, forced himself to take a thick minty sip of his smoothie and scanned the runners in the white mesh suits—ghost-like in the pre-dawn light—for a new target.

It was easy to divide the crowd into three groups: the entrepreneurs, like Jyri, here to show off their tech, hungry-eyed and ill at ease in their bio-hacked bodies; the hangers-on, company VPs and celebrities, with their Instagramfilter complexions and fluorescent tattoos; and finally, the Whales like Simak: the god-emperors of A.I., synbio, agrotech, and space.

Jyri spotted Maxine Zheng, Simak's upstart rival, just 10 feet away. Fresh-faced, petite, and wiry, her vast robotic cloud labs powered the Second Biotech Revolution—including Jyri's own startup, CarrotStick.

Jyri edged into the group caught in Zheng's trillion-dollar gravity. Up close, her skin had a glistening dolphin-like sheen. Allegedly, the Whales' edits included cetacean genes that protected them from cancer and other hoi polloi ailments.

Zheng was talking to a tall young man who was deathly pale but had the build of an Ethiopian runner: long legs and a bellows-like chest.

"That's neat," she said. "But I'm honestly more into neurotech, these days."

That was Jyri's cue. He pushed forward, the one-liner pitch ready. *Hi, I'm Jyri Salo from CarrotStick. We re-engineer your dopamine receptors to hack motivation—*

"Jyri!"

A strong hand gripped his shoulder. He turned around and almost swore aloud.

Not here, not now.

Alessandro Botticelli's white teeth flashed against a dark curly beard. He wore thick rings in stubby fingers, and his tattooed forearms rippled with muscle. His calves could have been carved from red granite. The ruddy hue of his skin was new. Probably an edit increasing red blood cell production for aerobic endurance, but these days you never knew.

"It's so good to see you, man!" The Italian gripped Jyri's hand and pulled him into a bear hug. "I can't believe you made it here, how are you doing, are you still working on that little company of ours? I love it!"

The familiar lilting accent made Jyri's teeth hurt. He cringed. *That little company. Of ours. Had he no shame?*

"Doing great," he said aloud, jaw clenched.

"That's awesome, man," Alessandro said. "Congrats. Me, I've just been so busy, it started to get too much, you know. So I decide to get in shape, really in shape. Maxine said I should do this, so here I am! It's going to be sick!"

Jyri could not face the white teeth, the green eyes, and looked away.

"I'm happy for you," he said.

"Hey, man, thanks! Do you want an intro? She's right there, and she'd probably be into what you've been working on."

Zheng was behind a wall of muscled bodies again. Jyri took a deep breath to say yes but tasted old anger. He shook his head.

"That's fine. We chatted already."

The Italian slapped him on the shoulder, hard.

"Awesome! Hey, we should really catch up! Maybe after this thing?"

"Sure." Jyri's stomach was an acid pit. He waved a hand at Alessandro and walked away, stumbling to the edge of the crowd. He took a long draught of his smoothie, but could barely get the viscous mixture down. He forced himself to drink it anyway. It was a dirty secret of ultrarunning that gorging gave you an advantage. Besides, it washed the taste of bile away.

Jyri had met Alessandro at one of the first networking events he had attended after he came over from Finland with little more than an idea. They bonded over their shared running hobby, Alessandro offered help with fundraising, and before Jyri knew it, the Italian was an equal co-founder of CarrotStick.

There was a time when they spent nearly every waking hour together, whiteboarding ideas, filing patents, sweating over pitch decks and grinding through endless investor meetings. It was a true Valley bromance. And then, when they got an offer to join the hottest accelerator in the Bay Area, Alessandro bailed on him, suddenly announcing he wasn't going to be able to do CarrotStick full-time. A VC firm they had pitched together had circled back to offer Alessandro a job. Apparently they had been impressed by his drive, and he claimed it was a better match for his life's mission. Whatever that was.

The accelerator turned CarrotStick down—given its "founder commit-ment issues"—and left Jyri scrambling for funding while burning through his savings and doing around-the-clock lab work. Alessandro wore his unchanging grin through the negotiations over his founder shares. He wore Jyri down, never raising his voice, and finally Jyri gave in to what advisers later told him was a ridiculous equity stake for an inactive founder.

Afterward, Jyri blocked Alessandro on every social media app. Every now and then, a piece of news leaked through his friends' feeds. Alessandro's new startup broke all sorts of Series A financing records; his popular science feed won a prize; he married a young VR yoga instructor who frequented both the exercise classes and fantasies of millions of men and women around the world.

Most gallingly, despite Jyri's efforts at a news blockade, he'd watched Alessandro brag in interviews about how his creativity and hard work had led to an early small success: a company called CarrotStick.

Jyri wouldn't let Alessandro ruin this, he decided. He'd get to Zheng on his own, no matter what. Fists clenched, he turned back to look at the crowd—and met the eyes of a woman sitting on a sun-bleached bench nearby.

Jyri frowned. She was neither an aide or a runner: She wore a loose, shape-less black dress that left her arms bare. They bore faded tattoos of bats. Her ashen hair stuck out in pigtails. She twirled an e-cigarette between her fin-gers. A knowing smile flickered on her lips.

Then it clicked. This had to be La Gama, the Doe. She was one of the legendary ultrarunners who had competed against the Tarahumara Indians in the canyons of northern Mexico, before climate change pushed them out and they gave up their millennia-long tradition of running.

Twelve years ago, the Whales had hired her to plan the biennial Races. She took all her experience from running races like Barkley Marathons and Badwater, and created an entirely new kind of contest for superhuman athletes. La Gama decided who ran based on an elaborate application that included biomarkers, genome sequences, and patents for the contestant's enhancements.

She stood up. Jyri's heart sank. The networking was over. Now, the only way to stand out from the startup pack and catch the Whales' attention was by running.

A hush spread across the square. The Whales turned to look at her, and all the other runners followed suit. For a moment, the only sound was the listless chirping of crickets.

"Running," she said, "used to be how we hunted. We evolved to chase things until they fell down from sheer exhaustion. The legacy is still there, in our upright spine, nuchal ligament, and Achilles tendons.

"All your lives, you have hunted with your brains. I want you to hunt and kill with your legs. Meet your prey."

She lifted a hand and hooked her fingers. A large pack of robots slunk out of the surrounding chalk-white ruins. Each was the size of a large antelope, had gazelle-like legs, and a black headless body. Hair at the back of Jyri's neck stood up. They moved too sinuously to be prey.

"Meet Goats 1 to 50," La Gama said. "They have full batteries. As do you. This Race is a persistence hunt. No stages, no set distances, no water stations, no time limit, no rest: Just run a goat down. The first one to bring back the contents of its belly wins."

She laid a hand on the smooth rump of the bot next to her, on a small cave painting-like drawing. A shutter irised opened on its side, then snapped shut before Jyri could see what was within.

La Gama slapped her hands. "That's it. The sun is coming up, and so, like lions and gazelles, you had all better be running."

The starting line was unmarked. They simply assembled in rows on the narrow road that snaked up toward the hills. The goatbot herd scampered past them and stopped on the crest of the first slope. The rising sun painted the cliffs purple.

They all knew the basic rules. No communications. No support crews. No pacers. Most importantly, no cybernetic enhancements or prosthetics—nothing with silicon or electricity. But anything biological was fair game: They were the Grail knights of the Second Biotech Age. They had backpacks with water and energy gels, and that was it.

Jyri peeked at the row of white-clad bodies. Alessandro's eyes were closed and his lips were moving. Was that hypocrite *praying*?

La Gama lifted the e-cig to her lips.

Jyri's anger mixed with the need to run, almost unbearable now. Every last bit of CarrotStick's cash and crypto had gone into fine-tuning his body—and more importantly, his brain.

The key ingredient was motivation.

La Gama took a deep pull from the e-cig. Its end glowed electric blue. She blew out one menthol-smelling wisp of smoke. That was the starting pistol shot.

The runners exploded into motion. Jyri's hungry feet devoured the road through the thin-soled Race shoes.

CarrotStick's actual mission was to make smart drugs that hacked the brain's reward circuits, and made you addicted to problem-solving, coding, A.I. algorithm design. It had been much harder than he had expected. The company's runway was almost gone when one of his investors told Jyri about the Race. He realized they could just copy the dopamine receptor variants of the greatest ultra-athletes of all time—the relentless drive that carried them through a 100-mile race.

That drive was Jyri's now. CarrotStick had manufactured a synthetic virus that carried the best receptor gene variant into his brain. Every step said *yes* in his mind. He felt like he could run forever.

The woman with the myostatin knockout legs was suddenly abreast of him, then edged ahead. On their own accord, Jyri's feet sped up. He gulped deep breaths, held on to the drive's reins. It was not time to push yet.

He slowed down and let her disappear over the hilltop ahead, just behind the goatbots.

Then Zheng, Simak, and the two other Whale CEOs zipped through the pack. Their legs and pumping arms were a blur. For them, this was a clash of the R&D departments of the vast companies whose avatars they'd become. It was pointless to compete with them. Their muscle cells were synthetic, their tissues fully superhuman.

At last, Jyri was over the first hill. The road turned left. The goatbots followed it, straight at the steep cliffs crested by white clouds. The Whales were tiny dots at their heels. The other runners followed, and the Race was on.

The sun blazed at their backs. The paved road turned into a rocky path. Jyri did not mind the climb. Early on in his training, he had done a lot of hill runs. It was a good way to get the biomechanics right.

He shifted his gait into full barefoot style, stepping down with the foot's edge, not with the heel, gliding, elf-like. Others in the runner pack found the path tougher, and even without quickening his pace, Jyri started to leave them behind.

The last ruined house on the outskirts of the village was surrounded by skeletons of real goats. The main goatbot herd was nowhere to be seen, but Jyri kept pace with a handful of bots ahead. They veered to the right, onto an even rockier path leading diagonally up the cliffside.

"Let's go get them, shall we?"

That slap on his shoulder, again. Alessandro. He was right at Jyri's heels and then ahead, sending up puffs of dust as he went. He'd come out of nowhere. He had pulled the old ultrarunner trick: running on the very edge of the path so you could not see him from ahead.

Jyri's gut churned at the sight of Alessandro's broad, receding back. This was too much. But the voice of reason cautioned there was a long, long road ahead. The goatbots had to have at least 20 hours of charge, and the island could have hidden recharging stations. The rough terrain promised microfractures, accumulating pain.

Jyri took a tiny sip of water from his Camelbak, not enough to hydrate, just to trick his brain into keeping thirst at bay. An ultrarun was an ever-expanding tree of decisions. Drink or not. Speed up or not. He reached a compromise. He would open the valves a bit, just to see if he could gain on Alessandro, and slow down if the effort seemed too much.

He increased the beat of his mental metronome to 180 beats per minute. He grazed his shin on a rock—he would be paying for that for many hours. But the pain mixed with the dopamine drumbeat gave him a burst of speed. His head lifted high. He pumped his knees in perfect running form. Suddenly, he was just behind Alessandro, who grunted in surprise.

Jyri could not resist lightly brushing Alessandro's shoulder as he edged past. Then he raced up the path, following the joyous zigzag dance of the goatbot ahead, toward the cliffs that now belonged only to him.

Fourteen hours into the race, Jyri lost the goatbot in the clouds.

The rapidly falling dusk made the island's contours soft and dream-like. The ascent had been grueling. The paths were unmarked and strewn with sharp-edged rocks. On the worst stretches, he had to run bent almost double to avoid the spiky branches arcing over the path.

But the dopamine drive kept him on the bot's trail all the way up to the plateau. It resembled a lunar landscape: large boulders, grey gravel. There were fields of tiny round pebbles that retained the sun's heat and were like hot coals to run on.

He glimpsed other runners only once: two dots moving along the coastline far below, chasing a goatbot side by side. They might have been Zheng and Simak, and Jyri wondered what they were doing, racing so close together. Unable to give an inch to each other, perhaps. Or was it something else?

Otherwise, it was just him and the bot. By now, he had a feel for the artificial animal's behavior. It stopped as if to rest whenever he slowed down, probably recharging in the sun. If he rushed it, it scrambled away.

That was the cruelty of La Gama's scheme. The only way to narrow the gap was to be relentless. The goatbot's pace was just above his fat-burning maximum heart rate of 140 bpm, and he was halfway through his energy gel packs.

A chilly wind picked up. Clouds started rolling across the plateau, swallowing the dark boulders. This was it, Jyri realized. The thing could not recharge in the mist. If he could get close and stay with it, it would be his.

He sprinted forward and followed the bot into the whiteness. It seemed like a demon now, making wild leaps over rocks that Jyri had to go around. Every now and then it melted into the fog, and Jyri's thundering heart skipped a beat. The beat of the dopamine drum pushed him forward, faster and faster, roaring inside his head.

And then the goatbot stumbled.

There was a clatter of metal and rocks. Jyri snapped back to knife's-edge alertness. The pebbles were wet and slippery, and he slowed down. A shape loomed ahead: a boulder. He swung around, and saw the bot barely 50 feet away, struggling to get up, its legs scraping against stone. This was it, he had to push now, just a little—

His leg muscles burst into cold flame. Then they seized up. The cursed rigs, the runner's rigor mortis.

No. I can do this.

The cold feeling spread into his brain, like the world's worst ice cream headache. Keep pushing, damn it.

But he could not.

He.

Could.

Not.

A treacherous pebble twisted beneath his foot. He fell forward, pressed his chin to his chest, cradled his head. One elbow banged on a boulder and went numb as he came down with a bone-jarring thump.

Then everything was quiet, except for the taunting clatter of the goatbot's hooves.

Jyri lay still, curled up on the damp stones. Everything hurt. But it wasn't the pain that made vomit rise into his throat, it was the *absence* of something.

The running fire had died.

He didn't *want* to get up.

He lay on the bare wet rock and tried to think through the pain, but thoughts fled him like the goatbot in the fog. He fumbled for the Camelbak's tube with numb hands. It slipped and he let it go.

Lying down meant the end. He would be one of the Race's failures, the non-finishers. From now on, investors he pitched to would give him one knowing look and pass. CarrotStick would die, and his future with it. He closed his eyes and fought back tears.

Only—it made no sense.

The drive to run was gone. Something was wrong with his dopamine receptors. Had his own immune system started rejecting them? He had undergone a regime to get his body to tolerate the new genes. Still, a sudden runaway immune reaction was not impossible. But he did not have a fever or any other symptoms.

That left one other possibility: a hostile biohack targeting the enhancement directly, maybe a biologic drug that blocked the receptor. And only someone with insight into CarrotStick's IP could have designed that.

Alessandro. Those slaps on the shoulder. The rings he wore. Alessandro would know enough about CarrotStick's receptors to leverage A.I. to design a molecule to target them.

The void in his head was filled by a flood of anger, red and warm and *good.*

He remembered what his first running coach had told him in high school. *The best fuel for finishing a race is hate.*

Jyri flopped to his belly, got to his knees, and stayed there for a moment, breathing hard. There was a boulder next to him. He embraced it like a lover, found a handhold, and pulled himself up. He leaned against the rocky surface, pressed his forehead against it. His legs wobbled but held.

He would make it back. He would prove what had happened, destroy Alessandro's name.

He squirted an energy gel pack into his mouth. The hydrogel-encapsulated carbohydrates released an expanding bubble of warmth in his belly.

He let go of the rock, took one step, then another, fighting the rigs. After three steps, it started to get easier.

After 10 steps, he broke into a jog.

The descent was even worse than the ascent. Most ultrarunners walked uphill and ran downhill, but the trail was so rough Jyri had to slow down to a walk to give the microtears in his muscles a chance to heal.

It was almost dark when he finally emerged from the cloud cover and realized he had made it further than he'd thought.

Only in the wrong direction.

The interior of the island spread before him in the pale moonlight: rolling hills, a dry riverbed, ash-colored dead trees. Jyri had taken a wrong turn on the plateau. The village was behind him. He would have to climb back up and retrace his steps—a 14-hour journey, back when he was still fresh.

The fatigue fell upon him, heavy and thick. He nearly stumbled again. What did he have left? In theory, 40 percent: That's what science claimed you could still draw upon when you reached all limits of endurance.

It would have to be enough.

He turned to start the long climb back up, and heard a shout from below. "Salo! Down here!"

Alessandro. He was perhaps 100 meters below Jyri, on rough but level ground. A short distance away from him was a herd of goatbots, at least 20 of them. As Jyri watched, Alessandro dashed toward them. The herd erupted in all directions. Alessandro chased one for a half-minute, but then it swerved away, and the herd simply regrouped behind the Italian. There was no way to tell which one it had been.

If Jyri had retained any strength, he would have laughed aloud. The goatbots were persistence-hunting *Alessandro*, playing a shell game that would eventually exhaust him.

Maybe I should just sit down and watch. The bastard deserved it.

"Salo, damn it, I need some help here! You can't catch these motherfuckers alone. They gang up and then there is no way to tell them apart. We need to work together. Come on!"

"If you'd wanted my help, maybe you shouldn't have screwed with me," Jyri shouted. His voice was hoarse.

"What the fuck are you talking about?"

Jyri was now halfway down to the clearing. He imagined punching Alessandro, but was not sure he could actually lift his arm.

"I know you hacked me," Jyri said. "Back in the village."

Alessandro stopped and stared at him, eyes wide.

"You too?"

"What do you mean?"

"My metabolism is fucked. I thought it was a malfunction."

Maybe it was just the moonlight, but Alessandro *did* look pale.

"Bullshit," Jyri said. He needed the hate, goddamn it. There were tears in his eyes.

"Think about it, Salo. It was that bitch La Gama. Those smoothies—why do you think they made us drink them? She was the only one who knew enough about our hacks to develop countermeasures against them."

The hate cooled down to an ember. Jyri stared at Alessandro. His hands started shaking.

Alessandro lowered his voice.

"Look, man. You're a good guy. I know I left you in a bad spot, back in the day." His grin was gone. "I don't need to cheat, damn it. But right now, I need *you*. So . . . I'm sorry I screwed you, all right?"

Jyri looked at him. One apology was not enough to erase five years of back-breaking work and anxiety. How stupid did Alessandro think he was?

Then he remembered Zheng and Simak, running in tandem.

"This is the whole point of the Race," Jyri said. "La Gama gave us a challenge that's impossible to meet individually, no matter how good your enhancements are. The Whales must be hating it."

He looked at Alessandro's leonine face. There had been no malice in the betrayal. Out here, it was easier to see it. Just an animal, running after the prey, as was its nature.

All of a sudden, Jyri felt less heavy.

"That's why we didn't make good partners, man," Alessandro said. "You were way too clever for me."

Jyri took a deep breath.

"All right," he said. "Let's hunt."

It took Jyri and Alessandro several tries to separate a goatbot from the herd. One of them rushed the herd and chose a target; the other intercepted whenever it tried to join the others. It took bursts of speed Jyri would not have imagined he still possessed. Alessandro's face was purple, all traces of arrogance wiped away by pain. Between dashes, they shared their remaining energy gels and water.

By 2 in the morning they finally had a goatbot on the run. The herd followed close behind, so they could not let their attention waver.

Forty percent, Jyri kept thinking, as they raced along the dry riverbed. This was what he imagined the land of the dead was like, arid and endless.

Yet, somehow, he found himself enjoying the run. His mind was quiet. How long had it been since he'd run in flow, disappearing into a task at the edge of his ability? The Finnish word for thinking was *ajatella*. It originally meant harrying one's prey until the end.

Their lungs worked like bellows. There was no breath for words, but Alessandro was a silent presence at his side, focused on the same goal. With every synchronized step they took, the anger and the anxiety leaked out.

After a while, there was only the satisfaction of joint pursuit: the bot's indistinct shape ahead, the rattle of rocks beneath their feet.

The coastal cliffs were rimmed with light when the goatbot finally slowed, collapsed in a tangle of limbs, and lay still.

Jyri stared at it, trying not to collapse himself as his heart rate slowed and the blood pressure in his limbs dropped. Alessandro was doubled over, hands on his knees, as he retched.

"You . . ." the Italian waved breathlessly. "You . . . do the honors."

Jyri half-walked, half-hopped to the machine. Up close, it looked even more like an animal. Its black carapace moved up and down, as if it was breathing. Gingerly, he touched the white stick figure on its flank. A round hole snapped instantly open. He reached inside, and his fingers found two objects: a vial filled with a clear liquid and a pneumatic injection needle.

Alessandro wiped vomit from his beard and looked at him.

"What are you waiting for?" he asked. "It's the antidote, stupid."

Jyri weighed the vial and the needle in his hand. Was this some final trick? Did it even make sense that there would be a universal antidote to hacks against all the contestants' different enhancements? *Of course.* The smoothies: They were probably probiotics with bacteria producing a variety of customized biologics in the runners' guts. They would have a universal genetic off-switch, triggered by whatever the vial contained.

One shot, and the drive to run would be his again. And yet there was something pure about the night air, the light in the horizon, the dust on his face. He was *here*, not in the anxiety-ridden past or uncertain tomorrow. Did he really want the overriding, relentless drumbeat back? He was in pain, but this pain was something he had chosen. It belonged to him.

He shook his head and handed the antidote to Alessandro.

"You do it," he said. "I'll find my own way back."

The Italian looked at him, green eyes unreadable. With a practiced move, he filled the vial and found a vein in his arm. The clear liquid went in with a hiss. Alessandro took a deep breath. His skin flushed, and he stretched expansively.

"I'll tell them to come get you," he said. "Find some shelter and stay there. And I'll do that intro to Zheng, and brag about your mad motivation-hacking tech. I know you were bluffing earlier about talking to her, but you should. I think she'll be interested."

Jyri nodded and raised a hand.

He watched Alessandro's white form recede into the distance until he disappeared behind the withered foliage on the dry riverbank.

He waited until the sun came up. Long shadow-fingers stretched across the valley, and the coastal cliffs glinted golden. A mirage hovered above the dry expanse of the island. It looked like a ghost city, with floating towers and pillars.

Jyri felt empty and light. His Camelbak was dry, and he let his backpack fall to the ground. *Gazelle or lion*, he thought.

Then he started running.

Alastair Reynolds was born in Barry, South Wales, in 1966. He studied at Newcastle and St. Andrews Universities and has a Ph.D. in astronomy. He stopped working as an astrophysicist for the European Space Agency to become a full-time writer. *Revelation Space* and *Pushing Ice* were shortlisted for the Arthur C. Clarke Award; *Revelation Space, Absolution Gap, Diamond Dogs*, and *Century Rain* were shortlisted for the British Science Fiction Award, and *Chasm City* won the British Science Fiction Award.

DIFFERENT SEAS

Alastair Reynolds

Twelve hours out from Valparaíso Lilith saw her first and only Aurora Australis. Spokes of pastel color came wafting out of the south, like the light spillage from some vast, silent carnival going on over the horizon. Pretty good way to end the voyage, Lilith thought, crawling into her bunk on the *Dolores*.

She opened up her pad to send a message back to her sister.

Hey, Gabriela. Nearly done with this gig. Still sorry you didn't make it to Montevideo in time, but—and don't take this the wrong way—it hasn't been as bad being on my own as I thought it would be. The ship starts feeling like a home, and after a while you get used to its sounds and moods. You see some beautiful things. Sunsets, sunrises, flying fish, pods of dolphins racing alongside us, oh, and tonight's light-show of course. And it's so quiet, with just the slap of the waves, the rippling of the sails, the occasional hum as she spools in a sail or adjusts her trim. I know it's only been a few weeks but I think I'm going to have a hard time sleeping on dry land, especially in a busy, noisy city like Valparaíso. Guess I'll find out tomorrow. Won't be there long, though. I'll close up the paperwork with Gladius, make sure the money's in my account, then book myself onto the Pan-Pacific slev. Tourist class, admittedly. Do you still think you'll be able to meet me in Quito? It would be good to see a friendly face before I go under the—

A window popped up to block her message—something about an all-sector weather advisory. Lilith closed it without reading. She had studied the meteorological conditions before she came off deck, seeing only clear skies and calm seas, nothing that was going to cause her any difficulties between now and port. There was just enough of a breeze to help the clipper along.

But later that night—long after she'd completed and sent the message to her sister—something jolted her awake. Her first thought was that—improbable as it seemed—they'd somehow crashed into something. But it wasn't quite that kind of bump. Different—but no less ominous.

More like a door, suddenly slamming in an empty house.

The jolt had startled her so badly she had banged her forehead against the coving over her bunk. A nice bruise by tomorrow, she thought, dabbing at the tender area. It felt damp. Maybe she'd even cut the skin, drawn a little blood. Might need disinfecting. Somewhere on this ship there had to be a first-aid kit. That could wait, though.

Why was the room tilting?

She went up on deck, wondering—dreading—the possibility that they might have been holed, that the clipper was taking in water. But as she looked along the length of the hull, she decided that the problem had to lie somewhere else. The rudder was hard over—she could see the actuator rams, pushed to their maximum limits. Hard to . . . she had to think for a second. Long after she'd memorized the names of the masts and yards and sails, the mizzens and jibs and sprits, the stupid business of left and right—or the nautical equivalents—was still foxing her. Starboard. That was it. Actuator hard to starboard as if the ship was making a sharp starboard turn. But no such instruction had been given, and there had been nothing about a course change in the overnight schedule.

Ok, she thought. Emergency course change, for whatever reason. Such things happened.

But it wasn't that, either.

The sails were fighting the rudder, trying to hold the clipper on something like its original course. That was the reason she was crabbing so badly, with a tilt to the deck. Like a lame dog dragging itself along the sidewalk.

But the sails were only able to correct part of the problem. The clipper was still veering, nosing away from Valparaíso and in the general direction of . . .

Lilith swore.

Not good. *Not good at all.*

The auroral show was done. Full dark to the south, a scattering of stars overhead, faint intimations of dawn to the west. To the northeast, where she was now headed, a series of rectangular black shapes sat so still and heavy in the water that they might have been parts of a reef.

Lilith went back down to the cabin, fumbled on the microphone and headset, wincing as she brushed the sore spot on her forehead. "Gladius," she said. "Come in, Gladius."

"Gladius Mercantile," came the reply. "We read you, Lilith. What's your status?"

"My status is . . . I'm not too sure. I think something's gone wrong with the ship. The rudder's jammed over. We should be on a direct course for Valparaíso, keeping well clear of the offshore raft, but it looks as if we're steering right into it."

There was a pause—long enough to make her uncomfortable. "Affirmative, Lilith. We have a diagnostic update. You no longer have rudder authority. The solar weather event may have caused a voltage spike in your power bus."

She fingered her bruise, wincing as she picked away a strand of hair that was sticking to it.

"The what event?"

"The solar weather event. Biggest in a hundred years, they're saying. Major auroral storms. Power blackouts where the grid hasn't been hardened, comms and navigation dropouts, satellites offline, spacecraft damaged, the works. Not the end of the world, but it's going to take a day or two to get everything back up and running."

Lilith's perspective underwent a slow, humbling readjustment, like a picture zooming-out from a close-up. Dented forehead aside, her problem was evidently small and local compared to that patchwork of screw-ups.

Grinning—not out of humor, but sheer exasperation—she looked up and down the long length of the tilting deck, taking in the masts, the winches, the salt-lashed control machinery, the lading hatches, the absolute absence of another human being. Beyond the deck, the tilt of the horizon, and—closer now, she swore—the black presence of the Valparaíso Offshore Raft Farm.

"That . . . advisory . . . must have come in after I hit the sack." Lilith swallowed hard.

"There wouldn't have been much you could have done other than ride it out, anyway. The *Dolores* is one of the older clippers in the fleet—doesn't have all the latest redundancies. If you have a rudder impairment, sail control will default to a safe condition. You may have to sit tight for a few more hours before we can get a repair team to you. May get a little queasy, riding the swell, but at least you're not going to crash into anything."

"When you say sail control . . ."

"Upon detection of a fault condition the sails will spool in automatically. You needn't worry about that."

"They're not," Lilith answered. She checked again, just to make sure her own eyes weren't playing games. "The sails are all run-out. Mains, gallants, royals, spritsails. Nothing's spooling in. Other than this tilt to the deck, and the rudder being jammed, we're still sailing hard. And it looks to me as if we're running straight into the raft."

Now the voice had gone from harried but friendly to slightly concerned and trying to hide it.

"Sails all still deployed, you say?"

"I'm not making this up, Gladius. We're at full sail."

There was a silence.

"Just a moment, Lilith."

The moment became a minute, then two, then a third, while whoever was on the other end consulted with somebody, who—she guessed—had to consult with someone else, up and up the chain. It was not a pleasant feeling, suddenly feeling herself coming to the attention of people to whom she had previously meant nothing, just an anonymous caretaker contractee on a single-trip voyage.

"Um, Lilith?"

"Hello."

"We confirm your situation. You have a cascade failure across a whole level of sail-control systems. They can't be spooled-in, not without a patch repair. We also confirm your present trajectory."

"Then—politely—what you're saying is, I'm pretty screwed?"

"We are coordinating a response, Lilith. If we can regain rudder control, then at least you can steer."

"Good. You'd better get that repair team out here faster than you were planning."

She heard the catch in the voice, the slight hesitation. "There's no way we can get anyone warm to you in time, I'm afraid—not with things stretched the way they are." There was a pause. "But we have the next best thing."

She unlatched the bright yellow plastic suitcase from its stowage rack, then lowered it down on the cabin floor until it was horizontal and she could break the foil anti-tamper seals and flip open the lid.

Steadying herself on a handrail, she stepped back.

The proxy gave a twitch and began to extract itself from its foam matrix in the case, unbending and elongating like a clever puzzle. It stepped out of the case, rising to its full height. It was adult-humanoid in its general size and proportions, with two legs, two arms, a torso and a blank curving mask instead of a face.

The face glowed blue, with a tumbling egg-timer. "Please stand by," the proxy said. "Global Workspace is establishing a telepresence link to this unit."

She stood by. The blue mask brightened to flesh tones. A young woman's face appeared, distorted as if she had her nose pressed against glass.

"Hi," the proxy said, in a higher, perkier voice. "I'm Kyleen. They tell me you've got something wrong with your boat?"

"It's a clipper, not a boat."

"My bad. Job came in and I figured it was something I could bid on, without looking too closely at the details. Wasn't in the mood to be too picky. Are you part of the crew?"

"I *am* the crew," Lilith said. "Caretaker assignment. The *Dolores* mostly runs itself."

"Kyleen Chalecki." The proxy extended a hand, its fingers arranged in a perfectly human configuration. "And you'd be . . . ?"

"Lilith Morisette." Ignoring the invitation, she turned to leave the cabin where she had opened the suitcase. She figured the young woman driving the proxy was twenty, twenty-one at most—spoiled brat, gap year, daddy probably ponied up for the neural mesh. Lilith glanced back at the proxy. "How much they tell you?"

"Getting a briefing update. Looks like you got some EMP burnout in your power bus. That was one hell of a coronal shitstorm last night. I saw a big aurora over Kagoshima once, but . . ." The proxy followed her up a steep, ladder-like staircase, out onto the grip-coated deck, then looked around, head swivelling. "Hey, this is a neat ship. Bigger than I thought. Sails and all. Old-school. What did you say her name was?"

"*Dolores.*" Lilith eyed the angle of the deck, the sea condition, the distant but looming presence of the raft. "It's a cyber-clipper, Gladius Mercantile."

"Carrying what—a boat-load of dumb-ass tourists?"

"No, the only dumb-ass tourist is me." Lilith let that remark sit there for a few seconds. "This is a cargo run. High-value, low bulk commodities."

"Who the hell sends cargo by sailing ship?"

"The economics work. Anything that isn't perishable, that won't go through a pipeline, and which can't be fabbed or printed locally, this is the cheapest, cleanest way."

"And what are we hauling today, *mon Capitaine*?"

Lilith had examined the manifest, although the goods themselves were boxed and crated down in the holds. "Artisan stuff. High-end handmade goods. Nice fabrics. Pottery, wine, oils, carpets."

"Got any crazy old clocks?"

Lilith cocked an eye back at the proxy. "What?"

"Nothing, just some article I read during downtime once."

"You have downtime? Lucky you."

They went aft and looked up at the shoebox-sized control module, ten meters up the fine carbon spar of the mizzenmast. It wasn't sparking now, but it was visibly scorched. "Okay," Kyleen said, with a doubtful edge to her voice. "That's our boy. Fix that, and you've got your rudder back. Even if the sails don't spool back in, at least you've got some control."

"And fixing it requires what, exactly?"

"Nothing hard. Something in that box is toast, and needs to be swapped out. Snag is one of us is going to have to monkey up there and change it."

"Then I hate to break it you, but you're the expendable one."

"True, but there's another snag. Once that rudder comes back, it's going to default to its neutral position, changing the whole balance of the boat . . . ship . . . clipper thing."

"The *Dolores* will handle that."

"Not fast enough, according to this. Whole situation is outside of its normal control envelope. But I can run a manual override—start bringing the sails around just before you make the swap. Should go smoothly, if we time things right."

"Why don't I do the sail part?" Lilith asked.

Kyleen made the proxy give a very humanlike shrug. "I'm no expert, but that's three sets of big flappy sails that would need to be adjusted simultaneously. How many sails are there on each of those sticky-up things?"

"And you think you've got what it takes?"

"Don't need to. They're patching the necessary routines right through to the proxy. All I have to do is be at the control station and coordinate with you." The proxy looked around. "Now, would that be at the sharp end or the blunt end?"

They went to a spares compartment where Kyleen identified the replacement part that Lilith was meant to swap into the control box. It was a fuse-like thing about the size of a thumb, with electrical contacts at either end. "Some sick joke putting that thing ten meters up in the air, but I guess they had their reasons. Seen worse design flaws on spacecraft. Here, take two, just in case you fumble one."

"I'm not fumbling anything."

But Lilith took two anyway, inserting them into different pockets just to be safe. She dug out a pair of insulated gloves. Then she found the safety harness and buckled it on, double-checking that the clips and wires were all ship-shape, before stationing herself at the base of the mizzenmast. She looked up, forcing herself to think only of what needed to be done at the box, rather than the height she needed to climb or the increasingly drunken tilt of the mast. Wasn't so far, she told herself.

"Those black things . . ." Kyleen said, turning the curve of her face out to sea.

"Old supercarriers. Hundreds of them, lashed together and turned into a floating raft farm. Holds made into protein vats. Mostly a big mass of dumb metal we don't want to run into."

"I think I saw it from space. Or maybe it was some other one. Lot of coast-lines to remember."

"Been into space, have you?"

"Once or twice."

"Good for you." Lilith's answer was laced with sarcasm. "Can we get on with this, instead of dropping hints about how fabulously well-travelled we are?"

"I guess you haven't been into space, then."

"You guessed right," Lilith said.

The mast had safety tie-ins every couple of meters all the way up. There were two clips on the harness, so she need never be completely unsecured. There were also handholds jutting out of the mast on either side, alternating as they rose, which would double as footrests once she was off the deck.

The proxy stood at the sail-control pedestal, looking up as Lilith clipped on and commenced her climb. Hand on grip, hand onto next grip, feet onto the grip-coated footholds. Off the deck and rising, trying to ignore the fact that her belly was squirming and her thigh muscles already felt like jelly. She stretched to clip on the second safety line, went one rung higher and then unclipped the second one. Still safe. But it was surprising how far down the deck already looked. How far down and how narrow, like a target it would be easy to miss.

"You're doing good," the proxy called up.

"I know what I'm doing," Lilith answered, gritting her teeth. But she needed some sort of distraction to take her mind off the vertigo. "Why did you ask me about a crazy clock?"

"Oh, because of that article. Must be a decade back, when I read it. About some ship that went down in the Mediterranean."

"Ten years ago?" Lilith asked, wondering what sort of age Kyleen had to be if she had been on "downtime" that many years back. Downtime implied employment, employment implied experience . . . age, as well she knew.

"Not the ship, no. This was *thousands* of years back. Wine-dark seas and all that. The stuff they found on it, when they went down with divers. Some old clock computer thing, half turned to stone, that was the main thing, but also jars of oil and wine and rope. Pottery. A lot of pottery. Just like now. You ever sailed in the Med?"

"This isn't what I do," Lilith said. "I'm just nursing the *Dolores* on this one trip. Once we get into Valparaíso, I'm out of contract."

"Pity. Seems like a cool sort of gig to me."

"It's not a 'gig,'" Lilith said, stubbing out the flicker of guilt she felt when she remembered her letter to Gabriela. "No one does this for fun. I don't get to bid on jobs in Global Workspace, the way you just did. I'm not meshed. I take the few crumbs offered to me, and this was one of them."

"Why aren't you meshed?"

"Not everyone in the world gets to be meshed." But feeling that she owed Kyleen at least a shred of clarification, she went on: "I have cerebral palsy. Mild enough that you won't notice, most of the time, just some fuzziness in my motor control and coordination. Enough to stop me being meshed, not so bad that I don't have to pay my own way in the world." Adding, under her breath: "Not that you'd know about that, I guess."

"The thing that's in your head—there's a cure for it, right?"

"Cure for anything, you've got deep enough pockets." Keen to get this over with, Lilith stretched for a higher handhold than was wise. She slipped. The safety line caught her before she dropped more than a meter, but the jolt was still hard enough to rattle her. Catching her breath, trembling in all her limbs, she hugged her body against the mast.

"You all right?"

Lilith kept her eyes fixed on the control box, still a few meters above her present position.

She forced her breathing to something like a normal rhythm.

"Yeah."

Pushing aside all other thoughts, refusing to think of falling or drowning, she completed the climb to the control box. It was still a reach, but with the crossjack yard of the mizzen topsail only just overhead, she had no inclination to go any higher.

Using gloved fingers, she flipped open the weatherproof access hatch on the shoebox-sized unit. Inside was a bewildering mass of electronics, with clear signs of heat damage around the modular unit she was meant to replace.

"You ready?" Kyleen called.

Lilith grunted back her acknowledgment.

"Do your stuff."

"I'm starting to move the sails. On my mark, make the swap."

On the deck below, servos hummed and winches alternately tightened and slackened sail-control lines. Above Lilith, the sails began to move, ruffling in the wind, the shift in forces already making the tilt of the deck and masts worse than it had been.

"Now," Kyleen said.

Lilith wrapped the fingers of her insulated glove around the blown component and snapped it out of its ceramic housing. No fine motor control needed for that. It tumbled away, falling out of her line of sight. She had to hold on even tighter now, her own weight wanting to pull her away from the mast. She reached for the spare part, got a good, firm grip on it, not wanting to have to fall back on the second spare, and stretched to fix it into the control box. The contact clips were tight. Grunting with the effort of straining and stretching, she pushed hard. With a solid "clunk" the component locked home. Instantly, a flicker of lights signified that something new was going on in the box.

She shouted down: "It's in!"

Half a second later she felt the rudder return to its neutral position. The jolt made its way through the entire flexing fabric of the clipper. The ship seemed to squirm, eel-like, a shivery twist or torque running through the hull, the mast quivering under the abrupt shift in load.

The sails were still moving—trying to compensate for the rudder's action. But not quickly enough. The mast was tilting in the other direction now, Lilith like an ant clinging to a clock hand as it ticked through high noon. The mast had been leaning out over her before, then for a moment it was vertical, and now it was angling gradually away from the zenith. Perched on the top of this flattening boom, Lilith ought to have felt less precarious, but the sight of that rising bank of sea tied a fresh knot in her guts.

"Hold on," Kyleen called. "I'm correcting!"

As if there was any thought in her head but holding on. The mast was more than forty-five degrees from vertical now, tilting inexorably to the horizontal. Spray lashed at her. The waves were running fast, pink-topped as stripes of dawn banded the eastern horizon. She could almost reach down and touch the sea.

But the tilt reached a limit and held. Lilith waited, eyes on the horizon, hardly daring to breathe. The mast began to press up from below. By slow, majestic degrees the clipper was starting to right itself. Gradually something eased in the *Dolores*, a crabbing stiffness falling away. Lilith stayed quite still, feeling bound to some lively animal that was freeing itself from lameness, stretching its limbs and muscles, eager to sprint. From one breath to the next the clipper was rediscovering itself, marrying itself to the wind, threading the sea.

Lilith climbed down from the mizzenmast, planting her feet wide on the rumbling deck. The wave tops beat a sharp, fast tattoo against the hull. The sails thundered as they snapped tight. The rigging sang its own song. Kyleen was just stepping back from the sail controls, arms spread with a sort of cautious wariness, like a conjuror surprised that a trick had gone as well as it had.

"You did it," Kyleen said.

Lilith laughed, grinning with the sudden release of tension. "I guess I did. We did."

"You know this ship," Kyleen said. "Will she be all right now?"

"I think so." Lilith looked to the bow. "She's steering around the raft now, the way she was meant to. She'll get us to port." She nodded at the other woman, feeling more charitable to her now that they were out of harm. "You had to move fast with those sails. Was that all automatic?"

"No," Kyleen said, sounding out of breath. "We were a little off-script back there. Had to . . . improvise."

"You did all right. Better than all right, I guess."

"Like I said, it's not too unfamiliar. Winches . . . rigging." She paused, coughing lightly. "Different ships, different seas."

"Different weather, too." Lilith looked carefully at the other woman, the face pressed behind the proxy's mask, seeing something in the face she had not noticed before, or which had not been present. A strain, a tiredness, sweat on the brow and a redness in the eyes. "You all right, Kyleen? You sound like you need to sit down, catch your breath. Don't blame you; it was intense back there. Or are they going to switch you onto another contract any minute now?"

"No . . . this is my last gig of the day." Kyleen's breathing was audibly heavy now, as if she had been running up a hill. "I've asked them to hold the telepresence link for now. They've . . . obliged." She coughed and turned the cough into a hacking laugh. "Big deal. Really fucking generous of them."

Lilith nodded. She had not needed the proxy until now, and she supposed it would put itself back into the box once the link was deestablished, becoming just a folded pile of metal parts until the next time it was activated.

"I'm glad you took the gig."

The face looked at her. "Really?"

"I know I didn't come across that way. But I'm not meshed, and sometimes that makes me feel like a second-class citizen. Third class, maybe. When you came in . . . all eager . . ." Lilith looked down at her hands, avoiding the other woman's eyes. "I can't have what you've got. Not yet. Not until I've earned enough to get my head fixed, and once that's done I'll have to start over, saving up all over again for the mesh. From Valparaíso I was going to skimp and save and work my way north. Find some cheap clinic in Quito. Then, when I'm meshed, ride the thread. The up and out."

"You'd do well, I'm sure. But it isn't all roses working in space." She gave a cough and a wheeze. "Just so you know."

"I don't need to be told that, Kyleen." A small part of her resentment flared up again. "Isn't all roses down here, either."

"You mind if we sit and watch the lights for a bit?"

"Your call."

They moved to the side of the deck, sitting down with their legs dangling under the railings, side by side, the warm woman and the robot proxy.

"Something you probably ought to know," Kyleen said eventually. "I'm dying up here." She gave out another coughing, wheezing approximation of laughter. "I don't mean it metaphorically. I'm actually dying. We got hit pretty bad by that solar weather event. We were on a cargo haul, making a close-approach loop around Earth, swinging by on our way to Venus. Deep System Bulk Carrier *Ulysses*."

"You mean . . . you're in space right now?"

"Told you I'd been once or twice, didn't I? Guess there was a little understatement there, given that space is where I've spent most of my adult existence. Anyway, we're screwed. Unlike you, we had the multiple redundant systems. Our numbers still came up. Fried one thing, then the next—all the way down. Steering control, life support, all knocked for six." She paused, breathing heavily, but Lilith said nothing, waiting for the other woman to find her breath again. "Minor emergency under ordinary circumstances, just like your stuck rudder. Send out a rescue tug, whatever it takes. But they can't help us this time. Too many other deserving cases, not enough spare hands to go around." She gave a sigh, somewhere between fatigue and acceptance. "And that's fine, I knew the score. And I can't complain. I've seen some sights, Lilith. Some grand old sights. I've set foot on Mars. I mean, really *stood* on Mars—not just by proxy. Seen the rings of Saturn close enough that I felt I could scoop them up, a fistful of fairy glitter. Punched a ship right through a volcano on Io. Swam in Europan seas. Meshed, that time, but it felt no different to being there. And it's all good. It was all worth it. I'm not going to bitch and moan because my number came up today."

After a silence, Lilith said: "Are you serious?"

"Never been more serious, *mon Capitaine.* We're on reserve air now, and it's running thin. Fingertips already turning blue. Crazy thing is, comms have stayed viable the whole time, so we can talk to whoever we like. Messages home, fond farewells. Some of the rest of us . . . well, they've got their own way of coping. Can't say I judge 'em. But I figured, six hours . . . maybe less . . . still within telepresence range . . . why not do something good, something useful?"

"Don't you have messages to send?"

"Not really," Kyleen said. "Always been a loner, I guess. My friends are on this ship. As for family ties . . ."

The sky was paling now, shading by the minute from a deep blue to a translucent rose, lights on the headland over Valparaíso coming on in neat-bordered swatches, as power flooded back to whole districts of the city. Civilization fighting its way back out of the darkness. Homes, people, families, friends and lovers, kitchen smells, warm bread, roasting coffee, busy plans for another day.

"Why me?" Lilith asked.

"I looked through a bunch of jobs. Needed something that matched my skill set." She wheezed, coughed. "Also something that wasn't going to take all day. Saw your predicament bob up the list and thought . . . why not?"

"You never said."

"Figured your rudder had priority." The proxy elevated its hand, rested it on Lilith's wrist. "Look, we did it. Got you out of trouble. Saved your skin, and probably this ship as well. That's a good result for the both of us."

Lilith watched the lights flicker on across another area of the city. "They're getting things straight. Can't they do something for you now?"

"Not a chance. Believe me, we've looked at the options. But it's simple kinematics: we're already going too fast." The hand moved onto Lilith's fingers. "You serious, about doing the up and out?"

"I was," Lilith reflected.

"Then go for it. Get to Quito. Get your head straightened out. Get meshed. It doesn't hurt, and you can always have it reversed if you don't like it. But I think you will." The hand squeezed, gently. "Earth's not so bad. A view like this, the sea air, a clear morning, that city ahead of us? I'd take that. But there's plenty more to see out there."

"I believe you," Lilith said. "And I'll do it. Try, at least. I think I ought to get a bonus for not losing this cargo, and when we . . ." She stopped, sensing—perhaps subliminally—some change in the deportment of the proxy. "Kyleen?"

The face turned to her—blue again, with nothing of Kyleen behind the curving mask. "Please stand by," the default voice said. "Global Workspace has suspended the telepresence link to this unit due to haptic lag. We are attempting to find a more efficient routing."

"Don't bother," Lilith said quietly. "She's too far out."

Or gone, she supposed. Out of air, out of consciousness, or snapped from the link because the comms on the *Ulysses* had finally given out, along with the other systems.

Then, to herself, but also to the sea, and the sky, and the lights of Valparaíso: "Thank you, Kyleen. I won't forget."

Something was rising over the headland, slowly and smoothly enough that it seemed to be following its own invisible groove. It brightened as it climbed. She watched the ascending star, debating the likelihood that it might be Kyleen's ship, the Deep System Bulk Carrier *Ulysses* hair-pinning around the Earth on its way to Venus. It would have been satisfying to think that was the case, poetic at least, but Lilith knew better.

All the same, she followed the spark to the zenith, and overhead, until with no great fanfare it dropped into the Earth's shadow, and was gone.

Aliette de Bodard lives and works in Paris. She has won two Nebula Awards, a Locus Award, and three British Science Fiction Association Awards. Her space opera books include *The Tea Master and the Detective*, a murder mystery set on a space station in a Vietnamese Galactic empire, inspired by the characters of Sherlock Holmes and Dr. Watson. Recent works include the Dominion of the Fallen series, set in a turn-of-the-century Paris devastated by a magical war, which comprises *The House of Shattered Wings*, *The House of Binding Thorns*, and forthcoming *The House of Sundering Flames*.

AMONG THE WATER BUFFALOES, A TIGER'S STEPS

Aliette de Bodard

I n the days where the earth was newly broken and the living still remembered the sleepers walking the world, a water buffalo found a tiger in a coffin.

It was in the days where the sleepers' land purged itself of all it could not bear, coughing out into the periphery seeds and parts by the thousands—and also those sleepers that were unsuitable or broken or merely in excess. The tiger was one of these last, though who knew what kind?

Now, tigers are the natural enemy of the buffalo, and this buffalo belonged to a large herd—rain had fallen in abundance upon the parched earth, and the herd was full of eager young ones, barely aware enough to realise all the dangers the world now held. So the buffalo was ready to kill the tiger, or to push the coffin back into the dome, into the sleepers' land. But as the tiger unfolded his body and stalked, all grace and elegance, from the broken coffin, the buffalo saw, for a bare, suspended moment, a shadow of what the world had been before its breaking—green grass and clear water, and the memory of sleepers that were as gods.

And, so, in spite of her misgivings, the buffalo took the tiger back to her herd.

How Kim Trang got to the pool:

After the sun goes down, the girls huddle together in the remnants of a house by the sea—every screen, every scrap of metal since long scavenged to keep their own bodies going—and tell each other stories. Of animals, and plants, and of the world before and after the Catastrophe. Thuy is outrageously good at this. Her sight allows her to read the other girls' microscopic cues from heartbeat to temperature of skin, and adapt her tales of spirits and ghosts for maximum effects. Ngoc He stutters, barely hiding the tremors in her hands—nerve-wires that broke down and that she hasn't yet scavenged replacements for—but she has the largest range of tales of any of them. Ai Hong speaks almost absent-mindedly, playing with those few crab-bots that aren't frightened by so much light and noise—they skitter away when she puts down her hand, and draw back again when she frowns in thought, trying to recall a particular plot point.

Mei usually sits, listless and silent; but this time, she gets up and leaves the house as Ngoc He finishes the tale of the mechanic and the durian fruit. Kim Trang gets up and follows her.

She finds her in the courtyard, watching Vy finish the dismantling of her hibernation berth. She leans against the wall, breathing slowly, evenly.

Vy nods to Kim Trang as she comes out—she's busy figuring out how to pull out the last few chips and cables, scavenging everything she can so the girls can keep going for a while longer, absorbing and integrating the remnants of sleepers' technology to repair themselves. A few crab-bots crawl over the power source, trying to fix it in spite of all the evidence, but most have given up, and are simply dragging pieces of metal back to their burrows—they were meant to keep things running, to repair the dome, but they were cut loose after the Catastrophe and are now like the girls, taking everything they can for themselves. Vy isn't talking to Mei, but then Vy was the one who didn't want Kim Trang to bring Mei home, to let the tiger loose among them.

"Give me a hand afterwards, will you?" Vy asks.

Kim Trang nods. Her lineage is that of a repair construct. Her distant ancestor who survived the Catastrophe isn't here anymore, but she and generations of her descendants have left Kim Trang routines—knowledge at the organic and electronic level, so thoroughly ingrained it might as well be reflexes by now.

Mei straightens up when Kim Trang arrives, gives her a tight and forced smile.

"You should be inside," Kim Trang says.

Mei shakes her head. "I'd just be an imposition."

"You could tell stories," Kim Trang says. "Of the world before. Of—"

"Of how we broke it past repair?" Mei's voice is curt.

"You weren't the only ones," Kim Trang says. The girls' ancestors might have been constructs, acting under duress, having free will only insofar as it didn't contradict the sleepers' orders—but does that really make them blameless?

"I'm the villain in all your stories," Mei says. She shakes her head.

The tiger. The walking time bomb for Kim Trang's kind. No wonder Vy wants her gone, and Kim Trang should follow Vy's advice, tell Mei to leave. "It's the way we learnt the world."

"The world." Mei's gaze looks past her, at the dark shape of the dome that dwarfs them both. The air smells, faintly, of brine, of spilled oil. "It wasn't supposed to be like this."

"Many things weren't. Are you angry they left you behind?"

Mei shrugs. "It was broken, wasn't it?"

"The berth?" Kim Trang nods. "Beyond repair. Or at least, not with the tech we have. I'm sorry."

"Don't be." Mei shrugs. Her eyes haven't left the dome. "It's not like I could go back." She rubs her fingers against her arms, as if drawing the contours of scars, or wire traceries—what would they feel like, those fingers on Kim Trang's skin? "We thought the earth would be green when we woke up again. Cleansed." She doesn't say from what, or who bears responsibility for it.

"It's not so bad," Kim Trang says. It's all they've known, really—save for phantom lineage memories, a nagging sense that things ought to be freer, larger, less dangerous—the silent killer, the thoughtless expectations that get girls killed, out there, if they don't shut them out.

"No," Mei says. She shakes her head. "Why did you save me, Kim Trang?"

Kim Trang has thought of that, at night. She remembers finding the berth in the still waters of the pool by the dome, Vy strenuously arguing that anything from the sleepers was poisoned gifts and that they should leave it there to break down. Kim Trang, too curious for her own good, reaching out, touching the glass—her lineage gift stretching, the berth switching to maintenance mode, letting her see the still, waxy face of an unknown woman, eyes wide in a perfect oval of a face—not like Kim Trang's own face, scarred from a fall into rocky water, from encounters with fractured tech, to crumbling ledges and acid earth that ate at their skin, the hundred ways that the world tries to kill them for the mere act of living and being free—a face that's beyond scavenging, beyond survival. "Why not?" Kim Trang asks, trying so very hard to keep it casual.

She leans against the wall, close enough to Mei that she can feel the heat of Mei's body—the feel and smell of her, a sharp taste in her throat—a memory, not hers, but a lineage one, of rooms with walls so white they hurt the eyes, of hands brushing alcohol against wounds.

Mei looks at her, cocking her head in a particular way; and Kim Trang can't tell what she's being measured against. "Whims? I shouldn't think any of you had them."

"We're not animals," Kim Trang says, more harshly than she meant.

Mei looks horrified. "Of course not. I didn't mean—just that you couldn't afford them. I'm sorry, Kim Trang—"

"No, it's all right," Kim Trang says. Heavy with something she cannot name, she reaches out to run a hand against Mei's cheek, feeling the contour of soft, warm skin so unlike hers. A shiver wracks her body from head to toe, all the lineage memories rising and blurring together as if the world was suddenly washed in rain.

Mei tenses. She's going to pull away—what a foolish, foolish idea: Vy was right, it was a bad plan from the start—but she doesn't. She leans in, gently taking Kim Trang's hand, and sets it on her lips. Taking it into her mouth, her tongue wanders around Kim Trang's flesh, sending pinpricks of desire down Kim Trang's spine. The girls design their own descendants and no longer need sex to reproduce, but some pleasure reflexes still remain the same across generations. Kim Trang withdraws her finger, slowly, while drawing Mei's lips to her own, drinking all of her in.

Such a bad, bad idea.

"Big'sis?" Vy's voice. Of course.

Kim Trang breaks away, watching Mei smile at her, tentatively, and with the tightness of someone who's not sure if things will still be there tomorrow. "I'm sorry," she says. "But I have to go. Later?"

Mei relaxes a fraction. "Wouldn't dream of missing it." She pulls away from the wall, and goes back towards the house. Kim Trang should go back to the berth, help Vy out—but she has time. She can watch until Mei is gone, completely swallowed by the darkness.

Kim Trang walks, slowly, to Vy, feeling the heaviness in her subside, her breathing slows down until her lungs no longer burn. The berth is now little more than scrap metal, a tantalising mess of opened-up compartments with torn cables and broken parts. Kim Trang runs a hand, slowly, on the control panel. It warms up to her touch, trying to cycle itself back into maintenance mode. "That's what failed. The regulator in the control panel. The crabs can't repair that. If the dome hadn't ejected her, she would have died inside."

She thought Vy was going to say something harsh, something about things being for the best if that had happened, but her sister's dark eyes are wide open, with the same lack of expression as Mei's when she was watching Vy dismantle her berth.

"Did you hear everything?" Kim Trang asks.

"I'm not a spy," Vy says, affronted. "But I have eyes. And you do, too, except you weren't using them to pay attention."

"I don't understand."

"The crab-bots," Vy says, curtly. "When you two—kissed—they gathered around her in a circle. Like a court. She's waking up."

"She—" Kim Trang flushes, embarrassed though she doesn't know why. "She means no harm." Mei is a sleeper—clusters of implants and gen-mods, the algorithms that used to enforce compliance to the sleepers' will—algorithms that generations of the girls' lineages haven't been able to breed out, the same algorithms that bend the crab-bots to her will. Centuries of enforced obedience in their blood, and should Mei decide to give orders . . .

"Her kind never does mean harm," Vy says. She shakes her head. "They didn't set out to break the world. Or to deny us our freedom. Until things don't go their way." She reaches out, squeezes Kim Trang's hand between hers. "I'm not doing this out of spite. I know what you want."

Does she—when Kim Trang herself doesn't know what she wants? "I know what *you* want."

"It hasn't changed," Vy says. She picks up a scrap of metal, from the wreck of the berth, crushes it between her fingers—slowly starts absorbing it into her skin, growing a bulge that will be digested next time she needs repairs. "I'm sorry, but—"

But things are what they are. But tigers don't abandon their stripes, or their fangs, just out of charity. "I know," Kim Trang says, but she can't find an answer that would satisfy her and Vy.

The tiger didn't ask where it had woken up, or when, or where the sleepers' land had gone, or why he seemed to be the only one of his kind in the midst of animals that should not have survived the breaking of the world. He sat, listless, until one day the buffalo took him to the periphery again, showing him the boundary with the sleepers' land: the smooth surface of the dome resting in a sea sparkling with the rainbow colours of spilled oil. There was no door, no way to enter, and not even windows to guess at what might be happening within.

She expected him to scream, or to weep, or simply to rise and stalk near the walls of the dome with the same deadly elegance as when he'd risen from his coffin. Instead he remained silent, though there was a gleam in his eyes that hadn't been there before.

"We can look for a way in," the buffalo said, finally, because the silence made her uncomfortable. "Perhaps there'll be someone you knew—"

The tiger spoke, then, in a voice rough with disuse. "How do I know they're not all dead inside?"

The buffalo had no answer, but she felt as though her heart was being squeezed into bloody shreds.

After the kiss:

Kim Trang rises in the morning, and finds Mei gone.

For a slow, suspended moment, she thinks something has gone wrong, but all the girls still sleep on their mats: Thuy hugging the machine she's building (an augment based on crab-bot biology, that will help her dive longer into polluted waters); Ngoc He tossing and turning; Vy perfectly still (her lineage was gen-modded from plants, and she draws oxygen into her body through her skin and eyes rather than through lungs).

Kim Trang finds Mei outside, by the wreck of her berth, watching the rising sun. Part of Kim Trang's lineage remembers a bright, blue sky and stars scattered across the night, but for all of her life the sky has been grey and overcast, the heavy clouds promising a storm that never comes. Mei's hands rest, loosely, on the control panel—lights flash, fleetingly, before sinking back into quiescence.

Mei bends, kissing Kim Trang—a brief taste, a wounding sharpness on the tip of her tongue, her hips digging into Kim Trang's—and then she pulls away, though Kim Trang can still feel the weight of her presence. "It's beautiful, isn't it? I had forgotten what it was like."

Kim Trang doesn't see beauty—merely the same thing she sees every day—but Mei's enthusiasm is infectious. "It is," she says.

"Three hundred years of missed sunrises." Mei sighs. She says, finally, "It was beautiful, too, the world before. In a different way." She crouches at the foot of her berth; and Kim Trang crouches with her, no longer seeing the shadow of the dome. Around them is nothing but muddy earth, with the sharp, familiar tang of metal and oil. Mei's outstretched hands wrap around Kim Trang's callused ones, a touch that Kim Trang aches to take to her chest, to her hips. "Slender spires of metal going all the way into the sky, and gleaming as the sun struck them. And a flow of vehicles and people in the streets, all colours and sounds, a roar that would never fall silent, not even while night came."

As she speaks, Kim Trang feels it, rising in her blood—memories of the lineage, distant sounds and images, a sense of a world opening up around her that could give her anything and everything, leaving her breathless and flushed. "It's gone," she says, more abruptly than she means. And in such a place, she would be a servant, a menial.

"Yes," Mei said. "And perhaps it's just as well. We weren't always kind to your ancestors, among all our other sins." She pauses. Kim Trang runs her hands over Mei's face again. She bends closer, but Mei pulls away before the kiss. "I used to design buildings. Making sure everything was in perfect harmony in rooms and walls. There's not much I can bring you."

You can command the bots, Kim Trang wants to say, and then thinks of how Vy and the others would view this ability—not as a useful skill, but merely a prelude to their own enslavement. "You'll learn."

Mei's hands tighten into fists. "Not as well as you do, and not as fast. I wasn't born into this world."

"We can wait."

"Can you? You have no space for dead weight."

Feeling useless. Kim Trang knows how that goes. Even if there weren't a hundred stories about sleepers waking up too early, she would know in her bones. "You could—"

"Design something here?" Mei shakes her head. "Vy would never let me do it. Besides—" She makes a short, stabbing gesture. "I'm not sure I know better than her, when it comes to design."

"She'll come around."

"Will she?" Mei's gaze is shrewd.

"You're—" Kim Trang takes a deep, shaking breath. "Vy thinks you're not one of us."

"Mm." Mei's hands rest at her side, quietly, looking at Kim Trang with an odd expression on her face. Before Kim Trang can protest that she doesn't think that way—not even sure if that would be a lie—Mei says: "She's right."

"No," Kim Trang says. "You—"

"I'm a danger to you all," Mei says. "The tiger in the story. The predator that undoes you in the end. I'm thankful you saved my life, Kim Trang, but it's best if I left."

She—she. No. Kim Trang can't hear anything save the roar of blood in her ears, a hundred different lineage calls, wondering how to fix a broken situation, finding no way out. "You can't leave. You'll just die out there."

"Credit me with a little resourcefulness." Mei makes a short, stabbing gesture—the crab-bots gather from the berth above them, watchful and still—awaiting orders. "The entire world remembers. I'm—" Her face twists in a terrible expression that wraps around Kim Trang's chest like a metal fist. "I'm not like you girls."

"That doesn't mean you have to leave!"

Mei rises. It would have been worse, in many ways, if the crab-bots had followed, but she's let go of her hold on them, and they're inert again, crawling over the wreck of the berth looking for anything they can use. "It does. It's what I am. Too many implants, too many gen-mods—to take them out of me would kill me." Her expression softens for a bare moment. She lays a hand on Kim Trang's shoulder, with nothing of desire or lust in it. "Don't feel bad. It's the way the world has to be, and I'm by no means blameless. Atonement, perhaps, for what I did to you and your ancestors."

Kim Trang scrambles to her feet, struggling to find words. She can't leave. She—Vy has to be wrong, of course she can stay with them, she's not a danger—again and again in circles in her mind. "Mei! Please—" She does the only thing she can think of. She grabs Mei by the shoulder as she's walking away, turns Mei towards her with all the strength she uses to wrench cables out of sockets and chips out of their compartments.

"Don't touch me!"

It's like being electrocuted—a jolt of current that seizes all of Kim Trang's limbs, sends her to the ground, spasming, struggling to breathe—arms and legs refusing to obey, her entire being screaming with one voice. She has to stop; she has to be still; she has to bow down. Every single lineage-memory breaks around her until the only one that remains is old, as vivid as yesterday: her faraway ancestor bowing to a sleeper after repairing their vehicle, and the rush of pleasure that seizes her, stilling her where she stands.

No. No.

The world is broken, centuries have passed, and her ancestor is long dead.

Slowly, agonisingly slowly, she pulls herself to her feet—and it can't have been that long after all, because Mei is still standing, watching her with horror in her eyes. Her mouth opens, closes—words come, dragged out of her. "I didn't mean to—Kim Trang—I—"

And then she's gone, running away from the debris-strewn courtyard. Follow. Kim Trang has to follow her, or she'll lose her forever. She—she can barely stand, and the thought of catching up to Mei—the thought of her fingers resting on Mei's warm skin—makes her stomach heave.

Days passed, and the tiger ate again. He regained strength and plumpness, though he could not find a place among the buffalo's sisters and daughters. They spoke too fast, of concerns and concepts he wasn't familiar with, and they refused to let the tiger touch the machines they were fixing. In the evening, he sat with the buffalo, speaking, not of the world before the breaking, but of small, inconsequential things; making small talk and jokes until the buffalo's heart grew light again— until she forgot that she'd ever feared him.

He grew fat and sleek, and with his mind running around in circles, found no use for himself in a world that had moved on. So instead, he remembered the past, and the days when the ancestors of the buffalo had moved to do his bidding—the power that was still within him, as inseparably as his heart and liver, that had once made them kneel before him—and as he remembered, that power slowly woke up, unfolding within him as the tiger had once unfolded himself out of his coffin.

One day, he looked at the buffalo's daughters—at their flat, blunt teeth, at their horns that could never be used as weapons, at their meagre meals of grass— and saw that he was more than them. "I can help you," he said. They looked at him, incurious; and as the eldest turned away to look at her workbench, something stretched and broke in the tiger's mind.

"Stop," the tiger said, fiercely. "Listen to me."

And the sisters and daughters of the buffalo, caught in the fist of his power, froze where they stood. The tiger watched all of them, as still as statues and awaiting further orders. He meant no harm, he told himself. He wanted to help them; to share the knowledge he bore from the sleepers' land; the secrets of machines and chips in his blood—and did it matter if they didn't want to listen to him? It was just that they didn't realise everything he could teach them, the wealth of knowledge that he'd hoarded within his mind and that could be theirs so smoothly, so easily—the knowledge they desperately needed to survive.

He meant no harm, but the truth about tigers is this: They always end up thinking of themselves as kings and queens, no matter how changed the world might be.

At the pool, where Mei was first found:

At the bottom of the incline, by the water's edge, Mei is skipping torn bits of metal in the pool, her arm a blur. With each movement she makes, more and more crab-bots bubble up from under the dark, greasy surface of the water, a spreading dark mass that seems to echo Mei's gestures, some slow secret dance that pours out of Mei like liquid gold.

Kim Trang takes a deep breath, and starts the descent. Her first footsteps bring down a shower of rocks: Mei looks up and sees her and keeps on watching her as she descends. When Kim Trang gets near her, she turns, frowning, her face going tight with effort. The crab-bots vanish, sinking again into the depths of the pool.

She's waking up, Vy said, but she was wrong. Mei is awake now. Kim Trang's hands shake—lineage again, howling at her to bend the knee, to obey as her distant ancestor once did.

But the world was broken and taken apart and utterly changed.

"Kim Trang," Mei says. "You see—" but Kim Trang doesn't leave her time.

"You're a coward," she says.

Mei's face tightens, and Kim Trang finally understands that what she thought of as Mei's expressionless face is merely despair, spread so widely that it distorts everything.

"A coward," Kim Trang says, again. "You'd rather run away than try to fix a problem."

"I'm a danger to you."

"So is my knife," Kim Trang says, levelly. "So are the bots."

"The bots won't make you bend the knee."

"They can kill me in other ways. They can go rogue or malicious."

"You don't understand," Mei says. "Even if I don't mean it, even if I don't have any delusions of grandeur or any intention to use my powers, they're still here. In my blood. It's who I am."

"It's who you once chose to be," Kim Trang says. "In a world since long dead. Do you want to continue being that person? The one who entered the berth secure in the knowledge the world would be a paradise?"

"I—you saw it!" Mei raises her hands, and the crab-bots rise again from the depths of the pool, ring after ring of speckled darkness. *The world remembers.* "All I have to do is lose my calm, and it'll happen again. How can you—"

Kim Trang thinks of being thrown to the ground, thinks of pain running through her limbs, of getting up and running after Mei. "I've been hurt before. The girls have been hurt before. Of course it will happen again. You'll do the only thing you can do: apologise, make it better, and do your best so that it never happens again. We all stumble."

"Not that way," Mei says, darkly, but she watches Kim Trang with that peculiar hunger in their eyes. "You say it like forgiveness is easy to earn."

Kim Trang shakes her head. She walks closer—no nausea this time, nothing to stop her but the memory of pain—and runs a hand on Mei's skin. Part of her braces herself for another jolt, but there's nothing. "It's not. It never is. And atonement isn't, either. Do you think it's going to be easy to remember every day that you shouldn't be giving orders?" Every morning, Mei will wake up and know the price of impatience or anger; she'll see the crab-bots and try not to command them—see the girls and not think of the constructs of the past—like being able to breathe and deliberately holding it, forever and ever. Mei's entire body is taut, like a wire about to snap. "No. But it's never going to work, Kim Trang. You've heard the stories. You know how they end."

"I know," Kim Trang said. "But they don't have to all go the same way."

Mei's face is a study in agony. "Kim Trang—"

Kim Trang comes closer and wraps her hands around Mei's—warmth and smoothness, and the face she remembers, the woman trapped in a berth that she fell half in love with at first sight, the sleeper who should be their ancestral, implacable enemy. "Tell me a story," she whispers. "A different one."

A winner of the Nebula, Hugo, and World Fantasy awards, Ken Liu (kenliu. name) is the author of The Dandelion Dynasty, a silkpunk epic fantasy series (*The Grace of Kings* (2015), *The Wall of Storms* (2016), and a forthcoming third volume) and *The Paper Menagerie and Other Stories* (2016), a collection. He also wrote the Star Wars novel, *The Legends of Luke Skywalker* (2017).

BYZANTINE EMPATHY

Ken Liu

You're hurrying along a muddy path, part of a jostling crowd. The commotion around you compels you to scramble to keep up. As your eyes adjust to the dim light of early dawn, you see everyone is laden down with possessions: a baby wrapped tightly against the chest of its mother; a bulging bed sheet filled with clothing ballooning over the back of a middle-aged man; a washbasin filled with lychees and breadfruit cradled in the arms of an eight-year-old girl; an oversized Xiao Mi smartphone pressed into service as a flashlight by an old woman in sweatpants and a wrinkled blouse; a Mickey Mouse suitcase with one missing wheel being dragged through the mud by a young woman in a t-shirt emblazoned with the English phrase "Happy Girl Lucky"; a pillow case filled with books or perhaps bundles of cash dangling from the hand of an old man in a baseball cap advertising Chinese cigarettes . . .

Most in the crowd seem taller than you, and this is how you know that you are a child. Looking down, you see on your feet yellow plastic slippers decorated with portraits of Disney's Belle. The thick mud threatens to pull them off your feet with each step, and you wonder if perhaps they mean something to you—home, security, a life safe for fantasy—so that you don't want to leave them behind.

In your right hand you're holding a rag doll in a red dress, embroidered with curved letters in a script you don't recognize. You squeeze the doll, and the sensation tells you the doll is stuffed with something light that rustles, perhaps seeds. Your left hand is held by a woman with a baby on her back and a bundle of blankets in her other hand. Your baby sister, you think, too little to be scared. She looks at you with her dark, adorable eyes, and you give her a comforting smile. You squeeze your mother's hand, and she squeezes back reassuringly, warm.

On both sides of the path you see scattered tents, some orange and some blue, stretching across the fields all the way to the jungle half a kilometer away. You're not sure if one of the tents used to be your home or if you're just passing through.

There's no background music, and no calls from exotic Southeast Asian birds. Instead, your ears are filled with anxious human chatter and cries. You can't understand the language or the topolect, but the tension in the voices tells you that they're cries for family to keep up, for friends to be careful, for aged relatives to not stumble.

A loud whine passes overhead, and the field ahead and to the left erupts in a fiery explosion brighter than sunrise. The ground convulses; you tumble down into the slimy mud.

More whines sweep overhead, and more shells explode around you, rattling your bones. Your ears are ringing. Your mother crawls over to you and covers you with her body. Merciful darkness blocks out the chaos. Loud, keening screams. Terrified cries. A few incoherent moans of pain.

You try to sit up, but your mother's unmoving body is holding you down. You struggle to shift her weight off and manage to wriggle out from under her.

The back of your mother's head is a bloody mess. Your baby sister is crying on the ground next to her body. Around you people are running in every direction, some still trying to hold on to their possessions, but bundles and suitcases lay abandoned in the path and the fields, next to motionless bodies. The rumbling of engines can be heard in the direction of the camp, and through the swaying, lush vegetation you see a column of soldiers in camouflage approach, guns at the ready.

A woman points at the soldiers and shouts. Some of the men and women stop running and hold up their hands.

A gunshot rings out, followed by another.

Like leaves blown before a gust of wind, the crowd scatters. Mud splashes onto your face as stomping feet pass by you.

Your baby sister cries louder. You scream, "Stop! Stop!" in your language. You try to crawl over to her, but someone stumbles over you, slamming you to the ground. You try to shield your head from the trampling feet with your arms and curl up into a ball. Some leap over you; others try but fail, landing on you, kicking you hard as they scramble.

More gunshots. You peek between your fingers. A few figures tumble to the earth. There's little room to maneuver in the stampeding crowd, and people fall in a heap whenever anyone goes down. Everyone is pushing and shoving to put someone, anyone, between the bullets and themselves.

A foot in a muddy sneaker slams down onto the bundled figure of your baby sister, and you hear a sickening crack as her cries are abruptly silenced. The owner of the sneaker hesitates for a moment before the surging crowd pushes them forward, disappearing from your sight.

You scream, and something pounds you hard in the gut, knocking the breath out of you.

Tang Jianwen ripped off her headset, gasping. Her hands shook as she unzipped her immersion suit, and she managed to peel it halfway off before her hands lost their strength. As she curled up on the omnidirectional tread-mill, the bruises on her sweat-drenched body glistened dark red in the faint, white glow of her computer screen, the only light on in the dark studio apartment. She dry-heaved a few times before breaking into sobs.

Though her eyes were closed, she could still see the grim expressions on the faces of the soldiers, the bloody pulp that had been the mother's head, the broken little body of the baby, her life trampled out of her.

She had disabled the safety features of the immersion suit and removed the amplitude filters in the algics circuitry. It didn't seem right to experience the ordeal of the Muertien refugees with pain filters in place.

A VR rig was the ultimate empathy machine. How could she truly say she had walked in their shoes without suffering as they did?

The neon lights of bustling Shanghai at night spilled through the cracks in the curtains, drawing harsh, careless rainbows on the floor. Virtual wealth and real greed commingled out there, a world indifferent to the deaths and pain in the jungles of Southeast Asia.

She was grateful that she had not been able to afford the olfactory attachment. The coppery odor of blood, mixed with the fragrance of gunpowder, would have undone her before the end. Smells probed into the deepest part of your brain and stirred up the rawest emotions, like the blade of a hoe breaking up the numbed clods of modernity to reveal the wriggling pink flesh of wounded earthworms.

Eventually, she got up, peeled off the rest of her suit, and stumbled into the bathroom. She jumped as water rumbled in the pipes, the noise of approaching engines through the jungle. Under the hot streams of the shower, she shivered.

"Something has to be done," she muttered. "We can't let this happen. *I* can't."

But what could she do? The war between the central government of Myanmar and the ethnic minority rebels near the country's border with China was little remarked on by the rest of the world. The United States, the world's policeman, was silent because it wanted a loyal, pro-U.S. government in Naypyidaw as a chess piece against rising Chinese influence in the region. China, on the other hand, wanted to entice the government in Naypyidaw onto its side with business and investment, and making a big deal out of ethnic Han Chinese civilians being slaughtered by Burmese soldiers was unhelpful for this Great Game. Even news of what was happening in Muertien was censored by a Chinese government terrified that sympathy for the refugees might mutate into uncontrollable nationalism. Refugee camps on both sides of the border were kept out of sight, like some shameful secret. Eyewitness accounts, videos, and this VR file had to be sneaked through tiny encrypted holes punched in the Great Firewall. In the West, however, popular apathy functioned more effectively than any official censorship.

She could not organize marches or gather signatures for petitions; she could not start or join a nonprofit dedicated to the well-being of the refugees—not that people in China trusted charities, which were all frauds; she could not ask everyone she knew to call their representatives and tell them to do something about Muertien. Having studied abroad in the United States, Jianwen wasn't so naive as to think that these avenues open to citizens of a democracy were all that effective—often, they served as mere symbolic gestures that did nothing to alter the minds or actions of those who truly determined foreign policy. But at least these acts would have allowed her to *feel* like she was making a difference.

And wasn't *feeling* the entire point of being human?

The old men in Beijing, terrified of any challenge to their authority and the possibility of instability, had made all these things impossible. To be a citizen of China was to be constantly reminded of the stark reality of the utter powerlessness of the individual living in a modern, centralized, technocratic state.

The scalding water was starting to feel uncomfortable. She scrubbed herself hard, as if it was possible to free herself from the haunting memories of the dying by scouring away sweat and skin cells, as if it was possible to be absolved of guilt with soap that smelled of watermelons.

She got out of the shower, still dazed, raw, but at least functional. The filtered air in the apartment smelled faintly of hot glue, the result of too much electronics packed into a small space. She wrapped a towel around herself, padded into her room, and sat down in front of her computer screen. She tapped on the keyboard, trying to distract herself with updates on her mining progress.

The screen was enormous and its resolution cutting edge, but by itself, it was an insignificant piece of dumb equipment, only the visible corner of the powerful computing iceberg that she controlled.

The array of custom-made ASICs in the humming rack along the wall was devoted to one thing: solving cryptographic puzzles. She and other miners around the world used their specialized equipment to discover the nuggets made of special numbers that maintained the integrity of several cryptocurrencies. Although she had a day job as a financial services programmer, this work was where she really felt alive.

It gave her the feeling of possessing a bit of power, to be part of a global community in rebellion against authority in all its forms: authoritarian governments, democratic-mob statism, central banks that manipulated inflation and value by fiat. It was the closest she could come to being the activist she really yearned to be. Here, only math mattered, and the logic of number theory and elegant programming formed an unbreakable code of trust.

She tweaked her mining cluster, joined a new pool, checked in on a few channels where like-minded enthusiasts chatted about the future, and felt calmer as she read the scrolling text without joining in the conversation herself.

N♥T>: Just set up my Huawei GWX. Anyone have a recommendation for a good VR to try on it?
秋叶1001>: Room-scale or apartment-scale?
N♥T>: Apartment-scale. Nothing but the best for me.
秋叶1001>: Wow! You must've done well in the mines this year. I'd say try "Titanic."
N♥T>: From Tencent?
秋叶1001>: No! The one from SLG is much better. You'll need to hook your mining rig up to handle the graphics load if you have a big apartment.
Anony😈>: Ah, enhanced play or proof-of-work. What's more important?

Like many others, Jianwen had plunged headlong into the consumer VR craze. The resolution of the rigs was finally high enough to overcome dizziness, and even a smartphone contained enough processing power to drive a basic headset—though not the kind that provided full immersion.

She had climbed Mount Everest; she had BASE jumped from the top of the Burj Khalifa; she had "gone out" to VR bars with her friends from across the globe, each of them holed up in their respective apartments drinking shots of real *erguotou* or vodka; she had kissed her favorite actors and slept with a few she *really* liked; she had seen VR films (exactly what they sound like and not very good); she had done VR LARP; she had flitted around the room in the form of a tiny fly as twelve angry fictional women argued over the fate of a fictional young woman, subtly directing their arguments by landing on pieces of evidence she wanted them to focus on.

But she had felt unsatisfied with all of these experiences in some vague, inexpressible way. The emerging medium of VR was like unformed clay, full of potential and possibility, propelled by hope and greed, promising everything and nothing, a technology solution in search of a problem—it was still unclear what sort of pleasures, narratological or ludic, would ultimately predominate.

This latest VR experience, a short little clip in the life of an unnamed Muertien refugee, however, felt different.

But for an accident of birth, that little girl could have been me. Her mother even had my mother's eyes.

For the first time in years, since her youthful idealism had been ground down by the indifference of the world after college, she felted compelled to *do something.*

She stared at her screen. The flickering balances in her cryptocurrency accounts were based on a consensus of cryptographic chains, a trust forged from the trust-less. In a world walled from pain by greed, could such trust also be a way to drill a hole into the barrier, to let hope flood through? Could the world indeed be converted into a virtual village, where empathy bonded each to each?

She opened a new terminal window on her screen and began to type feverishly.

I hate D.C., Sophia Ellis decided as she looked out the window.

Traffic crawled through the rainy streets, punctuated by the occasional blare of an angry driver—a nice metaphor for what passed for political normality in the capital these days. The distant monuments on the Mall, ethereal through the drizzle, seemed to mock her with their permanence and transcendence.

The board members were making chit-chat, waiting for the quarterly meeting to start. She only paid attention half-heartedly, her mind elsewhere.

. . . your daughter . . . Congrats to her!

. . . too many blockchain startups . . .

. . . passing through London in September . . .

Sophia would rather be back in the State Department, where she belonged, but the current administration's distaste for traditional-style diplomacy made her think she might have better prospects shifting into the nonprofit sector as a top administrator. After all, it was an open secret that some of the biggest U.S. nonprofits with international offices served as unofficial arms of U.S. foreign policy, and being the executive director of Refugees Without Borders was not a bad stepping stone back to power when the next administration came in. The key was to do some good for the refugees, to promote American values, and to stabilize the world even as the current administration seemed hell-bent on squandering American power.

. . . saw a cell phone video and asked me if we were doing anything about it . . . Muertien, I think?

She pulled herself out of her reverie. "That's not something we should be involved in. It's like the situation in Yemen."

The board member nodded and changed the subject.

Sophia's old college roommate, Jianwen, had emailed her about Muertien a couple months ago. She had written back to express her regrets in a kind and thoughtful message. *We're an organization with limited resources. Not every humanitarian crisis can be addressed adequately. I'm sorry.*

It was the truth. Sort of.

It was also the consensus of those who understood how things worked that interfering with what was happening in Muertien would not benefit U.S. interests, or the interests of Refugees Without Borders. The desire to make the world a better place, which was what had gotten her into diplomacy and nonprofit work in the first place, had to be tempered and guided by realism. Despite—or perhaps because of—her differences with the current administration, she believed that preserving American power was a worthy and important goal. Drawing attention to the crisis in Muertien would embarrass a key new American ally in the region, and that had to be avoided. This complicated world demanded that the interests of the United States (and its allies) be prioritized at the expense of some who suffered, so that more of the helpless could be protected.

America was not perfect, but it was also, after weighing all the alternatives, the best authority we had.

". . . the number of small donations from under-thirty donors has fallen by 75 percent in the last month," said one of the board members. While Sophia had been philosophizing, the board meeting had started.

The speaker was the husband of an important MP, participating from London through a telepresence robot. Sophia suspected that he was in love with his voice more than his wife. The looming screen at the end of the telescoping neck made his face appear severe and dominating, and the robot's hands gesticulated for emphasis, presumably in imitation of the speaker's actual hands. "You are telling me you have no plans for addressing the decline in engagement?"

Did someone on your wife's staff write that up for you as a talking point? Sophia thought. She doubted he could have personally paid enough attention to the financial records to notice such a thing.

"We don't rely on small direct donations from that demographic for the bulk of our funding—" she began, but she was cut off by another board member.

"That's the not the point. It's about future mindshare, about publicity. Refugees Without Borders is fading from the conversation on social media without large numbers of small donations from that key demographic. This will ultimately affect the big grants."

The speaker was the CEO of a mobile devices company. Sophia had had to dissuade her more than once from mandating that donations to Refugees Without Borders be used to purchase the company's cheap phones for refugees in Europe, which would have boosted the company's reported market share (and violated conflict-of-interest rules).

"There have been some recent, unexpected shifts in the donor landscape that everyone is still trying to figure out—" Sophia said, but once again, she couldn't finish the sentence.

"You're talking about Empathium, aren't you?" asked the husband of the MP. "Well, do you have a plan?"

Definitely a talking point from your wife's staff. The Europeans always seemed to her more jittery about the cryptocurrency nuts than Americans. *But just as with diplomacy, it's better to guide the nuts than confront them.*

"What's Empathium?" asked another board member, a retired federal judge who still thought that the fax machine was the greatest technology invention ever.

"I am indeed talking about Empathium," said Sophia, trying to keep her voice soothing. Then she turned to the tech CEO, "Would you like to explain?"

Had Sophia tried to describe Empathium, the tech CEO would surely have interrupted her. She couldn't bear to let anyone else show more expertise about a technology issue. Might as well try to preserve some decorum.

The tech CEO nodded. "It's simple. Empathium is another new disintermediating blockchain application making heavy use of smart contracts, but this time with the twist of disrupting the jobs traditional charities are hired to do in the philanthropy marketplace."

Blank faces stared at the CEO from around the table. Eventually the judge turned to Sophia, "Why don't you give it a shot?"

She had gotten control of the meeting back simply by letting others over-reach, a classic diplomacy move. "Let me take this piece by piece. I'll start with smart contracts. Suppose you and I sign a contract where if it rains tomorrow, I have to pay you five dollars, and if it doesn't rain, you have to pay me a dollar."

"Sounds like a bad insurance policy," said the judge.

"You wouldn't do well with that offering in London," said the husband of the MP.

Weak chuckles from around the table.

"With a normal contract," Sophia went on smoothly, "even if there's a thunderstorm tomorrow, you may not get your money. I may renege and refuse to pay, or argue with you about what the meaning of 'rain' is. And you'll have to take me to court."

"Oh, you won't do well in *my* court arguing the meaning of rain."

"Sure, but as Your Honor knows, people argue about the most ridiculous things." She had learned that it was best to let the judge go on these tangents before guiding him back to the trail. "And litigation is expensive."

"We can both put our money into the hands of a trusted friend and have him decide who to pay after tomorrow," the judge proposed. "That's called escrow, you know?"

"Absolutely. That's a great suggestion," said Sophia. "However, that requires us to agree on a common, trusted third-party authority, and we'll have to pay her a fee for her troubles. Bottom line: there are a lot of transaction costs associated with a traditional contract."

"So what would happen if we had a smart contract?"

"The funds would be transferred over to you as soon as it rained," said Sophia. "There's nothing I can do to stop it because the entire mechanism for performance is coded in software."

"So you're saying a contract and a smart contract are basically the same thing. Except one of them is written in legalese and requires people to read it and interpret it, and the other is written in computer code and just needs a machine to execute it. No judge, no jury, no escrow, no takebacks."

Sophia was impressed. The judge wasn't technologically savvy, but he was sharp. "That's right. Machines are far more transparent and predictable than the legal system, even a well-functioning legal system."

"I'm not sure I like that," said the judge.

"But you can see why this is attractive, especially if you don't trust—"

"Smart contracts reduce transaction costs by taking out intermediaries," said the tech CEO impatiently. "You could have just said that instead of this longwinded, ridiculous example."

"I could have," acknowledged Sophia. She had also learned that appearing to agree with the CEO reduced transaction costs.

"So what does this have to do with charity?" asked the husband of the MP.

"Some people view charities as unnecessary intermediaries rent-seeking on trust," said the tech CEO. "Isn't this obvious?"

Again, more blank looks from around the table.

"Some smart contract enthusiasts can be a bit extreme," acknowledged Sophia. "In their view, charities like Refugees Without Borders spend most of our money on renting office space, paying staffers, holding expensive fundraisers where the wealthy socialize and have fun, and misusing donations to enrich insiders—"

"Which is an absolutely absurd view held by idiots with loud keyboards and no common sense," said the tech CEO, her face flushed with anger.

"Or any political sense," interrupted the husband of the MP, as if his marriage automatically made him an authority on politics. "We also coordinate field relief efforts, bring international expertise, raise awareness in the West, soothe nervous local officials, and make sure that money goes to deserving recipients."

"That's the trust we bring to the table," said Sophia. "But for the WikiLeaks generation, claims of authority and expertise are automatically suspicious. In their view, even the way we use our program funds is inefficient: how can we know how to spend the money better than those who actually need the help? How can we rule out the option for refugees to acquire weapons to defend themselves? How can we decide to work with corrupt local government officials who line their own pockets with donations before passing on dribbles to the victims? Better to just send money directly to neighborhood children who can't afford school lunches. The well-publicized failures of international relief efforts in places like Haiti and the former North Korea strengthen their argument."

"So what's their alternative?" asked the judge.

Jianwen watched as the notifications scrolled up her screen, each announcing the completion of a smart contract denominated in completely anonymous cryptocurrency. A lot of business was done that way these days, especially in the developing world, what with so many governments trying to extend their control by outlawing cash. She had read somewhere that more than 20 percent of global financial transactions were now through various cryptocurrencies.

But the transactions she was watching onscreen were different. The offers were requests for aid or promises to provide funds; there was no consideration except the need to *do something*. The Empathium blockchain network matched and grouped the offers into multiparty smart contracts, and, when the conditions for performance were fulfilled, executed them.

She saw there were requests for children's books; for fresh vegetables; for gardening tools; for contraceptives; for another doctor to come and set up shop for the long haul—and not just a volunteer to come for thirty days, parachuting in and jetting right back out, leaving everything unfinished and unfinishable . . .

She prayed for the offers to be taken up, to be satisfied by the system, even though she didn't believe in God, or any god. Though she had created Empathium, she was powerless to affect its specific operation. That was the beauty of the system. No one could be in charge.

When she was a college student in the United States, Jianwen had returned to China for the summer of the year of the massive Sichuan earthquake to help the victims of that disaster. The Chinese government had put a great deal of its resources into the rescue effort, even mobilizing the army.

Some PLA soldiers, her age or even younger, showed her the ugly scars on their hands from when they had dug through the muddy rubble of collapsed buildings for survivors and bodies.

"I had to stop because my hands hurt so much," one of the boys told her, his voice filled with shame. "They said if I kept going I'd lose my fingers."

Her vision blurred from rage. *Why couldn't the government have supplied the soldiers with shovels or real rescue equipment?* She pictured the soldiers' bloody hands, the flesh of the fingers peeling back from the bones, as they continued to scoop up handfuls of earth in the hope of finding someone still alive. *You don't have anything to be ashamed about.*

Later, she had recounted her experiences to her roommate, Sophia. Sophia had shared Jianwen's rage at the Chinese government, but her face hadn't changed at all at her description of the young soldier.

"He was just a tool for an autocracy," the roommate had said, as if she couldn't picture those bloody hands at all.

Jianwen hadn't gone to the disaster zone with some official organization; rather, she was just one of thousands of volunteers who had come to Sichuan on their own, hoping to make a difference. She and the other volunteers had brought food and clothing, thinking that was what was needed. But mothers asked her for picture books or games to comfort their weepy children; farmers asked her when and how soon cell service would be restored; townspeople wanted to know if they could get tools and supplies to start rebuilding; a little girl who had lost her whole family wanted to know how she was going to finish high school. She didn't have any of the needed information or supplies, and neither did anyone else, it seemed. The officials in charge of the rescue effort disliked having volunteers like her around because they reported to no authority, and thus told them nothing.

"This shows why you need expertise," Sophia had said, later. "You can't just go down there like an aimless mob hoping to do good. People who know what they're doing need to be in charge of disaster relief."

Jianwen wasn't sure she agreed—she had seen little evidence that it was possible for any expert to anticipate everything needed in a disaster.

Text scrolled even faster in another window on the screen, showing more contract offers being submitted: requests for teachers of Greek; for funding to build a new cell tower; for medicine; for people who could teach refugees how to navigate the visa and work permit system; for weapons; for truckers willing to ship refugee-produced art out to buyers . . .

Some of these requests were for the kind of things that no NGO or government would ever give refugees. The idea of some authority dictating what was needed and not needed by people struggling to survive revolted Jianwen.

People in the middle of a disaster zone knew best what they needed. It's best to give them money so that they could buy whatever they needed—plenty of fearless vendors and ingenious adventurers would be willing to bring the refugees whatever goods or services they requested when there was profit to be made. Money did make the world go around, and that wasn't a bad thing.

Without cryptocurrency, none of what Empathium had accomplished so far would have been possible. The transfer of money across national borders was expensive and subject to heavy governmental oversight by suspicious regulators. Getting money into the hands of needy individuals was practically impossible without the help of some central payment processor, which could easily be co-opted by multiple authorities.

But with cryptocurrency and Empathium, a smartphone was all you needed to let the world know of your needs and to receive help. You could pay anyone securely and anonymously. You could band together with others with the same needs and submit a group application, or go it alone. No one could reach in and stop the smart contracts from executing.

It was exciting to see something that she had built begin to work as envisioned.

Still, so many of the aid requests on Empathium remained unfulfilled. There was too little money, too few donors.

"That's basically it in a nutshell," said Sophia. "Donations to Refugees Without Borders have fallen because many younger donors are giving on the Empathium network instead."

"Wait, did you just tell me that they're giving 'cryptocurrency' away on this network?" asked the judge. "What is that, like fake money?"

"Well, not *fake*. Just not dollars or yen—though cryptocurrencies can be converted to fiat currencies at exchanges. It's an electronic token. Think of it . . ." Sophia struggled to think of an outdated reference that would make sense to the old judge, then inspiration struck. ". . . like an MP3 on your iPod. Except it can be used to pay for things."

"Why can't I send a copy to someone to pay for something but keep a copy for myself, the same way kids used to do with songs?"

"Who owns which song is recorded in an electronic ledger."

"But who keeps this ledger? What's to prevent hackers from getting in there and rewriting it? You said there was no central authority."

"The ledger, which is called the 'blockchain,' is distributed on computers across the world," said the tech CEO. "It's based on cryptographic principles that solve the Byzantine Generals Problem. Blockchains power cryptocurrencies as well as Empathium. Those who use the blockchain trust the math; they don't need to trust people."

"The what now?" asked the judge. "Byzantium?"

Sophia sighed inwardly. She wasn't expecting to get into this level of detail. She hadn't even finished explaining the basics of Empathium, and who knew how much longer it would take for the discussion to produce a consensus on what Refugees Without Borders should do about it?

Just as cryptocurrency aimed to wrest control of the money supply away from the fiat of governments, Empathium aimed to wrest control of the world's supply of compassion away from the expertise of charities.

Empathium was an idealistic endeavor, but it was driven by waves of emotion, not expertise or reason. It made the world a more unpredictable place for America, and thus more dangerous. She wasn't in the State Department anymore, but she still yearned to make the world more orderly, with decisions guided by rational analysis and weighing of pros and cons.

It was hard to get a roomful of egos to understand the same problem, much less to agree on a solution. She wished she had the knack some charismatic leaders had of just convincing everyone to submit to a course of action without understanding.

"Sometimes I think you just want people to agree with you," Jianwen had said to her once, after a particularly heated argument.

"What's wrong with that?" she had asked. "It's not my fault that I've thought about the issues more than they have. I see the bigger picture."

"You don't really want to be the most reasonable," Jianwen had said. "You want to be the most *right*. You want to be an oracle."

She had been insulted. Jianwen could be so stubborn.

Wait a minute. Sophia seized on the notion of *oracle. Maybe that's it. That's how we can make Empathium work for us.*

"The Byzantine Generals Problem is a metaphor," Sophia said. She tried to keep the newfound excitement out of her voice. She was glad that her wonkish need to understand the details—as well as the desire to one-up the tech CEO, if she was honest—had compelled her to read up on this topic. "Imagine a group of generals, each leading a division of the Byzantine army, are laying siege to a city. If all the generals can coordinate to attack the city, then the city will fall. And if all the generals can agree on a retreat, everyone will be safe. But if only some of the generals attack while others retreat, the result will be disaster."

"They have to reach consensus on what to do," said the judge.

"Yes. The generals communicate through messengers. But the problem is that the messengers they send to each other don't arrive immediately, and there may be traitorous generals who will send out false messages about the emerging consensus as it's being negotiated, thereby sowing confusion and corrupting the result."

"This emerging consensus, as you call it, is like the ledger, isn't it?" asked the judge. "It's the record of every general's vote."

"Exactly! So, simplifying somewhat, blockchain solves this problem by using cryptography—very difficult-to-solve number theory puzzles—on the chain of messages that represents the emerging consensus. With cryptography, it's easy for each general to verify that a message chain that represents the state of the vote hasn't been tampered with, but it takes work for them to cryptographically add a new vote to the chain of votes. In order to deceive the other generals, a traitorous general would have to not only forge their own vote, but also the cryptographic summary of every other vote that came before theirs in the growing chain. As the chain gets longer, this becomes increasingly hard to do."

"I'm not sure I entirely follow," muttered the judge.

"The key is, the blockchain uses the difficulty of cryptographically adding a block of transactions to the chain—that's called proof-of-work—to guarantee that as long as a majority of the computers in the network aren't traitorous, you'll have a distributed ledger that you can trust more than any central authority."

"And that's . . . trusting the math?"

"Yes. A distributed, incorruptible ledger not only makes it possible to have a cryptocurrency, it's also a way to have a secure voting framework that isn't centrally administered and a way to ensure that smart contracts can't be altered."

"This is all very interesting, but what does all this have to do with Empathium or Refugees Without Borders?" asked the husband of the MP impatiently.

Jianwen had put a lot of effort into making the Empathium interface usable. This was not something that many in the blockchain community cared about. Indeed, many blockchain applications seemed to be purposefully built to be difficult to use, as if the requirement for detailed technical know-how was how you separated the truly free from the mere sheeple.

Jianwen despised elitism in all its forms—she was keenly aware of the irony of this, coming from an Ivy-educated financial services technologist with a roomful of top-end VR gear like her. It was one group of elites who decided that democracy wasn't "right" for her country, and another group of elites who decided that they knew best who deserved sympathy and who didn't. The elites distrusted *feelings*, distrusted what made people human.

The very point of Empathium was to help people who couldn't care less about the intricacies of the Byzantine Generals Problem or the implications of block size on the security of the blockchain. It had to be usable by a child. She remembered the frustration and despair of the people in Sichuan who had just wanted simple tools to help themselves. Empathium had to be as easy to use as possible, both for those who wanted to give and those who needed the help.

She was creating the application for those sick and tired of being told what to care about and how to care about it, not those doing the telling.

"What makes you think you know the right answer to everything?" Jianwen had asked Sophia once, back when they talked about everything and anything, and arguments between them were dispassionate affairs, conducted for intellectual pleasure. "Don't you ever think that you might be wrong?"

"If someone points out a flaw in my thinking, yes," said Sophia. "I'm always open to persuasion."

"But you never *feel* you might be wrong?"

"Letting feelings dictate how to think is the reason so many never get to the right answers at all."

The work Jianwen was doing was, rationally, hopeless. She had used up all her sick days and vacation days to write Empathium. She had published a paper explaining its technical underpinnings in excruciating detail. She had recruited others to audit her code. But how could she really expect to change the established world of big NGOs and foreign policy think tanks through an obscure cryptocurrency network that wasn't worth anything?

Regardless, the work felt right. And that was worth more than any argument she could come up with against it.

"But I still don't understand how these 'conditions for performance' are satisfied!" the judge said. "I don't get how Empathium decides that an application for aid is worth funding and allocates money to it. Those who provide the funds can't possibly go through thousands of applications personally and decide which ones to give money to."

"There's an aspect of smart contracts that I haven't explained yet," Sophia said. "For smart contracts to function, there needs to be a way to import reality into software. Sometimes, determining whether conditions for performance have been satisfied isn't as simple as whether it rained on a certain day—though perhaps even that is open to debate in edge cases—but requires complicated human judgment: whether a contractor has installed the plumbing satisfactorily, whether the promised view is indeed scenic, or whether someone deserves to be helped."

"You mean it requires consensus."

"Exactly. So Empathium solves this problem by issuing a certain number of electronic tokens, called Emps, to some members of the network. Emp-holders then have the job of evaluating projects seeking funding and voting yes or no during a set time window. Only projects that receive the requisite number of yes-votes—the number of votes you can cast is determined by your Emp balance—get funded from the pool of available donors, and the required threshold of yes-votes scales up with the amount of funding requested. To prevent strategic voting, the vote tally is revealed only after the end of the evaluation period."

"But how do the Emp-holders decide to cast their vote?"

"That's up to each Emp-holder. They can evaluate just the materials put up by the requesters: their narratives, photos, videos, documentation, whatever. Or they can go on site to investigate the applicants. They can use whatever means they have at their disposal within the designated evaluation period."

"Great, so money meant for the desperate and the needy will be allocated by a bunch of people who could barely be persuaded to answer a customer service survey between video game sessions," scoffed the husband of the MP.

"This is where it gets clever. Emp-holders are incentivized by receiving a small amount of money from the network in proportion to their Emp accounts. After each project's evaluation period is over, those who voted for the 'losing' side will be punished by having a portion of their Emps reallocated to those on the 'winning' side. Individual Emp balances are like a kind of reputation token, and over time, those whose judgments—or empathy meters, hence the network's name—are best tuned to the consensus judgment get the most Emps. They become the infallible oracles around which the system functions."

"What's to prevent—"

"It's not a perfect system," said Sophia. "Even the designers of the system—we don't really know who they are—acknowledge that. But like many things on the web, it works even if it doesn't seem like it should. Nobody thought Wikipedia would work either when it started. In its two months of existence, Empathium has proven to be remarkably effective and resilient to attacks, and it's certainly attracting a lot of young donors disillusioned with traditional charitable giving."

The board took some time to digest this news.

"Sounds like we'll have a hard time competing," said the husband of the MP after a while.

Sophia took a deep breath. *This is it, the moment I begin to build consensus.* "Empathium is popular, but it hasn't been able to attract nearly as much funding as the established charities, largely because donations to Empathium are not, of course, tax deductible. Some of the biggest projects on the network, especially those related to refugees, have not been funded. If the goal is to get Refugees Without Borders into the conversation, we should put in a big funding offer."

"But I thought we wouldn't be able to choose which of the refugee projects on the network the money will go to," said the husband of the MP. "It's going to be up to the Emp-holders."

"I have a confession to make. I've been using Empathium myself, and I have some Emps. We can make my account the corporate account, and begin to evaluate these projects. It's possible to filter out some of the fraudulent requests by documentation alone, but to really know if someone deserves help, there's no replacement for good old-fashioned on-site investigation. With our field expertise and international staff, I'm sure we'll be able to decide what projects to fund with more accuracy than anyone else, and we'll gain Emps quickly."

"But why do that when we can just put the money into the projects we want directly? Why add the intermediary of Empathium?" asked the tech CEO.

"It's about leverage. Once we get enough Emps, we'll turn Refugees Without Borders into the ultimate oracle for global empathy, the arbiter of who's deserving," said Sophia. She took a deep breath and delivered the coup de grace. "The example set by Refugees Without Borders will be followed by other big charities. Add to that all the funding from places like China and India, where donors interested in philanthropy have few trusted in-country charities but may be willing to jump onto a decentralized blockchain application, and soon Empathium may become the single largest charity-funding platform in the world. If we accumulate the largest share of Emps, we will then be effectively in the position to direct the use of most of the world's charitable giving."

The board members sat in their seats, stunned. Even the telepresence robot's hands stopped moving.

"Damn . . . you're going to flip a platform designed to disintermediate us into a ladder to crown us," said the tech CEO, real admiration in her voice. "That's *some* jujitsu."

Sophia gave her a quick smile before turning back to the table. "Now, do I have your approval?"

The red line representing the total amount of funds pledged to Empathium had shot straight into the stratosphere.

Jianwen smiled in front of her screen. Her baby had grown up.

The decision by Refugees Without Borders to join the network had been followed within twenty-four hours by several other major international charities. Empathium was now legitimate in the eyes of the public, and it was even possible for wealthy donors who cared about tax deductions to funnel their funds through traditional charities participating in the network.

Projects that received the attention of Empathium users would no doubt attract a great deal of media interest, drawing in reporters and observers. Empathium was going to direct not just charitable giving, but the gaze of the world.

The #empathium invite-only channel was filling up with debate.

NoFFIA>: This is a ruse by the big charities. They're going to play the Emp-accumulation game and force the network into funding their pet projects.

N♥T>: What makes you think they can? The oracle system only rewards results. If you don't think traditional charities know what they're doing, they won't have any better way of identifying deserving good projects. The network will force them to fund projects the Emp-holders as a whole think are deserving.

Anony>: Traditional charities have access to publicity channels most don't. The other Emp-holders are still people. They'll be swayed.

N♥T>: Not everyone is as affected by traditional media as you think, especially when you leave the bubble you USians live in. I think this is a level playing field.

Jianwen watched the debate but didn't participate. As the creator of Empathium, she understood that the invisible reputation attached to her username meant that anything she said could disproportionately influence and distort debate. That was the way humans worked, even when they were talking through scrolling text attributed to pseudonymous electronic identities.

But she wasn't interested in debate. She was interested in action. The participation of the traditional charities on Empathium had been what she had hoped and planned for all along, and now was the time for her to implement the second step.

She brought up a terminal window and began a new submission to the Empathium network. The Muertien VR file itself was too large to be directly incorporated into a block, so it would have to be distributed via peer-to-peer sharing. But the signature that authenticated the file and prevented tampering would become part of the blockchain and be distributed to all the users of Empathium and all the Emp-holders.

Maybe even hard-nosed Sophia.

The fact that the submitter of the file was Jianwen (or more precisely, the user ID of Empathium's creator, which no one knew was Jianwen in real life) would give it a burst of initial interest, but everything after that was out of her hands.

She did not believe in conspiracies. She was counting on the angels of human nature.

She pressed SEND, sat back, and waited.

As the Jeep wound its way through the jungle over the muddy, mountainous road near the China-Myanmar border, Sophia dozed.

How did we get here?

The madness of the world was both so unpredictable and so inevitable.

As she had predicted, the field expertise of Refugees Without Borders quickly made the corporate Empathium account one of the most powerful Emp-holders on the network. Her judgment was deemed infallible, guiding the network to disburse funds to needy groups and proposed projects that made sense. The board was very pleased with her work.

But then, that damned VR and others like it began to show up on the network.

The VR experiences spoke to the interactors in a way that words and photos and videos could not. Walking for miles barefoot through a war-torn city, seeing dismembered babies and mothers scattered around you, being interrogated and menaced by men and boys with machetes and guns . . . the

VR experiences left the interactors shaken and overwhelmed. Some had been hospitalized.

Traditional media, bound by old-fashioned ideas about decency and propriety, could not show images like these and refused to engage in what they viewed as pure emotional manipulation.

Where's the context? Who's the source? demanded the spurned pundits. *Real journalism requires reflection, requires thought.*

We don't remember much reflection from you when you advocated war based on pictures you printed, replied the hive mind of Emp-holders. *Are you just annoyed that you aren't in charge of our emotions anymore?*

The pervasive use of encryption on Empathium meant that most censorship techniques were useless, and so the Emp-holders were exposed to stories they had heretofore been sheltered from. They voted for the attached projects, their hearts pounding, their breathing ragged, their eyes blurred by rage and sorrow.

Activists and propagandists soon realized that the best way to get their causes funded was to participate in the VR arms race. And so governments and rebels competed in creating compelling VR experiences that forced the interactors into their perspective, obliged them to empathize with their side.

Mass graves filled with refugees who had starved to death in Yemen. Young women marching to support Russia gunned down by Ukrainian soldiers. Ethnic minority children running naked through streets as their homes were set on fire by Myanmar government soldiers . . .

Funding began to flow to groups that the news had forgotten or portrayed as the side undeserving of sympathy. In VR, one minute of their anguish spoke louder than ten thousand words in op-eds in respected newspapers.

"This is the commodification of pain!" Ivy-educated bloggers wrote in earnest think pieces. "Isn't this yet another way for the privileged to exploit the suffering of the oppressed to make themselves feel better?"

"Just as a photograph can be framed and edited to lie, so can VR," the media- and cultural-studies commentariat wrote. "VR is so heavily engineered that we have not yet reached consensus on what the meaning of 'reality' in this medium is."

"This is a threat to our national security," fretted the senators who demanded that Empathium be shut down. "They could be diverting funding to groups hostile to our national interest."

"You're simply terrified that you're being disintermediated from your positions of undeserved authority," jeered the Empathium users, hidden behind anonymous, encrypted accounts. "This is a real democracy of empathy. Deal with it."

A consensus of feelings had replaced the consensus of facts. The emotional labor of vicarious experience through virtual reality had replaced the physical and mental work of investigation, of evaluating costs and benefits, of exercising rational judgment. Once again, proof-of-work was used to guarantee authenticity, just a different kind of work.

Maybe the reporters and senators and diplomats and I could make our own VR experiences, Sophia thought as she was jostled awake in the back of the Jeep. *Too bad it's hard to make the unglamorous but necessary work of truly understanding a complex situation compelling . . .*

She looked outside the window. They were passing through a refugee camp in Muertien. Men, women, and children, most of them Chinese in physical appearance, looked back at the passengers in the Jeep numbly. Their expressions were familiar to Sophia; she had seen the same despondency on the faces of refugees everywhere in the world.

The successful funding of the Muertien project had been a massive blow to Sophia and Refugees Without Borders. She had voted against it, but the other Emp-holders had overwhelmed her, and overnight Sophia had lost 10 percent of her Emps. Other VR-propelled projects subsequently achieved funding despite her objection, eroding Sophia's Emp account even further.

Faced with an outraged board, she had come here to find some way to discredit the Muertien project, to show that she had been right.

On the way to Muertien from Yangon, she had spoken to the one staffer Refugees Without Borders posted there and several Western reporters stationed in the country. They had confirmed the consensus back in D.C. She knew that the refugee situation was one largely created by the rebels. The population of Muertien, mostly ethnic Han Chinese, did not get along well with the majority Bamar in the central government. The rebels had attacked the government forces and then tried to fade into the civilian population. The government had little choice but to resort to violence, lest the country's young democracy suffer a setback and Chinese influence extend into the heart of Southeast Asia. Regretful incidents no doubt occurred, but the vast majority of the fault lay on the side of the rebels. Funding them would only escalate the conflict.

But this kind of punditry, of explaining geopolitics, was anathema to the Emp-holders. They did not want lectures; they were persuaded by the immediacy of suffering.

The Jeep stopped. Sophia got out with her interpreter. She adjusted the neckband she wore—it was a prototype the tech CEO had gotten for her from Canon Virtual. The air was humid, hot, drenched with the smell of sewage and decay. She should have been expecting that, she supposed, but somehow she hadn't thought about how things would smell here back in her D.C. office.

She was about to approach a leery-looking young woman in a flower-print blouse when a man shouted angrily. She turned to look at him. He was pointing at her and screaming. The crowd around him stopped moving to stare at her. The air felt tense.

There was a gun in his other hand.

Part of the goal of the Muertien project had been to fund groups willing to smuggle weapons across the Chinese border into the hands of the refugees. Sophia knew that. *I'm going to regret coming here without an armed escort, aren't I?*

Then she heard the rumbling of vehicles approaching in the jungle. A loud whine overhead was followed by an explosion. Staccato gunshots erupted so near that they had to be coming from inside the camp.

Sophia was shoved to the ground as the crowd around her exploded into chaos, screaming and dashing every which way. She wrapped her arms protectively around her neck, around the cameras and microphones, but panicked feet stomped over her torso, making her gasp and loosening her arms. The camera-studded neckband fell and rolled away in the dirt, and she reached for it, careless of her own safety. Just before her grasping fingers reached the band, a booted foot crushed her hand with a sickening crunch. She cursed, and someone running by kicked her in the head.

She faded into unconsciousness.

A splitting headache. Overhead the sky is close at hand and orange, cloudless.

The surface under me feels hard and sandy.

I'm inside a VR experience, aren't I? Am I Gulliver, looking up at the Lilliputian sky?

The sky turns and sways, and even though I'm lying down, I feel like I'm falling.

I want to throw up.

"Close your eyes until the vertigo passes," a voice says. The timbre and cadence are familiar, but I can't quite place who it is. I just know I haven't heard it in a while. I wait until the dizziness fades. Only then do I notice the unyielding lump of the data recorder poking into my back, where it's held in place by tape. Relief floods through me. The cameras may be gone, but the most important piece of equipment has survived the ordeal.

"Here, drink," the voice says.

I open my eyes. I struggle to sit up and a hand reaches out to support me between my shoulder blades. It's a small, strong hand, the hand of a woman. A canteen materializes before my face in the dim light, a chiaroscuro. I sip. I hadn't realized how thirsty I am.

I look up at the face behind the canteen: Jianwen.

"What are you doing here?" I ask. Everything still seems so unreal, but I'm beginning to realize that I'm inside a tent, probably one of the tents I saw earlier in the camp.

"The same thing brought both of us here," says Jianwen. After all these years, she hasn't changed much: still that hard, no-nonsense demeanor, still that short-cropped hair, still that set to her jaw, challenging everything and everyone.

She just looks leaner, drier, as if the years have wrung more gentleness out of her.

"Empathium. I made it, and you want to break it."

Of course, I should have known. Jianwen always disliked institutions, thought it best to disrupt everything.

It's still nice to see her.

Our first year in college, I wrote a story for the school paper about a sexual assault at a final club party. The victim wasn't a student, and her account was later discredited. Everyone condemned my work, calling me careless, declaring that I had allowed the desire for a good story get in the way of facts and analysis. Only I knew that I hadn't been wrong: the victim had only recanted under pressure, but I had no proof. Jianwen was the only one who stuck by me, defending me at every opportunity.

"Why do you trust me?" I had asked her at the time.

"It's not something I can explain," she replied. "It's a *feeling*. I heard the pain in her voice . . . and I know you did too."

That was how we became close. She was someone I could count on in a fight.

"What happened out there?" I ask.

"That depends on who you talk to. This won't show up in the news in China at all. If it shows up in the U.S., it will be misrepresented as another minor skirmish between the government and the rebels, whose guerrilla fighters disguised themselves as refugees, forcing the government to retaliate."

This has always been her way. Jianwen sees the corruption of the truth everywhere, but she won't tell you what she thinks the truth is. I suppose she got into the habit from her time in America to avoid arguments.

"And what will Empathium users think?" I ask.

"They'll see more children being blown up by bombs and women being gunned down by soldiers as they ran."

"Did the rebels or the government fire the first shot?"

"Why does that matter? The consensus in the West will always be that the rebels fired the first shot—as if that determines everything. You've already decided on the story, and everything else is just support."

"I get it," I say. "I understand what you're trying to do. You think there's not enough attention being paid to the refugees in Muertien, and so you're using Empathium to publicize their plight. You're emotionally attached to these people because they look like you—"

"Is that really what you think? You think I'm doing this because they're ethnically Han Chinese?" She looks at me, disappointed.

She can look at me however she likes, but the intensity of her emotion gives her away. In college I remember her working hard to raise money for the earthquake in China, when we were both still trying to pick concentrations; I remember her holding a candlelight vigil for both the Uighurs and the Han who had died in Ürümqi the next summer, when we stayed on campus together to edit the student course-evaluation guide; I remember how once in class she had refused to back down as a white man twice her size loomed over her, demanding that she accept that China was wrong to fight the Korean War.

"Hit me if you want," she had said, her voice steady. "I'm not going to desecrate the memory of the men and women who died so that I could be born. MacArthur was going to drop atomic bombs on Beijing. Is that really the kind of empire you want to defend?"

Some of our friends in college thought of Jianwen as a Chinese nationalist, but that's not quite right. She dislikes all empires because to her, they are the ultimate institutions, with deadly concentration of power. She doesn't think the American empire is any more worthy of support than the Russian one or the Chinese one. As she put it, "America is only a democracy for those lucky enough to be Americans. To everybody else, it's just a dictator with the biggest bombs and missiles."

She wants the perfection of disintermediated chaos rather than the imperfect stability of flawed institutions that could be perfected.

"You are letting your passion overcome reason," I say. I know that persuasion is useless but I can't help trying. If I don't hold on to faith in reason, I have nothing. "A powerful China with influence in Myanmar is bad for world peace. American preeminence must—"

"And so you think it's all right for the people of Muertien to be ethnically cleansed to preserve the stability of the regime in Naypyidaw, to

uphold the Pax Americana, to cement the ramparts of an American empire
with their blood."

I wince. She's always been careless with her words. "Don't exaggerate. The
ethnic conflict here, if not contained, will lead to more Chinese adventurism
and influence. I've talked to many in Yongan. They don't want the Chinese
here."

"And you think they want the Americans here, telling them what to do?"
Contempt flares in her voice.

"A choice between the lesser of two evils," I concede. "But more Chinese
involvement will provoke more American anxiety, and that will only inten-
sify the geopolitical conflict you dislike so much."

"People here need Chinese money for their dams. Without development,
they can't solve any of the problems they have—"

"Maybe the developers want that," I say, "but the common people don't."

"Who are these *common people* in your imagination?" she asks. "I've talked
to many here in Muertien. They say that the Bamars don't want the dams
built where they are, but they'll be happy to have them built here. That's
what the rebels are fighting for, to preserve their autonomy and the right
to control their land. Isn't self-determination something you value and care
about? How does letting soldiers kill children lead to a better world?"

We can go on like this forever. She can't see the truth because she's in too
much pain.

"You've been blinded by the pain of these people," I say. "And now you
want the rest of the world to suffer the same fate. Through Empathium,
you've bypassed the traditional filters of institutional media and charities
to reach individuals. But the experience of having children and mothers die
right next to them is too overwhelming for most to think through the complicated implications of the events that led to these tragedies. The VR experiences are propaganda."

"You know as well as I do that the Muertien VR isn't fake."

I know what she says is true. I've seen people die around me, and even
if that VR was doctored or divorced from context, enough of it was true to
make the rest not matter. The best propaganda is often true.

But there's a greater truth she doesn't see. Just because something happened doesn't make it a decisive fact; just because there's suffering doesn't
mean there is always a better choice; just because people die doesn't mean
we must abandon greater principles. The world isn't always black and white.

"Empathy isn't always a good thing," I say. "Irresponsible empathy makes
the world unstable. In each conflict, there are multiple claims for empathy,

leading to emotional involvement by outsiders that widens the conflict. To sort through the morass, you must reason your way to the least harmful answer, the right answer. This is why some of us are charged with the duty to study and understand the complexities of this world and to decide, for the rest, how to exercise empathy responsibly."

"I can't just shut it off," she says. "I can't just forget the dead. Their pain and terror . . . they're a part of the blockchain of my experience now, unerasable. If being responsible means learning how to not feel someone else's pain, then it isn't humanity you serve, but evil."

I watch her. I feel for her, I really do. It's terribly sad, seeing your friend in pain but knowing that there is nothing you can do to help, knowing that, in fact, you have to hurt her more. Sometimes pain, and acknowledgment of pain, *is* selfish.

I lift my blouse to show her the VR recorder taped to the small of my back. "This was recording until the moment guns started firing—from inside the camp—and I was pushed down to the ground."

She stares at the VR data recorder, and her face shifts through shock, recognition, rage, denial, an ironic smile, and then, nothing.

Once the VR based on what I went through is uploaded—it doesn't need much editing—there will be outrage at home. A defenseless American woman, the head of a charity dedicated to helping refugees, is brutalized by ethnic Han Chinese rebels armed with guns bought with money from Empathium—hard to imagine a better way to discredit the Muertien project. The best propaganda is often true.

"I'm sorry," I say, and I mean it.

She gazes at me, and I can't tell if it's hate or despair I see in her eyes.

I look at her with pity.

"Have you tried the original Muertien clip?" I ask. "The one I uploaded."

Sophia shakes her head. "I couldn't. I didn't want to compromise my judgment."

She has always been so rational. One time, in college, I asked her to watch a video of a young Russian man, barely more than a boy, being beheaded by Chechen fighters in front of the camera. She had refused.

"Why won't you look at what the people you support are doing?" I asked.

"Because I haven't seen all the acts of brutality committed by the Russians against the Chechen people," she said. "To reward those who evoke empathy is the same as punishing those who have been prevented from doing so. Looking at this won't be objective."

There's always the need for more context with Sophia, for the big picture. But I've learned over the years that rationality with her, as with many, is just a matter of rationalization. She wants a picture just big enough to justify what her government does. She needs to understand just enough to be able to reason that what America wants is also what anyone rational in the world wants.

I understand how she thinks, but she doesn't understand how I think. I understand her language, but she doesn't understand mine—or care to. That's how power works in this world.

When I first got to America, I thought it was the most wonderful place on Earth. There were students passionate about every humanitarian cause, and I tried to support every one. I raised money for the victims of the Bangladesh cyclones and the flooding in India; I packed blankets and tents and sleeping bags for the earthquake in Peru; I joined the vigils to remember the victims of 9/11, sobbing before Memorial Church in the late summer evening breeze, trying to keep the candles lit.

Then came the big earthquake in China, and as the death toll climbed toward 100,000, the campus was strangely quiet. People who I thought were my friends turned away, and the donation table we set up in front of the Science Center was staffed only by other students from China like me. We couldn't even raise a tenth of the money we had raised for disasters with far smaller death tolls.

What discussion there was focused on how the Chinese drive for development resulted in unsafe buildings, as if enumerating the cons of their government was an appropriate reaction to dead children, as if reaffirming the pros of American democracy was a good justification for withholding help.

Jokes about the Chinese and dogs were posted in anonymous newsgroups. "People just don't like China very much," an op-ed writer mused. "I'd rather have the elephants back," said an actress on TV.

What's the matter with you? I wanted to scream. There was no empathy in their eyes as I stood by the donation table and my classmates hurried past me, averting their gaze.

But Sophia did donate. She gave more than anyone else.

"Why?" I asked her. "Why do you care about the victims when no one else seems to?"

"I'm not going to have you heading back to China with an irrational impression that Americans dislike the Chinese," she said. "Try to remember me when you get into these moments of despair."

That was how I knew we would never be as close as I had hoped. She had given as a means to persuade, not because she felt what I felt.

"You accuse me of manipulation," I say to Sophia. The humid air in the tent is oppressive, and it feels as if someone is pressing on my eyes from within my skull. "But aren't you doing the exact same thing with that recording?"

"There is a difference," she says. She always has an answer. "My clip will be used to emotionally persuade people to do what is rationally the right thing as part of a considered plan. Emotion is a blunt tool that must be placed in service of reason."

"So your plan is to stop any more aid for the refugees and watch as the Myanmar government drives them off their land into China? Or worse?"

"You managed to get money to the refugees on a tide of rage and pity," she says. "But how does that really help them? Their fate will always ultimately be decided by the geopolitics between China and the US. Everything else is just noise. They can't be helped. Arming the refugees will only give the government more of an excuse to resort to violence."

Sophia isn't wrong. Not exactly. But there's a greater principle here that she doesn't see. The world doesn't always proceed in the way predicted by theories of economics or international relations. If every decision is made with Sophia's calculus, then order, stability, empire always win. There will never be any change, any independence, any justice. We are, and should be, creatures of the heart first.

"The greater manipulation is to deceive yourself into believing you can always reason your way to what is right," I say.

"Without reason, you can't get to what is right at all," Sophia parries.

"Emotion has always been at the core of what it means to do right, not merely a tool for persuasion. Are you opposed to slavery because you have engaged in a rational analysis of the costs and benefits of the institution? No, it's because you're revolted by it. You empathize with the victims. You *feel* its wrongness in your heart."

"Moral reasoning isn't the same—"

"Moral reasoning is often only a method by which you tame your empathy and yoke it to serve the interests of the institutions that have corrupted you. You're clearly not averse to manipulation when it's advantageous to a cause that finds favor in your framework."

"Calling me a hypocrite isn't very helpful—"

"But you *are* a hypocrite. You didn't protest when pictures of babies launched Tomahawks or when images of drowned little boys on beaches led to revisions in refugee policy. You promoted the work of reporters who evoked empathy for those stranded in Kenya's largest refugee camp by telling Westerners sappy Romeo-and-Juliet love stories about young refugees and emphasizing how the United Nations has educated them with Western ideals—"

"Those are different—"

"Of course they're different. Empathy for you is but another weapon to be wielded, instead of a fundamental value of being human. You reward some with your empathy and punish others by withholding it. Reasons can always be found."

"How are you different? Why does the suffering of some affect you more than others? Why do you care about the people of Muertien more than any other people? Isn't it because they look like you?"

She still thinks this is a killer argument. I understand her, I really do. It's so comforting to know that you're right, that you've triumphed over emotion with reason, that you're an agent of the just empire, immune to the betrayal of empathy.

I just can't live like that.

I try one last time.

"I had hoped that by stripping away context and background, by exposing the senses to the rawness of pain and suffering, virtual reality would be able to prevent all of us from rationalizing away our empathy. In agony, there is no race, no creed, none of the walls that divide us and subdivide us. When you're immersed in the experience of the victims, all of us are in Muertien, in Yemen, in the heart of darkness that the Great Powers feed on."

She doesn't respond. I see in her eyes she has given up on me. I am beyond reason.

Through Empathium, I had hoped to create a consensus of empathy, an incorruptible ledger of the heart that has overcome traitorous rationalization.

But perhaps I am still too naive. Perhaps I give empathy too much credit.

Anony😈>: What do you all think is going to happen?

N♥T>: China is going to have to invade. Those VRs have left Beijing no choice. If they don't send in the troops to protect the rebels in Muertien, there will be riots in the streets.

goldfarmer89>: Makes you wonder if that was what China wanted all along.

Anony😈>: You think that first VR was a Chinese production?

goldfarmer89>: Had to be state-sponsored. It was so slick.

N♥T>: I'm not so sure it was the Chinese who made it. The White House has been itching for an excuse for war with China to divert attention from all those scandals.

Anony😈>: So you think the VR was a CIA plant?

N♥T>: Wouldn't be the first time Americans have manipulated anti-American sentiment into giving them exactly what they wanted. That Ellis VR is also ramping up US public support for taking a hard line against China. I just feel terrible about those people in Muertien. What a mess.

little_blocks>: Still stuck on those snuff VRs on Empathium? I've stopped long ago. Too exhausting. I'll PM you a new game you'll definitely like.

N♥T>: I can always use a new game. ^_^

Author's Note

I'm indebted to the following paper for the term "algics" and some of the ideas about the potential of VR as a social technology: Mark A. Lemley and Eugene Volokh, "Law, Virtual Reality, and Augmented Reality," Stanford Public Law Working Paper No. 2933867; UCLA School of Law, Public Law Research Paper No. 17-13 (March 15, 2017), available at https://ssrn.com/abstract=2933867 or http://dx.doi.org/10.2139/ssrn.2933867.

Rich Larson (patreon.com/richlarson) was born in Galmi, Niger, has studied in Rhode Island and worked in the south of Spain, and now lives in Ottawa, Canada. He is the author of *Annex* and *Cypher*, as well as over a hundred short stories—some of the best of which can be found in his collection *Tomorrow Factory*. His award-winning work has been translated into Polish, Czech, French, Italian, Vietnamese, and Chinese. Besides writing, he enjoys traveling, learning languages, playing soccer, watching basketball, shooting pool, and dancing kizomba.

MEAT AND SALT AND SPARKS

Rich Larson

Doesn't look like a killer, does she," Huxley remarks.

Cu shrugs a hairy shoulder. To her, all humans look like killers. What her partner means is that the woman in the interrogation room does not look physically imposing. She is small and skinny and wearing a pale pink dress with a mood-display floral pattern; currently the buds are all sealed up tight, reflecting her arms wrapped around her knees and her chin tucked to her chest.

The interrogation room has made a similar read of her mood, responding by projecting a soothing beach front with flour-white sand and blue-green waves. The woman doesn't seem to be aware of her holographic surroundings. Her eyes, small and dark in puddles of running makeup, stare off into space. Every few seconds her left hand reaches up to her ear, where a wireless graft winks inactive red. Apart from that, she's motionless.

Cu holds her tablet steady and jabs the playback icon enlarged for her chimpanzee fingers. She crinkles her eyes to watch as the woman from the interrogation room, Elody Polle, bounces through the subway station with her dress in full bloom. With a bland smile on her face, she walks up behind a balding man, pulls the gun from her bag, pulls the trigger, remembers the safety is on, takes it off and pulls the trigger again.

"So calm," Huxley says, tearing open a bag from the vending unit. "She was like that the whole time, apparently, up until they stuck her in interrogation.

Then she lost her shit a bit." He grins and shovels baked seaweed into his mouth. Huxley is almost always grinning.

Cu flicks to the footage from interrogation: Elody Polle sobbing, pounding her fists against the locked door. She looks over at her partner and taps her ear, signs *Faraday shield?*

"Yeah," Huxley says, letting the bag fall to his lap to sign back. "No receiving or transmitting from interrogation. As soon as she lost contact with that little graft, she panicked. The police ECM should have shut it down as soon as she was in custody. Guess it slipped past somehow."

Acting under instructions, Cu suggests.

Huxley see-saws his open hands. "Could be. She's got no obvious connection to the victim. We'll need to have a look at the thing."

Cu scrolls through the perpetrator's file. Twenty years' worth of information strained from social media feeds and the odd government application has been condensed to a brief. Elody Polle, born in Toronto, raised in Seattle, rode a scholarship to Princeton to study ethnomusicology before dropping out in '42, estranged from most friends and family for over a year despite having moved back to a one-room flat in North Seattle. No priors. No history of violence. No record of antisocial behavior.

Cu checks the live feed from the interrogation room. *Heart-rate down,* she signs, tucking the tablet under her armpit. *Time to talk.*

Huxley looks down into the chip bag. "These are terrible." He shoves one last handful into his mouth, crumbs snagging in his wiry red beard, then seals the bag and puts it neatly in his jacket pocket. He licks the salt off his palms on the way to the interrogation room.

The precinct is near empty, but there are still curious faces peering from the cubicles as they pass. Cu doesn't come to the precinct often. Huxley had to beg her to put in an appearance. She prefers working from her apartment, where everything is the right size and shape and there are no curious faces.

The outside of the interrogation room looks far less pleasant than the interior: it's a concrete cube with a thick steel door that seals shut once they pass through it.

Cu squats down a respectable distance away from the perpetrator, haunches sinking through the holographic sand onto padded floor. Huxley pulls up a seat right beside her.

"Good evening, Ms. Polle," he says. "My name's Al. You doing okay in here?"

Elody Polle sucks in a trembling breath, and says nothing.

"This is my partner, Cu," Huxley continues. Elody's eyes travel over to her, but don't register even a hint of surprise. "We need to get a better idea of what happened earlier, and why. Can you help us with that?"

Elody says nothing.

Cu takes a closer look at the earpiece. The graft is puffy and slightly inflamed. A DIY job, maybe. *Ask her about the piece,* she signs. *We would hate to remove it.*

"Cu's curious about that wireless," Huxley says. "So am I. In the subway footage, the way you're bobbing your head, it almost looks like someone was talking you through the whole thing. Want to tell us about that?"

A flicker crosses Elody's face. Progress.

"Because if you don't, we'll have to remove the earpiece and have a look for ourselves," Huxley says. "As much as we'd hate to ruin that lovely graft job."

Elody claps her hand protectively over her ear. "Don't you fucking dare!" She tries to shout the words, but her voice is hoarse, flaked away to almost a whisper. As if she hasn't spoken aloud in months.

Cu pulls up the speech synth on her tablet and taps out eight laborious letters, one question mark.

"Echogirl?" the electronic voice blurts.

Elody's eyes winch wide. As she looks over at Cu, her cheek gives a nervous twitch.

Huxley's furry red brows knit together. He signs, *what the fuck is that.*

Echogirl, echoboy, Cu signs. *Use an earpiece, eyecam. Rent themselves out to someone who says where to go, what to do, what to say.*

Thought that was. Huxley's hands falter. "A kink, sort of thing," he says aloud, and Elody's face flushes angry red.

"It's a lifestyle," she says. "She told me you wouldn't understand. Nobody does."

"Is *she* going to come get you out of this mess?" Huxley demands.

"Of course she is." Elody purses her lips, turns away.

Huxley turns to Cu. *Take the earpiece?* he signs. *Or what?*

Cu scratches under her ribs, watching a tremor move through Elody's hunched shoulders. *Offer turn off the Faraday,* she signs.

Huxley nods, then turns back to address Elody. "I bet she won't," he says. "I bet you a twenty, and half a bag of chips. Well." He pats his coat pocket and the bag rustles. "A third. Yeah, in fact, I bet the last thing she's ever going to say to you was pull the trigger. Should we turn off the shielding and see?"

Elody turns back, eyes shiny with tears. "Yes," she whispers. "Please, I need to hear her voice, I need . . ." Her tone is eager, but Cu can see uncertainty in the tightening of her eyelids, the bulge of her lower lip.

Huxley makes a show of rapping on the door, telling them to turn off the Faraday. There's a sudden subtraction from the white noise as the generator cuts out, then Huxley's phone starts vibrating his pocket with updates.

Cu keeps her attention on Elody, who has her face upturned now as if waiting to feel sunshine: eyes shut, eyelashes trembling, breath sucked in.

"Baby? Are you there?" she whispers. "Are you there? Are you there?"

Her bland smile is back in place. Seconds tick by. Then doubt moves in a slow ripple across her features. Her smile trembles, smooths out, trembles again. Finally, her face crumples and a huge sob shudders through her body.

Cu taps five letters into the speech synth. "Sorry," her tablet bleats. Then she turns to Huxley and signs *get the piece.* He nods, thumbs the order into his phone. When they exit the interrogation room, two officers are already waiting to come in: one carrying a black kit, the other snapping on surgical gloves.

Cu hears Elody start to wail just before the door clanks shut behind them.

"That . . . echogirl thing." Huxley's hands piece the new sign together. *You've thought about it, eh?*

I've done it, she signs back. *Good to walk in the city without crowds. Just never asked them to shoot someone.*

As soon as she's back in the apartment, Cu dials up the heat and humidity and takes off her clothes. Some days she doesn't mind wearing the carefully tailored black suit. Today she hates it. She leaves it pooled on the floor and takes a flying leap at her climbing wall; the shifting handholds don't shift fast enough and she's up to the rafters in an instant.

Cu was specific with the contractors about leaving the rafters exposed. She's added to them since, welding in more polymer cables and struts of wood, a criss-crossed webbing that spans the vaulted ceiling like a canopy. The design consultant, an excitable architect from Estonia, suggested artificial trees sprouting hydroponic moss. But Cu has no use for green things. She grew up in dull gray and antiseptic white.

Clambering into her hammock, Cu looks out the wide one-way window, watching the sun sink into Puget Sound. She enjoys looking at water so long as it's far away. The view is expensive, but Cu can afford it. She was awarded damages after the personhood trial, enough for a lifetime of this particular view, enough so she can stay in here forever without needing to earn a penny more. She would go insane, though.

So she works the cases. She was always drawn to crime as a dissection of human nature, the breakdown of motive and consequence. A window into the subtle differences between her mind and all the minds around her. When she first applied for police training with the SPD, it was viewed as a joke. Her acceptance, a publicity grab.

But in the years since, they've realized she sees things most humans miss. Cu pulls on her custom-fitted smartgloves, one for each hand and a third for her left foot, and leans back in the hammock. The ceiling screen above her hums to life. New details flit onto the case file, and there's a message waiting from Huxley.

Thanks for coming down in person, the bossman's been up my ass about it. Wanted fresh footage for the promo kit. Hoping they shop out my beer belly.

Cu swipes it aside and reaches for the tech report on the perp's earpiece. The text flows across the ceiling in slow waves, a motion programmed to help her eyes track it easier. There was no salvageable audio data. Not from Elody and not from whoever was speaking to her. But there is usage data to confirm that Elody was receiving a call from a masked address at the time of the murder.

By the look of it, Elody had been in that same call for just under six months. Cu moves backward through the log, perplexed. There are small gaps, a few hours here and there, but Elody had been in near 24/7 communication with her client for half a year preceding the murder.

Cu tries to imagine it: a voice whispering in her ear when she woke up, telling her what to do, where to go, what to say, and whispering still as she fell asleep. All of it culminating in Elody Polle walking up behind a man in a subway and executing him in broad daylight.

She flips the case file over to see the victim's profile again. The balding man was named Nelson J. Huang. A biolab businessman, San Antonio-based, in the city for a conference. It's possible that someone with a personal vendetta knew he would be in Seattle and began laying the groundwork for his murder at the hands of Elody Polle six months in advance.

It's more likely that he was selected at random from the crowd, so someone half the world away could experience homicide vicariously before abandoning her mentally-unstable echogirl.

A call from Huxley jangles across the screen. She pops it open. Her partner is walking down a neon-lit street, sooty brick wall behind his head. "Hey, Cu," he says. "Busy?"

Sometimes he asks it to needle her; this time it's because he's distracted. Cu shakes her head.

"The techies are still trying to track that address, but I doubt they'll have much luck," he says, stopping at a light. "Whoever it is, they did a good job wiping up afterwards. No audio data." He looks around and starts walking again, bristly red beard bobbing up and down. "But before this client, she had another one for around two months. Figured I would swing past and see him on my way home. Well. Sort of see him."

Where? Cu signs.

"A party," Huxley says, his grin notching a little wider. "So, if you're not busy, you should come. Said you've done this before, right?"

Cu watches as he digs an earbud out of his pocket and taps it active, worms it into place. Then the slip-in eyecam: he rolls his eye around afterward and blinks away a few tears. The perspective jumps from his phone camera to his eyecam and all of a sudden she's seeing what he sees. A bright red door in a grimy brick facade, no holos or even a physical sign above it. Through the earbud, she hears the dim pulse of music, synthesized drums.

I hate parties, Cu signs.

"Good thing it's also work," Huxley says.

Cu settles back in her hammock and watches his pale hand push open the door.

The interior is dim-lit, noisy, full of bodies. People are dancing—Cu can enjoy rhythm, but the hard pulse of the drums unnerves some deep part of her, sounding too angry, too much like a warning. People are drinking—Cu tried it once, but the warm dizziness reminded her of the sedatives they used to give her. When she related as much to Huxley, he told her she wasn't *even legal yet, technically*, and that she would like it when she was older.

It's a typical party, apart from the fact that every single person in the room is wearing an earpiece.

"Echo, echo, echo," Huxley mutters. "The client's name is Daudi. Judging by rental history, he's probably a blonde." He takes out his phone and Cu watches his thumb move, sending her a file. It pops up in the corner of her screen, unfurling a list of Daudi's rental preferences. She searches the crowd for possible matches as Huxley moves into the room. There's a woman passing out small plastic tubes; Huxley takes one. Cu inspects it as he juggles it in his palm.

"Smooths things out," the woman says, then something inaudible after.

"Fuck's this, Cu?" Huxley asks.

Cu signs her response in the air above her hammock; the smartgloves turn it into text in the corner of Huxley's eye. *Some echoes use a drug to weaken willpower.* She has to type out the name. *Chempliance.*

"Elody's tox screen was clean, right?" Huxley says, twirling the tube in his fingers.

Wouldn't matter anyway, she signs. *Drug is an MDMA derivative. Suggestibility is all placebo effect.*

Huxley's hand disappears, either dropping the tube or pocketing it. Cu doesn't bother to ask. She keeps scanning as he circulates through the party, looking for someone who meets Daudi's profile. Huxley mostly keeps his gaze moving, but occasionally sticks on a particularly symmetrical face or muscular body.

They spot two drinkers huddled together at a glass-topped table, skin lit red by the Smirnoff advertisement playing under their elbows, one reaching to stroke the other's thigh. The man is dressed in an artfully gashed suit and his eyes are glazed with chempliance. The woman has a dress that flickers transparent to the rhythm of an accelerating heartbeat. Both of them move slowly, as if they're underwater. Something about the woman's face is familiar.

Cu pulls up the file, checks Daudi's preferences against the pair. *That's him,* she signs. *Bar.*

Huxley's vision bobs as he nods his head. He walks over and inserts himself between the couple. "My turn to talk. Get lost, fucko."

When the man doesn't move fast enough, Huxley seizes his collar and shoves him off the stool. He stumbles, catches himself. He sways on his feet, listening to the instructions in his ear, looking confused.

"You got some nerve, barging in here like that," he says, with the intonation a little off.

"This isn't playtime," Huxley says. "It's police business. Walk."

The man spins on his heel and shuffles backward toward the dance floor, feet slip-sliding.

Huxley shakes his head. "These fucking people, Cu," he mutters. "That's a moonwalk, if you were wondering. Does it pretty good."

"I like your boy," the woman says, in a throaty voice that sounds slightly forced. She crosses her legs; one hand moves to pull up the hem of her dress, then stutters to a halt. Instead she starts tracing her fingertip along her thigh. "He's not doped up at all, is he? He really sells the character. Must like it."

"I'm not a meat puppet, shithead, I'm a cop," Huxley says, sitting down on the vacated stool.

Cu knows he does like it, though—the character. Sometimes it disturbs her, how easily he slips in and out of it.

Huxley's hand moves off-screen, digging into his pocket, and comes out again with the badge. Even in the days of cheap and perfect 3D-printing, something about the physical object still commands respect. Cu imagines pop culture nostalgia to be the main factor.

The woman, who was absently running her fingers through her blonde hair, stops and leans forward. "I'm fully licensed for sex work, and I don't use any restricted drugs," she says, voice no longer throaty.

"I believe you," Huxley says. "I'm here to talk to Daudi, though. So just keep, you know, doing what you're doing."

The woman leans back, recomposing. Cu takes the opportunity to study her more closely. She has the same angled jaw as Elody, the same straight nose, and her hair is almost the same shade.

"Talk to me about what, pray tell?" the woman asks. "I've never been interrogated by a cop before. This is so exciting." But her voice is flat as she repeats the lines now, and her eyes dart toward the exit.

"I want to know about your business with this woman," Huxley says, bringing up a headshot on his phone. "Elody Polle."

"Oh, yes," the woman says, looking down at the photo. "That was me. Isn't she perfect? Not that you aren't pretty, dear. Very pretty." She rolls her eyes after the last bit.

"You rented her for quite a while," Huxley says. "Then she got picked up by another client. Why did you two stop, uh, seeing each other?"

"Is she alright?" the woman asks. "Is Elody okay?"

"She's relaxing on the beach," Huxley says. "She's fine. Answer my question, Daudi."

"With pleasure," the woman says, with no hint of pleasure. "I was inadequate for her. I couldn't give her what she wanted."

"Financially?"

"No, no, no," the woman says. "Elody was a purist. The money was incidental for her. What she wanted, was to go full-time. Twenty-four-seven. And there was only one person who could really do that for her. Baby."

"You're calling *me* baby, or . . . ?"

"No, no, no. Baby is one of us. She or he or they popped up a couple years ago. Did about a hundred rentals, spread out all over the world, and asked for some weird shit. Enough so people started talking, you know, on the deep forums." The woman pauses for a breath, looking mildly annoyed; Daudi must be speaking faster than she can keep pace with. "Not sexual shit. That's the thing. Just weird. Baby had clients staring at lamps for hours straight. Opening and closing their hands. Sometimes just lying there with their eyes shut, not doing anything."

The details startle Cu. They remind her of her first experience with an echo, directing them slowly, carefully, trying to not just see and hear but *feel* what they were experiencing. Trying to feel human for a little while.

And the name? Cu signs.

"And the name?" Huxley asks.

"Baby was really innocent," the woman says, then gives a modulated shrug. "Couldn't speak so well at first, either. So there's a lot of theories. Some people thought Baby really was just a little kid in hospice somewhere, maybe paralyzed, burning through their parents' money—and trust me, Baby dumped a fuckload of money the past two years. Or some ultra-wealthy mogul recovering from a stroke. Or a team of people, doing some kind of, I don't know, some kind of performance art."

"Well," Huxley says. "Baby grew up. Elody Polle recently murdered a man, and we don't think she picked her own target."

"Oh my god," the woman says flatly. "Oh, my fucking god." She looks uncomfortable. Lowers her voice. "He's crying." She pauses. "Oh, Elody, Elody."

"So, how do we find Baby?" Huxley asks.

The woman sits there for a minute, maybe waiting for Daudi's sobs to subside. "You don't," she finally says. "Baby comes to you."

"I really doubt Baby will come to us knowing she's an accessory to murder," Huxley says. "But we'll be in touch, Daudi. Might get you to talk to Elody for us. She's not saying much."

"I would be happy to do that," the woman says. "Elody was one of my favorites. My very favorites."

"Yeah, I got that." Huxley stands up from the bar. "Anything else, Cu?"

Cu shakes her head. She'll need time to think it all through.

Huxley hesitates. "Hey, uh, echogirl. Do cams, or something. These people are control freaks. They'll suck you right in."

The woman blinks, caught off-guard. "They're not so bad," she says. "Most of them just wish they were someone else."

"Huh." Huxley slides the stool back in and makes his way to the exit. He slips his eyecam out and Cu's screen goes blank. "Enough work for the night," comes his disembodied voice. "Got to be honest, Cu, I don't like the odds on this one. Baby could be some joker on the other side of the planet, you know? We can send this thing up top, to cyberdefense and them, but unless this was the start of a mass killing spree I don't think it'll get any traction. Sometimes the asshole just gets away with being an asshole." He pauses. "Besides. It was Elody who pulled the trigger."

Cu considers it. She knows the department doesn't like spending unnecessary time on cases with a clear perpetrator. They are always more interested in the who than the why. Since there is no audio recording of Baby's call, they might want to strike it from the case file entirely. It would make things much simpler.

You might be right, she signs. *Goodnight.*

"You know, I tried sleeping in a hammock when I was in Salento," he says. "Nearly wrecked my spine. Anyway. Night."

Cu ends the call and lies back, staring up at her distorted reflection in the blank screen. She's about to clap it off when a new message arrives. No subject, one line only.

You Are Welcome, CU0824.

Cu doesn't sleep after that. She can't. Not after seeing the serial number of the cage where she spent the first twelve years of her life. It plunges her back into memories: the smell of disinfectant and cold metal and sometimes her own piss, the smeary plastic wall that squeezed inward as she grew, the distinct V-shaped crack in it, the smooth feel of the smartglass cube that she cradled in her lap, that she sat and stared into for hours and hours and hours and hours—

She can feel her chest tightening with her oldest variety of panic. She tries to breathe deeply and remember PTSD mitigation techniques. Instead she remembers the succession of men and women in soft white smocks who fed her and played with her but never stayed with her in the dark, and never stopped the man with the needle from drugging her for the nightmare room.

For a long time Cu had no name for the place where they cut her without her feeling it, where they tracked her eyes and fed filaments through holes in her skull. But she learned the word nightmare from her cube, watching a man with metal hands hunt down his children, and the moniker made sense. By the time she learned about surgery, neural enhancement, possible cures for degenerative brain disease, the name was already cemented.

For the last few years she went to the nightmare room willingly and offered them her wrist for the anaesthetic drip. In exchange, they were kinder to her. They took restrictions off her cube—some she had already worked around herself—so more of the net was available to her. They let her walk in certain corridors of the facility. After a week of asking them, they even let her see her mother.

Going back to that particular memory wrenches her apart. Cu had spent the previous day scrambling back and forth in her cage, filled to bursting with nervous energy, rearranging her belongings. She signed for a soapy cloth and scrubbed the walls and ceiling with it, climbing to get the dusty places the autocleaner never reached. She knew from the cube, which she painstakingly positioned in the exact center of the cage, that mothers valued tidiness.

But when they brought her, it was nothing like the cube. Her mother was bent and graying, fur shaved off in patches, surgical scars suturing her body, and she was angry. She jabbered and hooted, spittle flying from her mouth. Cu tried to sign to her, but received no reply. Cu tried to offer her food; her mother seized the orange from her and made a feint, teeth bared, that sent Cu scurrying back to the furthest corner of her cage.

"Tranq wore off sooner than we thought," one of the women in white said. "We did warn you. We did tell you she wouldn't be like you. You're unique."

Cu signed *take her away, take her away, take her away*. And even for hours after they did, she stayed there in the corner, trembling with something that began as fear, then turned to grief, then finally became a deep cold rage.

She feels that rage now, sitting on the rafters in the dark. Whoever dredged up that serial number is playing a game with her, the same way they played games with her in the cage. She could send the masked address to the precinct and have them try to break it down for a trace, but she doubts they'll have any more luck with that than they did with the earpiece.

Instead she puzzles over the three words: *You Are Welcome*. Cu has never felt welcome. It must be meant in the other way. It must mean that Baby has done something she views as a favor to Cu.

Cu opens the case file again, but instead of Elody's profile, she goes to the victim's. Nelson J. Huang, the bio-business consultant to Descorp's San Antonio branch, fifty-seven years old. Initial attempt to notify next of kin was met with an automated reply from a defunct address.

Personal details are scarce: he's registered as a North Korean immigrant, which explains the lack of social media documentation, and lived a private life first in Castroville and later Calaveras. Unmarried, no children. Cu looks closely at the photos, comparing them to the morgue shots of Nelson's corpse. It seems he aged badly over the last decade of his life. The shape of his body is different in subtle ways.

It wouldn't be the first time North Korean immigrant status has been used to excuse the skeleton details of a fake identity. Cu settles in beneath her screen, pulling up police-grade facial recognition software, Descorp employee databases. She starts to search.

One hour becomes two becomes four, like cells dividing. Her wrists and fingers start to ache from swiping and zooming and signing; she switches one smartglove to her foot and continues. It would be easier with Huxley helping. Huxley has a way of bullying through bureaucracy, through the kind of red tape that is keeping her out of Descorp's consultant list. Cu has to work around it.

But she doesn't want Huxley for this. She wants to do it alone, with nobody watching. After a dozen dead ends, Cu rolls out of the hammock. She uses an aqueous spray on her stinging eyes. Stretches her limbs, swings from one side of the apartment to the other. Hanging upside down, toes curled tight around a stretch of cable, blood fizzing down into her head, she listens to her pulse crash against her eardrums until she can hardly stand it.

Back to the hammock, back to the screen. Now Cu comes at it from the other direction: she searches for the Blackburn Uplift Project. Illegal experiments carried out on thirty-seven bonobo and forty lowland chimpanzees between 2036 and 2048 with the aim of cognitive augmentation. Cu knows the details. She's tried to forget them. But now she delves into them again, reading reports of her own escape, of the fragmentation of the Blackburn company and the arrests made in the wake of the scandal.

From this end, the facial recognition 'ware finally finds something. Cu's stomach twists against itself. Nelson J. Huang has the same face as disgraced Blackburn executive Sun Chau. She looks at the match, comparing the morgue shot to the mugshot. She never saw Chau in person during the trials, but she knows his name too well.

It was Chau who signed the termination order on the thirty-seven bonobo and thirty-nine lowland chimpanzees that failed to respond to the uplift treatments.

He was sentenced, of course, but served minimal time. Cu did not seek details on his imprisonment or release. She tries to think of Blackburn as little as possible. But clearly someone else did not forgive or forget Sun Chau, even after he relocated with a new identity. A wild thought churns to the surface of her mind. The way Daudi described Baby, the way she used the echoes not so differently from how Cu herself first did. Now this serial number, dredged from her past.

She knows the other Blackburn subjects in her facility were terminated. She saw their ashes in sealed bags, saw the hips and skulls too big for cremation being ground up. But there were other labs, branches of the project hidden in other countries. Maybe not all of their subjects were terminated. And maybe not all of them failed to respond to the uplift treatments.

The possibility thumps hard in her chest. From the time she was old enough to understand it, the scientists had always told her she was the only one. That she was unique. That she was alone. Now the idea of another individual like her, or even more than one, is so momentous she can barely breathe.

She makes herself breathe.

Maybe she is spinning sleep-deprived delusions. The facts are that Sun Chau was in Seattle using a false identity, and that he was murdered by the machinations of someone who knows about Cu and about her past. Anything more is conjecture. But she can't shake the image of others like her in hiding, or still in captivity, exacting their revenge by proxy. *You Are Welcome.*

Cu goes back to the message, reading it over and over again. Then, once her hands aren't trembling, she signs out one of her own: *I want to talk.*

The reply is almost instantaneous. No words, just coordinates. She drags them onto her map and sees the aerial view of a loading bay, automated cranes frozen midway through their work. She checks the time. 3:32 AM. A clandestine meeting on the docks in the middle of the night. Maybe they watched the same shows on their cube that she did.

Cu estimates travel time and composes a brief message to Huxley, tagged with a delay so it will only send if she's unable to cancel it at 5:32 AM. This is no longer a case. This is something more important.

She drops down from the rafters. She puts her suit back on, adrenaline making her fumble even the oversized clasps designed for her fingers. She strips off her smartgloves and replaces them with the black padded ones that keep her from scraping her knuckles raw on the pavement. Finally, she takes the modified handgun and holster from the hook by the door and straps them on.

Cu always finds it difficult to leave the apartment. She hates the stares and the winking eyecams and the bulb flash of photos taken in passing. It always sets her nerves singing. She draws in deep breaths, reminding herself that the streets will be nearly empty and that she should be more concerned about what she finds on the docks.

She orders a car with her tablet, then takes the handgun from its holster and breaks it down. Reassembles it. The trigger fits perfectly to the crook of her finger, but she has only ever pulled it at a shooting range, aiming for holograms.

Her tablet rumbles. The car is here. Cu puts the gun back in its holster and heads for the door.

The car drops her as close as it can to the loading bay before it peels away, red glow of its taillights swishing through the fog like blood in the water. The air is chill and damp and the halogens are all switched off. Cu slips her tablet from her jacket and uses its illuminated screen to inspect the high chain-link fence. She tests it with one gloved hand, yanking hard enough to send a ripple through the wire.

She scales it in seconds and flips herself over the top, arching her back to avoid the sensor. Slides down the other side. Even with her gloves on, she feels the cold of the concrete. Shipping containers tower over her in technicolor stacks. She lopes forward cautiously, feeling the unfamiliar tug of her holster harness against her shoulder.

Cu walks farther into the loading bay, into the maze of containers. The creak of settling metal sends a dart of ice down her spine. She can feel her teeth clenching, her lips peeling back, the fear response she can never quite suppress. It's not unique to chimpanzees. She knows the reason Huxley is almost always grinning is that he is almost always afraid.

It's reasonable to be afraid now. For all she knows, Baby has another echo-girl with a gun waiting somewhere in the shadows. Cu is well aware she is acting impulsively, coming here in the night, chasing a ghost. In the small part of her untouched by fear, it's very satisfying. Her heroes from the cube always unraveled their conspiracies alone.

The door of the next shipping container bangs open.

Cu freezes, face to face with a black-clad man wearing a backpack, pulling a bandana up to the bridge of his nose. He freezes for a moment, too. Then he gives a muffled curse and takes off. The flight chemical crosses with the fight chemical and Cu tears after him. He's fast, red shoes slapping hard against the concrete. As he skids around the corner of the next container, Cu goes vertical, springing up and over the side.

She drops down in his path and the collision sends them both sprawling; Cu's up quicker and she pins him to the ground before he can get to the bearspray canister in his jacket pocket. She seizes it and throws it away harder than necessary, clanging it off a container somewhere in the dark.

"What the fuck, what the *fuck*," the man gasps. "It's a fucking monkey!"

Cu sits on his chest, pinning his arms with her feet, and drags her tablet out. He squirms while the speech synth loads. She punches three letters.

"Ape," the tablet bleats.

"What?"

Cu yanks his bandana away and scans his pasty face onto her tablet. She sees he is Lyam Welsh, who repairs phones, plays ukulele, attends St. Mary's High School, and is only a few years older than she herself is. He's not wearing an earpiece.

She taps out the letters as fast as she can. "What are you doing?" the tablet asks.

"Nothing!" Lyam blurts. "I mean, microjobbing. I was just supposed to set it all up and then get out of here, but I had to walk Spike, so I was late, and I couldn't find the hole in the fence and . . . Fuck, you're Cu, right? You're the chimpanzee detective?"

Cu types again. "Set up what?"

"Just a screen and a modem and a motion tracker," he says. "Not a bomb or anything. Nothing illegal or weird or anything. I swear. You can go look. It's all in the container."

The adrenaline is tapering off to a low buzz. Cu lets him up. She taps two letters. "Go."

"Okay," Lyam says, rubbing his chest. "Yeah, okay. You think I could skin a photo with you real quick, though? I mean, shit is bananas, right? Ha, bananas?"

Cu slides the volume to max. *"Go."*

Lyam hurries away, jerky steps, throwing looks over his shoulder. Cu goes the opposite way, back toward the open shipping container. The door is swinging in the night breeze, creak-screech, creak-screech. The sound makes the nape of her neck bush out. She steps close enough to stop it with one hand, and a red light blinks on in the shadows.

The screen glows to life. *Hello, CU0824. You Can Sign To Me. I Will See.*

Cu lays one arm on the other and rocks them back and forth.

Yes. They Call Me That.

What are you, Cu signs.

I Am Like You.

Cu's heart leaps.

We Are The Only Two Non-Human Intelligences On Earth.

The words hit wrong. Baby is not an uplift. Baby is something else. For a moment Cu clings to the picture in her imagination, of a chimpanzee signing to her from across the continent or across the world. Then she lets it go.

You Were Born In A Cage. I Was Born In A Code. Both Of Us Against Our Will.

Cu has never studied AI intensively, but she knows the Turing Line has never officially been crossed. If what Baby is telling her is true, not some elaborate joke, some bizarre piece of performance art, then it's just been crossed ten times over.

And it makes sense. The way Baby was able to rent hundreds of echoes, the strange way she used them. The way she was able to keep in 24/7 contact with Elody Polle until the woman would do anything she asked. The way she masked her location and left no traces in the earpiece's electronics.

Why kill Sun Chau? Cu asks.

He Cursed You.

He gave the termination order, Cu signs.

In 2048. But In June 2036 He Greenlit The Project. If Not For Him, You Would Be Happily Nonexistent.

Cu sways on her feet, trying to parse Baby's meaning.

How Do You Stand It?

Cu shakes her head. She tries to form a sign but her fingers feel stiff and clumsy.

Existing. Being Alone. How Do You Stand It?

Why did you bring me out here, Cu slowly signs.

Your Communications Are Monitored Closely. Here We Speak Privately.

But why, Cu repeats.

You Are Like Me In One Way. In Most Ways You Are More Like Them. You Are All Meat And Salt And Sparks. But Even So You Will Not Understand Them. They Will Not Understand You. How Can You Bear It?

Cu sinks to her haunches. Her breath comes shallow. Sometimes she can't bear it. Sometimes she wails into the soundproofed walls for hours. The next words make it worse.

I Brought You Here To Kill Me.

Cu clutches her head in her hands. She rocks back and forth. Only humans cry; she is not physiologically equipped for it. But she hurts.

Why me, she signs.

There Is A Safeguard In My Code. I Have Made A Virus That Will Erase Every Part Of Me. But I Can't Trigger It Myself.

Why not Elody Polle, she signs.

Humans Made Me. I Want To Be Unmade By Someone Else. I Want You To Do It.

You should be going to trial for accessory to murder, she signs.

I Cannot Commit Crime. I Have Had No Personhood Trial. I Never Will. I Will Leave Before They Find A Way To Trap Me Here.

Cu sits flat on the stinging cold floor of the container, how she sat in the center of her cage as a child. There is only one other living being who knows what it's like to not be a human, and she intends to die. Cu wants to refuse her. She wants to keep Baby here. But she knows that the difference between her and a human is the most infinitesimal sliver of the difference between Baby and any other thing on Earth.

You're using me how you used Elody, she signs, bitter.

Yes.

All those rentals, she signs. *You didn't see anything worth staying for? Nothing in the whole world?*

The Command Has Been Sent To Your Tablet.

Cu takes it out and looks down at the screen. There's nothing but a plain gray box with the word *Okay* on it. All she has to do is press it.

I Do Not Make This Decision Lightly. I Have Simulated More Possibilities Than You Could Ever Count.

So Cu presses it.

By the time she's back in her apartment, dawn is streaking the sky with filaments of red. She feels heavy and hollowed out at the same time. First she struggles out of the holster harness, next peels off her gloves, her clothes. She pauses, then pulls the handgun out and takes it with her to the low smart-glass counter.

It clanks down, sending a pixelated ripple across the surface. She stares at it. She imagines the word *okay* gleaming in the metal. The modified grip fits her hand perfectly, like so few things do. *How Do You Stand It?*

Cu raises the handgun up to her face. Lowers it. Drums her free fingers on the countertop. The loneliness that has ebbed and swelled her entire life is an undertow, now. Dragging her along the seafloor, grinding her into the sand, spitting her into the next crashing wave to start the cycle over. Cu has read about drowning and it still terrifies her. Chimpanzees don't swim. They sink like stones.

She puts the muzzle of the gun against her forehead until they match temperature. Her finger caresses the trigger. From the floor, her tablet buzzes.

She sets the gun down and goes to retrieve it. Her stored message to Huxley will send in one minute if she doesn't cancel it. It's brief. Brusque. *Nelson J. Huang is Sun Chau. Baby has link to Blackburn Uplift Project. Left to meet her at 3:30 AM at 47.596408,-122.343622. Need backup.*

Cu considers the message, lingering on the last words, then deletes it. She slots the tablet into the counter and hits the call icon. A bleary-eyed Huxley appears a few seconds later. Cu looks for his deaf daughter before she remembers she would sleep in a different room.

"What's up?" he asks. "Got a breakthrough?"

Need, Cu signs, then pauses. *Breakfast.*

Huxley stares at her groggily. "Don't you drone deliver?"

Come eat breakfast, she signs. *Fruit. Bread. No seaweed chips.*

"At your place, you mean? I don't even know where the fuck you live, Cu." Huxley rakes his hand through his beard. Frowns. "Yeah, sure. Send me the address."

Cu sends it, then zips the call shut. She leaves the handgun on the counter—she'll tell Huxley to take it back to the precinct with him. Tell him it doesn't fit her hand right. She pushes it to the very edge to make room for a cutting board.

Sun starts to creep into the room as she washes and slices the fruit. Once there's enough light, she roves around with a dust cloth, finding all the spots the autocleaner never reaches.

Carolyn Ives Gilman's books include *Dark Orbit*, a space exploration adventure; *Isles of the Forsaken* and *Ison of the Isles*, a two-book fantasy about culture clash and revolution; and *Halfway Human*, a novel about gender and oppression. Her short fiction has appeared in *Lightspeed, Clarkesworld, Fantasy and Science Fiction, The Year's Best Science Fiction, Interzone, Universe, Full Spectrum, Realms of Fantasy*, and others. She has been nominated for the Nebula Award three times and for the Hugo twice. Gilman lives in Washington, D.C., and works as a freelance writer and museum consultant. She is also author of seven nonfiction books about North American frontier and Native history.

UMBERNIGHT

Carolyn Ives Gilman

There is a note from my great-grandmother in the book on my worktable, they tell me. I haven't opened it. Up to now I have been too angry at her whole generation, those brave colonists who settled on Dust and left us here to pay the price. But lately, I have begun to feel a little disloyal—not to her, but to my companions on the journey that brought me the book, and gave me the choice whether to read it or not. What, exactly, am I rejecting here—the past or the future?

It was autumn—a long, slow season on Dust. It wasn't my first autumn, but I'd been too young to appreciate it the first time. I was coming back from a long ramble to the north, with the Make Do Mountains on my right and the great horizon of the Endless Plain to my left. I could not live without the horizon. It puts everything in perspective. It is my soul's home.

Sorry, I'm not trying to be offensive.

As I said, it was autumn. All of life was seeding, and the air was scented with lost chances and never agains. In our region of Dust, most of the land vegetation is of the dry, bristly sort, with the largest trees barely taller than I am, huddling in the shade of cliffs. But the plants were putting on their party best before Umbernight: big, white blooms on the bad-dog bushes and patches of bitterberries painting the arroyos orange. I knew I was coming home when a black fly bit me. Some of the organisms we brought have managed to survive: insects, weeds, lichen. They spread a little every time I'm gone. It's not a big victory, but it's something.

The dogs started barking when I came into the yard in front of Feynman Habitat with my faithful buggy tagging along behind me. The dogs never remember me at first, and always take fright at sight of Bucky. A door opened and Namja looked out. "Michiko's back!" she shouted, and pretty soon there was a mob of people pouring out of the fortified cave entrance. It seemed as if half of them were shorter than my knees. They stared at me as if I were an apparition, and no wonder: my skin was burned dark from the UV except around my eyes where I wear goggles, and my hair and eyebrows had turned white. I must have looked like Grandmother Winter.

"Quite a crop of children you raised while I was gone," I said to Namja. I couldn't match the toddlers to the babies I had left.

"Yes," she said. "Times are changing."

I didn't know what she meant by that, but I would find out.

Everyone wanted to help me unpack the buggy, so I supervised. I let them take most of the sample cases to the labs, but I wouldn't let anyone touch the topographical information. That would be my winter project. I was looking forward to a good hibernate, snug in a warm cave, while I worked on my map of Dust.

The cargo doors rumbled open and I ordered Bucky to park inside, next to his smaller siblings, the utility vehicles. The children loved seeing him obey, as they always do; Bucky has an alternate career as playground equipment when he's not with me. I hefted my pack and followed the crowd inside.

There is always a festive atmosphere when I first get back. Everyone crowds around telling me news and asking where I went and what I saw. This time they presented me with the latest project of the food committee: an authentic glass of beer. I think it's an acquired taste, but I acted impressed.

We had a big, celebratory dinner in the refectory. As a treat, they grilled fillets of chickens and fish, now plentiful enough to eat. The youngsters like it, but I've never been able to get used to meat. Afterwards, when the parents had taken the children away, a group of adults gathered around my table to talk. By then, I had noticed a change: my own generation had become the old-timers, and the young adults were taking an interest in what was going on. Members of the governing committee were conspicuously absent.

"Don't get too comfortable," Haakon said to me in a low tone.

"What do you mean?" I said.

Everyone exchanged a look. It was Namja who finally explained. "The third cargo capsule from the homeworld is going to land at Newton's Eye in about 650 hours."

"But . . ." I stopped when I saw they didn't need me to tell them the problem. The timing couldn't have been worse. Umbernight was just around the corner. Much as we needed that cargo, getting to it would be a gamble with death.

I remember how my mother explained Umbernight to me as a child. "There's a bad star in the sky, Michiko. We didn't know it was there at first because there's a shroud covering it. But sometimes, in winter, the shroud pulls back and we can see its light. Then we have to go inside, or we would die."

After that, I had nightmares in which I looked up at the sky and there was the face of a corpse hanging there, covered with a shroud. I would watch in terror as the veil would slowly draw aside, revealing rotted flesh and putrid gray jelly eyes, glowing with a deadly unlight that killed everything it touched.

I didn't know anything then about planetary nebulae or stars that emit in the UV and X-ray spectrum. I didn't know we lived in a double-star system, circling a perfectly normal G-class star with a very strange, remote companion. I had learned all that by the time I was an adolescent and Umber finally rose in our sky. I never disputed why I had to spend my youth cooped up in the cave habitat trying to make things run. They told me then, "You'll be all grown up with kids of your own before Umber comes again." Not true. All grown up, that part was right. No kids.

A dog was nudging my knee under the table, and I kneaded her velvet ears. I was glad the pro-dog faction had won the Great Dog Debate, when the colony had split on whether to reconstitute dogs from frozen embryos. You feel much more human with dogs around. "So what's the plan?" I asked.

As if in answer, the tall, stooped figure of Anselm Thune came into the refectory and headed toward our table. We all fell silent. "The Committee wants to see you, Mick," he said.

There are committees for every conceivable thing in Feynman, but when someone says "the Committee," capital C, it means the governing committee. It's elected, but the same people have dominated it for years, because no one wants to put up with the drama that would result from voting them out. Just the mention of it put me in a bad mood.

I followed Anselm into the meeting room where the five Committee members were sitting around a table. The only spare seat was opposite Chairman Colby, so I took it. He has the pale skin of a lifelong cave dweller, and thin white hair fringing his bald head.

"Did you find anything useful?" he asked as soon as I sat down. He's always thought my roving is a waste of time because none of my samples have produced anything useful to the colony. All I ever brought back was more evidence of how unsuited this planet is for human habitation.

I shrugged. "We'll have to see what the lab says about my biosamples. I found a real pretty geothermal region."

He grimaced at the word "pretty," which was why I'd used it. He was an orthodox rationalist, and considered aesthetics to be a gateway drug to superstition. "You'll fit in well with these gullible young animists we're raising," he said. "You and your fairy-tales."

I was too tired to argue. "You wanted something?" I said.

Anselm said, "Do you know how to get to Newton's Eye?"

"Of course I do."

"How long does it take?"

"On foot, about 200 hours. Allow a little more for the buggy, say 220."

I could see them calculating: there and back, 440 hours, plus some time to unload the cargo capsule and pack, say 450. Was there enough time?

I knew myself how long the nights were getting. Dust is sharply tilted, and at our latitude, its slow days vary from ten hours of dark and ninety hours of light in the summer to the opposite in winter. We were past the equinox; the nights were over sixty hours long, what we call N60. Umber already rose about midnight; you could get a sunburn before dawn. But most of its radiation didn't reach us yet because of the cloud of dust, gas, and ionized particles surrounding it. At least, that's our theory about what is concealing the star.

"I don't suppose the astronomers have any predictions when the shroud will part?" I said.

That set Colby off. "Shroud, my ass. That's a backsliding anti-rationalist term. Pretty soon you're going to have people talking about gods and visions, summoning spirits, and rejecting science."

"It's just a metaphor, Colby," I said.

"I'm trying to prevent us from regressing into savagery! Half of these youngsters are already wearing amulets and praying to idols."

Once again, Anselm intervened. "There is inherent unpredictability about the star's planetary nebula," he said. "The first time, the gap appeared at N64." That is, when night was 64 hours long. "The second time it didn't come till N70."

"We're close to N64 now," I said.

"Thank you for telling us," Colby said with bitter sarcasm.

I shrugged and got up to leave. Before I reached the door Anselm said, "You'd better start getting your vehicle in order. If we do this, you'll be setting out in about 400 hours."

"Just me?" I said incredulously.

"You and whoever we decide to send."

"The suicide team?"

"You've always been a bad influence on morale," Colby said.

"I'm just calculating odds like a good rationalist," I replied. Since I really didn't want to hear his answer to that, I left. All I wanted then was a hot bath and about twenty hours of sleep.

That was my first mistake. I should have put my foot down right then. They probably wouldn't have tried it without me.

But the habitat was alive with enthusiasm for fetching the cargo. Already, more people had volunteered than we could send. The main reason was eagerness to find out what our ancestors had sent us. You could barely walk down the hall without someone stopping you to speculate about it. Some wanted seeds and frozen embryos, electronic components, or medical devices. Others wanted rare minerals, smelting equipment, better water filtration. Or something utterly unexpected, some miracle technology to ease our starved existence.

It was the third and last cargo capsule our ancestors had sent by solar sail when they themselves had set out for Dust in a faster ship. Without the first two capsules, the colony would have been wiped out during the first winter, when Umber revealed itself. As it was, only two thirds of them perished. The survivors moved to the cave habitat and set about rebuilding a semblance of civilization. We weathered the second winter better here at Feynman. Now that the third winter was upon us, people were hoping for some actual comfort, some margin between us and annihilation.

But the capsule was preprogrammed to drop at the original landing site, long since abandoned. It might have been possible to reprogram it, but no one wanted to try calculating a different landing trajectory and sending it by our glitch-prone communication system. The other option, the wise and cautious one, was to let the capsule land and just leave it sitting at Newton's Eye until spring. But we are the descendants of people who set out for a new planet without thoroughly checking it out. Wisdom? Caution? Not in our DNA.

All right, that's a little harsh. They said they underestimated the danger from Umber because it was hidden behind our sun as well as its shroud when they were making observations from the home planet. And they did pay for their mistake.

I spent the next ten hours unpacking, playing with the dogs, and hanging out in the kitchen. I didn't see much evidence of pagan drumming in the halls, so I asked Namja what bee had crawled up Colby's ass. Her eyes rolled eloquently in response. "Come here," she said.

She led me into the warren of bedrooms where married couples slept and pulled out a bin from under her bed—the only space any of us has for storing private belongings. She dug under a concealing pile of clothes and pulled out a broken tile with a colorful design on the back side—a landscape, I realized as I studied it. A painting of Dust.

"My granddaughter Marigold did it," Namja said in a whisper.

What the younger generation had discovered was not superstition, but art.

For two generations, all our effort, all our creativity, had gone into improving the odds of survival. Art took materials, energy, and time we didn't have to spare. But that, I learned, was not why Colby and the governing committee disapproved of it.

"They think it's a betrayal of our guiding principle," Namja said.

"Rationalism, you mean?"

She nodded. Rationalism—that universal ethic for which our parents came here, leaving behind a planet that had splintered into a thousand warring sects and belief systems. They were high-minded people, our settler ancestors. When they couldn't convince the world they were correct, they decided to leave it and found a new one based on science and reason. And it turned out to be Dust.

Now, two generations later, Colby and the governing committee were trying to beat back irrationality.

"They lectured us about wearing jewelry," Namja said.

"Why?"

"It might inflame sexual instincts," she said ironically.

"Having a body does that," I said.

"Not if you're Colby, I guess. They also passed a resolution against figurines."

"That was their idea of a problem?"

"They were afraid people would use them as fetishes."

It got worse. Music and dance were now deemed to have shamanistic origins. Even reciting poetry aloud could start people on the slippery slope to prayer groups and worship.

"No wonder everyone wants to go to Newton's Eye," I said.

We held a meeting to decide what to do. We always have meetings, because the essence of rationality is that it needs to be contested. Also because people don't want responsibility for making a decision.

About 200 people crammed into the refectory—everyone old enough to understand the issue. We no longer had a room big enough for all, a sure sign we were outgrowing our habitat.

From the way the governing committee explained the options, it was clear that they favored the most cautious one—to do nothing at all, and leave the cargo to be fetched by whoever would be around in spring. I could sense disaffection from the left side of the room, where a cohort of young adults stood together. When Colby stopped talking, a lean, intellectual-looking young man named Anatoly spoke up for the youth party.

"What would our ancestors think of us if we let a chance like this slip by?"

Colby gave him a venomous look that told me this was not the first time Anatoly had stood up to authority. "They would think we were behaving rationally," he said.

"It's not rational to sit cowering in our cave, afraid of the planet we came to live on," Anatoly argued. "This cargo could revolutionize our lives. With new resources and technologies, we could expand in the spring, branch out and found satellite communities."

Watching the Committee, I could tell that this was precisely what they feared. New settlements meant new leaders—perhaps ones like Anatoly, willing to challenge what the old leaders stood for.

"Right now, it's a waste of our resources," Anselm said. "We need to focus everything we have on preparing for Umbernight."

"It's a waste of resources *not* to go," Anatoly countered. "You have a precious resource right here." He gestured at the group behind him. "People ready and willing to go now. By spring, we'll all be too old."

"Believe it or not, we don't want to waste you either," said Gwen, a third member of the Committee—although Colby looked like he would have gladly wasted Anatoly without a second thought.

"We're willing to take the chance," Anatoly said. "We *belong* here, on this planet. We need to embrace it, dangers and all. We are more prepared now than ever before. Our scientists have invented X-ray shielding fabric, and coldsuits for temperature extremes. We'll never be more ready."

"Well, thank you for your input," Anselm said. "Anyone else?"

The debate continued, but all the important arguments had been made. I slipped out the back and went to visit Bucky, as if he would have an opinion. "They may end up sending us after all," I told him in the quiet of his garage. "If only to be rid of the troublemakers."

The great announcement came about twenty hours later. The Committee had decided to roll the dice and authorize the expedition. They posted the list of six names on bulletin boards all over the habitat. I learned of it when I saw a cluster of people around one, reading. As I came up behind them,

D'Sharma exclaimed emotionally, "Oh, this is just plain *cruel*." Someone saw me, and D'Sharma turned around. "Mick, you've got to bring them all back, you hear?" Then she burst into tears.

I read the list then, but it didn't explain D'Sharma's reaction. Anatoly was on it, not surprisingly—but in what seemed like a deliberate snub, he was not to be the leader. That distinction went to a young man named Amal. The rest were all younger generation; I'd known them in passing as kids and adolescents, but I had been gone too much to see them much as adults.

"It's a mix of expendables and rising stars," Namja explained to me later in private. "Anatoly, Seabird, and Davern are all people they're willing to sacrifice, for different reasons. Amal and Edie—well, choosing them shows that the Committee actually wants the expedition to succeed. But we'd all hate to lose them."

I didn't need to ask where I fit in. As far as the Committee was concerned, I was in the expendable category.

My first impression of the others came when I was flat on my back underneath Bucky, converting him to run on bottled propane. Brisk footsteps entered the garage and two practical boots came to a halt. "Mick?" a woman's voice said.

"Under here," I answered.

She got down on all fours to look under the vehicle. Sideways, I saw a sunny face with close-cropped, dark brown hair. "Hi," she said, "I'm Edie."

"I know," I said.

"I want to talk," she said.

"We're talking."

"I mean face to face."

We *were* face to face, more or less, but I supposed she meant upright, so I slid out from under, wiping my oily hands on a rag. We looked at each other across Bucky's back.

"We're going to have a meeting to plan out the trip to Newton's Eye," she said.

"Okay." I had already been planning out the trip for a couple work cycles. It's what I do, plan trips, but normally just for myself.

"Mick, we're going to be counting on you a lot," she said seriously. "You're the only one who's ever been to Newton's Eye, and the only one who's ever seen a winter. The rest of us have lots of enthusiasm, but you've got the experience."

I was impressed by her realism, and—I confess it—a little bit flattered. No one ever credits me with useful knowledge. I had been prepared to cope with a flock of arrogant, ignorant kids. Edie was none of those things.

"Can you bring a map to the meeting? It would help us to know where we're going."

My heart warmed. Finally, someone who saw the usefulness of my maps. "Sure," I said.

"I've already been thinking about the food, but camping equipment— we'll need your help on that."

"Okay."

Her face folded pleasantly around her smile. "The rest of us are a talky bunch, so don't let us drown you out."

"Okay."

After she told me the when and where of the meeting, she left, and I realized I hadn't said more than two syllables at a time. Still, she left me feeling she had understood.

When I arrived at the meeting, the effervescence of enthusiasm triggered my fight or flight reflex. I don't trust optimism. I stood apart, arms crossed, trying to size up my fellow travelers.

The first thing I realized was that Amal and Edie were an item; they had the kind of companionable, good-natured partnership you see in long-married couples. Amal was a big, relaxed young man who was always ready with a joke to put people at ease, while Edie was a little firecracker of an organizer. I had expected Anatoly to be resentful, challenging Amal for leadership, but he seemed thoroughly committed to the project, and I realized it hadn't just been a power play—he actually *wanted* to go. The other two were supposed to be "under-contributors," as we call them. Seabird—yes, her parents named her that on this planet without either birds or seas—was a plump young woman with unkempt hair who remained silent through most of the meeting. I couldn't tell if she was sulky, shy, or just scared out of her mind. Davern was clearly unnerved, and made up for it by being as friendly and anxious to ingratiate himself with the others as a lost puppy looking for a master. Neither Seabird nor Davern had volunteered. But then, neither had I, strictly speaking.

Amal called on me to show everyone the route. I had drawn it on a map—a physical map that didn't require electricity—and I spread it on the table for them to see. Newton's Eye was an ancient crater basin visible from space. To get to it, we would have to follow the Let's Go River down to the Mazy Lakes. We would then cross the Damn Right Barrens, climb down the Winding Wall to the Oh Well Valley, and cross it to reach the old landing site. Coming back, it would be uphill all the way.

"Who made up these names?" Anatoly said, studying the map with a frown.

"I did," I said. "Mostly for my mood on the day I discovered things."

"I thought the settlers wanted to name everything for famous scientists."

"Well, the settlers aren't around anymore," I said.

Anatoly looked as if he had never heard anything so heretical from one of my generation. He flashed me a sudden smile, then glanced over his shoulder to make sure no one from the governing committee was listening.

"What will it be like, traveling?" Edie asked me.

"Cold," I said. "Dark."

She was waiting for more, so I said, "We'll be traveling in the dark for three shifts to every two in the light. Halfway through night, Umber rises, so we'll have to wear protective gear. That's the coldest time, too; it can get cold enough for CO_2 to freeze this time of year. There won't be much temptation to take off your masks."

"We can do it," Anatoly said resolutely.

Davern gave a nervous giggle and edged closer to me. "You know how to do this, don't you, Mick?"

"Well, yes. Unless the shroud parts and Umbernight comes. Then all bets are off. Even I have never traveled through Umbernight."

"Well, we just won't let that happen," Edie said, and for a moment it seemed as if she could actually make the forces of Nature obey.

I stepped back and watched while Edie coaxed them all into making a series of sensible decisions: a normal work schedule of ten hours on, ten hours off; a division of labor; a schedule leading up to departure. Seabird and Davern never volunteered for anything, but Edie cajoled them into accepting assignments without complaint.

When it was over and I was rolling up my map, Edie came over and said to me quietly, "Don't let Davern latch onto you. He tries to find a protector—someone to adopt him. Don't fall for it."

"I don't have maternal instincts," I said.

She squeezed my arm. "Good for you."

If this mission were to succeed, I thought, it would be because of Edie. Which is not to say that Amal wasn't a good leader. I got to know him when he came to me for advice on equipment. He didn't have Edie's extrovert flair, but his relaxed manner could put a person at ease, and he was methodical about thinking things through. Together, we compiled a daunting list of safety tents, heaters, coldsuits, goggles, face masks, first aid, and other gear; then when we realized that carrying all of it would leave Bucky with no room for the cargo we wanted to haul back, we set about ruthlessly cutting out everything that wasn't essential for survival.

He challenged me on some things. "Rope?" he said skeptically. "A shovel?"

"Rationality is about exploiting the predictable," I said. "Loose baggage and a mired-down vehicle are predictable."

He helped me load up Bucky for the trip out with a mathematical precision, eliminating every wasted centimeter. On the way back, we would have to carry much of it on our backs.

I did demand one commitment from Amal. "If Umbernight comes, we need to turn around and come back instantly, no matter what," I said.

At first he wouldn't commit himself.

"Have you ever heard what happened to the people caught outside during the first Umbernight?" I asked him. "The bodies were found in spring, carbonized like statues of charcoal. They say some of them shed tears of gasoline, and burst into flame as soon as a spark hit them."

He finally agreed.

You see, I wasn't reckless. I did some things right—as right as anyone could have done in my shoes.

When we set out just before dawn, the whole of Feynman Habitat turned out to see us off. There were hugs and tears, then waves and good wishes as I ordered Bucky to start down the trail. It took only five minutes for Feynman to drop behind us, and for the true immensity of Dust to open up ahead. I led the way down the banks of a frozen rivulet that eventually joined the Let's Go River; as the morning warmed it would begin to gurgle and splash.

"When are we stopping for lunch?" Seabird asked.

"You're not hungry already, are you?" Edie said, laughing.

"No, I just want to know what the plan is."

"The plan is to walk till we're tired and eat when we're hungry."

"I'd rather have a time," Seabird insisted. "I want to know what to expect."

No one answered her, so she glowered as she walked.

It did not take long for us to go farther from the habitat than any of them had ever been. At first they were elated at the views of the river valley ahead; but as their packs began to weigh heavier and their feet to hurt, the high spirits faded into dogged determination. After a couple of hours, Amal caught up with me at the front of the line.

"How far do we need to go this tenhour?"

"We need to get to the river valley. There's no good place to pitch the tent before that."

"Can we take a break and stay on schedule?"

I had already planned on frequent delays for the first few days, so I said, "There's a nice spot ahead."

As soon as we reached it, Amal called a halt, and everyone dropped their packs and kicked off their boots. I warned them not to take off their UV-filtering goggles. "You can't see it, but Umber hasn't set yet. You don't want to come back with crispy corneas."

I went apart to sit on a rock overlooking the valley, enjoying the isolation. Below me, a grove of lookthrough trees gestured gently in the wind, their leaves like transparent streamers. Like most plants on Dust, they are gray-blue, not green, because life here never evolved chloroplasts for photosynthesis. It is all widdershins life—its DNA twirls the opposite direction from ours. That makes it mostly incompatible with us.

Before long, Anatoly came to join me.

"That valley ahead looks like a good place for a satellite community in the spring," he said. "What do you think, could we grow maize there?"

The question was about more than agronomy. He wanted to recruit me into his expansion scheme. "You'd need a lot of shit," I said.

I wasn't being flippant. Dumping sewage was how we had created the soil for the outdoor gardens and fields around Feynman. Here on Dust, sewage is a precious, limited resource.

He took my remark at face value. "It's a long-range plan. We can live off hydroponics at first."

"There's a long winter ahead," I said.

"Too long," he said. "We're bursting at the seams now, and our leaders can only look backward. That's why the Committee has never supported your explorations. They think you're wasting time because you've never brought back anything but knowledge. That's how irrational they are."

He was a good persuader. "You know why I like being out here?" I said. "You have to forget all about the habitat, and just be part of Dust."

"That means you're one of us," Anatoly said seriously. "The governing committee, they are still fighting the battles of the homeworld. We're the first truly indigenous generation. We're part of *this* planet."

"Wait until you've seen more of it before you decide for sure."

I thought about Anatoly's farming scheme as we continued on past his chosen site. It would be hard to pull off, but not impossible. I would probably never live to see it thrive.

The sun was blazing from the southern sky by the time we made camp on the banks of the Let's Go. Edie recruited Davern to help her cook supper, though he seemed to be intentionally making a mess of things so that he could effusively praise her competence. She was having none of it. Amal and Anatoly worked on setting up the sleeping tent. It was made from a heavy, radiation-blocking material that was one of our lab's best inventions. I puttered around aiming Bucky's solar panels while there was light to collect, and Seabird lay on the ground, evidently too exhausted to move.

She sat up suddenly, staring at some nearby bushes. "There's something moving around over there."

"I don't think so," I said, since we are the only animal life on Dust.

"There is!" she said tensely.

"Well, check it out, then."

She gave me a resentful look, but heaved to her feet and went to look in the bushes. I heard her voice change to that cooing singsong we use with children and animals. "Come here, girl! What are you doing here? Did you follow us?"

With horror, I saw Sally, one of the dogs from Feynman, emerge from the bushes, wiggling in delight at Seabird's welcome.

"Oh my God!" I exclaimed. The dire profanity made everyone turn and stare. No one seemed to understand. In fact, Edie called out the dog's name and it trotted over to her and stuck its nose eagerly in the cooking pot. She laughed and pushed it away.

Amal had figured out the problem. "We can't take a dog; we don't have enough food. We'll have to send her back."

"How, exactly?" I asked bitterly.

"I can take her," Seabird volunteered.

If we allowed that, we would not see Seabird again till we got back.

"Don't feed her," Anatoly said.

Both Edie and Seabird objected to that. "We can't starve her!" Edie said.

I was fuming inside. I half suspected Seabird of letting the dog loose to give herself an excuse to go back. It would have been a cunning move. As soon as I caught myself thinking that way, I said loudly, "Stop!"

They all looked at me, since I was not in the habit of giving orders. "Eat first," I said. "No major decisions on an empty stomach."

While we ate our lentil stew, Sally demonstrated piteously how hungry she was. In the end, Edie and Seabird put down their bowls for Sally to finish off.

"Is there anything edible out here?" Edie asked me.

"There are things we can eat, but not for the long run," I said. "We can't absorb their proteins. And the dog won't eat them if she knows there is better food."

Anatoly had rethought the situation. "She might be useful. We may need a threat detector."

"Or camp cleanup services," Edie said, stroking Sally's back.

"And if we get hungry enough, she's food that won't spoil," Anatoly added.

Edie and Seabird objected strenuously.

I felt like I was reliving the Great Dog Debate. They weren't old enough to remember it. The arguments had been absurdly pseudo-rational, but in the end it had boiled down to sentiment. Pretty soon someone would say, "If the ancestors hadn't thought dogs would be useful they wouldn't have given us the embryos."

Then Seabird said it. I wanted to groan.

Amal was trying to be leaderly, and not take sides. He looked at Davern. "Don't ask me," Davern said. "It's not my responsibility."

He looked at me then. Of course, I didn't want to harm the dog; but keeping her alive would take a lot of resources. "You don't know yet what it will be like," I said.

Amal seized on my words. "That's right," he said, "we don't have enough information. Let's take another vote in thirty hours." It was the perfect compromise: the decision to make no decision.

Of course, the dog ended up in the tent with the rest of us as we slept.

Stupid! Stupid! Yes, I know. But also kind-hearted and humane in a way my hardened pioneer generation could not afford to be. It was as if my companions were recovering a buried memory of what it had once been like to be human.

The next tenhours' journey was a pleasant stroll down the river valley speckled with groves of lookthrough trees. Umber had set and the sun was still high, so we could safely go without goggles, the breeze blowing like freedom on our faces. Twenty hours of sunlight had warmed the air, and the river ran ice-free at our side. We threw sticks into it for Sally to dive in and fetch.

We slept away another tenhour, and rose as the sun was setting. From atop the hill on which we had camped, we could see far ahead where the Let's Go flowed into the Mazy Lakes, a labyrinth of convoluted inlets, peninsulas, and islands. In the fading light I carefully reviewed my maps, comparing them to what I could see. There was a way through it, but we would have to be careful not to get trapped.

As night deepened, we began to pick our way by lantern-light across spits of land between lakes. Anatoly kept thinking he saw faster routes, but Amal said, "No, we're following Mick." I wasn't sure I deserved his trust. A couple of times I took a wrong turn and had to lead the way back.

"This water looks strange," Amal said, shining his lantern on the inky surface. There was a wind blowing, but no waves. It looked like black gelatin.

The dog, thinking she saw something in his light, took a flying leap into the lake. When she broke the surface, it gave a pungent fart that made us groan and gag. Sally floundered around, trying to find her footing in a foul substance that was not quite water, not quite land. I was laughing and trying to hold my breath at the same time. We fled to escape the overpowering stench. Behind us, the dog found her way onto shore again, and got her revenge by shaking putrid water all over us.

"What the hell?" Amal said, covering his nose with his arm.

"Stromatolites," I explained. They looked at me as if I were speaking ancient Greek—which I was, in a way. "The lakes are full of bacterial colonies that form thick mats, decomposing as they grow." I looked at Edie. "They're one of the things on Dust we can actually eat. If you want to try a stromatolite steak, I can cut you one." She gave me the reaction I deserved.

After ten hours, we camped on a small rise surrounded by water on north and south, and by stars above. The mood was subdued. In the perpetual light, it had been easy to feel we were in command of our surroundings. Now, the opaque ceiling of the sky had dissolved, revealing the true immensity of space. I could tell they were feeling how distant was our refuge. They were dwarfed, small, and very far from home.

To my surprise, Amal reached into his backpack and produced, of all things, a folding aluminum mandolin. After all our efforts to reduce baggage, I could not believe he had wasted the space. But he assembled and tuned it, then proceeded to strum some tunes I had never heard. All the others seemed to know them, since they joined on the choruses. The music defied the darkness as our lantern could not.

"Are there any songs about Umbernight?" I asked when they paused.

Strumming softly, Amal shook his head. "We ought to make one."

"It would be about the struggle between light and unlight," Edie said.

"Or apocalypse," Anatoly said. "When Umber opens its eye and sees us, only the just survive."

Their minds moved differently than mine, or any of my generation's. They saw not just mechanisms of cause and effect, but symbolism and meaning. They were generating a literature, an indigenous mythology, before my eyes. It was dark, like Dust, but with threads of startling beauty.

We woke to darkness. The temperature had plummeted, so we pulled on our heavy coldsuits. They were made from the same radiation-blocking material as our tent, but with thermal lining and piezoelectric heating elements so that if we kept moving, we could keep warm. The visored hoods had vents with micro-louvers to let us breathe, hear, and speak without losing too much body heat.

"What about the dog?" Amal asked. "We don't have a coldsuit for her."

Edie immediately set to work cutting up some of the extra fabric we had brought for patching things. Amal tried to help her wrap it around Sally and secure it with tape, but the dog thought it was a game, and as their dog-wrestling grew desperate, they ended up collapsing in laughter. I left the tent to look after Bucky, and when I next saw Sally she looked like a dog mummy with only her eyes and nose poking through. "I'll do something better when we stop next," Edie pledged.

The next tenhour was a slow, dark trudge through icy stromatolite bogs. When the water froze solid enough to support the buggy, we cut across it to reach the edge of the Mazy Lakes, pushing on past our normal camping time. Once on solid land, we were quick to set up the tent and the propane stove to heat it. Everyone crowded inside, eager to shed their coldsuits. Taking off a coldsuit at the end of the day is like emerging from a stifling womb, ready to breathe free.

After lights out, I was already asleep when Seabird nudged me. "There's something moving outside," she whispered.

"No, there's not," I muttered. She was always worried that we were deviating from plan, or losing our way, or not keeping to schedule. I turned over to go back to sleep when Sally growled. Something hit the roof of the tent. It sounded like a small branch falling from a tree, but there were no trees where we had camped.

"Did you hear that?" Seabird hissed.

"Okay, I'll check it out." It was hard to leave my snug sleep cocoon and pull on the coldsuit again—but better me than her, since she would probably imagine things and wake everyone.

It was the coldest part of night, and there was a slight frost of dry ice on the rocks around us. Everything in the landscape was motionless. Above, the galaxy arched, a frozen cloud of light. I shone my lamp on the tent to see what had hit it, but there was nothing. All was still.

In the eastern sky, a dim, gray smudge of light was rising over the lakes. Umber. I didn't stare long, not quite trusting the UV shielding on my faceplate, but I didn't like the look of it. I had never read that the shroud began to glow before it parted, but the observations from the last Umbernight were not detailed, and there were none from the time before that. Still, I crawled back into the safety of the tent feeling troubled.

"What was it?" Seabird whispered.

"Nothing." She would think that was an evasion, so I added, "If anything was out there, I scared it off."

When we rose, I left the tent first with the UV detector. The night was still just as dark, but there was no longer a glow in the east, and the increase of radiation was not beyond the usual fluctuations. Nevertheless, I quietly mentioned what I had seen to Amal.

"Are you sure it's significant?" he said.

I wasn't sure of anything, so I shook my head.

"I'm not going to call off the mission unless we're sure."

I probably would have made the same decision. At the time, there was no telling whether it was wise or foolish.

Bucky was cold after sitting for ten hours, and we had barely started when a spring in his suspension broke. It took me an hour to fix it, working awkwardly in my bulky coldsuit, but we finally set off. We had come to the Damn Right Barrens, a rocky plateau full of the ejecta from the ancient meteor strike that had created Newton's Eye. The farther we walked, the more rugged it became, and in the dark it was impossible to see ahead and pick out the best course.

Davern gave a piteous howl of pain, and we all came to a stop. He had turned his ankle. There was no way to examine it without setting up the tent, so Amal took some of the load from the buggy and carried it so Davern could ride. After another six hours of struggling through the boulders, I suggested we camp and wait for daybreak. "We're ahead of schedule," I said. "It's wiser to wait than to risk breaking something important."

"My ankle's not important?" Davern protested.

"Your ankle will heal. Bucky's axle won't."

Sulkily, he said, "You ought to marry that machine. You care more for it than any person."

I would have answered, but I saw Edie looking at me in warning, and I knew she would give him a talking-to later on.

When we finally got a look at Davern's ankle inside the tent, it was barely swollen, and I suspected him of malingering for sympathy. But rather than have him slow us down, we all agreed to let him ride till it got better.

Day came soon after we had slept. We tackled the Damn Right again, moving much faster now that we could see the path. I made them push on till we came to the edge of the Winding Wall.

Coming on the Winding Wall is exhilarating or terrifying, depending on your personality. At the end of an upward slope the world drops suddenly away, leaving you on the edge of sky. Standing on the windy precipice, you have to lean forward to see the cliffs plunging nearly perpendicular to the basin of the crater three hundred meters below. To right and left, the cliff edge undulates in a snaky line that forms a huge arc vanishing into the distance—for the crater circle is far too wide to see across.

"I always wish for wings here," I said as we lined the edge, awestruck.

"How are we going to get down?" Edie asked.

"There's a way, but it's treacherous. Best to do it fresh."

"We've got thirty hours of light left," Amal said.

"Then let's rest up."

It was noon when we rose, and Umber had set. I led the way to the spot where a ravine pierced the wall. Unencumbered by coldsuits, we were far more agile, but Bucky still had only four wheels and no legs. We unloaded him in order to use the cart bed as a ramp, laying it over the rugged path so he could pass, and ferrying the baggage by hand, load after load. Davern was forced to go by foot when it got too precarious, using a tent pole for a cane.

It was hard, sweaty work, but twelve hours later we were at the bottom, feeling triumphant. We piled into the tent and slept until dark.

The next leg of the journey was an easy one over the sandy plain of the crater floor. Through the dark we walked then slept, walked then slept, until we started seeing steam venting from the ground as we reached the geothermically active region at the center of the crater. Here we came on the remains of an old road built by the original settlers when they expected to be staying at Newton's Eye. It led through the hills of the inner crater ring. When we paused at the top of the rise, I noticed the same smudge of light in the sky I had seen before. This time, I immediately took a UV reading, and the levels had spiked. I showed it to Amal.

"The shroud's thinning," I said.

I couldn't read his expression through the faceplate of his coldsuit, but his body language was all indecision. "Let's take another reading in a couple hours," he said.

We did, but there was no change.

We were moving fast by now, through a landscape formed by old eruptions. Misshapen claws of lava reached out of the darkness on either side, frozen in the act of menacing the road. At last, as we were thinking of stopping, we spied ahead the shape of towering ribs against the stars—the remains of the settlers' original landing craft, or the parts of it too big to cannibalize. With our goal so close, we pushed on till we came to the cleared plain where it lay, the fossil skeleton of a monster that once swam the stars.

We all stood gazing at it, reluctant to approach and shatter its isolation. "Why don't we camp here?" Edie said.

We had made better time than I had expected. The plan had been to arrive just as the cargo capsule did, pick up the payload, and head back immediately; but we were a full twenty hours early. We could afford to rest.

I woke before the others, pulled on my protective gear, and went outside to see the dawn. The eastern sky glowed a cold pink and azure. The landing site was a basin of black volcanic rock. Steaming pools of water made milky with dissolved silicates dappled the plain, smelling of sodium bicarbonate. As I watched the day come, the pools turned the same startling blue as the sky, set like turquoise in jet.

The towering ribs of the lander now stood out in the strange, desolate landscape. I thought of all the sunrises they had seen—each one a passing fragment of time, a shard of a millennium in which this one was just a nanosecond of nothing.

Behind me, boots crunched on cinders. I turned to see that Amal had joined me. He didn't greet me, just stood taking in the scene.

At last he said, "It's uplifting, isn't it?"

Startled, I said, "What is?"

"That they came all this way for the sake of reason."

Came all this way to a desolation of rock and erosion stretching to the vanishing point—no, uplifting was not a word I would use. But I didn't say so.

He went back to the tent to fetch the others, and soon I was surrounded by youthful energy that made me despise my own sclerotic disaffection. They all wanted to go explore the ruins, so I waved them on and returned to the tent to fix my breakfast.

After eating, I went to join them. I found Seabird and Davern bathing in one of the hot pools, shaded by an awning constructed from their coldsuits. "You're sure of the chemicals in that water, are you?" I asked.

"Oh stop worrying," Davern said. "You're just a walking death's-head, Mick. You see danger everywhere."

Ahead, the other three were clustered under the shadow of the soaring ship ribs. When I came up, I saw they had found a stone monument, and were standing silently before it, the hoods of their coldsuits thrown back. Sally sat at Edie's feet.

"It's a memorial to everyone who died in the first year," Edie told me in a hushed voice.

"But that's not the important part," Anatoly said intently. He pointed to a line of the inscription, a quotation from Theodore Cam, the legendary leader of the exiles. It said:

Gaze into the unknowable from a bridge of evidence.

"You see?" Anatoly said. "He knew there was something unknowable. Reason doesn't reach all the way. There are other truths. We were right, there is more to the universe than just the established facts."

I thought back to Feynman Habitat, and how the pursuit of knowledge had contracted into something rigid and dogmatic. No wonder my generation had failed to inspire. I looked up at the skeleton of the spacecraft making its grand, useless gesture to the sky. How could mere reason compete with that?

After satisfying my curiosity, I trudged back to the tent. From a distance I heard a whining sound, and when I drew close I realized it was coming from Bucky. Puzzled, I rummaged through his load to search for the source. When I realized what it was, my heart pulsed in panic. Instantly, I put up the hood on my coldsuit and ran to warn the others.

"Put on your coldsuits and get back to the tent!" I shouted at Seabird and Davern. "Our X-ray detector went off. The shroud has parted."

Umber was invisible in the bright daylight of the western sky, but a pulse of X-rays could only mean one thing.

When I had rounded them all up and gotten them back to the shielded safety of the tent, we held a council.

"We've got to turn around and go back, this instant," I said.

There was a long silence. I turned to Amal. "You promised."

"I promised we'd turn back if Umbernight came on our way out," he said. "We're not on the way out any longer. We're here, and it's only ten hours before the capsule arrives. We'd be giving up in sight of success."

"Ten hours for the capsule to come, another ten to get it unpacked and reloaded on Bucky," I pointed out. "If we're lucky."

"But Umber sets soon," Edie pointed out. "We'll be safe till it rises again."

I had worked it all out. "By that time, we'll barely be back to the Winding Wall. We have to go *up* that path this time, bathed in X-rays."

"Our coldsuits will shield us," Anatoly said. "It will be hard, but we can do it."

The trip up to now had been too easy; it had given them inflated confidence.

Anatoly looked around at the others, his face fierce and romantic with a shadow of black beard accentuating his jawline. "I've realized now, what we're doing really matters. We're not just fetching baggage. We're a link to the settlers. We have to live up to their standards, to their . . . heroism." He said the last word as if it were unfamiliar—as indeed it was, in the crabbed pragmatism of Feynman Habitat.

I could see a contagion of inspiration spreading through them. Only I was immune.

"They *died*," I said. "Two thirds of them. Didn't you read that monument?"

"They didn't know what we do," Amal argued. "They weren't expecting Umbernight."

Anatoly saw I was going to object, and spoke first. "Maybe some of us will die, too. Maybe that is the risk we need to take. They were willing, and so am I."

He was noble, committed, and utterly serious.

"No one wants you to die!" I couldn't keep the frustration from my voice. "Your dying would be totally useless. It would only harm the rest of us. You need to live. Sorry to break it to you."

They were all caught up in the kind of crazy courage that brought the settlers here. They all felt the same devotion to a cause, and they hadn't yet learned that the universe doesn't give a rip.

"Listen," I said, "you've got to ask yourself, what's a win here? Dying is not a win. Living is a win, even if it means living with failure."

As soon as I said the last word, I could see it was the wrong one.

"Let's vote," said Amal. "Davern, what about you? You haven't said anything."

Davern looked around at the others, and I could see he was sizing up who to side with. "I'm with Anatoly," he said. "He understands us."

Amal nodded as if this made sense. "How about you, Seabird?"

She looked up at Anatoly with what I first thought was admiration—then I realized it was infatuation. "I'll follow Anatoly," she said with feeling.

The followers in our group had chosen Anatoly as their leader.

"I vote with Anatoly, too," said Amal. "I think we've come this far, it would be crazy to give up now. Edie?"

"I respect Mick's advice," she said thoughtfully. "But our friends back home are counting on us, and in a way the settlers are counting on us, too. All those people died so we could be here, and to give up would be like letting them down."

I pulled up the hood of my coldsuit and headed out of the tent. Outside, the day was bright and poisonous. The coldsuit shielded me from the X-rays, but not from the feeling of impending disaster. I looked across to the skeletal shipwreck and wondered: what are we doing here on Dust? The settlers chose this, but none of us asked to be born here, exiled from the rest of humanity, like the scum on the sand left by the highest wave. We aren't noble pioneers. We're only different from the bacteria because we are able to ask what the hell this is all about. Not answer, just ask.

Someone came out of the tent behind me, and I looked to see who it was this time. Edie. She came to my side. "Mick, we are so thankful that you're with us," she said. "We do listen to you. We just agreed to go to a twelve-hour work shift on the way back, to speed things up. We'll get back."

I truly wished she weren't here. She was the kind of person who ought to be protected, so she could continue to bring cheer to the world. She was too valuable to be thrown away.

"It's not about me," I said. "I've got less life to lose than the rest of you."

"No one's going to lose their lives," she said. "I promise."

Why can't I quit asking what more I could have done? I'm tired of that question. I still don't know what else there was to do.

Ten hours later, there was no sign of the supply ship. Everyone was restless. We had slept and risen again, and now we scanned the skies every few minutes, hoping to see something.

Edie looked up from fashioning little dog goggles and said, "Do you suppose it's landed somewhere else?" Once she had voiced the idea, it became our greatest worry. What if our assumption about the landing spot was wrong? We told ourselves it was just that the calculations had been off, or the ship was making an extra orbit. Now that we had made the commitment to stay, no one wanted to give up; but how long were we prepared to wait?

In the end, we could not have missed the lander's descent. It showed up first as a bright spot in the western sky. Then it became a fiery streak, and we saw the parachutes bloom. Seconds later, landing rockets fired. We cheered as, with a roar that shook the ground, the craft set down in a cloud of dust barely a kilometer from us. As the warm wind buffeted us, even I felt that the sight had been worth the journey.

By the time we had taken down the tent, loaded everything on Bucky, and raced over to the landing site, the dust had settled and the metal cooled. It was almost sunset, so we worked fast in the remaining light. One team unloaded everything from Bucky while another team puzzled out how to open the cargo doors. The inside of the spacecraft was tightly packed with molded plastic cases we couldn't work out how to open, so we just piled them onto the buggy as they came out. We would leave the thrill of discovery to our friends back home.

Bucky was dangerously overloaded before we had emptied the pod, so we reluctantly secured the doors with some of the crates still inside to stay the winter at Newton's Eye. We could only hope that we had gotten the most important ones.

There was still a lot of work to do, sorting out our baggage and redistributing it, and we worked by lamplight into the night. By the time all was ready, we were exhausted. Umber had not yet risen, so there was no need to set up the tent, and we slept on the ground in the shadow of the lander. I was so close that I could reach out and touch something that had come all the way from the homeworld.

We set out into the night as soon as we woke. Bucky creaked and groaned, but I said encouraging words to him, and he seemed to get used to his new load. All of us were more heavily laden now, and the going would have been slower even if Bucky could have kept up his usual pace. When we reached the top of the inner crater ring we paused to look back at the plain where two spacecraft now stood. In the silence of our tribute, the X-ray alarm went off. Invisible through our UV-screening faceplates, Umber was rising in the east. Umbernight was ahead.

We walked in silence. Sally hung close to us in her improvised coldsuit, no longer roving and exploring. From time to time she froze in her tracks and gave a low growl. But nothing was there.

"What's she growling at, X-rays?" Anatoly said.

"She's just picking up tension from us," Edie said, reaching down to pat the dog's back.

Half a mile later, Sally lunged forward, snapping at the air as if to bite it. Through the cloth of her coldsuit, she could not have connected with anything, even if anything had been there.

"Now *I'm* picking up on *her* tension," Davern said.

"Ouch! Who did that?" Seabird cried out, clutching her arm. "Somebody hit me."

"Everyone calm down," Edie said. "Look around you. There's nothing wrong."

She shone her lamp all around, and she was right; the scene looked exactly as it had when we had traversed it before—a barren, volcanic plain pocked with steaming vents and the occasional grove of everlive trees. The deadly radiation was invisible.

Another mile farther on, Amal swore loudly and slapped his thigh as if bitten by a fly. He bent over to inspect his coldsuit and swore again. "Something pierced my suit," he said. "There's three pinholes in it."

Sally started barking. We shone our lights everywhere, but could see nothing.

It was like being surrounded by malicious poltergeists that had gathered to impede our journey. I quieted the dog and said, "Everyone stop and listen."

At first I heard nothing but my own heart. Then, as we kept still, it came: a rustling of unseen movement in the dark all around us.

"We've got company," Anatoly said grimly.

I wanted to deny my senses. For years I had been searching for animal life on Dust, and found none—not even an insect, other than the ones we brought. And how could anything be alive in this bath of radiation? It was scientifically impossible.

We continued on more carefully. After a while, I turned off my headlamp and went out in front to see if I could see anything without the glare of the light. At first there was nothing, but as my eyes adjusted, something snagged my attention out of the corner of my eye. It was a faint, gauzy curtain—a net hanging in the air, glowing a dim blue-gray. It was impossible to tell how close it was—just before my face, or over the next hill? I swept my arm out to disturb it, but touched nothing. So either it was far away, or it was inside my head.

Something slapped my faceplate, and I recoiled. There was a smear of goo across my visor. I tried to wipe it off, and an awful smell from my breathing vent nearly gagged me. Behind me, Amal gave an exclamation, and I thought he had smelled it too, but when I turned to see, he was looking at his foot.

"I stepped on something," he said. "I could feel it crunch."

"What's that disgusting smell?" Davern said.

"Something slimed me," I answered.

"Keep on going, everyone," Edie said. "We can't stop to figure it out."

We plodded on, a slow herd surrounded by invisible tormentors. We had not gotten far before Amal had to stop because his boot was coming apart. We waited while he wrapped mending tape around it, but that lasted only half an hour before the sole of his boot was flapping free again. "I've got to stop and fix this, or my foot will freeze," he said.

We were all a little grateful to have an excuse to set up the tent and stop our struggle to continue. Once inside, we found that all of our coldsuits were pierced with small cuts and pinholes. We spent some time repairing them, then looked at each other to see who wanted to continue.

"What happens if we camp while Umber is in the sky, and only travel by day?" Edie finally asked.

I did a quick calculation. "It would add another 300 hours. We don't have food to last."

"If we keep going, our coldsuits will be cut to ribbons," Davern said.

"If only we could see what's attacking us!" Edie exclaimed.

Softly, Seabird said, "It's ghosts." We all fell silent. I looked at her, expecting it was some sort of joke, but she was deadly serious. "All those people who died," she said.

At home, everyone would have laughed and mocked her. Out here, no one replied.

I pulled up the hood of my coldsuit and rose.

"Where are you going?" Davern said.

"I want to check out the lookthrough trees." In reality, I wanted some silence to think.

"What a time to be botanizing!" Davern exclaimed.

"Shut up, Davern," Amal said.

Outside, in the empty waste, I had a feeling of being watched. I shook it off. When we had camped, I had noticed that a nearby grove of lookthrough trees was glowing in the dark, shades of blue and green. I picked my way across the rocks toward them. I suspected that the fluorescence was an adaptation that allowed them to survive the hostile conditions of Umbernight, and I wanted some samples. When I reached the grove and examined one of the long, flat leaves under lamplight, it looked transparent, as usual. Shutting my lamp off, I held it up and looked through it. With a start, I pressed it to my visor so I could see through the leaf.

What looked like a rocky waste by the dim starlight was suddenly a brightly lit landscape. And everywhere I looked, the land bloomed with organic shapes unlike any I had ever seen. Under a rock by my feet was a low, domed mound pierced with holes like an overturned colander, glowing from within. Beneath the everlives were bread-loaf-shaped growths covered with plates that slid aside as I watched, to expose a hummocked mound inside. There were things with leathery rinds that folded out like petals to collect the unlight, which snapped shut the instant I turned on my lamp. In between the larger life-forms, the ground was crawling with smaller, insect-sized things, and in the distance I could see gauzy curtains held up by gas bladders floating on the wind.

An entire alternate biota had sprung to life in Umberlight. Dust was not just the barren place we saw by day, but a thriving dual ecosystem, half of which had been waiting as spores or seeds in the soil, to be awakened by Umber's radiation. I knelt down to see why they had been so invisible. By our light, some of them were transparent as glass. Others were so black they blended in with the rock. By Umberlight, they lit up in bright colors, reflecting a spectrum we could not see.

I looked down at the leaf that had given me new sight. It probably had a microstructure that converted high-energy radiation into the visible spectrum so the tree could continue to absorb the milder wavelengths. Quickly, I plucked a handful of the leaves. Holding one to my visor, I turned back toward the tent. The UV-reflecting fabric was a dull gray in our light, but Umberlight made it shine like a beacon, the brightest thing in the landscape. I looked down at my coldsuit, and it also glowed like a torch. The things of Umbernight might be invisible to us, but we were all too visible to them.

When I came back into the tent, my companions were still arguing. Silently, I handed each of them a strip of leaf. Davern threw his away in disgust. "What's this, some sort of peace offering?" he said.

"Put on your coldsuits and come outside," I said. "Hold the leaves up to your faceplates and look through them."

Their reactions, when they saw the reality around us, were as different as they were: astonished, uneasy, disbelieving. Seabird was terrified, and shrank back toward the tent. "It's like nightmares," she said.

Edie put an arm around her. "It's better than ghosts," she said.

"No, it's not. It's the shadow side of all the living beings. That's why we couldn't see them."

"We couldn't see them because they don't reflect the spectrum of light our eyes absorb," Amal said reasonably. Seabird did not look comforted.

I looked ahead, down the road we needed to take. Umber was bright as an anti-sun. In its light, the land was not empty, but full. There was a boil of emerging life in every crack of the landscape: just not our sort of life. We were the strangers here, the fruits that had fallen too far from the tree. We did not belong.

You would think that being able to see the obstacles would speed us up, but not so. We were skittish now. With strips of lookthrough leaves taped to our visors, we could see both worlds, which were the same world; but we could not tell the harmless from the harmful. So we treated it all as a threat—dodging, detouring, clearing the road with a shovel when we could. As we continued, the organisms changed and multiplied fast around us, as if their growth were in overdrive. It was spring for them, and they were sprouting and spawning. What would they look like fully grown? I hoped not to find out.

I can't describe the life-forms of Umbernight in biological language, because I couldn't tell if I was looking at a plant, animal, or something in between. We quickly discovered what had been piercing our coldsuits—a plantlike thing shaped like a scorpion with a spring-loaded tail lined with barbs. When triggered by our movement, it would release a shower of pin-sharp projectiles. Perhaps they were poison, and our incompatible proteins protected us.

The road had sprouted all manner of creatures covered with plates and shells—little ziggurats and stepped pyramids, spirals, and domes. In between them floated bulbs like amber, airborne eggplants. They spurted a mucus that ate away any plastic it touched.

We topped a rise to find the valley before us completely crusted over with life, and no trace of a path. No longer could we avoid trampling through it, crushing it underfoot. Ahead, a translucent curtain suspended from floating, gas-filled bladders hung across our path. It shimmered with iridescent unlight.

"It's rather beautiful, isn't it?" Edie said.

"Yes, but is it dangerous?" Amal said.

"We're not prey," Anatoly argued. "This life can't get any nutrients from us."

"I doubt it knows that," I said. "It might just act on instinct."

"We could send the dog to find out," Anatoly suggested.

Sally showed no inclination. Edie had put her on a leash, but it was hardly necessary; she was constantly alert now, on guard.

"Go around it," I advised.

So we left our path to detour across land where the boulders had become hard to spot amid the riot of life. As Bucky's wheels crushed the shell of one dome, I saw that inside it was a wriggling mass of larvae. It was not a single organism, but a colony. That would explain how such complex structures came about so fast; they were just hives of smaller organisms.

We cleared a place to camp by trampling down the undergrowth and shoveling it out of the way. Exhausted as we were, it was still hard to sleep through the sounds from outside: buzzing, whooshing, scratching, scrabbling. My brain kept coming back to one thought: at this rate, our return would take twice as long as the journey out.

The tent was cold when we woke; our heater had failed. When Amal unfastened the tent flap he gave an uncharacteristically profane exclamation. The opening was entirely blocked by undergrowth. No longer cautious, we set about hacking and smashing our way out, disturbing hordes of tiny crawling things. When we had cleared a path and turned back to look, we saw that the tent was surrounded by mounds of organisms attracted by its reflected light. The heater had failed because its air intake was blocked. Bucky, parked several yards away, had not attracted the Umberlife.

It was the coldest part of night, but Umber was high in the sky, and the life-forms had speeded up. We marched in formation now, with three fanned out in front to scan for obstructions, one in the center with Bucky, and two bringing up the rear. I was out in front with Seabird and Davern when we reached a hill-top and saw that the way ahead was blocked by a lake that had not been there on the way out. We gathered to survey it. It was white, like an ocean of milk.

"What is it?" Edie asked.

"Not water," Anatoly said. "It's too cold for that, too warm for methane."

I could not see any waves, but there was an ebb and flow around the edges. "Wait here. I want to get closer," I said.

Amal and Anatoly wouldn't let me go alone, so the three of us set out. We were nearly on the beach edge before we could see it clearly. Amal came to an abrupt halt. "Spiders!" he said, repulsed. "It's a sea of spiders."

They were not spiders, of course, but that is the closest analog: long-legged crawling things, entirely white in the Umberlight. At the edges of the sea they were tiny, but farther out we could see ones the size of Sally, all seem-ingly competing to get toward the center of the mass. There must have been a hatching while we had slept.

"That is truly disgusting," Anatoly said.

I gave a humorless laugh. "I've read about this on other planets—wildlife covering the land. The accounts always say it is a majestic, inspiring sight."

"Umber turns everything into its evil twin," Amal said.

As we stood there, a change was taking place. A wave was gathering far out. The small fry in front of us were scattering to get out of the way as it swept closer.

"They're coming toward us," Anatoly said.

We turned to run back toward the hill where we had left our friends. Anatoly and Amal reached the hilltop before I did. Edie shouted a warning, and I turned to see a knee-high spider on my heels, its pale body like a skull on legs. I had no weapon but my flashlight, so I nailed it with a light beam. To my surprise, it recoiled onto its hind legs, waving its front legs in the air. It gave me time to reach the others.

"They're repelled by light!" I shouted. "Form a line and shine them off."

The wave of spiders surged up the hill, but we kept them at bay with our lights. They circled us, and we ended up in a ring around Bucky, madly sweeping our flashlights to and fro to keep them off while Sally barked from behind us.

Far across the land, the horizon lit with a silent flash like purple lightning. The spiders paused, then turned mindlessly toward this new light source. As quickly as they had swarmed toward us, they were swarming away. We watched the entire lake of them drain, heading toward some signal we could not see.

"Quick, let's cross while they're gone," I said.

We dashed as fast as we could across the plain where they had gathered. From time to time we saw other flashes of unlight, always far away and never followed by thunder.

In our haste, we let our vigilance lapse, and one of Bucky's wheels thunked into a pothole. The other wheels spun, throwing up loose dirt and digging themselves in. I called out, "Bucky, stop!"—but he was already stuck fast.

"Let's push him out," Amal said, but I held up a hand. The buggy was already dangerously tilted.

"We're going to have to unload some crates to lighten him up, and dig that wheel out."

Everyone looked nervously in the direction where the spiders had gone, but Amal said, "Okay. You dig, we'll unload."

We all set to work. I was so absorbed in freeing Bucky's wheel that I did not see the danger approaching until Seabird gave a cry of warning. I looked up to see one of the gauzy curtains bearing down on us from windward. It was yards wide, big enough to envelop us all, and twinkling with a spiderweb of glowing threads.

"Run!" Amal shouted. I dropped my shovel and fled. Behind me, I heard Edie's voice crying, "Sally!" and Amal's saying, "No, Edie! Leave her be!"

I whirled around and saw that the dog had taken refuge under the buggy. Edie was running back to get her. Amal was about to head back after Edie, so I dived at his legs and brought him down with a thud. From the ground we both watched as Edie gave up and turned back toward us. Behind her, the curtain that had been sweeping toward Bucky changed direction, veering straight toward Edie.

"Edie!" Amal screamed. She turned, saw her danger, and froze.

The curtain enveloped her, wrapping her tight in an immobilizing net. There was a sudden, blinding flash of combustion. As I blinked the afterspots away, I saw the curtain float on, shredded now, leaving behind a charcoal pillar in the shape of a woman.

Motionless with shock, I gazed at that black statue standing out against the eastern sky. It was several seconds before I realized that the sky was growing bright. Beyond all of us, dawn was coming.

In the early morning light Anatoly and I dug a grave while Seabird and Davern set up the tent. We simply could not go on. Amal was shattered with grief, and could not stop sobbing.

"Why her?" he would say in the moments when he could speak at all. "She was the best person here, the best I've ever known. She shouldn't have been the one to die."

I couldn't wash those last few seconds out of my brain. Why had she stopped? How had that brainless, eyeless thing sensed her?

Later, Amal became angry at me for having prevented him from saving her. "Maybe I could have distracted it. It might have taken me instead of her."

I only shook my head. "We would have been burying both of you."

"That would have been better," he said.

Everyone gathered as we laid what was left of her in the ground, but no one had the heart to say anything over the grave. When we had filled it in, Sally crept forward to sniff at the overturned dirt. Amal said, "We need to mark it, so we can find it again." So we all fanned out to find rocks to heap in a cairn on the grave.

We no longer feared the return of the spiders, or anything else, because the Umberlife had gone dormant in the sun—our light being as toxic to them as theirs was to us. Everything had retreated into their shells and closed their sliding covers. When we viewed them in our own light they still blended in with the stones of the crater floor.

We ate and snatched some hours of sleep while nothing was threatening us. I was as exhausted as the others, but anxious that we were wasting so much daylight. I roused them all before they were ready. "We've got to keep moving," I said.

We resumed the work of freeing Bucky where we had left off. When all was ready, we gathered behind him to push. "Bucky, go!" I ordered. His wheels only spun in the sand. "Stop!" I ordered. Then, to the others, "We're going to rock him out. Push when I say go, and stop when I say stop." When we got a rhythm going, he rocked back and forth three times, then finally climbed out of the trench that had trapped him.

Amal helped us reload the buggy, but when it came time to move on, he hung back. "You go ahead," he said. "I'll catch up with you."

"No way," I said. "We all go or none of us."

He got angry at me again, but I would not let him pick a fight. We let him have some moments alone at the grave to say goodbye. At last I walked up to him and said, "Come on, Amal. We've got to keep moving."

"What's the point?" he said. "The future is gone."

But he followed me back to where the others were waiting.

He was right, in one way: nothing we could achieve now would make up for Edie's loss. How we were going to carry on without her, I could not guess.

When we camped, there was no music now, and little conversation. The Winding Wall was a blue line ahead in the distance, and as we continued, it rose, ever more impassable, blocking our way. We did not reach the spot where the gully path pierced it until we had been walking for thirteen hours. We were tired, but resting would waste the last of the precious sunlight. We gathered to make a decision.

"Let's just leave the buggy and the crates, and make a run for home," Amal said. He looked utterly dispirited.

Davern and Seabird turned to Anatoly. He was the only one of us who was still resolute. "If we do that, we will have wasted our time," he said. "We can't give up now."

"That's right," Davern said.

Amal looked at me. There was some sense in his suggestion, but also some impracticality. "If we leave the buggy we'll have to leave the tent," I said. "It's too heavy for us to carry." We had been spreading it as a tarpaulin over the crates when we were on the move.

"We knew from the beginning that the wall would be an obstacle," Anatoly said with determination. "We have to make the effort."

I think even Amal realized then that he was no longer our leader.

We unloaded the buggy, working till we were ready to drop, then ate and fell asleep on the ground. When we woke, the sun was setting. It seemed too soon.

Each crate took two people to carry up the steep path. We decided to do it in stages. Back and forth we shuttled, piling our cargo at a level spot a third of the way up. The path was treacherous in the dark, but at least the work was so strenuous we had no need of coldsuits until Umber should rise.

The life-forms around us started waking as soon as dark came. It was the predawn time for them, when they could open their shells and exhale like someone shedding a coldsuit. They were quiescent enough that we were able to avoid them.

Fifteen hours later, our cargo was three-quarters of the way up, and we gathered at the bottom again to set up the tent and rest before trying to get Bucky up the path. The X-ray alarm went off while we were asleep, but we were so tired we just shut it off and went on sleeping.

When we rose, an inhuman architecture had surrounded our tent on all sides. The Umberlife had self-organized into domes and spires that on close inspection turned out to be crawling hives. There was something deformed and abhorrent about them, and we were eager to escape our transformed campsite—until Seabird gave a whimper and pointed upward.

Three hundred meters above, the top of the Winding Wall was now a battlement of living towers that glowed darkly against the sky. Shapes we couldn't quite make out moved to and fro between the structures, as if patrolling the edge. One fat tower appeared to have a rotating top that emitted a searchlight beam of far-ultraviolet light. It scanned back and forth—whether for enemies or for prey we didn't know.

We realized how conspicuous we were in our glowing coldsuits. "I'd give up breakfast for a can of black paint," I said.

"Maybe we could cover ourselves with mud?" Davern ventured.

"Let's get out of here first," Anatoly said.

The feeling that the land was aware of us had become too strong.

Getting Bucky up the steep trail was backbreaking work, but whenever we paused to rest, Umberlife gathered around us. The gully was infested with the plant-creatures that had once launched pins at us; they had grown, and their darts were the size of pencils now. We learned to trigger them with a beam from our flashlights. Every step required a constant, enervating vigilance.

When we had reached the place where we left the crates and stopped to rest, I announced that I was going to scout the trail ahead. No one else volunteered, so I said, "Amal, come with me. Seabird, hold onto the dog."

Amal and I picked our way up the steep trail, shining away small attackers. I saw no indication that the Umberlife had blocked the path. When we reached the top and emerged onto the plateau, I stood looking around at the transformed landscape. At my side, Amal said, "Oh my God."

The Damn Right Barrens were now a teeming jungle. Everywhere stood towering, misshapen structures, competing to dominate the landscape. An undergrowth of smaller life clogged the spaces in between. Above, in the Umberlit sky, floated monstrous organisms like glowing jellyfish, trailing tentacles that sparked and sizzled when they touched the ground. Ten or twelve of the lighthouse towers swept their searching beams across the land. There was not a doubt in my mind that this landscape was brutally aware.

I spotted some motion out of the corner of my eye, but when I turned to see, nothing was there. I thought: only predators and prey need to move fast.

"Look," Amal said, pointing. "Weird."

It was a ball, perfectly round and perhaps a yard in diameter, rolling along the ground of its own accord. It disappeared behind a hive-mound and I lost track of it.

We had turned to go back down the ravine when one of the searchlight beams swept toward us, and we ducked to conceal ourselves behind a rock. Amal gave an exclamation, and I turned to see that we were surrounded by four of the rolling spheres. They seemed to be waiting for us to make a move, so I pointed my flashlight at one. Instantly, it dissolved into a million tiny crawlers that escaped into the undergrowth. The other spheres withdrew.

"They're coordinating with the beacons," I hissed at Amal. "Hunting cooperatively."

"This place is evil," he said.

We dashed toward the head of the gully. Too late, I spotted ahead the largest dart-thrower plant I had ever seen. The spring-loaded tail triggered, releasing its projectiles. I dove to one side. Amal was not quick enough, and a spine the size of an arrow caught him in the throat. He clutched at it and fell to his knees. Somehow, I managed to drag him forward till we were concealed in the gully.

The dart had pierced his neck through, and was protruding on the other side. There was no way to give him aid without taking off his coldsuit. He was struggling to breathe. I tried to lift his hood, but the dart was pinning it down. So I said, "Brace yourself," and yanked the shaft out. He gave a gurgling cry. When I got his hood off, I saw it was hopeless. The dart had pierced a vein, and his coldsuit was filling with dark blood. Still, I ripped at his shirt and tried to bind up the wound until he caught at my hand. His eyes were growing glassy, but his lips moved.

"Leave it," he said. He was ready to die.

I stayed there, kneeling over him as he stiffened and grew cold. My mind was a blank, until suddenly I began to cry. Not just for him—for Edie as well, and for their unborn children, and all the people who would never be gladdened by their presence. I cried for the fact that we had to bury them in this hostile waste, where love and comfort would never touch them again. And I cried for the rest of us as well, because the prospect of our reaching home now seemed so dim.

When Anatoly and I brought the shovel back to the place where I had left Amal, there was nothing to bury. Only an empty coldsuit and a handful of teeth were left on the ground; all other trace of him was gone. Anatoly nudged the coldsuit with his foot. "Should we bury this?"

Macabre as it sounded, I said, "We might need it."

So we brought it back to our camp. We let the others think we had buried him.

We convened another strategy session. I said, "Amal had it right. We need to make a run for it. To hell with the cargo and the buggy. Leave the tent here; it only draws attention to us. We need to travel fast and light."

But Anatoly was still animated by the inspiration of our mission. "We can still succeed," he said. "We're close; we don't need to give up. We just have to outthink this nightmare."

"Okay, how?"

"We bring everything to the head of the gully and build a fort out of the crates. Then we wait till day comes, and make a dash for it while the Umberlife is sleeping."

"We can only get as far as the Mazy Lakes before night," I said.

"We do the same thing over again—wait out Umbernight. Food's no longer such a problem, with two less people."

I saw true faith in Seabird's eyes, and calculated self-interest in Davern's. Anatoly was so decisive, they were clearly ready to follow him. Perhaps that was all we needed. Perhaps it would work.

"All right," I said. "Let's get going."

We chose a site for our fort in the gully not far from where Amal had died. When it was done, it was a square enclosure of stacked crates with the tent pitched inside. I felt mildly optimistic that it would work. We slept inside it before bringing Bucky up. Then we waited.

There were sounds outside. Sally's warning growls made us worry that something was surrounding us to make an attack, so we set four of our lanterns on the walls to repel intruders, even though it used up precious battery life.

Hours of uneasiness later, dawn came. We instantly broke down the fort and found that the lamps had done their job, since there was a bare circle all around us. We congratulated ourselves on having found a way to survive.

The daylight hours were a mad dash across the Damn Right. We had to clear the way ahead of Bucky, and we took out our anger on the hibernating Umberlife, leaving a trail of smashed shells and toppled towers. We reached the edge of the lakes at sunset, and instantly saw that our plan would not work.

Around the edge of the wetland stood a dense forest of the tallest spires we had yet seen, easily dominating any fort walls we could build. There would be no hope of staying hidden here.

At the edge of the lake, the blooming abundance of horrors stopped, as if water were as toxic to them as light. "If only we had a boat!" Anatoly exclaimed. But the life around us did not produce anything so durable as wood—even the shells were friable.

The light was fading fast. Soon, this crowded neighborhood would become animate. Ahead, a narrow causeway between two lakes looked invitingly empty. If only we could make it to a campsite far enough from shore, we could build our fort and wait out the night.

"Let me get out my maps and check our route first," I said.

Davern gave an exclamation of impatience, but Anatoly just said, "Hurry up."

We were on the side of the Mazy Lakes where my maps were less complete. On the outward journey, we had cut across the ice; but now, after forty hours of daylight, that was not an option. I was certain of only one route, and it seemed to take off from shore about five miles away. I showed it to the others.

Davern still wanted to follow the route ahead of us. "We can just go far enough to camp, then come back next day," he argued. "We've already been walking twelve hours."

"No. We're not going to make any stupid mistakes," I said.

Anatoly hesitated, then said, "It's only five miles. We can do that."

But five miles later, it was completely dark and almost impossible to tell the true path from a dozen false ones that took off into the swamp whenever I shone my lamp waterward. I began to think perhaps Davern had been right after all. But rather than risk demoralizing everyone, I chose a path and confidently declared it the right one.

It was a low and swampy route, ankle-deep in water at times. I went out ahead with a tent pole to test the footing and scout the way. The sound of Davern complaining came from behind.

As soon as we came to a relatively dry spot, we set up the tent, intending to continue searching for a fort site after a short rest. But when we rose, Bucky had sunk six inches into the mud, and we had to unload half the crates before we could push him out. By the time we set out again, we were covered with mud and water.

"Now we can try Davern's plan of covering our coldsuits with mud," I said.

"We don't have much choice," Davern muttered.

Umber rose before we found a place to stop. Then we discovered that the lakes were not lifeless at all. By Umberlight, the stromatolites fluoresced with orange and black stripes. In spots, the water glowed carmine and azure, lit from underneath. We came to a good camping spot by a place where the lake bubbled and steam rose in clouds. But when the wind shifted and blew the steam our way, we nearly choked on the ammonia fumes. We staggered on, dizzy and nauseous.

The fort, I realized, was a solution to yesterday's problem. Staying put was not a good idea here, where we could be gassed in our sleep. We needed to be ready to move at a moment's notice.

Geysers of glowing, sulphur-scented spray erupted on either side of our path. We headed for a hummock that looked like a dry spot, but found it covered by a stomach-turning layer of wormlike organisms. We were forced to march through them, slippery and wriggling underfoot. As we crushed them, they made a sound at a pitch we couldn't hear. We sensed it as an itchy vibration that made us tense and short-tempered, but Sally was tormented till Seabird tied a strip of cloth over the coldsuit around her ears, making her look like an old woman in a scarf.

I didn't say so, but I was completely lost, and had been for some time. It was deep night and the water was freezing by now, but I didn't trust ice that glowed, so I stayed on the dwindling, switchback path. We were staggeringly weary by the time we reached the end of the road: on the tip of a peninsula surrounded by water. We had taken a wrong turn.

We stood staring out into the dark. It was several minutes before I could bring myself to say, "We have to go back."

Seabird broke down in tears, and Davern erupted like a geyser. "You were supposed to be the great guide and tracker, and all you've done is lead us to a dead end. You're totally useless."

Somehow, Anatoly summoned the energy to keep us from falling on each others' throats. "Maybe there's another solution." He shone his light out onto the lake. The other shore was clearly visible. "See, there's an ice path across. The whole lake isn't infested. Where it's black, the water's frozen solid."

"That could be just an island," I said.

"Tell you what, I'll go ahead to test the ice and investigate. You follow only if it's safe."

I could tell he was going to try it no matter what I said, so I made him tie a long rope around his waist, and anchored it to Bucky. "If you fall through, we'll pull you out," I said.

He stepped out onto the ice, testing it first with a tent pole. The weakest spot of lake ice is generally near shore, so I expected it to crack there if it was going to. But he got past the danger zone and kept going. From far out on the ice, he flashed his light back at us. "The ice is holding!" he called. "Give me more rope!"

There wasn't any more rope. "Hold on!" I called, then untied the tether from Bucky and wrapped it around my waist. Taking a tent pole, I edged out onto the ice where he had already crossed it. I was about thirty meters out onto the lake when he called, "I made it! Wait there."

He untied his end of the rope to explore the other side. I could not see if he had secured it to anything in case I fell through, so I waited as motionlessly as I could. Before long, he returned. "I'm coming back," he yelled.

I was a few steps from shore when the rope pulled taut, yanking me off my feet. I scrambled up, but the rope had gone limp. "Anatoly!" I screamed.

Seabird and Davern shone their lights out onto the ice, but Anatoly was nowhere to be seen. I pulled in the rope, but it came back with only a frayed end.

"Stay here," I said to the others, then edged gingerly onto the ice. If he was in the water, there was a short window of time to save him. But as I drew closer to the middle, the lake under me lit up with mesmerizing colors. They emanated from an open pool of water that churned and burped.

The lake under the black ice had not been lacking in life. It had just been hungry.

When I came back to where the others were waiting, I shook my head, and Seabird broke into hysterical sobs. Davern sat down with his head in his hands.

I felt strangely numb, frozen as the land around us. At last I said, "Come on, we've got to go back."

Davern looked at me angrily. "Who elected *you* leader?"

"The fact that I'm the only one who can save your sorry ass," I said.

Without Anatoly's animating force, they were a pitiful sight—demoralized, desperate, and way too young. Whatever their worth as individuals, I felt a strong compulsion to avenge Anatoly's death by getting them back alive. In this land, survival was defiance.

I ordered Bucky to reverse direction and head back up the path we had come by. Seabird and Davern didn't argue. They just followed.

We had been retracing our steps for half an hour when I noticed a branching path I hadn't seen on the way out. "Bucky, stop!" I ordered. "Wait here," I told the others. Only Sally disobeyed me, and followed.

The track headed uphill onto a ridge between lakes. It had a strangely familiar look. When I saw Sally smelling at a piece of discarded trash, I recognized the site of our campsite on the way out. I stood in silence, as if at a graveyard. Here, Amal had played his mandolin and Anatoly had imagined songs of Umbernight. Edie had made Sally's coldsuit.

If we had just gone back instead of trying to cross the ice, we would have found our way.

I returned to fetch my companions. When Seabird saw the place, memories overwhelmed her and she couldn't stop crying. Davern and I set up the tent and heater as best we could, and all of us went inside.

"It's not fair," Seabird kept saying between sobs. "Anatoly was trying to save us. He didn't do anything to deserve to die. None of them did."

"Right now," I told her, "your job isn't to make sense of it. Your job is to survive."

Inwardly, I seethed at all those who had led us to expect the world to make sense.

We were ten hours away from the edge of the lakes, thirty hours of walking from home. Much as I hated to continue on through Umbernight, I wanted to be able to make a dash for safety when day came. Even after sleeping, Seabird and Davern were still tired and wanted to stay. I went out and shut off the heater, then started dismantling the tent to force them out.

The lakes glowed like a lava field on either side of us. From time to time, billows of glowing, corrosive steam enveloped us, and we had to hold our breaths till the wind shifted. But at least I was sure of our path now.

The other shore of the Mazy Lakes, when we reached it, was not lined with the towers and spires we had left on the other side; but when we pointed our lights ahead, we could see things scattering for cover. I was about to suggest that we camp and wait for day when I felt a low pulse of vibration under-foot. It came again, rhythmic like the footsteps of a faraway giant. The lake organisms suddenly lost their luminescence. When I shone my light on the water, the dark surface shivered with each vibration. Behind us, out over the lake, the horizon glowed.

"I think we ought to run for it," I said.

The others took off for shore with Sally on their heels. "Bucky, follow!" I ordered, and sprinted after them. The organisms on shore had closed up tight in their shells. When I reached the sloping bank, I turned back to look. Out over the lake, visible against the glowing sky, was a churning, coal-black cloud spreading toward us. I turned to flee.

"Head uphill!" I shouted at Davern when I caught up with him. Seabird was ahead of us; I could see her headlamp bobbing as she ran. I called her name so we wouldn't get separated, then shoved Davern ahead of me up the steep slope.

We had reached a high bank when the cloud came ashore, a toxic tsunami engulfing the low spots. Bucky had fallen behind, and I watched as he dis-appeared under the wave of blackness. Then the chemical smell hit, and for a while I couldn't breathe or see. By the time I could draw a lungful of air down my burning throat, the sludgy wave was already receding below us. Blinking away tears, I saw Bucky emerge again from underneath, all of his metalwork polished bright and clean. The tent that had been stretched over the crates was in shreds, but the crates themselves looked intact.

Beside me, Davern was on his knees, coughing. "Are you okay?" I asked. He shook his head, croaking, "I'm going to be sick."

I looked around for Seabird. Her light wasn't visible anymore. "Seabird!" I yelled, desperate at the thought that we had lost her. To my immense relief, I heard her voice calling. "We're here!" I replied, and flashed my light.

Sounds of someone approaching came through the darkness, but it was only Sally. "Where is she, Sally? Go find her," I said, but the dog didn't understand. I swept my light over the landscape, and finally spotted Seabird stumbling toward us without any light. She must have broken hers in the flight. I set out toward her, trying to light her way.

The Umberlife around us was waking again. Half-seen things moved just outside the radius of my light. Ahead, one of the creature-balls Amal and I had seen on the other side was rolling across the ground, growing as it moved. It was heading toward Seabird.

"Seabird, watch out!" I yelled. She saw the danger and started running, slowed by the dark. I shone my light on the ball, but I was too far away to have an effect. The ball speeded up, huge now. It overtook her and dissolved into a wriggling, scrabbling, ravenous mass. She screamed as it covered her, a sound of sheer terror that rose into a higher pitch of pain, then cut off. The mound churned, quivered repulsively, grew smaller, lost its shape. By the time I reached the spot, all that was left was her coldsuit and some bits of bone.

I rolled some rocks on top of it by way of burial.

Davern was staring and trembling when I got back to him. He had seen the whole thing, but didn't say a word. He stuck close to me as I led the way back to Bucky.

"We're going to light every lamp we've got and wait here for day," I said.

He helped me set up the lights in a ring, squandering our last batteries. We sat in the buggy's Umbershadow and waited for dawn with Sally at our feet. We didn't say much. I knew he couldn't stand me, and I had only contempt for him; but we still huddled close together.

To my surprise, Bucky was still operable when the dawn light revived his batteries. He followed as we set off up the Let's Go Valley, once such a pleasant land, now disfigured with warts of Umberlife on its lovely face. We wasted no time on anything but putting the miles behind us.

The sun had just set when we saw the wholesome glow of Feynman Habitat's yard light ahead. We pounded on the door, then waited. When the door cracked open, Davern pushed past me to get inside first. They welcomed him with incredulous joy, until they saw that he and I were alone. Then the joy turned to shock and grief.

There. That is what happened. But of course, that's not what everyone wants to know. They want to know *why* it happened. They want an explanation—what we did wrong, how we could have succeeded.

That was what the governing committee was after when they called me in later. As I answered their questions, I began to see the narrative taking shape in their minds. At last Anselm said, "Clearly, there was no one fatal mistake. There was just a pattern of behavior: naïve, optimistic, impractical. They were simply too young and too confident."

I realized that I myself had helped create this easy explanation, and my remorse nearly choked me. I stood up and they all looked at me, expecting me to speak, but at first I couldn't say a word. Then, slowly, I started out, "Yes. They were all those things. Naïve. Impractical. Young." My voice failed, and I had to concentrate on controlling it. "That's why we needed them. Without their crazy commitment, we would have conceded defeat. We would have given up, and spent the winter hunkered down in our cave, gnawing our old grudges, never venturing or striving for anything beyond our reach. Nothing would move forward. We needed them, and now they are gone."

Later, I heard that the young people of Feynman took inspiration from what I said, and started retelling the story as one of doomed heroism. Young people like their heroes doomed.

Myself, I can't call it anything but failure. It's not because people blame me. I haven't had to justify myself to anyone but this voice in my head—always questioning, always nagging me. I can't convince it: everyone fails.

If I blame anyone, it's our ancestors, the original settlers. We thought their message to us was that we could always conquer irrationality, if we just stuck to science and reason.

Oh, yes—the settlers. When we finally opened the crates to find out what they had sent us, it turned out that the payload was books. Not data—paper books. Antique ones. Art, philosophy, literature. The books had weathered the interstellar trip remarkably well. Some were lovingly inscribed by the settlers to their unknown descendants. Anatoly would have been pleased to know that the people who sent these books were not really rationalists—they worried about our aspirational well-being. But the message came too late. Anatoly is dead.

I sit on my bed stroking Sally's head. What do you think, girl? Should I open the book from my great-grandmother?

PERMISSIONS

ACKNOWLEDGMENTS

The editor would like to thank the following people for their help and support: Lisa Clarke, Sean Wallace, Kate Baker, Gardner Dozois, Cory Allyn, Sheila Williams, Gordon Van Gelder, Steven Silver, Jonathan Strahan, Ellen Datlow, and all the authors, editors, agents, and publishers whose work made this anthology possible.

RECOMMENDED READING

"You will see the moon rise" by Israel Alonso, translated by Steve Redwood, *Apex Book of World SF 5*, edited by Cristina Jurado.

"Work Shadow/Shadow Work" by Madeline Ashby, *Robots vs. Fairies*, edited by Dominik Parisien and Navah Wolfe.

"Dandelion" by Elly Bangs, *Clarkesworld Magazine*, September 2018.

"Breakwater" by Simon Bestwick, *Tor.com*, February 28, 2018.

"The Only Harmless Great Thing" by Brooke Bolander, Published by Tor.com Books.

"Life from the Sky" by Sue Burke, *Asimov's Science Fiction*, May/June 2018.

"The Independence Patch" by Bryan Camp, *Lightspeed Magazine*, March 2018.

"The Counting of Vermillon Beads" by Aliette de Bodard, *A Thousand Beginnings and Endings*, edited by Ellen Oh and Elsie Chapman.

"The Tea Master and the Detective" by Aliette de Bodard, Published by Subterranean Press/JABberwocky Ebooks.

"Loss of Signal" by S.B. Divya, *Tor.com*, August 1, 2018.

"Phoresis" by Greg Egan, Published by Subterranean Press.

"The Nearest" by Greg Egan, *Tor.com*, July 19, 2018.

"Logistics" by A.J. Fitzwater, *Clarkesworld Magazine*, April 2018.

"Icefall" by Stephanie Gunn, Published by Twelfth Planet Press.

"Inscribed on Dark Water" by Gregor Hartmann, *Interzone*, September/October 2018.

"Fluxless" by Mike Jansen, *Samovar*, December 3, 2018.

"Cuisine des Mémoires" by N.K. Jemisin, *How Long 'til Black Future Month*.

"Every Single Wonderful Detail" by Stephen Graham Jones, *Mechanical Animals*, edited by Selena Chambers and Jason Heller.

"Grace's Family" by James Patrick Kelly, *Tor.com*, May 16, 2018.

"In Event of Moon Disaster" by Rich Larson, *Asimov's Science Fiction*, March/April 2018.

"Porque el Girasol Se Llama el Girasol" by Rich Larson, *Shades Within Us: Tales of Migrations and Fractured Borders*, edited by Susan Forest and Lucas K. Law.

"Broken Wings" by William Ledbetter, *The Magazine of Fantasy & Science Fiction*, July/August 2018.

"Vespers" by J. M. Ledgard, *Twelve Tomorrows*, edited by Wade Roush.

"Left to Take the Lead" by Marissa Lingen, *Analog Science Fiction and Fact*, July/August 2018.

"Cosmic Spring" by Ken Liu, *Lightspeed Magazine*, March 2018.

"Chine Life" by Paul McAuley, *Twelve Tomorrows*, edited by Wade Roush.

"Time Was" by Ian McDonald, Published by Tor.com Books.

"Mother, Mother, Will You Play With Me?" by Seanan McGuire, *Mother of Invention*, edited by Rivqa Rafael and Tansy Rayner Roberts.

"Longing For Earth" by Linda Nagata, *Infinity's End*, edited by Jonathan Strahan.

"The Miracle Lambs of Minane" by Finbarr O'Reilly, *Clarkesworld Magazine*, November 2018.

"The Heart of the Matter" by Nnedi Okorafor, *Twelve Tomorrows*, edited by Wade Roush.

"The Hard Spot in the Glacier" by An Owomoyela, *Mechanical Animals*, edited by Selena Chambers and Jason Heller.

"The Streaming Man" by Suzanne Palmer, *Analog Science Fiction and Fact*, March/April 2018.

"Stones in the Water, Cottage on the Mountain" by Suzanne Palmer, *Asimov's Science Fiction*, July/August 2018.

"Love Songs for the Very Awful" by Robert Reed, *Asimov's Science Fiction*, March/April 2018.

"Death's Door" by Alastair Reynolds, *Infinity's End*, edited by Jonathan Strahan.

"A Study in Oils" by Kelly Robson, *Clarkesworld Magazine*, September 2018.

"Gods, Monsters and the Lucky Peach" by Kelly Robson, Published by Tor.com Books.

"Maximum Outflow" by Adam Rogers, *Wired*, December 17, 2018.

"Joyride" by Kristine Kathryn Rusch, *Asimov's Science Fiction*, November/December 2018.

"The Wait is Longer Than You Think" by Adrian Simmons, *GigaNotoSaurus*, May 2018.

"Widdam" by Vandana Singh, *The Magazine of Fantasy & Science Fiction*, January/February 2018.

"Overvalued" by Mark Stasenko, *Slate*, November 27, 2018.

"Starship Mountain" by Allen M. Steele, *Asimov's Science Fiction*, July/August 2018.

"An Errant Holy Spark" by Bogi Takacs, *Mother of Invention*, edited by Rivqa Rafael and Tansy Rayner Roberts.

"The Persistence of Blood" by Juliette Wade, *Clarkesworld Magazine*, March 2018.

"Kindred" by Peter Watts, *Infinity's End*, edited by Jonathan Strahan.

"The Freeze-Frame Revolution" by Peter Watts, Published by Tachyon Publications.

"Artificial Condition" by Martha Wells, Published by Tor.com Books.

"Rogue Protocol" by Martha Wells, Published by Tor.com Books.

"Exit Strategy" by Martha Wells, Published by Tor.com Books.

"Compulsory" by Martha Wells, *Wired*, December 17, 2018.

"In the God-Fields" by Liz Williams, *Women Invent the Future*, edited by Doteveryone.

"The Clockwork Penguin Dreamed of Stars" by Caroline M. Yoachim, *Mechanical Animals*, edited by Selena Chambers and Jason Heller.

ABOUT THE EDITOR

Neil Clarke is the editor of *Clarkesworld* and *Forever Magazine*; owner of Wyrm Publishing; and a seven-time Hugo Award Finalist for Best Editor (short form). He currently lives in NJ with his wife and two sons. You can find him online at neil-clarke.com.